The Generals

SIMON SCARROW

headline
review

First published in 2007 by HEADLINE REVIEW
An imprint of HEADLINE PUBLISHING GROUP

First published in paperback in 2008 by HEADLINE REVIEW
An imprint of HEADLINE PUBLISHING GROUP

1

978 0 7553 3688 3 (A format)
978 0 7553 2436 1 (B format)

Typeset in Bembo by Avon DataSet Ltd,
Bidford-on-Avon, Warwickshire

Printed and bound in Great Britain by
Mackays of Chatham plc, Chatham, Kent

Headline's policy is to use papers that are natural, renewable and recyclable
products and made from wood grown in sustainable forests. The logging
and manufacturing processes are expected to conform to the environmental
regulations of the country of origin.

HEADLINE PUBLISHING GROUP
An Hachette Livre UK Company
338 Euston Road
London NW1 3BH

www.reviewbooks.co.uk
www.hodderheadline.com

For Pat and Mick

Thanks for the good craic over the years

Egypt and Syria, 1799

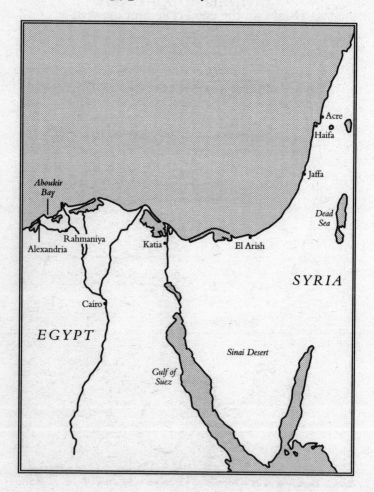

The territories and chief cities of India 1795–1804

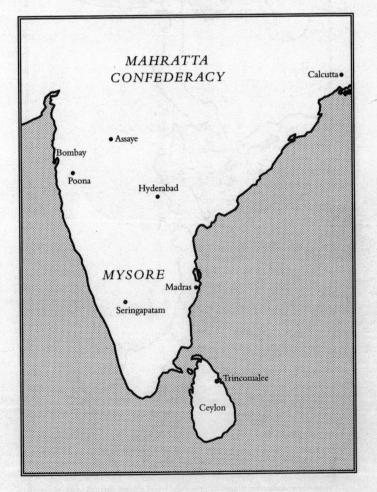

MAHRATTA CONFEDERACY

Calcutta

Assaye

Bombay

Poona

Hyderabad

MYSORE

Madras

Seringapatam

Trincomalee

Ceylon

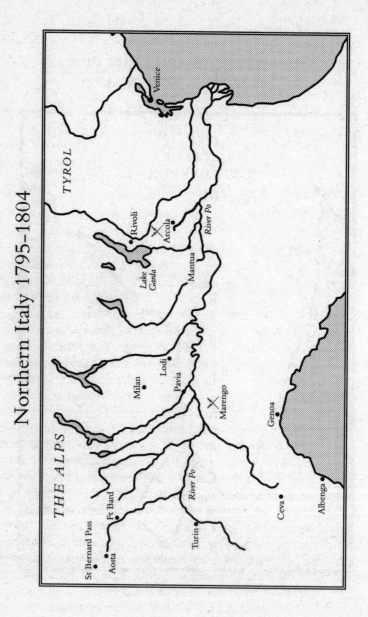

Northern Italy 1795–1804

Chapter 1

Napoleon

Paris, 1795

It was a hot day early in August and the heat lay across the tiled roofs of Paris like a blanket, smothering the still air with the odours of the city: sewage, smoke and sweat. In his office at the corner of the Tuileries Palace, Lazare Carnot sat at a large desk piled with paperwork arranged in labelled trays. Each tray's contents had been prioritised by his staff, so that Citizen Carnot – as he styled himself – could expedite the most pressing documents concerning the French armies struggling to defend the infant Republic. Ever since the execution of King Louis the enemies of France had regarded her as a monstrous aberration. Monarchs and aristocrats across Europe would not rest easy until the revolution had been mercilessly crushed and the Bourbons returned to the throne. So war raged across the continent as great armies clashed beneath the standards of Austria and the tricolour flags of France. And it was Carnot's duty to see that his country-men were organised and supplied to achieve the victories that would guarantee the survival of the ideals of the revolution.

The armies were ever hungry for more recruits, more uniforms, boots, gunpowder, muskets, cannon, remounts for the cavalry and the minutiae of military equipment that was necessary for an army to march and fight. Every day Carnot had to cope with the urgent demands of the generals, meeting their needs as best he could from the finite resources available. There

1

were shortages of everything the armies needed, most of all money. The treasury was all but empty and the National Assembly had been forced to issue paper currency – assignats – that were openly traded at a fraction of their face value. Carnot smiled grimly at the thought as he initialled a requisition for artillery uniforms from a textile mill at Lyons. At least it cost the government nothing to print yet more assignats to pay for the uniforms. If the mill-owner made a loss trading them on that was his own affair. Carnot reached for his pen, dipped it in the inkwell and signed his name with a flourish: Citizen Carnot, on behalf of the Committee of Public Safety.

An ironic name for a committee, he reflected, given that its members had been responsible for the deaths of thousands of their fellow citizens in order to safeguard the principles of liberty, equality and fraternity. The Committee ruthlessly suppressed any symptom of dissent inside France even as it directed the war against external enemies. Yet membership of the Committee carried its own danger, as Robespierre and his hardcore Jacobin followers had discovered, and paid for it with their heads. Carnot sighed as he slipped the signed requisition into the out tray.

Unless the fortunes of war changed and the political situation in France stabilised, then the revolution would fail, and all that had been gained, and all that might be gained, for the common people would be lost. Then the retribution of the monarchists, the aristocrats and the church would be even more terrible than the very worst of the excesses of the early years of the revolution.

Carnot leaned back in his chair and tugged at the collar of his shirt. The heat had made his skin feel prickly and a trickle of perspiration ran down his back. Even though he wore a dark coat over his shirt there was no question of removing it. Carnot was a soldier of the old school and discomfort had always been part of the profession.

A soft knock at the door broke his concentration and he sat up stiffly as he responded. 'Yes?'

The door opened and through the gap Carnot could see to the far end of the much larger office outside. His staff sat on stools behind their desks in neatly regimented rows. Carnot's secretary was a thin man with cropped grey hair, who had worked in the War Office since he left school and still served his new masters with the deference he had learned under the old regime. He stepped into Carnot's office and creased into a bow.

'Sir, Brigadier Bonaparte has arrived.'

'Bonaparte?' Carnot frowned. 'Does he have an appointment?'

'So he says, citizen.'

'Does he now?' Carnot could not help smiling. Though he had never met the young brigadier, he had dealt with a steady stream of correspondence with the man ever since Napoleon Bonaparte had taken command of the artillery outside Toulon nearly two years ago. The quality of Brigadier Bonaparte's mind shone through the operational plans he had drafted for the Army of the Alps and the Army of Italy. So, too, did his impatience and his insistence on having his way. For a moment Carnot was tempted to make the officer wait. After all, his time was precious and Bonaparte had not made an appointment to see him through the proper channels. Perhaps the young pup should be reminded of his place in the grand scheme of things, Carnot mused. Then he relented, partly from a desire to see if the man matched the mental image Carnot had constructed from Bonaparte's voluminous correspondence.

'Very well.' He shrugged. 'Please show the brigadier in.'

'Yes, citizen,' the secretary replied and automatically bowed again on his way out, closing the door quietly behind him. Carnot had time to scan another requisition and was dashing off his signature when he heard the door open again and the scrape and creak of boots on the floorboards.

The secretary coughed. 'Brigadier Bonaparte, sir.'

'Very well,' Carnot replied without looking up. 'You may leave us.'

As the door closed Carnot read back over the document he had just signed and nodded with satisfaction before he slipped it across the desk into the out tray. Then he raised his head.

On the other side of the desk stood a slight figure, short and thin with dark hair that fell to his collar. The fringe was cut severely across the top of his pale head in a straight line. The grey eyes gleamed and darted round the office, seeming to take in every detail before they settled on Carnot. The young officer's nose was fine and narrow and his lips reposed in a faint pout, then parted in an impulsive smile before he forced his features into an impassive expression and stiffened to attention.

Carnot stared at the brigadier, rueing the fact that so many young men had achieved such rapid advancement through the ranks in the space of a few years. Many officers had fled the country during the revolution and Robespierre had culled the ranks of those that remained. Inevitably, a shortage of officers had arisen and promotion was thrust upon any man who demonstrated raw courage, or the least indication of a sound military brain. Brigadier Bonaparte was one of the few who possessed both.

'Welcome, Bonaparte. I've been wanting to meet you for some time.'

'Thank you, citizen.'

The voice was soft, and agreeable to Carnot's ear, and he relaxed his face into a smile. 'I had not expected you to arrive in Paris so soon. How long have you been here?'

'We arrived last night, citizen.'

'We?'

'My staff officers and I. Captain Marmont and Lieutenant Junot.'

'I see. And you have found comfortable quarters?'

The brigadier tilted his head to one side and shrugged. 'I have taken some rooms in a hotel in the Latin quarter. It's cheap, but comfortable enough. I might find something more suitable,' Bonaparte paused to add emphasis to the words that followed, 'once I am returned to full pay, citizen.'

Carnot shifted in his chair as he recalled the circumstances of the brigadier's reduction in pay. Bonaparte had been a protégé of the Robespierre brothers and when they had fallen many of their followers had been executed. Others, like Napoleon's fellow Corsican, Antoine Saliceti, had gone into hiding. Others, like Napoleon Bonaparte, who openly espoused Jacobin politics, had been proscribed. Trumped-up charges of corruption and selling information to foreign powers had been enough to see

Bonaparte sent to prison for several days. Even though the charges had been dismissed, Bonaparte had been only provisionally released on half-pay to continue his service in the army. No wonder the brigadier sounded bitter, Carnot reflected.

'I assure you, I am doing what I can to restore your rights.' Carnot opened out his hands. 'It's the least France can do for one of its most promising young officers.'

If he expected a modest expression of gratitude at the remark, he was instantly disappointed. Napoleon simply nodded.

'Yes, citizen . . . the very least. I have given good service to France, and I have been loyal to the revolution, and it is still my ambition to serve both as well as I can.'

'France and the revolution are one and the same, Bonaparte.'

Napoleon gestured towards the window. 'You might say that, citizen, but there are plenty of voices on the streets that do not. I must have passed a score of royalist notices plastered across the walls as I walked here. Not to mention a man selling royalist pamphlets, not a hundred paces from the entrance to the Tuileries. I doubt he would consider that France and the revolution are the same thing.'

'Then he is a fool.'

Napoleon's eyebrows rose. 'I wonder how many more fools are out there, citizen?'

'Enough to provide encouragement for the enemies of the republic,' Carnot admitted. 'Which is why they must be crushed without mercy. It is the duty of every officer in the French army to assist in the process, distasteful as that no doubt seems to you. Do you find such a duty distasteful, Bonaparte?'

'I do. As you will know from my letter.'

'Ah, yes, I recall. It seems that you do not wish to take up your post with the Army of the West.'

'I am certain that my talents could be put to better use in other armies, citizen. There is no glory to be had in fighting one's countrymen, no matter how misguided their politics. What chance have they got against professional soldiers? They will be slaughtered like innocents. Yes, I find that distasteful.'

Carnot leaned forward and lowered his voice. 'For a bunch of innocents they are raising merry hell in the Vendée. Attacking our patrols, burning supply depots and poisoning the hearts and minds of simple peasants and workers. And who do you think is backing them? England, that's who. English ships land spies and troublemakers on our coasts almost every day, their pockets loaded with English gold. Do not delude yourself, Bonaparte. The war we fight inside France is every bit as vital as the war we wage against foreign enemies. Perhaps it is more important. Unless we win the battle for France it does not matter what happens on the plains of Italy, or along the banks of the Rhine. If we lose the battle for control of our country then all is lost.' He leaned back in his chair and forced a smile. 'So you can understand why the Committee wants to appoint its best officers to the army facing the most difficult task.'

Napoleon looked faintly amused. 'I wonder how much this posting has to do with my ability, citizen.'

'What do you mean?'

'I am an artillery officer. My speciality is the movement and disposition of cannon. Find me a fortification to lay siege to, or the massed ranks of an army to shatter with my batteries. I can do that as well as any other artillery officer in the service. What use would I be to the Army of the West? Unless they want me to bombard every barn in the Vendée, or fire grapeshot at shadows flitting along the edges of woods.'

'You will not be required to command artillery, as you already know. You have been appointed to an infantry brigade.'

'Precisely, citizen. You make my point for me. I am a gunner. I should be placed in command of cannon, not cannon fodder.'

'You have demonstrated other talents,' Carnot replied tersely. 'I've read the reports of your work at Toulon. You lead from the front. That's the kind of inspiration our men need in taking on the rebel scum in the Vendée. Also, you know how to organise. Most of all, you are single-minded and perhaps ruthless. That's why you are needed in the Army of the West.'

Napoleon was silent for a moment before he replied. 'Even if that is true, I can conceive of another reason why the Committee wants to send me to the Vendée.'

'Oh?' Carnot stared back at him and said acidly, 'Do please explain yourself.'

'It would appear that my loyalty is still doubted. At a time when good artillery officers are desperately needed in the other armies, why else would the Committee send me to fight Frenchmen, except to prove that I have no common purpose with the rebels?'

'The Committee has its reasons, and it is not obliged to share them with you, Bonaparte. You have your orders. You are a soldier; it is not your place to question orders. So you will join the Army of the West as soon as possible. That is the end of the matter.'

'I see.' Napoleon nodded. 'Unless the Committee has cause to reconsider its decision.'

'It won't.' Carnot raised his hands and folded the palms together beneath his chin. 'There's nothing more to be said. Now, if you don't mind, I have work to do.'

Napoleon was still for a moment before he replied. 'Of course, citizen. I will take my leave.'

Carnot's shoulders relaxed a moment as the tension eased slightly. He had feared that the brigadier would prove more obdurate than this, and felt that he ought to offer some last word of encouragement. 'If you serve us as well in the Vendée as you served us at Toulon, then I'm sure you will find that the next posting will be more agreeable, more . . . glorious.'

Napoleon fixed him with an even stare. 'I understand, citizen.'

'Then, good day to you.' Carnot quickly reached for his pen and pulled another requisition off the pile.

Napoleon turned and strode to the door, then paused and looked back. 'Before I take up my new command, there are a few personal matters I need to attend to. I have not had any leave for over a year. I would appreciate some time to get my affairs in order, citizen.'

'How long?'

Napoleon pursed his lips for a moment. 'A month. Perhaps two.'

'Two months, then. No more. I'll have my secretary inform the Committee.'

'Very well. Thank you, citizen.' Napoleon bowed his head and stepped out of the office, closing the door loudly behind him.

Carnot winced and muttered, 'Damn the man . . . Just who the hell does he think he is?'

Chapter 2

'I've sold my carriage,' Napoleon said as he poured more wine into the cups of his two friends. They were sitting in one of the bars on the Palais-Royal. The thoroughfare was beginning to fill with those who were looking for their evening's entertainment.

Marmont and Junot exchanged a look before Junot took a healthy swig from his cup and set it down softly. 'What did you get for it, sir?'

'Three thousand francs.'

Marmont pursed his lips. 'That's a fair enough price.'

Napoleon shook his head. 'I was paid in assignats.'

'Ah . . . That's not so good.'

'No,' Napoleon agreed. 'But there's no helping it. I need the money. I haven't been paid a sou since we left Marseilles and the owner of the hotel won't wait much longer for the rent. At least we'll have a roof over our heads and wine in our cups for a few weeks yet. So drink up, but not too fast, eh, Junot?'

The other men smiled but there was a lingering expression of guilt on Junot's face as he stared into the dregs of his cup. He glanced up. 'Sir, it's not right that you should have to pay for us. My family has a little money. I could ask—'

'That's enough, Junot. You are on my staff. Part of my military family. It is only right that I should pay for us all. What kind of commanding officer would I be if I didn't take care of such things?'

'A richer one,' Marmont cut in with a bleary smile. He reached

9

over and patted Napoleon's shoulder. 'Cheer up. Something will come up. There's a war on. They need us. Our time will come. In the meantime let's hope Carnot lets your leave run a while longer yet.'

'Yes, I hope so.'

Napoleon reflected that it had been over a month since the Minister of War had granted him leave. Fortunately for him, Carnot's attention had been diverted from military matters for much of that time. A new constitution was being debated in the chamber of deputies and every political faction was fighting to have its views enshrined in the document. While the debate preoccupied Carnot, Napoleon had been pleading his case with the officials at the Ministry of War to find him another command. But time was running out. Unless the military situation changed, he would be forced to leave Paris and join the thankless fight against the rebels in the Vendée. And possibly very soon. That morning he had received a message from the Ministry, summoning him to a meeting the following day.

Napoleon raised his glass and took another sip of the cheap wine, then gazed for a moment at the surrounding scene.

Now that the days of the Great Terror were over the capital had quickly recovered much of its gaiety. The wealthier citizens no longer dressed down when they walked abroad for fear of being singled out as aristocrats. Ostentatious carriages had reappeared on the streets and those ladies who could afford it paraded their fashions openly. The cheaper theatres once again played comedies and sketches that dared to poke fun at the more tolerant, or ridiculous, members of the national assembly, though as yet those who sat on the Committee for Public Safety were studiously overlooked by Parisian playwrights. Every day, it seemed, a new newspaper appeared on the streets, taking an increasingly critical line on those who ruled the republic. Every social ill was laid at the door of the government: inflation, the failure of the harvest, the black market, the apparent political anarchy and the poor management of the war. Some newspapers even dared to argue for the restoration of the monarchy and there had been angry confrontations between rival crowds of republicans and monarchists on the streets. Even though the high temperatures of summer had dissipated, the mood in Paris was heated and strained, like the air before the breaking of a storm, and Napoleon, like everyone else, was filled with a sense of foreboding. With good reason. He drained his glass and muttered, 'I am to present myself at the Ministry at noon tomorrow. I was informed this morning.'

'Why?' asked Junot.

'I don't know, but I fear my leave is about to come to an abrupt end.' Napoleon shrugged. 'So I might as well as make the most of this evening. Come on. Let's be off. I've heard that there are some new girls at Madame Marcelle's place.'

The Palais-Royal was lit from one end to the other by the orange glow of lanterns. Madame Marcelle's establishment was in the far corner, and as the three officers threaded their way through the evening throng of friends, families, lovers, hawkers and all manner of street entertainers, Napoleon noticed a crowd gathered round a man speaking from a large wine cask outside a café. He was screened from his audience by four men carrying long staves. As Napoleon drew closer he could hear the first words of the speaker, strident against the good-humoured tone of the wider crowd.

'Citizens! You are in grave danger – your complacency threatens to kill you! Do you not know that even as you stand there, the Bourbon agents are plotting to overthrow the revolution? It is they who are behind the price rises and food shortages. They are the ones who are trying to undermine the new constitution. Trying to steal the liberty that we have taken into our own hands.' The speaker raised his fists. 'All that we have fought for. All that those gallant martyrs of the Bastille died for – all, ALL will be torn from us and we will be as slaves again. Is that what you wish?'

'No!' called a resonant voice. Napoleon sensed the theatrical tone of the cry, and he smiled. A supporter planted in the crowd. 'No! Never!' the voice cried out again, and others joined in.

The speaker nodded and raised a palm to quieten them before he continued. 'You are good patriots. That I can tell at once. Not like those Bourbon scum who would sell their souls to foreign powers and their mercenary hordes. They are traitors!'

'Damned liar!' a shrill voice called out. 'Royalists are not traitors. We seek to free France of the tyranny of the godless!'

Napoleon paused, straining his neck and rising on his toes as he tried to see over the heads of the crowd towards the protester. He saw a tall thin man standing on a pediment at the far side of the crowd. As soon as he had spoken he turned and gestured towards the colonnade. At once a swarm of men emerged from the shadows of the tall columns. Each wore a scarf across his face and carried a wooden club.

A woman screamed. Her cry was taken up and the people surged as one away from the onrushing men.

'Death to the murderers of the King!' the voice shrilled out. 'For God and monarchy!'

He jumped down from the pediment and joined his followers as they charged into the terrified crowd, swinging their clubs at victims without any regard for age or gender. Suddenly a dense mass of bodies surged against Napoleon, thrusting him back against his companions. Junot grabbed hold of his arm and held him up while Marmont stepped forward with a roar and brandished his fists, daring any of the panicked crowd to come any closer to them. As the bodies flowed past on either side and the evening air filled with cries of fear, pain and anger Napoleon growled, 'Come on! We'll teach those royalists a lesson.'

'What?' Junot turned to him in surprise. 'Are you mad? They'll cut us down in no time.'

'He's right.' Marmont eased himself back towards his friends. 'Three against twenty or more. What can we do?'

'Three right now,' Napoleon conceded, his voice betraying his nervous excitement. 'But once we fight back, so will others. Come on!'

He thrust his way past Marmont and pushed through the people streaming away from their attackers. Then, over the heads of those at the back of the crowd, he saw the raised clubs and scarved faces of the men beating a path through to the original speaker and his guards. Napoleon paused, fists bunched and heart pounding, not for the first time uncertain about the wisdom of what he was doing. Then he saw on the ground the prone figure of an old man, sprawled on his face, blood gushing from his scalp on to the cobbles. Beside him lay a crutch. Napoleon snatched it up, instinctively grasping it as if it were a musket, armpad clutched to his side and the base held out like a muzzle. His confidence returned and he stepped forward again, swerving round a woman clutching a young boy to her breast, long skirts flowing as she fled. A short distance behind her was the first of the royalists. Above the scarf he wore to conceal his features, his wide excited eyes turned and fixed on Napoleon, widening still further with surprise. He hesistated for an instant before he began to raise his club, and Napoleon swept forward, throwing all the weight of his slight figure behind the crutch as he rammed the base into the man's chest, and hissed 'Bastard!' through clenched teeth.

The blow drove the man back with an explosive grunt and his head struck the ground as he tumbled, knocking him cold.

'Marmont! Take his club!'

Now that two of them were armed, they made for the next target, a short distance off in the gathering gloom. Napoleon feinted at him and as the man moved to block the blow Marmont charged forward and felled him with a vicious strike to the head. As Junot seized the man's weapon Napoleon turned to shout over his shoulder.

'Citizens! Citizens, hear me! Are you cowards or patriots?'

A few faces turned to look and Napoleon seized the moment, charging towards the middle of the body of men fighting their way towards the meeting's speaker. He filled his lungs and shouted, 'Death to tyranny!'

Marmont and Junot raced after him, adding their cries to his. An instant later they were amongst the royalists, slashing out with their clubs. Since they were soldiers and more accustomed to the madness of battle, and the need to strike hard and fast, they had an advantage over the casual bullies who had been expecting an unarmed crowd and not this fierce counter-attack. Napoleon thrust out again with his crutch, and struck a man's shoulder. The blow was not disabling and the man at once swung his club at Napoleon's head. Napoleon snatched the crutch back and up into the path of the club and there was a sharp crack, the force of the blow jarring his hands. Marmont abruptly swung his boot into the man's crotch, hard enough to lift the royalist off his feet, and the man tumbled back with a deep groan and rolled on the ground vomiting. Marmont hissed at Napoleon, 'Hold the other bloody end, you fool! Use it like a club.'

As he reversed his hold Napoleon heard the speaker shout out to his bodyguards. 'Help those men! Help them!'

Napoleon, Marmont and Junot stood back to back in a loose triangle, swinging their makeshift weapons at the men about them, trying to keep them at a distance. Marmont growled, 'Come on then, you bastards! If you have the stomach for it.'

'Girondin scum!' someone shouted back.

'Girondin? Girondin!' Marmont roared. 'I'm a Jacobin, you bastard! And you're dead!'

He hurled himself into their midst, knocking two of the royalists to the ground, and then he was laying about him in great sweeping arcs with his club, shattering bones, battering muscles into nerveless jelly and driving the breath from his enemies with his blows.

Junot edged closer to Napoleon. 'They really shouldn't have called him a Girondin. I almost feel sorry for them.'

'No time for that,' Napoleon replied. Taking a deep breath he moved off in Marmont's wake. The speaker and his bodyguards joined the fight and as the royalists were forced to stop and defend themselves the crowd stopped fleeing. Some edged towards the fight and then the first of them walked, then ran, back to the melee. 'Death to tyrants!' he called out, then again, his voice strengthening. Others joined in, emboldened by his confidence.

Napoleon glanced back and felt his heart lift. 'Citizens! Help us!'

Some heeded his call, and charged into the fight, throwing themselves on to the royalists. But some were struck down by the royalists' clubs and brutally beaten to the ground. Edging round a crumpled body, Napoleon raised the crutch and looked for another opponent. But in the growing darkness, the civilians around him all looked the same, until he saw a face half hidden by a scarf, and at once smashed his crutch down on the man's head. The blow never landed. Suddenly the dusk exploded in a blinding flash of light and Napoleon reeled back. He shook his head, trying to disperse the fading white flashes that obscured his sight.

'Run for it!' a voice shouted. 'Royalists! On me!'

Several figures turned and bolted, running back for the dark shadows beneath the colonnade. The crowd pursued them for a moment and then gave up, jeering and shouting insults after the defeated enemy. Even though he was aware of a searing pain high on his forehead Napoleon felt awash with elation. Finding Marmont, he gave his friend a hearty slap on the back.

'Auguste Marmont, I swear you are half man, half wild animal.'

'Bastards had it coming to them,' Marmont muttered. 'Call me a Girondin, would they?' Then he caught sight of the dark smear streaming down Napoleon's temple. 'Sir, you're bleeding.'

Napoleon drew out his handkerchief and clasped it to his head with a wince. Then he looked down at the crutch still in his hands, and turned to find its owner. The old man was sitting up, nursing a tear in his scalp.

'My thanks, citizen.' Napoleon helped the man up and returned his crutch to him.

The man nodded his gratitude. 'Just wish I'd been able to help you out, sir.'

'You made your contribution.' Napoleon smiled and patted the crutch. 'Which is more than can be said for most of the people here tonight.'

Junot emerged from the gloom, a thin-faced man at his side, whom Napoleon recognised as the speaker who had been addressing the meeting before it had been broken up. He approached the three officers, glanced over them and turned to Marmont.

'I must thank you, and your friends, sir.'

Marmont looked embarrassed, and nodded towards Napoleon. 'Don't thank me. Our brigadier led us into the fight. I just followed.'

The speaker stared at Napoleon more closely with his hooded eyes and Napoleon sensed that he was not impressed by what he saw. 'Brigadier?' He recovered from his surprise and proffered his hand. 'Joseph Fouché at your service.'

Napoleon took the hand and felt the man's cold skin. He nodded. 'Brigadier Napoleon Bonaparte, at yours.'

'Well, it seems I must thank you for saving my skin. Though not without some cost to yourself.'

'A scratch,' Napoleon replied. 'We were glad to help you. I'll not let any royalists drive our people off the streets. Not whilst I live.'

'I see.' Fouché's lips flickered into a thin smile. 'I like your spirit. The republic needs more men like you. Especially now. Paris seems to be infested by nests of royalist sympathisers. It is time that good men recognised the growing threat and stood up to them. Before it's too late.'

Napoleon laughed. 'Come now, they were no more than a gang of thugs. A rabble.'

'You think so? Then look here.' Fouché squatted down over one of the men who had attacked the crowd, now lying senseless on the cobblestones. Fouché pulled the scarf away from his face, and then flicked open the dark coat. Underneath it the man was wearing a smartly tailored jacket and waistcoat. Fouché stood up.

'A common thug? I think not. He's an aristo.' Fouché swung his foot into the side of the man's head. 'An aristo and a traitor. And there are many more like him out there, scheming and plotting to place a Bourbon back on the throne. Mark my words, Brigadier Bonaparte, we have to watch our backs. The revolution is not quite as safe as our government would like us to think.' He smiled. 'Now I must go. I have another speech to make, in the Place Vendôme.' Fouché suddenly looked tired and anxious. 'The people have to be convinced to vote for the new constitution. If it fails to win their support then all is lost . . . Anyway, I hope we meet again, sir.'

Napoleon nodded faintly, not relishing the prospect.

As Fouché and his bodyguards strode away towards the Rue Saint-Honoré Napoleon glanced round at the people in the Palais-Royal. Now that the excitement was over, most were drifting back to their earlier entertainments. Only a small proportion of them had come to Fouché's aid. As for the rest, Napoleon could not say where their loyalties lay. Perhaps Fouché was right, Napoleon conceded. Perhaps the situation in Paris was more dangerous than he had supposed.

Chapter 3

The Minister of War gestured to the chair that had been positioned on the opposite side of his desk. 'Please, Brigadier Bonaparte, sit down.'

Napoleon complied, and Carnot leaned forward. 'You've injured your head.'

For a moment Napoleon considered relating the events of the previous evening, and then realised it might be thought unseemly for a senior officer to be involved in a street brawl. He cleared his throat. 'I had a dizzy spell, citizen. I tripped and fell down some stairs.'

'But your head's clear enough, I trust.'

'Yes, sir. Of course.'

'Just as well, since I have been asked by the Committee for Public Safety to pick your brains.' Carnot smiled. 'It seems that you are regarded as something of an expert on military affairs in Italy.'

Napoleon's mind raced. It was true that he had been asked to draft some plans for the campaigns of the Army of Italy, and he had written some assessments of the war capability of Genoa, but did that qualify him as an expert? If he assumed the role too readily he risked being thought impudent. On the other hand, this might be a chance to improve his prospects. He straightened his back and nodded modestly as he replied.

'It is true that I have a thorough knowledge of the Italian theatre, citizen. Though I have been out of touch with operations for some months now.'

'Then you are not aware of the latest reports from the front?'

Napoleon shrugged. 'I read the newspapers, citizen.'

'The newspapers are hardly intelligence reports.' Carnot sniffed. 'Besides, even they don't yet know of the latest situation. But they will soon enough. Some fool or other on the Committee will blurt it out to one of his friends and it'll be round Paris quicker than a dose of the clap.' Carnot eased himself forward and stared directly at Napoleon. 'General Kellermann and his men have suffered another defeat. The Army of the Alps is in full retreat, and I wouldn't be surprised if Kellermann had scurried halfway back to Paris by now.'

Napoleon was irritated to hear the hero of Valmy spoken of so dismissively and instinctively rallied to a fellow officer's defence. 'The general must have his reasons for withdrawing, citizen.'

'Oh, I'm sure he does.' Carnot wafted a hand. 'But let us call a spade a spade, Bonaparte. This is no withdrawal, it is a retreat pure and simple. The man has been beaten. What the Committee wants to know is whether it is worth renewing our efforts to take Italy from the Austrians, or whether we should be content with just defending the frontier. Now, you know the terrain, you know the enemy's strengths and weaknesses and you know what our men are capable of achieving. So, then, which course of action would you advise?'

Napoleon hurriedly marshalled the knowledge he had of the Italian front and mentally composed his response before he spoke. There was only a short pause before he began, ticking the points off with his fingers.

'We need Italy. France's treasury is almost empty. There's plenty of wealth to be had from seizing Austria's Italian provinces. We might even be able to exact enough money to pay for the war. Besides, it's not as if the Italians are keen to stay under the Austrian yoke. If France promises them freedom and political reform, then we can be sure of winning over all but the most entrenched of their aristocrats. We could also make good use of the enmity that exists between Genoa, Lombardy, Venice, Rome and Naples. Play them off against each other and we can take each one in turn.'

'But first we have to defeat the Austrians.'

'Yes, citizen. I believe it can be done. Their soldiers are tough enough. But they've been serving in Italy for a long time. Many of them are far older than our men. All our soldiers need is the right kind of leader. Someone who can fire their patriotism . . .' Napoleon paused a moment, to allow Carnot to reach the inevitable conclusion of this line of rhetoric. Then he drew a breath and continued. 'A man of General Kellermann's reputation is more than adequate for the task.'

'Such faint praise.' Carnot smiled. 'For a moment there I thought you were going to volunteer for the job.'

'No,' Napoleon protested and tried to sound sincere. 'I'm not ready to command an army. The idea's preposterous.'

'I know it is. That's why I am glad that you didn't suggest it. Please continue.'

'Yes. Well then, leaving aside the morale issue, the Austrians lack mobility. They never advance anywhere without long supply columns. If our men can live off the land they will march many times faster than the Austrians. We could cut their communications at will, fight a war of manoeuvre.' The ideas were spilling out of his mind in a rush and Napoleon forced himself to slow down. If his words were to have any effect on the members of the Committee he must not appear to be some cavalier adventurer. He must present his case in a balanced manner. He continued.

'Those would be the arguments for going on to the offensive, citizen. Of course, one must consider the opportunities and risks of the alternative strategy; merely defending our frontier. It would require a large body of men tied up in a line of static defences. They would have to be supplied regularly – an expensive undertaking. And garrison duty would dull the edge of their fighting potential. Then there's the issue of handing the initiative to the Austrians. If they wished to attempt an invasion along our southern coast they could pick the time and place to launch the attack and France would be compelled to counter-attack in strength just to restore the frontier.'

Carnot held up his hand to stop Napoleon. 'I can see where

your analysis is heading, Bonaparte. Your advice would be to go on the offensive?'

'Frankly, citizen, I can't see any profitable alternative. General Kellermann goes on the offensive now, or else France will be forced to go on a more costly counter-offensive later on, with far more limited goals.' He leaned back in his chair. 'I say we should make every effort to knock the Austrians out of the war, in the Italian theatre at least.'

Carnot stared back at him, his face creased into a faint frown as he pondered Napoleon's words. 'Your views are most interesting, and I will be sure to share them with the other members of the Committee. There is one last matter which requires some thought, namely who would be best suited to command the army, whether it sits on the defensive or is sent forward. General Kellermann is no longer a young man . . .'

Napoleon studiously ignored the invitation to pass comment, and at length Carnot was forced to continue. 'Then, let us say his experience might be better engaged in more administrative functions. Wouldn't you agree?'

'It is not fitting for a subordinate officer to make such judgements, citizen. I am a simple soldier and I speak only in terms of facts.'

The other man smiled. 'It is true that you are a soldier, just as it is manifestly untrue that you are simple. I think that if you were to deploy your talents on the political field as shrewdly as you do on military matters then you would be a man I would be wise to watch closely. Particularly at a time when so many soldiers seem to be carrying their political ambitions in their knapsacks.'

'I'm not sure what you mean, citizen.'

'If I'm any judge of character, you know exactly what I mean,' Carnot reflected wearily. 'Now then, I'm grateful for your insights. And it may be that I will need to consult you again on these matters. Which means I have to find some way of keeping you out of the clutches of the Army of the West.'

Napoleon felt his pulse race and he sat still and waited for the Minister of War to continue.

'There's a position available in the Ministry's bureau of

topography. They need a senior officer to co-ordinate the movements of our armies. It's an administrative post, and it needs a good head for detail and quick calculations. I'm certain you could cope with it. I want you to take the job. Of course it has the added virtue of keeping you close at hand, in case a combat command should fall vacant. I'm not promising anything, you understand?'

'I understand, sir.'

'Good. In the meantime I will see to it that someone is found to replace you on the strength of the Army of the West.'

'Thank you, citizen,' Napoleon replied. 'I am in your debt.'

'Yes, you are. And I will show you no pity if I have misjudged your potential, Bonaparte. Make sure you remember that. Now you may go.'

'Yes, citizen.' Napoleon rose from his chair and strode towards the door.

'One last thing,' Carnot called after him.

'Yes?'

'Keep your wits about you. The word is our royalist friends are brewing something up. It could be just a rumour, but I'm not so sure. Keep your ears open. Don't leave the city and be ready to act if something happens.'

'Something?'

Carnot lowered his voice ominously. 'Just be ready.'

Chapter 4

One morning, late in September, Napoleon was taking his usual morning stroll through the gardens of the Tuileries. The air was crisp and fresh and the slight chill hinted at the coming change of season. The gardens were scattered with people enjoying the clear skies and Napoleon felt his spirits rise. The appointment to the bureau of topography had saved him from the bitter struggle against the Vendée insurgents and, at last, he had been restored to full pay. His debts had been cleared, and now that Marmont had been posted to the Army of the Rhine his expenses had been reduced to maintaining only himself and Junot.

On the far side of the gardens a crowd had gathered outside the hall of the National Assembly. As Napoleon made his way round the gravel path and approached the building he saw that the crowd had swelled in size and angry shouts filled the air. He approached and caught the eye of a man in an expensively tailored coat.

'Citizen, what's happening here?'

The man turned and stabbed his finger towards the National Assembly. 'They've just released the details of the new constitution.'

'Oh? And?'

'It's a disgrace, that's what. Those bastards of the Convention are taking seats in the Legislative Assembly. The scum just want to cling on to their jobs.'

Napoleon couldn't help smiling. 'What did you expect? They're politicians.'

The man faced Napoleon and glared. 'That's as maybe, but the people won't stand for it.' He gestured to the surrounding crowd and Napoleon could see that many faces wore expressions of anger and the air was filled with cries of 'Fraud!' and 'Down with the government!' Some even cried out for the restoration of the monarchy.

The man turned back towards the National Assembly and added his voice to the angry chants. Napoleon glanced over the crowd one last time and then resumed his walk, making his way back to his lodgings with a heavy heart. The new constitution was supposed to restore political order, but the self-interest of the politicians meant that none had lost any power, or their jobs. What had been lost was the chance to unite the country, and Napoleon's heart filled with contempt for the political class that simply looked to its privileges and its purses and couldn't give a damn about the rest of the nation.

Over the following days the outrage over the proposed constitution swelled. Large crowds gathered in the streets to protest and at night shots were fired at the National Assembly and the headquarters of the Jacobin and Girondin parties. Fearing for their lives, the deputies granted the leading member of the Committee for Public Safety, Paul Barras, temporary powers to defend the government. And so the entrances to the Tuileries palace were barricaded and manned by troops still loyal to the government.

On the morning of the third day in October Junot shook Napoleon awake.

'Get dressed. We have to get out of here.'

'What?' Napoleon shook his head. 'Junot, what's going on?'

'The royalists. They're on the move. They have squads of men out on the streets arresting any deputies they can find, and any army officers. They're already searching the hotels in the next street.'

Napoleon threw back his bedclothes and dressed quickly. He pulled a plain grey coat over his uniform jacket and thought for a moment about taking his sword, then decided against it. If they came across a search party the best thing to do would be to run for it. The sword would only be an encumbrance. Instead, he picked up an old plain coat and tossed it to his friend. 'Wear that over your jacket.'

Shortly afterwards, the two men left the hotel, cautiously glancing down the narrow street, still gloomy in the thin light of dawn.

'Where are we going?' Junot asked.

'The Tuileries.'

'Why there? That's the first place the royalists will attack. We'll be trapped.'

'Barras will need every man to defend the government.'

Junot recalled the last days of the monarchy and its futile attempt to defend the palace against the Paris mob. 'We'll be slaughtered.'

'It's possible,' Napoleon replied coolly. 'This is the hour of the republic's greatest danger. If we lose, then the revolution fails. But if we win, then, my dear Junot, we will be the heroes of the hour and our fortunes will be made.'

As they strode swiftly along the cobbled streets, they heard a sudden crackle of musket fire in the distance. Junot turned to his friend. 'Somehow, I think that the other side has exactly the same thought.'

They avoided the main boulevards as they hurried towards the Tuileries, while the sounds of musket fire became more general, accompanied by distant shouts. At last they reached the edge of the square called the Carrousel in front of the grand gates of the palace. Several wagons had been dragged into the square and overturned and armed men took cover behind them, keeping watch on the government troops defending the palace.

'Damn,' Napoleon muttered. 'We'll have to try another approach closer to the gates.'

Beside him Junot looked out over the square. 'We'll still have to cross the open ground.'

'Of course, but the range is long. They'll never hit us, even if they do shoot.'

'Really? That's a comfort.'

'Come on, Junot!' Napoleon punched his shoulder. 'Where's

that spirit you showed at Toulon? We'll be safe enough, provided we can find a way through.'

They retreated down the street and picked a narrow alley running closer to the palace. It was still very early and only the rebels had taken to the streets. Most of the Parisians remained in their homes, and prayed that the trouble would not come close to their door. At length the two officers found a narrow passage cutting between two tenements. At the far end the Carrousel lay clearly visible, with the gates of the palace a hundred paces beyond. Napoleon crept to the end of the passage, with Junot close behind. Then they crouched down and Napoleon took a deep breath. 'Ready?'

Junot nodded.

They burst from cover and sprinted across the cobblestones towards the gates. For a few seconds no one seemed to have noticed them. Then there was a shout from one of the men sheltering behind the nearest wagon.

'You there! Stop!'

As they kept running Napoleon saw some of the soldiers on the gates raise their heads to look in their direction. Then one of them snatched up his musket, snapped the cock back and took aim. There was a flash and a puff of smoke, followed by a loud crack and the high-pitched whirr as the ball passed close overhead.

'Don't fire!' Napoleon cried out. 'We're army officers!'

But his shouts were lost in the confusion of other voices as the royalists rose up and hurled insults at them. Another shot was fired, low, ricocheting off the stones between Napoleon and Junot. At once, Napoleon tore at the buttons of his coat as he ran and then shivered free of the coat to expose his uniform jacket. 'Don't fire!'

To his relief the soldiers lowered their weapons. Then the sound of further shots filled the air and he turned and saw that some of the royalists were attempting to shoot the officers down before they reached the safety of the palace gates.

The soldiers began to provide some covering fire, and Napoleon and Junot sprinted for the army barricades as musket balls cracked off the ground and cut through the air like angry hornets. Then they were at the gates and desperately scrambling over the line of barrels and meal bags that formed the barricade. They rolled over the top and dropped down on the far side, breathless. A sergeant scurried along the line of the barricade towards them. 'Who the hell are you?'

'Brigadier Bonaparte and Lieutenant Junot. We're here to help.'

'Help?' The sergeant frowned. 'Then you could have brought some men with you, sir. A battalion or two of line infantry wouldn't go amiss.'

'Sorry.' Napoleon smiled grimly. 'We're all there is.'

'Pity.'

'Where is Paul Barras?'

'Barras?' The sergeant turned and pointed towards the old royal quarters in the centre of the Tuileries. 'In there, with the other officers, sir.'

'Fine. Come on, Junot.'

Keeping low, they hurried across the courtyard and up the steps to the main entrance. Behind them the exchange of musket fire kept going a moment longer and then eased off into the odd desultory shot. Inside the palace a young orderly escorted them up the grand staircase to the first floor suite that Barras had chosen for his headquarters. The door was open and the two officers strode in. It was a large chamber, decorated with gilt and fine wallpaper. Little of the original furnishings had survived the mob's assault on the royal palace a few years earlier and Barras sat at a plain desk. Around him stood or sat several officers, only one of whom Napoleon recognised, and his heart sank.

'That's General Carteaux,' Junot whispered.

Napoleon nodded. The last time they had met, Carteaux had been commanding the army laying siege to Toulon – until the Committee of Public Safety had relieved him of the post for his complete incompetence. Napoleon turned his gaze towards Barras as the latter stood to greet the new arrivals.

'And who may you two be?'

Once Napoleon had introduced himself and Junot Barras nodded. 'Any combat experience?'

'Yes, sir. We served with the army that took Toulon. I commanded the artillery.'

Barras raised his eyebrows. 'Ah! I remember. So you are *that* artillery officer. Robespierre could not have praised you more highly. Still, given the way things turned out I'm not so sure how much stock I should place in his judgement.'

The other officers laughed. There was a harsh nervous edge to the sound that made Napoleon's spirits sink. If this was a sign of how far morale had fallen then the odds against their beating the royalists had lengthened. Barras sat back down.

'Well then, Brigadier, I expect you want me to tell you about our little predicament?'

Napoleon nodded.

'From the latest reports it seems that General Danican has gone over to the royalists. My agents tell me that at first light tomorrow over twenty thousand militia men and royalist sympathisers are going to march on the Tuileries. They intend to massacre every soldier and member of the government that they find here.'

Chapter 5

'How many men do you have under your command?' Napoleon asked.

'Five thousand,' Barras replied. 'Although a thousand of those are volunteers and have no weapons and another five hundred are reservists. They don't have weapons either.'

'So, three and a half thousand muskets against twenty thousand.' Napoleon shook his head. 'Not good odds. Not unless we can restore the balance some other way. What about cannon? How many pieces do you have?'

'None.' Barras shrugged. 'This is the seat of government, not a bloody arsenal.'

'Then we'll have to find some guns and bring them here.' Napoleon turned to Junot and snapped an order. 'There are cannon at the artillery park at Neuilly. Find some men – two companies should do – and bring back ten light pieces. We only need them to fire grapeshot.'

'It's too late for that,' Barras cut in. 'A royalist column is already on its way there.'

'Then we must beat them to it!' Napoleon's eyes flashed angrily. 'Unless you want to surrender the palace to them right now, citizen.'

'Of course not!' Barras drew himself up and placed a hand on his chest. 'I have dedicated my life to defending the republic.'

Napoleon drew a deep breath before he continued. 'We are not in the debating chamber now, citizen. We need actions not words. Better still, we need those guns.'

Carteaux jabbed a finger at him and sneered. 'And just how do you think we can get them? We're not at Toulon now, boy. You can't just pull the guns out of thin air. We've already done all we can.'

'So we sit on our arses and wait for them to come for us, eh?' Napoleon mocked him.

Carteaux jumped up from his chair and strode towards Napoleon, towering over him. He spoke through clenched teeth. 'Your Jacobin masters are not here to protect you now. I put up with your insolence far too long before. Now it's time we settled this.'

'Gentlemen!' Barras shouted. 'That's enough. We have enough enemies out there without making more in here. Sit down, Carteaux.'

The old general glared at Napoleon for a moment before he returned to his chair. There was a tense silence while tempers cooled a little and Napoleon realised that not one of the other officers had spoken since he had entered the office. Clearly the fight had already been knocked out of them. Someone needed to take charge of the palace's defences. They needed a plan if they were to stand any chance of beating General Danican and his rebels.

His thoughts were interrupted by the harsh clatter of heavy boots and he turned towards the sound as a cavalry officer swaggered into the office. He was a tall man with broad shoulders, long curly hair and bearded cheeks. Approaching the table he glanced round.

'Who is in command here?'

'I am,' Barras replied.

'No, I mean who is really in command?'

Napoleon took a step forward and cleared his voice. 'Citizen Barras has been charged by the assembly to defend the palace. But I have assumed command.' He turned to the other officers. 'Unless there are any objections?'

There was no reply, not even from Carteaux who stared fixedly at his long boots. Napleon nodded. 'Very well then. And who might you be?'

'Major Joachim Murat, of the hussars. I came as soon as I got word that the royalist scum were up to no good. I have brought two squadrons of my men with me.'

Napoleon's eyes lit up. 'Cavalry! Your men are ready to ride?'

'Well, yes.' Major Murat was taken aback. 'But we've only just got here.'

'There's no time to discuss this, Major. You must do exactly as I say. Do you know the artillery park at Neuilly?'

'Yes, sir.'

'Good. Take your men and ride there immediately. You must stop for nothing. Cut down anyone who gets in your way. Citizen Barras will write an order while you are gone to cover that. When you get there find me some guns – four-pounders – and plenty of powder and ammunition, particularly case shot. Then bring it straight back here. Have you got that?'

'Yes, sir.'

'Then go at once, Murat. The fate of France rests on your shoulders today. Remember that.'

'Yes, sir.' With a scrape of his boots Murat stood to attention and saluted Napoleon. Then he turned and strode from the room.

'Murat!'

'Sir?'

'Run, don't walk.'

Napoleon turned back to Barras. 'Citizen, if you would permit me, I would like to walk round the defences and see to the best disposition of our men.'

'Of course.' Barras nodded. 'Whatever you think best.'

'Once that's done, these officers will be assigned to the key points we are defending. They will need to hold them at all costs.' Napoleon turned to address them all. 'It is as I said to Major Murat. The fate of France is in our hands. Our hands, gentlemen. We must not fail. And we must not let our men think there is any doubt in our minds that we will beat the royalists. Do you understand me? Our men will look to us in the coming hours. Do not fail them. Show no fear and accept no dissent. Is that clear?'

The other officers nodded their agreement and Napoleon clapped his hands. 'Good. That's settled. Come, Junot. We have work to do.'

As they strode out of the room, Junot leaned towards his friend and muttered, 'Did you see their faces? You made them look like scared rabbits. Now they're eating out of your hand.'

Napoleon shrugged. 'They just needed someone to give them an order. Now I just hope they'll do their duty.'

The two of them made a thorough inspection of the defences of the Tuileries and Napoleon gave orders for the boarding up of the lowest windows and doors and the barricading of all but a few of the smaller entrances. Nearly all of the men looked nervous and he could understand their fear at the overwhelming odds they faced. But he did his best to inspire them, telling them again and again of the significance of the next few days, and that when it was over they would have stories to tell their grand-children and make them proud to be the bearers of an honoured family name. He also saw to it that the stores of powder and musket balls in the magazine were distributed to each strong-point, together with food and water to last each several days. Every time he glanced out into the streets surrounding the palace, Napoleon could see more and more of the royalists around the Tuileries as they prepared for the coming attack. But, other than the cautious figures moving behind cover, the streets were empty and silent.

Napoleon returned to Barras' office at noon and quickly assigned the officers to their positions. Even those senior to him in rank readily nodded their assent and hurried off to their posts. As the last of them left, Napoleon turned to Barras and saw that behind the earlier bluster of a politician the man was anxious, fearful even, and seemed resigned to defeat.

'Don't worry, citizen. We're in a strong position and the men are prepared to fight. When Danican makes his move in the morning he'll get far more than he bargained for. If we can cut down his men quickly enough, then they'll break and run for it.'

'And if they don't?'

'Then we will just have to defend the palace room by room.'

'I see.' Barras gave him a searching look. 'And are you prepared to die for the republic, Brigadier Bonaparte?'

'I am,' he replied firmly, then smiled. 'In any case, it makes no difference if I am willing to die for the republic or not. Our lives are in the hands of fate now. But I have to admit, I am intrigued to know what the outcome will be, once this fight is settled.'

'Intrigued?' Barras laughed. 'Good God, man! You're a cool one. And if we're both still alive at the end of it, then I will make sure that the nation knows your name.'

As the afternoon wore on, the royalists began to be more bold. Individual men crept closer to the Tuileries through the gardens, or climbed to the upper floors of neighbouring buildings, and took pot shots at any faces they saw at the palace windows. When the sun started to sink towards the distant rooflines Napoleon was squinting out across the gardens as Junot muttered, 'Doesn't look as if Murat managed to reach the guns. Danican's men must have got there first.'

'You'd better pray that they didn't. Otherwise they'll pound the Tuileries into rubble. In any case, you're being unfair to Murat.'

'Really, sir? I thought he looked like a typical cavalryman. Spoiling for a fight. All mouth and no mind.'

'Right now, perhaps that makes Murat the best man for the job. He's—'

Napoleon was interrupted by the crackle of gunfire from the far end of the Tuileries gardens. Through the trees lining the central avenue he glimpsed figures running to each side. Moments later a handful of mounted men charged down the avenue, brandishing the silvery curves of their sabres. Behind them came the guns, each limbered up and drawn by teams of horses. At the rear came the main body of Murat's cavalry. They halted halfway down the avenue to discharge their pistols and carbines as the braver souls amongst the royalists rose up to take a shot.

Napoleon turned to Junot. 'There, I was right about him. Come on!'

In the safety of the courtyard Murat had dismounted and was waiting by one of the guns he had snatched from under the noses of the rebels. As Napoleon and Junot approached he slapped the breech of the cannon with his leather gauntlets.

'Here are the cannon you requested.'

Napoleon laughed and grasped Murat's hand. 'Well done! Now we have them!'

'Was there any trouble?' Junot asked.

'Trouble? Oh, nothing much.' Murat shrugged indifferently. 'The other side almost beat us to it. There must have been three companies of militia. But they scattered at the first sign of a blade.'

Napoleon's gaze fell to the bloody gash on Murat's thigh, and he noticed that several of the other riders were injured as well. Clearly, there had been more to it than Murat had implied, but Napoleon had been in the army long enough to know that the best of the cavalry were inclined to such studied understatement. He turned to inspect the guns. Eight of them, all light pieces as he had ordered.

'Major, have your men position two of the guns on the terrace to cover the gardens and have the others taken to the courtyard at the front of the palace. I'll site each one personally.'

'Yes, sir.'

Before Murat turned away, Napoleon grasped his shoulder. 'That was a fine piece of work, Major. When this is over, you can be sure that everyone will know of Joachim Murat's role in the defeat of the traitors.'

'Yes, sir. Thank you, sir.' Murat could not contain a boyish smile. Then he saluted and turned to stride off and carry out his orders.

Night had fallen as the last of the cannon was eased into position behind the barricades at the main gateway leading out on to the Carrousel. The sky was thick with clouds and the air was cold and clammy, and as the first chill flecks of rain began to fall Napoleon gave orders for the powder kegs to be covered with waxed canvas. It was vital that the guns have dry powder ready for the next morning. Without artillery support the thinly spread government forces would not stand a chance.

Light glowed round the edges of the shutters of the royal suite where Barras had settled in for the night with his closest political associates, but Napoleon did not begrudge the man his creature comforts. It was better that Barras kept away from the men protecting the palace, in case he felt tempted to give any orders. A grenadier had found Napoleon a sword and another man lent Napoleon his greatcoat. At midnight, as the drizzle turned into steady, freezing rain, Napoleon settled with his back to the wheel of a gun carriage and pulled the thick woollen folds of the garment tightly about his shoulders. He willed himself not to sleep, in case the royalists attempted an attack under cover of the foul weather. But there was no sound other than the steady hiss as rain struck the cobbles in a shimmering film of tiny explosions.

The rain continued through the night and into the dawn as the men on watch duty stared into the gloom, tense and alert for any sign of attack. As the thin milky light spread across the Carrousel and revealed a handful of the royalists still sheltering behind their wagons, Napoleon roused Junot, who had fallen asleep an hour or so earlier, and told him to pass the word along the line to stand to. Sodden, shivering forms of men rose up stiffly behind the barricades and reached for their muskets. Their ears strained to pick up any sound of the approach of the royalist assault columns. But the streets were still as dawn gave way to dull daylight hemmed in beneath a thick blanket of dark rain clouds.

Junot returned from his errand and crouched down beside Napoleon.

'There's little sign of any movement around the palace, sir. Seems that Barras's information wasn't accurate.'

'Maybe not.' Napoleon scratched his chin and glanced up at the sky as the rain cleared away. For a moment a single shaft of light angled across the Carrousel from a fleeting gap in the clouds, and then it was gone. He smiled. 'Perhaps the rain has doused their spirits a little. After all, most of them are just part of the mob. Even the militia have little field experience. On a day like this, it'll be as much as they can bear to stick their noses outside the door.'

The morning wore on, and the defenders waited for the royalist attack with increasing impatience. Then, just before noon, the sound of drums drifted across the Carrousel. The men around Napoleon raised their muskets and levelled the muzzles on the barricades as they waited for the first of the rebels to appear. The beating of the drums gradually increased in volume and now they could hear the sounds of cheering, rising and falling in waves. Before the noise was loud enough to drown out his orders Napoleon rose up and cupped his hands to his mouth.

'No man will fire until the order is given! If blood is to be shed today, then let it be the fault of the royalists!'

There was a puff from behind the nearest wagon in the Carrousel and Napoleon ducked as a ball whined past his head.

'Well.' Junot grinned. 'That's the culpability issue settled. We can start killing the bastards as soon as we like.'

'Only when I give the order!' Napoleon snapped irritably, and was at once angry with himself for letting his nervous exhaustion reveal itself. He turned and called down the line. 'Gun crews! Stand to! Load with canister!'

The canvas covers were whipped back immediately as the gunners opened ammunition cases and took out the charges. As soon as they had been rammed home the packs of lead balls secured in tin containers were thrust down the muzzles up against the charge and the crews stood by their weapons.

The sound of the drums and the cheers of the approaching royalists echoed round the buildings facing on to the Carrousel, and then one of the men close by Napoleon thrust out his arm.

'Here they come!'

Chapter 6

The royalists spilled out of the avenue leading from the Rue Saint-Honoré and flowed into the Carrousel. At the head of the mob came a white-coated officer in a gaudy feathered hat. He was clutching a standard from which the sodden Bourbon colours hung limply. Behind him were a score of drummer boys, beating out a deafening rhythm. The men following them made no attempt at holding a formation as they strode boldly across the square towards the palace. The blue-coated militiamen were armed with muskets, as were many more of the royalist volunteers. The rest of the mob were armed with staves, axes, clubs and knives. Their cheering reached a climax now that their enemies were in sight.

Napoleon stood up and drew his sword, raising it high above his head. 'Prepare to fire!'

On either side the muskets came up, thumbed back to full cock, and the defenders squinted down the long length of their barrels towards the dense mass of rebels advancing towards them. The royalists made no attempt to stand in line and fire a volley. All along the front of the crowd there was a constant stabbing of flames and puffs of smoke as they fired freely. There was no chance to reload as those behind pressed the first rank on.

'Hold your fire!' Napoleon bellowed, keeping his arm erect. On either side musket balls whipped through the air, or splintered the wooden material in the barricade with sudden loud crashes. Close by, a young grenadier's head snapped back in a welter of blood that spattered across Napoleon's cheek as the body tumbled back on to the cobbles.

'Hold steady!' Junot shouted from nearby.

The crowd surged forward, the white-coated officer waving the banner from side to side to try to loosen its waterlogged folds and inspire his men. They were now close enough for Napoleon to see that he was an older man with a powdered wig beneath his bicorn hat.

When they were a scant fifty paces from the palace gate, Napoleon swept his sword arm down and roared out the command. 'OPEN FIRE!'

As the muskets spurted flame and smoke in a rolling volley the gun crews lowered their portfires on to the firing tubes and the cannon roared out, belching fire and great plumes of acrid smoke as they discharged a torrent of grapeshot into the mob. At once the infantry and the gun crews hurried to reload their weapons.

For a moment all sight of the rebels was lost in a thick bank of rolling gunpowder smoke. Then as the breeze dispersed it Napoleon could see the terrible impact of that first volley. The four cannon had cleared great lanes into the mob and left scores of dead and injured sprawled on the ground, and all along the front of the crowd many more of the rebels had been struck down by musket fire. Only one of the drummers was still beating his instrument. The others, like most of the crowd, stood aghast at the devastation around them. The cheering had died in their throats and they stopped dead. As the cries and screams of the wounded filled the air the spell was broken and the white-coated officer thrust his banner above his head.

'Charge! For France and the monarchy!'

He broke into a run, and the braver souls in the crowd surged forward after him, heading straight towards the barricaded gate, and Napoleon beyond. The two officers' eyes met for an instant and then Napoleon turned to give a fresh order to his men. 'Fire at will!'

The defenders fired on the crowd in a long, rolling crackle of shots that echoed back from the surrounding buildings and then the cannon boomed out again, dashing swaths of men to the ground. Miraculously the royalist officer still lived, and he paused at the barricade to plant his banner before he drew his sword and swept it overhead to rally his nearest men.

'Come on! One charge and the palace is ours!'

Junot calmly drew and cocked his pistol, stepped up to the barricade, thrust the weapon towards the man's chest, and fired. The royalist fell back, a livid red stain spreading across his white coat. His sword clattered to the ground as the standard slipped and fell into Junot's grasp. At once he snatched it and threw it on to the ground a short distance behind the barricade.

'First blood to us, and one colour already taken,' he called out to Napoleon.

But Napoleon's attention was fixed on the enemy. He was standing with the nearest cannon directing the crew to aim to the left, where a section of the mob, having managed to escape the earlier blasts of grapeshot, was edging towards the barricade. The sergeant in charge of the gun stepped back and fired the weapon. The concussion from the blast punched into Napoleon's ears as the cone of deadly lead shot cut the leading ranks to bloody shreds. All the time the infantry on either side of Napoleon loaded and fired their muskets into the mob at point-blank range, cutting the rebels down. Slowly, the mob stopped moving forward. A few amongst them still had the presence of mind to fire back, and some of them just waved their weapons and screamed with fury or tried to sound defiant as they cried their royalist slogans. But already scores of them were falling back, wide-eyed with horror at the slaughter and terrified of sharing the fate of the dead and mangled littering the cobbles of the Carrousel. The panic spread through the crowd like a wind rippling across a field of wheat and then they were all in retreat, more falling all the time as Napoleon's men continued to fire after them.

He waited until only a handful of the rebels were left, huddled down behind the wagons in the square, before he gave the order to cease fire. The last patches of smoke cleared and revealed to the defenders the full scale of the destruction they had caused. The ground in front of the palace was covered with the still forms of the dead and the writhing bodies of the injured. Blood pooled around them, and lay splashed over clothes and flesh. Thin cries of agony and low moans rose from the carnage.

'Good God, what have we done?' muttered one of the gunners.

'Our duty,' Napoleon responded curtly. 'And when they come back for more we must do it all over again. And again, until we break their will to continue this treachery. Now then, reload the cannon and stand by.'

The gunner nodded, still dazed by the awful scene stretching across the square, but carried out his orders as efficiently as if he were on an exercise. Napoleon rose up and called out to the rest of his command.

'Reload!'

The sound of ramrods rattling in the musket barrels briefly interrupted the cries of the injured and then all was still once more along the barricade in front of the palace. A quick glance either side showed that only five of his men were down, with a handful of wounded who were being helped inside the palace to the dressing station in the grand entrance hall. Napoleon quietly summoned Junot.

'Go to Barras. Tell him that we've repulsed the first attack. My guess is they'll try one of the other strongpoints next. Barras is to send runners to the other commanders to let them know we've beaten off the first attack. That should help to stiffen their resolve.'

Junot ran across the courtyard and disappeared into the palace, and Napoleon settled down to wait for the enemy to make their next move. The royalists wasted little time, and half an hour later there was a sudden burst of musket fire from the direction of the Riding School, punctuated by the dull blasts of cannon. For a moment the soldiers around Napoleon turned to face the noise with anxious expressions. The sounds of the assault soon faded away with a last crash of cannon fire that told them the defenders still held their position.

A few moments later Junot came hurrying back to Napoleon. 'They're coming back this way! Up the Rue Saint-Honoré.'

Napoleon thought for a moment, pulling at his ear lobe. The

royalists had been driven back twice already, and much of the fight must have been beaten out of them. Very well, this attack must be the last. This was the decisive moment, and when they broke they had to be pursued without mercy so that the rebellion would be utterly crushed.

Napoleon snapped an order to Junot. 'Find Major Murat. I want him and his men mounted and ready in the courtyard, out of sight of the barricades. They are to wait there for my order to move. Once they have the order they are to clear the Carrousel and pursue the enemy as far as they can. They are to take no prisoners and show no mercy to those traitors. Make sure he understands it. I want that mob out there to be in no doubt about the cost of defying the government.'

'Yes, sir.' Junot nodded, then ventured a question. 'And what if we don't hold them back? What are the major's orders then?'

Napoleon shook his head. 'It won't come to that . . . But, if it does, then Murat is to cover our withdrawal to the palace, and then look to his own survival.'

'Very well, sir.' Junot saluted and ran off, leaving Napoleon staring out across the barricade. It was possible that they might not beat off another attack, Napoleon considered briefly, then he shook his head irritably. No. There was no question of defeat. Junot was a fool to even think it.

The sound of the royalists marching back along the Rue Saint-Honoré grew louder and then the head of the column entered the Carrousel again. It was clear that someone had taken charge of the attackers this time, as a line of militia men formed across the square and, at the command, advanced steadily towards the palace. The rest of the mob spilled into the space behind the front line and cheered them on. Napoleon drew a deep breath.

'One last effort, lads! Make every shot count. Aim true and kill as many of the bastards as possible! Long live the republic!'

Some of the soldiers echoed his call before turning to face the enemy with intent expressions. The militia battalion reached the edge of the zone carpeted with bodies and discarded weapons and slowed down as they stepped over their fallen comrades. They halted fifty paces from the barricades and then their commander bellowed the order to prepare their weapons. The cocks clicked back, and the weapons came up at the order to present.

'Keep down!' Napoleon called out.

The defenders ducked behind the barricade. The order to fire was instantly drowned out by the crash of the volley and smoke immediately obliterated the militia as their musket balls rapped home against the barricade or whirred overhead. A sharp cry sounded to Napoleon's right but he ignored it and rose up to give his orders.

'Make ready! Open fire!'

Once again the muskets and cannon crashed out into the square, and so thick was the bank of smoke this time that the effect of the volley was not visible. As his men reloaded their weapons Napoleon heard the militia commander give the order to charge. Most of the defenders fired blindly into the smoke, until vague shapes flitted into sight and then burst through the smoke right in front of the barricade. Five or six men appeared directly before the cannon beside Napoleon and drew up wide-eyed at the sight of the muzzle gaping before them. An instant later the portfire touched the fuse and the men were shredded into bloody ribbons by the grapeshot.

The militia appeared all along the barricade, bayonets thrusting towards the defenders as the government troops rose up and defended themselves, using their bayonets or wielding their muskets like clubs. Napleon's sword was in his hand and his heart beat wildly as he stepped up to the barricade. To his left a grenadier was locked in a duel with a stocky man in a black cap, their bayonets scraping as each tested the other's strength. With a snarl the militiaman thrust the other's weapon aside and made to thrust his point home. Napoleon slashed his sword down on to the barrel and the point thudded harmlessly into a meal bag, tearing the material open instantly. The grenadier swung his butt up, smashing it into the militiaman's face, and he collapsed with a grunt. The grenadier grinned and nodded his thanks to Napoleon before turning to face the next attacker.

For a moment Napoleon found that he had no one to engage.

He glanced to both sides and saw that, even though his men were holding the line, the rest of the mob were piling into the rear of the militia battalion and soon the sheer weight of numbers must overwhelm the defenders.

Junot appeared beside him. 'Hot work.'

'Where's Murat?'

'He's entering the courtyard, over there.' Junot gestured with his arm.

'Then tell him to charge now. Now, or the fight is lost!'

When Junot had gone, Napoleon stepped back from the line and filled his lungs. 'Grenadiers! Gunners! Fall back to the palace! Fall back!'

His men obeyed at once, as best as they could. Some ran back from the barricade, others retreated with their weapons levelled, ready to fight off their pursuers. In the thick smoke along the fighting line the militia did not immediately realise what was happening and there was a moment's delay before a triumphant cheer swept through their ranks and they began to clamber over the rough barricade and charged after the government troops. Napoleon raced at the head of his men, making for the stairs that led up to the main entrance. He sprinted to the top and turned round to face his soldiers.

'Form up here! Quickly, damn you!'

The men turned and hurriedly shuffled into several ranks, bayonets lowered to receive the royalists streaming across the courtyard. More and more of them filled the open space, anxious to butcher the men who had caused them such grievous losses earlier on. But they never made it as far as the stairs. The sound of horses' hooves clattering across the courtyard stopped them in their tracks, the cries of triumph dying in their throats as they turned to see a line of hussars sweeping towards them, long curved blades resting on the riders' shoulders as they picked up more speed. At their head rode Murat, tall and imposing in his saddle. A short distance from the fringe of the loose mob he raised his sword into the air, then arced it down and leaned forward as he spurred his mount on.

The royalists turned and fled for their lives, throwing down their weapons as they ran, fighting with their comrades to get away from the dreadful fate carving its way through their ranks. From the stairs the defenders jeered their enemy. True to their orders Murat's men showed no mercy as they hacked and slashed at the men running before them, cutting them down in droves. Then they reached the line of the barricade and the slowly dissipating powdersmoke, leapt their mounts over the barrels and meal bags, and were swallowed up in the haze. And the sounds of the pursuit drifted away from the palace, across the square and back up the avenues running between the Rue Saint-Honoré and the River Seine.

Napoleon was suddenly aware of how cold and tired he felt and his sword hand trembled as it struggled to retain its hold on the hilt. As he sheathed the blade there was a clatter of footsteps behind him and Napoleon turned to see Paul Barras hurrying down the steps towards him, arms stretched as he smiled widely.

'Bonaparte! My dear Bonaparte! You've done it! They're running like the treacherous cowards they are. Murat will cut them down like vermin.' He reached Napoleon and flung his arms round his shoulders. 'France is saved. Thanks to you. All thanks to you.'

Around them, the soldiers turned away from the grisly carnage of Murat's pursuit and cheered, some of them raising their hats up into the air on the ends of their bayonets as they joined in the cheers for their commander standing a few steps above them, in the embrace of the most powerful man in France.

Chapter 7

Over the next two days the royalists' rebellion crumbled as the government troops hunted them down. Most had already fled into the suburbs and surrounding countryside where they could do no more harm. With the centre of Paris back under government control Barras moved quickly to disarm every quarter of the city, even those that had stayed loyal. All firearms, pikes and swords were to be handed in to the local town halls. As the people of Paris began to emerge back on to the streets Paul Barras announced his triumph to the National Assembly. He paraded the officers responsible for crushing the attempted coup, and publicly thanked them for their assistance in defeating the royalists. But even as he did so, Napoleon suddenly realised that not one of them had been singled out by name. Barras was determined to seize all the glory for himself, and would have done without an intervention from one of the deputies, who rose to his feet to propose a vote of thanks to 'General Bonaparte'. Struggling to hide his irritation, Barras conceded the vote. By the end of the next day all Paris knew of the brilliant officer who had saved France from the Bourbons, and to spare the people the confusion of explaining that Bonaparte was only in fact a brigadier, Barras rushed through his promotion to full general.

So it was that, a week after the storms of grapeshot had swept clear the ground in front of the Tuileries palace, Napoleon was sitting in a large, comfortably appointed office overlooking the same square. He found it hard to believe the improvement in his fortune that had occurred in the last few days. Barras had appointed him second in command of the Army of the Interior. On his greatly enhanced pay he had been able to move out of his squalid rooms in the slum quarter, and into a fine official residence in the hôtel de la Colonnade in the centre of the city. He had servants, a new carriage and horses and a beautifully cut new uniform, albeit lacking in the ostentatious gold braid that Major Murat seemed so fond of. No longer the obscure officer of artillery, Napoleon was now the most talked about man in Paris, invited to almost every ball and salon in the capital. Napoleon smiled to himself. Even the conceited Madame de Staël had condescended to send him an invitation to visit her house. Life was good, he mused. All he lacked now was an army posting worthy of his talents and ambition. That, and perhaps a wife.

There was a knock at the door and Napoleon pulled himself up in his chair and called out, 'Come!'

His secretary, a thin man with glasses, entered the office. 'General, there's a boy outside wishing to see you.'

'A boy? What's his name?'

'Eugène Beauharnais, he says.'

'Beauharnais?' Napoleon frowned. 'I don't know the name. Did he say what he wants to see me about?'

'A personal request, with regard to his late father's sword.'

Napoleon's curiosity was piqued by this information. He had been on the verge of sending the boy away, but he decided to spare this Eugène Beauharnais a moment of his time. 'Very well, I'll see him now.'

'Yes, General.'

The secretary disappeared and a minute later the door opened again to reveal a tall, handsome boy in his early teens. He had wide clear eyes, and a high forehead capped with curly brown hair. He bowed gracefully. 'Good morning to you, General Bonaparte.'

Napoleon nodded without rising from his chair. 'And to you, Citizen Beauharnais. How can I be of service? I'm told it's some matter relating to your father's sword?'

'Yes, sir. My mother has sent me with the request that the

family might be able to retain the sword.'

'I'm sorry, but you must know the terms of the Assembly's disarmament decree?'

'Indeed I do, sir.' The boy looked pained. 'But the sword is one of the few keepsakes that my family has to remember my father by.'

'What happened to your father?'

'He was guillotined last year, sir.'

'For what reason?'

'He was in command of the garrison of Metz when it fell. The Committee of Public Safety charged him with treason. And, well, you know how it was under Robespierre, sir.'

Indeed Napoleon did. Any military reverse was treated with suspicion and the representatives of the Committee were merciless in their punishment of failure in order to inspire other commanders to achieve success. And here was the human cost of such a strategy – the grief of a blameless family. Napoleon felt some compassion for the boy and his mother. They had already sacrificed enough for France without having to give up a precious memento of what they had lost.

'Very well, young Beauharnais. You shall keep the sword. It has already been surrendered, I presume.'

'It was taken from our house yesterday.'

'Then it will be at the nearest praefecture. Leave your address with my secretary and I will see that the sword is returned to you as soon as possible.'

The boy bowed his head. 'My sincerest gratitude, General. And my mother's as well.'

Napoleon smiled. 'Your mother must be proud of you, Beauharnais. I'm sure you'll grow up to be a fine soldier, and wear your father's sword at your side.'

'That is my ambition, sir.' Eugène smiled back before he turned to the door and made his way out of the office.

The next day, at noon, Napoleon received another visitor. Madame Josephine Beauharnais was shown into the general's office, and he automatically rose to his feet and bowed as gracefully as he could. His keen eyes examined her thoroughly the moment he straightened up. She had a tall, long-limbed body and a finely boned face with a small nose, slightly turned up. Her eyes were lively and scrutinised him in return.

'Madame, what can I do for you?'

She smiled. 'You have done enough for my family, General, by permitting us to keep my late husband's sword.'

Her voice was low and warm and Napoleon immediately felt himself intrigued by her tone and measured way of speaking. He waved a hand dismissively.

'It was the least I could do for the family of a fellow soldier. Just make sure that fine boy of yours follows in his father's footsteps.'

Josephine smiled faintly. 'Not as far as the guillotine, I would hope.'

Napoleon was taken aback by her morbid jest and laughed nervously. 'No. Of course not. Your family has already suffered enough for France,' he added grandly and mentally winced at his pompous tone.

'Well, yes, I suppose it has.' Josephine nodded. 'But times are hard when the nation is at war and death sweeps up everyone in its embrace, regardless of age, gender and innocence. And if the death of Robespierre had come much later, then I would surely have gone the way of my dear Alexandre, leaving my children helpless orphans.'

The woman had an artful turn of phrase, Napoleon decided. There was a very nicely worked huskiness to her last words. Unless it was genuine. He felt a flush of shame at his ungallant thoughts, and tried to cover his feelings by hurrying round the desk to pull out a chair for his guest. 'Please, madame, take a seat.'

'Thank you, General,' she replied, with a small catch in her voice. 'I'm sorry to appear before you like this. I assure you that I am not in the habit of being so . . . emotional.' She lowered her head, and Napoleon saw her shoulders trembling. As she leaned forward his eyes fell upon the smooth white flesh of her cleavage and as her chest heaved slightly with a sob he forced his embarrassed gaze away and stared fixedly at the top of her neatly pinned hair.

'Madame, please. There is no need to apologise. Not after all that you must have been through.'

'No, no! I must apologise. I only came here to thank you for your kindness, and I'm taking up your valuable time with my nonsense.' With a delicate flick of her hand she pulled out a lace handkerchief and dabbed at her eyes. 'I must go. I have no right to impose upon a man with such grave responsibilities. I'm sorry.'

Abruptly she rose from the chair, and Napoleon found himself suddenly looking directly into her eyes. There was intelligence in her expression, and a sensuality in the smooth curve of her lips. Scent filled his nostrils with a musky sweetness that stirred his loins. He took a step back and bowed his head.

'As you wish, madame. Do you wish me to have your carriage called for you?'

'Carriage?' She looked up and he saw the faint look of distress in her expression. 'I have no carriage, General. I walked here.'

'Ah . . . Then, please, allow me to call for mine. It will take you home.'

The corners of her lips lifted into a grateful smile. 'You are a most gallant man, my general. Once again, I am in your debt. Perhaps I might repay you by asking that you call on me?'

'Yes, I should like that. If it's not imposing?'

'It will be I who imposes, on the valuable time of France's hero.'

Napoleon opened his mouth to speak, but for once no words emerged and he strove for a reply before he blurted out, 'I'll come as soon as I can.'

Josephine smiled faintly. 'I'll look forward to it. I'll make sure your driver makes a note of my address.'

Then she turned and left, and as the door closed behind her Napoleon received one last waft of her scent. He breathed it in deeply before it had faded away, leaving only a memory of her that made his blood warm and his heart beat fast as he recalled the creamy whiteness of her breast.

Chapter 8

The following week Napoleon made sure that the malcontents of Paris realised that their uprising was over. Soldiers were posted at all the main road junctions and public buildings, and artillery pieces were openly positioned so that the main boulevards lay under their muzzles. At the same time he summoned regular troops from the Army of the Vendée and some of the depots to supplement the National Guard units in Paris.

But he did not forget his promise to the Beauharnais boy, and as soon as the sword was located Napoleon had it delivered to his office. Early the next day he set off in his carriage to the address on the Rue de la Chaussée-d' Antin. As the carriage pulled up outside a generously proportioned building Napoleon felt his pulse racing. He descended from the carriage carrying the sword, and hurriedly smoothed down his coat jacket and breeches, glancing at his boots to ensure that the glassy polish he had demanded from one of his servants was still unbesmirched. Then, taking a breath, he strode up to the door and rapped the large iron knocker. There was a short delay in which he had time to imagine that Josephine Beauharnais might not be at home, even this early in the day.

But then the door was opened by a mulatto woman wearing a bright red headcloth. She stared at him with narrowed eyes.

'Sir?'

'Is Madame Beauharnais at home?'

'She is.' The woman's voice had a peculiar sing-song lilt to it that Napoleon could not place. 'Who may I say is calling for her?'

'General Bonaparte.' Napoleon tilted his head back as he announced himself.

'General, you say?' The woman looked at him with an amused expression. 'Please wait in here, General, and I'll see if Madame will receive you.'

He was ushered to a low couch in the hall, just to the side of the door. There were two more seats against the opposite wall and Napoleon realised with a sinking feeling that Josephine must be in the habit of receiving many visitors. The light slap of bare feet on the staircase at the end of the hall drew his attention and he turned to see a young girl hurrying down the stairs towards him. Josephine appeared behind her and called out, 'Hortense! Back up here right now. I must comb your hair before you go out.'

'But Mother, I want to see the hero!'

Josephine looked past her daughter and flushed as she saw Napoleon. 'I'm so sorry. Please bear with me a moment.'

'Of course.' Napoleon could not help smiling. 'It seems you have a mutiny to suppress.'

Josephine raised her eyes. 'If you only knew. Now then, Hortense, back to your room.'

Her daughter took a last look at the visitor and trotted back up the stairs. Josephine took her hand firmly and nodded towards the couches. 'Please take a seat. I'll be with you in a moment.'

Once she had gone Napoleon waited in the hall, noting the faded curtains and worn thread of the rugs on the cracked tiles of the floor, clear signs of the declining fortunes of the Beauharnais family. At length the faint sounds of the girl's excited chatter faded and a door closed somewhere at the back of the house. A moment later he heard footsteps descending the stairs and looked up.

Josephine was wearing a silk gown, and looked to have little on beneath it from the way it clung to the curves of her body. Her hair had been carefully pinned back. Napoleon had to swallow before he could return the greeting she called out to him.

'So, my general has come to see me after all.' Her lips parted in a smile. 'I had feared we had been forgotten amid the public clamour for your attention.'

'I promised to bring your husband's sword, and here it is.' He offered the sword to Josephine. Her gaze passed over the scabbard and then she tenderly lifted it and held it to her chest.

'My thanks, General. You have no idea how much this simple blade means to me, to my family. I shall be for ever in your debt.'

There was an awkward silence before Napoleon coughed. 'Well, I suppose I had better take my leave.'

'Oh . . .' Her smile faded.

'Unless—'

'Please take some refreshment with me,' Josephine gushed. 'I mean, if you can spare me the time.'

Napoleon nodded. 'I will, thank you.'

Josephine glanced at the sword, looked round and then quickly lowered it, with a clatter, on to a marble-topped side table. Then she thrust open a door into a small, sparsely furnished parlour. 'In here, if you please.'

Napoleon entered the room and crossed to one of the pair of softly upholstered two-seater couches and eased himself down. It was even softer than it looked and he sank into the cushions. Josephine turned to face down the hall and called out, 'Hesther! Coffee in the small parlour.'

Then she entered the room and closed the door behind her, before crossing to the same couch as her guest and taking the spare cushion, so that their thighs were almost touching.

She looked at him with a concerned expression. 'General, are you quite well?'

'Yes. Fine. Why?'

'It's just that you look a little feverish.'

'I'm very well, thank you. It's warm in here.'

'So? That must be it.' She patted his knee. 'No need for me to worry then.'

He shook his head and forced a smile; then, aware that his gaze was lingering on her body for longer than was seemly, he glanced away, around the room, and saw a miniature portrait in a frame on the mantelpiece. He stood up and approached it.

'Isn't that Paul Barras?'

'Yes. He's a good friend of mine.'

'I thought I recognised the face,' Napoleon responded. In truth the miniature flattered Barras. 'Your friend, you say?'

'Paul has been good to me. Since my husband was executed, he has been my gallant protector. It was Barras who returned most of the property that was confiscated after Alexandre's death. I owe him a lot. And now he owes you far more, it seems.'

'Nonsense. I was just doing my duty.'

'Of course. But that does not change the fact that without your intervention it was more than likely that Paul would have lost his head.'

Napoleon shrugged.

The door opened and Hesther entered the room with a silver tray bearing two steaming cups of coffee. She set the tray down on a side table and left the room. Josephine patted the cushion next to her.

'Come. Sit down and have your coffee. I have it made strong and sweetened with two spoons of sugar. Black as the devil and sweet as a stolen kiss, as they say in Martinique. I hope you like it.'

Easing his back into the cushions, Napoleon took the proffered cup and cautiously sipped the dark contents. It was hot, but not too hot, and the flavour was surprisingly smooth and pleasing.

'It's good. Very good.'

Josephine smiled. 'I'm so pleased you like it. I think we shall discover that we have a great deal more in common in the future . . .'

As autumn gave way to winter Napoleon found as much time as he could to see the woman who had such a hold over his emotions and his desire. A few days after he had delivered the sword he was invited to dinner and arrived to discover that he was the only guest. The meal was a fascinating example of a cuisine she called Creole, far more spicy and exotic than the fare Napoleon normally allowed himself. They dined by the light of a handful of candles and a small fire in the grate and the conversation flowed as freely as the hands of the clock standing in the corner, which seemed to Napoleon to fly round the hours until it was past midnight. Napoleon called for his carriage, and as they stood on the short flight of steps outside her house Josephine suddenly raised her hands to his shoulders and gently drew his face towards hers for a kiss.

As their lips touched Napoleon felt a warm quiver of delight ripple through his breast. At first he dared not move his lips too insistently, but as she pressed hers against his mouth his lungs filled with her scent and the aroma of her hair and body. He felt her soft body against his and gave in to his passion for this bewitching woman, reaching his hands round to the small of her back and pulling her into his embrace. Then he felt her tongue, softy searching between his lips, and he closed his eyes, knowing that nothing had ever been more perfect than this moment, nor ever would be.

As their lips parted, he nuzzled her cheek, then her neck, and whispered into her ear, 'Josephine . . . my love.'

'No more Madame Beauharnais?' she teased him with a whisper.

'You are Josephine now. My Josephine.'

'I like that.' She kissed him again, and murmured, 'Don't leave now. Stay until morning . . .'

In November, the rest of Napoleon's family arrived in Paris. He had sent word of his success to his mother, Letizia, at the house she had been renting near Marseilles. She was still bitter at having lost her home and possessions when the family had been forced to flee from Corsica two years earlier. Napoleon and his brothers, who shared his revolutionary politics, had taken a stand against Pascal Paoli, who – with English backing – was now virtual dictator of the island, and the family had only just escaped the murderous rage of a Paolist mob. Napoeoln knew that his mother blamed their misfortune on France in general, and the revolution in particular. Yet it was the same revolution that had given Napoleon the chance to prove himself and he was keen to show his mother, and the rest of his family, the results of his fame and good fortune. Now he could afford to keep them all in comfort.

When his older brother, Joseph, stepped through the door of Napoleon's new home and beheld him in the uniform of a general, tears of selfless pride pricked at the corners of his eyes before he hugged his brother.

'If only Father could see you now!'

Napoleon nodded. Their father, Carlos, had sacrificed much to send his two oldest sons to good schools in France. It had been a cruel fate that he died too soon to see their success.

Joseph released Napoleon and stood aside to allow Letizia and the other brothers and sisters to crowd round. There was Lucien, the next boy, who had already made a reputation for himself in Marseilles, espousing the radical politics of the Jacobin party. Louis and Jérôme were already attending a school near Paris. His sisters, Caroline, Pauline and Élisa, stood round him, admiring his best uniform coat with the gleaming braid that marked him out as a general.

Letizia held off until the last before she kissed her son formally on each cheek. 'I knew you had it in you to achieve greatness. But keep your feet on the ground, my boy. There are people in this world who will try to use you and your new position for their own ends.'

'Mother!' Napoleon laughed. 'I am a grown man now. I know how to look after myself.'

'You are your father's son,' she replied wearily. 'And I know how easily led he was.'

Napoleon frowned. 'I am no fool, Mother.'

'We'll see.'

In view of her smothering attitude it was nearly a month before Napoleon revealed to his family that he intended to get married.

Chapter 9

'Congratulations, sir!' Murat grinned as he strode up to them in the hall of Madame Sinoir's house. 'She's a lucky woman.'

Napoleon's blood froze and he sensed his mother bristle beside him as he replied, 'Thank you, Murat.'

'Well, can't stop, sir. Some of us bachelors still have a busy love life.'

'Yes.' Napoleon glared. 'I shan't keep you.'

Whistling off key to himself, Murat strode away and Napoleon quickly steered his mother to the doorway leading through to the salon.

'You're getting married?' Letizia said loudly as they entered the crowded room. 'To whom?'

Some of the other guests at the salon turned briefly to look at Letizia before returning to their conversations. Napoleon winced and his mother instantly noticed the gesture.

'It was your idea to bring me here. Kindly do me the courtesy of not being embarrassed by my presence. Especially since it is only now that you tell me this news.'

'Yes, Mother.' Napoleon had been putting the moment off for as long as possible, even after he had arranged to bring her to the salon to be introduced to Josephine.

'So then. Who is this woman you think you want to marry?'

'Her name is Josephine Beauharnais.' Napoleon replied calmly. 'She's a widow with two children, well connected, intelligent and witty. She will be a fine wife, and one day I hope she will be the mother of my children. And she's over there.'

Napoleon nodded to a table where Josephine was playing cards with Paul Barras and two young cavalry officers.

Letizia squinted for a moment. 'She looks older than you.'

'She is,' Napoleon admitted.

'And she's flirting with that man.'

'That's Paul Barras. He's an old friend of hers.'

'More than that, I should say,' Letizia muttered.

Napoleon frowned, and then abruptly turned and waved a hand to attract Josephine's attention. She looked up from her cards and smiled at him. Napoleon beckoned, and after a brief word of apology to her male companions she rose from her seat and crossed the room to join him.

'You wanted me, my love?'

'Yes.' Napoleon felt his heart lift at her words. 'I'd like you to meet my mother.'

Josephine smiled graciously and bowed her head. 'I have heard so much about you, and the rest of the family, from Napoleon. I feel I almost know you already.'

'And I know almost nothing of you,' Letizia replied flatly, in her heavy Coriscan accent. 'But I will make sure that I find out everything I can about you.'

'Mother . . .'

'Oh, don't fret!' She turned back to Josephine with a forced smile. 'I'm just keen to know more about any person who might join our family. I'm sure you understand?'

'Of course,' Josephine replied. 'It's a natural instinct for any mother. Especially the mother of one of France's most promising soldiers.'

'Precisely. It is important that Napoleon marries well. To someone deserving of his fame.'

Napoleon felt his insides clench with embarrassment. He wished he had never suggested this meeting. But it had to happen, he realised. A man's family and his wife could not be kept apart for ever. Unfortunately. He glanced at Josephine and gave a slight shake of his head to indicate that she should not take his mother's brusqueness to heart.

'I see,' Josephine replied evenly. 'Madame Bonaparte, I can

assure you that my family is as respectable as any in France, and has been for many generations.' She paused, then continued in a warm tone, 'As I am sure you will come to realise once you have settled into Paris. You must be finding it difficult to adjust to such a sophisticated world after spending a lifetime in Corsica, no?'

Letizia glared back at her, as Josephine went on, 'I should be delighted to introduce you and your family to Paris, if you would like. It can be quite bewildering to provincials, and of course it would be a pleasure to help the family of my husband to settle into polite society.' She smiled sweetly, then turned towards Napoleon and slipped her hand through his arm.

'Napoleon,' Letizia said hurriedly. 'I find that I am tired. Please would you take me home.'

'But we've only just arrived.'

'Well, it seems I am not well. Come,' she said.

Napoleon nodded and gave Josephine's hand a gentle squeeze. 'I'll see you later.'

She nodded, and turned back to Letizia. 'It was a pleasure to meet you, Madame Bonaparte. However briefly.'

'Oh, I am sure that we will have plenty of time to become thoroughly acquainted with each other,' Letizia replied as she took hold of Napoleon's arm. 'Please excuse us. I am sure your gentlemen friends are missing your company.'

Josephine smiled a farewell and turned away. As soon as she was out of earshot Napoleon whispered to his mother, 'What do you think of her?'

'I don't think she is for you.'

'She is for me,' Napoleon replied earnestly. 'She is all I ever wanted in a woman.'

'I will not discuss this here, in front of these people. Later, when we get home.'

Napoleon folded his arms and leaned against the window frame as he faced his mother, Joseph, Lucien, Caroline and Élisa, sitting in the chairs of his small study.

'What is the reputation of this woman?' Letizia shot at him. 'If we were in Ajaccio I would know of her at once and be able to decide if she was worthy of you. But here in Paris? Hardly anyone has a good reputation from what I have seen. Women disport themselves like whores. So, I ask you again, Napoleon, what is her reputation?'

Napoleon felt a stab of anger tear through his heart and had to bite down hard to stop himself from swearing. The moment passed and he responded quietly, 'This is not Ajaccio, Mother. This is Paris, and life is lived differently here. The old ways are gone, and people express themselves in a more liberal manner now.'

'Liberal manner, indeed. Pouf! It's licentiousness, pure and simple, and Corsicans are better than that.'

'Mother,' Joseph intervened. 'For better or worse, we are French now. We have to live by a different standard.'

'Lower our standards, you mean.'

Joseph ignored her and turned to his younger brother. 'The important question is, does Napoleon love her? And does she love him?'

'Love?' Letizia laughed. 'What do either of you know of love? Sound reasons for marriage come first, love grows later. Depend upon it, that's how marriages work. If you do it the wrong way round it is merely a childish infatuation that quickly passes and all that is left is a marriage certificate and a lifetime of duty. Napoleon!'

'Yes, Mother?'

'This Beauharnais woman, what do you know of her?'

Before Napoleon could reply, Lucien coughed and stirred. 'I have heard something of her.' He smiled. 'I've been spending some time at the Jacobin club, finding out as much as I can about the political terrain, as it were.'

'Really?' Letizia stared at him. 'Is that wise, given your nose for trouble?'

Lucien looked down at his shoes, shamed by the memory of the ill-timed radical pamphlet he had written that had done so much to ruin the family's fortunes in Ajaccio.

His mother tapped her foot impatiently. 'Well? What do you know of this woman? Speak up.'

'She is well connected indeed, just as Napoleon said. Until very recently she was the mistress of Paul Barras.' His eyes flickered towards his brother leaning against the window frame. 'Some say that she still is.'

'Then they are fools,' Napoleon replied tersely. 'She is mine and mine alone, and she wants to be my wife.'

'Of course she does,' Letizia said. 'Who else would be fool enough to have her?'

'Enough!' Napoleon took a stride forward, his hand cutting through the air. 'I have decided to marry her and that is an end to it! You will not question my decision, Mother.'

'I will do what I like, my boy. And when is this farce going to be made legally binding?'

'I don't know,' Napoleon admitted. 'We haven't settled on a date yet.'

'Well I should, and soon. I imagine that Paris folk are not inclined to respect the sanctity of the marriage bed. Best to get yourself married before any bastards spoil things.'

'We are already lovers, Mother.'

There was no expression of surprise or horror on Letizia's face, just a look of disdain and disgust. 'I see. In that case you leave me no choice. Marry the woman and be done with it. Just never expect me to be her friend, or to approve your choice. You've soiled your bed. Now you must lie in it.'

Napoleon forced a smile. 'You give your blessing then?'

'Yes,' she replied through clenched teeth.

Joseph stood up and grasped his brother's hands. 'May I be the first to offer my congratulations?'

His face was sincere and for the first time in years Napoleon felt the grateful affection he had known as a small child at the school in Autun where Joseph had done everything in his power to protect his prickly young brother.

'Thank you,' he said.

After a moment's hesitation Lucien rose to his feet and joined his brothers. 'I offer my best wishes as well. If she's as well connected as I hear, she will be a useful ally to have in Paris. Don't worry about what I said about Paul Barras. Most of those

I spoke to said he had grown tired of her and was grateful to have her off his hands.'

Napoleon stared at him for a moment before replying in a tone of strained calm. 'Thank you for that, Lucien. It's a comfort to know.'

Letizia snorted and rose from her chair. 'Good luck and good riddance. I'll leave you three fools to yourselves, then.'

She stormed from the room, shutting the door loudly behind her. The brothers exchanged a look and then Napoleon burst into laughter.

Even as he wooed Josephine Napoleon did his best to ingratiate himself with her children. Despite his gifts and the efforts he made to befriend them Napoleon sensed their reserve. It was only natural, he reflected. The memory of their father's arrest, trial and execution was still fresh in their minds and their mother's latest suitor must compare unfavourably with the tall, well-mannered soldier whose cultured tones and noble bearing were fixed in their memories. On the other hand, Napoleon comforted himself, they could not but prefer him to the glib politician, Barras.

Napoleon saw Josephine almost every day, even though he was embroiled in organising the morass of details that needed to be drawn together and given shape so that the armies of the republic could fight and defeat the enemy. His particular field of expertise related to the Army of Italy and the problem of driving Austria out of the northern areas of the Italian peninsula and claiming them for France. The more he considered the matter the more Napoleon convinced himself that Austria could be beaten, provided his plans were carried through with sufficient dash by the officer who was entrusted with command of the Army of Italy.

One day, as he was walking in the Tuileries garden with Josephine and had just dealt with yet another group of well-wishers, overawed to meet the soldier who had saved the government from the mob, he turned to her and said sadly, 'Your children, I think, would rather you did not marry me.'

'They are children.' Josephine shrugged. 'Their hearts will

change, given time. They will come to know you well enough to appreciate your qualities.' She slipped her hand under his arm and squeezed it. 'Be patient, my dear.'

'I would be patient, if I could only control my heart. I want you so much that I would marry you this day if I could. But I am afraid that if your children bear me any ill will it will act as a wedge in your affections. Perhaps we should delay our wedding for a while.'

She stopped and turned on him quickly. 'Delay? Why?' Her eyes narrowed. 'What is it, Napoleon? Do you no longer love me?'

'Yes! Yes, of course I do.' He cupped her cheek in his hand. 'Never doubt that. I just want to be sure that nothing stands between us when we become man and wife. I swear that's all I meant. I should like to have the chance to achieve something that Eugène and Hortense could be proud of, so that they would be pleased that you married me.'

Josephine smiled briefly.

'What is it?'

'Oh, just something I heard the other day. A rumour,' she added quickly. 'You might get that chance sooner than you think.'

'Why?'

'I will not say. I am sworn to secrecy.'

'Tell me.'

'No.' She pressed a finger to his lips. 'You'll see. I won't say any more for now. But we must not worry about the children. When they see how happy I am I promise you they will be happy for me, and accept you.'

'I hope so,' Napoleon replied, but his mind had already moved on to other things. What was this rumour that Josephine had mentioned?

Early in the new year they settled on a June date for their wedding. Napoleon would be busy until then co-ordinating the military effort in Italy. After that he would take leave and they would honeymoon in Normandy. Or so they thought, until Napoleon was summoned to the Tuileries for an interview with

Paul Barras. It was late in January and cold rain swept the streets of the capital. As his coach drew up in the courtyard Napoleon pulled up his collar and dived out, trotting quickly up the steps into the entrance hall. Barras was alone in his office when the young general was ushered inside. He dispensed with formalities and waved Napoleon to the chair opposite his desk.

'How are the preparations coming for the new campaign?'

Napoleon instantly collected his thoughts as he made his report. 'The operational plan is complete. My staff has calculated the logistical requirements and rations and ammunition should be arriving at the forward depots this week. However, General Masséna reports that all three divisions of the army urgently require fresh drafts of replacements as well as boots, uniforms, muskets and their back pay. Otherwise he cannot guarantee the success of the campaign.'

Barras nodded his head and smiled indulgently. 'That's all I seem to hear from our generals these days. Constant demands for more men and more supplies or all is lost. The army appears to have been struck down by an epidemic of exaggeration. Tell me, General, if you were in Masséna's boots, and you could not count on all the things he has asked for, what would you do?'

Napoleon raised his eyebrows. 'If France could not supply what I needed then I would take my supplies from somewhere else. The north of Italy is a prosperous land. They have productive farms and wealthy cities. An army could live off the land very comfortably indeed.'

'I see. Then you would make the people we saved from Austrian domination pay for the privilege. Hardly an ethical proposition.'

'War is not ethical, citizen.'

Barras took a deep breath. 'Perhaps it is best for both of us that you are a soldier, Bonaparte. As it is you have become something of an idol for our people. Perhaps it would be best if you were found employment outside Paris. Your fame is making the politicians nervous.'

'Citizen, I am loyal to the republic.'

'I know that,' Barras replied with a quick smile. 'But there are some men who have always been unnerved by the popularity of our military heroes, and they are watching you carefully, even now. As much for your own protection then, you must be found a position some distance from the centre of power.'

Napoleon sensed the direction the discussion was about to take and leaned forward to tap his finger loudly on Barras's desk. 'I will *not* be sent to the Army of the West.'

'You will do as you are ordered, General,' Barras said firmly. He held up his hand to forestall any angry response. 'However, that is not the decision I have made. As it happens, I want to offer you the command of the Army of Italy.'

Napoleon was stunned. This was the opportunity that his entire military career so far had been working towards. The chance to put all his ideas to the test, to ensure that the planned campaign was conducted precisely according to his intentions. Then a cold suspicion filled his thoughts and he looked at Barras with narrowed eyes.

'Why me? There are plenty of other men to choose from.'

'You drew up the plans for the coming campaign, and I think you have the qualities that will ensure the best chance of success. This campaign may make your reputation. If you succeed, then, of course, I will take credit for choosing you for the command.'

'And if I fail?'

'Then it will be the end of any military or political ambitions you may have. Do you accept the post?'

'Yes,' Napoleon replied at once. 'And I will not fail France.'

'Very well,' Barras replied with a relieved expression. 'I will have the necessary papers drafted. There's little time before the campaign season begins. You must take up the command before April. Can you be ready by then?'

'Of course, citizen. I will need to brief my subordinates at the bureau and select my staff officers. There are some personal matters that need to be attended to as well.'

'So I have heard. Congratulations.'

'Thank you.' Napoleon smiled ruefully. 'Though I dare say Josephine will not thank me for pre-empting our plans.'

'I think you will find that Madame Beauharnais is sufficiently adaptable to cope. I know her well enough to assure you of that.'

★

In the short time that was left Napoleon flew through the many tasks that required his attention before he could take up the command. He offered posts on his headquarters staff to Murat and Junot and requested the recall of Marmont from the Army of the Rhine. The position of Chief of Staff was given to General Berthier, a colleague from the bureau of topography who had sound administrative skills. Uniforms were ordered, horses purchased, a travelling library selected and arrangements made for the care of his family while he was away on campaign. More important still was the need to bring forward the wedding and find a home for his new wife.

Late in the afternoon of 9 March, in a register office close to the new house Napoleon had leased on the Rue Chantereine, there was a small gathering of family and friends. Josephine arrived first, accompanied by Paul Barras who had offered to be one of the witnesses. Napoleon was over an hour late, delayed by the need to reply to some urgent dispatches. He hurried into the register office, flushed and breathless, still in his plain uniform coat. Letizia, who had been enjoying the delay, hoping that her son had at last seen reason, slumped back on her chair in dejection.

'If we may proceed?' the registrar said impatiently.

'By all means,' Napoleon panted, and the official went through the procedure in a weary monotone.

Josephine dug him in the ribs and whispered fiercely, 'Thanks for making me look a fool in front of my friends.'

Napoleon glanced round and could see only Barras and a handful of others. He whispered back, 'Those who could be bothered to come, at least.'

'You swine.'

'We're here,' Napoleon whispered softly. 'That's all that matters, my love.'

'I had hoped for something grander than this.'

'There was no time to organise anything else,' Napoleon protested. 'Some day, we'll make it more formal, I swear it. A ceremony you can be proud of to your dying day.'

The registrar coughed and leaned towards them. 'If you don't mind, I'd rather complete the formalities before you have your first matrimonial row.'

'Yes, of course.' Napoleon blushed. 'I'm sorry.'

The registrar glared at him for a moment before returning to his script and continuing with the ceremony. When it was over, Napoleon and Josephine signed their names, witnessed by Barras and Joseph. There was a small reception in the new house before the guests left and the newly wed couple retired to their bedroom and closed the door behind them.

'Still angry with me?' Napoleon smiled, his fingers gently untying the straps of her bodice. She stood stiffly before him, trying to keep her face fixed in a stern expression of rebuke.

'Of course.'

'Well then, let us see whether I can persuade you to forgive me . . .'

Two days later, as dawn broke over Paris, Napoleon stepped out of the house he had lived in for barely a week. Outside in the street Junot was waiting for him, holding the reins of their horses. The rest of the staff and his baggage had been sent ahead a few days earlier and there would be a long hard ride before they caught up with them. Napoleon swung up into his saddle, adjusted his reins and then turned to look at the bow window on the first floor. Through the glass he could see Josephine gazing down at him, her arms clasped about her body as if she were cold. Their eyes stayed fixed on each other for a moment, and Junot, sensitive to their need, turned his horse away and made for the end of the street. Napoleon mouthed words of his love, then waved one hand in a gentle gesture of farewell and rode off to war.

Chapter 10

Arthur

Dublin, 1795

After the frozen horrors of the campaign in the Low Countries, Lieutenant Colonel Arthur Wesley returned to Dublin with a warm sense of familiarity and comfort. He was gaunt and thin after the harrowing experience of the campaign and his eyes seemed sunken on either side of his large hooked nose. Exercise and hearty eating would soon restore him to his normal athletic build, but the callowness of youth had been left behind on the battlefield and he was filled with determination to improve himself, and defend his country from the ravenous appetite of revolutionary France.

Even though he had been glad to quit his role as aide-de-camp at the castle to lead the 33rd regiment of foot against the French, the terrible reality of war had taught Arthur to appreciate the easy-going life he had lived before. There would be no more of the stomach-gnawing hunger, no more of the cold that penetrated to the core of his being and made surrendering to its final embrace so tempting. For the present he was at home, amongst friends, and most important of all he would have the chance to see Kitty Pakenham again. Since moving into the family house in Rutland Square, Kitty had become a frequent visitor to the court in Dublin Castle, and Arthur, like many other young gentlemen, had quickly fallen under the spell of her gentle, teasing nature and indefinable charm. He had not seen her for several months, and as he made his way from his modest lodgings in Fostertown to the new Lord Lieutenant's suite of offices in Dublin Castle, he indulged in the memory of the light brown curls that surrounded the delicate features of her face. He recalled, with a quickening pulse, the fine whiteness of her complexion and the faint scent of her skin as he had kissed her on the balcony outside the ballroom of Dublin Castle one night the previous summer.

Then the spell was broken as he recalled the harsh rebuff he had received from Kitty's brother, Tom, when he had asked for her hand in marriage. As a younger brother of the Earl of Mornington, Arthur had no inheritance and lived on his army pay, an allowance from his eldest brother, Richard, and whatever he could borrow from the family's land agent in Dublin. Hardly a decent prospect for Kitty, he conceded. Unless he could make a name for himself as a soldier or a statesman he was doomed never to win her. Just as fate had denied him an inheritance, it had also withheld the intellectual brilliance that had been so generously apportioned to his brothers, especially Richard and young Henry. While Richard was a rising star in Pitt's government, and had recently been appointed to the Board of Control of the Indian Colonies, Henry had already embarked on a promising diplomatic career. Arthur felt a stab of frustration at his lack of advancement.

Even though England was at war, her army was small and dispersed across the world and there were few opportunities to win swift promotion and fame. The situation of his rivals in France was very different, Arthur reflected. With the aristocrats swept away the field was open for men of talent. Like that fellow Arthur had read of in a newspaper account of the siege of Toulon. He frowned for a moment and then recalled the name of the artillery officer who had masterminded the French victory. Bonaparte. A man of the same age as Arthur, and already a brigadier. If their situations had been reversed Arthur felt certain he would have achieved as much, and for a moment he was aware of a bitter resentment of the enemy officer's good fortune. Then he pulled his heavy army coat more tightly round his shoulders, and exchanged a salute with the sentries guarding the castle entrance, as he trudged inside.

In addition to his light duties as an aide to the Lord Lieutenant, Arthur had resumed his seat as member of parliament for Trim, and was resolved to make something of a political career for himself, since the army provided little opportunity of advancement for the moment. He had requested this interview with Lord Camden with a view to being given a prominent office in the Irish parliament. It would be an opportunity to gain the experience he would need when he followed his older brother Richard into the English parliament and on to the first rung of the political ladder at Westminster. In the shorter term it would also lead to a significant increase in his income, enough perhaps to impress Tom Pakenham.

Making his way into Lord Camden's suite of offices, Arthur presented himself to the Lord Lieutenant's duty aide, a young cavalry lieutenant in a smartly cut jacket and long, gleaming boots. His face, thin and fresh, was unfamiliar and Arthur realised that he must be a recent appointment, enjoying his first posting. For a moment Arthur felt a twinge of envy as he saw himself several years earlier – free of the burdens of mounting debt and anxiety over the dwindling prospects of a worthy career.

'Sir?' The lieutenant addressed him. 'May I help you?'

'I have an appointment with his lordship. Lieutenant Colonel Wesley.'

The aide bent over the diary on his desk and ran a finger down the entries until he found the name, and the note beside it. 'Ah, yes. Please follow me, sir.' He rose from his chair, crossed to a door and knocked sharply before opening it. 'Lieutenant Colonel Wesley, my lord.'

'Send him in.'

Lord Camden was standing at the window, gazing down into the courtyard and sipping from a brandy glass. He turned as Arthur entered and frowned.

'Let me guess. You want me to find you some lucrative employment. Well? Since I've arrived here I've been deluged with office-seekers. So what's your claim on me, eh?'

Arthur was taken aback by the instant incivility of the man. 'My lord, I merely wish to serve my country in some capacity that will be mutually rewarding. I see no wrong in that.'

'You wouldn't. I'm the one who has to field all the requests from ambitious young men like you. If that wasn't bad enough, I'm bombarded with letters of recommendation from mothers, brothers, fathers, friends of fathers and fathers of friends and so on and so on, caught like a fly in a web of nepotism. No laughing matter, I can assure you.'

'I can imagine,' Arthur replied tactfully.

Lord Camden fixed him with narrowed eyes. 'Oh really? I shouldn't think you would have to exert your imagination. Your brother has already written to humbly request an office worthy of your qualities of . . . of . . .' He paused, paced over to his desk and fanned through a pile of letters until he found the one he wanted. 'Ah! Here it is . . . your qualities of industry and integrity. Hardly a ringing endorsement, is it? But since your brother is racing up through the political ranks in London and I may well have need of his patronage for my own family and friends one day, I'll see what I can do for you, Wesley. Did you have a position in mind?'

'Yes, my lord,' Arthur replied evenly. But inside his heart was beating swiftly and he felt the anxious excitement of any man about to request the most generous of favours.

'Well, spit it out, man.'

'My lord, since the office of Secretary at War is not yet filled, I would like to be considered for it.'

Lord Camden raised his eyebrows and stared at Arthur for a moment before he recovered from his surprise enough to reply. 'Upon my soul, you don't ask for much, do you? Secretary at War? What on earth makes you think I should consider you for such an important position?'

It was Arthur's turn to be shocked by open candour. 'I believe I am well matched to the duties and responsibilities of the post, my lord. I have several years of military experience.'

Lord Camden wagged a finger at him. 'You have several years' experience as an aide. Drinking, dancing, gambling and whoring. What bloody good is that?'

'I served under the Duke of York in the Low Countries. I have been under fire, my lord, and led my men to safety in the following retreat.'

'So you were roundly thrashed? And you think that is supposed to support your application? I'm looking for a Secretary at War, not a Secretary at Retreat, Wesley. Face facts, man. You are too young and too inexperienced for the job. Besides, even if you were the best soldier in Ireland it still wouldn't matter. I need an experienced politician, not a soldier. Bloody country is on the verge of revolt. I have Grattan and his cronies pushing for reform on one side and the rump of the Tories pressing me to stamp down on the reformers on the other. I have to find a man who can handle both camps with aplomb. Do you really think you could do that?'

He stared hard at Arthur and the latter knew that his bluff had been called. And it wounded his pride painfully to accept that Lord Camden was right in his judgement of him.

'I see that you understand me, Wesley. Don't take it badly. Besides, it's not as if you're the first man to apply for the post. Half these letters are in support of far better candidates than you, and many of their sponsors are much better connected than your brother Richard.'

Arthur felt a pit of despair open inside as he took in the implications of what Lord Camden was saying. Arthur lacked the connections that would give him a chance to secure the position, and he was dismayed, not just by this rebuff, but by his longer term prospects within a system so bound up with mutual favours exchanged between powerful families. It was not fair, but he forced his expression to remain composed. Even though there was no justice or logic to the system, there was no profit in protesting against it. Arthur needed employment now. He cleared his throat.

'Very well, my lord, if I am not to be Secretary at War, then perhaps I might be considered for another position. A seat on the treasury or revenue boards would be well within my capabilities.'

'I'm sure it would,' Lord Camden agreed. 'I will see what I can find for you. As a favour to Richard. I'll let you know the instant I have anything.' He stood to one side and stretched his arm out loosely in the direction of the door, and Arthur took the hint and bowed his head in farewell.

'My thanks to you for seeing me at such a busy time, my lord.'

'My pleasure, Wesley,' Lord Camden replied automatically. 'Do please pass on my very best wishes to your brother when you next write to him.'

'Yes, my lord.' Arthur nodded and turned to leave the office. He marched out stiffly.

As he left the castle it began to rain and Arthur pulled up his collar and wedged his bicorn down tightly over his head. It was time, he told himself, to speak to Kitty. He had not seen her since he had left for the ill-starred campaign in the Low Countries. Even if her brother had refused to let them marry, he could at least find out if her heart was still his.

Chapter 11

Arthur could not face going to see Kitty in her own home, in case Tom was there. It was not that he had any fear of Tom. On the contrary, he held the man in contempt for his boorish obsession with money. It was just that Arthur's presence would only aggravate an already difficult situation, and make the chance of any improvement in relations with Tom less likely. The longer it took to win Tom's approval the more chance there was that Kitty would lose interest in him or, worse, have her head turned by another suitor. There were plenty of other young men in Dublin who were far more attractive propositions than an impecunious lieutenant colonel of foot.

As the first blossoms of spring appeared Lady Camden held a ball at the castle, the first of the season, and everyone of consequence was invited. If Kitty was still in Dublin, she would surely be at the ball, and Arthur resolved to seek her out and ask her what she felt for him.

On the night of the ball, Arthur stood in front of the mirror in his wardrobe room. His best uniform was spotless and his buttons, boots and epaulettes gleamed brilliantly, as they should given the amount the corporal on the castle staff had charged him for the work. As yet he had won no rewards for bravery, and the only decorations on his jacket were the looped lanyards. Still, he ate sensibly and exercised regularly and his body was trim as a consequence. Arthur was pleased with the image he presented, and hoped that Kitty would judge him as favourably – if she was at the ball.

★

The illumination from the candelabras in the ballroom gleamed through the windows and projected long, fading slants of light into the street as Arthur strode up towards the entrance. A guard of corporals was standing to attention in the arched doorway and Arthur presented his invitation.

The ballroom was already crowded with women in elaborate gowns that still owed much to Paris fashions despite the war. The older ladies sat to the side of the room while the younger women dominated the centre, where they mixed with young men in neatly cut jackets and breeches. As usual for such occasions, many of the men wore uniforms, with the cavalry being the most ornate and the Navy the most prosaic. As an officer of foot, Arthur felt himself to be smart without being distastefully ostentatious. An orchestra was tuning at the far end and men in livery moved through the crowd serving refreshments. Arthur stood with his back to one of the columns that supported the arched ceiling. He glanced over the crowd looking for Kitty, but could not see her and felt a moment's relief that he would not have to confront her about her feelings after all. Then he felt something tap his arm and turned quickly to see Kitty smiling at him as she withdrew her fan. Her other hand was tucked under the arm of a tall naval officer with broad shoulders that seemed intent on bursting out of his uniform coat.

'Hello, Arthur.'

'Good evening, Kitty.' There was a slight hesitation in his use of her name and Kitty's fine eyebrows narrowed for a moment.

'I do hope you aren't going to revert to calling me Miss Pakenham all over again.'

'Of course not, Kitty.' Arthur smiled. 'After all, we are close friends, are we not?'

'Indeed.' She turned to her companion. 'May I introduce Captain Charles Fenshaw? Apparently he is one of the youngest post captains in the Navy. A protégé of my uncle, Captain Pakenham. Although that was some years back, before he retired and became Surveryor General of the Ordnance, whatever that means.'

Captain Fenshaw smiled modestly. 'Captain Pakenham was kind enough to offer me a berth on his ship when I was a midshipman. Since then I have done my best to be worthy of his patronage.' He raised his hand and offered it to Arthur.

'Glad to make your acquaintance,' Arthur responded. 'Colonel Wesley, at your service.'

'Arthur has been away from Dublin fighting the French in the Low Countries,' Kitty explained. 'He returned some weeks ago, as I discovered from his brother William. It seems that he is such a good friend of mine that he neglected to let me know that he had returned from the war safe and well.'

The words were barbed, but the tone was light hearted and Arthur made a rueful face. 'My duties have kept me busy, Kitty. What else could prevent me from attending on you? Apart from your dear brother.'

Kitty laughed. 'Touché, Arthur.'

Captain Fenshaw ignored the jibing between the two of them and concentrated on Arthur. 'My brother was in the same campaign.'

'Indeed?' Arthur turned his gaze away from Kitty.

'He was injured and sent home back in January,' said Fenshaw. 'He wrote to tell me of the conditions there. It seems he was lucky to have survived most of the winter, when many others did not.'

'You have a funny notion of luck to think that any man who experienced that winter was in any way fortunate.'

'Yes, I suppose so,' Fenshaw replied quietly. 'Especially since he succumbed to his wounds only a week after writing to me.'

'Ah . . .' Arthur bowed his head. 'Forgive me, Captain. I did not mean to seem flippant.'

'I am sure of it, sir. You know well enough what my brother endured.' Fenshaw turned to Kitty. 'Allow me to fetch some drinks while you and the colonel exchange your news.'

Kitty nodded gracefully and the naval officer turned away, gliding through the crowd with a surprising grace given his imposing physique. Kitty stared after him with a calculating expression.

'What do you think of him, Arthur?'

For a moment Arthur said nothing. He hardly knew the man, but Fenshaw seemed decent enough at first glance. It would be a great shame if he should prove to be a rival for Kitty's affection. 'I've only just met him, Kitty. What can I say?'

'That he has a handsome appearance.'

'I suppose so. Any other qualities that I should be aware of?'

'Oh yes!' She turned towards Arthur with a glint in her eyes. 'He is the nephew of a rear admiral, and is in line to inherit a sizeable estate in Somerset, as well as a large holding of six per cents. He studied classics at Oxford and writes poetry.'

'Poetry?' Arthur glanced across the room to where Fenshaw had turned to make his way back to them, with three glasses between his hands. 'Really?'

'Oh, yes! Quite the romantic.'

The enthusiasm in her voice cut into Arthur's heart like a knife and he took her hand in his.

'What is it, Arthur?' Kitty frowned.

'Tell me, Kitty. What is this man to you?'

'A friend, for now. His family have some land to sell near Castlepollard and Charles has come to Dublin to arrange the sale. My uncle provided him with an introduction to my brother. Tom thought that I might show him the sights in Dublin. Since then, we've become quite attached. Tom likes him too.'

'I bet he does,' Arthur muttered. 'He would be quite a catch for you.'

'Yes he would,' Kitty replied, and then squeezed Arthur's hand lightly. 'But he is not you. Did you think I would abandon you so readily, Arthur? I had hoped you would have more faith in me.'

'Oh, Kitty . . .' Arthur's despair was swept away and he made to move closer to her, but she backed away and slipped her hand free of his.

'All the same, he is a good catch. Good enough to please Tom.'

Arthur shook his head. 'Don't do this, Kitty.'

'Do what? I'm not doing anything. That's the trouble. But there will come a time when I must find a husband if I am not to be an old maid. Unless you can make something of yourself,

Tom will not consent to your marrying me. It's up to you, Arthur, but I don't think I can wait for ever.'

Arthur spared the naval officer a quick glance. He would be rejoining them in a moment, and Arthur spoke quickly. 'Say you won't marry him, Kitty. Promise me.'

'I shall do no such thing. Besides, I like him.'

'But you love me.'

'For now.' Kitty smiled sweetly and turned towards the looming hulk of Fenshaw as he eased past a small group of young ladies, who glanced at him sidelong and then whispered amongst themselves.

'Here you are, Kitty!' Fenshaw handed her a glass of punch, then gave one to Arthur and raised the last glass. 'A toast. To the meeting of old friends.'

'Old friends,' Arthur and Kitty chorused. Arthur sensed that the other man was watching him closely, as if he were trying to discern the true nature of the friendship between them.

The orchestra struck up the first dance of the night and at once Captain Fenshaw turned to Kitty. 'My dance, I believe. Here, Wesley, take the drinks.'

Arthur reached out and awkwardly clutched the three glasses as the others moved out into the centre of the ballroom and took up their positions with the other couples. Glancing round, Arthur caught the eye of a servant and nodded to the glasses. Once he had been relieved of them he turned round to see Kitty and Fenshaw join in the first movements of a reel, smiling at each other as they linked arms and swirled round. Arthur felt sick. And angry. That Kitty should be so mercenary . . . Then again, what right had he to insist on her affection when he had no hope of marrying her for some years yet, the way his life was heading? For now, it all depended on Lord Camden. If only he could find a profitable position for Arthur, then there was hope.

For the rest of the evening, Kitty danced with each of them in turn. In between dances she was unscrupulously flirtatious with both men. Try as he might, Arthur found it hard to dislike Fenshaw, who seemed to be as professional as himself, and in the few snatches of more serious conversation that Kitty permitted them it was clear that he was a thoughtful man with considerable charm, much intelligence and a ready wit. In short, the sort of man who would make an admirable brother-in-law for Tom Pakenham. At the end of the evening, after the orchestra had finished playing and the guests made to leave in order of their social standing, Kitty turned to them.

'Well! I've had a fine evening. To be the object of the undivided attention of two such fine beaux has made me the envy of almost every unmarried woman at the ball. What more could a girl ask for?' She laughed, and the others joined in politely. 'We should do more of this. I think the three of us could become fast friends.'

Arthur nodded faintly, hiding his disappointment.

'Yes,' Fenshaw agreed. 'It would be a pleasure to see you again, Colonel.'

When the carriage which was to take himself and Kitty home had been called, Captain Fenshaw insisted on giving Arthur a lift back to his lodgings in Fostertown. Arthur had been on the verge of politely declining the offer, in order to deny his rival the chance to see the unfashionable neighbourhood where he had his lodgings, but that would mean denying himself the chance of spending a little longer in Kitty's company, and he reluctantly accepted.

As he descended from the carriage Arthur kissed her hand and bid Captain Fenshaw good night. He stood and watched as the carriage rattled down the street, turned the corner and disappeared. He heard Kitty laugh one last time, a light joyful sound that had once been as music to him, but now felt like an open taunt.

Chapter 12

'I'm sorry, Wesley, but there are no seats available for you on either the treasury or the revenue boards.' Lord Camden opened his hands in a helpless gesture. 'As you know, I have many political favours to repay and, regretfully, I had to give them priority over any consideration of who might be best qualified for a job. I wish it were not so, but that's how the system works.'

'I see,' Arthur replied, trying to keep his disappointment from showing. 'Thank you for being honest with me, my lord.'

'The least you deserve. And rest assured, I will be tireless in my efforts to secure you a post where you can prove your mettle. I know that you will serve me well.' He smiled. 'It is merely a question of time, Wesley. Your star will rise.'

'It feels as if it is already waning, my lord.' The words were out before he could check himself and Lord Camden frowned irritably.

'Look here, there is an order to these things. Patronage is a well-tried system. Without it we might as well give up the fight and embrace the principles of the revolution in France. And we've seen where that leads. Chaos and tyranny. Patronage works. When the needs of patronage have been satisfied then we can appoint people on merit. That usually comes with experience, young Wesley, and at the moment that is what you lack. I have heard fine things about you from various sources, particularly concerning your aptitude for military command. However, in the sphere of politics and office-holding you are something of an ingénu, wouldn't you agree?'

'It is true that I lack experience,' Arthur conceded. 'But as you say, I show promise and I am very keen to learn. In any case, how is a man to acquire the necessary experience if he is denied the chance to gain it in the first place?'

Lord Camden shrugged. 'It may seem like something of a conundrum, but something will turn up. I am sure of it.'

'And if it doesn't, my lord?'

'Then perhaps you would be best advised to pursue a purely military career. You might win promotion, decorations and a title if you cover yourself in glory, and live long enough. Then you could enter politics at some advantage. It's worth considering.' Camden clapped his hands. 'Come now! Surely a young man like you must be longing for adventure and the chance to win his spurs?'

Arthur smiled bitterly. 'It sounds as if there is already considerable doubt that any public office will be found for me.'

'I said I would do what I can for you,' Camden replied coolly as he picked up a pen. 'You cannot ask for more than that, Wesley. In any case, you are not in a position to. Now, if you don't mind, I have other duties to attend to.'

The meeting was over, Arthur realised. He turned away from the desk and strode out of the office seething with indignation, which swiftly gave way to new depths of hopelessness. There was one last thing he could try, even though it stuck in his throat like a fishbone. He could write to Richard and ask for more assistance. A direct recommendation from the Earl of Mornington would surely open some doors.

Once the letter had been composed, carefully written out and sent to Richard in London, Arthur turned his attention back to Kitty. Now that he had renewed their acquaintance at the ball, he felt able to call on her at home. After all, with a handsome and financially well-endowed suitor like Captain Fenshaw on the scene, there was no reason for Tom Pakenham to be concerned over the presence of Arthur. So he was able to join Kitty and Fenshaw for evenings at the theatre, or various soirées and castle picnics once the summer managed to shoulder its way through the persistent rainclouds of the Irish climate. It pained him when Kitty used Fenshaw's first name. He had not been on first name terms with Kitty for some months after he had met her.

His feelings towards Fenshaw were mixed. Fenshaw told a good story, and hinted, in terms discreet enough for Kitty's ears, about the bawdy life of officers in the Navy. At the same time, he had a natural philosophical sensitivity and knew his Locke thoroughly. In all, a fine man, who would be a pleasure to know, were it not for his affection for Kitty.

Every smile she bestowed on Fenshaw, every touch of her hand on his and every meeting of their eyes filled Arthur with such jealousy that he instinctively wished for divine intervention of the most fatal and instant kind. Then he felt shamed by the thought, and less of the man that he wanted to be. It did not take long for Arthur to realise that these moments of hatred for Fenshaw were due to his having precisely the personal qualities and social connections that Arthur felt himself to lack. That added a most bitter and distasteful edge to the baser sentiment of jealousy.

One day in July, the three of them took a carriage out to the hills south of Dublin at Dundrum. It was a fine summer's day and thin skeins of white cloud drifted across a deep blue sky. They spread a blanket down in the shade of an ancient oak tree and began to unpack the basket.

'A fine spread.' Fenshaw smiled. 'Fit for a king.'

'While we still have one,' Arthur added wryly.

The naval officer looked at Arthur curiously and Kitty chuckled. 'You'll have to excuse Arthur. He thinks that the French will be invading us at any moment, red in tooth and claw as they lay waste our cities and slaughter our people, though not without ravaging the womenfolk first.'

'Oh, I doubt that will happen,' Fenshaw replied, and helped himself to a chicken leg.

'Not with the heroes of the Navy standing, or floating, between us and the enemy, I suppose,' said Kitty, then glanced at Arthur. 'And the heroes in the army as well.'

Fenshaw shook his head. 'That's not what I meant. I just don't think that the French can be as bad as our newspapers, and our government, would have us believe.'

'Really?' Arthur stared at him. 'What makes you think that?'

Fenshaw delicately took a bite from his drumstick and chewed it for a while before he responded. 'It's a question of what motivates the revolutionaries. From the outset their goal was to improve the condition of their people. The commoners had a far harder time of it than our people in England, with little hope of any reform at the hands of the aristocrats and those who ran the Catholic church. Given what they had to put up with I would say that there is some justification for responding to their condition as they did. If the common people are oppressed too severely then some day they will rise up and overthrow their rulers.'

'So you would justify regicide?' Arthur cut in.

'No, I think they were wrong to execute their king. But it would be hard not to justify almost anything short of that.'

'Including the abolition of the monarchy?'

Fenshaw shrugged. 'Maybe, given how far their kings had moved away from the needs and desires of their subjects. The revolutionaries are simply shifting the balance of government back in favour of the people. That is why I do not think that they should be regarded as some elemental force of chaos and evil.'

Arthur shook his head in astonishment. 'You can't be serious, Fenshaw. Look at what they have been doing to their own countrymen. Sending them to the guillotine in their thousands. Waging war on their compatriots in the Vendée, in Normandy and in the south of the country. And what of the lands they have invaded? How is that proof of their good intentions to the common man?'

'They are fighting to keep the revolution alive, Wesley. No monarchy in Europe dares to allow the French republic to succeed for fear of the precedent it would set. It is a beacon to oppressed people everywhere – that is why other powers are bent on destroying the revolution by waging war from without, and by spreading lies and insurrection from within. Faced with that, they do what they must to defend the revolution.'

'So the end justifies the means?' Arthur sniffed. 'That's been the excuse of tyrants through the ages. The means and end are indistinguishable and only fools and charlatans pretend that they aren't.'

'Sometimes sacrifices have to be made for the greater good.'

'Oh, come now, Fenshaw! You can't really believe that. The scum who have risen to the top of the heap in France aren't killing their own people, and those of other nations, for the sake of an ideal. They are doing it to protect themselves alone, and to extend their tyranny to other nations. A tyrant is a tyrant no matter what noble cause he may profess to serve. Revolution only breeds chaos, and chaos can only be resolved by a cruel and ruthless tyrant. That is not a fate I want for my country and my people, should the French invade.'

Fenshaw smiled slightly. 'Wesley, you shouldn't believe everything that you read in Edmund Burke's vile pamphlets.'

'And you should not be fooled by the wretched scribblings of Thomas Paine,' Arthur snapped back.

There was a dangerous tension hanging over the picnic blanket and Kitty grabbed a small pot from the basket and thrust it between the two men. 'Goose liver terrine? You really should try it. Our cook makes it. Quite delicious.'

Arthur turned to her with raised eyebrows, then took a deep breath and held out his plate. 'That would be nice, Kitty. Thank you.'

Fenshaw continued to nibble at his chicken leg as he shifted to take in the view of Dublin, for once free of the usual brown haze of smoke, sprawling either side of the Liffey.

'It's such a lovely day, isn't it?' Kitty gushed. 'Far too nice to waste on talking about those wretched Frenchmen. Please let's not mention them again today. Let's not give them the satisfaction of ruining our picnic. Come now, Arthur and Charles, eat up.'

There was no attempt to continue the disagreement for the rest of the afternoon and the two men were scrupulously polite to each other as they made small talk, but the friendly ambience had gone and despite Kitty's best efforts to revive it the atmosphere remained strained. Late in the afternoon, as the sun's angled rays burnished the slope of the hill and the fields below in red and yellow hues, they packed up the picnic basket and loaded it on to the carriage. Fenshaw strode away to help the groom lead the horses back into their traces. Kitty waited until he was out of earshot before she turned on Arthur.

'What did you do that for?' she whispered fiercely.

'To what do you refer?'

'Don't treat me like a fool, Arthur. You know precisely what I'm talking about. Why did you provoke him?'

'I did no such thing. If anything, he provoked me, Kitty. All that nonsense about the revolutionaries and their principles. The man is a damned fool if he really believes any of that.'

'He was just being sensitive. I thought he spoke quite well about the unjust way their common people were treated.'

'What does he know about common people?'

'Arthur, what do any of us know about them?'

Arthur opened his mouth to reply, but could say nothing. Kitty was right. There was as wide a gulf of incomprehension between the classes as there was between nations. He felt shamed by that knowledge. He was a lieutenant colonel of foot, and yet he knew little of those he led. Something must be done about that, if he was to be trusted with the command of hundreds of his countrymen. He must not only command them, but command their respect and their willingness to serve him to the best of their ability. In the recent campaign Arthur had seen the terrible consequences when officers distanced themselves from their soldiers and took no interest in their well-being.

Kitty nudged him. 'Charles is coming back. Don't say another word on the subject.'

Fenshaw flashed a warm smile at Kitty as he joined them, and kept the expression fixed in place as he nodded to Arthur. 'All ready? Then let's be off.'

He graciously handed Kitty up into the carriage and stood aside to allow Arthur to go next, but Arthur stood his ground.

'You first, Fenshaw.'

'After you, sir. I insist.'

Arthur was about to protest when Kitty began to drum her fingers on the side of the carriage. 'If you boys have quite finished . . . Arthur, get in.'

He hesitated a moment, then did as she had asked and took the seat next to her. Fenshaw climbed up and sat opposite, his stout knees pressing between Arthur's boots and the folds of Kitty's skirt. The groom clambered up on to the driver's bench, took up the reins, and gave them a deft flick as he clicked his tongue. The carriage lurched into motion and rumbled back down the track towards Dublin.

For a while no one spoke, not even Kitty, and they gazed unseeingly across the passing countryside, until at length Fenshaw cleared his throat.

'Colonel, I must apologise if I offended you in some way. It would distress me to think that a good friend of Kitty's was discomfited by something I had said.'

Arthur flapped a hand. 'Think nothing of it. I was in an intemperate mood. I shouldn't have reacted as I did. It was just that your remarks surprised me, coming as they did from a king's officer. I imagine that you were playing devil's advocate for the sake of debate.'

Fenshaw stiffened. 'Indeed, sir, I was not. I stand by my opinions.'

'And how do your opinions stand beside your duty to your king and country? Surely sympathy for the enemy must lead to some conflict of interest, given that you may be forced to kill them?'

Kitty slapped her hand down on her thigh. 'Arthur! You go too far.'

Fenshaw raised a hand to calm her. 'It's a fair question, Kitty. Let me answer.'

'Oh, very well, then!' She turned away from them and rested her chin on her knuckles, staring fixedly into the middle distance.

Fenshaw looked at Arthur. 'It is true that my politics are on the radical side. Even for a Whig. But I am first and foremost an Englishman and I know that my first duty is to my country. If France tries to invade England then she will tangle with the Royal Navy first, and I swear to you that I will fight to the last drop of my blood to prevent French soldiers from setting foot on our shores. That is how things stand with me, Wesley. So do not doubt my loyalty. Do not think me a traitor. May we leave it at that?'

Arthur glanced at Kitty, profoundly wishing that he had bitten his tongue earlier in the afternoon, when it would have made a difference. But it was too late now, and he would not be satisfied until he had tested the other man's point of view, and hopefully shown Kitty that her new beau was playing fast and loose with his principles.

'We could, sir, but I confess I am intrigued to discover how one who has such perverse obligations will cope with them should he come into contact with French forces.'

'Trust me, sir. I have thought this through, and my mind is clear on the matter. I will fight them as tenaciously as the next man. And given that it is the Navy who forms our country's first line of defence, it is likely that I shall be called upon to prove myself far sooner than you are.'

It was a point well made and Arthur saw no further profit in continuing the debate, not least because he sensed Kitty's growing fury and had the good sense not to strive for a Pyrrhic victory over his rival.

It was dark when the carriage dropped him at his lodgings in Fostertown and he politely bade the others good night before mounting the steps to the front door. As he entered the hall Arthur discovered a letter waiting for him in the mail rack, and at once recognised the hand of his brother Richard. He broke the seal and began to read. Richard was as terse as ever, and informed Arthur that he had managed to persuade Lord Camden to appoint him to a useful position within the government of Ireland. To be sure it was not as significant a post as Arthur might hope for, but it would provide a sound basis for further advancement.

Arthur read on, then frowned and read the last paragraph again before lowering the letter with a sick feeling.

'Oh, Richard,' he muttered. 'What have you done to me?'

Chapter 13

'This is just what I needed first thing on a Monday morning,' Lord Camden grumbled. He leaned forward in his chair and continued testily, 'It was my understanding that you wanted a government appointment. And yet here you are, bearding me in my bloody office on a matter of some vital urgency – so your note said – and now you tell me that you don't want the job.'

'That's not quite it, sir,' said Arthur anxiously. 'Of course I want the position, and I'm very grateful that you have considered me worthy of it.'

'I haven't, but your brother was a most eloquent advocate on your behalf.'

Arthur did not doubt it, and wondered what political favour had been promised in return for his appointment as Surveyor General of the Ordnance. It did not matter. There was no question of his taking the post. Not if he wanted to stand any chance of finally winning Kitty as his wife.

'My lord, may I explain?'

'Please do.'

'The present Surveyor General is Captain Pakenham.'

'I know that, thank you.'

'His niece is Kitty Pakenham.'

Lord Camden stared back at him for a moment and shook his head. 'Never heard of her.'

'She is the woman I intend to marry, my lord. As soon as circumstances permit.'

Lord Camden's eyes widened as he grasped the point. 'Ah!

I see, young man. It would not be good form to depose your lady's relative.'

'No, my lord, it would not. Particularly as I have to seek her brother's permission to marry Kitty, and he already thinks ill of me. So, as you can see, I am forced to decline the offer.'

'A bad business, Wesley,' Camden said sadly.

'Yes, my lord.'

'And it's about to get worse.'

Arthur's eyebrows rose questioningly, even as a sick feeling of dread welled up in his guts. But what could be worse than his current predicament?

'I've already informed Captain Pakenham that he is to be replaced. The letter was sent three days ago.'

Arthur lowered his head, and the nausea within briefly made him feel as if he was teetering on the edge of a precipice. *Three days ago.* Even if it hadn't been delivered already there was no hope of overtaking the message. More likely Captain Pakenham had fired off a bitter protest to Lord Camden and sent a letter to the other members of his family to denounce the move. Good God, he thought in a panic, it might already have arrived. For a moment Arthur visualised the scene as Kitty opened the letter, read the contents and turned her face for ever away from him. It was too bleak a vision to entertain and he shook it off, and concentrated his thoughts once again.

'My lord, I most humbly request that you rescind the decision to replace Captain Pakenham with me. Even though I know the damage is already done, I cannot allow other people to think that I was complicit in this matter. I must be able to defend myself against any accusations of dishonourable conduct. You must see that.'

'Of course I do!' Lord Camden shouted. 'What do you take me for, an idiot? Once this gets out I think you'd be lucky if some young man in that family didn't call you out to eat grass before breakfast.'

'That's my fear. If it should be Kitty's brother . . .'

'Then you're damned if you win, and dead if you lose.'

'Quite.'

'Blast you and that interfering brother of yours!' Lord Camden slapped his hand down on his desk. 'How do you imagine this is going to look for me? First I take the man's job away from him, to give to someone less than half his age, then I toss it back to him as if I'm teasing a damned hound. It won't do, sir!'

'No, my lord.'

For a moment neither spoke as the Lord Lieutenant glared at his aide, and Arthur stood and endured the burden of disapproval, and the dread of the consequences of Richard's intervention. If only Richard had consulted him first . . .

'I'll have to write another bloody letter to Captain Pakenham now. Only this time I shall have to humbly ask the man to take his job back. I hope for both our sakes that he doesn't go off in high dudgeon, broadcasting his shabby treatment to one and all.' He leaned forward and wagged a finger at Arthur. 'And I think that you can forget any notion that I will help you find another post in my government. Now get out of my sight, Wesley. I've got a letter to write.'

'Yes, sir.' Arthur snapped to attention, saluted and then turned and quickly marched out of the office as Lord Camden bellowed for his secretary.

Arthur hurried from the castle and made straight for Russell Square. There was no time to waste. He had to find Kitty and explain the situation before she heard the news from her uncle. When he reached the house Arthur bounded up the stairs, paused to catch his breath, remove his hat and straighten his jacket, and then rapped the gleaming knocker. An elderly servant answered the door, smiling when he recognised the caller, and Arthur felt his spirits rise as he realised that the staff could not have been instructed to cold-shoulder him yet.

'Is Miss Pakenham at home?'

'I'm afraid not, sir. She left over an hour ago.'

'Do you know where she has gone?'

'Shopping, I would imagine, sir. Miss Pakenham has most likely gone to buy some materials from Thorns, the haberdashers on Fitzroy Street.'

'Are you sure?'

The servant smiled again. 'Miss Pakenham is a creature of habit, sir.'

'Thank you.' Arthur turned away and descended two steps, then paused and turned back. 'If she returns before I find her, please tell her that I have something very important to relate to her. I'd be obliged if she stayed here and I'll come back once I've looked for her.'

'Yes, sir. Any other words you wish me to convey to her?'

'No. I'll tell her everything.'

'Yes, sir.' The servant nodded and closed the door.

Arthur hurried back into the centre of the city, weaving through the morning shoppers and stepping nimbly round the beggars as he made for Fitzroy Street. He entered Thorns and scoured the store, with no luck. He returned to Russell Square, but she had not yet returned home. In exasperation Arthur left a message requesting Miss Pakenham to send word to his lodgings the moment she got back, so that he might come and speak to her on a matter of great urgency.

Feeling his world tumbling into turmoil around him, he walked slowly home, head down, hands clenched tightly behind his back as he tried to frame the words he would use to attempt to persuade Kitty of his blamelessness in this whole sorry mess. It began to rain, and he realised that he had left his cape at the castle in his haste to find Kitty. By the time he reached his lodgings in Fostertown he was soaked through. The caretaker of the house frowned as he saw Arthur dripping in the hall. He began to speak but Arthur cut him off. 'Earnshaw, how much to draw me a bath?'

'Cold will cost you threepence, sir. Hot will be sixpence.'

'I'll give you a shilling if you can have a hot bath ready within the half-hour.'

'Yes, sir.'

Arthur started towards the stairs but the caretaker called out to him. 'Sir!'

'What is it?'

'There's someone waiting to see you, sir. In the parlour.' The caretaker smiled. 'A proper lady, sir.'

'Oh, Christ . . .' Arthur muttered. For an instant he desperately hoped it was a coincidence. Then he cursed himself. Of course it wasn't. Kitty had already received the news. He stared down at the floor for a moment before he summoned enough resolve to straighten up and walk steadily towards the parlour door. He opened the door and saw Kitty sitting in a chair by the window. Over her shoulder the rain streaked the cheap glass and made the outside world waver indistinctly. She stared at him, lips drawn in a tight line across her ashen face.

'Hello, Kitty.' Arthur nearly let himself smile, but stopped just in time. 'I tried to find—'

'How dare you?' she interrupted harshly.

'Kitty!' Arthur took a step towards her, and she flinched as before a vile serpent.

'Stay back, Arthur. I think I should be sick if you came any closer. In all the time I have known you I never once suspected that you could behave in such a low, calculating, ungentlemanly manner. There's a good man, I told myself. Honest, charming and intelligent. Well, now you've made the stupidest, most wretched mistake of your life. To think that I loved you. That I wanted to marry you! The very thought makes my flesh creep. I . . .' Her head lowered and she angrily cuffed away a tear. But it was not enough to stop the raw emotion pouring from her body and her shoulders shuddered as more tears came.

Arthur looked at her, torn by the desire to go and comfort her, and knowing that she would be repelled by the act. He swallowed nervously. 'Kitty, let me explain. Please.'

She shook her head violently, quickly brushed her eyes and looked up at him defiantly. 'What is there to explain, Arthur? I know everything. Most of all, I know how you have betrayed me and my family. I feel like such a fool not to have seen through you.'

'There is nothing to see through, Kitty. I am the same Arthur as I ever was. The same man you once said you loved.'

'Don't you dare say that! You worm.'

'Let me speak. Hear me out, Kitty. Then you can call me what you will if your heart is still turned against me. But listen to me first.'

She pursed her lips, and glowered at him, red-eyed, and then nodded slowly. 'Have your say, Arthur, for all the good it might do.'

For the first time that day his heart lightened a fraction, and he drew a breath to calm himself before he told her about his letter to Richard, and its unfortunate consequences.

'I told Lord Camden that under the circumstances there was no question of my taking the position,' he concluded. 'I've been looking for you ever since, because I wanted to tell you the truth about it, before you heard what had happened and perhaps misunderstood.'

'Misunderstood? It's a bit more serious than that, Arthur.'

'Don't you think I know?' Arthur struck his chest. 'Kitty, I realise I am within a hair's breadth of losing the person I love more than any other in this world, but I swear I am telling you the truth. I had no part in this.' He took a step closer and sank down on to his knees in front of her. 'I swear I have not done anything to be ashamed of. I have told Camden I cannot take the job and I pleaded with him to return it to your uncle. I have acted as honourably as the situation allowed.'

She stared at him in silence, and he saw the conflicting emotions in her expression. Slowly, he reached for her hand and held it gently. Her lips trembled and she lifted his hand to her cheek and pressed her flesh against his.

'Oh, Arthur, I want to believe it. Tom said some dreadful things this morning. He had an urgent meeting today. Afterwards I feared he might come to find you, to demand satisfaction. That is why I had to speak to you first.'

'I'll have to explain it to him.'

'Not now. He would as soon shoot you as see you. Let me speak to him first. I'll send a message when it's safe to tell him in your own words.' She released his hand and dried her eyes on the sleeve of her coat. 'I had better get back. He may be at home and wonder where I have gone.'

Arthur eased himself up on to his feet. 'Yes, of course. I'll wait until I hear from you.'

He escorted her to the door, and as they stood on the

threshold Arthur held her shoulders and looked down into her eyes. 'I love you, Kitty. I would never do anything to endanger or dishonour that love.'

She smiled briefly. 'I know. And I love you. I think I always will.'

Then she turned and hurried away.

Even though Captain Pakenham accepted Arthur's explanation, he was understandably angry about Richard's role in the affair. Kitty's brother was less forgiving and refused to have anything further to do with the Wesley family, forbidding Arthur to visit his home, and warning Kitty to steer clear of him. Worse still, the affair had soured Arthur's relations with Lord Camden and it was clear that there would be no chance of preferment from that quarter for a long time.

Accordingly Arthur swallowed his pride and his bitterness and wrote to Richard to see what his brother could do by way of finding him a field command, since only a career in the army still lay open to him. The orders came swiftly. Lieutenant Colonel Wesley was to rejoin the 33rd regiment of foot in Plymouth where the regiment was preparing for service in the West Indies. Arthur packed his meagre belongings into travel chests, and made his farewells.

He managed to get a message to Kitty through Captain Fenshaw, who was more than happy to convey a note from his soon to be departing rival. They met, late in August, at a small coffee house close to the castle. For the first time in over a week the sky was clear and Dublin was bathed in warm sunshine that raised the spirits of the city's inhabitants, so that there was a marked contrast between the expressions of the two figures sitting at a table in a corner and those of the other customers, who chatted together in cheerful tones.

'I've no idea how long I will be away this time,' said Arthur. 'It may be for some years.'

'Years?' Kitty winced. 'Why so long? The last campaign was over in a matter of months.'

'I know. But this time it will be different. The government

wants to take the war to the French colonies. So it's going to be a question of subduing one island at a time. That might take much longer than anyone thinks, particularly with conditions as they are in the West Indies.'

'Conditions?' Kitty frowned. 'You mean the dangers to health, don't you? Charles told me about all the diseases: yellow fever, dysentery . . . oh, I don't want to remember the rest.' She reached her hand across the table and interlaced her fingers with his. 'Arthur, promise me you will take care of yourself.'

'I'll do my best, Kitty. But in any case I imagine that I won't be able to see you again for a long time. By then, you will have forgotten me, and be married to someone else. Charles perhaps.'

'Don't say such things.' She looked down and shook her head. 'I want you.'

'It would be the height of folly for us to marry as things stand, Kitty. Just know that my feelings for you will never change. Whatever happens. And if I do return one day, having made my fortune, and by some miracle you have not wed, then . . .'

She looked up and forced a smile. 'I'll still be here. If you still want me.'

Arthur felt a raw flood of emotion fill his heart, only to turn to a terrible aching agony at the cruel knowledge that in a short time they would be parted, perhaps for ever.

'Kitty. On my life, I will still want you. I promise.'

Chapter 14

December, 1795

It was a fine, clear winter day and the harbour at Southampton was filled with shipping. The masts, spars and rigging looked like a vast, intricate spiderweb from where Arthur observed the scene from the main quay. In amongst the coasters and small trading vessels were the large Indiamen flying the East India Company's flag. Further out lay the warships of the Royal Navy, from small sloops up to the stately ships of the line. The vessels were anchored to one side of the channel as several ships, taking advantage of a favourable breeze, glided into Southampton, passing those setting sail for other destinations. Their topsails were sheeted home and bulged as they filled under the pressure of the wind, canting the vessels gently to leeward.

The quay was filled with men unloading cargo from the merchant ships, and others loading supplies and equipment aboard the troopships berthed near the naval yard. Arthur watched as his officers and sergeants marshalled the red-coated men of his regiment, the 33rd Foot, and marched them up the ramps on to the decks of the vessels that would be their cramped quarters for the next few months. The harsh shouts of the sergeants competed with the breeze singing through the rigging and the shrill cacophony of seagulls. Once the last of the men were aboard, Arthur turned away and made his way back to his lodgings at the Crown and Anchor inn to settle his personal affairs before joining his men. If the wind direction remained constant, the regiment would sail on the noon tide of the following day. So he worked hard to complete the remaining tasks before he quit England.

He still owed the family's land agent over a thousand pounds and had arranged for his mother, Lady Anne Wesley, to guarantee the debt until he should return from foreign service to repay it. He owed Richard considerably more once he had reckoned up all the loans advanced to him by his brother to purchase commissions and pay for the costs of his election to the seat at Trim. Lastly, he wrote a final letter to Kitty, in which he set down his intention to make a name and a fortune for himself, and should she still be unmarried on his return to honour his pledge to marry her. Arthur had given much thought to this letter. Time could change a man's feelings, yet he felt sure enough of the permanent nature of his love for Kitty to commit himself to her in writing.

He signed the letter, folded it carefully, wrote Kitty's name and address on the front and then sealed it. Then he sat back in his seat and poured himself a large glass of Madeira. It was dusk and the light was fading. The rooms he had rented at the Crown and Anchor were comfortable enough, but the windows were small and stained and looked down into the coach yard. Not that there had been a moment to contemplate a view had there been one.

As soon as Arthur had arrived in Southampton he had been overwhelmed by the host of tasks demanding his attention. He had to ensure that the regiment was fully equipped for the coming campaign, and that all the men with families had made arrangements for a proportion of their pay to be sent directly to their wives. Wills had to be written and countersigned before being sent back to the battalion's depot. A small number of men were in jail for sundry offences and debts and Arthur had had to humbly request their release, or cajole the local magistrates into believing that it was their patriotic duty to return the miscreants to their colours so that they could atone for their sins by fighting for King and country. One of his officers had run up a large gambling debt which Arthur had borrowed money to pay off rather than lose the young man's services. The debt would be recouped from his pay, eventually. The letter to Kitty had been the final task, and one that had been put off until there were no lingering distractions to interfere with the composition of what might well be his last message to her.

Now it was finished, and there was nothing more to do. As soon as the wind was favourable Arthur would board his ship and sail away from England. As he sipped, sparingly, from his glass Arthur realised how tired he was. Frantic weeks of activity had taken their toll and he felt drained of energy. His head was pounding and his body ached. He rose from his seat wearily and undressed. Leaving his clothes hanging over the back of his chair, he climbed into his bed and closed his eyes.

He woke early, cold and shivering. Outside the wind moaned across the roofs of the port and when Arthur made his way down to the quay it was clear that a gale was blowing directly up the channel. The weather remained foul for several more days and while the men sat aboard their ships, struggling to find their sea legs, Arthur spent his time walking and riding along the shores of the Solent, watching and waiting for the shift in the wind that would make it possible for the convoy to leave Southampton. In the evenings he returned to his room to read the books he had bought about the West Indies. He had also borrowed some French newspapers from the harbour master so that he might learn the latest news of the conflict in Europe. As he perused the articles he once again came across the name of Bonaparte. It seemed that France's hero of Toulon had now added to his laurels by crushing a royalist uprising in Paris and had been promoted to full general. Arthur sighed wearily. It seemed that luck favoured some men far more than others. While this man Bonaparte seemed to have every good fortune strewn in his path, every possible obstacle was being placed between Arthur and any measure of success. Much as he abhorred the revolution in France and all that it stood for, he could not help feeling envious of Bonaparte's situation. One day perhaps Arthur's luck would change, and he would strive to match, and possibly outdo, the achievements of men such as General Bonaparte.

At last, in the middle of December, on a bitingly cold day, the wind veered round to the east and the captain of the frigate *Hermione*, charged with escorting the transports, sent word to Arthur that the convoy would set sail the next morning.

The wind howled across the surface of the sea, whipping foam off the crests of the waves. On the ships the rigging moaned and shrilled as the deck rolled one way and then the other beneath Arthur's boots. Overhead thin strips of sail were stretched taut beneath the furled material hanging from the spars. Two small triangles of jib sails above the bowsprit helped to thrust the transport ship on as it followed the loose line of vessels ahead, steering south-west away from the coast of the Isle of Wight. Half a mile off the starboard bow the *Hermione* surged forward, bursting through the waves in great showers of spray that were blown back over her foredeck.

Wild as the weather was on deck, Arthur was enjoying himself, wrapped up in a thick coat and covered with oilskins to protect him from the icy squalls that blew in every so often, almost blotting out the coast of England when they struck. The wild fury of nature filled him with a sense of awe, mingled with an all too human pride in man's triumph over the elements as the ships ploughed defiantly through the waves towards the open sea. Ahead he could just make out the Needles: tall columns of white rock stretching out from the end of the Isle of Wight. The lead transport was sticking to Captain Shelby's orders and, as Arthur watched, began to pass well clear of the rocks. As the last of the transports beat past the Needles he could hear the boom and roar of waves striking the columns even above the wind. Then they emerged from the partial shelter of the island and the ship was exposed to the full force of the wind. The deck canted over alarmingly and he clung to the side rail.

'Colonel! Colonel Wesley!'

He turned and saw a figure making his way forward along the quarterdeck. A fluke of wind blew the rim of the newcomer's oilskin hat flat against his forehead, and Arthur recognised Captain Hodges. Hodges was an experienced sailor and strode forward comfortably enough as the deck heaved and swooped beneath his boots. As he closed up on Arthur he cupped a hand to his mouth and shouted, 'I'd advise you to get below, sir!'

Arthur shook his head. 'Not yet! I want a last look at England!'

Hodges stared back for a moment and then shrugged as he turned back towards the quarterdeck. 'It's your funeral, sir.'

In truth Arthur just wanted to delay returning to the narrow cabin that had been allocated to him close to the stern of the ship. The soldiers had been ordered to stay below and keep out of the way of the sailors, but the world below deck was a hellish chaos. There was no fixed point of reference for the eye relative to the motion of the ship and within minutes the wild motion had stricken scores of men with nausea and several were vomiting into the first slop bucket that came to hand. Their suffering was made worse by the stink wafting up from the ship's bilges. Some of the men were too terrified to feel unwell and sat wedged in corners against the great compass timbers of the ship that groaned and creaked with the strain of battling the storm. Their lips moved in silent prayer, or curses, and the cumulative effect of it all drove Arthur up on deck where he had sought Hodges' permission to stay there a while, out of the way of the crew.

But now it was growing dark, and already the lead ship was no longer visible, just the bright spark of the heavy lantern lashed halfway up the mizzen mast. As night closed in round the transport, Arthur finally picked his way back towards the gangway that led to the cabins, and with a final glance at the black mass of the sea surrounding the transport he ducked down and carefully descended the steep stairs into the narrow passage. His cabin was one of the more spacious, but even so it was not very much larger than the cot it held. Arthur stripped off his oilskins and cloak, placed them over his sea chest, and then called for one of the ship's servants to bring him a drink. As he settled into his blankets to go to sleep his ears were filled with the protesting creaks of stressed timbers, the deep moan of the wind, and the thud-crash of the waves.

★

The morning brought fresh problems. The convoy had been scattered during the night, and when Arthur joined Hodges on the deck in the wan glow of the light filtering through the dark grey clouds rolling overhead he could see the pale streaks of the sails of only two ships on the surrounding sea.

'Are any of the other transports in sight?'

'Lookout reports two more, hull down to the south of us.'

'What's happened to the others?'

'Could be many miles away by now. If they haven't foundered.'

'Deck there!' a voice cried out, just audible above the wind. Arthur glanced up and saw a figure in the ratlines of the mainmast, clinging on as the mast inscribed crazy circles against the clouds. 'The *Hermione*'s hoisted a signal.'

'What does it say?' Hodges bellowed back through a speaking trumpet.

There was a delay as the lookout raised a telescope and tried his best to fix it on the frigate. At length he lowered the glass and called down, 'Make sail, course south-west, until further orders.'

'South-west?' Arthur frowned. 'Why south-west?'

'For safety. We head south and we might come up on Ushant. West and we might hit the Cornish coast.'

'In all this sea?' Arthur shook his head. 'Surely not. They are hundreds of miles apart.'

'True,' Captain Hodges admitted. 'But do you know where we are at this moment? Precisely where we are? Neither do I, and I won't until I can shoot the sun. In this weather who knows how long that will be. So until then, we play safe and steer south-west.'

The following dawn revealed a storm-tossed horizon clear of any ships and Captain Hodges kept to the course he had been given. More days passed with grinding monotony as the transport sailed with the wind on her port quarter, rising up on each wave, then lurching and swooping into the trough as the wave passed on ahead. Rain squalls constantly swept over the ship and water found its way between decks so that soon nothing seemed dry and it was almost impossible to keep warm.

One morning, as Arthur emerged for his regular attempt at a walk up and down the quarterdeck, Captain Hodges came over to greet him with a brief knuckle to the brim of his hat.

'Good day to you, Colonel.'

'Any sign of the other ships?'

'None, sir. Not for several days now.'

'Any idea how far we've come?'

'Difficult to say. We're making six knots through the sea, but over the ground?' He shrugged. 'But if the wind stays steady, it's fair for the West Indies and we'll make good time.'

'That's something of a comfort.'

'Yes, sir.' Hodges nodded and turned back to keep an eye on his ship, then paused and glanced back at Arthur. 'One other thing, sir.'

'Oh?'

'Merry Christmas.'

'Christmas? Oh, Christ, of course it is.' Arthur laughed. 'Merry Christmas to you too, Captain!'

The next day the wind began to veer. Slowly, degree by degree, until it had shifted far enough to the west to force the captain to change course and he tacked for six hours at a time before going about and clawing back with the wind on the opposite bow, pointing as close to the wind as the ship would steer. And still the storm continued, day after day, week after week, until nearly seven weeks into the voyage the lookout called down to the deck.

'Land ho!'

'Where away?' Hodges called back.

'Two points off the starboard bow!' The lookout thrust his arm out and the officers on the quarterdeck turned to scan the horizon in that direction. For a while they could see nothing; then the ship lifted on to the crest of a large ocean roller and there was the coast, a thin dark strip with flashes of white cliffs.

'What land's that?' Arthur squinted. Hodges was quiet for a moment, bracing his legs as he trained his glass on the distant coast before the ship slumped down into a trough and he snapped the telescope shut. He laughed bitterly.

'It's the Needles.'

'The Needles?' Arthur shook his head. 'Impossible! How can it be? We've been at sea for nearly two months.'

'It's this bloody storm. We've made no headway against it. Now it's blown us back to England.'

'What are you going to do?'

'What can I do? We've consumed two months' provisions, the rigging has been strained to breaking point and two of my sails have been torn to pieces in the wind. We're heading back to port.'

The next morning the transport eased its way up Southampton Sound on reduced sail. Hodges joined Arthur at the rail and pointed to a cluster of ships moored in the sound. 'Recognise them? That's the rest of the convoy. Wonder how long they've been here?'

As soon as the transport had taken on the mooring line and reefed in all the sails Arthur went ashore in one of the ship's boats. Stepping on to dry land was a strange experience after seven wild weeks at sea. The very cobbles beneath his boots seemed to cant and tilt as wildly as the deck of the ship and Arthur frowned angrily as his sea legs took him clumsily down the quay to the harbour master's headquarters. The current office-holder was Rear Admiral Porter, a relic of a bygone age in his powdered wig. As Arthur was ushered into his office Porter eased himself stiffly up from his chair and pumped Arthur's hand.

'Good to see you again, Colonel. Just beginning to wonder if your ship had foundered. Rest of the convoy's been in port for the best part of a month.'

'A month?' Arthur shook his head. While Hodges and his crew had been battling the elements to win every scrap of distance they could to the west, the other crews had been sitting snug in the sound.

'Ah!' Porter raised a hand. 'While I think of it, you have new orders. Arrived from London last week. Over there on the table. Go and get them, man, and I'll order you a drink. What's your poison, Wesley?'

'Tea, please, sir. A nice hot pot of tea.'

Porter chuckled. 'I'll see to it.'

As the old sailor bustled to the door to order the refreshment, Arthur crossed to the table indicated and ran his eyes over the correspondence resting there. He saw his name almost at once and picked up a slender package and broke the seals. Removing the outer waxed covering, he unfolded the letter and began to read a tersely written missive from a staff officer at Horseguards. As of the start of the year Lieutenant Colonel Wesley had been promoted to full colonel. He was further requested and required to make preparations for a fresh voyage. As soon as the convoy's supplies were replenished it was to set sail and make best time to Fort William in Calcutta.

'Calcutta!' Arthur could not believe his eyes. India?

'What did you say, Colonel?' Porter headed back towards him cupping a hand to his ear.

'Calcutta,' Arthur repeated. 'The War Office is sending the 33rd to India.'

'India?' Porter mused. 'You're in luck, Colonel. Many's the man who has made his fortune in India. Now, it seems, your turn has come.'

Chapter 15

Napoleon

Italy, April 1796

'I don't think they're going to be happy about the situation,' Major Junot muttered as they watched the three division commanders of the Army of Italy dismount outside the merchant's house that had been commandeered for Napoleon's headquarters in Nice. Like many of the fine houses that Napoleon had seen in Northern Italy, it was filled with ancient sculptures and the finest paintings of the Renaissance.

Napoleon smiled at his recently promoted aide. 'No one is asking them to be happy. Just to obey orders.'

Their gaze followed the three commanders as they strode across the courtyard towards the entrance to the house. It was not difficult to work out who was who. Napoleon had read through the records of each man on the journey from Paris. The smallest in stature was Masséna, who was described as a brave soldier and a good tactician. He was also a flagrant womaniser and there were frequent comments about his larcenous approach to any private property that took his fancy whilst on campaign. General Augereau at thirty-eight was the same age as Masséna, but tall, well built and a gifted fencer. The representative of the Committee of Public Safety who had compiled the report had obviously been a sensitive soul since he drew attention to Augereau's penchant for constantly swearing. He too was not above the occasional spree of looting, but the representative had concluded, grudgingly, that the general was very brave and was loved by the men he led. The third general was Serurier. He had served in the army for over thirty years. He was tall and lean with a humourless countenance. He was strict with his men, and they served him well enough, but Serurier had yet to prove himself as a commander.

Napoleon could understand Junot's concern. Each of the divisional commanders would have been hoping to become the new commander of the Army of Italy. Instead the post had gone to a man eleven years junior to the youngest of them. Moreover, Napoleon had never commanded any force larger than the artillery train which he had used to bombard the defences of Toulon two and a half years earlier. They were bound to regard him as a political appointment. The puppet of Paul Barras and the other Directors at the head of the government in Paris. Well let them think that, Napoleon mused. The more wrong-headed they were the easier they would be to impress once the campaign began and he won his first victories against the Austrians and their rag-tag allies in the Italian peninsula.

He turned away from the window and took his seat at the head of the long table in the merchant's finely decorated dining room. The members of his personal staff, Junot, Berthier, Murat and Marmont, were seated either side of him as they waited for the three generals to be admitted to the first meeting of the army's senior officers.

The double doors at the end of the room were opened by a pair of corporals and Napoleon and his staff rose graciously as the divisional commanders entered the room in their fine dress coats, laced with gold braid. They handed their hats and swordbelts to the corporals and took their places at the table. Napoleon made the introductions before resuming his seat to begin the briefing.

'Well then, gentlemen, Paris has asked us to drive the Austrians from Italy. At the same time we are to make allies of any Italian kingdom that we can, and overawe or crush the rest. All in a day's work for the soldiers of France, I think you'll agree.'

The officers chuckled easily enough at the remark and Napoleon continued. 'However, I have to say that the task will not be quite so easy given the current condition of the Army of Italy. I was told in Paris that there were forty-two thousand men in the army. What I discover when I get here is that there are no more than thirty thousand, and most of them are hungry and poorly equipped and haven't been paid for months. In one unit I passed through yesterday the men were wearing goatskins for coats and many of them did not even have boots. The army's artillery train consists of twenty light mountain guns and a handful of transport mules. That's not going to frighten any enemy. Small wonder that the morale of the officers and men is as low as it is.'

General Augereau laced his fingers together and leaned back in his chair. 'Well, you can't believe everything you hear in Paris, it would seem. Perhaps you should return there and tell them the truth, sir.'

'There is no time for that, General. We must act now. We shall have to work hard to get the Army of Italy ready for the coming campaign. We need reinforcements, we need supplies and equipment, and above all we need to raise morale. And for that we need victories. So I have decided to open our campaign against the Austrians by the middle of April.'

'But that's just over two weeks away!' Serurier protested. 'That's impossible. You said it yourself, sir. The army's in no condition to fight. The best we can hope for is to defend our positions, and marshal resources for a campaign later this year, or early next year.'

Napoleon shook his head. 'You're thinking like an Austrian, General Serurier. It is true that the Army of Italy is not ready to fight in a conventional manner, so we must wage war in an unconventional way. Since the army has no supply train, we will do without. Our men will have to live off the land. That means we can outmarch the enemy. The Austrian armies march like snails, hauling vast supply columns with them. They stop to establish depots and then move on again. They make us a present of the initiative, Serurier. It is true that they outnumber us, but by virtue of our greater mobility we will be able to mass superior forces against their weak points and beat them every time. A few such victories and our men will be as lions, ready to leap on their prey. I tell you, gentlemen, by the end of this year the Austrians will be in full retreat, and every man in this room will be regarded as a hero in Paris.'

He paused to let the impact of his words sink in, then turned to Junot. 'Major, the map if you please.'

Junot unrolled a large map across the table and weighted the corners down. The staff officers and the generals leaned forward to examine the features of northern Italy while Napoleon picked up a cane and stood at the head of the table.

'In brief, the plan is for the army to march down the coast as far as Savona, then cut inland to threaten the Austrian supply lines. True to form, the Austrians will fall back to the north-east. We'll hold them there while a strong force turns on the Piedmontese forces. Without their Austrian friends they will crumble very quickly. Then we take Lombardy and Milan before turning our attention back to the Austrians. My final aim for this campaign season is to take the fortress at Mantua. So there it is, gentlemen. Any questions?'

Serurier shook his head. 'You ask too much of the men, sir.'

Napoleon looked at him shrewdly. 'Or is it that I am asking too much of my generals?'

Serurier's eyes widened angrily and he thumped his hand down on the table. 'You insult me, sir! Let me remind you I was a soldier long before you were born, and these other generals were fighting the enemies of France while you were still a schoolboy. What makes you think you have the right to question my judgement?'

Napoleon glanced at all three of his divisional commanders. 'It's simple, gentlemen. I obey the Directory . . . and you obey me. The Directory has told us to take the war to the Austrians and that is precisely what we shall do. If you wish to protest, Serurier, then you must resign your command and take the matter up in Paris. Is that clear?'

Serurier glared at him for a moment, before nodding mutely.

'Very well then,' Napoleon continued in a warmer tone. 'Then let's discuss the details. And tomorrow, Serurier, I will inspect one of your brigades.'

★

It was a dull morning, and a faint drizzle speckled the hats and uniforms of the men assembled on the field a short distance outside Oneille. At first it was difficult to believe that these men belonged to an army. Only a handful of them still had their complete kit; the rest were missing backpacks, gaiters, and boots, and some even lacked muskets and bayonets. Several were coughing badly and the majority were thin and gaunt for lack of food.

'Hardly the stuff of victories,' Junot said quietly as they approached. Napoleon had temporarily dismissed the senior officers of the brigade and a sergeant major called the soldiers to attention as the commander of the army and his aide marched towards them. The men did their best to straighten their backs and thrust their chests out, but it was as miserable a display of drill as Napoleon had ever seen and for the first time he felt a stab of fear that the command of the Army of Italy was going to be the death of his ambitions. He shook off the doubt as he approached the front rank. He walked slowly past the first dozen soldiers and then stopped in front of an older man, who still had his full kit, albeit worn out.

'Name?'

'Private Dunais, General,' the man replied, with a pronounced accent that Napoleon picked up at once. He smiled.

'You are a Gascon, then. Good. I need men with the fighting spirit of Gascony. How long have you served in the army?'

'Four years in this army, General, then twelve years in the Russian army, and before that eight years in the Bourbon army.'

'I see. What kind of trouble were you in, Dunais? To make you quit France for Russia?'

'I didn't like my officers, sir. All breeding and no brains.'

'And you thought it would be better in the Russian army?'

'I hoped it would be. I was wrong, General.'

'And what of the French army today, Dunais? How does it compare with the old Bourbon army? Be honest with me – your officers are not here.'

For the first time Dunais looked him in the eyes. 'Not well, sir. The lads are keen enough to fight, and would make good enough soldiers . . .'

'But?'

'They've been given a raw deal by those bastards in the government. And they've been cheated by the army contractors. Worst of all, there's some of the officers who treat us as bad as the contractors, or owe their rank to political friends and know nothing about soldiering, sir.' Dunais realised he might have said too much, and suddenly clamped his mouth shut and stared straight ahead once more.

'Private Dunais, your comments are noted, and I give you my word that your grievances will be addressed as soon as possible.' Napoleon raised his voice so that more men could hear him. 'If France wants us to fight, then France is going to make sure that her soldiers get the best of what's available. It's the very least that her soldiers deserve. Major Junot, make a note of this man's complaints.'

'Yes, sir.'

Napoleon continued down the line, stopping every so often to question one of the men and find out where he had come from, and what his grievances were. Once the inspection was over he climbed into a light supply wagon that had been brought forward to act as a podium. He waited until there was almost total silence and stillness in the ranks, and then began to address them.

'Soldiers! You are hungry and short of equipment. Your government owes you everything but can afford to give you nothing. The patience and courage which you have shown so far has been admirable – but it has not brought you any glory. Not one shred of glory. That is about to change. I will lead you into the most fertile lands in Europe. There are rich provinces with fine towns and cities in Italy, all of which will be yours for the taking. There you will find honour, glory and riches.' Napoleon paused to draw breath and then thrust his arm out and pointed at them. 'Soldiers of the Army of Italy! With all this before you, will you be lacking in courage or endurance?'

'No!' a voice cried out. 'We will fight!'

'Fight!' another shouted. 'Fight for General Bonaparte!'

Others picked up the mood and soon they were all chanting his name. Napoleon indulged them for a moment and then turned to Junot and smiled. 'Now we have an army!'

The date set for the opening of the campaign was 15 April and in the days leading up to the start of the offensive Napoleon and his staff worked every possible hour to remedy the army's problems. Local banks were forced to make loans to the army so that the men could be paid and supplies purchased. The complaints of the soldiers were investigated and corrupt and incompetent officers were relieved of their commands or sent far to the rear on garrison duty, or even dismissed from the service. The supply contractors were threatened with the loss of their army business if the men were not properly fed. Napoleon visited as many of the units as he could in the early days of April to make rousing speeches to the men, and he set up an army newspaper to provide news from home as well as morale-boosting accounts of the progress of the war with Austria. At the end of every day he sat down and wrote a letter to Josephine, telling her of his exhausting duties, and of the deep love and fiery passion for her that made every day of separation a torture. He asked her, with increasing frustration, to write and let him know when she would come and join him.

The Army of Italy moved forward towards Savona to mass in readiness for the campaign. Napoleon was in a fine mood; his time had come and soon his name would be known the length and breadth of Europe. The only lingering worry was the lack of precise intelligence about the main body of the Austrian army under General Beaulieu. He resolved to send Murat out with some light cavalry first thing in the morning to scout ahead and find the enemy. Then, eyes and limbs aching from his exertions, Napoleon climbed into his bed and fell asleep.

'Sir!' a voice called out, waking him. Napoleon rose stiffly and blinked his eyes. Major Junot was standing at the foot of the bed, still in his nightshirt. Behind him the first grey light of dawn was creeping across the roofs of Savona.

'Junot, what the devil's going on?'

'It's the Austrians. They've attacked one of Masséna's brigades.'

'Where?' Napoleon threw back the bedclothes and climbed out of bed. 'In what strength?'

'Near Voltri. The report from Colonel Cervoni is that his brigade is holding them back but the enemy is arriving in greater numbers all the time. He says he will be forced to fall back before long.'

'Voltri, eh?' Napoleon closed his eyes and recalled the details of the map of the coastal area towards Genoa. Voltri was a port a short distance from Genoa where Masséna's division was moving into position to attack. At once he grasped the danger. He opened his eyes and fixed his stare on Junot.

'Get Berthier and the others in my office. Then send an alert to all divisional and brigade commanders. I want the army ready to march at once. Tell them the campaign begins today. Today, understand?'

'Yes, sir.' Junot saluted and left the room as Napoleon reached for his clothes.

When he entered his office, a staff sergeant was already laying out a map, and Napoleon ordered him to find some coffee and bread. Leaning over the map he found Voltri at once and nodded as he saw the disposition of his troops that Berthier had marked in the night before. The Austrians were attempting to drive towards the coast to cut Masséna off from the rest of the army. If they succeeded, the campaign was over before it had begun. Just as Napoleon's career would be. On the other hand, he considered, unless the Austrians had changed their tactics the attack would proceed at a slow pace. Slow enough for Napoleon to turn the situation to his advantage.

Chapter 16

By the time the last of his senior staff officers had arrived Napoleon had formed his plan and was impatient to give the orders.

'I assume you've all the heard the news. It seems that the Austrians have got more balls than we thought.'

The officers chuckled and Napoleon raised a hand to quieten them.

'We have been saved the job of finding the Austrians, and it's time to take the battle to them. Cervoni's brigade is here.' He tapped his finger on the map. 'He's holding his position at the moment, and buying us time to move into the attack. General La Harpe is the closest to the Austrians' line of advance. Berthier, you will order him to attack at once. The Austrians will be forced to stop and turn to face the threat, which will free Masséna to march on their flank and rear. The rest of the army will be given orders to move up in support. Gentlemen, if we act swiftly, the Army of Italy will have its first victory of the campaign, courtesy of the Austrians. See to it. I'm riding ahead to join Cervoni. Send any messages to me there.'

As soon as the officers had been dismissed Napoleon called for a horse to be readied. Taking a handful of dragoons with him, he galloped down the coast road towards Voltri. He soon caught up with the rear elements of Masséna's division quick-marching to join their commander and strike at the Austrians. Some of the men cheered as he rode past and Napoleon raised his hat in acknowledgement. Then, four miles short of Voltri, he came to the junction that led up into the hills where Cervoni's brigade was fighting the Austrian vanguard. Already he could hear the faint boom of cannon and the crackle of musket fire echoing from the hills. Napoleon kicked his heels in, urging his mount up the track, and the dragoons struggled to keep up with their general.

As the small party of horsemen came up on to the ridge, they had a clear view down the far slope which dropped steeply towards a mountain stream crossed by a narrow stone bridge. Cervoni's men had formed up in solid ranks to contest the crossing. Ahead of them, clustered amongst rock outcroppings, were small parties of light infantry, keeping up a steady fire on the Austrians on the far side of the stream. Beyond the bridge, a battalion of the white-uniformed enemy stood in neatly dressed ranks, busily loading their weapons and then bringing them up to fire in company volleys at the French skirmishers as if they were on a parade ground. Each time the Austrian muskets rose to the shoulder the French ducked down, and nearly every shot rattled harmlessly off the rocks or whistled overhead. By contrast, the irregular fire of the skirmishers was whittling down the Austrians. Behind them a battery of artillery was unlimbering on a patch of even ground close to the stream, and beyond stood a long column of infantry waiting for the order to force their way across the bridge.

Colonel Cervoni had spotted his commander and trotted his horse up to Napoleon. He saluted. 'Good morning, sir.'

Napoleon nodded. 'Better than we could have hoped for. Must be three or four thousand men over there. I think you've managed to find the Austrian army for me, Cervoni. What's the situation?'

Cervoni turned to look down the slope as he stroked his stubbled chin. 'We've been falling back by battalions. Each time they've deployed just like that, as if they were following a manual and had all the time in the world. Our skirmishers have been shooting them up until their guns open fire, then withdrawing.'

'What are your losses?'

'No more than fifty men so far. A fraction of what they've lost, sir.'

There was a dull roar from the far side of the stream and Napoleon turned to see a puff of smoke swirling in front of one of the guns of the Austrian battery. Shortly afterwards a divot of grass and stone was thrown into the air a short distance in front of the foremost of Cervoni's line companies.

'I'm afraid that's about to change,' Napoleon said quietly. 'You must hold this ridge as long as possible. The Austrians must not reach the coast road. Augereau's division is moving forward to attack the Austrian column, and Masséna is marching round to the east.' Napoleon gestured to the hills on his right. 'But they won't come up for two or three hours. You have to hold this position until then. Whatever the cost.'

Cervoni nodded. 'I understand, sir.'

Napoleon looked over the ground below him. 'Where are your guns? You're supposed to have two six-pounders attached to your brigade.'

'There, sir.' Cervoni smiled as he indicated a thicket of reeds a hundred and fifty yards from the bridge. When Napoleon squinted he could just make out the crews crouched round two dark shapes. Cervoni explained. 'I had them smear the guns in mud so they wouldn't show. They have orders not to fire until the head of the column is on our side of the bridge.'

Napoleon nodded approvingly. 'That'll be a nasty surprise. You can return to your battle, Cervoni. I'll watch from here for a while.'

'Yes, sir.'

They exchanged a salute and Cervoni wheeled his horse round and trotted back to his small cluster of staff officers. Now the Austrian guns had found their range and a well-aimed shot ploughed a bloody furrow through the centre of the nearest company. More solid shot followed and several men were swept away before the order to take cover reached them. The enemy gunners reloaded with grapeshot and trained the guns on the skirmishers covering the bridge. Then the Austrian drums beat the advance and the light company peeled aside to let the main column approach the bridge. They came on at a steady, measured pace, up to the parapet and tramping over the slight hump in the middle of the bridge. They were led by a slender officer who rested his sword on his shoulder as he led his men towards the near bank of the stream.

The French gunners rose up, still half hidden by the reeds, and two tongues of flame ripped out, disgorging two cones of lead shot into the face of the Austrian column. The guns had been well laid and almost every man on the bridge was cut down to lie in twisted heaps, splattered with blood. The front of the column halted, dumbstruck, and then bulged forward as the men behind pressed into them. The men nearest the hidden guns had nowhere else to go and stumbled over the bodies of their comrades as they pressed on over the bridge.

Cervoni's guns discharged more grapeshot, adding further carnage to the scene on the bridge. The commander of the Austrian battery was frantically giving orders to his men to redirect their fire on to the French guns but they were obscured by the bridge and the gunners could not see their target. A third blast of grapeshot decided the issue and the Austrian column backed away, leaving at least forty of their comrades littered across the small span of ancient stones.

'Fine work.' Napoleon smiled with satisfaction as he turned his horse back towards the ridge and the road that led to his headquarters. Berthier was waiting for him when Napoleon reached Savona shortly before noon.

'What news?'

'Augereau's division are moving towards Montenotte, General. His forces have been sighted by the Austrians and the enemy are already turning to face him.'

'Excellent!' Napoleon slapped his hand down on the map. 'And Masséna?'

'Cutting round their flank, as ordered. He estimated that he would be ready to strike no later than four o'clock.'

'Then we should have trapped our Austrian friends very nicely.' Napoleon smiled excitedly. 'Our first victory!'

★

It was not until the following morning that the scale of the Austrian defeat at Montenotte was evident. Over fifteen hundred Austrians had been killed and wounded and another two and a half thousand were taken prisoner. The survivors fled towards the town of Dego, abandoning cannon, muskets and other equipment. The French seized the enemy's weapons eagerly. Over a thousand men in Augereau's division had had no muskets and these now shouldered Austrian weapons, ready for use against their former owners.

Napoleon seized the advantage at once, urging Masséna's columns forward in pursuit of the enemy, while Augereau and Serurier fell on the Piedmontese army and drove them from one town after another over the next ten days, until on the evening of 23 April the French army was on the road to Turin. A farmhouse had been found for the general's headquarters and as Napoleon sat hunched over a quick meal of cold chicken and bread it began to rain, the drops rattling on the roof tiles overhead. The door opened and Junot was briefly outlined against the steel glint of a curtain of rain as he ducked under the lintel and closed the door behind him. He stood dripping on the stone floor and smiled at his commander.

Napoleon set down the hunk of bread in his hand, and quickly swallowed. 'What's the matter, Junot?'

'There's a Piedmontese colonel standing outside. He carries a message from General Colli.'

'And?'

'General Colli is requesting an armistice.'

'An armistice?' Napoleon pushed his plate aside and folded his hands together, his mind racing as he considered the implications of the offer. He nodded at a spare chair on the other side of the plain country table and Junot sat down.

'What have you said to him, Junot?'

'As we were walking up to headquarters he asked me if I thought you would accept. I said nothing.'

'You didn't speak to him?'

'Not a word.' Junot shrugged. 'I thought it was presumptuous of him even to ask.'

'And so it was!' Napoleon laughed. 'Well then, Colli wants to break off the fighting, does he?'

'It's not difficult to see why, sir. We've been snapping at their heels since we turned on them after Montenotte. They're hungry and exhausted and need a breathing space. Same as our men. We could use the time to regroup.'

'Yes, but they don't know that.' Napoleon looked up sharply. 'This colonel, was he blindfolded as he passed through our lines?'

'Of course, sir.'

'Very well then, you'd better tell him that I reject the offer.'

Junot looked surprised, and hesitated a moment before he spoke. 'May I ask why, sir?'

'Junot, the fact that they have approached us for an armistice means they must think they have more to gain from it than we do. Turin is two days' march away. Why give them a chance to fortify it? Let's push on, and then offer them an armistice on our terms. Now, go and tell him.'

Over the next two days the French threw themselves after the retreating Piedmontese, driving them back from one village to the next and cutting them off from the Austrian army. Now it was Napoleon's turn to offer an armistice. General Colli reluctantly conceded the key fortress towns of Cuneo, Ceva and Tortona and signed the documents that Junot had drawn up.

The same night, Napoleon wrote a quick note to Josephine and gave it to Colonel Murat to take to Paris along with the provisional terms of the armistice for the Directors to consider. Then he sat down to compose the following morning's order of the day. Napoleon paused to take in the speed at which the campaign had moved. He had never felt such a sense of achievement and he was proud of his men. Yet, even now, he looked ahead. He dipped his pen into the inkwell and began to write.

Soldiers! In fifteen days you have taken twenty-one colours and fifty-five pieces of artillery, seized several fortresses and the richest lands of Piedmont. You have captured fifteen thousand prisoners and inflicted more than ten thousand casualties. The success I promised you has been fulfilled, yet this is only the beginning . . .

Chapter 17

'When will those damned Austrians turn and fight us!' Napoleon fumed, glaring at his senior officers by the light of the lanterns inside his tent. 'Every time we advance General Beaulieu falls back behind another tributary of the Po. We need to beat him decisively, yet all he offers us is one rearguard action after another.'

Masséna stretched his shoulders and replied, 'Then we'll just have to destroy them one rearguard at a time, sir.'

'That is not remotely funny, Masséna,' Napoleon snapped. 'They are falling back on their lines of communication, while we are extending ours. They grow stronger all the time and our men are tired and many of our battalions are well under strength. Time is on their side. A few more fights like today's effort and we will be ripe for an Austrian counter-attack.'

He was silent for a moment, reflecting on the bloody crossing of the River Adda at Lodi that had taken most of the day. Several times the grenadiers had advanced towards the bridge along a narrow causeway under murderous fire from the far bank and it was not until after six in the evening that his men had broken through and the French army had started to cross in strength. The pursuit of the Austrians had continued until darkness fell, and only then had the French made camp for the night. By the time the headquarters tents had been set up it was past midnight and the officers around Napoleon were bleary-eyed and exhausted. Like their men, he reflected. Well, it was too bad. The impetus had to be maintained to force the Austrians to turn and fight, and if they didn't then they must be chased right out of Italy, leaving only the massive fortress at Mantua to deal with. That could be starved into submission by a covering force while Napoleon led the rest of the army into the Tyrol. The Austrians would then be caught between the Army of Italy and the Army of the Rhine, which even now should be pushing towards Austria on the far side of the Alps, according to the Directory's grand strategy.

He rubbed his eyes and blinked, fighting back his desire for sleep. Then he pulled a map towards him and pointed out the next river barrier.

'If things run true to form, Beaulieu will fall back behind the Oglio. If we can force him back from that line, then we can cut off Mantua.'

Junot cleared his throat. 'Is that wise, sir? Shouldn't we consolidate our gains first? Now that Beaulieu has retreated, Milan must fall to us. Our troops need to rest. And, as you pointed out, thanks to the length of our supply lines we're running out of powder and rations. But most of all we need more men, sir.'

'He's right,' Serurier added. 'We've been promised reinforcements for months. So far I've not had one man to replace my losses. Sir, you said that there would be more men.'

'I've written to the Directory to request reinforcements on more occasions than I care to remember,' Napoleon said wearily. 'You would think that after all we have achieved they would give us the tools to win further victories. But it seems that the Directory has decided that all available men will be sent to the Army of the Rhine.'

'That's not quite what I've heard,' Masséna growled. 'We've been sent reinforcements, but that bastard Kellermann is creaming them off for the Army of the Alps as they march through his area of operations.'

'That is a rumour,' Napoleon said firmly. 'Those men must have been sent to him, not us.'

'You really think so, sir?' Masséna smiled bitterly.

'I know it. Kellermann is a man of honour. And he's intelligent enough to realise that we need reinforcements far more than he does.'

'Then why is he being reinforced and not us?' Masséna asked.

'Politics, that's why.' Junot sneered. 'This was supposed to be a sideshow to the main thrust across the Rhine.' He turned towards Napoleon. 'Sir, that's why they picked you for this command. After the victory over the royalists you became an embarrassment to the politicians. They needed you out of Paris, and the Army of Italy should have been the graveyard of your ambitions. The trouble is you keep winning battles and their plans have misfired. That is why we receive no help from them.'

Napoleon thought for a moment. It could be true. But surely not even a venal politician would put his own interests above the interests of his country? He had met and mingled with the Directors, and had sensed the ideals that had drawn them to the revolution and the need to build a new France. But it seemed that time had eroded those aspirations. He frowned. When the war was over, then maybe he would return to Paris and do what he could to force idealism back into public affairs. That was the future, he reminded himself. For the present he had more pressing problems to deal with. He looked at Junot.

'It is time we began to show the government why they should be reinforcing and resupplying us.'

'Sir?'

'What is it that our politicians want above all else, right now?'

'To beat the enemy and end the war,' Junot replied.

Napoleon shook his head. 'You are thinking too much like a soldier.'

Masséna chuckled. 'They want money. The treasury is empty, and gold and silver are the sinews of war. Not to mention politics.'

Napoleon nodded and laughed. 'And you, my dear Masséna, are thinking too much like a politician.'

Massena shrugged. 'No man is perfect, General.'

'Money.' Napoleon slapped his hand down on the table. 'Money is what they want and that is what we shall give them. Once it starts to flow into their coffers then we shall receive what we need. Junot, first thing in the morning, I want you to send messages to all our agents in the north of Italy. They are to assess the fortunes of every city and town. They are to try to find out how much is held in coin and how much might be raised from loans. We shall, of course, negotiate the most favourable terms when the time comes. I've never known a sword at the throat of a banker fail to produce fair repayment terms.'

The officers laughed, warming to the idea, and Napoleon continued. 'Send the messages in code and have them report back by the end of May.'

'Yes, sir.'

'Meanwhile, we'll take Milan and give the men a brief rest. The Austrians aren't going anywhere for now. We'll march on them again once the men are fed and in good spirits. That's enough business for tonight. Berthier will send you your orders at first light. Good night, gentlemen.'

They rose from their chairs and filed out of the room. Napoleon sat and stared at the map. The Austrians had retreated yet again, but they were running out of space to retreat into. Some time, in the coming weeks or months, there would be a reckoning. When it came, it was vital that the Army of Italy was strong enough to face a hard battle and win.

There was a knock on the door frame and Napoleon looked up to see Berthier holding a waterproofed document bag.

'Dispatches and papers from Paris, sir. Will you read them now, or wait until morning?'

'Now, please, Berthier.'

'Yes, sir.' His chief of staff crossed to the table and unfastened the straps. Inside was a carefully wrapped bundle of newspapers, a sealed packet from the War Office and a letter addressed to him in Josephine's hand. Napoleon warmed at the sight and he instinctively picked up the letter and ran his fingers gently over the writing. He smiled. It was typical of her to use her contacts to get a letter included in the official dispatch bag. For a moment he lingered over the letter, then set it aside and reached for the packet and broke the seal.

There were two documents inside, one from Carnot at the War Office and the other from Barras on behalf of the Directory. He read Carnot's letter first. The War Office was unable to send the requested reinforcements to the Army of Italy for the present, but assured General Bonaparte that he would be given priority the instant reinforcements were no longer needed on the Rhine. The letter concluded with an intelligence report revealing that Beaulieu was shortly to be joined by fifteen thousand fresh troops. Napoleon felt a cold rage flow through his veins. With fifteen thousand fresh men, he himself could sweep the enemy from Italy and chase them all the way back across the Tyrol to Vienna. He wondered, idly, who constituted the greater danger to his army. The Austrian forces, or the politicians back in Paris?

He opened the letter from Barras, glanced over the usual official preambles and started reading the substance of the wishes of his political masters. When he got to the end he lowered the document on to the table, his hand trembling with anger.

'Damn them,' he muttered through clenched teeth. 'Damn them all.'

Berthier stood silently, waiting for his superior to elucidate on the contents of the letter. At length Napoleon looked up, his brow creased into a furious frown.

'It seems that the Directory wants to split the command of the Army of Italy.'

'Sir?'

Napoleon stabbed a finger at the text. 'The Directory has ordered me to hand over half of the army to General Kellermann. I am not to continue the offensive. I am not to invade the Tyrol. I am not even permitted to occupy Milan. Those operations are to be carried out by Kellermann. Instead,' he continued icily, 'I am to take two divisions south to apply pressure to the papal states and the Kingdom of Naples to make peace with France. It seems that our leaders want to cut me down to size.' He shook his head as he glanced at the letter again. 'Apply pressure – what the hell does that mean? I think these politicians must mistake me for a fool.'

There was a short silence before Berthier nervously cleared his throat. 'Why is that, sir?'

'The phrase is far too vague, don't you agree? What kind of pressure am I supposed to apply? Diplomatic or military? If I apply the former and fail to secure an agreement then the Directors will say I should have used force. If I use force and fail, or if I antagonise other states in Italy, then they will say I was exceeding my orders and should have negotiated. So I must succeed or be damned. Of course, that's assuming that I do decide to relinquish half my army to Kellermann.' Napoleon looked up, eyes shifting rapidly as he examined the map on the table. His mind was racing.

If the Army of Italy moved swiftly enough he could seize Milan and Pavia. Once those cities were in French hands Napoleon could begin to exact loans and 'donations' from the wealthier classes, and perhaps some of the neighbouring states and principalities. Why stop at money, he reflected. The lands of northern Italy were awash with art treasures. Once the Directory received this booty they would think twice about replacing the man who was feeding badly needed wealth into France's empty treasury. He would gamble on that. Meanwhile he would also offer them a more reasoned and acceptable case for retaining him as the sole commander of the army.

'Berthier, send me my secretary.'

When Bourrienne had set out several sheets of paper and the inkwell and readied his pen, Napoleon began to dictate a reply to the Directors. He was careful to ensure that his tone was respectful and unemotional. It was essential that his arguments be seen as objective, well reasoned and in the vital interests of France. As the early hours dragged by Bourrienne scratched out the rough draft of the letter. Napoleon emphasised, as forcefully as he dared, that unity of command is the most important thing in war. While the Army of Italy was under one general it could be wielded in the most effective manner. He was careful not to disparage Kellermann, who still basked in the afterglow of being hailed as the saviour of the revolution following his victory at Valmy. Napoleon drew a deep breath as he dictated the concluding section.

'General Kellermann will command the army as well as me, for no one is more convinced than I am that the victories are due to the courage and audacity of the men.' He smiled at that touch:

underscoring his modesty with praise for the revolutionary zeal of his men. Then he continued, 'However, I consider that uniting Kellermann and myself in Italy will put all our gains at risk. I believe that one bad general is better than two good ones.'

He nodded contentedly at this conclusion and looked over at Bourrienne. 'There, that should do it. Draft a fine version and bring it here as soon as it's done.'

'Yes, General.' Bourrienne snapped the lid of his inkwell closed and began to clean the nib of his pen on an old rag. 'Do you want me to have a courier prepared to carry it to Paris?'

Napoleon thought a moment and then shook his head. 'No, we'll wait a few days. I want the news of any booty that I have seized to arrive close on the heels of this.'

'Very well, sir.' Bourrienne tucked the papers under his arm, bowed his head and left Napoleon alone.

For a long time he was still, staring at the map as his mind concentrated on the letter he had received from the Directory. It had come as a shock to him that the government was so insecure that it considered him a threat. Napoleon had been aware of some of the bad feeling directed towards him after the crushing of the royalist uprising, but had assumed that any jealousy of his acclaim could be countered by his own unswerving loyalty and good service. If this was how those in power in Paris treated successful generals, then perhaps Napoleon would be better off campaigning as far from the French capital as this war could take him.

For now he would have to fight the politicians in Paris to retain his command of the Army of Italy, every bit as hard as he had to fight the Austrians. A knife in the back would finish him just as surely as a bullet in the chest. He sighed wearily. This was no way to wage war. But unless he learned to fight on both fronts he could not hope to win the renown and respect that he craved.

The coming weeks were going to be more vital than ever. He must risk everything, even his life, to make the Directors believe that he was irreplaceable.

Chapter 18

Five days later the French army entered Milan. The people of the city thronged the streets to welcome the ragged soldiers who had come to liberate them from Austrian oppression. The aristocrats and the wealthy merchants and bankers were more circumspect in their greeting and Napoleon accepted their gifts and praise for what they were: attempts to bribe him and appeal to his vanity so that he would not subject Milan to the liberal values of the French revolution. Napoleon treated them courteously enough, before announcing his ambition to establish a democratic republic in Milan, allied to France. His proclamation was greeted by wild celebration that spilled out into the narrow streets of the poorer quarters of the city. Meanwhile, several battalions of infantry surrounded the small Austrian garrison that had been left behind to defend the citadel. The force, under the command of General Despinois, would not only contain the Austrians, but also ensure the loyalty of the Milanese.

The celebrations in the city were short lived. While Napoleon plundered the local banks, his troops roamed the city, taking food, wine and women as they wished. As soon as he heard what was happening Napoleon issued stern orders to his officers to stop their men from looting the city. But it was already too late. Discipline had broken down and there was nothing that could be done until appetites had been sated.

Napoleon waited impatiently for the men to return to their units and then, a week after the army had entered the city, it marched out to continue the war against Austria. But this time the streets were quiet as the Milanese cowered in their homes, waiting until the last sounds of marching boots had faded into the distance before they dared to emerge and stare in shock, and then bitter anger, at their ransacked city.

Napoleon and his staff paused on a low hill a short distance from the city and watched as the men marched past, haversacks bulging with looted goods.

'They're in good spirits, sir,' commented Berthier. 'I just hope it lasts until they go up against the Austrians, once we catch up with them.'

Napoleon glared at a passing column of infantry, sullenly acknowledging their cheerful greetings. 'What concerns me is that if they conduct themselves in this fashion again, then we'll be spending as much time putting down revolts in the lands we've taken from Austria as we do fighting the enemy.'

Berthier shrugged. 'I hope not, sir.'

Napoleon turned to him with a bitter smile. 'You hope not? I don't think we can avoid it. There's hardly a single Milanese, rich or poor, that we've not offended. Our men have had a free hand with the common folk, while I've thoroughly plundered the rich.'

In the last few days Napoleon had demanded over ten million francs from the dukes of Parma and Modena, the money to be paid into banks in Genoa before being transferred to Paris. More cash was being squeezed from the kingdom of Piedmont and every city and town under French control. Very soon it would be flowing into the treasury in Paris. Napoleon fervently hoped that it would convince the Directors not to meddle any further with his command in Italy. The bitter truth was that while he might buy them off, he would now be forced to continue his advance with an outraged population at his back. Still, he reflected, the army was grateful to him, especially as some of the money he had exacted from the local rulers had been used to make good the arrears in their pay. In his growing awareness of the need to think politically, Napoleon realised that a loyal army was as good a power base as any mob in Paris.

The army had only marched as far as Lodi when a message

arrived from General Despinois. The people of Milan had risen up against the French occupiers. Despinois assured his commander that the uprising would be put down swiftly. But there was also more disturbing news of a further uprising in the town of Pavia.

'Pavia?' Napoleon stared at the courier, a young officer of hussars. 'What's happened in Pavia?'

'Sir, the garrison there surrendered to the townspeople.'

'Surrendered?' Napoleon struggled to control his anger. 'Was there a fight?'

'Not as far as I know, sir. The commander, Captain Linois, agreed to lay down arms if he and his men were spared. They're being held in the citadel.'

'Are they, by God?' Napoleon balled his hand into a fist and rapped it against his thigh. 'Very well, Lieutenant. Return to General Despinois. Tell him that he has full authority to put down the revolt in Milan by any means necessary. Now go.'

The hussar saluted and swung himself back on to his mount before spurring it back towards Milan. Napoleon turned to his staff officers.

'Berthier, Junot, over here!' He led them to one side, out of earshot of any other officers, and explained the situation before giving his orders. 'The army will continue towards Brescia. Keep pushing the Austrians back as far as the Mincio river. If they fall back to the far bank it will buy me a little time.'

'Time?' Junot raised his eyebrows. 'Time for what, sir?'

Napoleon removed his hat and ran a hand over his dark lank hair. 'Time to teach the Italians a lesson. I have to make an example of those rebels in Pavia, and deal with Captain Linois. I'll need two thousand picked troops. Grenadiers are the best men for the job, and I need a good field officer. Someone brave and with the stomach for . . .' he paused and pursed his lips for a moment before continuing, 'the stomach for distasteful work. Whom can you recommend?'

'I know just the man for you, General,' Junot answered at once. 'There's a Gascon, Colonel Lannes. As fierce as they come.'

'Good. Then fetch him. I'll take Bourrienne with me as well.

Have the grenadiers ready to move. They're to take a day's rations, powder and shot. They're to leave everything else here, and pick it up when we march back to the main army. See to it.'

The small column covered the twenty miles to Pavia by dawn the following day and formed up behind a wood a short distance from the crumbling walls of the ancient town. Napoleon and Lannes crept forward and surveyed the defences from just inside the treeline. A handful of armed men were sitting on a bench to one side of the gate that bestrode the main road leading into the town. On the other side of the road stood several pens of pigs, their occupants still asleep in their filth. The men were sharing a loaf of bread and talking animatedly with scant regard for the surrounding landscape they should have been keeping watch on. Napoleon's gaze tracked along the edge of the town. Crude attempts had been made to block the gaps between the buildings with carts, wagons, barrels and pieces of furniture. Here and there he could see the head and shoulders of a defender. He turned his attention to the small citadel in the centre of the town. A green and red banner hung from the highest bastion. Napoleon did not recognise the design and guessed that the people of Pavia had ambitions towards some kind of independence.

'I don't think they present much of a danger,' Napoleon decided. 'If we bring the men up through these trees we can cross the open ground and be in the town before they can react.'

Lannes considered the defences for a moment and then nodded. 'And what then, General?'

'We disarm them, round up the ringleaders and make an example of them.'

Lannes lowered the telescope and turned to Napoleon. 'An example?'

'They will be hanged from the walls of the citadel. I have to be sure that the Italians know what will happen to those who rebel against us.'

'Yes, sir.' Lannes nodded. 'I'll see to it.'

'Off you go then. Have the men load their weapons, but none

are to be cocked. I'll flog any man who fires before the order is given. Understand?'

'Yes, sir.' Lannes rose to a crouch and hurried off between the trees, leaving Napoleon to watch the town. He waited a while longer, but there was still no sign that the alarm had been raised. Then he crept back a short distance and returned to his men.

A few minutes later Napoleon glanced to either side at the men waiting in the shadows, muskets poised at the advance, then nodded to Colonel Lannes. The big Gascon drew his sword and filled his lungs before bellowing out the order.

'Grenadiers! . . . Forward!'

The uneven blue line rustled through the undergrowth, twigs snapping and cracking beneath their boots as they emerged from the gloom of the wood and trotted across the open ground towards Pavia. Napoleon took up position behind the centre company and hurried forward with them, his heart pounding with excitement. The men at the gate saw them almost at once and jumped up from their bench, snatching at their weapons. One turned to shout out a warning and then, realising the need for a more urgent call to arms, raised his musket into the air and fired. The shot sounded dull and flat as it carried across the fields, but it was enough to alert the defenders to the danger, and Napoleon knew there was no further need to keep his men quiet. His sword rasped from its scabbard and he thrust it forward towards the town.

'Charge!' he shouted. 'Charge them!'

The officers and sergeants took up the call until the whole force surged towards the flimsy defences in a great roar of battle cries. The first shots from the defenders stabbed out from the barricades, but the grenadiers surged on heedlessly. Only one of the men on watch stood his ground, bayonet lowered and legs braced as he glared at the Frenchmen. The others simply turned and ran, fleeing back down the street into the town. Their comrade parried aside the first attacker and slammed his butt into the grenadier's face, and then he was knocked to the ground and the point of a bayonet punched into his chest. The Frenchman tore the blade free and ran on, leaving his victim squirming on the ground, staring wide-eyed at the blood pumping from his wound in a great hot rush of crimson.

Such was the momentum of the attack that the grenadiers had scrambled over the barricades and were streaming through the streets before they encountered the first organised resistance. Napoleon was at the head of a loose company of his men when they turned a sharp corner into a small piazza. He just had time to register a line of levelled muskets and throw himself to the ground before they disappeared in a thick swirl of smoke and flame. The musket balls whipped overhead and struck several of the attackers down. At once Napoleon thrust himself up, stretched out his sword and bellowed at his men. 'Forward! Forward! Get them!'

He rushed on, conscious of the grenadiers behind him stepping and jumping over their fallen comrades as they raced after their general. Napoleon ran into the swirl of gunpowder smoke and saw the dim grey shapes of the defenders ahead of him. The point of a bayonet pierced the gloom and stabbed forward towards his face. Napoleon let out a ragged gasp as he smashed the hilt of his sword against the bayonet and knocked the weapon away. Abruptly he was shouldered aside by one of the grenadiers who slammed his blade into the enemy's guts and pushed him back into the ranks of his comrades. More grenadiers swept past as Napoleon stood close to the wall of the house, chest heaving as he struggled to catch his breath. Ahead, the fight was already over, and when he moved on to catch up with his men he stepped over a dozen of the townspeople, cut down in the furious onslaught. Some were wounded and one was screaming as he clamped a hand tightly over the glistening guts protruding from his torn stomach.

When he reached the main square, Napoleon found Colonel Lannes and most of the men, already being re-formed into their units by their sergeants. In the far corner of the square, up against the side of the town hall, stood a small crowd of prisoners under close guard. Colonel Lannes was interrogating a tall thin man in fine clothes as Napoleon hurried up to him.

'Who's this?'

'The mayor, sir. He's offered to surrender the town. I told him, not until I have the garrison and Captain Linois safely in our hands. He's sent a man to order their release.'

'Good,' Napoleon replied in relief. 'Then it's over.'

He turned to the mayor. 'You must identify the ringleaders of this revolt.'

'I will not betray them,' the mayor replied in French.

'We'll see about that,' Napoleon said curtly. 'Take him over to the other prisoners.'

There was a sudden shout from one side of the square and the two officers turned to see what was happening. One of the grenadier companies had broken ranks and was running away from a tall house that overlooked the market. On the roof Napoleon could see a handful of men throwing tiles down on the French soldiers. Three men were already down and as Napoleon watched another tile thudded into the shoulder of a fourth man, and he collapsed with a sharp cry of agony.

'Don't just stand there!' Colonel Lannes bellowed. 'Shoot the bastards!'

Musket fire crackled in the square and the tiles around the men on the roof exploded into fragments. They hurriedly ducked back out of sight and after a few more shots the grenadiers lowered their weapons.

'Find those men,' ordered Napoleon. 'They can join the prisoners.'

Within moments the company that Lannes led down either side of the buildings that the men had fled across came under bombardment from more roof tiles. The example had been set and soon more of the townspeople were on the roofs, raining tiles down on the French soldiers. Napoleon watched with growing frustration as the injured men were carried back into the square. Meanwhile Bourrienne and the colour party had found a clear route through the streets to join their general, and the secretary looked round in shock at the number of men lying on the paving stones having their wounds dressed before he approached Napoleon.

Napoleon nodded a greeting and shook his head wearily. 'Christ, I hate fighting civilians. Reminds me of the time we had to put down that rebellion in Lyons.'

Bourrienne nodded at the memory of the first action that he and Napoleon had shared as junior lieutenants in the Régiment de la Fère. Napoleon took off his hat and mopped his brow. 'For most of them it's just some kind of game. They'll hurl insults at soldiers one day, rocks the next, and the moment we open fire they cry "massacre" and accuse us of committing some kind of atrocity.' Napoleon replaced his hat and gave it an extra push to fix it on his head, as if that might protect him from a stray tile. 'They're costing me too many men. It's time the Italians were taught a lesson. We can't afford to have this mess repeated in every major town behind our lines.'

He turned to a sergeant. 'Find Colonel Lannes. Tell him that every time a tile is thrown at his men they are to break into the house concerned and kill everyone inside and then torch the place.'

The sergeant smiled cruelly, saluted, and then turned to trot across the piazza, following the sounds of musket fire. Bourrienne looked at his general warily.

'Is that wise?' he asked softly.

'Wise?' Napoleon shrugged. 'I think so. Why? What are you thinking?'

'I'm thinking that if we start butchering the people of Pavia then you are setting a standard for the behaviour of our men. And once word of this spreads to the other cities we'll make enemies of all those who welcomed us as liberators.'

'That may be so,' Napoleon reflected. 'On the other hand, it might be argued that I am saving lives in the long term. Once people hear of the fate of Pavia it will surely dampen any rebellious flames that burns in their hearts. It will save the lives of our men as well, Bourrienne, and that's what really matters, is it not?'

'If you say so, General.'

The fighting continued through the town until early in the afternoon, when flames and thick clouds of dark smoke rose into the sky and a dirty pall lay across Pavia. The bodies of those killed inside the buildings were dragged out into the streets and left in heaps to serve as a warning to others. Not a man, woman or child was spared and Napoleon hardened his heart at the sight as he made his way round the town after the fighting had ended.

'They have only themselves to blame,' he muttered to Bourrienne. 'If they had not chosen to defy us, none of this would have happened. I swear it.'

Colonel Lannes was waiting for them in the main piazza once Napoleon had completed his inspection of the grenadiers' checkpoints. A small band of older and sickly-looking French soldiers stood to attention behind Lannes.

'Is this the garrison?' Napoleon asked.

'Yes, sir. They've been held in the cells beneath the citadel for the last three days. They've had no food and were left in their own filth.'

'Where's Captain Linois?'

Lannes turned and indicated a stoop-shouldered man with a thin moustache standing in front of the garrison.

'Linois!' Napoleon barked. 'Come here!'

'Yes, sir.' The captain saluted and trotted over. As he stood before his general Napoleon's nose wrinkled at the stench that hung round the man.

'Linois, do you have any idea how much damage you have done to our cause?'

The captain's gaze fell and Napoleon struck him on the side of the head and continued in a low harsh voice. 'Once word reaches other cities that a French garrison has surrendered to the local rabble without firing a shot, what do you imagine they will think? As a result of your cowardice I'm going to have to double the size of the garrisons, and bolster them with good combat troops, instead of this rubbish that you command. Troops that I am counting on to defeat the Austrians. Well, what have you to say for yourself, Linois?'

The captain shook his head and looked up at his general with a wretched expression. 'Sir, they surprised us. There were hundreds of them. What could we do?'

'You could have fought them! That's what!' He stepped up to the captain and thrust an arm into his chest, sending the man reeling back. 'God damn you, Linois, you useless bastard.' For a moment he sensed that he was on the edge of a great rage and he had to force himself to be calm. He breathed deeply, his nostrils flaring. 'So, what am I to do with you, Linois?'

Linois's eyes widened. He sensed his peril. 'Sir, break me to the ranks. It's the least I deserve.'

'Too true,' Napoleon muttered with contempt. 'By virtue of the power vested in me by the Directory and the War Office, I sentence you to death.' He turned to Lannes. 'Take ten men from the garrison. Arm them. They will serve as Captain Linois's firing squad. He will be shot here in the piazza at once.'

Linois dropped to his knees and reached out a hand imploringly. 'No, sir! Please spare me! Send me to the front. Let me die like a soldier!'

'It's too late for that,' Napoleon replied coldly. 'You had your chance, and you proved that you are no soldier. Take him away.'

Linois made a light keening noise and bit his lip as two soldiers pulled him to his feet and half led, half dragged him across the piazza to join the other prisoners. Napoleon turned away, sickened by the sight, and caught Bourrienne's eye. His secretary stared at him, then shook his head faintly.

'Are you questioning my judgement?' Napoleon asked softly.

'I would not presume to do that, sir,' Bourrienne replied.

'Good. Perhaps if you were a general you would understand.'

'Then I thank God I am not a general, sir.'

Napoleon stared at him briefly before he responded. 'Yes. Thank God. For the sake of France if no other reason.'

The men of the firing squad stood to attention facing the town hall. Opposite them Captain Linois leaned against the wall, his head covered with a piece of sacking and his hands bound behind his back. His body trembled and Napoleon hoped that he would spare himself the indignity of falling over before the sentence was carried out. He turned away from the man to address the three companies of grenadiers assembled to bear witness to the execution.

'Through his cowardice this man has endangered the lives of every one of his comrades in the Army of Italy. His death will act as a signal to every French soldier that betrayal of one's comrades is beyond contempt and will never go unpunished! Tell every soldier you meet what you witness here today so there will be no doubt about the fate reserved for those who fail France, fail their comrades and fail in their own duty as a soldier! Colonel Lannes, carry out the sentence.'

He moved to one side as Lannes drew his sword, raised it overhead, and barked out the commands.

'Firing party . . . present arms! Take aim!'

There was a final sob from Linois, a horrible animal noise from deep in his chest, and then Lannes swept his sword down.

'Fire!'

The volley thundered out, echoing off the tall walls of the town hall as the musket balls ripped into Captain Linois, flattening him against the wall before he tumbled to the side, twitched once, and was still. Colonel Lannes marched stiffly across to his commander.

'Sentence has been carried out. What are your orders, sir?'

Napoleon drew a breath to help strengthen his resolve. His work in Pavia was not yet complete. One final task remained to be carried out. He gestured across the Piazza to the prisoners. 'Hang them. All of them.'

There was only the faintest look of surprise in Lannes's face before he nodded solemnly and turned away to carry out his orders.

The grenadiers were in a subdued mood as they marched out of Pavia late in the afternoon. Napoleon did not want to linger in the devastated town overnight and resolved to let his men rest for the night only when they were some distance from the scene. Several wagons had been seized to carry the wounded back to the army, as well as the bodies of their fallen comrades. Napoleon did not wish to have them buried where the townspeople could desecrate their graves. They would be given full honours by the army once the column reached Brescia.

Behind them Pavia lay under its shroud of smoke, still and quiet as a ghost town. Napoleon drew rein and stared at the scene, feeling cold and tired. For a moment he yearned for a different life, or at least a period of respite away from the monstrous deeds that he had been compelled to carry out. Then he turned his horse away from the town and trotted forward to take up his place at the head of the column.

Chapter 19

As soon as he reached the army headquarters in the bishop's mansion in Brescia Napoleon dictated a letter for circulation to every town and city lying between his army and the border with France. There were to be no more uprisings. If any French soldiers were killed then the nearest town or village would be burned to the ground and any men caught under arms would be shot. Bourrienne took down his words in silence, and once his commander had finished he rose from his seat and left the room with a curt bow. Napoleon propped his head on his hands and stared at the far wall as the punitive attack on Pavia came back to him. The execution of civilians was not a new refinement, merely an inevitable feature of war. Bourrienne's distaste for the measures that Napoleon had felt forced to carry out in Pavia was misplaced, Napoleon reassured himself.

He raised his head and pulled over a fresh sheet of paper. He opened an inkwell, dipped his pen and wrote the opening words of a new letter, words that he had written a hundred times before, but which still gave him a small thrill when he saw them in his own hand on the page.

Dear Josephine.

He still marvelled that she had consented to be his wife, and the familiar longing to lie in her arms once again fired the passion in his veins. He readied his pen, wanting to burst into the flow of impassioned words that poured from him in a torrent whenever he wrote to Josephine. But tonight the words did not come. His mind was too weary and too occupied with the demands made upon him as commander of the Army of Italy. Napoleon sat for a moment, pen poised, wanting to unburden himself of all the concerns that weighed down on him. The Directory's criminal neglect of his soldiers; uniforms in tatters, boots worn to shreds and bellies frequently empty, and the men were still owed several months' pay. Then there was the need to close with the Austrian army and destroy them, but Napoleon was constantly frustrated by the enemy's refusal to stand and fight. And Napoleon still had to deal with the prospect of dividing his army with Kellermann. If Barras and the other Directors stood by their decision then Napoleon would be removed from the public's gaze. The Army of Italy would certainly lose the initiative in the war against Austria as the two generals struggled to co-ordinate their separate, weaker forces against an enemy who already outnumbered them even before a wave of fresh troops was added to its strength. He desperately wanted to confide all this to Josephine, and yet he dared not. All of his soldier's troubles would surely seem arcane and dull to someone who moved in the most exclusive circles in Paris. He feared she would find him boring. The only words which he felt confident of pleasing her with were words of love.

Josephine.

She was truly the first woman he had loved. To be sure, there had been women before her. Those who had satisfied his physical yearnings, or had been objects for his youthful veneration when, like all young men, he had desperately needed to practise his love, and be loved in turn by someone whose affection was not bound to him by family ties. With Josephine he had learned to enjoy the pleasures of the flesh without shame or embarrassment. So it had been easy to surrender to the flood of feelings: passion, loneliness, hope, anticipation and sometimes even jealousy when he received a rare letter from her in which she expressed even the slightest affection for another man. And from such feelings the words formed readily, written down as fast as his pen could manage, raw and intense.

But tonight he felt too tired, too drained, and the usual phrases of an ardent lover seemed stale and insufficient. It was no longer enough to commit his emotions to paper. He needed Josephine here and now. Dipping his pen in the inkwell, Napoleon wrote a terse note, asking why he had not heard from her for several days. If she truly loved him, he wrote, then she would do all in her power to be at his side without delay, and he expected that of her. He signed it with a formal expression of affection and then folded the paper and sealed it, tossing it on to the other correspondence to be sent to Paris in the morning.

Napoleon rose early the next day to read the latest intelligence reports. The Austrians had established a new line of defence stretching southwards from Lake Garda to the fortress town of Mantua. As ever, the key to driving the Austrians from Italy was taking Mantua, but to do that the fortress had to be cut off from the rest of the Austrian army. At the morning conference Napoleon outlined his plan.

'We must take Mantua before the end of the year. Once we have Mantua, Austria is finished this side of the Alps,' he began. 'Accordingly, we will have to force a crossing of the Mincio river and drive Beaulieu north, away from Mantua, which will be besieged by Serurier.'

Berthier raised his eyebrows.

'Do you object to my plan, Berthier?' Napoleon asked curtly.

'No, General, it's sound enough, provided we can get across the river. Where do you intend to cross?'

'At Valeggio.'

'But that's in the centre of Beaulieu's line. He'll be able to strike at us from either flank, even if we do manage to force a crossing.'

'That's why we must stretch his lines of defence to breaking point,' Napoleon smiled. 'Augereau is to take his division up the west shore of Lake Garda. He's to make a great show of it so that Beaulieu is fully aware of his movements. Beaulieu will recognise the threat to his supply lines and will be forced to shift his weight north to counter the threat. As soon as he does that we will cross the river.'

'And what if he doesn't take the bait, sir?' asked Berthier.

'Then Augereau's division will march east and cut Beaulieu's supply lines. Either way he has to react and move forces to his right flank. Then we cross the Mincio.'

'That still leaves Mantua, sir,' Junot pointed out. 'We don't have any siege artillery with the army. That means we will have to starve them out.'

'More than likely,' Napoleon conceded. 'But if the Directory won't provide us with siege guns we'll have to find some from another source. I gather that the armies of the papal states have a more than adequate supply of heavy guns. I am certain that His Holiness will be happy to part with them, and provide us with a decent settlement, in exchange for peace with France.'

'Blackmail,' Berthier muttered. 'How can we be sure it will work? What if the Pope decides to go to war? And if the King of Naples sides with him then we'll be caught between them and the Austrians. Not a good position to be in, sir.'

'No more dangerous than being caught between an old man and a weakling,' Napoleon replied. 'Trust me. The Pope is a realist. Even with God at his side he knows that victory generally goes to the bigger battalions. He will give us what we want.'

'And if he doesn't?'

'Then God have mercy on him, because I won't.'

Once the Army of Italy was in position between the Austrian army and the fortress at Mantua Napoleon turned his attention to the latter as Italy basked in the hot summer sunshine. As the French troops laid siege to the fortress Napoleon and his staff observed the proceedings from the top of a watchtower on a Venetian banker's mansion. It was a sultry day and the climb up the narrow flight of steps had left them hot and sweating under their uniforms. From the decorative battlements of the tower the officers could see the outer works of Mantua and examine the defences through their telescopes. Napoleon watched the French advance guard marching along one of the dykes that radiated from the fortress town. Mantua had been constructed in the middle of three lakes on its northern side. To the south it was protected by a great sprawl of marshes. The five dykes were the only means of approach and these were protected by great bastions. Behind their ditches and ramparts hundreds of cannon commanded the roads that ran along the dykes.

Napoleon lowered his telescope and snapped it shut.

'Not an easy task, I think.' He turned round, eyes searching out General Serurier. 'This job is for you, Serurier. There's no chance of taking the place by a direct assault. Not until the defences are battered down. And that can't happen until we secure the siege artillery. Your orders are to contain the Austrians. Nothing more. At least not until I can reinforce you. Are you clear on that?'

Serurier nodded. 'Yes, General. When might I expect to have the guns and the men?'

'Now that we have come to terms with the Pope, they will be on their way to us any day.'

Napoleon smiled at the thought. His representative, Saliceti, had made a fine job of the negotiations. All political prisoners, many of whom sympathised with the French republic, were to be released. The ports of the papal states were to be closed to the enemies of France and the Pope had been persuaded to offer France a settlement of over fifteen million francs in coin, as well as another five million in supplies. When news of the terms reached Paris the Directors would surely abandon their foolhardy notion of dividing the command of the Army of Italy, Napoleon reflected cynically. Money did not just talk, it positively shouted, and would be far more eloquent and forceful an advocate for Napoleon's cause than any argument he might raise by himself.

Of more immediate importance, the papal armies had given up enough heavy guns to provide a siege train with more than sufficient firepower to flatten the defences of Mantua. Even now, Junot was in Rome organising the drivers and draught animals necessary to haul the guns north to Mantua. When they were in position it should only be a matter of time before the French army pounded their way in, or the Austrian garrison was starved into surrender.

'Serurier, you have your orders. Establish your lines carefully. Let no one enter or leave Mantua.'

'Yes, sir.'

'Gentlemen, once Mantua falls, we will turn our full strength against the Austrians and drive them back across the Alps. You may pass that on to every officer and man in the army. Tell them their general gives his word that all their efforts will be rewarded before the year is out.'

The staff began to disperse, some continuing to survey the defences whilst others made for the staircase, passing a sergeant who had climbed the winding stairs, and stood aside deferentially as the officers squeezed past him. He strode across to Napoleon, hot and puffing.

'Message for you, sir. From Milan.'

Napoleon took the letter and broke the seal. General Despinois was pleased to inform the commander of the Army of Italy that the Austrian garrison in the citadel had finally surrendered. French troops now commanded the guns that governed the city of Milan. There was no question of any further uprising by the Milanese. Napoleon nodded with satisfaction before his eyes skimmed down to the last, brief, paragraph.

I am pleased to inform you that your wife, her children and her entourage arrived in Milan the day of the surrender. They have been found good accommodation and Madame Bonaparte begs me to tell you that her heart will break unless you come to her in Milan without delay.

Napoleon read the words again, and again, and each time it was as if a weight had been lifted from his shoulders. At last he lowered the note and turned to Berthier, eyes glittering with excitement.

'Have my horse and escort readied. I ride to Milan at once!'

Chapter 20

She arched her back and thrust against him as Napoleon groaned, his body shuddering as he climaxed. He pressed against her and held himself there until the moment had passed. Then he slumped forward on to Josephine with a gasp, his heart pounding and his breath swift and ragged from his exertions. She gently placed her arm round his clammy shoulder and kissed the top of his head.

'Worth waiting for?' she whispered, giving him a squeeze.

'What?' he murmured dozily, still awash with the warm bliss of their lovemaking. 'What did you say?'

'Was it worth waiting for? I just wondered, after all those letters you wrote to me. Quite the passionate husband – on paper. I just wondered if you felt the same here in the flesh.'

Napoleon eased himself up on an elbow and gazed down at her, grinning. 'What do you think? There hasn't been a day when I haven't imagined this moment. To be back together, making love, just like that. I feel whole again.' His expression became serious. 'Josephine, you are all the world to me. There is no other who moves me as you do. I love every inch of you.' His hand cupped her breast and he nuzzled her nipple, savouring the sensation of its budlike hardness against his lips.

'Oh, I'm sure you say that to all your women!'

He rolled off her, and frowned. 'There aren't any other women. I swear on my life.'

'Of course not.' She cupped his cheek in her hand and gave him a quick kiss. 'But I wouldn't really blame you if there were.

From what I understand of soldiers it is all part of your way of life. A wife at home and more than one kind of conquest when you are on campaign. And your campaign has been so successful, my darling. You are the toast of Paris.'

Napoleon ignored the flattering remark. 'I swear there has been no other.'

'If you say so.' She shrugged. 'All I am saying is that I wouldn't mind if there had been, as far as this is concerned.' She reached down and gave his penis a gentle tweak. 'Just as long as your heart is mine.'

'My heart, body and soul . . .' Napoleon whispered, and then a dark thought rose into his consciousness and he was seized by a sense of uncertainty and fear. 'And have you been faithful to me, Josephine?'

There was a brief pause before she replied. 'Of course I have. What do you take me for? One of your cheap army tarts?'

'Be serious with me. Tell me the truth.'

'I am telling you the truth.'

'On your life, swear it.'

'I will not swear it, Napoleon. You either trust me or you don't. What difference would swearing on my life make? I'm telling you, I have been faithful. That should be enough for you, if you really love me, as you say you do.'

Napoleon stared at her a moment longer, looking deep into her eyes for the slightest hint of betrayal, and then he rolled on to his back and shut his eyes.

'If I thought that you were unfaithful, Josephine, it would break my heart. I could not go on. I could not live knowing that another man has lain with you, like this. That another man has . . .' He could not say the words. Just the bare thought of it made his stomach clench into a knot. He tried to shake the feeling off by forcing himself to think of something else.

'Why did you stay in Paris for so long? I thought we had agreed that you would follow me as soon as possible.'

'I have come to you as soon as I was able,' Josephine replied evenly. 'But I had to sort out my travelling chests, and make sure that the house was left in good order for our return. Then I was ill for some weeks. Too ill to travel, at least.' She fumbled for his hand and squeezed it. 'I had hoped that I was with child, but nothing came of it. It was just a chill. But I hope we will be blessed one day, even though I will not remain in my childbearing years for ever. Besides,' her tone took on a lighter note, 'I am sure that I would have been an unwelcome distraction for the only general who seems to be winning any battles for France.'

'A distraction, yes. But not an unwelcome one.'

'A distraction all the same.' She laughed. 'I doubt France would ever forgive me if I caused your concentration to slip from the task of beating the Austrians. And forgive me for saying this, but I am not terribly interested in military matters. I am only really at home in society, and would rather share that world with you than a humble campaign tent and the rough company of your soldiers.'

'This is hardly a humble campaign tent.' Napoleon gestured round the room, a fine bedchamber in one of the best houses in Milan. It was far larger and more gracious than the bedroom they had shared in the brief period between their marriage and his departure to take up command of the Army of Italy. 'I can keep you far more comfortably here in Italy than in Paris. You would not want for anything.'

'Apart from all my friends.'

'I am sure you will make new friends here,' Napoleon said quietly. 'Besides, is being with your friends preferable to being with your husband?'

'Of course not! But you cannot expect me to so easily give up my home, my friends, everything that was part of my life long before you appeared. As it is, I have brought some of my friends with me. And Hortense and Eugène, I hope you will try to become a good father to them. They need one.'

'I will do my best.' Napoleon yawned, his weariness creeping up on him like a soft warm shroud. 'I will find a post for Eugène on my staff. As for your friends, I will make them feel welcome. While the campaign against Austria lasts we can create our own social life here in Italy. You'll be treated like a princess, I promise.

And I'll have my family join us. My mother, sisters and brothers.' He smiled fondly. 'To have all those I love close to me. I've not known that since I was a child. Not since I was sent away to school.'

Josephine shifted next to him, and he sensed a slight stiffening of her body.

'What's the matter, my love?'

There was a pause before Josephine replied. 'Your family is the matter. They've made little secret of their dislike for me, especially your mother and sisters. It seems that they don't consider me worthy to be your wife. As if I was some common slut.'

'That's the Corsican blood. They tend to see the rest of the world as somehow beneath them.'

'But not you?'

'My future is tied to that of France. Paoli and his henchmen threw us out of Corsica. I owe Corsica nothing. But my family still feel as if they belong to the island, particularly the women, and Mother most of all. You must try to ignore them, Josephine. All that matters is how I feel about you. You married me, not them.'

'I married into your family,' Josephine responded. 'That's how they see it. And for that they treat me like a trespasser, or a poacher.'

'A poacher,' Napoleon mused sleepily. 'Then I must be your game.'

'Oh, you!' She punched him playfully, then leaned over to kiss him on the lips, and rested her head on his shoulder as he drifted off to sleep.

Josephine's entourage was everything Napoleon had feared. A string of brightly dressed women, all big mouths and small talk – some of the smallest talk he had ever encountered. They proved to be an unwelcome distraction for his staff officers and senior generals, who found every excuse to visit the army's headquarters and stay long after the briefings and meetings were over. In addition to her female coterie a number of young men had travelled to Milan with her. Some were on official business: art specialists sent to select the finest works of art to be shipped to Paris under the terms of various treaties that had been imposed by France; scientists and topographers to select various papers and maps from the most prestigious academies of Italy; and a handful of officers in glittering uniforms that had never been near a battlefield, or a field of any kind, Napoleon mused. There was one in particular who caught his eye. A tall, fair lieutenant of hussars who seemed to follow Josephine everywhere, carrying her pug, Fortuné, tucked under his arm.

'Who is he?' Napoleon nodded towards the hussar as they walked with a small crowd of guests around the ornate gardens of the mansion he had chosen for his quarters.

Josephine turned to look in the direction her husband had indicated and smiled. 'That's Hippolyte Charles. Rather elegant, don't you think? Quite a catch for my salon in Paris. The ladies adore him.'

'Why is he not on active service?'

'He's incompetent as a cavalry officer, by all accounts – despite being what one might describe as a fine mount in other ways. Anyway, he has a private fortune, very few duties, and a desire to see how well my husband and his army are performing. So I invited him along. You don't mind? He's devoted to my dog.'

'No, of course not, my dear,' Napoleon replied evenly, though he could think of better uses to which he might put a cavalry officer than looking after a lap dog. On the other hand, anyone who kept that wretched pug away from him should be considered a blessing, he reflected, recalling a nasty bite that Fortuné had once inflicted on him when the little beast had refused to give up his space on Josephine's bed to him. Napoleon frowned at the memory. 'Would you like me to find a place for him on my staff?'

Josephine shrugged. 'If you like. But I warn you, the man has air for brains. I can't think that he would be of any value to you.'

'Perhaps not, but if it would please you?'

'You're very kind.' Josephine smiled. 'But I think a man of his intellectual pedigree is best suited to serving as my dog groom.'

Napoleon laughed. 'Very well. I cannot think of a man I'd rather wish Fortuné on.'

Josephine turned and swatted him on the shoulder with her fan. 'What is wrong with my darling dog?'

Napoleon glanced at the pug, which promptly bared its teeth at him. 'Let's just say his bite is worse than his bark.'

The time that Napoleon could spare for Josephine was as precious to him as any treasure, especially since the Austrians were intent on relieving the fortress at Mantua. Towards the end of July a new offensive was launched from the Tyrol under an old veteran, General Wurmser. Napoleon was roused from the bed he shared with Josephine in the early hours, and for several days he hardly left his saddle as the French army was driven back by the enemy advancing in three columns. For his men, so used to advancing, being forced on to the defensive was an unfamiliar and dispiriting experience. So dangerous was the situation that Napoleon was forced to summon Serurier from Mantua, with orders to spike all the siege guns that had just been laboriously positioned to bombard the fortress. With all his men concentrated into a single force, Napoleon fell on each enemy column in turn and defeated them all. The routes down which the Austrians retreated were choked with bodies, abandoned cannon and wagons. Muskets and other equipment had been cast aside as they fled, and all that remained were the stragglers and the wounded, sitting amid the wreckage of their proud army as they waited to be taken prisoner.

Even so, before falling back with his battered army Wurmser had managed to reinforce and resupply Mantua and now, to Napoleon's intense frustration, the fortress would be able to hold out for several more months. Serurier's men, who returned to the siege, rapidly began to succumb to the unhealthy conditions in the surrounding marshes and by August over fifteen thousand of his men were on the sick list. Every large building in the country around Mantua was packed with suffering soldiers, racked by fever and hunger, while outside the lines of the graves lengthened day by day. There was no question of an assault on the fortress.

The best that could be done was to blockade the garrison and hope to starve them out.

'It's impossible!' he raged at Berthier one evening in August, after reading the latest dispatches from his masters in Paris. 'They might have abandoned that absurd plan to split the army, but how can we defeat Austria when the Directory starves us of reinforcements? Now it seems they want us to launch an attack on Naples. With what?' He threw the letter aside with a look of bitter contempt. 'I have barely enough men to hold the line against Wurmser. Do they think I can conjure soldiers out of thin air?'

Berthier waited a moment for his general to calm down, and then spoke quietly. 'You must write to them, sir.'

'Another letter?' Napoelon shook his head. 'What use would it serve?'

'We have to keep trying, sir. Tell them that they must make peace with Naples. It is the price of victory against Austria. Once Wurmser is defeated there will be plenty of time to turn on Naples. But if we fight on two fronts now, we'll surely be defeated.'

Napoleon stabbed a finger towards the discarded letter. 'You think they don't know that? What's worse is that it seems they are intent on breaking the armistice with Rome. Already our agents tell me the Pope is negotiating with Naples and Venice to form a coalition against us. I tell you, Berthier, it's almost as if the Directory is hell bent on sabotaging all that I have achieved here in Italy.'

'It wouldn't be the first time that you suspected them of undermining you,' Berthier said quietly.

'Undermining me?' Napoleon laughed. 'Hardly that. They're betraying me. Me and every single soldier of the Army of Italy. And why do they do it? Do they imagine I have designs on their power? What cause have I given them to suspect that?' He paused, rose from his chair and crossed to the window to stare down into the garden. Josephine and her coterie were sitting listening to a string quartet. As usual Hippolyte Charles was at her side with Fortuné curled up on his lap. Napoleon frowned. He dearly longed to be as close to Josephine, yet the pressures of his command seemed to demand his attention to the exclusion of almost everything else. He turned back to his chief of staff wearily.

'I'll write to Barras. I'll tell him that unless we make peace in Italy, then it is only a question of time before the army collapses under assault from Austria and the papal allies. We need time to rest our men. Time for those who are ill to recover. If the Directory refuses to negotiate for peace, then I will resign from command of the Army of Italy.'

'Resign?' Berthier shook his head. 'You can't do that, sir. Without you, the army would still be wasting away in Piedmont. You must convince the Directors to come to terms with our enemies.'

'You and I know that,' Napoleon replied bitterly. 'But we don't make policy. That is the job of men who live far from the consequences of their decisions. That's what it means to be a politician. Sometimes I wonder if a nation at war can afford to be ruled by politicians.' He smiled quickly. 'Not a wise thought for a soldier to speak aloud, eh, Berthier?'

'That may be true, sir, but it's a thought that has occurred to most soldiers at some time or other.'

'Then it's just as well that our Austrian and Italian friends are keeping us occupied.' Napoleon waved Berthier towards the small writing desk in the corner. 'I'll send two letters. One to Paris, and one to Wurmser.'

'General Wurmser?'

Napoleon nodded. 'If we can't depend on our own government to make peace then let's see if we can make the enemy see sense. I'll ask them for terms for the surrender of Mantua and an armistice.'

'Do you really think they will accept, sir?'

'I don't know. All I can do is put it to them while we wait for a reply from Paris. We'll just have to wait and see if anyone comes to their senses.'

There was no response from the Austrians and Napoleon could understand why. Despite having been defeated in the recent campaign they could draw on more men for the next attempt.

At the same time their diplomacy with the Italian states hostile to France was bearing fruit. The King of Naples marched north at the head of his army to join Wurmser. Napoleon immediately sent a message to the King warning him that Naples would share the fate of Pavia if he advanced any further north than Rome, and for a while at least the Neapolitans halted, no doubt waiting to see how the French fared against the Austrian army, which was preparing to launch yet another attack. From the Directory came mere words of encouragement and a plea for Napoleon to retain his command.

Encouragement did not win battles, he fumed, and he dispatched another letter promising the Directory to squeeze further money out of the Italians, if he was sent thirty thousand more men. Otherwise, Napoleon might not be able to defeat the next Austrian army sent against him. Then, late in October, came the news he was dreading. A new Austrian commander had been appointed, General Alvinzi, and he had already advanced as far as the Piave river. While Napoleon gathered his men to counter the latest attack the Austrians drove into the first line of defence, at Corona, and forced Masséna to retreat. As early winter set in with cold rain and bitter winds the French troops continued to give ground, pressed by the Austrian vanguard.

Outnumbered almost two to one Napoleon finally saw a slim chance of snatching back the initiative in November.

'The enemy think they have us beaten,' he told his senior commanders in his headquarters tent. Overhead rain drummed steadily on the canvas, forcing him to raise his voice to ensure that everyone heard his words and no misunderstandings would occur. 'So, we will indulge them. Tomorrow we will continue the retreat towards Verona. As soon as night falls we will march back, round their advance units, and strike them in the rear, at Villanova. If we can destroy their baggage train and supplies Alvinzi will be forced to abandon his attack on Verona. I'll be taking Masséna's and Augereau's divisions. Masséna will cross the Adige near Ronco, then march north to attack the enemy flank. Meanwhile the main attack will come from Augereau's division.'

'Where will I cross the river?' General Augereau asked.

Napoleon turned to the map frame that had been erected at the head of the table. He ran his finger down the line of the river until it came to a bridge over the Alpone – a tributary of the Adige.

'Here, at Arcola.' Napoleon turned to Augereau. 'We have to secure the crossing or there will be no chance of surprising the Austrians. Arcola is the key. If we win the coming battle, gentlemen, then we win the campaign. If we lose, then the Army of Italy will be smashed and scattered and our men will be at the mercy of every Italian peasant with a grievance. It all depends on this battle.' He turned back to the map. 'It all depends on the crossing at Arcola.'

Chapter 21

The Bridge at Arcola

The crackle of muskets sounded flat through the dawn mist that had risen from the marshy land beside the Alpone river. Napoleon swore under his breath and urged his horse forward, breaking into a gallop as he passed beside the long narrow column of infantry and cannon marching down the track towards the crossing. Behind him rode a small group of staff officers: Major Muiron, Captain Marmont and Napoleon's brother Louis. Napoleon had given strict orders that there would be no firing until the first units had crossed the river at Arcola. The noise intensified as he approached. It could mean only one thing. The Austrians had recognised the threat and had posted some men at Arcola to guard the crossing. The question was, how many?

Up ahead, where the track rose a little above the surrounding landscape, the mist had thinned and Napoleon could see that the head of the column had halted and the leading units were deploying to either side of the track. As he reached General Augereau and his staff, Napoleon reined in.

'What's happening?' he snapped at Augereau.

'My skirmishers ran into some enemy outposts, sir,' Augereau explained, and then grinned. 'There was a brief exchange of fire and they ran like rabbits.'

'Where are they now?'

'The enemy?'

'Your skirmishers!'

Augereau frowned. 'They've taken up a position in a redoubt

they captured, while they wait for the main body to come up.'

'What the hell are they doing there?' Napoleon shouted. 'Get them moving. At once! Before the Austrians decide to make a stand on the far side. You keep after them, Augereau, do you hear? Drive them across the river. Don't stop for anything and don't let the enemy rest. If word gets back that the main weight of our attack is here then they'll have the chance to turn and meet us. Get your men forward, Augereau, now!'

'Yes, sir.' Augereau saluted and turned to bellow an order for his leading grenadier companies to prepare to advance on the crossing. While the attack column was forming up Napoleon saw a mill to one side of the track and rode over to it. He dismounted and entered the building. Even though there were still sacks of grain lining the walls the place was deserted, its owner having fled at the first sight of the French soldiers. There was a ladder leading up to the flour storage floor and, stuffing his telescope in a pocket, Napoleon clambered up. Like many of the older buildings in the area the mill had a fortified tower built on to the corner, and Napoleon pushed open the heavy studded door and climbed the steps up to the crenellated observation platform. There was a fine view of the ground towards Arcola. As the morning light strengthened and the first rays of the sun warmed the air, the mist had started to lift, enough to reveal an expanse of flat ground that narrowed as it reached the bridge. A short distance from the mill he could see the fascines of the small fortification that Augereau's skirmishers had taken. Just visible amid the threads of mist several figures in white uniforms were running across the bridge. Behind them chased the French skirmishers, eagerly closing for the kill. Then, when they were halfway across the bridge, scores of muzzle flashes flickered on the far side of the river and several of the skirmishers fell. The rest hesitated, until more of them here struck down by enemy fire, and then they melted back to the near bank.

Napoleon felt his heart sink as he saw more Austrian troops on the far bank, in amongst the buildings of the village. He snapped out the brass tube of the telescope and squinted to make out the enemy force in more detail. The houses and low walls closest to the bridge were lined with soldiers. Hundreds of them. Worse still, he could make out two artillery pieces, either side of the bridge, trained on the crossing and no doubt loaded with grapeshot. Further examination revealed a still more worrying factor. The far bank of the river bowed slightly around the bridge so that the defenders would be able to pour fire on to it from either flank as well as from the end. Below the bridge the surface of the river was just visible, glassy and grey, between stretches of reeds and mud on either bank.

'Shit,' Napoleon muttered, and snapped his telescope shut before climbing down to rejoin Augereau as the latter was giving orders to one of his officers. Napoleon recognised Colonel Lannes.

'Morning, sir.' Lannes saluted and smiled.

Napoleon nodded in response to the greeting and glanced over the leading companies of the column. The men had fixed their bayonets and stood ready to advance.

'Order them to drop their packs,' Napoleon said to Lannes. 'There's two hundred paces of open ground before you reach the near end of the bridge, then perhaps another hundred to the far side, all of it covered by the enemy. They have a couple of guns over there as well. Your men are going to have to cover the distance as quickly as possible, understand?'

'Yes, sir.' Lannes's smile faded as he turned to his men. The coming assault was going to cost his battalion dearly. He filled his lungs and bellowed out, 'Down packs!'

The order was relayed along the column and the men lowered their muskets as they wriggled out of their straps and placed their backpacks and other superfluous belongings in a low pile on each side of the track. The sergeants shouted at them to get back into formation and when the column was ready Lannes drew his sword and without any preamble swept it towards the bridge.

'Quick march! Forward!'

The head of the column lurched forward and Lannes turned to Napoleon with an excited grin. 'I'll see you on the far side, sir!'

'Good luck, Colonel. You'll need it.'

Napoleon walked with them a short distance, until he reached the small rise that gave out on to the open ground. Then he stopped to watch the attack, all the while conscious of the column held up on the track behind him. Even now, a messenger would be riding towards the Austrian commander to alert him to the force that had appeared behind the rearguard. When the column was halfway across the open ground Lannes ordered them to break into a run and with the grenadier company in the lead the men streamed towards the narrow span crossing the river. There was a blasting thud from the far side of the river as a plume of fire and smoke erupted from the muzzle of one of the enemy cannon. An instant later the grapeshot tore through the men at the head of the charge, cutting several down. Lannes was untouched and waved his sword above his head, calling out to his men to follow him as he covered the remaining distance to the bridge. There was no semblance of formation now as his men sprinted forward, heads instinctively lowered. As soon as they pounded on to the first stretch of the bridge the far bank erupted in a cloud of smoke as the infantry fired. More men fell, one tumbling over the low timber rail and out of sight into the reeds below. As Napoleon watched a ball plucked off Lannes's hat, yet the colonel did not flinch as he turned briefly to beckon his men on, then charged forward again. They reached the centre of the bridge before the second cannon fired, the grapeshot carving a bloody lane through the blue ranks pressing on. The grenadiers edged forward, the front ranks crouching low, holding up those behind them, and all the time musket fire whittled down their numbers. The charge ground to a halt as those at the front fired back and then made to reload.

Napoleon cursed. The moment a charge went to ground it was over. Lannes went from man to man, hauling them up and thrusting them towards the enemy. The next blast of grapeshot decided the issue as the men at the rear of the column started to step back, then move away across the open ground. Their officers and sergeants tried to stop them for a moment; then, as the mass of men hurried away from the storm of lead sweeping the bridge, they reluctantly gave way and joined the retreat. Lannes stood alone on the bridge for a moment, shouting after them; then he turned to shake his fist at the enemy before starting to follow his men. As he reached the end of the bridge he jerked forward, as a ball struck his shoulder. Lannes kept to his feet, hunched low and scrambled back across the open ground as the enemy musket fire died away. One last blast of grapeshot tore up a patch of earth and cut down another straggler before the Austrians ceased fire. The sound of jeering and whistles swelled from the far bank and Napoleon could see some of the enemy waving their hats in the air as the French soldiers retreated out of range.

Napoleon ran forward towards Lannes and took hold of the arm on his unwounded side, supporting it across his shoulder as he helped the much larger man make for the safety of the low rise on the fringe of the open ground. There he slumped down alongside Lannes. The Gascon officer was breathing hard and gritting his teeth against the pain. His uniform coat was stained with blood front and back where a musket ball had passed through the flesh under his arm.

'Over here!' Napoleon called out to two grenadiers passing by. The men paused for a moment, still numbed by the horror they had endured on the bridge, then hurried to their general's side.

'Get the colonel to the rear and find him a surgeon.'

The men nodded and led Lannes away. Napoleon turned back towards the bridge. Already the sun had risen above the horizon and with the coming of day there would be no hiding the movements of the French army. If the Austrians reacted swiftly they could deal a lethal blow to each of Napoleon's columns in turn. Napoleon smacked his fist against his thigh. They must cross the river as quickly as possible, whatever the cost. The plan depended on it. He cursed the enemy for having positioned a force to cover the bridge. Then, more bitterly still, he cursed himself for assuming that the Austrians would leave it undefended. It was his mistake, he admitted, as he looked across the open ground, scattered with dead and dying, and on to the carpet of bodies on the bridge. His miscalculation had cost these men their lives, and Lannes his wound. Their attack had been brave and he owed them a display of courage in return.

Turning round, he approached General Augereau and the colour party of the next battalion in the column. Napoleon gestured towards the sergeant holding the tricolour standard.

'Give me that!'

Augereau cleared his throat anxiously. 'Sir, what are you doing?'

'What every general should do,' Napoleon replied quietly, trying not to show the excitement and fear that gripped his body. 'I'm going to lead from the front. Have this battalion ready to advance. Packs down and bayonets fixed. Do it now!'

'But, sir.' Augereau looked horrified. 'What if you are killed?'

'Then, if this attack fails, you will need to lead the next charge. And you will stick to the plan. We have to cross the river. Understand?'

Augereau nodded reluctantly and turned away to issue the commands. The sergeant handed Napoleon the standard.

'Sir?'

Napoleon turned round and saw that Major Muiron had stepped forward. At his shoulder stood Marmont and Louis.

'What is it, Muiron?'

'We request permission to go with you.'

'No,' Napoleon replied in a harsh tone, and at once relented. It was hardly fair to men who had offered to risk their lives alongside his. He forced himself to smile and he clasped Muiron's shoulder with his spare hand. 'I would not want to be the cause of your deaths, my friends. Stay here, and then join me on the far bank when it's all over.'

Muiron shook his head. 'Sir, with respect, we know the dangers, and we know our duty is to be at your side. If we stay here while our general goes forward we shall be shamed for ever.'

'Nevertheless it is my order.'

'Sir, your order would dishonour us. What have we done to deserve that?'

'Nothing.' Napoleon smiled. 'But you have served me well enough not to deserve death on that bridge.'

Muiron shrugged. 'Death comes for us all, sir. I would sooner face it today at your side than die an old man, made infamous by remaining behind whilst his commander went into battle.'

Napoleon felt a flush of irritation. There was no time for this. He had given an order and the man should obey it. But then, there was truth in what Muiron said, and he knew he would make the same request for the same reasons if their positions had been reversed. So he nodded. 'Very well then. If this is the day, then there are no men I would be more proud to have at my side. Let's go.'

Raising the standard aloft where all the men of the battalion – and the Austrians – could see it, Napoleon walked steadily forward. Behind him the sergeants of the following battalion bellowed out the order to advance and the second attack headed towards the bridge. Major Muiron stepped into position to Napoleon's left and Louis and Marmont fell in on his right as the four officers reached the open ground and unconsciously quickened their pace. Then they passed the first of the bodies, a young lieutenant sprawled on his front with half his head blown off by grapeshot. They were in range of the Austrian cannon, Napoleon realised, and steeled himself for the first blast from the enemy guns. He took a deep breath and called over his shoulder.

'Advance . . . at the double!'

The French broke into a trot, buckles chinking as boots pounded across the open ground. As before, the Austrians held their fire until the attackers had passed well within killing range to maximise the effect of the first blast. Time seemed to slow and Napoleon found that he was seeing every detail in its full intensity of colour and form as he rushed on. He saw the Austrian artillery officer raise his arm, readying his gun crews for the first discharge, and his racing mind tried to calculate the chances of being hit by the cone of fire blasting from the muzzle of a cannon. The odds of coming out of this alive were not impressive and he laughed. Muiron shot him a questioning look. There was no time to explain as the flat detonation of the cannon echoed across the river. He was aware of a low hissing in the air around him and the sound of a soft, wet thud, and an explosive groan from a man behind him.

'Charge!' he shouted out. 'Charge! For France!'

The rough grass of the open ground gave way to the muddy ruts of the track leading up to the bridge and Napoleon ran to one side of the rail and paused, waving his men on.

'Forward!' he cried, thrusting his sword at the far end of the bridge. 'Keep moving! Keep moving!'

The men ran past him, heads hunched into their shoulders. Grim faced, they clutched their muskets vertically to avoid skewering their comrades. As they ran down the length of the bridge the Austrian infantry opened fire and the air filled with the low whip of musket balls, mixed with the splintering crack of shots striking the woodwork, and the soft thuds as they cut down men in the dense mass surging along the narrow bridge. Napoleon felt the concussion as one of the guns on the far side fired at the attackers and he stood up, craning his neck to see how his men were progressing. As before, the fire was murderous in the middle of the bridge and body piled upon body as the French were slaughtered. The charge faltered.

'No!' Napoleon shouted. 'Keep going! Keep going and victory is ours! Stop and we all die!'

He strode forward, pushing his way through the men until the mass thinned out and those ahead were going to ground, trying to find whatever cover they could from enemy fire. Napoleon stepped amongst them and held the standard high.

'Keep going!'

But the men around him refused to meet his eye and began to creep back.

'Bastards!' Napoleon screamed. 'Would you let your general die alone?'

He was about to step forward when someone grasped his arm and spun him round, shielding his body from the far bank. Muiron glared into his face.

'General! You will get yourself killed!' the major shouted above the din. 'If you fall we are lost! This is not your place. Get back!'

He pushed Napoleon through the men stalled on the bridge, just as some herd spirit made them all turn back towards their own lines.

'Make way for the general!' Muiron called out, and then his grip on Napoleon's arm spasmed. Napoleon turned and saw a shocked expression on the major's face. He was looking down and Napoleon followed his gaze and saw the hole in his jacket, over the heart, the blood pumping from the wound.

'Muiron?'

The major frowned, then his head slumped and his legs buckled as he fell on to the bridge. Napoleon paused and reached down to help his companion. As he did so one of his men thrust past, desperate to escape the slaughter. He was a large man and he sent his general reeling towards the edge of the bridge. The rail had been splintered by grapeshot and gave way with a crack the moment Napoleon fell against it. He flung his arms forward, dropping the standard as he desperately tried to keep his balance, but his momentum was too great and he tumbled backwards off the bridge. He landed on his back in the mud, the impact driving the breath from his body. For a second he was staring up at the clear sky, dazed. Then he rolled over and tried to push himself up, but the mud sucked his hands down. With great difficulty Napoleon scrambled upright and tried to take a step, but his boots just churned up the filthy mire and he sank up to his knees, far enough to hold him in place.

'General!' a voice cried from above and Napoleon looked up at the bridge.

'Sir? Where are you?' Marmont cried out.

'Here! Down here!'

A moment later Marmont's head appeared over the rail.

'Get me out!' Napoleon shouted.

Marmont nodded and his head disappeared from view. A moment later he leaped over the rail a short distance further along, closer to the bank, and landed in the reeds. Louis jumped after him and they thrust their way through the rasping stalks until they emerged at the edge of the mud. Napoleon leaned towards them, stretching out his arms.

'Shit! I can't reach.'

Marmont turned to Louis. 'Hold my legs!'

Then he fell forward on to the mud and grabbed at his

general's hands. As soon as he had a good hold he grunted over his shoulder, 'Pull us back.'

Louis wrapped his arms round one of Marmont's boots, and, digging his heels into the soft ground at the base of the reeds, he pulled with all his might. At first Napoleon did not feel himself budging, and then with a glutinous sucking he lurched towards Marmont.

'Keep pulling!' Marmont called back to Louis. 'He's coming!'

Napoleon kept as flat as he could to spread his weight, and slowly they drew him out of the mud. Just then there was a shout from the Austrian bank and glancing back Napoleon saw a handful of men pointing at them from behind a wall. One of the men levelled his musket and fired. There was a dull plop close by Napoleon's side and a plug of dark mud leaped into the air, leaving a furrow in the glistening brown surface. Marmont was back on solid ground now and wrenched Napoleon after him. He emerged from the mud, plastered in filth, as more shots slapped into the mud around them.

Napoleon clapped Marmont on the shoulder. 'I'll thank you properly later on. Let's go!'

They thrust their way into the reeds, out of sight of the Austrians who continued to take shots in their direction, cutting through the tall stems. Once they reached the bank Napoleon and Marmont waited until they had caught their breath and scraped as much of the thick, heavy mud from their clothes and boots as possible.

'Ready?' Napoleon asked. 'Then let's go!'

They burst from the reeds and scrambled up the bank. As they reached the flat ground before the bridge more shots rippled out from the Austrian side of the river, but at that range Napoleon knew there was very little chance of scoring a hit. Nevertheless they ran all the way to the safety of the low rise before they stopped, bent double and gasped for breath. General Augereau came over.

'Good God, sir! Are you all right?'

Napoleon nodded. Augereau's nose wrinkled at the stench of the filth that caked his commander. 'What the hell's that smell?'

'Mud,' Napoleon replied sourly. 'What do you think?'

He forced himself to stand upright, and stared back towards the bridge. 'We cannot cross there. That much is clear.'

He turned to Augereau. 'Send two brigades downriver to Albaredo at once. They are to cross and come up on the flank of Arcola. See to it. We may still have time to catch General Alvinzi in our trap.'

'Yes, sir. At once.' Augereau saluted and turned towards his small cluster of staff officers to communicate the new orders. Napoleon turned to his muddy companions and clasped their hands in turn.

'Thank you, gentlemen. I owe you my life.' He turned towards the bridge, now piled high with French bodies. 'You, and Major Muiron.'

As the day wore on, Napoleon received word from Masséna that he had cleared the Austrians out of Porcile and he had a clear view of the road between Verona and Villanova from the church tower in Porcile. There were signs that the enemy had recognised the threat to their baggage train. Several cavalry units had already returned along the road. Napoleon crumpled up the note with an exasperated curse. More messages followed reporting the return of a large infantry column to Villanova and Napoleon realised that the original target of his surprise attack was no longer available. Yet the Austrians were now in full retreat from Verona. Clearly Alvinzi was terrified of being cut off from his supplies.

As dusk gathered there was a sudden exchange of musket fire on the far bank and through his telescope Napoleon saw Augereau's detached brigades storm into Arcola, driving the Austrians from the village. The fighting ended as both sides ceased fire and the two armies camped for the night in and around the marshland that stretched between the Adige and Alpone rivers. Even though Napoleon knew that Alvinzi had rejoined his baggage train, there was still some advantage to be wrung from the situation. Only three narrow dykes crossed the marshland and the enemy would not be able to deploy superior numbers against Napoleon's forces if they attacked. His plan had been bold, and now he decided that he had to take one last risk. He sent for three thousand of the men blockading Mantua. If the force left under cover of darkness then, with luck, the enemy garrison would not detect their absence.

Once the reinforcements arrived Napoleon attacked Alvinzi down each of the routes through the marshland for the next two days. Then, on the third morning, as the exhausted men of the Army of Italy readied themselves for a third onslaught, reports began to arrive at headquarters from the patrols that had been sent out at first light.

Marmont hurried into the study of a small villa that served as Napoleon's field headquarters as the general was drafting his order of the day, exhorting his men to one last effort to send Alvinzi reeling back towards the Austrian border. They were bone tired, and had seen many of their comrades killed and wounded in the bitter skirmishes of the previous days. Napoleon doubted that they had much fight left in them. This day they must fight and win, or he would have to fall back and try to defend Verona with the forces that were left to him.

'Sir, they've gone!'

Napoleon looked up at him, pen poised over the paper. 'Gone?'

'The Austrians!' Marmont laughed and slapped his thigh in delight. 'Our patrols did not come up against any enemy pickets and went forward. Their positions are empty. They've gone. We've beaten them, sir! Alvinzi's running for it.'

Napoleon stared at him for a moment and then sat back in his chair with a deep sigh. It was over then, for now. No doubt the Austrians would fall back and ready themselves for yet another attempt, and the battered veterans of the Army of Italy would be called on to make yet another superhuman effort to defend the land they had won for France. Napoleon marvelled at what his men had achieved. But for now they had gained a desperately needed respite.

'Give the order for the men to stand down. Then find Murat. I want the cavalry to snap at the enemy's heels all the way to

Bassano. They are not to give Alvinzi a moment's rest. Is that clear?'

'Yes, sir.' Marmont saluted, and paused before he turned away to carry out his orders. 'My congratulations, sir.'

'Congratulations?' Napoleon shook his head. 'We've lost too many men, too many comrades for that, Marmont.'

Once Marmont had left the room and closed the door, Napoleon looked down at the order he had written, and then crumpled the piece of paper up and threw it aside. He pulled out a fresh sheet and began writing a new order of the day for his army.

Never has a field of battle been as disputed as that of Arcola. But nothing is lost as long as courage remains . . .

Chapter 22

February 1797

'It seems that the Directory has finally decided to reward our good work, gentlemen.' Napoleon could not help smiling as he addressed his staff and senior officers. 'After nearly a year of victories, won by half-starved men with rags on their backs, our masters have finally decided to honour their pledge to send us the reinforcements we need.'

Masséna snorted. 'Now that we've all but driven the Austrians from Italy!'

There was a murmur of bitter assent from the other officers, and Napoleon could well understand it. Only two weeks earlier the Army of Italy had turned back the last attempt by the Austrians to relieve Mantua. In five days of marching and fighting the French had defeated the enemy at Rivoli and La Favorita, destroying three quarters of the Austrian army. The final triumph of the swift campaign was General Wurmser's surrender of Mantua. Most of the garrison was starving and sick and once he had received news of the spectacular defeat at Rivoli Wurmser had realised that Mantua was doomed. He was accorded the honours of war by Napoleon and allowed to leave the fortress with his sword as a free man. The fall of the Austrian fortress had also marked an end to the incessant plotting between Venice, Naples and the papal states, now that Napoleon was free to turn his attention to his southern flank. In quick succession the Pope and the King of Naples had pledged loyalty to France, and sealed the pledge with thirty million francs. It was no wonder that Masséna and the others treated the news from Paris with such cynicism.

'Yes.' Napoleon raised a hand to quiet his fiery subordinate. 'Their timing is less than perfect, I grant you. But once Bernadotte and Delmas join us with their divisions the Army of Italy will have eighty thousand men on its strength. More than enough for the next, and I hope final, phase of the war against Austria . . .'

He paused, enjoying the keen concentration of his officers as they waited for him to continue. He clicked his fingers and Berthier crossed to the table and unrolled a map of the north of Italy, the Alps and Austria. Once the map was weighted down, Napoleon took up position at the head of the table and tapped his finger on the Austrian capital.

'Vienna, gentlemen. That is the goal for the coming campaign. The Army of Italy and the Army of the Rhine will be the two prongs of an attack on Austria. The enemy will no longer be able to shuffle men between the two fronts and for the first time we shall outnumber them. I aim to be in Vienna by summer at the latest. And there I shall dictate terms to the Emperor of Austria, while my officers and soldiers take the spoils of war that they have earned.'

There were broad smiles from the assembled officers, and Napoleon turned to Masséna. 'I imagine that meets with your approval, André?'

Masséna rubbed his hands together. 'Indeed, sir! I shall loot the place until the Viennese are begging for mercy.'

'Just as long as you leave a little something for the rest of us.'

The others laughed and Napoleon indulged them for a moment before he tapped the map again. 'Now to business: the plan for the campaign.'

Once the briefing was over and the field officers had returned to their commands to prepare their men for the months ahead, Napoleon went to Josephine at the house he had

169

commandeered at Montebello. It was a very grand affair, a palace truly fit for the man who ruled the whole expanse of northern Italy, from the border of France across the shores of the Adriatic Sea. Josephine's entourage had been swelled by a large number of local aristocrats and others seeking the favour of the young French general. As Napoleon rode up the long tree-lined avenue he was struck by the thought that the original coterie of family and friends now had more the appearance of some regal court, with its finely dressed guests served by hundreds of uniformed staff amid the stately halls, corridors and immaculately landscaped gardens of Montebello.

Josephine had gone for a ride with Lieutenant Charles and did not return until dusk. Napoleon was waiting for her in the stables when they returned, two riders emerging from the thin blue light that bathed the withered winter landscape. As Napoleon walked out of the shadows of the stable Josephine was talking in a quiet undertone. The hussar lieutenant caught sight of Napoleon at once, and reining in he snapped a salute at his superior. Josephine slid from her saddle and ran into Napoleon's arms and they exchanged a kiss. Napoleon released his wife and nodded to the hussar.

'You may go now, Lieutenant. My wife is quite safe, but I thank you for acting as her protector this afternoon.'

'My pleasure, sir.' Lieutenant Charles wheeled his mount, took up the reins of Josephine's horse, and led it away towards the waiting grooms. Napoleon stared at the man for a moment. He could see why the ladies might warm to the company of the tall, graceful cavalry officer with his finely sculpted features. Quite the Adonis, Napoleon reflected ruefully, suddenly conscious of his own slight frame and dark hair. Had he not been celebrated for his victory over the royalists in Paris he would still be an undistinguished officer of artillery languishing in the ranks of the Army of the Vendée. The kind of man that Josephine would never have married. The knowledge cut him like a knife and his wife sensed the sudden change.

'What is it?' she asked in an alarmed tone. 'What's the matter?'

Napoleon turned away from Hippolyte Charles. 'It's nothing.'

'What's happened, Napoleon?' She grasped his shoulders. 'You're scaring me.'

'Really, it's nothing,' he lied. 'It's just that I had hoped to spend more time with you here at Montebello. But there's to be a new campaign. I'm going away again, possibly for some months.'

'Is that it?' She looked relieved. 'I thought . . . Never mind. Then we must make the most of whatever time you have with me. It's cold. Come, let's get inside. I need to slip into some warm clothes.' Her eyes twinkled as she lowered her voice. 'Bedclothes, that is.'

'I don't know what it is that you see in her,' Napoleon's mother muttered as they sat by the fire. The evening meal had just finished and the intimate circle of family and close friends had retired to the library. Outside it had begun to rain, and the crack and hiss of the wood in the large iron grate mixed with the soft drumming of rain on the glass panes of the tall windows overlooking the gardens. Josephine was playing a simple card game with Eugène, Hortense, and several of her friends, and their bright chatter was frequently interrupted by sharp cries of surprise and glee at the turn of a card. The Bonapartes had retired to the chairs arranged around the fireplace and a footman had brought a gleaming silver pot of coffee and fine china cups and set them down on a low table in front of them. Napoleon reached for the pot and poured for his mother, then set the pot down and resumed his seat.

'Josephine is my wife, Mother. I love her. That should be good enough for you.'

'Well it isn't,' Letizia snapped back, and leaned closer to her son as she continued, 'I've heard the gossip from Paris. She has a reputation, you know.'

'So? I have a reputation too.'

'Not the same kind of reputation and you know it. So don't act the fool.' Letizia tapped his knee with her fan. 'She was the lover of Paul Barras before you.'

'I know. She told me. That was before we met.'

There was an awkward silence before Letizia smiled. 'I'm only thinking of you, my son. It would break my heart if that woman shamed you. If she humiliated you in public.'

'I see.' Napoleon smiled bitterly. 'This is about the family's honour, isn't it? That stiff Corsican morality you take such pride in.'

'Yes.'

'But we aren't in Corsica any more, Mother.'

'Maybe, but that does not make us any less Corsican.' She tapped him on the breast. 'In your heart you know this. Anyway, anyone listening to you speak could hardly fail to be aware of your origins.'

'This is beside the point. She is my wife and you will respect her as such. It is my will.'

'It may be your will,' Letizia nodded discreetly towards the card players, 'but do you really know her will? Does she really love you?'

'She says so.'

'Of course she would. But look at it from her point of view, Napoleon. She's some years older than you. Her looks are beginning to fade. She knew that it was only a matter of time before she no longer graced any Paris salon. Then you came along. Young, inexperienced, famous and, more important, unattached. You were her last chance of a good match.'

Napoleon glared at his mother. 'Enough. You go too far.'

He stood up abruptly, shook his head, and strode out of the room.

The Austrians appointed their most able general to command the forces opposing the Army of Italy. Archduke Charles had enjoyed some notable successes against the Army of the Rhine and now sought to bolster his reputation by humbling the young French general who had caused so much grief to Austrian interests in Italy. Napoleon gave him no time to prepare for the attack. As soon as the passes across the Alps were free of snow he led his men through the mountain ranges and fell upon the enemy in the broad valley through which the River Drave flowed. Nothing could check the Army of Italy in its advance, and it was only with the capture of the city of Klagenfurt that Napoleon halted.

There had been no news of the Army of the Rhine since Napoleon had launched his offensive and the further he advanced into Austria, the longer his lines of communication had become. If the Directory's strategy was being followed to the letter then the Army of the Rhine should be thrusting deep into Austria from the north. Yet there had been no word from General Moreau, nor any confirmation from Paris that Moreau's progress was going ahead as planned. As the days passed Napoleon became increasingly anxious about the silence. If Moreau had been thrown back then the Austrians would be able to reinforce Archduke Charles and any reverse that Napoleon suffered so far from his bases in northern Italy could lead to the destruction of the Army of Italy.

'What are those fools playing at, Berthier?' Napoleon muttered, hands clasped behind his back as he stared out of the window of Hochosterwitz castle at the distant mountains. 'It's nearly a month since I last had news of Moreau. I tell you, the Directors have betrayed us again. Just one last push, by both armies, and we'd have Vienna.'

'I've had a report from Murat, sir. One of our cavalry patrols reached the top of the Semmerling pass. They claim that they could see Vienna in the distance.'

Napoleon shook his head with disdain. 'Wishful thinking. But I know exactly how they feel. One last victory and the war would be over. Only we can't have that without Moreau. What am I to do?'

Berthier had come to know his commander well enough to realise the question was rhetorical, and he kept his silence as Napoleon continued.

'We dare not advance without Moreau in support. Yet we cannot remain here and permit the enemy to gather their forces and attack our supply lines . . .' Napoleon was still for a moment, and then nodded, his decision made. 'There is only one thing we can do.'

'Sir?'

'Offer the Austrians an armistice.' He turned away from the window. 'We must buy ourselves some time. But we must not look as if we need the ceasefire. We must be seen to be negotiating from a position of strength. I'll offer the Austrians a five days' armistice. Meanwhile we'll advance and take Leoben. That should put the spur to their thinking. They'll have to agree to terms then, just to stop us pressing even further into their homeland. Very well, Berthier, send a message to Archduke Charles.'

True to form, the enemy refused to reply at first, but with the fall of Leoben early in April the Austrians accepted the offer, and added that they would not be averse to negotiating a broader treaty. Napoleon delayed his response, still hoping for word that Moreau was closing in from the north. Finally, a messenger arrived from the Directory in Paris. Moreau had not even begun his advance. Worse still, there was news of uprisings in Tyrol and Venice where the people had seized a French ship and slaughtered its crew. Napoleon's full fury was directed at Moreau, and the Directory who had failed to make Moreau fulfil his part of the plan. It almost felt as if they had conspired against Napoleon, fearful of the public acclaim he would have won for capturing the enemy capital. As it was, he had no choice; he needed peace.

So he assented to the Austrian offer and sent them his terms. Austria was to cede Belgium to France, permit France to occupy the left bank of the Rhine and recognise the Cisalpine republic of Milan, Bologna and Modena. In return France would hand back Venice, Istria and Dalmatia.

For some days there was no reply from the court of the Austrian Emperor, and then on 18 April they sent formal notification that they would sign the preliminary treaty.

Napoleon received the news with far better grace than his chief of staff had anticipated and once they were alone Berthier cleared his throat nervously.

'What if Paris refuses to endorse the treaty, sir?'

'They won't,' Napoleon replied assuredly. 'France has much to gain from this treaty, and the Directory needs to give the people peace.'

'Some will say that you have exceeded your authority.'

'And I will say that the Directory abrogated theirs the moment they failed to see their plan through. I doubt that the people of France, or the army, would stand by and let me be disciplined for bringing a profitable peace.'

'I suppose not,' Berthier conceded, surprised at the political turn his commander's thoughts had taken. This was more than soldierly ambition. But there was an obvious flaw in Napoleon's peace. Berthier reflected for a moment. Perhaps Napoleon wasn't as cunning as he had thought.

'One thing bothers me, sir.'

'Oh?'

'This treaty leaves Austria with territory in Italy. It's hard to believe that there will be no more friction between France and Austria over those lands.'

'I know.' Napoleon smiled cynically. 'My treaty practically guarantees that there will be another war.' He clenched his fist. 'And next time, I *will* seize Vienna.'

Chapter 23

Arthur

Calcutta, February 1797

From the quarterdeck of the *Queen Charlotte*, anchored half a mile from the shore, the stench of human ordure was overpowering. The sides of the Indiaman were crowded with soldiers curious to have their first sight of the colony. Their excited chatter filled the air and competed with the cries of the beggars swimming in the water around the newly arrived ship. Amongst them, rowing with little regard for the people in the water, were scores of boats offering their services to anyone on board who needed to be transferred to the shore.

On the quarterdeck of the ship stood the paying passengers, equally curious about the new land that lay on either bank of the Hoogley. The river itself was broad and brown and scattered with flotsam, the odd bloated carcass of an animal, and the occasional human. Despite having read as much as he could about India during the six-month voyage round the southern cape, Arthur was shocked by the evident squalor on his first encounter with Calcutta. And he had not even set foot ashore, he reflected grimly. His first instinct was that he should have insisted on a different posting for his regiment. Most of the men of the 33rd Foot had been fed a diet of the most fanciful stories and legends about India. While it was true that a man from even the most humble origins could make a fortune – and a few did – in the employ of the East India Company or in the service of one of the numerous princes who ruled huge swathes of the subcontinent as absolutely as any Caesar, the chances of a man's surviving the climate and the other risks to health were one in two. Odds that Arthur did not find wholly encouraging, and he was resolved to do his utmost to see that he, and the men of his regiment, looked after their health as diligently as possible.

Six months at sea with little opportunity for exercise had already taken its toll on the fitness of the men of the 33rd, and the poor diet and copious drinking had made many of them stout and red-faced. As soon as he had them on dry land that would have to be remedied, Arthur decided. He turned to beckon to his adjutant, Captain Fitzroy, who was talking animatedly with one of the few female passengers who had been so much the centre of attention in the small closed world of the better class of passenger during the voyage. Fitzroy noticed his superior's summons on the second attempt. He graciously made his excuses to the lady and hurried across the deck to Arthur. 'Yes, sir?'

'I'd be obliged if you secured the services of one of those boatmen. I wish to pay my compliments to the Governor General as soon as possible.' He indicated the grey granite-like mass of Fort William standing on the eastern shore of the Hoogley. 'In the meantime, I want our men ashore as quickly as possible. They are to be quartered in the fort.'

'Yes, sir.'

'And do make sure that you negotiate a good price with the boatman,' Arthur continued. 'His Majesty's funds are not infinite.'

Captain Fitzroy grinned. 'Yes, sir.'

Arthur lowered his voice. 'I'd be obliged if you did not arrange any commission for yourself in the process. We're here to improve the lot of these people, and to serve our country, not just ourselves.'

'Yes, sir.'

Fitzroy's disappointment was evident in his tone and Arthur rather regretted that there was not a hint of shame there. 'Very well, Fitzroy. Carry on.'

'Yes, sir.' The adjutant saluted and strode off to carry out his orders.

Arthur could not help feeling a surge of irritation over the man's attitude. He was also worried about the magnitude of the task facing him, given his ambitions for India. Already he had written to Richard and gently suggested that he might put himself forward for the appointment of Governor General of India, and that Henry might be persuaded to join them. India might well be the making of the three brothers, if they could meet the challenges facing them. As far as the East India Company was concerned, their purpose was to make money out of the subcontinent. But now that war was being waged between the powers of Europe, it was vital for Britain's trade that the Company's possessions were given military protection. It was already clear that one day the Indian colonies would be run by the Crown, rather than private entrepreneurs, just as it was clear to Arthur that it was in the interests of the peoples of the subcontinent that England put an end to their endless wars and brigandage and bring peace and effective governance to India. That was his great ambition, and one he hoped to share with Richard and Henry if they decided to join him. But he was well aware that there were many obstacles between him and the achievement of his aim.

From the copious background reading Arthur had done, it was clear that corruption was rife amongst the Englishmen who served in the three presidencies that belonged to the East India Company at Calcutta, Madras and Bombay. It was hardly surprising given that they were only answerable to Parliament and the stockholders of the East India Company thousands of miles away in London. Any message sent from India took the best part of a year to elicit a reply from London and that meant that the local officials were left fairly much to their own devices. In such circumstances a culture where bribes were offered and readily accepted thrived in a way it did in no other place in the world. No man was immune from temptation. A King's officer might earn three hundred pounds a year at home in England. Here in India he might earn as much as ten thousand pounds a year through bribes or 'gifts' offered by the native princes and merchants in exchange for lucrative army contracts, or forcefully settling disputes between the patchwork of little states that dotted the continent.

While that remained the case, Arthur reflected, the British presence in India would never amount to much more than a distasteful leeching operation. If it was allowed to continue, then he firmly believed that Britain's greatest ever opportunity for enrichment and international prestige would be lost. With scrupulous governance, and an ethic of service to the people, India could be the brightest gem in any nation's crown.

Such had been his thinking on the long voyage out from England. But now that he was here, the raw truth of India made him lose hope. The view of Calcutta from the deck of the Indiaman was as nothing compared to the assault on the senses that greeted Arthur as he stepped out of the small boat on to the roughly constructed quay. Every kind of filth was impacted on the ground and at the entrance to the nearest street lay a dead dog, crushed by a cart so that its entrails had burst from its belly and were now covered in a dark droning cloud of flies.

'*Salaam, sahib!*' A thin native in a loincloth scurried up and struck his forehead as he bowed to Arthur. Bright white teeth flashed in a smile. 'I take your bags, *sahib*.'

'I don't have any,' Arthur replied. 'They're on the ship.'

The porter glanced over the English officer for anything else that might need carrying, but Arthur waved him aside.

'Out of my way, please.'

'*Acha, sahib!*' The porter bowed and hopped to one side as Arthur started along the quay towards the distant mass of Fort William. The squalor of the rapidly expanding town sprawled back from the banks of the river along filthy thoroughfares that Arthur glanced down as he made his way through the crowd of porters, beggars and merchants. The sounds of their cries, alien and shrill, the strangeness of their clothes and rags and the colour of their skins made Arthur keenly aware of how out of place he must seem. Indeed, as he glanced round, he realised that he was almost the only white man visible on the quay.

At length the quay gave way to a patch of mud at the river's edge where children were playing in the water, splashing each other in silvery spray that reminded Arthur how hot he was. He wore the uniform in which he had set off from England, made from a heavy wool that might be sensible for this time of year back in Europe but was a positive torment here in Calcutta. He resolved to find himself a good local tailor as soon as possible to have some uniforms cut from a lighter material. It would be good if the men of the 33rd could be similarly dressed, or a hard march and a fight in this climate might well finish them.

Arthur entered Fort William and made his way to the elegant whitewashed headquarters, surrounded by a wide walkway which was raised above the ground and shaded by an overhanging roof. Several officers were sitting on cane chairs round a low table, talking quietly as they drank. Behind them squatted a small figure in a linen robe operating a large canvas screen that fanned the officers as they sat. They stood up as Arthur approached, one or two of them unsteadily, and exchanged a salute with him.

'Good day, gentlemen. Colonel Arthur Wesley at your service. Is the Governor General at headquarters today?'

'Yes, sir,' the senior officer, an India Company major, replied. 'Sir John is in his office. Do you wish me to show the way?'

Arthur nodded. 'I'd be obliged. Might I know your name?'

'Harry Ball, sir.' He smiled readily. 'A regular, before I took the John Company bounty, and I ain't looked back since. If you'd follow me?'

He led the way inside the headquarters and Arthur took the chance to examine the man. So this was one of the East India Company officers. At first glance there was only the uniform to distinguish Ball from the officers in His Majesty's service. Ball seemed to be in his mid-forties, grey hair cropped short above a creased and tanned face. He looked competent enough, Arthur decided, hoping that he was typical of his kind. There were few enough King's regiments in India as it was. Without the white-officered Company units the lands held by the three presidencies could be swallowed up by any maharaja, nawab or nizam whose greed and ambition got the better of him.

Major Ball led Arthur up a wide flight of steps to the offices on the second floor. The corridors and rooms of the building were airy and spacious and the Europeans who worked there were bent over their desks, cooled by one of the ubiquitous fans worked by the silent figures squatting discreetly at the side of each room. The Governor General's office was on the corner of the building, looking out over the ramparts to the broad expanse of the river beyond where the *Queen Charlotte* lay peacefully at anchor amid the other shipping. A man dressed in a loose shirt was reading some papers that lay on top of an enormous desk of solid design. His plain coat rested on the back of his chair.

Ball tapped on the doorframe. 'Sir?'

The Governor General looked up and Arthur saw that he was an older man, in his fifties with a kindly face and keen eyes. He smiled. 'I assume you are off the ships that arrived this morning.'

'Yes, sir. Colonel Arthur Wesley. Officer commanding the 33rd Foot.'

'The 33rd?' Sir John Shore leaned back and scratched his chin. 'We were expecting you a bit earlier. By the new year at any rate. Your regiment set sail in June, did it not?'

'Yes, sir.'

'Slow going, Wesley,' he said in a vaguely irritated tone.

Arthur felt unfairly slighted. It was hardly his fault if the vagaries of wind and sea had delayed the arrival of his regiment. But there was little point in making an issue about it the moment he met his new superior.

'Yes, sir. I thought so. But I'm sure the captains of the Company ships were doing their best to make the swiftest possible passage.'

'I suppose so.' Sir John waved him towards one of the chairs arranged on the far side of his desk. 'Thank you, Ball. You may go.'

Major Ball nodded and turned away, his footsteps echoing along the corridor as he strode off to rejoin his comrades on the veranda.

'Good man, that.' Sir John nodded after him. 'Knows the country well, and his men even better. Wish there were more officers like him in the Company's battalions. They have caused me quite a bit of trouble since I was appointed. Some of the blackguards even had the audacity to threaten mutiny last January. Threatened to take charge of India and run it for themselves unless I turned a blind eye to their peculations, and pressed the Company to increase their pay.' Sir John shrugged the matter aside. 'Anyway, Colonel Wesley, I expect you didn't report to me just to hear about the grumbles of our discontented Company officers, eh?'

Arthur smiled. 'No, sir. But it is as well to garner any information that may be of use later on.'

'Yes, I believe so. Anyway, I imagine you would like to be briefed on the situation here, before we attend to the more mundane matters concerning the billeting of your men.'

'I should be grateful for that, sir.'

Sir John nodded. 'Very well, then. First, you will not be aware of it, but Spain has allied itself with France. We had the news from an overland dispatch that reached Calcutta last week.'

Arthur raised his eyebrows in surprise. The odds against England winning the present war had lengthened considerably.

'When was the alliance made?'

'Back in October. And for all we know it has already crumbled. That is the burden of living so far from London, I'm afraid. We are never less than several months behind events taking place in Europe, but we must operate on the basis of the last official dispatch from England. To that end we now find ourselves at war with three out of the four major powers who have influence in the far east, France, Holland and Spain. We are not at war with Portugal. Not yet. Not as far as I am aware, at least. Of course, the biggest threat to English interests in India comes from the French. We saw off the Compagnie des Indes some years back, but since the revolution they have been doing their best to stir up discontent in the subcontinent. That's one of the reasons for the 33rd's being sent out here.'

'Is there trouble brewing?'

'There's always trouble on one front or another,' Sir John replied wearily. 'The presidency of Calcutta is an area somewhat bigger than England, controlled by perhaps no more than two thousand of our people. If the natives ever took it into their heads to unite and crush us it could be done in an instant.' He stared at the new arrival. 'I tell you, Wesley, our remit here is a very delicate affair. We rule because we have what the locals call *iqbal*.'

'That's their word for good luck, or good fortune, isn't it?'

Sir John smiled with surprise and nodded. 'I'm impressed. Where did you learn that?'

'I had plenty of time to read about my new posting on the voyage over, sir,' Arthur explained. 'I have even made a little progress in one of the local tongues, though of course I will need some further tutoring.'

Sir John laughed. 'That's the damnedest thing I ever heard! I doubt that one in a hundred of my staff here can claim more than a few words of Hindoostani. What on earth did you do that for?'

Arthur shrugged. 'It seemed the sensible thing to do, sir. If a man is to serve to best effect he must be familiar with the geography and people amongst whom he is required to campaign.'

'That's a bloody odd notion, Wesley. But if you think it serves a purpose then stick with it.'

'I intend to, sir.'

'Ah . . . where was I?'

'*Iqbal*, sir. You said we ruled here because the locals believed in our good fortune.'

'Yes, that's it. That's the most important thing for you to learn while you are here, Wesley. Whatever else you do, you will be judged by the good fortune that attends you. Therefore it is vital that you suffer no reverses, that you build on a reputation for success. That means that you must plan for every eventuality, consider every detail of your operations so that they progress as if blessed by fate, rather than as a result of tireless staff work. You follow me?'

Arthur nodded.

'Good. Because you will need all the luck you can get to meet the challenges facing us here in India. Bombay, Madras and Calcutta are surrounded by the territories of powerful nations. Some of them are bitterly opposed to us. Take that fellow Tipoo Sahib, the Sultan of Mysore. Caused no end of trouble to my predecessor, Lord Cornwallis. We've had an uneasy peace with Mysore since then, but now I hear from my spies that Tipoo is negotiating with France to enter into some kind of alliance. Worse still, the Nizam of Hyderabad and the rulers of the Mahratta confederation are employing a large number of French officers to train and command their armies. Of course, we have had a number of English officers in the employ of such states, but lately they have been having their contracts cancelled and finding themselves thrown out by their former employers, and always replaced by a Frenchman. For now we have peace, but the French will be using their influence to do whatever they can to defeat us in India.'

'I imagine they would, sir,' Arthur responded. 'While the Navy keeps them from the shores of England, all the French can do is attack our trade. The loss of India would cost England dear.'

'Then make sure that your brother realises that as well as you do.' Sir John nodded. 'That's right, I've done a little research on you too, Colonel. Your brother Richard has been on the Board of Control for a few years now, hasn't he?'

'Yes, sir, that's right.'

'Then I urge you to make him aware of the dangers facing us here. God knows I have tried my best to wake London up to the situation, but perhaps a family connection might make a difference.'

'Trust me, sir. Richard knows how important India is to England's interests. But I will keep him abreast of events here, as I see them,' he added carefully.

'Very good. I appreciate that.' Sir John spoke with quiet sincerity. 'Now then, I imagine you'll want to make arrangements for your men?'

'Yes, sir.'

'For the present the 33rd is to be accommodated here in the fort. Barracks have been prepared for them. When I say prepared,

I mean that they have been emptied. You will of course have to spend a little time and effort to make them . . . habitable. But I would not make them too comfortable if I were you, Colonel.' Sir John smiled slightly as Arthur gave him a searching look.

'Sir?'

'Let's just say that the 33rd might well be afforded the chance to get to grips with the enemy sooner than you think. I can't give you the details yet, but you will be told in good time. Now, if you'll forgive me I have some tedious correspondence that demands my attention.'

'Yes, sir.' Arthur rose from his chair. 'Thank you, sir.'

Sir John looked at him for a moment in silence before he concluded. 'India might not be every Englishman's cup of tea, Wesley. But you're young and you look healthy enough. Who knows, India might be the making of you. After all, this is the land of the pagoda tree. Shake it hard enough and a fortune will be yours. There's plenty of money and fame for the taking for those with the courage, and the good fortune, to seize it.'

'*Iqbal*.' Arthur smiled.

'That's right. *Iqbal*. It means everything here. Make sure you have it.'

Arthur shrugged. 'Frankly, sir, I don't believe in luck. It is simply too fickle to trust. I place my faith in myself. I aim to make my own success, and leave fate to others.'

'Really? Nevertheless, I wish you good luck, Colonel Wesley.' He glanced down at his papers, and Arthur was turning to leave when the Governor General suddenly looked up. 'Oh! I forgot to say, welcome to India.'

'Thank you, sir.'

Sir John laughed. 'You might thank me now. But I promise you there will be times when you curse the moment you ever set foot here. When that happens, and it will, then you will find yourself reflecting that you really are welcome to India.'

Chapter 24

The barracks that had been allocated to the 33rd were in a deplorable condition, Arthur discovered. It was true that they had been emptied of their last occupants in readiness for the arrival of the King's regiment, but whether the last creatures to dwell there had been men or beasts was hard to discern. The rooms were filthy and some had clearly housed animals, from the musky smell and the presence of dried grass and traces of excrement.

As soon as the equipment and serge coats had been set down outside the men set to work scrubbing the barracks out with vinegar. The old bedrolls were taken out and burned. This immediately drew the attention of the quartermaster of the fort who angrily demanded to know who would be paying for a new issue. Arthur forced himself to respond calmly to the man and point out the need for his troops to live in the healthiest possible conditions. He indicated one of the bedrolls waiting to be added to the smoking pyre.

'Do you see that?' Arthur pointed. 'The damn thing is crawling with lice.'

'Lice?' The quartermaster snorted. 'Lice never hurt anyone, sir. That's a perfectly serviceable bedroll. I demand you stop this wanton destruction of Company property at once!'

'You're right.' Arthur nodded, with a slight smile. 'There's nothing wrong with it. You men!' He called over to two soldiers standing by the pile of bedrolls. 'Bring that one over here!'

They dragged the bedroll over and laid it on the bare ground between the two officers. The quartermaster's nose wrinkled as a waft of old sweat and decay rose up. The material of the bedroll was stained, worn and torn in places, and over it all scurried the numerous tiny slivers of lice.

'Perfectly serviceable, eh?' Arthur looked at the quarter-master, and his expression hardened. 'Let's see, shall we? Lie down on it.'

'What?' The quartermaster looked surprised, then horrified.

'I said lie down on that bedroll,' Arthur replied harshly. 'You say it's serviceable. I want you to demonstrate that to these men.'

The two soldiers watched the exchange in amusement, thoroughly enjoying the quartermaster's discomfort.

'You can't be serious, sir.' The quartermaster looked down at the bedroll and winced. 'It's practically alive with lice. I'm not going near it.'

'I see. Then I take it you're saying that it's not serviceable after all?'

The quartermaster squirmed miserably.

'Well?' Arthur pressed him. 'Speak up, man.'

'Perhaps not, sir.'

'Good. Now I want you to get back to your desk and make sure that my men are issued with new bedrolls. Before the end of the day, understand?'

The quartermaster looked round at the soldiers cleaning the barracks and those still carrying out more bedrolls for the fire. 'All of them, sir?'

'Every single man.'

'Who's going to pay for it?'

Arthur pointed at the bedroll. In the corner was a stencil: *Property of the East India Company.* 'Since they belong to the Company the Company can pay for the replacements. See to it. Now, please.'

The quartermaster puffed out his cheeks and shook his head, but Arthur glared at him, daring him to make any further protest, and the man turned away and walked stiffly back towards headquarters. Arthur smiled as he watched him leave, then turned and saw that the two soldiers were grinning at him.

He frowned. 'What are you standing there for? Get that

bedroll up and burn the damned thing before anyone catches anything from it.'

'Yes, sir!' The soldiers bent to their task at once, lifting the spoiled bedroll by the ends and carrying it over to the blaze before tossing it on to the pyre. There was a faint pop and crack as the lice started to burst in the flames.

The next day, Arthur began to drill his men in earnest. The Governor General's hint that the regiment would soon be seeing action was at the front of Arthur's mind as he watched the sergeants and officers putting the 33rd through its paces over the following weeks.

Sir John made sure that the newly arrived colonel was introduced to Calcutta society, such as it was, as soon as possible. Calcutta was as wild a town as Dublin; the officers drank and gambled to even greater excess than any of the young swells that Arthur had known at the castle. He did his best to partake of the social life of the small European community of Calcutta, and drank with the officers in moderation, but he tended to withdraw from their company once the high jinks began, as befitted a man with his senior rank.

The officers were not accommodated in the barracks and had to look to their own resources to find accommodation in the better housing that had grown up close to the fort, on raised ground overlooking the teeming ramshackle sprawl of Calcutta. While the junior officers shared chummeries, Arthur rented a one-storey building with a wide veranda running around it: what the locals referred to as a bungalow. It was far finer than anything he could have hired in Dublin for the same price, and it overlooked a neat garden planted with mango trees and enclosed in a white-washed wall. Often, when the day's duties were complete, Arthur sat on his veranda and wrote letters to Kitty describing his new life in India, and his longing to return to her as soon as he could. Even though it might be in several years' time, he assured her of his undying love and urged her to write to him as often as possible.

As his men trained, Arthur studied the campaigns of

Cornwallis, in particular the failed attempt to reduce Seringa-patam and end the threat from Tipoo Sahib. Cornwallis had been defeated by the monsoon season, and the failure to secure a steady supply of food for his army. He had been forced to spike his guns, abandon the siege and retreat, occasioning a serious decline of faith in the *iqbal* of the English. The difficulties of campaigning in India were immense: the terrible heat of the dry seasons and the torrential rains of the monsoons that turned tracks into glutinous mud and could transform dry river beds into raging torrents in a matter of hours. Then there was the lack of any roads worth the name, just a series of tracks that linked the fortified villages that dotted the landscape. Any modern army desiring to cross the subcontinent was further handicapped by the sheer distance it would be obliged to maintain its lines of communication. It was difficult to find horses strong enough to pull the guns and wagons of a baggage train. The mounts favoured by the Mahratta and other warrior nations were small and nimble and of little use as beasts of burden.

These were matters he took up with Harry Ball when the two officers were attending one of the numerous dinner parties that were held in the houses of Calcutta's tiny European population. When the meal was over, officers and Company officials retired to the veranda outside the house to drink in the light draught of the punkahs swaying overhead. Arthur sat himself down on the chair next to Ball with a brief exchange of pleasantries.

'So how are you finding life in Calcutta, sir?'

'It's pleasant enough provided one doesn't get too hot.' Arthur smiled. 'Not that there's any chance of avoiding the heat.'

'You think this is bad?' Ball looked amused. 'Just wait until you encounter the climate further inland. Sometimes it gets so hot that a man will lie under his camp bed covered with a wet sheet just to stop his brains from boiling and sending him insane. It's not good country for proper soldiers like yourself, sir.'

'Nevertheless, we are required to fight here. Especially if we are to protect our interests from the French. So we are obliged to find some means of waging war effectively in India. From what I've read so far, we've not had much success.'

'It is a problem,' Ball agreed. 'That is why our interests in India are confined to the lands immediately surrounding the three presidencies. That is the limit of our operations. Most attempts to campaign further afield have failed to achieve anything worthwhile, or ended in disaster.'

'Perhaps we are wrong to think of conducting war as we would in Europe,' Arthur suggested. 'As you say, the distances are too great. The only way an army could stay in the field for long enough to cover the necessary ground is to be resupplied on the march.'

Ball nodded. 'It would make sense, sir, but the supplies of grain that we would need could not be met by the villages in the *mofussil* – sorry, the hinterland.'

Arthur smiled politely. 'I understand the word, Major. But I wasn't thinking of gleaning what little the natives had grown for themselves. I was thinking that our columns could be supplied by the *brinjarris*.'

Ball raised an eyebrow at the suggestion, then considered it carefully for a moment. The *brinjarris* were almost a separate nation in India, raising huge herds of bullocks which they contracted out, or used to carry excess grain and rice across the subcontinent in search of a decent profit. Ball nodded. 'It might work, provided they could be assured that they would make money. Certainly it would relieve our commanding officers and their staffs of the burden of arranging supplies.'

'That's what I thought. Do you have any contacts with their headmen?'

'I know some of the local boys. I could arrange a meeting with them, if you wish, sir.'

'I'd be most grateful. One other thing. These bullocks that the *brinjarris* use, would they be suitable for drawing guns?'

'Cannon?' Ball pursed his lips for an instant. 'I don't see why not. We could arrange a trial and see.'

'Then let's do it.' Arthur nodded amiably. 'If the bullocks prove a success, then we may be a step nearer taking the fight closer to our enemies.'

'Very well, sir. I assume you'll want an intermediary when you meet the headmen, someone to translate for you.'

'I'd be grateful. My Hindoostani is coming along, but I would rather not rely on it at present.'

Ball raised his eyebrows. 'You're learning Hindoostani?'

'Yes. Why not? You seem surprised, Ball.'

'I am. It's a rare officer of the King's regiments who bothers to learn more than a handful of words. It's different for the officers in the Company battalions. We have to live with the sepoys. Makes sense for us.'

'I would have thought it makes sense for any Englishman serving here, whether he is employed by the Crown or the Company.'

'I agree. But you would have a hard time convincing most of the officers of that, sadly.' Ball considered the young colonel for a moment before he continued. 'Frankly, I wish there were more here like you, sir. It's what England needs in India if the place is ever to become more than an asset on the Company's balance sheet. If there were more men like you, then there'd be a fine future for India.'

'The future of India?' Arthur mused. 'I've been thinking of little else since I arrived here. Believe me, before I return home, I will have made my mark on these lands and their peoples.'

Chapter 25

Spring gave way to summer and the heat increased to stifling proportions, but Arthur continued to drill his men as often as possible until the 33rd moved with precision in response to his commands. They soon sweated off the extra weight they had gained on the voyage from England and became as fit and hardy as they had ever been. Arthur had persuaded the quartermaster at Fort William to provide his men with the lighter and looser uniforms issued to Company soldiers, but the men still grumbled under the weight of their backpacks, heavy boots and muskets.

He ordered that a firing range be set up in the fort, and once every fortnight he had the men perform a live fire drill, the sound of their muskets echoing round the fort and drawing curious glances from those not used to it. The cost of gunpowder was such that few armies anywhere in the world allowed their soldiers to discharge their weapons off the battlefield. But Arthur had no intention of putting the request for powder through official army channels. Instead, he drew on the stocks of the East India Company who had plentiful supplies of powder and ball in their Calcutta arsenal.

Naturally the quartermaster protested, and Arthur cordially invited him to write a letter of complaint to the board of directors in London, in the happy knowledge that time and distance would mean that any dispute over his actions would take years to resolve. At the same time, Arthur was writing long letters to his brother Richard, urging him to put his name forward when His Majesty's government and the Company decided to find a replacement for Sir John Shore. He filled the pages of his letters with detailed reports on any aspect of India that might be of use to his brother: descriptions of the geography, the natural resources that England might harvest, the loyalties or otherwise of its peoples and carefully judged assessments of any Europeans who might help or hinder the expansion of British influence in the subcontinent. Most important of all Arthur outlined the threats to British influence in India which would need to be overcome before any grand vision for the future could become a reality. In addition to the resurgence of French involvement in the area, there were a number of powerful native warlords who must be reduced to client status.

In the south, there was Tipoo Sahib, ruler of Mysore, whose lands stretched to the borders of the Madras presidency and dominated the Carnatic. Tipoo had long harboured a hatred of the English, as his father had before him. His capital at Seringapatam was a strongly fortified city built on an island in the Cauvery river. It would have to be taken by storm, and that meant the creation of a practical siege train and supply system to allow the English army to operate nearly three hundred miles from Madras.

Then, in the heart of India, there was the Nizam of Hyderabad. Though the Nizam was far less hostile to English interests, he was a weak man, easily manipulated, and his army was large and well trained, principally by French mercenaries. The Nizam, like Tipoo, was being deliberately cultivated by the French who no doubt hoped to provoke both rulers into an open confrontation with England and the East India Company.

North of Hyderabad was the vast sprawl of the Mahratta confederacy, composed of kingdoms ruled by warlords at the head of huge armies of mounted warriors. Here too the French were busy building their relationships with gifts, promises and military advisers.

All three powers would have to be brought to heel, Arthur wrote to his bother, by diplomacy if possible, by force if not. But the key to success lay in fighting them one at a time. If they ever united in common interest against English forces then they must surely succeed in driving the English out of India. It was a sobering prospect, yet much had to be risked in pursuit of the vast wealth and influence that England might gain from exerting itself in India and the far east.

'Manila?' Arthur's eyebrows rose. 'That's in the Philippines, isn't it?'

'Yes.' Sir John nodded. 'There will be a force leaving from Calcutta and another one from Madras. They're to rendezvous at Penang before proceeding to Manila. Now that we're at war with Spain our government wants us to extend the conflict into their colonies, and hit their trade. Manila's their largest trading colony in the area. If we can take Manila then only the French will present us with much danger on this side of the world.'

Arthur took a sharp breath. 'Not just the French, sir. You've read the reports. Tipoo is building up his forces. I can't believe he won't be tempted to wage war on us before too long. And if we send men to take Manila, then we're offering him a grand opportunity to attack us when we'll be at our weakest. In the present circumstances the last thing we should be doing is spreading ourselves too thinly.'

Sir John nodded. 'I agree with you, Wesley. But those are my instructions from London.'

'But they don't know the situation here, sir. They don't understand the risk.'

'And you do? You're what, twenty-seven, and a colonel. Do you really think you know better than far older and wiser heads?'

'I am here on the ground, sir. They are ten thousand miles away. I believe my view of conditions is somewhat better than theirs.'

'Perhaps.' Sir John shrugged. 'Nevertheless, we have our instructions. I'd like you to take charge of planning the operation.'

'Me?'

'You have a good head for detail and a flair for organisation. I've seen how you run the 33rd, and I've read your report on making greater use of the *brinjarris* and their bullocks. A fine piece of work, that.' Sir John eased himself back in his chair and continued. 'You'll take the 33rd and two battalions of the Company's sepoys. That's over two thousand men. Should be more than enough to overcome the dago garrison in Manila. The Company will provide the transports and all supplies.'

Arthur made a wry smile. 'Then I take it I will be seizing Manila in the name of the East India Company?'

'That's right. Now would you like the job, or not?'

'Let us be clear, sir. You'd like me to organise the operation.'

'Yes.'

'Then who is to command it? Me?'

'I haven't decided yet.' Sir John's gaze flickered away from Arthur and out through the window on to the gardens below. 'I certainly think you would be as fit a man for this command as any senior officer in India. But I will need to consult with the senior officer in the presidency, General St Leger. If we agree, then the command is yours. In the meantime, I'd be grateful if you took charge of organising the operation.'

'Very well, sir.' Arthur felt a surge of pride at being given such a responsibility, mingled with anxiety that he would be superseded before he was given the chance to wield the force once it was put together. He cleared his throat as he rose from his chair. 'Thank you, sir. I promise I won't let you down.'

Sir John nodded, without shifting his gaze from the gardens. 'Do your duty, Colonel. That's all anyone can ask of you.'

'I will, sir.'

Throughout the hot months of June and July, Arthur made preparations for the capture of Manila. The Indiamen assigned to the assault force were anchored opposite the fort and their boats made available for training the 33rd in landing procedures. The redcoats sweated in the searing sunlight as they were rowed from the ships to the river bank where they disembarked as quickly as possible and formed up in their companies on the shore, ready for action. Then they were drilled for an orderly withdrawal to the boats in the event that their attack on Manila might fail. After that, the boats were rowed back to the Indiamen and the soldiers clambered up the sides of the ships, only for the entire performance to be gone through again.

As the men went about their drills, Arthur and his small staff drew up lists of all the supplies and equipment that would be required for the voyage to Manila, the assault, and then a subsequent two months' rations in case the Spanish launched a counter-attack. Training and hygiene schedules had to be worked out for each vessel, since Arthur was adamant that his soldiers were not going to suffer the same debilitating conditions that had dulled their edge of the voyage from England.

When the first packet of letters from Kitty arrived, Arthur read through them again and again, briefly taking in her notes on the social life in Dublin before concentrating on the sections where she spoke of her feelings for him. Every nuance of every word was carefully weighed before he allowed himself to believe she still loved him as strongly as ever. He held the letters in his hand tenderly, as if they were an extension of her body, and then carefully put them away in his writing box before turning his mind back to his duties.

Then, at the start of August, when the preparations were complete, Arthur was summoned to Sir John's office early one morning. As he strode from his house up the track that led to the fort he glanced out across the river to where the flotilla lay serenely at anchor. Even at this distance the red coats of his men were visible on the ships they had finished boarding the day before. The expedition would be able to sail this very day, if Sir John gave the order.

For the first time in his life in uniform Arthur felt pleasure at the prospect of an independent command. With the capture of Manila, he would surely be granted ever greater responsibilities, and the beginnings of a reputation that would free him from the shadow of his oldest brother. Even Tom Pakenham would be forced to sit up and take notice of the name Arthur Wesley. And Kitty would surely be thrilled at his success. The brief flight of fancy ended abruptly as he reminded himself that the expedition had not even weighed anchor yet. He was fantasising like a young fool, he reflected bitterly. He must learn to control his feelings and thoughts more thoroughly.

Arthur entered headquarters and made his way up the stairs to Sir John's office. The Governor General was not alone. Seated in one of the chairs on the far side of his desk was the slight, dapper figure of General St Leger.

Sir John smiled warmly as he waved Arthur towards a spare seat. 'Wesley, I have some news for you! An overland dispatch arrived yesterday. Your brother, the Earl of Mornington, has been offered the post of Governor General.'

'Has he accepted, sir?' Arthur asked eagerly.

'The dispatch didn't say. But he'd be a damn fool not to, eh?' Sir John grinned for a moment, and then the expression faded quickly as his gaze transferred to the other officer present. 'There is one further piece of news. General, would you be so good as to explain.'

General St Leger nodded and turned to Arthur with a kindly smile that immediately made Arthur's heart sink as he guessed what was coming.

'The thing of it is, Wesley, that I'm going to assume command of the expedition.'

'Oh . . .'

'Now I realise that you've put a lot of work into this. The 33rd's a damned fine regiment, and so's their colonel. Everyone in Calcutta says as much. No one doubts that you've a fine career ahead of you, and you would have made a fine job of leading this operation.'

Arthur did not want to hear any more platitudes. His first big opportunity to make a name for himself was being taken away and he had to know the cause. 'Why are you taking command, sir?'

'Ah, well, I don't suppose you are unaware of the fact that the destination of your – my flotilla has become common knowledge in Calcutta. Moreover, a Danish merchant ship arrived a week ago and left yesterday, for Manila.'

Arthur felt cold rage course through his veins as he turned to the Governor General. 'Then why wasn't the order given to impound the ship until after the expedition sailed, sir?'

'I have no legal right to do that, Colonel.'

'But we are at war, sir!'

'Not with Denmark,' Sir John said firmly. 'Not yet, and I have no desire to go down in history as the man who provoked the Danes into fighting alongside France. I had to let the vessel sail.'

Arthur pressed his lips tightly together before he made another angry comment, and there was silence for a moment. Then General St Leger spoke.

'I think it's safe to assume that the Spanish will know we are coming. They might have had a little time to improve their defences, but given that they are Spanish that should not worry us unduly.'

His attempt at lightening the mood failed. Arthur continued to glare at him, and St Leger continued in a flat tone. 'Given that the odds have shifted somewhat in the enemy's favour I thought it was important the expedition be commanded by a senior officer with some experience, and I accept that responsibility. The Governor General is of the same mind, is that not so, Sir John?'

'Yes,' Shore replied with a guilty glance at Arthur. 'It makes sense.'

'So,' the general opened one of his hands towards Arthur, 'I'd like you to assume the role of my second in command. As I said, you're a fine officer and what's more you know the men and you know the plan better than anyone else in Calcutta. Do please do me the honour of serving with me on this expedition.'

For a moment Arthur was tempted by some churlish spirit to turn the offer down. If they were so keen to take the expedition away from him, then let them suffer the consequences of a last-minute change of command. But it would not be these officials who suffered if things went badly. It would be the ordinary men once again. Arthur knew that he must accept this latest humiliation. He owed the men of the 33rd that much at least for all the loyal service they had shown him.

'I'd be pleased to accept, sir.' He forced himself to smile.

General St Leger slapped his hand down on his thigh. 'Good man! I knew you'd see the sense of it. There'll be another chance for you, Wesley. Take my word for it, this war against France has the makings of another Iliad.'

'I hope that Manila falls more quickly than Troy did, sir.'

'What? Oh yes, of course.' St Leger frowned as his conceit was pricked. 'Now then, you can brief me fully on the plan and then we will set sail at once.' He turned to Sir John. 'Of course, that's once you give the order, sir.'

'Go,' Sir John replied eagerly. 'Go at once, by all means. God speed to you both, and come back with Manila in your pocket!'

Chapter 26

As the ships raised their anchors and were carried slowly down-river with the Hoogley's current the sailors went aloft and lowered the sails to catch the light breeze blowing across the river. There was just enough wind to provide steerage way and the Indiamen glided gracefully past the battlements of Fort William and the seething slums and warehouses of Calcutta. Fortunately the breeze was from the other shore and so those on board were spared the stench that had greeted them when they had arrived in Calcutta at the start of the year.

Arthur was standing at the stern of his transport, arms folded as he stared at the fort, still furious with Sir John for taking away his command. After all the hard work he had done to make sure that the expedition stood every chance of success, another man had stepped in to reap all the credit. It stuck in his throat like a stone, yet he knew he must not reveal his frustration and anger, and must do his utmost to help General St Leger win his victory.

Footsteps approached from behind and a moment later Captain Fitzroy was beside him, leaning on the stern rail.

'Action at last, sir. I can hardly wait to reach Manila.'

'We should be there soon enough, Fitzroy,' Arthur replied quietly. 'Provided the weather holds. It's late in the season. We don't want to be caught out when the monsoons start.'

For a while they watched the city give way to irrigated field systems, dotted with occasional water buffaloes and small clusters of huts. Then Fitzroy stirred. 'Do you think we'll be able to take Manila?'

'Of course,' Arthur replied automatically. 'You heard what the general said. The last report from our agent in Manila was that the garrison consisted of two battalions of veterans and the cannon in the forts are old and decrepit. They'll be no match for us.'

'If the agent is right.'

'He'd better be. We paid him enough.' Arthur smiled. 'Rest easy. We'll be back at Fort William before the year is out, and we'll have given the men a victory to celebrate.'

'Aye, and we'll be the heroes of the Manila campaign when word gets back to London.' Fitzroy smiled at the thought of the social capital he would be able to make out of his part in the expedition.

'Calling it a campaign is stretching the truth a bit,' Arthur countered.

'You know that, and I know that, but none of the debutantes in Dublin and London will be any the wiser.'

Arthur shook his head pityingly. 'You are a scoundrel, Captain Fitzroy.'

'Did you ever see a lady's man who wasn't, sir?'

For a moment Arthur pictured Kitty gazing adoringly up at a beau such as Fitzroy as he related to her how he had scaled the walls of Manila's defences, flag in one hand and sword in the other, laying into the Spaniards with heroic abandon until he had taken the city virtually single-handed. How could a woman resist such a hero? The thought made him angry and he was suddenly tired of Fitzroy and his self-centredness.

'Captain, the first company is scheduled to exercise this morning. Please see to it.'

Fitzroy was surprised by the sudden cooling in tone, then stood stiffly to attention and saluted. 'Yes, sir.'

'Carry on then.'

Once Fitzroy had left him alone, Arthur turned back to watch the landscape passing slowly by as the flotilla edged down the Hoogley, until at noon the river merged with the great expanse of the Ganges river which carried the transports out into the Bay of Bengal and the ocean beyond.

Arthur had made it clear to his officers that they were responsible for the well-being of their men. During the voyage hammocks were scrubbed down every ten days, fitness training was taken daily and a number of dumb-bells had been allocated to each vessel to ensure that the men were able to do strengthening exercises. Twice a week, the men were given live firing practice at empty barrels deposited in the sea from one of the ship's boats, while the sailors looked on from vantage points in the rigging and jeered poor shots, and grudgingly cheered each time the target was hit.

The flotilla from Calcutta was the first to arrive at Penang and anchored a safe distance offshore to wait for the transports from Madras. Arthur took the opportunity to hone the skills of his men with plenty of drilling on the sand. General St Leger remained on his vessel for most of the time, only making for the shore once in a while, to take a stroll in the dense forest that grew on the slopes of the hills a short distance inland. He usually took a pistol with him to obliterate any parrot or small mammal that strayed across his path.

Eleven days after the flotilla had arrived off Penang a lookout sighted sails approaching from the south-west. As word of the sighting spread from ship to ship the men on the decks scanned the horizon, shading their eyes against the glare coming off the surface of the sea. There was a tense atmosphere as the ships crept into view. The crews and soldiers aboard the transports had good reason to be nervous. Although the French navy had ceased to be much of a threat in the East Indies there were still plenty of privateers in these waters, a handful of which preferred to operate in small squadrons that would be more than a match for the Company vessels. Then the lookout aloft positively identified them as Indiamen and the tension was relieved, some of the men even cheering as the Madras squadron approached the flotilla and reduced sail. Even before the leading ship had dropped anchor a boat was launched and rowed hurriedly across to the transport carrying the general and his staff.

'Now, what do you suppose that is all about?' Fitzroy asked languidly.

Arthur shrugged. 'We'll know soon enough, I imagine. Someone's in a pressing hurry to tell St Leger some news.'

'I wonder what kind of news, sir?' Fitzroy asked with a tinge of alarm. 'Nothing that will stop us taking Manila, I trust. I sincerely hope the bloody Spanish haven't gone and changed sides again.'

'I wouldn't be too concerned,' Arthur responded easily. 'There are more than enough enemies of England in this part of the world. You'll still get your chance to fight, and win that glory you've set your heart on. Trust me.'

He turned away from the side rail and called down the gangway for his steward to fetch his coat, hat and sword. As he checked his appearance in the small mirror held out by his steward a string of flags broke from the halyard of St Leger's vessel.

The first mate of the Indiaman translated the signal. 'Officer commanding to captains and senior army officers, repair aboard immediately.'

The heat in the cabin was stifling, even though the stern windows stood open and the vents on the skylight had been raised to admit whatever breeze was wafting over the anchored vessel. General St Leger, wearing a loose shirt, raised the dispatch he had received.

'Bad news, I'm afraid, gentlemen. A French army, commanded by General Bonaparte, has knocked Austria out of the war. They've agreed preliminary terms and by now it is likely that the treaty is signed and sealed. The War Office in London has sent warnings to all our forces to expect increased French activity, now that they are free to concentrate their efforts outside Europe. A squadron of warships left Toulon back in April, and our spies claim that it was bound for Mauritius. If that is the case then they will be ready to operate against our naval and commercial shipping as early as September, a mere few weeks from now.'

'Then we must proceed to Manila at once, sir,' said Arthur. 'Before they can arrive in these waters.'

'Wait.' The general brandished the letter again. 'There's more. The French navy is not the only threat, nor perhaps the most dangerous. The Goveror General has had fresh intelligence from his sources in Mysore. It seems that a small party of French officers arrived in Seringapatam at the end of June. They offered an alliance to Tipoo and possibly some form of assistance, be it money or weapons. Soon after they arrived Tipoo issued orders for the massing of his forces at Seringapatam. In view of this new threat Sir John has instructed us to reconsider the assault on Manila. If Tipoo decides to attack then our forces will be needed to subdue him. So I must decide whether to return to India, or proceed with the attempt to take Manila.'

The general dropped the dispatch on to the table and sat down. His officers sat in silence for a moment as they considered the situation outlined to them. One of the commanders of the Company battalions, Colonel Stephens, leaned forward and rested his elbows on the table. 'What are your intentions, sir?'

'My intentions?' St Leger looked faintly bemused. 'Why, to listen to the advice of my senior officers, of course.'

'Sir, Manila is but a few days' sail from here. At the moment I am confident we could take the place easily enough. But the longer we sit here, the better their chances of frustrating us.'

'I'm aware of that, Stephens.'

'Then we must strike quickly, sir. Take Manila, garrison it, then return here to await further orders.'

'And what if Tipoo attacks while we are engaged at Manila?'

'You know how those native armies are, sir. It will be some months yet before Tipoo is ready to take the field against us.'

'That is true,' the general conceded, and Stephens, sensing that his commander was wavering, pressed home his opinion.

'Then continue with the operation against Manila, while we still have the advantage over the Spanish. Sir, we must not let Sir John's timidity overrule sound judgement. Manila is ripe for the plucking, and with it most of Spain's possessions in the East Indies. We'd be fools to let the chance of a great victory slip through our fingers for want of resolve – on the part of Sir John,' he added quickly. 'Strike now, sir, and snatch Spain's prize colony for England.' He slapped his hand down on the table. 'That's my advice, sir.'

Arthur had been listening to the exchange with a growing sense of despair at the fragility of his commander's authority, and now he cleared his throat and shook his head. The general spotted the gesture at once.

'What is your opinion, Colonel Wesley?'

Arthur quickly ordered his thoughts before he replied.

'Sir, it is true that the best chance of taking Manila is now. If there is a strong force of French warships in the area they could make good use of Manila as a base of operations, in which case it would be foolhardy for us to attempt any attack on the place. Their ships would blow these Indiamen out of the water long before we could land our troops. We may only have a short time left in which it is practical to continue the operation. If you are to attack you must do it swiftly.'

'There!' Stephens nodded approvingly. 'You see, sir? Now is the time for boldness.'

'I haven't finished,' Arthur cut in firmly. 'While there may be truth in what has been said, we have to consider other possibilities. What if we do take Manila, at great cost; or, worse, what if we are rebuffed and forced to retreat? Then we will have lost many men who may be needed if there is a war with Tipoo. Worse still, once word of our failure leaks out to the other principalities and states in India we will lose face, and that might be enough to spur the warlords who are still undecided about joining Tipoo to declare war on us. If you proceed to Manila, and fail, then you will be damned by those men back in England who will judge your actions.'

General St Leger stirred uncomfortably in his seat. 'Damned if I do and damned to be forgotten by posterity if I don't.'

'Sir,' Colonel Stephens leaned forward. 'You have Manila in your grasp. All that remains is to pluck it.'

The general sat back and rubbed his forehead wearily. 'I will let you know my decision as soon as I've considered the options. You may return to your ships.'

★

The men on the vessels anchored around the general's Indiaman did not have long to wait. Scarcely half an hour after Arthur had returned from the flagship, signal flags rose up the halyards. Arthur and Fitroy turned to the first mate for an explanation.

'All ships, prepare to make sail. Course, west by north,' the mate intoned.

'What does it mean?' Fitzroy asked as the first orders were bellowed across the deck of the transport and the sailors went to their stations.

The mate scratched his chin. 'It means that we're heading back to Calcutta.'

'Calcutta . . .' Fitzroy repeated quietly in a tone of disgust. 'What a bloody waste of time.'

Arthur pressed his lips together. Once again, another chance to win his spurs had been snatched away from him. The war was likely to be over long before he could prove himself, and the only prospect that the future would hold out for him would be an undistinguished oblivion. He cursed the latest twist of fate with all his heart, and bitterly began to wonder how much more he could have achieved if only he had been one of the blessed few young soldiers who were the darlings of fate, like that damned fortunate Frenchman, Bonaparte.

Chapter 27

Napoleon

Paris, December 1797

The treaty that France had signed with Austria at Campo Formio brought peace to Europe, for the moment. Only the old enemy, England, remained, watching warily from the other side of the Channel. When Napoleon and Junot returned to his modest home on Rue Chantereine Napoleon was surprised to see how quickly the people of Paris had responded to peace. The shop windows were full of luxury items and well-dressed dandies and their ladies walked the streets cheek by jowl with the dowdy masses, almost as if there had never been a revolution. Expensive carriages rattled over the cobbled boulevards, weaving through the pedestrians and sedan chairs.

'You'd never guess this was the same city described by Augereau,' Junot muttered. 'I thought the place was supposed to be simmering on the edge of a violent uprising.'

'Seems peaceful,' Napoleon agreed, his bright eyes flickering from side to side as they rode down a street close to his home. 'We'll find out soon enough.'

Once the armistice had been signed some months earlier, Napoleon had sent General Augereau back to Paris to represent his interests during the negotiations with Austria. Augereau wrote regularly, and somewhat alarmingly, of the precarious state of the government, warning Napoleon that he had enough enemies in the capital to make it too dangerous for him to return until the treaty was signed and Napoleon could claim the fruits of victory from the grateful citizens. That was why Napoleon had told Josephine to remain in Milan until he sent for her. As he entered the house that they had shared for only three days after they had been married, Napoleon felt her absence more keenly than ever. She was far from home, and the marriage bed, but at least her friends would keep her company in his absence.

Once he had bathed and rested Napoleon joined Junot in the small study and sat at his desk to dictate to his friend. There were letters to be written, and meetings to be arranged before he retired to bed. The first note was to Paul Barras and the other members of the Directory to notify them of his arrival in Paris. It was more than a courtesy, since the unannounced arrival of a successful and popular general in the capital would greatly alarm the politicians and cause them to suspect his motives even more than they already did. With that obligation out of the way Napoleon drew up a list of people he needed to see as soon as possible: the new foreign minister, Talleyrand; his brothers Joseph and Lucien; and some of the most prominent generals and politicians presently in the city. France would not endure the current constitution for much longer, and when the inevitable happened, and the Directory was replaced, then a new generation of men would decide the fate of France. When that time came, Napoleon reflected, he must be prepared to play his part, and seize any opportunity.

It was late in the evening before he had finished his tasks and told Junot to make sure that the messages were delivered immediately. As he left the study and made his way to the bedroom Napoleon was aware of a flickering glow through the windows at the front of the house, accompanied by the muted sounds of a gathered crowd. At once he feared that a mob had discovered his return and was bent on attacking his home. In the years of the revolution no man had been safe from the fickle attentions of the Parisians. He turned back to his study in alarm.

'Junot! Come quickly.'

His friend hurried from the study, clutching the sealed letters under his arm. 'What is it, sir?'

'There, look.' Napoleon pointed to the window and

beckoned to Junot to follow him as he padded cautiously towards the front of the house. Keeping to the shadows they peered round the curtains, down into the street outside. Over a hundred people were gathered there, some carrying torches, and all talking in an excited babble.

'What do they want?' Junot said quietly.

'Whatever it is, let's keep out of sight. Find the groom and send him out there to see what's going on. Better tell him to use the rear entrance. He can go along the alley to reach the end of the street. Got that?'

Junot nodded.

'Send him straight to me the instant he returns.'

'Yes, sir.'

As Junot retreated down the corridor Napoleon stayed at the window for a moment, taking care to keep hidden in the shadows. Then, realising that his presence there served no purpose, he returned to his study and waited. A short while later footsteps mounted the stairs and Junot entered the room, ushering in the groom.

'Well?' Napoleon said tersely.

The groom gave a nervous smile and gestured towards the front of the house. 'They've come to see you, sir.'

'Why?'

'Why?' The groom could not hide his surprise. 'Because you're a hero, sir. Everyone's talking about the treaty, and the war you won against Austria. The crowd started gathering as soon as they heard you had arrived in Paris.'

'What do they want?'

'To see you, sir. That's all. They want to be the first to see the man who won all those battles. The man who led the attack on that bridge at Arcola.'

Napoleon could not help smiling faintly. The reports of the charge he had led into the hail of Austrian grapeshot had clearly reached far beyond the army newspapers, as he had hoped. Seeing the smile, Junot nodded towards the window.

'Does the great general want to reveal himself to his adoring public?'

Napoleon frowned. 'Don't be a fool, Junot. Any one of them could be carrying a firearm. I'd make a fine target of myself the moment I stood at the window.'

'Then what do we do, sir?'

'Nothing. Let them stand there if they want to, but I'm not parading myself in front of them. Not yet, at least.' He turned to the groom and nodded to the door. The man bowed and left the two officers to continue their conversation alone.

'You deserve their acclaim, sir.' Junot waved a hand towards the window. 'No other general has won as much glory for France in recent years. Besides, the more popular you are with the people the more popular you will become with the politicians. They can hardly afford to offend you if you enjoy the support of the populace.'

'The support of the populace . . .' Napoleon snorted. 'What is that worth? I tell you, Junot, that mob would be baying for my blood if we had suffered a setback in Italy.'

'But you gave them victories instead. They are grateful. Perhaps it would be wise to recognise their gratitude, sir. And make full use of it.'

'It would hardly be wise. They might want to see me now, and their thanks will be genuine enough for a while at least. Then they will forget me and shift their acclaim to another general, or some actor or soprano. That is the way of fame.' Napoleon paused and stroked his chin for a moment before he continued. 'So I will not give them what they want. I will not satisfy their desire to pay their respects. I will ration my public appearances. Maybe that will make this fame of mine last as long as possible. Long enough for me to use it to win my next command.'

Junot looked at him questioningly and Napoleon laughed and patted his friend on the shoulder. 'You'll see.'

'See what, sir?'

'All in good time, Junot. Now we should get some sleep. We'll need it in the days to come.'

Napoleon glanced round the sitting room, richly decorated and flamboyant, like its owner, Charles Talleyrand, the recently appointed foreign minister. Napoleon had been here only once before, to attend a recital with Josephine over a year ago. Even then he had been struck by the proliferation of gold leaf and lacquer that glowed with a molten luminescence in the sunlight streaming in through the tall windows. Some of the furniture was chipped and the upholstery faded, a reminder that many of the aristocrats who had emerged from the revolution no longer possessed the same fortunes that their forebears had enjoyed. Maybe so, Napoleon thought to himself, but at least they had kept their heads.

He wondered if the men gathered around him were destined for a similar fate. Any meeting of men with military and political influence in Paris was rightly regarded with suspicion by the government. If this meeting came to the attention of the Directory, then Napoleon and the others would be closely watched for any signs of treason. If such evidence came to light then all of them would face banishment, prison or the guillotine after the briefest of trials.

There were only a few guests and they sat on ornately scrolled chairs in one corner of the room, facing Napoleon: his brothers Joseph and Lucien; Junot; General Poucelle, the military commander of Paris; and Marcel Foudrier, a leading radical in the Chamber of Deputies. They were waiting impatiently for their host so that the meeting could begin.

Poucelle glanced towards the double doors on the far side of the sitting room. 'What's keeping him?'

Napoleon smiled. 'Calm yourself, General. Talleyrand can be trusted.'

'Really?' Poucelle raised his eyebrows. 'What makes you think that? The man is a politician, after all.'

Poucelle had spoken without thinking, and glanced hurriedly at Lucien and Foudrier. 'I meant no offence, gentlemen. It's just that I trust some politicians less than others.'

'No offence taken.' Lucien shrugged. 'I feel the same way about most soldiers.'

Poucelle glared back at him, lips compressed into a thin line. Napoleon could not help laughing, and wagged a finger at his brother.

'Take care, Lucien. General Poucelle is more than a match for you, despite his years.'

The backhanded compliment made Poucelle add a frown to his expression as he grumbled, 'I did not come here to be insulted by a pair of young striplings. Be so good as to respect my rank and my experience, if not my person.'

Napoleon shot a warning look at his brother and Lucien nodded gently as he responded. 'I apologise, General. It's just that I don't think that soldiers have an exclusive claim on morality and honour. They have as much predilection to corruption and personal ambition as the rest of us.'

'Including your brother?' Poucelle shot back.

Lucien looked quickly at Napoleon and nodded. 'Including Napoleon. Otherwise we wouldn't be meeting here.'

They were interrupted by the sound of the doors being wrenched open and turned to see Talleyrand entering the room. He shut the doors firmly and turned to limp across the room towards his guests. A birth defect had crippled his foot and he walked carefully and hid his pain behind a fixed smile.

'Gentlemen, I apologise for keeping you waiting. I had a visitor who simply refused to leave my house until I had to be quite firm with her.'

'I can imagine,' Lucien muttered and Napoleon realised the implication in an instant, and looked more closely at Talleyrand. He was in his early forties, curly hair streaked with grey, yet he was the kind of fine-looking man Napoleon could imagine drawing admiring glances from the women of the salons Talleyrand frequented. He pulled up a chair and joined the others with polite nods of greeting.

'Are we all present? Good. Then perhaps we should waste no time in pleasantries, since we are drawn here by common interest and not friendship.' He turned to Napoleon. 'Now then, General, you have already spoken to me and some of the others, but perhaps you should explain the purpose of arranging this meeting to the rest.'

Napoleon nodded. He appreciated his host's directness. Talleyrand was clearly not one of those procrastinating politicians who were paralysing France. At first Napoleon had not been sure about including Talleyrand in his inner circle of friends and confidants, but Lucien had vouched for the foreign minister. Since arriving in Paris, soon after the armistice with Austria had been agreed, Lucien had quickly made some useful political connections. He had traded on his brother's reputation and used his astute judgement to foster friendships in the salons of the capital. Napoleon had been away from Paris for nearly a year and a half and the shifting alliances meant that his understanding of the political scene was tenuous. For the present he must rely on Lucien's word.

'Very well,' he began. 'Let's be blunt, gentlemen. France needs strong government. By that I mean a body of statesmen who can co-ordinate the policies necessary to guarantee that France is ruled efficiently, in peace and war. Even though we have defeated Austria, I have little doubt that our countries will be at war again in a matter of years. When that happens we cannot afford to have our military operations left to the whims of bungling amateurs. I would have beaten the enemy far more swiftly and conclusively if the Army of Italy had been properly supplied and reinforced. It occurred to me, more than once, that my efforts in Italy were being deliberately sabotaged by my political masters here in Paris.'

Deputy Foudrier cleared his throat. 'That's quite an accusation, General. Do you have any proof?'

Napoleon shrugged. 'No. But I know how men's minds work. There are many senior officers who have been withdrawn from active service and would like nothing better than for me to fail. There are many politicians who resent having to show gratitude to those of us who saved them from the royalist uprising two years ago. Then there are those, like General Pichegru, who despise anyone who embraces Jacobin sentiments.' Napoleon paused and patted his chest. 'I freely admit that I am proud of my Jacobin politics. The party is the true conscience of the revolution, and the best guarantee of its survival. Most of you are Jacobins. We shared the dangers when we stuck to our beliefs after the fall of Robespierre. That is why I can place my trust in you, my comrades.'

'All of us, except our host,' Foudrier cut in. 'He had the good fortune to be safely abroad while we risked our necks.'

'I was on diplomatic service,' Talleyrand replied evenly. 'I could not help that. But my sympathies were, and are, the same as yours. The difference is that I did not proclaim them from the rooftops and get myself arrested. That is why I am foreign minister today, and not a mere deputy, my dear Foudrier.'

Foudrier glared at him for a moment before continuing bitterly, 'When I am old, and people ask me what I did during the great crisis of the revolution, I will say I held fast to my beliefs and defended them in public, even when others were being dragged off to the guillotine. What will you be able to say, I wonder?'

'Me?' Talleyrand smiled faintly. 'I shall say that I survived.'

'Gentlemen!' Napoleon interrupted. 'This is not helpful. Foudrier, the past is the past. Leave it be. What matters now is the future, and what we can do to make sure that the revolution retains its hold on France.' He paused to make sure that he had their attention.

'Peace,' Joseph said quietly. 'Peace is the best way to ensure the success of the revolution. It's what the people want. We give them peace and they'll give us their gratitude and their loyalty. The principles of the revolution will live on.'

'Precisely, brother.' Napoleon nodded. 'Which is why England will never give us peace. How can they, while the revolution serves as an example of what common people can achieve against the tyrants who oppress them? Every day that the French republic lives on makes the rulers of England weaker. So they cannot rest until the republic is defeated. England or France must win the war, and the other must be utterly defeated. There is no third way. That is the vision that we must hold to, and must do our best to persuade other patriots to embrace. That is the purpose of this meeting.'

'And if we can't persuade them?' asked Lucien.

'Then we must be ready to take control of France . . . if ever the time comes.'

Poucelle stirred uncomfortably. 'Some would say that is treason.'

'No,' Napoleon replied sharply. 'Treason is a betrayal of your country and your people. We are protecting France.'

Talleyrand smiled at the use of the present tense. 'Not yet, we're not. Let us hope that we never have to assume dictatorial powers.' He turned towards Napoleon. 'That is what you are suggesting?'

'I'm suggesting that true patriots do what they must in the circumstances.'

'Good God!' Talleyrand laughed. 'For a soldier, you have an unnervingly sound grasp of the political tongue.'

Napoleon glowered. 'I meant what I said.'

'Oh, I'm sure you did. That's what worries me.' Talleyrand raised his hand to forestall any outburst from Napoleon or Lucien. 'But, as you pointed out, extreme situations demand extreme responses. The trick is making sure that power is surrendered when the crisis has passed.'

'It will be,' Napoleon replied. 'I give you my word.'

'Your word? Then that will have to do. What are your plans for us, General?'

Napoleon collected his thoughts. 'First, we must do all in our power to convince others of the need to defeat England. That can be achieved by one of two means. First, by the invasion of Britain. I drafted an outline on the journey from Milan. Of course it will require a large army, a huge number of transport vessels, supply depots, and not least of all the defeat, or diversion, of the Royal Navy.'

'Impossible,' General Poucelle cut in. 'Our ships are no match for theirs.'

'Not at present,' Napoleon conceded. 'But given time we might match their battle fleet.'

'What was the other means of defeating England?' asked Talleyrand.

'England's lines of trade are her lifeblood. If we can't invade England then we must stop her trading with other nations, and seize her colonies. Then we can bleed her to death. To that end we must take the war to the West Indies, to the Mediterranean and India. Not one of her overseas possessions must be spared. If we take control of Egypt then we can block overland communication with India, and one day open a route for the invasion of India by a French army.'

'And I thought the invasion of England was ambitious,' said Talleyrand. 'What you are suggesting is a war such as no man has ever seen. Armies and fleets locked in a fight right round the world . . . almost a world at war.' Talleyrand appeared momentarily awed by the vision and looked at the slight figure of the young general standing in his salon. 'Very well then. What must we do?'

'At the moment I can count on the loyalty of the Army of Italy, and the goodwill of the people of France will last a few months yet, if I do not let them become too used to the sight of me. But there are other generals that they look to. Men like Augereau who has been so assiduously building his reputation at the expense of my own. I gather that he has been taking much of the credit for our victories in Italy. We'll have to bide our time until I am pre-eminent amongst generals, and then our soldiers and our people will be ready to accept a leader who can bring them to victory, and peace. But for that to happen, I must be given new commands, new opportunities to win glory for France. Will you help me do that, Talleyrand?'

'Yes, I will.' The foreign minister's eyes gleamed. 'For France.'

'For France,' Napoleon agreed, and the others solemnly joined in the pledge.

'Good,' he concluded with a smile. 'Then I suggest we end the meeting. Lucien will act as our go-between from now on. We cannot afford to have any written proof of our ambitions. Write nothing down, and say nothing to anyone else, no matter how close. If we fail in what we aim to achieve, then France will fall with us. Never forget that.'

They left Talleyrand's house by a side entrance, two by two, with Lucien and Napoleon the last to depart. The streets were dark as they strode quickly back to the Rue Chantereine. Lucien frequently glanced over his shoulder to see if they were being followed, but the few people they saw seemed to pay them no attention. Once they had reached the house and the door was closed on the street Lucien relaxed his shoulders with a sigh of relief.

'Is it really that dangerous?' Napoleon asked.

'Believe me, brother, I've been in Paris long enough to know that the police regard everyone with suspicion. And they'd be more than a little interested in a meeting of some prominent officers and politicians at the house of the foreign minister. Make no mistake. From this time our lives will be in danger, constantly.'

Chapter 28

Napoleon's desire to hide himself from public view lasted until the ceremony held at the Luxembourg palace where he formally presented the treaty to the Directory. He stood in front of the dais where the five Directors sat on high-backed chairs, lavishly upholstered in red and gold. Barras and the others wore fine dress coats and the broad tricolour sash of their office. By contrast, Napoleon and Junot wore plain uniforms, without decorations. His brother Lucien, who had already made a name for himself in the Assembly as a fiery radical, had advised him to dress up for the occasion, to let all of Paris know that he was the equal of the Directors. But Napoleon had refused. It was far too early to try to upstage Barras and his companions. At the moment he enjoyed the popularity that the common people were inclined to lavish on their military heroes. However, that kind of popular acclaim was double-edged. The more the people expressed their approval of him, the more suspicion and jealousy was aroused amongst their political leaders. It was already clear to Napoleon that he was going to need the support of both elements if he was to win the prime army commands in the coming years. For the present he must ensure that he did not offend his political masters. Better to play the loyal servant of the state with a display of humility that was sure to create a favourable impression on the public, even as the Directors were reassured that the young general was content to live in their shadow.

Barras rose from his seat and approached the lectern in front of the Directors and raised a hand to quiet the deputies and the other guests. When all was still he drew a deep breath and began the address.

'Citizens! It is an honour to welcome General Bonaparte here today. Few words can begin to describe the debt that France owes to the young commander of our forces in Italy. Outnumbered and outgunned by the Austrians, nevertheless General Bonaparte defeated them in a string of victories that would have graced the record of Alexander the Great himself . . .'

Napoleon almost winced at the hyperbole, but had the presence of mind to stand stiffly and stare past Barras and the other Directors to the tapestry on the wall behind. It depicted a Roman triumph and Napoleon fixed his attention on it to avoid paying too much attention to the flowery phrases and craven appeals for support that tumbled from Barras's lips as the address went on, and on, as the Director indulged himself in the long-winded oratory that politicians were inclined to treat as a birthright.

'. . . so he has brought us peace with Austria and for the first time the people of France are unchallenged on our landward borders. Only England stands in the way of a general peace in Europe, and it is my supreme pleasure to announce that General Bonaparte has been appointed to command of the Army of England, with orders to prepare a large-scale assault across the channel.' He paused to sweep his arm out towards Napoleon and beamed.

Napoleon's lips twisted into a smile and he nodded his head, while inside he was furious with the Directory. The Army of England was little more than an aspiration. A few tired divisions of worn-out veterans gathered in camps scattered along the coast between Boulogne and Calais. Napoleon had little doubt that this was an attempt to lure him into obscurity, away from the battlefield and far from the gaze of the French people.

Barras rounded his speech off with a few more flowery phrases extolling the brilliance of the young warrior who had won the affection of his nation, and then stood aside and beckoned Napoleon towards the podium as the applause filled the audience chamber like a hailstorm clattering off roof tiles. As he approached the lectern Napoleon realised that it was higher than he had thought, and would make him look like a child as his shoulders and head would only just be visible over the top of it. Yet another clever ploy by Barras to undermine him, Napoleon realised. With a faint smile he stepped away from the lectern to the very edge of the podium so that behind him the audience would see the soldiers assigned to protect the Directors, and not the Directors themselves. From the corner of his eye he saw Barras frown as he realised that he had been trumped.

Napoleon drew a deep breath and placing his hands behind his back he waited until the audience chamber was quiet again. Then he gestured briefly towards Barras.

'I thank the Director for his generous praise, which I accept on behalf of the brave soldiers I had the privilege of commanding in Italy. They are the true heroes of the war against Austria and it is to them that we are greatly indebted.' He paused as a fresh outburst of applause filled the room. 'No general could have been served better and I was able to plan for victory in the full confidence that my soldiers would carry out their orders with no thought for their own safety. In battle after battle my comrades and I were fired by one ambition: to see that the principles and ideals of the revolution would not perish from this earth, but emerge from the flames and smoke of battle triumphant. We fought for France, and France fought for us. Victory was made possible by the keen intelligence of the Directors who well understood that the sinews of victory lay in the generous provision of supplies and reinforcements. To them I offer thanks, on behalf of the Army of Italy.' He turned and bowed towards the Directors as the audience cheered his gallant magnanimity. Napoleon noted with wry amusement the look of surprise that flashed across Barras's face before he acknowledged the applause. It was an obvious ploy, Napoleon reflected, but by praising the Directors he hoped to make them feel indebted to him, as well as considering him a loyal supporter of the present regime.

'Of course, we are all aware that the treaty with Austria does not mark the end of war, only the opening of a new phase, as France turns its attention towards defeating England. Today, I dedicate myself to that end. I will not rest until we have beaten the English and ended the fruitless agonies of war in Europe. Wherever I serve, I swear by all that I hold dear that I will not spare myself, or the men I command, until the enemies of France are crushed and compelled to accept peace on our terms!'

He folded his arms and tilted his head back to indicate that his brief reply to Barras was over. At once the audience erupted into wild cheers of adulation that echoed back off the walls and ceiling of the audience chamber in a deafening roar. Barras leaped up from his chair and strode over to Napoleon and embraced him, planting a moist kiss on either cheek. Then with his arm around Napoleon's shoulders Barras paraded him from one side of the dais to the other, encouraging further applause with waves of his spare hand. Napoleon had a smile fixed on his face, but inside he felt nothing but contempt for Barras, fully aware of the fear he provoked in the Director. Fear and jealousy. Especially since Napoleon had won not only the affection of the people, but also that of Barras's former lover, Josephine.

The ceremony over, Barras escorted Napoleon out of the audience chamber and down the long hall, flanked by footmen and soldiers who stamped to attention as they passed by. Outside the palace a huge crowd had filled the street and they roared with excitement as they caught sight of Napoleon.

Waving to the crowd as he stood beside Napoleon, Barras leaned closer and muttered into his ear.

'I rather fear that the mob would make you their king. It is as well that you are a soldier and not a politician.'

'Perhaps,' Napoleon replied quietly. 'Just as it is as well, for the sake of our armies, that you are a politician and not a soldier.'

Barras turned to look at him. 'Then we understand one another, Bonaparte. As long as I permit you to operate in your sphere, you will do me the courtesy of not interfering in mine. Agreed?'

'Very well, Director.'

'Good.' Barras smiled and gestured towards the cheering crowd. 'Then enjoy your moment of adulation, Bonaparte. While it lasts.'

★

That evening, Napoleon sat in his study with Lucien as they shared a bottle of wine. Napoleon had been pondering the day's events and his aside with Barras and had come to a decision.

'Lucien, I can't bear to remain here in Paris for much longer. I cannot play at politics. Not yet. Not until the patience of the people has been tested beyond endurance by Barras and his cronies. Only then will they be ready for something different. In the meantime I have a reputation to build, and the best place to do that is on the battlefield.'

Lucien frowned. 'I thought you said that the invasion of England was impossible.'

'It is. That's why I have to persuade the Directors to back an invasion of Egypt, and make me the commander of the expeditionary force.'

'Egypt?' Lucien shook his head. 'Are you mad? If you go to Egypt you'll disappear from public sight. How can you build any kind of popular support from Egypt?'

'Lucien, believe me, the way things are going in Paris, I'd better stay away from here. I do not want to be tainted by any association with Barras and his regime. When the people start getting disillusioned they will look for someone outside Paris, someone young enough to represent a new order. I'll fit their needs as well as any other. So Egypt it is.'

Lucien considered for a moment, and then he nodded. 'Maybe you're right, brother. It would be for the best. And I can imagine that Barras and the other Directors will be only too pleased to see the back of you.'

'Oh, yes.' Napoleon smiled. 'You can count on it.'

At the start of the new year Napoleon wrote to Josephine to ask her to return to Paris. While he waited for her, he embarked on a campaign to win the Directors over to his scheme for the invasion of Egypt. A quick tour of the army camps and ports of the Channel coast armed him with the ammunition to fill his reports on the unfeasibility of any invasion of Britain. At the same time he was busy planning for the expedition to Egypt, bombarding the Directors with analyses of the strategic advantages of a campaign to cut across England's trade with the east, with a view to eventually wresting India from the grasp of the East India Company.

Meanwhile, Talleyrand began his own manoeuvres, pointing out to Barras the diplomatic possibilities of moving an army into Egypt. The vast Ottoman empire was crumbling and the Sultan was near to losing any authority over the governors of his provinces. If the Sultan could be won over to the side of France then the entire Levant could be denied to English ships.

The Directory asked Napoleon to advise them on the scale of the forces needed. He replied early in March. Twenty-five thousand infantry, fifteen hundred gunners and three thousand cavalry, most of whom could be mounted once the army arrived in Egypt. A strong naval escort would be required to protect the convoy across the Mediterranean, and with good fortune they might be able to seize Malta on the way.

A few days after he submitted his report, Napoleon was called to the Luxembourg Palace to meet the Directors. He was there nearly all day and only returned home as dusk closed over the capital, bringing with it thick clouds and a heavy downpour of icy rain. Josephine was waiting for him and helped to take off his sodden cape when he entered the house. He strode through to the sitting room where a fire glowed in the grate, casting an orange hue over the room and causing Napoleon's blurry shadow to waver behind him, huge and brooding.

'They have appointed me to command the army.'

Josephine stood beside him, slipping her arm through his. 'It's what you hoped for.'

'Yes. I thought so.' Napoleon turned towards her, and cupped her cheek in his hand as he kissed her on the lips. 'Until now.'

'How long will you be away?'

Napoleon was silent for a moment before he replied. 'At least a year. I've offered Eugène an appointment on my staff.'

'I know. He told me.'

'I think it will be the making of him. His father would have been proud to see his son in uniform. You should be proud of him too.'

'Oh, I am. But it's hard not to think of him as my little boy.' A fond smile flickered across her lips. 'Do you want me to come with you?'

'Of course. But this campaign will be different. If we fail . . . if we are defeated, then there will be no pity for the survivors. Our enemies will not wage war in the manner we are used to. I will take as few women with us as possible. Certainly, I want to spare you the rigours of the campaign. It will be a comfort to know you are safe in Paris.'

'As you wish,' she replied flatly.

'I'll write as often as I can. I hope this time you will be as diligent in your replies.'

'I will. I swear it.' Josephine put her arms round his shoulders and drew him into her embrace. 'When do you leave?'

'In May. I wish there was more time.' He kissed her again. 'I wish that it was safe for you to come with me.'

She leaned towards his ear and kissed his neck, then whispered, 'I suppose I'd only be a distraction. If I were to cause your concentration to wander on the eve of battle, I don't know if I could bear to have that weighing on my conscience.'

'Then we'd better get the distractions out of the way now.' Napoleon kissed the smooth curve of her neck and pressed a hand on her breast. 'Let's go to bed.'

Chapter 29

Egypt, July 1798

The three-decker, *L'Orient*, loomed above the other ships of the fleet that lay at anchor off the coast of Egypt. Napoleon checked his pocket watch by the light of the brilliant moon, and swore. It was already three o'clock in the morning and barely five thousand of his men had been landed on the shore close to the village of Marabout. Alexandria lay less than ten miles to the east and Napoleon wanted to open his attack on the port at first light. Even though the order to begin landing had been given the previous afternoon, the men were thoroughly seasick and the rough waves and pounding surf had made loading the smaller craft a hazardous affair. Several men had been drowned and those that had made it to the shore were disorientated, drenched and already desperately thirsty. Their officers were scouring the shore for their men and trying to form them up ready to march on Alexandria. General Reynier had reported that only three hundred men from his division were assembled and waiting for orders. Worse news had followed. None of the horses or guns had been landed yet, and General Desaix and his soldiers had been landed on the wrong beach.

Napoleon saw an officer striding towards him and recognised Berthier in the pale light of the moon.

'Sir, what units we have are formed up and ready to advance. What are your orders?'

'We'll attack,' Napoleon replied at once. 'After I've addressed them. Get a platform set up, and light some torches. I want our men to see me, not just some vague shadow. Arrange it at once.'

'Yes, sir.' Berthier saluted and turned away. Napoleon watched him for a moment and then stared back out to sea. Despite his present difficulties, it was hard to believe how lucky the expedition had been in recent weeks. The fleet had stopped en route to seize Malta. The Grand Master of the Knights of St John, who had so rashly declared war on France a few months earlier, had surrendered the formidable fortresses of Valletta after a brief exchange of fire. If the Knights had shown the same resolve against France as they had against the Turks then hundreds, perhaps thousands, of lives would have been lost. As it was, Napoleon had been able to liberate two hundred galley slaves, who even now were making their way through Egypt with proclamations written in Arabic promising the *fellahin* – the peasants – that Napoleon and his army were here to liberate them from their Turkish overlords. Better still, the vast fortune of the Knights had been seized and divided, the main portion being returned to France while Napoleon added the rest to his war chest.

The slow progress of the fleet that had caused Napoleon so much anxiety had saved it from destruction by the squadron of English warships under Lord Nelson that had been sent to intercept the French fleet. Nelson had overshot his target and arrived at Alexandria three days ahead of Napoleon, before turning north to search the sea in the direction of Cyprus, just hours before the French fleet arrived.

Clearly his lucky star was burning with its usual brilliance, Napoleon reflected with a smile. But good fortune had played its hand and now it was up to Napoleon to seize the initiative and take full advantage of the situation. He had briefly considered delaying the attack on Alexandria until his scattered force could be gathered in when morning came. However, any advantage he gained in numbers would be offset by the advance warning the Mameluke garrison would have of the approach of the French invaders. Regardless of the lack of any guns or cavalry, the attack would have to be launched as soon as possible.

Berthier formed the men up along three sides of a platform hastily constructed from some water barrels and the door from one of the hovels in Marabout. A torch flared at each corner and Napoleon clambered up, illuminated by the flickering glare. He paused a moment to catch his breath and then filled his lungs and began to address his men.

'Soldiers! At first light you will be in sight of one of the wonders of the ancient world – the port of Alexandria. It is named after its founder, the greatest conqueror in history, Alexander the Great. Today we will take the first steps in following the route he took in conquering an empire that spanned the known world. But where the Greeks called a halt to their march we shall go on and claim an even greater empire for the glory of France!'

A cheer rose from the grey ranks facing him in the moonlight. He waited for it to subside before he continued. 'Although we are here to fight an enemy, it is vital that you remember we are far from our homeland. We must win over the local people, or we will never be able to rest at night. So you will respect their religion. You will respect their customs. Any man caught looting or raping will be shot on the spot. We are here to liberate the people, not their chattels or their chastity!' The men laughed good-naturedly and Napoleon nodded to himself. Despite the trials of the landing, their spirits were high and they would recover their fighting mettle the moment they closed on the enemy.

Napoleon snatched his hat off his head and thrust it aloft. 'For France! For liberty, equality and fraternity! And most of all, for victory!'

Once the cheers had died away Napoleon left orders that Desaix should be told to guard the beachhead as soon as he was located. Then he gave the order for the men to form a marching column and they set off, their boots shuffling quietly across the sand as they advanced on Alexandria.

Even though the distance was not great it was tiring ground to march over, and even the men of Napoleon's personal bodyguard began to mutter and grumble as the sand gave and shifted under their boots. At least the brilliant illumination in the star-scattered heavens made it possible to see clearly for some distance and there was none of the usual night march anxiety of an ambush or a sudden engagement. As dawn streaked the eastern sky with pastel pink and orange hues Napoleon caught his first glimpse of Alexandria from the crest of a dune. The image of the great city of Alexander that he had carried in his head since childhood bore little resemblance to the present reality. A grey wall stretched round the perimeter of what was no more than a minor town by European standards. Beyond the wall he could see a sprawl of flat and domed roofs and dun-coloured buildings. A large triangular fort lay to one side of the track that led up to the western gate, and as the head of the French column descended the far slope of the dune a dull thud made Napoleon look up to see a puff of smoke roll lazily along the nearest wall of the fort. A moment later a column of sand leaped up from the ground a short distance from the head of the column.

'Berthier!'

'Yes, sir.'

'Halt the men. Then find General Menou. Tell him to take a brigade and storm that fort.'

Berthier saluted and a moment later the officers and sergeants were bellowing their orders up and down the line. While the other soldiers waited, three battalions marched forward and deployed across the track in front of the fort. The gun on the wall continued firing steadily, scoring one hit on the attackers that swept away a file of six men. Menou immediately sent forward a screen of skirmishers to fire at any of the enemy that dared to show their heads above the parapet. Under cover of their comrades' fire the assault columns quick-marched across the packed sand and scrambled up the crumbling mud walls. From his position Napoleon could see the glint of bayonets and curved swords twinkling in the sunshine as Menou's soldiers fell upon the defenders. It was soon over and the green flag with a yellow crescent that had fluttered above the ramparts was hauled down and a moment later the tricolour rose in its place.

Napoleon nodded with satisfaction, then gave the order for the column to move forward. They marched past the fort and exchanged cheers with the men on the walls. Menou left a handful of men behind to guard the prisoners and then rejoined the tail of the column as it passed the fort and continued down the track towards Alexandria. By the time they had reached the town the sun had risen high enough to make the air stifling. The men were wearing the same uniforms that they had worn in Europe and were weighed down by five days' issue of rations and sixty rounds for each musket. Most had already emptied their canteens and their dry throats were further irritated by the dust kicked up by the marching column.

Napoleon and Berthier climbed up on to a pile of ancient masonry to observe the town's defences while the men deployed for the attack. Closer to the walls they could now see that the stonework was old and small sections around the main gates had fallen down. Napoleon pointed them out with his riding crop.

'We'll attack through those.'

Berthier unrolled the map of the town that he had obtained from a French merchant. 'Ah, yes, the Pompey and Rosetta gates. According to our source, once we're through those, there are no other defences in the town, sir.'

'Good. Then let's not waste any more time. Kléber can attack the Pompey gate, while Bon takes the Rosetta. Give the orders.'

As the French battalions tramped foward, kicking up yet more dust that billowed around and above them, at times obscuring Napoleon's view of the assault, the enemy began to fire from the walls and bastions, tiny flickers of flame and puffs of smoke indicating their positions. The sunlight beat upon the parched landscape and after a while Napoleon sat down on a small pile of pottery fragments to watch the proceedings. As he squinted into the dusty haze about the gates he irritably swiped at the potsherds with his riding crop. Eventually he could stand it no longer and scrambled down and strode towards the nearest gate, his staff hurrying to catch up with him. Berthier trotted forward and fell into step alongside his general.

'Excuse me, sir, but where are we going?'

'Where the fighting is,' Napoleon grumbled. 'Can't see a thing from back there.'

'Is that wise, sir? After what nearly happened at Arcola?'

Napoleon drew up abruptly. 'Berthier, never question my actions again.'

'Sir, with respect, you are the commander of an army sent to fight far away from France. If you die, unnecessarily, then you place all these men in danger.'

'And what if I die necessarily?' Napoleon shook his head. 'War is dangerous, Berthier. Would it really be safer for me to stay so far back from the fighting that I could not see the battle? How could I respond in time to the moves of the enemy? I have to go forward, understand?'

Berthier nodded. 'Very well, sir. But please be careful.'

'That I can promise with a clear conscience.' Napoleon grinned. 'Come on!'

They passed through the Pompey gate and at once Napoleon smelt the thick heavy odour of excrement and decay, a far more pungent and unpleasant stench than even the poorest quarters of Paris had to endure. Just inside the walls they came across the first bodies: two Frenchmen sprawled across the corpse of a well-muscled man in a turban and a flowing tunic. He had four pistols jammed into a wide band of cloth around his waist. In his hand was the scimitar with which he had cut down his two foes. Beside him lay a purse, split open, and a few silver coins still lay on the soiled street where the first wave of French troops had not had time to sweep them all up.

'One of their Mamelukes, I think.' Napoleon knelt down beside the body and gently took the blade from the dead man's hand. The Mamelukes were an elite cast of warriors who were well rewarded by their Turkish masters. The hilt was finely crafted and set with precious stones arranged around a dazzling ruby.

'Good God,' muttered Berthier. 'Is that what I think it is? I've never seen such a fine gem.'

Napoleon smiled as he rose and handed him the scimitar. 'Here. If this is the kind of wealth their soldiers are carrying around then there'll be rich pickings for France, and for us. Come on.'

They hurried down a narrow, filthy street, following the crackle of musket fire, and soon caught up with one of the attacking columns which had emerged into a large market place. The men had taken cover behind abandoned and upended stalls and carts and were exchanging shots with scores of the enemy defending the walls of a mosque. High up, in the tower, a robed figure shouted encouragement to his brethren, occasionally breaking off to wave his fists at the French troops and scream some kind of abuse at the invaders. Napoleon strode across to the nearest officer, a young captain, and grabbed his arm. 'What the hell is going on here? Why aren't you advancing?'

'Sir, it's General Kléber. He's been wounded.'

'Kléber? Where is he?'

The captain pointed across the market to a group of men huddled in the entrance to a large house.

'Right.' Napoleon nodded. 'Get your men forward, Captain. Tell them to concentrate their fire on that man in the tower. I want him shot down, then you take the mosque. Clear?'

'Yes, sir.'

'Then get on with it.'

He left the captain and ran over to the house he had indicated. A small party of soldiers stood guard at the entrance and they stiffened to attention as their commander swept past them.

'Kléber?' Napoleon called out.

'Over here, sir!'

Napoleon turned and saw a surgeon gesturing to him as he crouched over a body stretched out on the tiled floor. Kléber stirred weakly as Napoleon squatted down beside him. He had been shot in the thigh and shoulder and his white shirt and trousers were stained with blood. His eyes flickered for a moment as he tried to speak, and then he passed out.

'Will he live?' Napoleon asked.

'Yes, sir. If I can stop him losing any more blood.'

'Carry on then.'

As Napoleon and Berthier emerged from the building a loud cheer echoed across the market square, and looking up Napoleon saw the body of the muezzin draped over the parapet of the minaret. The defenders of the mosque stopped firing when they became aware of their leader's death and one by one they began to throw down their arms and wait to be taken prisoner.

'Good.' Napoleon nodded with satisfaction. 'Seems we killed the right man. Let's hope that's how things work here.' For a moment, seeing Berthier's shocked look, he chided himself for such cold-blooded musing, then he shook the feeling off and began to issue his orders for the capture of the rest of Alexandria.

By noon the last pockets of resistance had been mopped up and Napoleon surveyed the town from the tower of the mosque. He had tipped the body of the muezzin unceremoniously over the edge of the parapet and it had tumbled on to the roof below, lying on the whitewashed curve like a broken doll. Napoleon stepped over the pool of blood and gazed round the horizon. To the north, the sea sparkled like a sheet of tiny diamonds, cool and inviting. He could even see the masts of Admiral Brueys's fleet lying peacefully at anchor ten miles away, and hoped that the last elements of the expeditionary force had finally reached shore. To the south and east sand and dunes stretched away into the shimmering distance. In that direction, he knew, lay Cairo, and the Turkish overlord of Egypt – Pasha Abu Bakr. Even now news must have reached him that a French army had landed, and the Pasha would be gathering a host to overwhelm the French general and his men. Napoleon smiled. At least he would not have to hunt too far to find his enemy. If the maps he had were accurate Cairo was only a hundred miles away. An easy five days' march if his good fortune held.

Chapter 30

As dawn painted the sky pink two days later Napoleon and his staff departed Alexandria, leaving two thousand men behind to defend the city under the command of General Kléber, who was recovering from his wounds. The army was striking out towards the Nile, nearly fifty miles away, and then Napoleon would lead the advance along the banks of the great river to Cairo. Desaix and the main body of the army had set out two nights before – after joining their comrades at Alexandria – tramping into the moonlit desert to cover as many miles as possible before the sun rose and turned the arid landscape into a furnace.

The air was still cool and Napoleon felt comfortable as his staff and the guides followed in the tracks of the four divisions that had gone ahead. A wide swath of churned sand stretched out before them and Napoleon was keen to re-join his army even as he enjoyed the muffled sounds of their progress. He laughed and turned to Berthier.

'I think the sun must have got to Desaix's head. Those reports he sent to us yesterday about the harsh conditions can't have been true. Why, at the rate we're marching, we could reach the Nile by tomorrow night.'

Berthier shrugged. 'It's early in the day, sir. You know what the heat is like at midday. Besides, the men are in the wrong kind of uniform for this climate, and with the loads they're carrying, well, it's going be a struggle.'

Napoleon shook his head. 'You worry too much. You saw what our men could achieve in Italy. My God, they marched for days at a time, and then fought a battle at the end of it. And that was against a proper army – not the barbaric rabble that the Pasha will throw against us. This campaign will be over in a matter of weeks, Berthier, mark my words. Egypt is as good as ours.'

'If you say so, General.'

'I do. Now cheer up and enjoy the ride. You won't see landscape like this in Europe.'

'No,' Berthier muttered. 'Thank God.'

But as the sun climbed into the sky the temperature rose with it and soon the very air that he breathed seemed to scald Napoleon's lungs. By mid-morning the blazing intensity of the sunlight reflected off the sand began to hurt his eyes so that he had to squint as the small column trudged on. Shortly after midday they came across the first signs of the difficulties that Desaix and his men had encountered on the march across the desert. A knapsack lay abandoned beside the track. Napoleon was outraged.

'Half a day from Alexandria! That's as far as the owner of that has got before he weakened. Have one of our men pick that up. When we find who it belongs to I'll have him court-martialled on the spot.'

They had not marched more than another mile before they came across more discarded equipment: knapsacks, cooking pots, spare clothing, blanket rolls, even bayonets. Napoleon's gaze swept over the detritus and he felt the first pangs of anxiety for the fate of his men. The column stopped to rest late in the afternoon and the officers and men took off their jackets and rigged them over the ends of ramrods and swords to provide some shelter from the glare of the sun. Napoleon gave orders that they should drink sparingly of their water since the nearest town marked on his map was still several hours' march away. As dusk fell upon the desert the men struggled wearily back on to their feet and the officers mounted their horses, and the column continued its advance.

There was no conversation amongst the men. Their lips were too dry and their throats too parched to bear the weight of any words as they shuffled across the sand into the twilight. A short distance further on, in the gathering gloom, Napoleon spotted a shape lying across the track and he ordered the column to halt while he went forward with Berthier and ten of the guides. A naked man lay sprawled on his back, his eyes staring blankly into the heavens. His jaw gaped open, and as Napoleon leaned over the corpse he could see that something bloody had been stuffed into the man's mouth. As he glanced down the torso he saw a raw, dark gash where the man's genitalia had been cut off, and a wave of revulsion and nausea swelled up from the pit of his stomach.

'What kind of man would do that?'

'It's probably the work of the Bedouin,' Berthier replied quietly. 'According to the reports they've been shadowing our forces. Now they've started picking off our stragglers, like this poor fellow.'

'Savages,' Napoleon hissed through clenched teeth as he stared at the body.

'It's another world here in the east, sir. They fight by different standards, different values.' Berthier gazed down at the corpse with a sad expression. 'Shall I have the men take the body to one side and bury it?'

Napoleon was silent for a moment before he replied in a harsh tone. 'No. Let them see it. Let them know what happens to stragglers, and maybe it'll put some fire into their bellies. God knows, they'll need it over the next few days.' He straightened up and walked back to his horse. 'We're wasting time here. We need to get moving.'

The column shuffled forward again, and rippled warily round the body as the men stared at their dead comrade in fear and anger. He was only the first that they encountered that night. By the time the sky began to lighten, with promise of yet another day of unbearable heat, they had passed several more corpses. Some had been beheaded and all of them showed signs of torture and mutilation. The way ahead was strewn with abandoned equipment and Napoleon and his men began to nurse dreadful fears about the fate of the men who had marched before them.

Again, the searing heat and dazzling glare pinned them to the wasteland as they followed the tracks of Desaix and his divisions. Late in the morning there was a shout from the company of guides, as Napoleon's bodyguard had come to be called, who were screening their advance. Napoleon rose up in his saddle to squint in the direction indicated. A mile away, on the crest of a dune, a small party of dark-robed figures mounted on camels was shadowing the column.

'Looks like some of those Bedouin you mentioned.'

Berthier nodded as he stared at the distant riders. 'I'll pass the word back down the column. I don't imagine there'll be many stragglers today, sir.'

'No . . .'

Despite Napoleon's orders the men could not resist the thirst that tormented them and nearly every canteen was empty long before they stopped under the midday sun and rested until it had inched down towards the western horizon. Then they rose up and continued again, their shadows stretching before them thin and gaunt and obscured by the dusty haze kicked up by their heavy boots. The men were exhausted and marched at a monotonous pace, dazed expressions on their faces. Here and there a man passed a dry, tacky tongue over cracked lips and winced at the pain it produced. Napoleon and the other officers had spare canteens hanging from their saddles and drank from them as discreetly as possible. Even so, the eyes of the nearest men flickered towards them with an intensity born of desperation as their parched throats burned in agony.

They rested again shortly after midnight and sat huddled together against the cold night air. Away to the west a sand dune was dimly highlighted by the glow of a campfire and a dark silhouette kept watch over the intervening desert. Napoleon stared at the Bedouin for a long time, wondering at the hardiness of a people who could endure such a hostile environment. What kind of man would choose such a life? But if this wasteland was the kind of terrain over which the Egyptian campaign would be fought, then he would do well to recruit these desert warriors to his side.

At length, Napoleon stood up and gave the order for the column to prepare to march. 'Tell them, one more day and then we'll camp on the bank of the Nile. Then they can drink as much water as they want.'

As the men rose up stiffly and took their places in the marching column a rider suddenly crested the dune a short distance along the track and galloped towards Napoleon and his staff officers. He slewed his foaming horse to a halt and stretched out an arm towards Napoleon as he offered him a folded dispatch.

'From General Desaix, sir. He begs you to read it at once.'

Napoleon hurriedly broke the seal, opened the sheet of paper out and scanned the hurriedly composed message, then looked up at the messenger. 'Tell General Desaix we will reach him tomorrow night. Until then he is to do nothing but rest his troops. Understand?'

'Yes, sir.'

As the messenger turned his horse back down the track and spurred it into a trot Napoleon gestured to Berthier. 'Ride ahead with me.'

The two officers urged their mounts forward until they were well out of earshot of the others. Then Napoleon slowed the pace to a walk and spoke quietly. 'Desaix says his men are on the verge of mutiny.'

'Mutiny?'

'Quiet, you fool!' Napoleon glanced round anxiously and then continued. 'The men refuse to go on. Their representatives have demanded that the army retreats to Alexandria and abandons the campaign. Even worse, some of the senior officers are backing their demands.'

'Who, sir?'

'General Mireur, and two colonels.'

'What will you do, sir?'

Napoleon shrugged. 'I'm not sure, yet. By rights I should have them shot. Them and all the other ringleaders. I must restore discipline at any cost. But I'll need to handle the situation very carefully.' He thought a moment longer and then nodded to himself as he made a decision. 'Berthier, I'm going to ride on ahead. I'll take a small escort and find Desaix. I'm leaving you in command. Make sure the column does not stop until it reaches the Nile. Clear?'

'Yes, sir.'

They exchanged a salute and then Napoleon pointed back to the squadron of mounted scouts. 'You . . . and you. Follow me!'

He urged his horse into a trot and headed along the track towards Desaix. For the rest of the night and into the first pale light of dawn Napoleon's anger at the situation Desaix had allowed to flare up smouldered in his breast. Mutiny? So early in the campaign? It was unthinkable, Napoleon fumed. If only these men had one fraction of the endurance and courage of the Army of Italy this would never have happened. He spurred his horse on. As the three men rode across the sands they encountered ever more abandoned equipment and bodies, and finally, to Napoleon's rage, a gun and limber, with two horses still attached to their traces. Each had been shot through the head. All the while, Napoleon was aware of a small band of Bedouin trailing them some distance off to their right. They made no attempt to close in on the French riders; they were just waiting patiently for a horse to go lame or for one of the men to fall far enough behind to be easily picked off.

As on previous days they stopped at noon to rest and water the horses as sparingly as possible. Then they moved on again. It was not until mid-afternoon that Napoleon finally sighted the main body of the army, camped outside the village of Damanhur, little more than a clutch of squalid hovels gathered around a handful of small wells. Desaix was still a day's march from the Nile and Napoleon felt his dusty face flush with rage that the army had halted short of its goal. He galloped through the pickets surrounding Damanhur and headed into the centre of the village, noting the soldiers staring listlessly as they leaned against the walls of the mud-brick houses that lined the dirty streets. There was hardly any sign of the local people, just occasional faces peering out from windows and doorways with fearful expressions. In the heart of the village Napoleon found a small market area shaded by several palm trees. He reined in and jumped down from his horse, and strode towards a group of soldiers sitting round a small cooking fire as they fed the remains of a market stall into the flames.

One of the men, a sergeant, looked round and his eyes widened. 'Christ! It's Bonaparte . . . On your feet, lads!'

The soldiers rose wearily and shuffled to attention and Napoleon had to force himself not to rage at their slovenly and insolent manner.

'Where's General Desaix's headquarters?' he snapped.

The sergeant pointed to a side street leading off the square. 'There's a small mosque just down there, sir. It's the big house opposite. Can't miss it. Most of the officers in the army are there right now.'

'Really? What's going on, Sergeant?'

'They're debating whether or not to continue the advance. Least that's the rumour that's going round, sir.'

'Then we'd better put an end to that rumour. There will be no retreat,' Napoleon said firmly as he stared round at the group of soldiers. 'We're here to win this land for France. That is what we have been ordered to do and there will be no debate on the matter. Clear?'

The men nodded and saluted Napoleon as he turned and strode off in the direction the sergeant had indicated. The soldiers watched him for a moment, and then returned to tending their evening fire and began to mutter again.

When Napoleon found the building he strode past the astonished sentries outside and made for the sound of raised voices that echoed off the high walls of the interior. The officers were gathered in the courtyard garden and from the top of a covered well General Desaix was waving his hands to try to quiet them when Napoleon emerged from the entrance hall. As soon as he saw his commander Desaix froze and his hands sank slowly to his sides. Gradually the angry debate died away as the other officers became aware of Napoleon's presence. When all was still Napoleon made his way through the crowd and nodded to

Desaix to get down from the well. He climbed up and surveyed the officers with a hostile expression.

'What is the meaning of this meeting, gentlemen?'

At first no one dared to answer him, and most avoided his gaze, until, at last, General Desaix cleared his throat.

'Sir, the army cannot endure this godforsaken land. The heat and the lack of water are driving our soldiers mad. Nearly every well we have found has been fouled by the Bedouin. Some of our men have even been driven to take their own lives. And for what? There is nothing here but desert and a slow death. There is not even a proper enemy to fight. They flee into the distance the moment any of our lads turn on them, and then come back when it's safe and wait to pick off any stragglers like a pack of vultures. The men have had enough. It's the same with many of the officers.'

'Which officers?' Napoleon asked coldly. 'You?'

The blood drained from Desaix's face. 'No. Not me. Never.'

'Then who is it that wishes to defy me? Which of you fine men wants to take issue with your general?'

No one replied and Napoleon snorted with derision. 'You cowards! You are officers in name only. It's no wonder that your men are mutinous dogs. Not when they are commanded by such curs as you.'

One of the senior officers pushed himself forward. 'Since no other will speak, then let me!'

'Very well, General Mireur. Say your piece.'

Mireur stepped towards the well and looked up at his commander. 'The situation is as bad as Desaix said. If we continue any further into the desert our army will be little more than an armed rabble in a few days. I am no coward, sir. I would follow you anywhere.'

'Anywhere but here.'

Mireur nodded warily. 'This is no place for civilised men. There is nothing here of value to France, sir. We owe it to France to save our men further suffering so that they may fight another day.'

'That's your judgement, is it, Mireur?' Napoleon sneered.

'What the hell do you know, you fool? This land is everything to France. We take Egypt and we drive a wedge between England and her trade. Better still we open the way to India. Better minds than yours have considered the value of this campaign and decided what the army must achieve here, and how they must do it. And yet you would stop here, barely a day's march from the Nile and an open route to Cairo. On the very cusp of victory you would let your courage fail you and stand there and whine like a child. You disgust me, Mireur. You offend the very idea of French manhood. You and every man like you.'

Mireur opened his mouth to respond but could not think of anything to say that would make his situation look less contemptible. He lowered his head in shame and Napoleon turned to the others, drew a deep breath and continued in a calmer tone. 'I know that most of you share my contempt for the cowards who would run back to France with their tails between their legs at the first sign of discomfort. Some of you might doubt that we can conquer Egypt. But what cause have you to doubt? Have I not won battles against greater odds and in more difficult circumstances? Those of you who were with me at Rivoli – have you forgotten the cold and the snow and the ice we endured that day? You endured hardship then – why not now? Would you return to your families, to your country, and tell them you had to retreat because you were thirsty? They will laugh in your faces. They will spit with contempt, and you would deserve it.' Napoleon paused to let his words sink in and then his voice hardened. 'Enough of this! This meeting is over. You will return to your units, and you will prepare them to march the moment the rest of my column has come up. Tell your men they will slake their thirst in the Nile tomorrow night. After that we will march on Cairo and make it ours. Anyone who refuses to carry out their orders will be shot. Is that clear?'

The assembled officers mumbled their assent and Napoleon turned to the hapless General Mireur. 'Is that clear to you?'

'Y-yes, sir.'

'Then get out of my sight and re-join your units.'

★

As soon as word of Napoleon's dressing down filtered through the ranks the men returned to their duties shamefaced and keen to prove themselves. Even before Berthier and the others arrived the army had formed up and started its march due east towards the Nile. At first they marched in the same fatigued manner, but as the night wore on so their resolve stiffened and there was no more abandoning of equipment or comrades. At last, as the dawn broke over the desert, a mounted patrol sped down the long column of troops snaking across the dunes. They reported to Napoleon that they had seen the village of Rahmaniya on the bank of the Nile, an hour's march away. Word of this swept through the ranks and now they marched forward as eagerly as if they were on a parade ground.

Then, as the column passed over a tall dune, Napoleon saw a glittering ribbon of water ahead of them. The irrigated crops of small farmers stretched on either side. The soldiers broke ranks and ran the last steps down the bank and into the cooling, refreshing waters of the Nile, sinking to their knees as they drank from the river again and again.

Napoleon watched them with an amused expression for a while, until his attention was drawn by a squadron of cavalry galloping downriver from the direction of Cairo. As they reined in and the sergeant gave the word to dismount and tend to their precious horses, his officer approached Napoleon and saluted.

'Sir, I beg to report we've found the enemy.'

'Where?'

'A day's ride to the south. We found a rocky outcrop and climbed to the top for a better view . . .' His voice faltered.

'Go on.'

'Sir, there must tens of thousands of them. More men than I have ever seen. Mamelukes, Arabs, peasants, as if they were on a crusade, sir.'

'Hardly a crusade.' Napoleon smiled. 'But we'll give them a battle all the same. Send word to every unit in the army, Berthier, we march to battle.'

Chapter 31

'Over there, sir.' Berthier handed him the telescope and pointed to the south. It took a moment for Napoleon to steady the instrument and then slowly sweep the horizon as he sought the feature that his chief of staff had indicated. For a moment the circle of vision passed along the front of the enemy line: thousands of Mameluke cavalry, gorgeously arrayed for battle in their turbans and silk robes. Between them and the Nile the Pasha's general, Murad Bey, had stationed his infantry, perhaps fifteen thousand of them as far as Napoleon could estimate. Their flank was covered by the fortified village of Embabeh, garrisoned by a few thousand more Mamelukes. And there, on the far bank of the river, drawn up before the outskirts of Cairo, stood a vast mass of peasants armed with swords, spears, and antique firearms. Although there had to be nearly a hundred thousand of them, they were on the wrong side of the river and would take no part in the coming battle. A handful of French gunboats, anchored fore and aft, maintained a steady fire on the far bank to discourage any attempts to cross the river.

Through the cloud of dust hanging over the enemy host Napoleon finally caught sight of the objects Berthier wished him to see. Shimmering in the afternoon heat were the neat geometric forms of the pyramids rising up beyond the village of Gizeh. Napoleon caught his breath as he grasped the true scale of the structures, then he lowered the telescope and returned it to Berthier.

'Quite a vision. We'll have plenty of time to explore ancient monuments when the day's over.' He gestured to the five French divisions drawn up on the rolling plain below them. A mile beyond the Mameluke cavalry was moving towards Desaix's division on the right of the French line. 'Until then we have other matters to attend to. I think the enemy are finally ready to begin their attack.'

The French had been deployed since mid-morning and had sat in the sun waiting for the battle to begin. The heat and thirst had taken their usual toll, and the men were keen to fight, if only to end the torment of being forced to wait in the dazzling glare.

With only a limited force of cavalry under his command Napoleon had been obliged to deploy his army in five great rectangular boxes. It still amused him that the army insisted on referring to the formations as 'squares'. Each contained a division and an allocation of guns from the artillery reserve and they were arranged in a staggered line to minimise the danger that they might fire on each other in the confusion of an enemy attack. Provided his men could keep their formations intact they would be able to hold off the Mameluke cavalry. But if the enemy managed to break into one of the squares, then they would cut the Frenchmen to pieces.

Napoleon and Berthier mounted their horses and rode down the slope of the small hill towards the division in the centre of the line. The officers and sergeants had seen the dust rising around the dense mass of Mameluke horsemen and were already bellowing orders for their men to stand to and close up the formation. Napoleon reined in and called for a telescope. As he swung the glass to the right of the line he could not help swearing in astonishment at the speed with which the Mamelukes had moved to envelop the French right flank. Desaix's and Reynier's divisions were going to take the brunt of the enemy's main assault and Napoleon could only hope that his generals and their men would hold their ground. This was a battle unlike any they had fought back in Europe. There would be no assaults in columns behind a screen of skirmishers. The French were on the defensive and had to trust in firepower and good discipline.

The distant roar of cannon fire drew Napoleon's eye back to the extreme right of the French line where a powerful battery had been established in a small village. Through the lens the battlefield was foreshortened into a swirl of figures and smoke in tightly compressed planes. Then Napoleon saw the barrels of his guns belch smoke and flame as they cut down swathes of the enemy cavalry closing on them. An instant later his view was obscured by the Mamelukes as they charged the French divisions and converged on the gaps between the French squares. There was a distant roar as Desaix's men poured volley fire into the flank of the horsemen riding past the side of their square. Then Reynier's men joined in, before the sound of musket fire became more general, a continuous roar and crackle. The Mamelukes added to the growing din as they drew their horse pistols and fired into the dense masses of blue-coated infantry.

Napoleon made his way across to the right hand side of the centre formation to better observe the attack. A torrent of enemy cavalry had swept into the gap between Reynier's division and the centre of the French line and now charged home, seemingly straight at Napoleon and his staff officers.

'Fix bayonets!' the colonel of the right flank brigade bellowed out to his men and there was a metallic rasp and rattle down the line as his men drew out the long blades and slid the sockets over the ends of their muskets. When his men were still again the colonel shouted the order to advance their weapons and the long line of bayonets rippled down, towards the oncoming Mamelukes.

A cannon roared from the corner of the square and sent a blast of grapeshot scything through those at the head of the charge, bringing down several horses and their riders. Close to Napoleon a musket went off and he cupped a hand to his mouth and bellowed, 'Wait for the order! Don't fire until they are within fifty paces!'

The sergeants relayed the order along the line and the men stood still in grim anticipation as they watched the approaching enemy, so close now that their wild cries could be heard above the drumming of hooves. From behind Napoleon there came a flat thud as a mortar was fired and the shell arced up and then plummeted down amid the enemy before exploding with a great flash and a roar. A pall of smoke and dust filled the air. For a moment the charge faltered and then the colonel of the brigade bellowed the order to open fire and a hail of musket balls added to the slaughter. Men and horses went down like skittles, and still they came on, desperate to get close enough to use their pistols on the French. Only a few managed it and hurriedly discharged their weapons. Most shots went high, or kicked into the sand at the feet of Napoleon's soldiers. Then the Mamelukes wheeled their mounts away and spurred them out of range of the French weapons so that they could reload and charge again.

Within minutes the ground in front of the square was scattered with the bodies of horses and riders, many writhing as their cries of agony split the air. Still the muskets roared out, cutting even more of the enemy down. Despite their desperate bravery the Mamelukes could not stand up to the withering fire from the French line, and at last they wheeled their mounts away from Napoleon's formation and galloped across the rear of Reynier's and Desaix's divisions to fall upon the artillery battery on the far right of the line. As soon as the artillery crews saw the threat they abandoned their guns, clambered up on to the flat roofs of the village and fired down on the horsemen swirling between the houses.

Once he saw that the flank would hold off the enemy's cavalry host, Napoleon turned to Berthier with a grin. 'We seem to have got their attention on the right. Now's the time to strike at Embabeh and close the trap.'

He wheeled his horse about and galloped back across the centre of the square. Followed by Berthier and a handful of mounted guides, he made his way through a narrow gap between two battalions of the brigade stationed on the left of the division. They made for the bank of the Nile where General Bon and his men were standing ready to assault Embabeh. Napoleon thrust his arm out towards the earthworks encircling the village.

'Now's the time, Bon! Send your men in.'

'Yes, sir.' General Bon passed the order on at once and a

moment later the drums began to beat the advance. The French battalions rolled forward, their standards rippling out in brilliant colours as they caught the glare of the sun's rays. To their right three small squares moved to cover the attack in case the Mameluke cavalry attempted to intervene. Napoleon urged his horse forward and joined Bon in the main assault column tramping towards the mud-brick ramparts of Embabeh. Behind the breastwork on top of the rampart Napoleon could see the turbaned heads of the defenders as they levelled their muskets and opened fire. The range was long and only an occasional shot whistled past close enough for Napoleon to hear. Even so, the dense mass of men marching forward was a hard target to miss and as they neared the walls the first men began to fall. Their comrades stepped over them and continued relentlessly towards the ramparts, now shrouded with gunpowder smoke, so that only the stabs of flame showed where the defenders stood.

Cannon fire echoed across the surface of the Nile as the gunboats shifted their aim from the other bank and started to bombard Embabeh, pounding the ramparts. The enemy fusillade slackened as the Mamelukes took cover and the French columns quickened their step as they approached the fortifications. Napoleon ducked instinctively as a roundshot from one of the gunboats whirred overhead.

'Shit, that was close,' Berthier muttered.

Napoleon nodded. 'Hope those bastards on our boats don't get carried away and forget to cease firing. Time to continue on foot, I think.'

He slipped down from his saddle and handed the reins to one of his staff officers. An infantry battalion was marching past and Napoleon exchanged a few cheerful greetings with them before falling into step with the captain of the rear company.

'Mind if Berthier and I join you?'

The captain, a stocky youth, a few years younger than his general, flushed with pride as he saluted. 'It would be an honour, sir.'

'The honour is ours, Captain. Now, let's see what your men can do.'

The last cannon fired from the gunboats just as the colours of the leading battalion reached the foot of the rampart. The grenadier company immediately scrambled up the steep slope, struggling to keep moving in the shifting sand that had been piled up against the ramparts to slow the attackers down. Now that the bombardment from the gunboats had ceased the Mamelukes returned to the ramparts and renewed their fire on the French troops. But it was already too late for them, as the skirmishers in front of the ramparts raised their muskets and fired at any turbaned heads that appeared above the parapet, either side of the assault column. As Napoleon watched, the grenadiers swarmed up the slope, and then hauled themselves over the breastwork to fall on the defenders beyond. The sound of musket fire was replaced with the harsh scrape and ring of bayonets and swords and the wild cries of men fighting for their lives.

The companies following the grenadiers began to climb up and feed into the fight spreading out along the wall. As Napoleon made his way forward with the last company of the battalion the churned sand gave way beneath his boots and he was breathing hard by the time he reached the ramparts. The bodies of Mamelukes and French soldiers were sprawled on either side. A short distance ahead lay the nearest houses of the village and the Mamelukes were streaming back from the walls into the narrow alleys between the mud-plastered buildings, pursued by French soldiers wildly shouting out their cries of triumph and jeers of contempt.

Suddenly, there was a loud boom and a cannon ball cut a bloody path through the soldiers who had just entered a street right in front of Napoleon. An instant later the ball struck the inside slope of the rampart a short distance from Napoleon and Berthier, flinging sand over them. Napoleon blinked and brushed the dirt away from his face before running to peer round the corner of the street into the heart of the village, where a cloud of smoke eddied around the monstrous muzzle of a vast gun. Already the Mamelukes were busy ramming another charge down the barrel while two men approached, struggling under the burden of a huge ball. A fearsome weapon indeed, thought Napoleon, but its very size was its biggest weakness. It could cover the street, but it was far too large to be manoeuvrable.

'You!' Napoleon beckoned to a corporal. 'Find your company commander. Tell him I want him to work forward down a side street and take that gun. He's to place a man here to warn others to keep clear. Understand?'

The corporal saluted and turned away to find his captain, just as the gun boomed out again, this time with greater elevation, so that the ball roared close overhead and Napoleon felt the wind of its passage before it ploughed through a group of men and blew out a section of the breastwork on the rampart.

'Sweet Jesus . . .' Berthier said softly as he looked up and saw the mutilated bodies and torn limbs that marked the place where the ball had struck.

Napoleon ignored him, and the carnage behind Berthier, and started forward until he reached the men assembling at the edge of the village a short distance along from the street covered by the gun. The young captain had drawn his sword and was issuing his orders to his men.

'No firing. We go down this alley as fast as we can. Don't stop for anything. I'll shoot the first man I see looting. Once we are parallel to the cannon, we'll take them with the bayonet.' He paused as he caught sight of his general. 'Sir, what are you doing here? It's dangerous.'

Napoleon grinned. 'You tell me where it isn't dangerous today!'

The men laughed along with their officer and then, as the captain led them into the alley, they followed with bayonets raised. Napoleon and Berthier went after them and Napoleon felt his pulse racing with the familiar feeling of excitement that only came when his life was at risk. He thought briefly of Josephine, and how she might react if he fell in this battle. The idea of her sweet grief spurred him on and he ran headlong behind his soldiers. The captain halted his company at a broad intersection and motioned to them to take cover along the sides of the street. Napoleon crept over to him and squatted down at his side.

'The gun's down there, sir.' The captain nodded to the corner. 'Not far.'

'Then what are we waiting for?' Napoleon drew his sword. 'Give the order, Captain.'

The other man nodded, rose up and drew a deep breath. 'Company! On your feet!' He paused a moment as his men gathered themselves, clutching their muskets tightly. Then he raised his sword and swept it down towards the street that led to the gun. 'Charge!'

They dashed forward, and Napoleon ran with them, sword held low to prevent it from accidentally stabbing any of his men. As he rounded the corner, he saw the Mameluke artillery crew throw down their equipment and snatch out their curved swords and pistols. There was no time to organise a defence and only a few managed to fire their weapons before the French were in amongst them, thrusting with their bayonets and clubbing at the enemy with the heavy butts of their muskets. It was all over even before Napoleon reached the gun. The Mamelukes had been cut down in the rush and the soldiers finished off the wounded with quick thrusts to the throat or heart.

As in every other village Napoleon had seen in Egypt, a mosque faced on to the market square and he beckoned to Berthier to join him as he made his way through the arched entrance. Inside it was cool and gloomy and as his eyes adjusted Napoleon was aware of movement across the floor of the building, and saw bodies stretched out before him. A few of the enemy orderlies treating their wounded glanced up with frightened expressions, but Napoleon and Berthier ignored them and made for the base of the tower to climb the steps to the roof.

From that vantage point they could see out over the entire village and its line of defences. Here and there Napoleon caught sight of his men in the streets or on the roofs as they steadily fought their way through Embabeh. The Mameluke defenders were falling back towards the river bank, and would surely escape to join the rest of their army. If Murad Bey was beaten today, it was vital that he escaped with as few men as possible to continue the struggle. The future of France's interests in Egypt depended on winning an annihilating victory. Napoleon pointed to a narrow spur of rock jutting out parallel to the river.

'Berthier, see that high ground there? I want that taken as swiftly as possible.' He thought quickly. 'Send Marmont. He has a brigade just outside the village. Tell him to cover the bank and hold back any attempt the enemy makes to escape along the river.'

'Yes, sir.' Berthier hurried down the steps, leaving Napoleon to pull out his small pocket telescope. He snapped it out to its full extent and turned to see how Desaix was coping on the right flank. The enemy cavalry had drawn back to regroup, but even as Napoleon watched they edged forward, building up speed until they were galloping straight towards the unbroken French squares. He could not help admiring the courage of those gaudily dressed warriors. On another battlefield, against a less professional army, they would have swept all before them. But not today.

Napoleon turned to look at the men of Bon's division drawn up outside Embabeh. It was not long before he saw Marmont's brigade, nearest the ramparts, turn to the right and begin quick-marching round the perimeter of the village. As it passed the section of the fortifications still in enemy hands the Mamelukes opened fire on the French column and Napoleon saw several fall before Marmont gave the order for his men to break into a run and the column hurried on, kicking up a billowing haze of dust as they made for the low ridge Napoleon had spotted earlier. Already, the Mamelukes had been pressed back to the far side of the village and the first of them were hurrying along the bank of the Nile towards safety.

Marmont deployed his men into line at once, and then marched down from the ridge to cut off the enemy's line of escape. As the Mamelukes continued to emerge from the south end of the village they were confronted by a solid formation of French soldiers. One of the enemy commanders rallied his men and they charged Marmont's brigade. He let them close to within fifty paces before he gave the order to fire and a bank of smoke instantly hid the French from view. Napoleon saw the

Mameluke charge stumble to a halt as scores of the warriors were cut down, including the man who had led them. They stood their ground for a moment, drawing their pistols and firing into the smoke. Then another volley tore through them and they broke and ran, in their desperation heading for the only remaining means of escape, the Nile.

They streamed down the banks, discarding their weapons and as much of their heavy clothing as possible, then plunged into the muddy shallows, wading out to the deeper water before striking out towards the far bank. As Marmont's brigade advanced towards the desperate fugitives a breathless Berthier re-joined Napoleon on the roof. He looked towards the river, glittering with the spray splashed up by the hundreds of men fleeing into the current. Many were cut down by musket fire from Marmont's men.

Napoleon raised his telescope and through the magnifying lens he saw a dozen men chest deep in the muddy river. Some of them lurched forward, trying to swim to safety. A few strokes out and one began to sink, his arms flailing before the weight of his flowing robes and his equipment pulled him under. There was a brief swirl in the water and then no further trace of the man. Another got a little further before he too sank and drowned. Only one of the Mamelukes, more lightly burdened than the others, kept going. The rest, unable to swim, or not daring to, turned and raised their hands. But there was no mercy in the hearts of Marmont's men. They had seen, or heard of, the terrible fate of those Frenchmen taken by the enemy and were out for revenge. So they lined the bank and shot down the Mamelukes in the river, calmly taking aim, firing and reloading, until finally, as the sound of musket fire petered out, the edge of the Nile was dotted with the glistening hummocks of dead men floating in muddy water streaked with vivid red.

'May God forgive us,' muttered Berthier.

Napoleon shrugged. 'And may Allah forgive them. Do you really imagine they would have treated us any differently had they won?'

Berthier was silent for a moment and then shook his head.

'Quite.' Napoleon gazed to the right flank. 'Besides, it isn't over yet.'

Murad Bey was attempting one more attack on the French right, and the afternoon sun glittered on the curved blades of his horsemen as they thundered across the desert towards the French formations. As before, they were met with a shattering volley of musket and cannon fire, cutting down the foremost ranks and littering the ground with the bodies of men and horses, so that the impetus of the charge was broken. But still the Mamelukes came on, closing on the squares and then galloping at full speed along the sides of the formations as they brandished their swords and fired their pistols. All the time their numbers were thinned out by the solid ranks of French infantry firing from behind their impenetrable hedges of bayonets.

'How much longer can they take such punishment?' Berthier wondered. 'Surely they must know they cannot win?'

Napoleon was silent for a moment before he responded. 'They are as brave as any soldiers I have ever seen, but bravery is not enough to win a battle. As Murad Bey is in the process of discovering.' He suddenly felt very weary. 'Let's hope that he has learned his lesson, before he squanders too many more of those fine men of his. Perhaps he is brave enough to accept defeat.'

'I don't think that's possible, sir.'

'Why not, Berthier?'

'These are his lands he is fighting for. We're the invaders. I doubt he'll give in, any more than we would if we were defending France from an invader.'

Napoleon considered this for a moment. Berthier was right about Murad Bey, perhaps, but he had forgotten one thing. Napoleon was a Corsican, and even though he had bound his fate to that of France he knew that, if ever the time came, he would fight any invader with his brains and not his heart.

'They're breaking off,' Berthier said in a relieved tone.

Sure enough, the Mameluke cavalry was drifting away from the French squares, the last to fall back turning and firing their pistols from the saddle before spurring their mounts out of range of the French muskets and cannon that had claimed the lives of so many of their comrades. They withdrew half a mile before re-forming, and for a moment it seemed they might yet charge one more time. But as Berthier and Napoleon watched, the mass of horsemen turned their mounts round and melted away into the large cloud of dust to the south.

Napoleon pulled his watch from its fob and glanced down. Not even five o'clock, he noted with surprise. The battle had been fought and won in less than an hour and a half. As the sun hung low in the sky, the French army stood their ground on a wasteland, surrounded by thousands of dead and dying enemies. A few hundred of their own lay about them. Yet there were no cheers of triumph, no spirit of elation, just an exhausted sense of relief at being alive, and awe at the vast number of those who had fallen to their guns. Most of all they yearned to slake their thirst in the bloodstained waters of the Nile, and loot the finely dressed corpses that lay all about them in the gathering shades of dusk.

Napoleon nodded to the far bank of the river. 'It's over. Tomorrow Cairo will be ours. Who would have thought that an empire could be won so easily? Wait until all France hears of this!' He slapped Berthier on the shoulder.

His chief of staff forced a smile. 'A battle is won, sir. But the campaign is not yet over.'

'It might as well be. What can Murad Bey do now? Nothing. He is finished. I tell you, Berthier, this is the hour of my triumph. And nothing can diminish it.'

'I hope so, sir. With all my heart.'

Chapter 32

The enemy abandoned Cairo during the following night and two days later, on 24 July, Napoleon entered the Egyptian capital. The imams and other leaders anxious to win favour had urged their people to come out on to the streets to welcome the French general and his army. As Napoleon and his staff rode up to the open gateway that gave on to the city's main thoroughfare the religious leaders, the highest officials and the wealthiest merchants met him at the gate and formally offered him the surrender of the city. Napoleon listened to their speeches through an interpreter and then respectfully accepted the surrender. With the Egyptians leading the way and a smartly turned out battalion from each division following Napoleon and his staff, the procession wound its way through the main streets of Cairo towards the palace of the Pasha. The soldiers with their smart facings and brightly polished buttons marched to the tunes of their bands and sang as they tramped through the baking streets, made more uncomfortable still by the press of bodies of the city's inhabitants who had come to see the spectacle.

Napoleon bowed his head graciously to either side as he passed through the cheering crowds. He had been told that the natives measured a man's status by his finery and wore his best uniform coat, hurriedly adorned with ample gold lace, and a silk sash of red and blue tied about his waist. This was not France, where a man was obliged to demonstrate his pious devotion to duty with no thought of reward if he was to win the affection of the public. They were in a new land, far from home, and needed to win the support of the local people if the influence of France was to spread into the east and encroach upon the territory and trade routes of England.

Besides, he reflected with a faint smile as he progressed along the streets, he had liked the image he cut in his fine uniform as he had examined himself in a mirror earlier that day. And his pride in his achievements, and those of his army, merited this celebration. In less than a month he had won a new land for France, and his mind churned with phrases and grand figures of speech that he would deploy when he wrote the dispatch to France telling them of the magnificent victory gained in the very shadow of the great pyramids. A fine phrase, he thought. One to note down the moment he had time to return to his papers.

Of course, he admitted to himself, the remnants of the enemy army still had to be brought to battle and annihilated. But after losing their capital and melting away into the desert it was surely only a matter of time before the *fellahin* levies returned to their homes, and then Murad Bey would have only a few thousand Mamelukes and Bedouin allies to continue the fight. What chance had they to frustrate French ambitions? Napoleon had already decided to hunt them down and destroy them utterly. Then there would be peace and France could begin to milk her latest conquest, wringing wealth out of Egypt to finance the sinews of war back in Europe. The Directory would be in his debt more than ever. Parisian society would worship him alongside the greatest heroes of France, and – his heart warmed at the thought – Josephine would glow with pride in her husband. One day he would return to her embrace as the great conqueror and they would be the most dazzling couple in Paris.

At that moment he felt a yearning for her more deep and profound than any he had experienced before and his mind dwelt on her every feature and facet of character in adoring detail. He could recall the scent of her hair, and the sweetness of her favourite perfume, and the soft, yielding flesh of her body. The thought sparked a hot surge of lust and Napoleon hurriedly forced her from his mind as he stiffened his spine and bowed his head to a group of merchants raising their arms in greeting.

Napoleon cleared his throat and spoke as clearly as he could. '*Salaam aleikum.*'

There was an instant of surprise in their expressions and Napoleon feared he had got the greeting wrong, then they smiled in delight and bowed their heads as they replied.

Junot edged his horse forward and grinned. 'Seems to have gone down well, sir.'

'Yes. But we'll need to do far more than exchange a few pleasantries with them.'

'Sir? What do you mean?'

'Not now, Junot. We'll talk later. Just enjoy the moment.' Napoleon patted Junot's shoulder. 'Just think. In years to come, when you are old and grey, you will tell your grandchildren that you rode at General Bonaparte's side as he captured Cairo for France.'

Junot suddenly looked serious. 'I will treasure this moment, sir. Always.'

'As will I, Junot.' Napoleon nodded. 'I just wish Josephine was here to see it.'

Junot's expression became more strained for an instant, and he looked away, quickly waving his hand in response to a fresh chorus of cheers from the crowd.

That night Napoleon entertained his senior officers and the local dignitaries in the banquet hall of the Pasha's palace. The French band had played during the first part of the feast as the guests sat on cushions before low tables set with platters of an eastern design. What was music to European ears was clearly little more than a discordant racket to the Egyptians and in the face of their pained expressions Napoleon had the band dismissed for the rest of the night. In deference to the locals, and to the chagrin of his officers, there was no alcohol at the tables and the Frenchmen sat with glazed expressions of boredom as several long-winded speeches were made by Cairo's leading worthies. In his reply Napoleon set out the ambition of the revolution to free peoples across the world from oppression. No longer would they be tyrannised by Mameluke warlords. He promised that his men would respect the Muslim faith, local customs and property.

His words were received with polite applause and nodding of heads and then the guests returned to their meals, and a low hubbub of conversation echoed off the high walls of the chamber. Napoleon was seated on a raised dais at the end of the hall, with Berthier, Desaix, Junot and the most influential imam and sheikh of the city. Sheikh Muhammad el Hourad had made a small fortune from his dealings with French merchants who traded with Alexandria and had a good grasp of the language of his new masters. As he reached to pour Napoleon a fresh goblet of water he smiled and said, 'Tell me, General, this revolution of yours, does it truly seek to rid the world of oppression?'

'Of course.' Napoleon nodded. 'Its values are inspired by the greatest and most enlightened philosophies of the civilised world. No Frenchman today is required to demean himself before any other. We are all equal before the law and any man can forge his own path to success and greatness. What people of the world would not want to share in that vision?'

The sheikh nodded his head. 'A fine ambition, General, but I wonder if your vision will have much purchase in less . . .' he paused for a moment, then smiled faintly, 'less civilised lands, such as our own.' He gestured round the hall. 'These people are not of the *fellahin*; they would not welcome any change to our social order. I fear there would be much resistance to the values of your revolution.'

'I understand, but surely you would agree that all men should have the chance to free their talents from the chains of their social caste?'

'If that was the will of Allah, then it would be so.'

'If it is the will of men, then it is so,' Napoleon countered. 'And now that we have freed Egypt from the Mamelukes, it will be so here, as it is in France.'

There was a tense silence as Muhammad el Hourad digested this and then translated it to the imam. The latter's expression hardened into frank hostility and he muttered his reply to the sheikh.

'He says that it would seem we have lost one oppressor only to have gained another.'

Junot leaned forward and spoke earnestly. 'But we are not here to oppress. We are here to free your people.'

'Free our people?' The sheikh pursed his lips. 'Forgive me, but I am confused. You see, whenever Allah has been good enough to see that foreign newspapers reach us here in Cairo, I have read of the wars in Europe. I have heard of the exploits of the great General Bonaparte in Italy. I have heard how France has spread her rule over other countries and grown rich off the spoils of war.' He paused and turned his gaze to Napoleon. 'I ask myself how such conquests can spread liberty and – what are the words of your national motto?' He clicked his fingers. 'Ah yes, liberty, equality and fraternity. Is that not so?'

'Those are the words.'

'Then, forgive me, General. I am not a sophisticated man, and, as you have implied, this is not a civilised land, but I wonder how such fine principles can be delivered by the application of fire and the sword.' He looked at Napoleon and raised his eyebrows, inviting a reply.

Napoleon returned his gaze coldly. 'France is at war with the tyrannies of Europe because they fear the example we have set. France would live in peace, but for the desire of other nations for war. When we have finally defeated our enemies we will be free to fully embrace the ideals that gave birth to the revolution. And we will be free to extend our ideals to other lands, far from Europe. As you pointed out, this is not a civilised land. One day it will be, under French guidance.'

'*Inshallah* – if Allah wills it.'

'Of course.' Napoleon forced himself to smile. '*Inshallah*.'

'Perhaps we are thinking too far ahead, General. After all, Murad Bey and his men are still in the field. Egypt is not con-quered – pardon me, liberated – until Murad Bey and his Mamelukes are crushed. I fear that you will find he has many allies amongst the Arab tribes that he can call on to reinforce his army.'

'Perhaps.' Napoleon shrugged. 'But as you saw the other day, courage and numbers are no match for the discipline and fire-power of a modern army. I have given orders for General Desaix here to complete the destruction of Murad Bey and his army.'

Desaix bowed his head in acknowledgement and added confidently, 'It will be the work of a few weeks, a few months at most.'

'It is true that your men are more than a match for the Mamelukes,' the sheikh agreed. 'But I fear you will find that our land and our climate will be your real enemy. Yours is not the first European army to be defeated by the sun and the sand. You march in the shadow of the crusaders, and perhaps you will share their fate. It is possible that Allah has deemed these worthless lands to be the domain of less civilised peoples.'

'We are here to stay,' Napoleon replied firmly. 'Desaix will defeat Murad Bey and the people of Egypt will embrace the opportunities that France extends to them.'

'And for those who don't accept those opportunities?'

Napoleon's expression hardened. 'There will be no place for such men in the new order.'

'I see.' The sheikh nodded thoughtfully. 'It occurs to me that should you drive Murad Bey out of Egypt, what is to stop him raiding us from neighbouring lands?'

'There will be no safe haven for him, or any who resist the changes here in Egypt. If the need arises I will lead my army across the Sinai and up into Palestine and Syria.'

'And on to Constantinople, perhaps?'

'No. Even now, the French foreign minister, Monsieur Talleyrand, is concluding a treaty with the Sultan. Our two empires will soon become allies.'

'If Allah wills it, though the Sultan might well regard the presence of French troops in Egypt, let alone Syria, with some concern, General. But, as you say, the French are a peace-loving people. I am sure the Sultan will see you for what you really are. Now, if you will permit me, I will take my leave. It has been a fine day, and a long day, and I am tired.' The sheikh rose to his feet, and Napoleon and his officers quickly followed suit. There was a formal exchange of statements of friendship before the sheikh left the hall, followed by the other local men of influence, and the French officers were left to themselves.

Berthier muttered, 'That seemed to go well enough, sir. I didn't get any sense they would cause us any trouble.'

'It hardly matters if they do,' Napoleon replied casually. 'What could they achieve against muskets and cannon? No, they'll soon see that any thought of resistance is futile, and once we begin to bring some order and efficiency to the public affairs of Egypt they'll be only too pleased that we took control of their land.'

Junot puffed out his cheeks. 'Well, let's hope so, sir. But I can't help thinking that opposition to France might just give them a cause to rally round.'

Napoleon laughed. 'Come now! They are a backward people, long accustomed to bowing before a constant flow of foreign overlords. They will bow to France just as readily. Gentlemen, I've had quite enough ceremony and polite behaviour today. It's time to celebrate like soldiers!'

The mess servants cleared away the remains of the banquet and brought out the wine and brandy that had been landed from the ships safely anchored in Aboukir Bay and brought up the Nile to Cairo. With the warmth of the eastern night and several rounds of toasts, Napoleon and most of his officers were soon quite drunk. And why not, he thought. The campaign was as good as over. Only the remnants of Murad Bey's army needed to be tracked down and crushed and Egypt would be the latest conquest to adorn the map of the French empire.

As the night drew on, the conversation became more reflective as the officers began to remind themselves of all the comforts that had been denied to them since coming ashore.

Berthier raised his glass. 'A good bath, clean sheets and a woman to take your mind off soldiering. That's my toast.'

The other officers chorused their agreement. Then they grew quiet as their commander held up his glass. 'Gentlemen, to French women. They have no peer when it comes to beauty, grace and wit. And they make love with a passion that makes men their slaves.'

As his companions roared their approval and clashed their

glasses together Napoleon felt his heart ache with longing for Josephine. His hand fumbled for the minature that hung round his neck and he stared at the image, gently caressing it with his thumb. The artist had captured her lively spirit in the eyes that seemed to glint mischievously as he stared at them. However, he knew that if he indulged in such reflection for too long he was in danger of becoming melancholy, so he forced himself to smile and raise his glass again.

'To our lovers, to our wives and to my beautiful, adoring wife Josephine.'

Again the officers cheered and drank. Junot refilled his cup, and blearily turned to some nearby officers and said, too loudly, 'To our wives, whoever they adore!'

Some of the officers exchanged embarrassed looks while others heedlessly drank to Junot's toast. Junot turned to Napoleon with a broad smile, and froze. Napoleon was looking at him with an angry expression.

'What did you say?'

'Sir?'

'Just now. What did you say?'

'To our wives . . .' Junot mumbled. 'Whoever they adore.'

'And what exactly do you mean by that?'

'Nothing, sir. It was a joke. Nothing more.'

'A joke?' Napoleon sat his glass down with a sharp rap. He felt light headed and his mind concentrated with difficulty. Slowly the conversation of the other officers died away as they turned towards their general with curious faces. Napoleon stepped up to Junot and stabbed a finger into his chest. 'Are you insulting my wife, Junot? You dishonour her. How dare you say that about her?' The fond affection of a moment earlier had gone. In its place was an injured drunken pride, and Napoleon clenched his fist and thrust it behind his back where it could not be so readily used. 'Say it again, if you dare.'

Junot shook his head as the blood drained from his face. 'Sir, I wasn't thinking. I meant no offence.'

'No offence!' Napoleon spat. 'You imply my wife is being unfaithful, and you say that you mean no offence.'

'I'm sorry, sir.' Junot attempted to stand stiffly to attention. 'I beg you to accept my apology.'

'No. I will not. You slander the woman I love, who loves me, and you think a mere apology will suffice? I think not, Junot. I think that you should leave me. Leave my staff. Leave my army and take yourself home. I will not have you near me.' Suddenly, his temper snapped and his clenched fist swept out, and he punched Junot hard in the face.

Everyone stood quite still, shocked by the confrontation and the sound of the impact that echoed back from the walls. Napoleon was drawing his arm back to hit him again when Berthier intervened, thrusting Junot aside and standing between him and Napoleon.

'Sir! That's enough!'

Napoleon glared at him, wide eyed. 'You dare to come between me and this foul-mouthed brute? I'll break you with him. You and anyone who dishonours my wife with such lies. Anyone who can think that of Josephine.'

'Then you will have to find a replacement for every man at headquarters,' Berthier said desperately.

'What?' Napoleon felt a sick feeling well up in his stomach. 'What are you saying? What are you saying about my wife?'

Berthier's face twisted into a pained expression and for a moment words failed him. Then he swallowed and spoke. 'Sir . . . she has a lover.'

'A lover?'

'Yes.'

Napoleon thought he was going to be sick, and bit down, clamping his lips together. His first instinct was to reject the idea, but then doubts rushed in to fill his mind like winter shadows. 'Who, then? Who is this lover? Tell me!'

'His name is Hippolyte Charles.'

'Charles? The cavalry officer who came with her to Italy?'

Berthier nodded.

Napoleon's mind instantly leaped back to those times where he had encountered Josephine in the young officer's company, and his heart felt as if it was locked in a cold vice. Doubt edged towards certainty and he looked round the hall at the other officers. 'Who else knows?'

Berthier shifted uncomfortably. 'It is known to most of Paris, sir. Has been for several months.'

'Months . . .' Napoleon lowered his head. All hope was fading, and in its place a tide of rage and, worse, shame engulfed him. If Paris society knew of this infidelity, had known of it for months, then he would be a laughing stock. They would look at him with the same cruel, amused contempt that was reserved for all cuckolded husbands. They would be laughing at him behind his back. He felt his cheeks burn as he realised that the grand reputation he had been trying to build for himself, and for Josephine, was worthless if she was so openly entertaining a lover while her husband was away at war. Then he raged at himself for not seeing it before. For being blinded by his love for her, his unquestioning belief in her devotion to him. He was worse than any lovesick boy and the knowledge burned into him like a heated iron and he slumped down on a cushion.

Berthier glanced round at the other officers and nodded towards the entrance to the banquet hall. Silently, the men began to drift away, slowly emptying the chamber until at last only Berthier and Junot remained with him. Junot, who had served with Napoleon through so many dangers and adventures, felt compelled to offer some comfort to his friend. He reached his hand tentatively towards Napoleon's shoulder and then hesitated, horrified by the enormity of what he was on the verge of doing. No general could show weakness. Before Junot could commit such an unpardonable transgression of the written and unwritten codes that exist between a commander and his subordinate officers, Napoleon glanced up, eyes red and glistening as he struggled to fight back the grief that threatened to overwhelm him.

'Get out. Both of you.'

Junot withdrew his hand. 'Sir, I just wanted—'

'Get out!' Napoleon screamed at him. 'You heard me! Get out and leave me alone! Now!'

Junot recoiled nervously and made his way over to the great doors at the entrance to the chamber. For a moment Berthier tried to think of some words of consolation, but what can one man say when faced with another's betrayed love? It was too painful, too personal, for tokens of comfort. So he turned to follow Junot, and closed the door softly behind him, leaving Napoleon sitting on his cushion, nursing his head on his arms. For a long time he stared at the floor tile between his boots and then his vision blurred as the first tears, which he had failed to fight off, welled up in his eyes. He pressed the palms of his hands against his face and at last gave in to his grief and rage.

For several days Napoleon rarely emerged from his quarters in the palace. It was hard to bear the shame of being almost the last man to know the truth about Josephine's treachery. He sensed that those around him regarded him with a mixture of pity and amusement, even though they struggled to hide their feelings. Soon the rest of the army would hear the rumours, if they hadn't already, and their laughter would echo that of Paris society. The great general who commanded France's armies and conquered her enemies, yet could not control his wife. Nor satisfy her as a man should. That Josephine should prefer a foolish, vacant-headed cavalry officer to him fell on his heart like a great weight. The recent victory, and all the others before, seemed no more than insignificant details now, and his immediate ambitions seemed futile and pointless. In an attempt to work through the dark thoughts whirling through his mind, Napoleon forced himself to write a letter to Joseph.

The words came slowly and painfully as he set down his feelings. 'Glory is stale when I am only twenty-nine. I have achieved everything a man can in this life. And now there is nothing left for me but to become really and completely selfish . . .'

He looked at the last word on the page with loathing and despair. He must not let himself sink into a well of self-pity. There would be time for that later, when he returned to Paris and confronted Josephine. Meanwhile an army stood by, waiting for his orders. The fate of twenty-five thousand Frenchmen, and the future of an empire, lay in his hands.

Very well then, he decided. He would harden his heart and pursue his goals with utter ruthlessness. Every enemy he killed, every army he crushed, would be dedicated to Josephine and those who mocked him.

Napoleon led the army out of Cairo early in August. Ignoring Murad Bey and his Mamelukes for the moment, he tracked down the large host of ragged and poorly armed foot soldiers under Ibrahim Bey. Napoleon's men had been issued with new, lighter uniforms and were accompanied by hundreds of commandeered carts and camels carrying casks of water. He marched them hard, driving Ibrahim Bey before him, until he caught up with the enemy at Salalieh. There was no battle to speak of, merely a bloody massacre as wave after wave of the *fellahin* conscripts were cut down by musket fire and grapeshot, until their bodies covered the ground before the ranks of the French soldiers. When, at last, the shattered remnants of Ibrahim Bey's army broke and ran, there were few cries of triumph from the French ranks. Most men simply stared out across the piles of peasant bodies and blood-spattered sand in numbed horror.

'This is not war,' Berthier said quietly. 'It is murder.'

Napoleon sniffed. 'It is neither. This is what victory looks like. The sooner our men get used to this the sooner our task in the east will be complete and they can go home. To which end, give the order for the pursuit of the enemy. Take command here, Berthier. Keep after them. Push the men as hard as you can, and there must be no mercy shown to the enemy. None, do you hear? I want the survivors to spread word of what happens to those who choose to oppose us. Then next time this can be avoided.' He gestured towards the battlefield. 'Now I must return to Cairo. Send me word of your progress.'

'Yes, sir.' Berthier saluted.

Napoleon wheeled his horse round and rode back to headquarters. He ate quickly as his mounted escort was assembled, and then they set off along the route back to Cairo. They had only ridden for two hours when they saw a small dust cloud on the track ahead of them. Napoleon reined in as the guides fanned out around him, ready to draw their sabres. As the other group approached Napoleon realised it was merely a dispatch rider accompanied by a handful of dragoons, and the tension eased amongst his men as they resumed their formation at his back. As the horses galloped up, foaming at the mouths and flanks heaving from their hard ride, the messenger made straight for Napoleon. His expression left no doubt that something terrible had occurred.

'Urgent message from General Kléber at Alexandria, sir.'

'What's happened?' Napoleon snapped. The rider was breathing heavily and struggled to find the words to relate the news. Napoleon frowned. 'Well? Speak up, man!'

'The English fleet attacked our ships at Aboukir Bay ten days ago, sir . . .'

'Go on.'

'Our fleet was defeated. Admiral Brueys is dead. The flagship blew up.'

'Who's in command now?'

'Admiral Villeneuve, sir.'

'Where is the rest of the fleet?'

The messenger looked confused for a moment. 'Sir, there is no fleet. The English sank or took all but two of our ships.'

Napoleon stared at him, as the full import of the man's words struck home. There was no longer a lifeline to France. No way home for the Army of the Orient. 'Dear God . . . We're on our own now. Completely on our own.'

Chapter 33

Arthur

Calcutta, May 1798

'By God! It does my heart good to see you again!' Henry clasped his brother's hand and smiled broadly at Arthur. 'It's been what, nearly two years.'

'It seems longer.' Arthur grinned. 'How does it feel to be the private secretary of the Governor of India?'

'Tolerable.'

'I trust the voyage from England went well?'

Henry gestured to the seats lining the wall either side of the door to the Governor General's office in Fort William and they sat down. 'Not the most comfortable way to spend six months of one's life. I don't think Richard enjoyed it much either. Spent most of the time fretting like a cat on heat. He couldn't wait for the ship to reach India, so he could take charge of our interests here. He has some pretty ambitious designs for the future of the subcontinent.'

'So do I.' Arthur nodded towards the door. 'Any idea how much longer he'll be?'

Henry laughed. 'Patience, Arthur! He's enduring a speech of welcome from the local John Company representative. There'll be plenty of time to exchange fraternal greetings before we discuss how far we aim to change the world.'

'Time is something of a luxury,' Arthur replied quietly. 'I'm twenty-nine years old. There's a war on, and I'm still plain Colonel Arthur Wesley.'

Henry frowned. 'You still go by that name then? The rest of the family has followed Richard and returned to the family's traditional name, Wellesley. Why haven't you?'

'I have had other matters to think of.'

'Given that the three of us are to work together in the coming years, it might be best if we shared a common name. To save confusion.'

'I'll consider it,' Arthur grumbled. 'But I've a hard enough time building a reputation under the name of Wesley. I don't want to have to start all over again as Arthur Wellesley.'

'I was under the impression that a man could get on swiftly and make his fortune in India.'

'So was I. But the former governor, and the local represent-atives of John Company, weren't exactly anxious to extend British rule in India. I just hope Richard grasps the opportunity, for all our sakes, or we'll never amount to anything.' Arthur smiled self-consciously. 'There I go again! But tell me, Henry, what of the rest of the family?'

'William is busy building his political connections, Anne is making inroads into society, Gerald is being groomed for a position in the church.'

'And Mother?'

'You know her, living as comfortably as only she knows how and complaining bitterly about the cost of it all.'

'Did she mention me last time you saw her?'

'Of course,' Henry replied quickly. 'She's very proud of you.'

'Liar.'

'Very well, then, she did say to pass on her greetings, and hopes that you will, in due course, find a proper career.'

'Now that I can believe!' They both chuckled for a moment before Arthur became serious again. 'She never changes. Always the harshest of my critics. I don't think I will ever meet with her approval.'

'You will, Arthur, you will. It's early days. Now that Richard is in charge here, you can be sure that there will be chances for you to prove yourself. Fame and honour are within your grasp.'

'God, you sound like some ghastly political pamphlet.'

'Alas!' Henry feigned a hurt expression. 'That's the price of associating with far too many diplomats and statesmen. I confess it all.'

The door opened and they turned to see a stout, red-faced man who appeared to be in his middle age. Like so many Europeans in India, he had succumbed to the temptations of alcohol. The man bowed, turned away and strode past the two brothers with a curt nod of the head.

'Charming . . .' Henry muttered.

'You'll have to get used to that. Conduct counts for little here.'

'Really? Then what does matter?'

'Money and position. As you will see all too soon.'

Footsteps approached from inside the office and Richard emerged into the corridor and held out his hand. Not much had changed in his features since the last time Arthur had seen him back in England. A little more grey around the temples, and a few lighter streaks in his hair, but no more than one might expect in a man just two years short of forty. But there was an excited glint in his eye and a restlessness that Arthur recognised from childhood. As they shook hands Richard examined his younger brother.

'Arthur, you are looking very well, I must say.'

'Thank you. India is not the healthiest of environments. I do what I can to ensure I remain fit enough to survive the experience. As should you, and Henry.'

'Yes, well, thank you for the advice. Now, won't you come into the office? There's much we have to discuss.'

He stood aside to allow his brothers to pass. Arthur and Henry crossed over to the desk and sat opposite the imposing chair behind it as their brother closed the door and joined them.

'Arthur, are you free to join Henry and me for dinner tonight?'

'Of course.'

'Good. We can keep the pleasantries until then. Meanwhile,' Richard gestured to a stack of reports and documents spread across his desk, 'we have more pressing matters to deal with. The French influence in India is on the rise, and I think it's safe to assume that they will be directing ever more attention towards us in the coming months and years.'

Arthur raised his eyebrows. 'I assume the situation in Europe is favouring the enemy then?'

'Very much so. When we left England there was little hope of enticing any of the continental powers back into the fray. That means that the French will have a free hand to concentrate their efforts against England, and our colonies. Our latest intelligence was that the enemy was planning an overseas operation. Perhaps to the West Indies, maybe Egypt, or even here. But that was months ago. Anything could have happened by now. So we must focus on what we can do for England in India and the far east. I've read the reports from the other presidencies at Bombay and Madras, as well as the military assessments of the French threat in the subcontinent.' He looked at Arthur. 'You've been here long enough to get a feel for the place and its politics. I'd be interested to hear your thoughts.'

Arthur had been expecting the request, but was still flattered to have his views placed on the same plane as the opinions of more senior officials. Even though Richard was his brother, Arthur was conscious that family ties had been pushed aside. The matter before them was serious. Richard would weigh what he had to say very carefully and Arthur was determined to prove himself worthy of being consulted by the Governor General of India. He cleared his throat, conscious that both Henry and Richard were watching him closely.

'I've given this a lot of thought, Richard. If we are to make advances in India, then we must do all we can to build strong relations with the local rulers. Most can be swayed over to our side, but there are others, such as Sultan Tipoo of Mysore, who I fear will need to be crushed. Once we have Company battalions garrisoned in their capital cities we will have effective control of India. The main danger, at present, is that French agents are doing their damnedest to undermine our relations with the locals. I'm sure you have already read the latest report from Kirkpatrick at Hyderabad. John Company has two battalions there, but some of the Nizam's other troops are marching under tricolour flags and sporting revolutionary cockades. The Nizam is clearly falling under the spell of his French military adviser, Colonel Piron. Even though Piron is a mercenary, there's every reason to suppose he is doing his utmost to further his country's interests.'

'Then we must rid the Nizam of his French advisers.'

'That's not going to be easy.' Arthur raised his eyebrows wearily. 'His army is the only thing that stands between the Nizam and his Mahratta enemies, and he's not certain how far he can trust his French-officered battalions.'

'What is their strength? Compared to the two East India Company battalions you mentioned.'

'The Nizam has twenty-three battalions in his army.'

'Ah. Not very good odds, then, should it come down to a fight.'

'Not as bad as you'd think,' Arthur replied. 'The Company battalions are larger, and far better trained and equipped than the others. Even so, they could not hold their ground for long if the other battalions turned on them. The Nizam knows the quality of the Company troops and knows that his best chance is to have us on his side. Especially if an alliance with us might lead to the return of those lands already seized by the Mahrattas.'

Richard stroked his chin thoughtfully. 'Tricky . . . We have to find some way of removing those French officers, and increasing our military presence in Hyderabad.'

'Precisely.' Arthur nodded. 'And the Nizam is only the most immediate of our concerns. Our intelligence people tell me that the rulers of the Mahratta lands covet our territory. More worrying is the threat that Tipoo is preparing for war with us. We must resolve the problem in Hyderabad without making war. If there is a war, and Tipoo throws his lot in with our enemies in Hyderabad, then things could become decidedly tricky for British interests in India.' Arthur paused and looked steadily at his brothers. 'We must proceed very carefully and deal with one threat at a time.'

'I understand,' Richard replied. 'I must do all I can to keep the peace with Tipoo while we deal with the Nizam. Meanwhile we'll make all the necessary preparations for war with him.'

'That would be prudent,' said Arthur. 'I just hope we have enough time to gather an army powerful enough to deal with Tipoo.'

'Have you any other bad tidings for us?' Henry asked in exasperation.

'I fear so.' Arthur paused a moment to collect his thoughts. 'India has been beset by warlords of one kind or another for many centuries and the East India Company is in grave danger of simply looking like the latest oppressor. I have to confess that the natives have every reason to judge us alongside their own rulers. There's a tendency amongst some of the Europeans of the lower orders – the *gora log* as the Indians call them – to treat the natives like slaves, and to act as if they are above the law. They will cheat them out of money and goods, and beat them mercilessly if the whim takes them. The situation is little different amongst the better class of European. Many of the Company's senior officials are equally corrupt. Hardly surprising given the fortunes that can be made from trading, bribery and straightforward theft. It seems that almost every Englishman who sets foot in India wants to return home as rich and powerful as Clive.'

'Well, there's not much we can do about that.'

'But we must do something,' Arthur protested. 'Otherwise we will never win the common people over to the idea that British rule is in their best interest. Moreover, I believe it is our duty to set a new standard. While you are the Governor General, Richard, there is a chance to change things here for the better. And you can count on Henry and me to support you. There is a great opportunity for England here in India, a great opportunity indeed. If we can rule by good example, if we can deal with the natives in an open and honest way, and bring them peace and order, then they will welcome British intervention, even British rule. To which end, I beg you to lead by example, Richard. If we can only convince the natives that we are motivated by an instinct for public service and fairness, then who knows how much of the subcontinent will come over to us.'

'That will mean stepping on quite a few toes,' Richard responded shrewdly. 'If the spirit of larceny is as widespread as you imply. We'll have to weed out the incompetent as well as the dishonest if we are to achieve anything worthwhile. And we'll have to make sure that we do what we can to improve the lot of the common people. It's not going to be cheap.'

'No more than John Company can afford, surely?'

The brothers laughed for a moment before Richard continued. 'Very well then, it seems that we three have a mountain to climb. But, for now, that concludes our business.' He stood up. 'I'm afraid that I still have several more people to see today. We'll speak again at dinner.'

Arthur was a little surprised, and hurt, by his curt dismissal. Richard might well be the highest ranking English official in India, but he was still Arthur's brother, and Arthur found it difficult to reconcile their relationship with his role as a subordinate. A junior one at that.

Henry escorted Arthur to the door and nodded a farewell as he held the door open.

'Arthur!' Richard called after him, and he turned back. Richard stared at him a moment before he continued. 'It is good to see you again. I can think of no man I'd rather have as my military right hand.'

Arthur smiled faintly. 'Thank you, Richard. I promise, you will not be disappointed in me.'

He strode out into the corridor and heard the door close behind him. Outside the Governor's headquarters he squinted as he emerged into the blistering midday heat. There was stillness in the grounds of the fort as everyone who could took shelter from the sun. A sole redcoat tramped slowly along the battlements above the main gate as Arthur made his way back to his rented house. The peace and quiet of the presidency would soon be a thing of the past, he mused. One way or another, war was coming to India and there was no telling if England would prevail, or Tipoo and his French allies.

Chapter 34

In the following weeks there was a constant stream of communications between the new Governor General and the Company's resident at the court of the Nizam, Captain James Kirkpatrick. Kirkpatrick was told to relay the message that England strongly desired closer relations with Hyderabad and would guarantee to support the Nizam, by force if required, against any threat to his position. It was Richard's conviction that the French officers in the Nizam's employ might have sufficient sway over their men to unseat the Nizam and replace him with a more compliant ruler.

These thoughts were very much on Arthur's mind as he drew up plans for removal of the French threat in Hyderabad, as well as the initial draft of a plan for the invasion of Mysore and the defeat of Tipoo. The difficulties presented by such an operation were the same as those that had faced General Cornwallis when he had attempted to bring Tipoo to heel seven years earlier. Cornwallis had managed to bring his army up to the enemy capital of Seringapatam and lay siege to the heavily fortified city. But then his food supplies had run short and he had been forced to retreat, with the added humiliation of having to abandon his heavy guns. This lack of mobility had bedevilled every attempt by English forces to push into the heart of India, and was the reason why the three presidencies were anchored to the coast and forced to communicate with each other by sea.

Colonel Wellesley, as he called himself now, and his small staff pondered the problem for nearly a month before hitting upon a solution that would be as simple as it was effective, and he at once sought a meeting with his brothers to explain his ideas. The instant he entered the office of the Governor General he sensed the tension.

'What's happened?'

Richard gestured to a document lying on the desk between him and Henry. 'The governor of the French colony on Mauritius has announced a formal alliance with Tipoo. He claims that French soldiers will be sent to Mangalore as soon as possible.'

Arthur leaned over the desk and quickly read through the document. 'Do you think it's true?'

'No doubt about it,' said Henry. 'A Portuguese ship came up the Hoogley yesterday. The captain had called in to Mauritius on his way north from the Cape. I interviewed him as soon as I could. He saved me this copy of the proclamation. He also said that he had seen Tipoo's ambassadors, and that they were given full honours by the French. Rather worrying, don't you think?'

'Quite,' Richard agreed.

Arthur was not so sure, and he sat down for a moment to reflect on the news before he responded. 'It's clear that the French aim to establish some kind of base of operations in Mysore, but there's no chance of capitalising on it for a while at least.'

'Explain yourself,' Richard said curtly.

'As far as we know, the French have no significant land forces in the Indian Ocean at the moment. True?'

Henry nodded.

'And if France is intending to send an army out to India then why announce it so publicly? Why give us so much warning? It doesn't make sense.'

Richard frowned and tapped the proclamation. 'So what is the meaning of this? What are they up to?'

'It seems to me that the Governor of Mauritius is trying to encourage Tipoo to make war on us. It won't cost France much more than encouraging words and a handful of supplies and advisers. If Tipoo wins the day then France can share in the spoils. If Tipoo is defeated then the French can at least hope that he has inflicted enough damage on us to significantly undermine our reputation.'

Richard smiled. 'Ah yes, it's that question of *iqbal* again.'

'Precisely. If our prestige is undermined it might be a long time before we win back the respect of the natives. Long enough at least for the French to gather forces to intervene more decisively.'

'I see.' Richard crossed to the window and gazed out across the ramparts towards Calcutta and the Hoogley river. 'Arthur, are we ready for a war against Tipoo?'

'No. And we won't be for some months yet. Our forces are too widely dispersed and we would need time to amass the necessary equipment and supplies to support an army.'

'When is the earliest that we could be ready to fight?' asked Henry.

'Not until next year. Spring, I'd say.'

'Spring . . .' Richard sighed and turned away from the window. 'In the meantime, I think we should move some forces closer to Mysore to show him that we will defend what's ours.'

'That would be wise.'

Richard sat down. 'Now then, to relieve the atmosphere of some of its gloom, I have some good news to relate. Concerning the Nizam.'

'Oh?'

'He has agreed terms for a treaty. I've persuaded him that a new alliance with England would be in his best interest. In exchange for removing his French officers the Nizam will permit us to increase the number of Company battalions at Hyderabad to six. More than enough to make him comfortable.'

Arthur raised his eyebrows. 'This is the first I've heard of any treaty.'

'Of course it is,' said Henry. 'It's still a secret. If word of it got out the Nizam's life would be in danger. Besides, he has yet to sign the treaty.'

Richard wagged a finger at Arthur. 'The moment the treaty's concluded I want our men in Hyderabad, and those French officers out. Do you think you can handle the task?'

'Me?' Arthur was surprised at the question. There were several officers senior to him who could easily have been offered the job. 'Why me?'

'Because you are my brother. I can trust you to keep your lip buttoned. Besides, you need a chance to prove your mettle. It was unfortunate that you were not given command of the Manila expedition, and doubly unfortunate that it was recalled before you had the opportunity to demonstrate your command skills. This time there will be no recall, and if you pull this off then no one can doubt my wisdom in choosing you for other commands in India. Do you understand, Arthur?'

'Yes.'

'Then don't let me down.'

Arthur left the four Company battalions to make camp for the night and rode on to Hyderabad. The treaty with the Nizam had finally been signed and the ruler of Hyderabad was well aware of the approach of the Company reinforcements, even if many of his courtiers and palace officials were not. Before the new-comers entered the city, it was vital that Arthur find out what was waiting for them. Kirkpatrick had sent a trusted agent to meet the advancing column and guide Arthur to the residency without attracting any unwelcome attention. The agent was a *hircarrah*, a member of an old guild employed in India to carry messages and act as scouts or spies. As they rode up towards the crest of a low hill in the fading light the agent raised his hand to halt Arthur.

'We must go most carefully from here, *sahib*.'

'How far are we from the residency?'

'Not so far, *sahib*. I know a safe route. Trust me.'

Arthur stared at the man in the gathering gloom, but the face was old and impassive and did not betray the slightest hint of what the *hircarrah* was thinking. There was nothing for it but to trust the man. It was possible that Arthur was being led into a trap, but he was well aware of the guild's reputation for fair dealing. The scout would have been paid by Kirkpatrick, and would stick to the bargain.

'Very well.' Arthur nodded. 'Let's go.'

They rode over the crest of the hill and Arthur saw the city of Hyderabad sprawling across the plain below him: a dark mass of buildings and minarets, illuminated here and there by the twinkling of small flames that cast a faint loom about them. The guide led Arthur down the far slope into a dried river bed that looped across the ground towards the city, and their horses' hooves scraped on the gravel loudly enough to make Arthur wince and glance anxiously into the surrounding shadows to see if they had been detected. But there was only the occasional crack and rustle from the undergrowth betraying the movement of small creatures. Eventually the banks of the river bed levelled out a little as they approached the city outskirts. The air was filled with the braying of goats and deeper bellows of cattle in wicker pens stretching out on either side. The sharp tang of their odour was mixed with the rich earthy smell of manure and Arthur instinctively wrinkled his nose as they rode on, a safe distance from the dark buildings from which the sing-song voices of their inhabitants occasionally sounded.

Then ahead of them Arthur saw a cluster of larger buildings outside the city and the scout clicked his tongue and pointed at them to indicate they were nearing their destination. He led Arthur to the largest of the houses, a single-storey dwelling surrounded by a wide, colonnaded veranda. A torch burned over the main entrance and, from within, faint slivers of light outlined the shutters closed across the windows. They made for the small cluster of stables and store sheds behind the bungalow and the scout called out softly towards the shadows. At once two men emerged and padded across to the horses to take the reins as Arthur and the scout dismounted. A door opened on to the veranda and a figure emerged.

'Colonel Wellesley?'

'Yes.'

'This way please, sir.' The figure beckoned to them and Arthur and the scout climbed the steps to the veranda. Arthur could now vaguely make out the features of the man in the doorway. He was a young man, perhaps the same age as Arthur, with closely cropped hair and a solid build. He turned to Arthur's guide and muttered to him in Hindoostani to wait outside.

Arthur cleared his throat. 'Captain Kirkpatrick?'

'Yes, sir. Please come inside. The others are waiting for you.'

Once Arthur had entered the house, Kirkpatrick closed the door behind him and picked up a small lamp on a side table, then led him down the corridor to where it opened out on to a formal reception room. Two men were sitting at a small table, lit by another lamp. Above them a punkah hung lifelessly and the air inside the room was still and stifling. The men stood up at the sound of approaching footsteps.

'Gentlemen, this is Colonel Wellesley.' Kirkpatrick spoke softly as if he feared that they might be overheard. 'Sir, may I introduce you to colonels Dalrymple and Malcolm, commanders of the two Company battalions stationed in Hyderabad.'

'Good evening, gentlemen.' Arthur shook their hands in turn and then eased himself down into one of the seats. 'I trust everything has been prepared for the arrival of the reinforcements tomorrow morning.'

There was a short silence while the other officers glanced at each other. Then Malcolm spoke. 'We have something of a problem, sir.'

'Problem? What kind of problem?'

'It's the Nizam, sir. I spoke to him this afternoon, as soon as we got word of your approach from the scout. He's decided that he does not want to disband the units commanded by French officers – not immediately, at least. It seems that word of the new treaty has got out and the officers and men are saying that he has betrayed them.'

'Which, of course, he has,' Arthur said acidly. 'That was the whole point of the treaty. If he backs down now the Governor General will be furious. Did you explain that to him?'

'I did, sir. Volubly.'

Arthur breathed deeply and exhaled to ease his tension. 'And?'

'The Nizam was courteous enough, sir, and expressed his loyalty to his English allies at some length. But he said that it would be too great a risk to disband the French battalions without any warning. However, now that they are aware of his plans he says they are threatening to overthrow him and kick the Company battalions, and the resident, out of Hyderabad.'

'Damn,' Arthur muttered. 'Damn the man. If his nerve fails now, then we face disaster. At the very least there'll be many lives lost if we have to disband those French units by force. If it goes badly for us we will have to fight our way out.'

'It's not all bad news, sir,' said Kirkpatrick. 'The other battalions in the Nizam's army are still loyal to him. They're not as numerous as the French-officered units, nor as well trained and equipped, but they'll not lift a finger to help any attempt to displace the Nizam. In fact, there's not much love lost between the native and the French officers.'

'That's something.' Arthur conceded. 'But it's vital that the Nizam himself gives the order for the units to disband. If he doesn't and we are forced to do the job, it can only cause considerable ill will amongst the Nizam's people.'

Kirkpatrick glanced at the other officers and then nodded. 'That's our fear, sir.'

'Then we must confront the Nizam again. Can you take me to him tonight?'

'It's dark, sir. He'll have retired to his private quarters by now.'

'Perfect. Then there's less chance of anyone seeing us.'

Kirkpatrick pursed his lips. 'I suppose we can give it a try, sir.'

'We have to, if we're going to prevent any bloodshed.' Arthur stood up. 'Let's go, then. You and me. Dalrymple and Malcolm can return to their commands.' Arthur turned to the two Company officers. 'Have your men fed, armed and ready to move as soon as I give the order. Understood?'

'Yes, sir.'

'Then I'll bid you good night, gentlemen. I'm sure I'll see you again tomorrow.' He turned back to Captain Kirkpatrick. 'It's time to beard the Nizam in his den.'

'Tonight? Now?' The Nizam's chamberlain shook his head. 'I am sorry, *sahib*, it is not possible. The Nizam—'

'Then make it possible,' Arthur said firmly. 'At once.'

The chamberlain glanced anxiously over his shoulder at the imposing entrance to the Nizam's private quarters. He turned back to the two English officers and raised his hands imploringly. 'The Nizam is entertaining guests. He would not be pleased to be interrupted, *sahib*. It would not go well with me if I dared to disturb him.'

'It will not go well for you, or the Nizam, if you don't. I have ridden here on the orders of the Governor General to speak with the Nizam on a matter of the utmost importance.' Arthur softened his tone and smiled. 'Now then, I am sure that you would not want the Nizam to hold you accountable for any offence caused to the most powerful Englishman in India.'

The chamberlain squirmed for a moment and clasped his hands to his forehead. '*Ayoo* . . .'

'Do as we ask,' Arthur insisted. 'Many lives hang in the balance.'

The chamberlain lowered his hands and stared at Arthur for a moment and then slumped his shoulders and nodded. 'Very well, *sahib*. Come with me.'

They followed him towards the double doors and the two guards standing on either side watched warily as the English officers approached. The chamberlain clapped his hands and called out an order. At once the guards grasped the heavy brass handles and pulled open the great slabs of intricately carved and painted wood. Beyond was a wide corridor and from the far end came the nasal notes of native music. There were voices too, men's and women's: high spirited and punctuated with bursts of laughter and joyful shouting.

'What kind of entertainment is the Nazim enjoying tonight?' asked Arthur.

'The usual, *sahib*. Our ruler is a man of the people, if you take my meaning. That is why I do not think it wise to interrupt him.' The chamberlain paused and looked at Arthur hopefully. '*Sahib*, I really do think it might be best if we didn't. I could arrange a meeting tomorrow morning.'

'Tonight.' Arthur steered the chamberlain towards the end of the corridor. 'I cannot wait until morning. Keep moving.'

The trio reached the end of the corridor and emerged into a garden courtyard. Through a thin screen of trees they could see the flickering glint of torches and Arthur led the way along a tiled path towards the voices of the Nizam and his companions. As they emerged into the lighted area at the heart of the courtyard Arthur sucked in his breath and muttered, 'Upon my soul . . .'

A dozen dancing girls were swaying to the music played by four men in a small arbour to one side of the open space. The dancing girls were clad only in flimsy loincloths and the flames of the torches glimmered off their bangles and earrings. In front of them, in a semicircle, a group of men sat on low couches and watched the dancers with fixed expressions. In the middle was a couch decorated in gold leaf and studded with jewels. The couch was set on a raised dais and squatting on its richly embroidered cushions was an old man in a loose robe that hung open to reveal a round stomach covered in grey hair. Nestled against his thigh was another young girl, as scantily clad as the dancers, and the man absent-mindedly kneaded one of her breasts as he watched the performance in front of him.

Arthur drew himself up to his full height and nodded to Kirkpatrick, and they marched into the loom of the light cast by the torches. The musicians stopped playing and the dancers ceased their sinuous movement as everyone turned towards the sharp rap of boots crossing the polished tiles of the Nizam's private pleasure garden. The old man seated on the dais, who Arthur realised must be the Nizam, released the girl's breast and rose to his feet with a shocked expression. As soon as he caught sight of his chamberlain, his expression became angry and he bellowed at the hapless official. Arthur and Kirkpatrick stopped a short distance in front of him and gave a stiff, formal bow.

'Captain Kirkpatrick,' said Arthur.

'Sir?'

'You speak the language far better than me, so you can translate what I have to say. Tell the Nizam I wish to speak to him alone.'

As the old man listened to Kirkpatrick his eyes widened in

outrage and he snapped something back, clenching his fist and waving it at the two Englishmen.

'He says, how dare we enter his private quarters, and issue such an outrageous order. He says his chamberlain is a mangy son of a whore who deserves to be torn in two for letting two infidels enter the gardens of his master.'

Arthur ignored the quaking chamberlain, who had dropped to his knees and buried his head in his hands as he muttered a string of appeals for mercy.

'Tell him to dismiss these people. We must speak to him at once.'

Again the Nizam shouted and blustered, until Arthur sharply held up a hand to silence him. The Nizam shrank back from the sudden gesture before recovering his poise, folding his arms and glaring back defiantly. His guests, the dancers and the musicians watched in silence, hardly daring to move.

'Tell him that he must do as I say, and that I speak on the direct authority of the Governor General. If he refuses, then the treaty with England is forfeit . . .'

As Kirkpatrick translated the Nizam stared at Arthur, his lips compressed into a thin line. Then there was silence and at last the Nizam's gaze faltered. He swung round to his followers and shouted an instruction, clapping his hands to send them away as speedily as possible. The guests scrambled up from their cushions and joined the dancers and the musicians as they stumbled through the trees towards the entrance to the Nizam's garden. As the last sounds of their departure faded away Arthur gestured towards the couches closest to the Nizam dais.

'Ask him if we might sit at his side.'

The civility of the sudden request caught the Nizam off guard and he nodded and indicated that they should sit with a graceful sweep of his hand. Then, gathering up his robe, he sat on his couch and poised himself for a private audience with the two Englishmen. The chamberlain remained where he lay, crouched and quite still, trying his hardest to be forgotten. Arthur took a deep breath and began.

'I have heard that the Nizam is considering going back on his agreement. Regardless of all previous treaties he may have made with representatives of the Company and England, he should be aware that the new Governor General is a man of his word. Which means he will do his utmost to guarantee the safety of the Nizam, whatever the cost to England in men, money or prestige. In return, the Governor General expects the Nizam to honour his side of the treaty with equal diligence.' Arthur waited for this to be translated and fully digested before he continued. 'Therefore, the Nizam will understand my frustration, as representative of the Governor General, when I learned that he had decided not to disarm the French battalions by the time specified in the treaty.'

The Nizam burst into a torrent of explanation which Kirkpatrick struggled to keep up with.

'Sir, the gist of it is that we do not understand how delicate the situation has become in Hyderabad. He requests that we give him ten days to negotiate a peaceful disbanding of the battalions, and that your column remain encamped outside the city until then. He gives his word that he remains a loyal ally of England and that his soldiers still hold him in sufficient regard and affection to bend to his will. He also says that the concessions he made in the treaty were far greater than those demanded by French representatives who seek an alliance with Hyderabad.'

'Is that so?' Arthur steeled his expression. 'Then tell him that if I even remotely suspect him of trying to cut a deal with the French, the treaty is forfeit and the four Company battalions camped outside Hyderabad, together with the two garrisoned within the city, will quit his kingdom and march back to Madras at first light tomorrow. And then he will have to deal with his French-officered battalions by himself. I know that those soldiers are verging on mutiny over the prospect of being disbanded. I imagine that without the Company battalions to protect him the Nizam's reign might be ended within a matter of days, at the very most.'

The Nizam heard the translation with growing agitation, but before he could respond Arthur held up a hand. 'If the Nizam is not willing to give the order for the disbanding of the French battalions, then it is my duty to handle the matter myself. If the Nizam attempts to interefere with this process in any way, then once I have finished dismantling the French battalions I will start to dismantle his kingdom.'

Kirkpatrick drew in a sharp breath and looked at his superior with a warning expression. But Arthur was adamant. This was a test of nerves. The Nizam's had clearly failed him and now, for the first time, all the gambling instincts that Arthur had once possessed at Dublin Castle served him well. He knew that the stakes were high and had already calculated the risk of the plan he had formed in his mind. He had called the Nizam's bluff. Of course, all that stood between Arthur and winning the round was several thousand soldiers under the command of men from a nation that had sworn to destroy England and all she stood for.

'We're leaving now. Just let the Nizam know that by this time tomorrow his difficulties will all be over.'

The Nizam muttered a reply as they rose to their feet, and Arthur turned to his subordinate for a translation.

'And if they are not?'

Arthur smiled. 'Then, more than likely, all three of us will be dead.'

Chapter 35

The streets were bathed in the fitful light of the moon as scattered shreds of cloud passed slowly across the night sky. Dark figures padded down the streets winding through the outskirts of Hyderabad. They moved quietly, having abandoned their boots a short distance from the city. They carried the minimum of equipment and the only sounds above the soft slap of their feet were the occasional whispered orders, passed from man to man. Arthur was leading the sepoy companies in person, since he could not trust any other officer with the task at hand. Kirkpatrick, who knew the route through the city well enough, even under the cloak of darkness, jogged along with the advance guard, a short distance ahead of Arthur. Both men had exchanged their military boots for soft-skinned shoes and were bareheaded, carrying only a brace of pistols and their swords. For Arthur's plan to stand any chance of succeeding it was vital that the small column remained undetected until it reached its goal. The rest of the men from the Company battalions were out of sight just outside the city, waiting until the hour before dawn to enter Hyderabad.

The men of the advance guard stopped and knelt down. Arthur raised his hand to halt the rest of the column and went forward to squat beside Kirkpatrick.

'Why have we stopped?'

'We're there, sir.' Kirkpatrick pointed down the street ahead of them. A short distance away the street gave on to a large open space. Arthur realised this must be the vast parade ground that

Kirkpatrick had described to him earlier. On the far side Arthur could see the low ramparts of the Nizam's army camp.

'Where's the arsenal?'

'You can't see it from here, sir. It's in a fortified bastion on the far corner of the camp, away from the city.'

'And the water gate?'

'At the end of a side street, not far from the square. We turn off here and join the street close to the parade ground.'

'All right then, lead on.'

Kirkpatrick nodded, then turned to his men and whispered the order to move. They rose up like ghosts and advanced a little further down the street before turning into a narrow alley. Arthur marked the spot carefully and then went back to the rest of the men and waved them on. The alley wound down a small slope and the hot night air became even more humid as the rank smell of dung fires and sewage filled Arthur's nostrils. They had nearly reached the small crossroads at the bottom of the slope when a door opened just ahead of Arthur and a man stepped into the street, shouting angrily as he spied the men moving through the shadows towards him. At that moment the moon cleared a thicker cloud and the alley was bathed in moonlight, revealing not only the number of men moving down the alley, but also their uniforms, and Arthur's white skin. The man's tirade was cut off abruptly, then he muttered some curse and dived back through the doorway.

'Damn!' Arthur growled and jumped after him, thrusting his weight against the door closing in his face. The door crashed inwards and he heard a grunt as the man inside fell back against the wall. Arthur drew out one of his pistols, holding it tightly by the muzzle. The man stumbled out from behind the door, clutching his hand to his nose, and Arthur swung the butt of his pistol down hard on his head. It connected with a soft thud and the man grunted with pain and then collapsed, out cold. There was a shrill call of panic from further within the house and Arthur glanced up and saw the dim shape of a woman watching him from an interior doorway. A child was clutching her leg.

'Shhhh!' Arthur raised the pistol and reversed the grip so the barrel was now pointed at the ceiling. He whispered to them in Hindoostani. 'Not a word, or I'll shoot. Understand?'

The woman nodded vigorously and backed away into the darkness, drawing her child after her. Arthur looked down for a moment at the man he had felled, then leaned over and shifted him into a more comfortable position on the floor. He closed the door as he stepped back into the alley. His heart was beating fast, the pounding in his ears making it hard to listen to the streets around him. There was no sound of any disturbance, no cry of alarm or challenge from the direction of the camp.

'Christ, that was close,' he muttered, wiping the perspiration from his brow. He eased the pistol back into his belt and waved his men forward again. Kirkpatrick had left a man at the junction to indicate the route to those who followed and Arthur and his column turned towards the camp. One of the advance guard whistled softly and the column halted at once, the men freezing as they hugged the shaded side of the alley. A short way off Arthur could see the ramparts looming above the crazy angles of the rooflines each side of the alley. The faint outline of a sentry crossed Arthur's field of vision and he let out a sigh of relief as the man passed from sight.

The column eased forward again. Just ahead the alley widened out to accommodate a long trench, that had been covered over with slabs of stone where it passed under the alley which led up to a small, grated arch at the foot of the wall. A foul stench filled the air and Arthur wrinkled his nose as he glanced down at the stinking trickle of filth that ran along the bottom of the trench: the outflow from the main latrine block of the camp. Kirkpatrick and his men stole forward on either side of the trench until they reached the wall, and then carefully clambered down into the channel. A moment later the soft sounds of gentle scraping carried back up the alley.

Arthur and the sepoys remained silent and motionless as Kirkpatrick's men worked away at the bars of the grille, loosening one after the other and placing them carefully at the base of the rampart. Work had to stop each time the sentry returned to this stretch of the wall. He crossed above the sewage outflow with a maddening measured tread, and as soon as the sounds of his boots faded away the work began again. It took far longer than Arthur had anticipated and he found himself glancing repeatedly at the skyline above the roofs of the city for the first sign of the coming dawn.

Eventually a dim shape climbed up over the side of the trench and trotted back towards Arthur.

'Colonel *sahib*?'

'Here,' Arthur responded softly. 'Keep your voice down.'

'A thousand pardons. Kirkpatrick *sahib* says the grate is cleared. He's sending a small party of men to deal with the sentry.'

'Very good. Tell him to let me know the instant the way is open.'

The sepoy nodded and hurried back towards the rampart. A short while later Kirkpatrick's voice called out, as loudly as he dared, 'All clear, sir.'

Arthur emerged from the shadows into the middle of the alley where his men could see him clearly. He raised his arm and then swept it down in the direction of the ramparts. The men hurried forward, down into the stinking trench, and doubled over as they splashed beneath the wall of the camp and emerged on the far side, spreading out to either side of the latrine drain. Arthur was one of the first men through, and made his way over to Kirkpatrick. Behind him the sepoys filed under the wall and spread out in the shadows beneath the ramparts.

Arthur glanced towards the eastern horizon. 'We have to move fast. It'll be light soon. You know what you have to do. Any last questions?'

'None, sir.'

'Good. Then you'd better go. Remember, there's to be no killing, if you can avoid it. There's to be no blood on British hands.'

Kirkpatrick nodded solemnly. 'I understand, sir.'

'Then I'll see you afterwards.'

'In this life or the next, eh, sir?' Kirkpatrick grinned nervously.

'If it comes to that. Now go.'

Kirkpatrick saluted and turned to trot away to the two companies under his command. He gestured to them to follow him and led the way along the foot of the wall towards the arsenal. Arthur waited a moment, listening for any indication that the alarm had been raised. But the camp was silent and Arthur whispered the order for his men to advance in the opposite direction. They passed several huge barrack blocks that stretched into the heart of the Nizam's camp before they reached the stabling for the officers' horses that Kirkpatrick had told him of. On the other side of a generous riding ring was the fine two-storey officers' mess and sleeping quarters. A large lantern cast a pool of light over the entrance, either side of which a guard sat on a bench, musket in hand. Again Arthur glanced to the east, and this time there was an unmistakable smear of light along the horizon. There was no time left to attempt an indirect approach. Already, the first men would be stirring.

Arthur realised at once that he had only one chance. He turned to the subadar at the head of the two companies stretched out behind him. 'I need a good man to help me. Quickly.'

The subadar called along the line and a moment later a burly man with a square-cut beard emerged from the darkness and stood to attention before Arthur.

'Come with me,' Arthur ordered in Hindoostani. 'When we reach the entrance to that building we must silence the sentries. When I give the order and not before.'

'Yes, *sahib*.'

'All right, then . . . Subadar, when you see me wave, bring the sepoys over on the double.' He turned back to the thickset man. 'Come with me.'

Arthur took a deep breath and set off across the riding ring, striding boldly towards the entrance to the headquarters building. His heart was beating fast and his mind raced, and he was aware of every detail around him, every sound and smell, as his senses acquired an extraordinary acuity that he had experienced only a handful of times before in his life. As they neared the sentries, the two men finally caught sight of them and stood up, grasping their muskets in both hands and making ready to challenge the two figures striding towards them. Then, as Arthur had hoped, they noticed his pale skin and officer's shell jacket, and quickly stood to attention, grounding their muskets. He maintained his pace as he approached the entrance, as if he was just returning from some duty in the camp. As they passed between the sentries Arthur whipped out his pistol and called out, 'Now!'

The sepoy suddenly lurched to the side, ramming the butt of his weapon into the side of the sentry's head and felling him with an explosive grunt. Arthur swung his pistol at the other man's head, but at the last moment the sentry detected the coming blow and scrambled back so that it brushed past his head harmlessly. Arthur was momentarily caught off balance and the sentry instinctively swung his musket butt towards him. Arthur felt a blow to his chest as the enemy musket caught him in the ribs, winding him. Then, before the shortage of air crippled him, he dropped his pistol and balled his right hand into a fist and punched it into the man's face, driving his head back against the headquarters wall.

Arthur helped the sepoy to drag the sentries to some nearby shrubs and roll the unconscious men into the undergrowth, out of sight. Then he returned to the wavering glow beneath the lantern, drew his sword and beckoned to the men on the far side of the riding ring. A moment later the darkness was filled with swarming shadows as the sepoys swept forward.

Arthur strode inside the building, into the grand entrance hall lined with a dark wood wainscot above which hung various hunting trophies: the skins of tigers and the stuffed heads of boar and deer. A double doorway to the right opened on to a huge banqueting hall and to the left another opened on to an equally large space filled with tables and chairs with a bar at the far end. An officer sat in a chair sound asleep, head slumped back as he snored gutturally. Footsteps pounded across the wooden floorboards of the hall as the sepoys joined their commander. Arthur called the subadars of the companies to him and issued their orders.

'Upstairs. Take every officer that you can find and bring them all down here. I want French officers taken to the banqueting hall. The rest go into the mess lounge. Remember, no harm is to be done. You understand?'

'*Acha, sahib!*' They saluted, and then called their men after them as they pounded up the staircase at the end of the hall and entered the first floor sleeping quarters of the Nizam's officers. At once there was the crashing of doors being flung open and the first of the sleepy shouts of anger and outrage. A small door opened at the end of the hall and a stout, bleary-eyed man in a silk dressing gown fastened with a wide leather belt stumbled into the hall.

'What the bloody hell is the meaning of this?' he bellowed at Arthur, then blinked. 'Who the hell are you, sir?'

'Colonel Arthur Wellesley, of His Majesty's 33rd Foot,' Arthur said formally. 'And you, sir?'

'Major MacDonald, quartermaster to the Nizam and president of the officers' mess. Now then, what's going on here?' He glanced up the stairs as the thud of footsteps and shouting reverberated down the length of the hall. 'Sounds like we're being invaded.'

'In a manner of speaking,' Arthur replied. 'I'm here on the orders of the Nizam. He requires the temporary detention of all the officers of his battalions garrisoned in Hyderabad city. That includes you, so if you wouldn't mind?' Arthur gestured to the mess lounge.

MacDonald folded his arms and puffed out his chest. 'I think not, sir. How do I know you are speaking the truth?'

Arthur drew his sword. 'That's how. Now move.'

MacDonald stumbled back a pace then edged towards the lounge door and hurried across to one of the cane chairs and slumped down. With a loud chorus of shouts the first of the officers taken from their rooms were escorted downstairs and separated into the two large rooms overlooking the riding ring. The officers continued to shout their angry protests at their treatment as the grinning sepoys thrust them into chairs and kept them covered with their bayonets. When the last of them had been brought downstairs Arthur pulled a chair into the hall and climbed on to it so that he could be seen by all in both rooms, and raised his hands to quiet them.

'I need your attention, gentlemen!'

The protests continued as loudly as ever and Arthur had no wish to seem like some ineffectual schoolteacher. He drew one of his pistols, cocked it, raised it towards the ceiling and fired. In the enclosed hall the detonation of the powder charge was thunderous and silenced the men at once. A moment later a large lump of plaster crashed to the floor, missing Arthur by inches.

He glanced at the shattered fragments on the floor with raised eyebrows, then looked up and drew a deep breath to begin his address before the officers recovered from their shock and began to protest again.

'Gentlemen! My apologies to you for this rude awakening. The Nizam requires that you are held here for a short time while a small piece of business is attended to. You are quite safe, provided that you sit still and make no attempt to escape or resist my men.'

'What is going on here?' a voice demanded. 'What's happening?'

'Your questions will be answered in good time. But for now, I would be obliged if you would keep your mouths shut, or my men will be obliged to do it for you.'

The threat was understood well enough and the sepoys lining the rooms held their weapons ready to reinforce their commander's words. When he was satisfied that the officers were subdued Arthur beckoned to one of the subadars.

'I'm taking four of your men. Keep this lot under control. No one is to leave the rooms under any pretext.'

'Yes, *sahib*.'

There was a thin grey light in the sky as Arthur trotted away from the headquarters building and made for the arsenal on the far side of the camp. A few early risers were sitting outside their barracks and laying the morning cooking fires. They stood up with vaguely confused expressions as the officer and sepoys passed by, and then returned to their fireplaces. The only shot that had been fired was from Arthur's pistol and there was no reason for the Nizam's men to suspect that anything was amiss. As far as they were concerned he was just another European officer up early on some official business, as Arthur had hoped they would think. They reached the squat mass of the camp's arsenal without being challenged and Arthur was relieved to see that Kirkpatrick had stationed his men inside the building, out of sight, so that only a few figures were visible on the ramparts above the arsenal, and on guard at its entrance. As Arthur and his men approached Kirkpatrick appeared in the doorway to meet them.

'Any problems?'

'No, sir. The guards didn't put up a fight. Went down into one of the storerooms as meek as lambs.'

'Good work.' Arthur looked up at the sky and saw that there was now enough light to see clearly across the camp. More men and women were emerging from their barracks, ready to prepare their morning meal. Outside the city the four Company battalions would be beginning their march, as Dalrymple and Malcolm led their men from their barracks towards the camp of the Nizam's army. 'Now we just have to wait for the others, and pray that the Nizam's men don't guess what is happening right under their noses.'

The sun rose over the camp and soon thousands of men, women and children had emerged from their quarters and gathered round their fires to eat. Arthur watched from the ramparts of the arsenal. Only a handful of his men were visible from outside the building and the two sepoys guarding the entrance wore jackets taken from the men imprisoned in the storeroom.

Kirkpatrick was squatting next to him and chewing the end of his thumb as he kept glancing towards the nearest gateway into the camp. 'They should be here by now. What's keeping them, damn it?'

Arthur glanced round and saw that one of the sepoys was looking at them. He turned back to gaze over the camp and muttered, 'Keep your voice down. What kind of effect do you think your fretting will have on the men?'

Kirkpatrick started guiltily. 'Sorry, sir.'

'I understand you are nervous.' Arthur smiled. 'So am I. The trick is not to let it show. Think on that and you'll be fine.'

'Yes, sir . . . Thank you.'

They were interrupted by a chorus of shouts from over by the barracks. Arthur squinted his tired eyes and saw a group of men running from the direction of the headquarters building, shouting and gesticulating wildly as they ran. The Nizam's soldiers hurried back into their quarters and began to emerge with their weapons to join the growing crowd.

'They're headed this way,' Arthur said quietly. 'Damn . . . All right, then, Kirkpatrick. The time for stealth is over. Call those two sentries in and close and barricade the doors and windows of the arsenal. We may have to hold them off for a while before the other columns turn up.'

'Yes, sir.' Kirkpatrick hurried away to carry out his orders and a moment later Arthur heard the heavy timber door thud home below him. The sepoys who had been hidden below came padding up on to the ramparts and took up position, muskets loaded and ready at half-cock. There was a roar from the crowd as they saw the arsenal being closed up, and then scores of heads appearing at the battlements. The mob surged forward and started battering at the door with their muskets, to no effect. One of Arthur's men rose up and took aim with his weapon.

'Lower your gun!' Arthur bellowed at him in Hindoostani. 'Now!'

When the man had dropped down again Arthur stood up so that all his men could see him and drew a deep breath so that he would be heard over the din of the crowd. 'We're safe enough here. They have no powder or shot for their weapons. They can't hurt us, so hold your fire.'

That was not entirely true, he reflected. That mob would do more than hurt Arthur and his men if they found a way into the arsenal. But it was a solid enough building and would keep the Nizam's men at bay for a while yet. Long enough for the other columns to arrive.

Then he saw some of the men at the rear of the crowd take up a solid-looking water trough. They emptied the water out of it, then lifted it up and bore it through the crowd towards the arsenal. A makeshift battering ram, he realised with a sick feeling. He must not let them have a chance to use it against the doors.

'Stand up!' Arthur shouted to his men. 'Present!'

The muskets swung up and levelled as the sepoys took aim on the mob. At once there were cries of terror and men flinched and fell back. Arthur leaned over the ramparts and stretched his arms open.

'Hear me! Hear me, I say!'

It took a while for the frightened protesters to grow silent, and still scores of them were slipping back into the heart of the crowd.

'I am Colonel Wellesley. I am here on the authority of the Nizam. He has given orders for the disbandment of the French-officered battalions. You will lay down your weapons and return to barracks now!'

This provoked a fresh outburst of rage from the crowd and the makeshift battering ram surged forward again. Arthur turned to the section of men covering the rampart over the entrance. 'Take aim on those men carrying the water trough!'

The muskets went up to their cheeks as the men squinted down the barrels towards the approaching crowd.

'Cock your weapons, but do not fire unless I give the order!'

The sepoys thumbed back the cocks, ready to fire a volley of heavy lead balls into the crowd in front of the arsenal. The ram came on, and there was a jarring thud as it struck home against the wall.

'Shoot over their heads!' Arthur called to the nearest men and they raised their barrels. 'Fire!' The volley roared out with a series of stabs of fire and a small rolling bank of gunpowder smoke. The crowd paused for only an instant before they realised the shots had been fired wide deliberately. Then they came forward again and there was another thud from below. Arthur swallowed. The time had almost come when he would have to open fire on the crowd in order to survive.

'Reload, and prepare volley fire!'

As his men bit off the ends of the tallow paper cartridges and spat the ball down the muzzles of their muskets a sudden movement drew Arthur's eye to the main gateway into the camp. A column of men was emerging through it, the colours of the East India Company at their head. At once he was giddy with relief. 'They're coming!' He thrust his arm out in the direction of the new arrivals. 'They're here!'

His men raised a cheer now, and down below as word of the relief column flew through the crowd they turned away from the arsenal and clutched their unloaded weapons restlessly, making little sound as they faced the new threat.

There was another shout from the men on the ramparts and Arthur saw a sepoy excitedly pointing to another column emerging between the barracks of the Nizam's army. Arthur indulged the sepoys for a moment before he ordered them to still their tongues. A silence hung over the camp as Arthur turned to the crowd.

'Lay down your weapons and return to your quarters.'

'What? And let you slaughter us like dogs!' A voice cried back.

'No! There will be no killing. Lay down your arms and get back to your quarters, now. If not, you will be fired on.'

One of the men tried to defy him, standing on an upturned washing tub to harangue his comrades. It was clear from the crowd's reaction that they would be easily stirred into action by their speaker and Arthur realised that now was the time for ruthlessness.

'Take aim. Prepare to fire . . . on my word . . .' He leaned forward to address the crowd again. 'This is your last warning. Lay down your weapons and return to the barracks or you will be shot down!'

For a moment none of them reacted and Arthur was aware that the other columns had entered the camp and were already forming a firing line. Then one of the Nizam's men on the fringe of the crowd lowered his weapon to the ground and hurried away. Another man followed his lead, then another, until the edges of the crowd were melting away and then those at the heart of mob also began to surrender their weapons, leaving their provocatory leader alone on his tub, still imploring them to come back and take the arsenal. Eventually, he too gave up, shoulders slumping as he climbed down from the upended tub and beat a retreat back to the barracks. Arthur watched him go, and saw that the others were gathering up their comrades, the women and the children and disappearing into the barrack blocks. Soon there was little sign of life around the camp and wisps of steam and smoke from the fires lifted lazily into the morning air. Arthur felt the tension of the last few moments drain from his body to be replaced by a blessed sense of relief that the crisis had passed and he had won the day, without any bloodshed. He idly hoped that all his victories could be as bloodless as this, then cursed himself for being such a naïve fool.

The plan had been good, and carried out to the letter. All that remained was to carry out the terms of the treaty the Nizam had signed.

The column that had entered by the main gate was led by Colonel Malcolm, who doffed his hat to Arthur as he approached the arsenal and called out, 'Good day to you, sir!'

Arthur nodded. 'And to you.'

'Bloody fine piece of work.' Malcolm laughed as he surveyed the abandoned muskets carpeting the ground in front of the arsenal. 'We've done it! Just wait till word of this gets back to Calcutta! Fine work, sir! Fine work.'

Arthur stretched his back and smiled to himself. He could already imagine Richard's delight at hearing that the plan had gone so smoothly. The French officers would be ousted, the Nizam would be in the debt of England and, best of all, not one life had been lost in achieving this result. For that, Arthur felt his heart swell with pride as he gazed out across the camp and let the warm rays of the rising sun wash over his face.

Chapter 36

'Egypt?' Arthur's eyebrows rose in astonishment. 'When did they invade?'

'At the start of July,' Henry replied. 'A large army, well over twenty thousand men according to our agents' reports. The commander is one of their rising stars, a General Bonaparte.'

'Bonaparte,' Arthur mused wryly. Once again the young French general was making his mark. 'What do we know of his intentions?'

Henry smiled. 'Not a great deal. It seems the French are set on turning Egypt into a province. This man Bonaparte is busy setting up a new government in Egypt, levying taxes, building roads and so on. It's not difficult to see what the longer term goal might be. With Egypt in their pocket the French will have a base from which to seize the whole of the Levant. Of course, our fear is that such a move would ultimately constitute a threat to us here in India. They will be in a far better position to send men and supplies to the aid of our enemies, like Tipoo.'

Richard leaned forward and stabbed his finger down on the desk. 'What I want to know is what our bloody Navy was doing while Bonaparte and his army were swanning around the Mediterranean. That glory-chaser, Nelson, was supposed to intercept and destroy any French fleets that left port. Instead, he's somehow managed to let the entire enemy battle fleet slip past him. The bloody man must be blind.'

'Well, now that you mention it . . .' Henry muttered.

'In any case, it doesn't matter,' Richard interrupted. 'We can't do anything about it now. The thing is, we have to be aware that this news will encourage Tipoo. I think that the time is fast approaching when he will move against us, unless we act first. I'm just glad that we have settled the situation in Hyderabad. At least we can count on the Nizam's support for a while yet. And there'll be no more Frenchmen drip-feeding their revolutionary bile into his ear.'

'What happened to the French officers?' asked Henry. 'How many did you take prisoner?'

'Over a hundred of them,' Arthur replied. 'I had them escorted to Bombay and put aboard an Indiaman. They're on their way to England where I imagine they'll spend the rest of the war on a prison hulk.'

Richard sniffed. 'Good riddance to 'em. At least that's put an end to the French influence in Hyderabad.'

'For now at least,' Arthur agreed. 'But they'll find other ways to try to exert their influence in India. Mark my words.'

'I don't have to. It's already happening.' Richard leaned over his desk and tapped a pile of intelligence reports. 'Tipoo and his army are daily becoming the proxies of the revolutionaries back in Paris. At the moment the French offer encouragement and promises, but it won't be too long before they back that up with guns, gold and men. Tipoo can hardly wait to have a crack at us. The problem is that we're not yet ready to fight him. The situation in Madras is a mess. The new Governor General, Lord Clive – the son,' he added, in response to a raised eyebrow from Arthur, 'is still learning the ropes and depends too much on his advisers, especially his chief of staff, Josiah Webbe. Webbe has sent me a memorandum demanding that we do nothing to provoke conflict with Tipoo, or indeed any of the other powers in India. According to my sources Webbe plays continually on Clive's desire to keep the books balanced. He's fighting every step to prepare the Madras presidency for war on the pretext that the Company cannot afford to fight Tipoo.'

'How can we afford not to fight him?' asked Arthur with exasperation. 'If we don't take the fight to Tipoo then you can be sure that he will take the fight to Madras. And that would be just the start. None of England's possessions in India would be safe.'

'Quite.' Richard nodded. 'If Tipoo can capture Madras then the natives will have no faith in our *iqbal*, and my fear is that they will flock to his side. If that happens then our days are numbered in the other presidencies.'

'What are we to do, then?' asked Henry. 'We're not ready for war, but it seems that we are compelled to fight one.'

'Indeed,' Richard mused. He rose from his chair and paced over to the large map of India that adorned one of the walls. He studied the area between Madras and Seringapatam for a moment before he continued. 'The main difficulty facing us will be one of distance. It defeated Cornwallis last time round. We must ensure that the same fate does not befall us.' He turned round to face his brothers, then fixed his gaze on Arthur. 'You've been thinking about this matter, I understand.'

'Yes. I've had some ideas about what we can do to give us a decent chance of defeating Tipoo once and for all.'

'Go on.'

Arthur quickly set his thoughts in order. 'Tipoo knows that his men stand little chance of defeating a large army of King's regiments and Company battalions. His cavalry, while numerous, is no match for ours, and his infantry lack training and experience compared to our men. He has a distinct advantage in artillery, but many of his guns are too large for mobile warfare and will have to be left at Seringapatam.

'It's my belief that Tipoo will follow the same strategy as last time. He will fight a series of delaying actions, destroying as much food and forage as he can in the path of our men, before he falls back on Seringapatam and holds out there until our supplies are finished, or the monsoon season comes. The rains will make the rivers around Seringapatam unfordable, and afterwards the pestilence will cause our men to drop like flies.'

Henry nodded. 'And how do you intend to counter his strategy, Arthur?'

'It won't be easy,' Arthur admitted readily enough. 'But the key to it is to find a new way of supplying our army once the campaign begins.'

'How do you propose to do that?'

'The main thing is to make our forces as mobile as possible. What limits the size and depth of our offensive ability at present is the need to build roads wherever we go so that we can bring up our wheeled transport – the supply wagons and artillery. The solution is obvious enough. We don't bother with lines of communication. And, as far as possible, we don't bother with roads, or even wheels for that matter.'

Richard looked confused. 'So, what are you suggesting? That we dispense with feeding our men, and not use artillery to support them?'

Arthur smiled. 'It's simple. We'll use bullocks and elephants to carry and haul our heavy equipment. They can go almost anywhere a man can go, and they can live off the land as they march. They move at about the same speed as draft horses so they will not slow the army down. Of course, we will need thousands of them, and that's where the second part of the solution comes in. We'll use the *brinjarris* to supply our needs.'

'*Brinjarris?*' Henry frowned for an instant. 'Please refresh my memory.'

'They're grain merchants. They buy and sell grain the length and breadth of India and breed vast herds of bullocks to carry their goods. My suggestion is that we subcontract the supply of our army to the *brinjarris*. We offer them the right to set up a bazaar to supply the soldiers' needs in return for paying a fair price and offering protection to them and their families. We also hire as many bullocks as we need from their stock, to draw our guns, and if the ground isn't suitable for wheeled traffic, then we can disassemble the guns and have the components carried forward by bullocks or elephants. If we do all that, then we can invade Mysore quickly, push the Tipoo's forces back to his capital and then lay siege to it, confident that there will be enough supplies, and time, to carry out the task.' He looked directly at Richard. 'Which leaves one question. Who is to command the army when the time comes to tackle Tipoo?'

Richard turned back to the map and scratched his chin for a

moment. 'Well, it's clearly a general's command, which rules you out.'

Arthur felt an instant stab of disappointment and then cursed himself for even thinking that there was any chance that he might have such a responsibility placed in his hands, brother of the Governor General or not. He cleared his throat. 'Of course it does. I wasn't for a moment suggesting myself for the post.'

Richard turned to him with a quizzical look. 'Don't over-react, Arthur. I know your quality, and you proved it well enough with that business in Hyderabad. Your time will come. I promise.'

The conversation was embarrassing Arthur and he waved a hand, as if sweeping it aside. 'We were discussing which general would be best for the command.'

'Yes we were. What is your opinion? As the professional soldier in the room.'

'Sir Alured Clarke's the obvious choice. He's the most senior officer in India, and the most capable.'

'So I've heard. However, when the war begins, I will move to Madras to be closer to events. In which case Clarke will be needed here, in Calcutta. He's about the only man I trust enough to leave in charge.'

Arthur shrugged. 'In that case, it should be General Harris, the ranking officer at Madras.'

'Harris?' Richard frowned for a moment and then nodded to himself. 'I remember him. Nice fellow, but too quiet and unassuming. Is he up to it?'

'Assuredly. He's organised and hard working. You can be sure that Harris will plan the operation thoroughly and see it through. After Clarke, he's the best choice.'

'All right then.' Richard nodded. 'I'll consider him. But on one other matter, I have already made a decision.'

'Oh?'

'I'm transferring the 33rd Foot from Calcutta to Madras. I want you down there to make sure that the necessary preparations for war are being carried out. And I want you to put into effect those ideas you had for making the field army more self-sufficient. You will, of course, have my full authority to obtain what you need in that regard.'

'Thank you, Richard.'

'There's one other thing. Unofficially, you are my eyes and ears in Madras, until such time as I move my headquarters down there when the war begins. Keep an eye on Lord Clive. I'm not sure that he has grasped the delicacy of the situation. I don't want him provoking Tipoo or making any deals with him before we're good and ready. At the same time, he must not be allowed to put the interests of the shareholders of the Company above the safety of the presidency. This war is going to be a costly affair. More than the Madras treasury can afford. But we cannot allow the likes of Josiah Webbe to undermine our military needs on the eve of war. So you will keep me informed of everything that happens in Madras. Use a code. Henry will provide you with a private cipher. Do you understand what's required of you?'

'Yes.' Arthur nodded solemnly. 'In polite circles it's called spying.'

'Call it what you like, Arthur. I do not have the time to bandy euphemisms about. Our interests in India are facing the gravest threat. I'll do whatever I must to ensure that we defeat Tipoo.'

Once again, the 33rd Foot took ship and the small flotilla of East Indiamen weighed anchor and slipped down the Hoogley into the Bay of Bengal before coasting south towards Madras. Unlike the placid waters of the Hoogley, the sea off the city of Madras was an unending expanse of surf rolling in from the ocean. There was no harbour, no breakwater, and the only means of landing men and equipment was by the strange local boats that looked more like rafts. Constructed from light timber, they were designed to bob above the waves rather than keep their passengers and cargo dry. It was an unnerving experience for many of the men of Arthur's regiment, and he himself was filled with nervous excitement as he squatted on the reed-woven bed of the craft hired to take him ashore. The natives paddled furiously through the rolling waves, shouting out instructions to each other in their sing-song tongue as spray drenched those aboard.

With expert skill they perfectly timed their approach to the glistening sand of the beach and, with a final flurry of powerful strokes at the paddles, the raft swept forward on the crest of a wave and crashed down on the shore with a jarring thud that knocked Arthur on to his knees. At once the boatmen were over the side and gripping the raft as they waited for the next wave to run it further up the beach, where it grounded solidly and Arthur and the other passengers could clamber ashore, grateful that the experience was over.

Arthur left the rest of his officers to marshal the men as they came ashore and take them to the barracks assigned to them, and made his way directly to the offices of the Governor of Madras at Fort St George. Despite the fact that both Mysore and Madras were supposed to be arming for war he was surprised to note little sign of any military activity in the fort. Most of the barrack blocks were empty and those few soldiers he did encounter were gambling or sleeping in the shade of the narrow thatched verandas that ran round the outside of the barracks.

Lord Clive and General Harris were in conference in the latter's office when an aide escorted Arthur into their presence. The Governor was wearing a light cotton coat while his senior military officer was stripped to his shirt and breeches. Clive was in his early forties, generously built; perhaps too generously, thought Arthur. His hair was neatly cut and curled and his lips had a slight arrogant lift to them.

'Who the deuce are you?'

'Colonel Wellesley, my lord. Of the 33rd Foot. We've just arrived from Calcutta.'

'So I can see. You might have dried yourself before coming in here.'

'In this heat I'll soon be dry enough, my lord.'

The comment was meant to be jovial and help lighten the mood, but Clive pursed his lips and tilted his head back as he looked over the new arrival without a trace of self-consciousness. 'So you're Mornington's little brother.'

'I have that honour.'

'Yes you do. But while you are here in Madras, there will be no special favour accorded to you because of the family connection.'

'I would not have it any other way, my lord.'

'I'm sure.' Clive smirked momentarily. 'You say you've only just arrived? Then you can't have heard the news?'

'What news?'

'Admiral Nelson has defeated a French fleet in Aboukir Bay. We received the report last night. It seems that only a handful of the enemy ships escaped destruction or capture, for no loss of our own. A striking success.'

'Some might argue that it would have been more striking still if it had occurred while Bonaparte was en route to Egypt, my lord.'

Lord Clive glared at him. 'Do you criticise the man's victory, Colonel?'

'Not his victory. I just question his timing.'

'Hmmm.' Clive frowned for a moment, then blinked as if he had just remembered some prior obligation. 'Can't stand here all day sharing the good news.' He stuck out his hand. 'I bid you welcome then, Colonel Wellesley. Glad to have with you with us. Another King's regiment is bound to stiffen the spines of our sepoys.'

'Yes, my lord. I imagine so.'

'Fine. Well, I'm sure I'll see you again soon. Now I have to go. Have a meeting with the finance committee. Until later then.'

Harris's chair scraped as he stood up and bowed his head as Lord Clive quit his office. The footsteps faded down the corridor outside and Harris gestured to Arthur to take a seat.

'Don't worry about Clive. He's still getting used to his role as Governor. He means well, and he'll be fine once he stops trying so hard to impress everyone. Meanwhile, I manage to keep both the army and the government of Madras on an even keel.' General Harris smiled. 'Don't worry. I'm not being indiscreet. There's nothing I've said that I haven't already reported to Mornington.' He looked at Arthur shrewdly. 'I imagine that one of your tasks here is to represent the interests of your brother.'

'He asked me to write to him from time to time, sir.'

'I'm sure he did. Well now, I imagine you want me to brief you on the latest situation here.' Harris eased himself back and interlaced his fingers beneath his chin. 'The truth is that my attempts to prepare our forces for war have been somewhat hampered by Webbe and his companions on the Madras Council. Those forces that I already have at my disposal have been sent forward, close to the border with Mysore, to discourage any attempt by Tipoo to stir up trouble along the frontier. I have other units in training, but the Company is refusing to release weapons and gunpowder from their arsenal until they are guaranteed payment by the War Office in London.' He caught Arthur's eye and sighed. 'I know, it's farcical. But what can one expect when control of our Indian possessions is divided between the government and a private concern? John Company treats Tipoo as if he was a business rival.'

Arthur laughed. 'There aren't many business rivals I know of who throw the competition to their pet tigers to be eaten alive.'

'Precisely.' Harris nodded. 'But perhaps that wouldn't be a bad idea. Might buck their ideas up a bit.'

'I can imagine, sir.'

'Anyway, I had better introduce you to the rest of my small planning staff. If you'd follow me.'

Harris led the way down the corridor to another office where two officers were busy at their desks as they entered. Arthur recognised the younger man instantly. He had met Henry Ashton briefly in England before setting out for India. Ashton was, like Arthur, a full colonel, and commanded the King's 12th Foot. He had a few days' seniority over Arthur. That meant he would always be the superior whenever the two of them served together.

'Hello, Arthur.' Ashton stood up with a broad smile and offered his hand. 'Haven't seen you for a while. I understand you've come to join us in the crusade against the Tipoo.'

'I had no idea that this was to be a religious struggle.'

Ashton laughed and Harris exchanged a look with the other officer, a much older, weathered-looking man in the uniform of the East India Company.

'Young bloods,' Harris muttered in an exasperated tone. 'Will they never grow up? Arthur, since you obviously know Ashton, let me introduce you to Lieutenant Colonel Barry Close – the real brains behind the staff work here in Madras. Close knows as much about the languages and customs of the natives as any white man in India and I'm damned lucky to have his services.'

Close nodded modestly and thrust out his hand. 'Colonel, glad to meet you, sir.'

'My pleasure.'

Harris backed away and turned towards the door. 'Yes, well now that you're introduced, Close can tell you what your responsibilities will be. I'll leave you in his hands.'

'Very good, sir.'

Once the door had shut behind the general, Close quickly scrutinised the new arrival before he continued. 'Right then, you're the *wallah* who is going to be in charge of organising the army's siege train. I'll have a desk brought in here for you, and arrange a few reliable orderlies and a secretary. Ashton there is dealing with the re-arming and training of our Company battalions and I'm responsible for food supplies and ammunition. If what I have heard about you is true, then I imagine you'll be keen to get to work.'

'Yes, I am.'

'Oh, Arthur.' Ashton winced. 'Surely you still have some of the rakish temperament about you that you were only too keen to display back in England? There will be some time for pleasure, you know.'

Close frowned. 'Don't listen to the young pup, Wellesley. The time for play is over. The threat from the Tipoo is very real.'

Arthur looked at the veteran and saw that the man was quite serious. He moved over to Close's desk and pulled out a chair and sat down. 'I'd be grateful if you briefed me on my duties at once.'

Close grinned. 'A man after my own heart.'

'What a tragedy,' said Ashton. 'Already I have lost a friend and gained a drone.'

Arthur turned towards him. 'I've read all the intelligence, Henry. There's no avoiding a war with Tipoo. And if we lose, then you'll have your tragedy for sure.'

Chapter 37

While Arthur attended to his duties the 33rd Foot was sent forward to Wallajabad. Ashton's regiment had already advanced to Arnee, much nearer to the border with Mysore. Both officers would re-join their commands when the preparations for war were complete. Meanwhile Arthur diligently attended to his duties by day and joined Ashton and the other officers at dinners and parties given by the limited social circle of Europeans in the city by night.

Arthur quickly discovered that the Military Board of Madras, the body in charge of co-ordinating the presidency's armed forces, had done nothing to assemble and supply the siege train needed to reduce Seringapatam. At once he descended on their offices and requested a meeting with the secretary of the Board, Josiah Webbe.

Webbe's office was large but felt cramped due to the proliferation of records, reports and correspondence crammed into cubbyholes that lined three of the walls. The fourth was taken up by a shuttered window that stood open to admit the faint breeze blowing in from the sea. Even though all his documents were weighted down the corners of the paperwork occasionally lifted and fluttered as they were stirred by wafts of air. Arthur discovered that Webbe was a man of his own age, neatly dressed, slim and healthy in appearance. He lowered his pen and rose to shake Arthur's hand, smiling warmly.

'Ah, the colonel of the newly arrived 33rd, I presume. Good morning to you, sir. What can I do for you?'

'Good morning, Mr Webbe. Please excuse me if I pass over any pleasantries and get down to business.'

A look of irritation flitted over Webbe's expression before he replied. 'Indeed. I am a busy man too, as you can see.' He gestured to the paperwork that surrounded him.

'Then I'll be brief. I have been charged with forming and equipping the siege train. This was the responsibility of the Military Board, until now.'

'Until now? I was not aware that the situation had changed, Colonel.'

'It has.' Arthur pulled a document out of his jacket and placed it on the table. 'This is my authority to assume control of the task, signed by Lord Clive and General Harris. I am empowered to do all that is required to organise the siege train.'

'Really?' Webbe raised his eyebrows. Then he leaned forward and picked up the document, opened it and began to read. At length he set it down and looked at Arthur. 'It seems that I am to co-operate with you as fully as is possible in accordance with the guidelines of the Military Board's responsibilities.'

'That is what the document says.'

'I feel it only fair to point out to you that, in principle, ratification of decisions by the Board is required from the directors of the Company.'

Arthur struggled to contain his irritation at the man's obstructive attitude. Instead he nodded. 'So I understand. But what you must understand is that by the time you receive any response from the directors in London, Tipoo may have rendered any reply rather academic. Wouldn't you agree?'

'Sir, I am only stating that I am bound by certain rules.'

'Sir, you are not bound. As you pointed out, you are merely obliged to be guided by certain principles. Now is not the time for principles, but practicalities. The army of Madras needs a siege train, and I would urge you to co-operate with me so that General Harris goes to war with the means to actually win.'

Webbe stared back at him for a moment and Arthur hoped that the man had seen reason. Then the secretary spoke again, in a lower tone. 'Don't think I don't know why your brother sent you here, Wellesley. He wants a war with Tipoo and means to get one whatever it takes. You are here to apply pressure to Harris, Lord Clive and officials like me. It's painfully obvious why Mornington wants this war. He embraces the highest political ambitions and sees a victory over Tipoo as being a means to that end. Is that not so?'

Arthur folded his arms and smiled faintly. 'Do you deny that Tipoo is a threat?'

'No. That's not it at all. I just want peace in India. Peace, so that the Company can go about its business in an orderly and profitable manner. That's why we are in India, Colonel. For profit, not political or diplomatic advantage. War is an expensive business and we would do well to avoid it by any and all means necessary, as I have explained to your brother and Lord Clive. Fortunately, the new Governor of Madras is a man who shares my vision on this matter.'

'This isn't about my brother's glorification,' Arthur responded. 'He no more wants war with Tipoo than you do. If Tipoo wasn't expanding his army, or going to such great lengths to win the favour of the revolutionaries in France, then we could ignore him and go about our business here, just as you would wish. Did you know that our latest intelligence is that he now goes by the title of Citizen Tipoo?'

Webbe waved his hand dismissively. 'A childish indulgence. Nothing more than that.'

'Really? And what about the rapid growth of his army? The encroachment on our border? His hatred of England is implacable. He will not rest until we are driven out of the subcontinent. He hates us just as his father did before him, and just as his sons will do when they inherit the kingdom.' Arthur paused a moment, before moderating his tone. 'Mr Webbe, please, listen to me. England is the only chance India has to become something better than it is. For hundreds of years its people have been ground down by one wave of warlords after another. Any opportunity that these people have had to develop their lands against a background of peace and order has been stolen from them by warlords and brigands. It's time that their situation changed. If England can exert its influence over the entire expanse of India, then in the long term its people, and the East India Company, can only profit from the results. Men like Tipoo stand in our way, and in the way of his own people. The Governor General does not want this war. I swear it, on my honour. He would far rather achieve his ambitions by peaceful means.'

'Then why prepare so ardently for war?'

'Because the Tipoo is firmly resolved to fight us.' Arthur suppressed the anger that was welling up inside him and took a deep breath before he resumed. 'I imagine you've placed a wager at some point in your life, Mr Webbe.'

'Yes. What of it?'

'Then hear me out. Tipoo may or may not intend to declare war on us, agreed? If we prepare for war and it turns out that he has no desire to attack us, then what has it cost us? Money. That's what. A lot of money, I grant you, but nothing the Company won't recover from future profits. But if it is Tipoo's intention to attack us, and we are not ready to face him, because we have not made the necessary preparations, however costly, then we lose everything. Not just the chests of gold and silver in the vaults beneath Fort St George, but also the priceless reputation England currently enjoys amongst the natives. Not to mention tens of thousands of lives – yours and mine amongst them. Now then, on that basis, what would a reasonable gambling man decide to do?'

'All very neatly argued, Wellesley, but what of the third possibility? That he might have no intention of attacking us, and that we might therefore save ourselves a considerable sum of money by not preparing for an attack that won't happen.'

'It's possible,' Arthur admitted. 'But what are the odds of that? Would you bet your life on such odds?'

Webbe turned his head and stared out of the window for a while. Below the building stretched the warehouses of the East India Company and the bungalows of its managers and their families, basking peacefully in the sunshine of a clear sky. He

313

turned back to Arthur with a resigned expression. 'Very well, Colonel. I'll do what I can to help you.'

With the Military Board behind him Arthur was able to put together the siege train, and by the end of the year the heavy artillery was sent forward to Vellore with twelve hundred rounds for each gun. As Arthur carried out the assembling of the train he soon discovered that his fellow staff officers were men of high calibre. Barry Close proved to be a mine of useful information about the terrain the guns would have to be moved over, while Henry Ashton deployed great charm and tact when dealing with civilian officials and senior officers in order to obtain what he and the other staff officers needed. If Ashton had a fault, it was his tendency to treat subordinates with studied indifference.

'Look here, Arthur,' he fumed one day as they sat in their office. He was brandishing a letter. 'Here I am trying to prepare the army for war and two witless officers in the 12th are stirring up trouble to waste my time.'

'What's the matter?' Arthur asked patiently, looking up from the requisition form he was completing.

'One of my lieutenants is registering an official complaint against Major Allen, my quartermaster, for billing him for equipment he has not received. Apparently it's caused quite a lot of fuss at Arnee and now the bloody major has asked me to intervene. Christ, as if I hadn't got enough to deal with.'

'What are you going to do?'

'Do?' Ashton snorted. 'Nothing. I will tell Allen to leave me alone and sort it out himself, or if he can't, to find someone more competent to do the job for him.'

Arthur lowered his pen and stared at Ashton. 'Good God, you can't say that to him. Certainly not in those terms.'

'Why not? It's true. He should not be bothering me with such trivialities.' Ashton plucked out a fresh sheet of paper and began to compose his response. Arthur watched him for a moment, then shook his head and turned his attention back to the requisition form.

A few weeks later, at the end of November, Ashton was

ordered to leave Madras to take up temporary command of the army forming up around Arnee. As he said his farewells to the staff at Fort St George Arthur regarded him with a touch of envy. Ashton would have the chance to take command of an army while Arthur remained behind in Madras dealing with paperwork.

Some days later Arthur was preparing to go to bed when a corporal arrived at his house. The man carried an urgent summons to the office of Lord Clive.

Arthur lowered the hurriedly written note from General Harris and turned to the messenger. 'Do you know what's happened?'

'No, sir. I was just told to deliver the message.' The man's chest was still heaving after his run from the fort. 'But the Governor, General Harris and Mr Webbe were all there.'

'Right!' Arthur dismissed the corporal and dressed quicky, and made for the fort as fast as he could run. It was infuriating that the messenger had not been able to provide more details, and Arthur wondered what could be important enough for Lord Clive to summon his senior officials at this time of night. With a chill of anxiety in his gut, Arthur wondered if Tipoo had decided to declare war on Madras. If that was it, then the situation was indeed perilous. The army was not yet ready to fight Tipoo's host. As he ran, Arthur's mind was haunted by the spectre of such an attack and its dreadful consequences.

There were lights burning in the offices of the Governor and when Arthur entered the building and raced up the stairs he saw a number of officers and civil officials talking in agitated tones in the corridor outside Lord Clive's room. The door was open so Arthur strode straight in. Lord Clive was seated behind his desk. General Harris stood at his side and both looked up as Arthur entered, drew himself up in front of the desk and saluted.

'You sent for me, sir.'

'Yes.' Clive replied, then nodded to Harris. 'Tell him.'

General Harris cleared his throat. 'You're to ride forward to Arnee tonight and assume command of the forces there. Your orders are being prepared by my secretary. I want you to leave the moment they're ready. You can send instructions for the rest of your kit to be sent on once you reach the army.'

'Excuse me, sir. I don't understand. What about Colonel Ashton? He's—'

'Ashton's been shot. More than likely he's already dead.'

Chapter 38

'Dead?'

'Or as good as,' General Harris continued. 'The fool got himself into a duel over some business with his quartermaster. He was shot through the side.'

'Is there any hope that he might live, sir?'

General Harris indicated the dispatch on the desk in front of Lord Clive. 'From what he says, it doesn't seem likely. So you're to take his place. Given our current relations with Tipoo we cannot afford to leave our troops on the frontier without a commander.'

'What are my orders when I reach Arnee, sir?'

'If Ashton is alive, send word of his condition. In any case, you will take charge of the equipping, training and disposition of our troops in the area. If Tipoo attacks you will hold him back for as long as possible and then conduct a fighting withdrawal to Madras. As for Ashton's shooting, I want the culprit confined to quarters and you're to see if we have enough evidence to warrant a court martial. I will not have any more duelling amongst the officers in my command. A man's honour is one thing, but if upholding it compromises his obligations to his country, then his honour must go and hang. Make sure they all understand that, Wellesley. There's to be no more of it!'

'Yes, sir.'

'Very well then. Now find a horse and go.'

Arthur rode alone through the night. Fortunately the moon was showing enough of its pallid face to light his way and he spurred

317

his mount along the track from Madras towards the field headquarters of the army at Arnee. He rode through sleeping villages, silent and dark, and only the occasional sullen barking of a woken dog heralded his passing.

He reached Arnee early the next morning. Entering the army camp outside the town, Arthur made for the cluster of large tents that marked the headquarters and dismounted. A staff officer emerged from the nearest tent at the sound of his arrival.

'Where's Colonel Ashton?' Arthur demanded.

'This way, sir.' The lieutenant beckoned and as Arthur followed him inside he continued, 'Have you come from Madras, sir?'

'I've been sent to assume command. How's the Colonel?'

'Difficult to say, sir. He seems calm enough to me, but the surgeon's concerned that the wound will go bad. If that happens he'll be gone in a matter of days.'

'Sounds like an optimistic fellow, your surgeon.'

The lieutenant turned and managed a grim smile. 'Despair comes naturally to him, sir. He's from Scotland.'

As Arthur entered his tent, Ashton struggled to prop himself up on his camp bed, and smiled weakly as he reached out a trembling hand. 'Really . . . you shouldn't have.'

'Don't be a bloody fool.' Arthur shook the hand and found his friend's flesh hot and sweaty. The fever was already taking hold then, he thought sadly. 'Rest yourself, Henry.'

'Rest?' Ashton chuckled and then winced, gritting his teeth as he fought off a wave of agony. It passed and he looked up at Arthur, his face pale and glistening with perspiration. There was a dressing strapped round his stomach, on which a dark stain showed over his side. 'I rather think I'll be resting peacefully enough quite soon.'

'Rubbish!' Arthur said loudly. 'You'll be on your feet in a few days. I'm well enough acquainted with you to know that you simply will not be able to resist the urge to be back on your feet committing further mischief.'

'Ah, is it possible that I am so transparent?'

'Evidently.'

They exchanged a smile, and then Arthur continued quietly. 'I've been sent here by Harris to take over from you and to investigate the incident. What happened, Henry?'

'It was Major Allen. He took offence at my letter to him, and called me out soon after I arrived here.'

'I warned you.'

'You did, Arthur. I am sorry I paid you no heed. It was foolish of me.'

'Yes, it was. But continue. He called you out. Why did you accept?'

Ashton looked surprised. 'It was a matter of honour. There was no question of avoiding the issue. Allen fired first and hit me. I shot into the air.'

'Why?'

'He had wounded me. If it proves fatal what would it profit me to have killed him? The army would have lost two officers instead of one.'

Arthur stared at him for a moment and then shook his head. 'Madness. That's what it is, pure madness.'

'You may be right, Arthur, but what's done is done.'

'Where is Allen now?'

'I sent him to Vellore. He can train the men there until this blows over.'

'I have orders to arrest him and prepare for a court martial.'

Ashton reached over and grasped Arthur's hand. 'No, I will not have Allen tried for this. He's a good officer, and we need such men at the moment. He just needs to curb his temper, that's all.'

'Henry, I have my orders,' Arthur said gently.

'And I have my honour. Major Allen and I have had our satisfaction and the matter is closed. I pray you, do not pursue this any further.' He stared at Arthur with blazing intensity and at length Arthur nodded.

'Very well.'

He left the tent and found the lieutenant waiting outside. 'Assemble the officers. I have an announcement to make.'

*

Arthur set to work on his new command at once. There were nearly twenty thousand men in the area surrounding Arnee, four thousand European troops and the rest made up from East India Company soldiers. The Company's men had grown used to being dispersed on garrison duties across the territories ruled by Madras. Now they had been concentrated in their battalions and needed to be trained to fight and march in large formations. Ashton had begun the task and Arthur saw to it that his regimen continued to be carried out, and then turned his attention to the issue of supplying the army in the coming campaign. He sent word to every *brinjarri* chief in the south of India, inviting them to Arnee to bid for contracts to carry the army's food and equipment.

He saw Ashton every spare moment. Any hope of the colonel's recovering from his wound faded a few days after Arthur's arrival. The army's chief surgeon had done all that he could to save Ashton's life, but the wound became inflamed and a foul-smelling pus had begun to exude from the puckered flesh where the ball had penetrated his side. Ashton's agonies increased steadily and Arthur sat helplessly by as his friend's pallid skin turned waxen and his breathing became more and more laboured. Two days before Christmas Arthur saw him at first light, before the day's duties began. Ashton was no longer even able to raise his head and his eyes rolled towards Arthur when he entered the tent and pulled up a stool beside the bed. The sickening stench from the wound filled the air and Arthur had to fight off the nausea it induced in his stomach.

He made himself smile. 'How are you today, Henry?'

'Dying, as usual.' Ashton's lips flickered into a grin for an instant. 'Arthur, it's too bad. There was still so much I wanted to do . . . so much.' His hand slithered across the sheet and reached for Arthur's. 'Don't waste your life, Arthur.'

'I'll try not to.'

'Good. I have one last favour I would ask of you.'

'Anything.'

'My horse, Diomed, she's a fine Arab. Best mount in the whole of India. Take care of her for me. She deserves only the finest of riders. I'd hate to think of her being sold to some fat, rich Company official after I'm gone.'

'I'll look after Diomed.'

A bugle sounded morning parade and Arthur glanced to the sliver of light piercing the tent flap. 'I have to go. I'll see you this evening.'

'Yes . . . I'll look forward to it.'

Arthur stood up and replaced the stool at the end of the bed before making for the entrance to the tent.

'Arthur!'

He paused and turned back. With a great effort Ashton raised a hand and pointed a trembling finger at his friend. 'Remember, whatever else you do, I beg of you, don't waste your life.'

'I have no intention of wasting it.' Arthur smiled at him, and ducked outside into the fresh dawn air, relieved to be free from the cloying, sickly-sweet stench inside Ashton's tent. He went straight to the army commander's administration tent and sat at his desk. The morning passed slowly as he worked through the terms of the contracts he would offer the *brinjarris*. As far as possible they were to operate independently of the army, policing themselves and maintaining their stocks of food. In exchange Arthur promised to protect them from the enemy and to pay them in staged cash sums for each phase of the army's advance into Mysore. The contracts were guaranteed to run until the onset of the monsoon season, whether the campaign was over by then or not. Just after noon he set his pen down and read over the draft with a critical eye. The terms were more than fair and he could not see how the *brinjarris* could turn down the opportunity presented by such a favourable deal. He smiled with satisfaction, and looking up he saw through the entrance to the tent the surgeon approaching across the parade ground. Their eyes met and Arthur knew at once what the man's presence portended. He stood slowly and met the surgeon at the threshold to the tent.

'Ashton's dead.'

'Yes, sir. I'm afraid so.'

'When did it happen?'

'A moment ago. He lost consciousness an hour or so earlier.'

'Thank God.' Arthur lowered his head to conceal the grief that theatened to break down his calm expression. 'Thank you. I'm grateful to you for doing what you could for him. I'll give the orders to prepare for his burial.'

'Yes, sir.'

'Now please go.' Arthur waved him away, then went back to his desk and covered his face with his hands. Ashton had died needlessly . . . pointlessly. His promise had been evident to all who knew him. One day he might have been a great general. Instead he had died for no better reason than hurting a man's pride. It was too cruel, especially at a time when his country needed its finest officers more than ever. Arthur swore to himself that, as far as it was in his power to make it so, he would never permit such a waste of life and potential to occur again while he held a military command.

As the new year of 1799 dawned, Arthur received news that Richard and Henry had arrived in Madras to oversee the preparations for the war with Tipoo and to be ready to respond to any military or diplomatic emergency that might occur. Even though Richard had instructed Lord Clive to continue running the presidency as if Richard was still in Calcutta, he sent a coded message to Arthur to see what his younger brother felt about the idea of Richard's accompanying General Harris on the coming campaign, in an advisory role. Arthur read the letter with a sinking heart. Much as he respected Richard's administrative abilities, his brother was no soldier, and had little appreciation of the niceties of etiquette as regarded the military hierarchy. Harris would need to concentrate all his efforts on manoeuvring his army and fixing and destroying Tipoo's forces. The last thing the general needed was a civilian official looking over his shoulder and offering helpful suggestions.

He picked up a pen and flicked open the cap of his inkwell, and paused. How should he phrase his response to Richard? Then he smiled to himself. Richard was family, and deserved to be addressed as such. He neatly wrote a brief note:

My dear Richard, all I can say is that if I were Harris, and you joined the army, I should quit it!

There, he thought, that summed it up nicely. He folded the paper, sealed it and added the letter to the correspondence to be sent back to Madras the following day.

Throughout January Arthur continued to drill his troops regularly and gave instructions that the men were to practise live firing. This at once drew down the wrath of the Military Board in Madras who fired off an angry complaint, copied to Lord Clive and General Harris, about his wanton profligacy with the property of the East India Company. With more than a hint of delight in the poetic justice of the situation, Harris wrote to Arthur to tell him that Richard had referred the matter back to Parliament and the Company's board of directors for a decision.

Richard made one last attempt to negotiate with Tipoo, and sent him a letter warning him of the perils of being allied to France and earnestly entreating him to keep peace with England and the East India Company. There was no reply and the army of Madras continued to prepare for war throughout January. At the end of the month General Harris arrived in Arnee to take command of the army, and relieve Arthur.

'No officer could have done more to prepare his men in so little time,' he concluded after Arthur had briefed him on the measures he had taken to ensure that the army was ready to march against Tipoo.

'Thank you, sir.' Arthur was proud of his achievement, but now that Harris and his staff had arrived Arthur was seventh in seniority amongst the higher-ranking officers and it galled him that others would take credit for his labours. Worse still, he was now commanding only the men of his regiment, once again. A lowly line officer far removed from the direction of the war.

General Harris was watching him closely, and could not help smiling. 'You will have your chance to win recognition, Wellesley. Sooner than you think. I will not say any more at present, for fear that it might cause bad feeling amongst some of the other officers.'

'I don't understand, sir.'

'You will. But you must be patient for just a little longer.'

Two days later General Harris summoned his senior officers to his headquarters. When all were present he produced a dispatch from inside his jacket.

'Gentlemen, I have today received orders from the Governor General. The army is to break camp tomorrow and march on Seringapatam. The war has begun.'

Chapter 39

Napoleon

Alexandria, August 1798

Aboukir Bay reeked of death and destruction even several days after the battle. The beach was littered with shattered timbers and severed cordage. Bodies were still being washed up on the shore, blotched and bloated and often mutilated by the effects of cannon fire and explosions. What was left had been worried by the fish gorging themselves in the bay. In the now calm waters, wreckage floated on the surface and the masts of the ships that had been sunk rose stark and bare from their watery grave.

'Sweet Jesus . . .' Berthier muttered as he gazed across the scene. He opened his mouth to continue and then closed it again with a slight shake of the head. There were no words to describe the scale of the defeat that France had suffered at the hands of Lord Nelson and his fleet.

'What was the final cost?' asked Napoleon.

Berthier took a moment to collect his thoughts and reached for his pocket book. He flicked the pages open to the notes he had made earlier that morning after consulting the army's chief surgeon, Dr Desgenettes. 'Nearly two and a half thousand killed or wounded. Over three thousand taken prisoner when their ships were captured.'

Napoleon waved his hand dismissively. 'What about the ships? How many did we lose?'

'The *L'Orient* blew up. Three ships of the line were taken and burned by the Royal Navy, another nine ships of the line were captured and two frigates were sunk.'

'And how many survived?'

'Two ships of the line and two frigates. They escaped to the east. We haven't heard anything from them yet.'

Napoleon shut his eyes for a moment. With one blow the English had shattered French naval power in the Mediterranean, and severed the link between Napoleon's army and France. Very well then, he concluded, that was the situation. What mattered now was surviving the consequences. His eyes flickered open.

'Berthier, take a note.'

His chief of staff hurriedly opened a fresh page of his pocket book and fumbled in his jacket for a pencil. He sat down on a rock and waited for Napoleon to begin.

'Tell Kléber to have some boats armed to patrol the harbours at Alexandria. If the Royal Navy is still out there, it's possible they will attempt a cutting-out raid against what is left of our fleet. Have Marmont's brigade moved up to Rosetta in case the English attempt any landings there. Then find a small ship, something fast, and have a warning sent to our forces in Malta. The ship is then to continue to France to convey the news of Admiral Brueys's defeat. Got all that?'

'Yes, sir.'

'There's one other matter to deal with. I must write a letter to the Sultan in Constantinople. Talleyrand should be close to concluding a treaty with Turkey by now. If I can reassure the Sultan that we are operating in his interests, then he might not be tempted to take advantage of this temporary setback.'

Berthier paused and looked up. 'Temporary setback, sir?'

'This.' Napoleon gestured vaguely towards the bay. 'The fleet had already served its purpose, in getting my army here safely. We can, and shall, manage without them.'

'Yes, sir.' Berthier turned his attention back to his pocket book. 'Anything else?'

Napoleon nodded. 'A message needs to be sent to Ahmad Pasha at Acre. He needs to be warned off any plans he might have for joining forces with what's left of the Mamelukes in Egypt. If we can secure an alliance with him so much the better. In the meantime,' he turned away from the bay and gazed back in the direction of Alexandria, 'we had better do what we can to settle the army into Egypt and win over the locals. It's possible we may be here for quite a while.'

Leaving Kléber and Marmont to guard against any attempts by the English to further exploit Nelson's victory, Napoleon and his staff mounted up and swiftly returned to Cairo. News of the battle had reached every corner of the city and there was a palpable tension in the streets of the capital as those who still opposed the French occupation openly rejoiced. The morale of the French troops was dangerously low now that their lifeline to their homeland was cut. Napoleon knew that the only cure for their malaise was to be kept occupied and fed a diet of rewards and propaganda. He immediately set out a list of public works and administrative measures to be carried out as soon as possible.

Chambers of commerce were set up in the largest towns of the delta, and register offices established to record land ownership and to issue birth certificates in an attempt to provide the basis of a new tax system. Napoleon was mindful that, despite the defeat at Aboukir Bay, Paris would still be anticipating fresh spoils from its army in Egypt. French engineers began projects to improve the economy of the new province by building roads and windmills, and work began on dredging the canal that linked Alexandria to Cairo. In the capital itself, Napoleon decreed that street lighting would be provided and a local police force set up. A hospital was established for the city's poorest inhabitants and the French historians, artists and scientists who had accompanied the expedition were finally rewarded for all the discomfort and danger they had endured. The Institute of Egypt for Arts and Sciences was inaugurated in Cairo with Gaspard Monge as its president. Napoleon added his lustre to the proceedings by accepting the post of vice-president.

He commandeered the mansions of the Mameluke leaders and handed them over to his senior officers. The soldiers, distressed by the hot climate, and lacking the wine and bread they had been raised on back in France, were even more disgruntled by the lack of available women. In order to distract them from their grievances Napoleon set up a soldiers' social club and two light-hearted newspapers. Gradually, the troops began to adjust to their new setting, discovering the pleasures of native *chebouk* pipes, steam baths and spiced native food enjoyed from the comfort of divans.

In order to impress upon the local worthies the technical superiority of the French regime, Napoleon ordered the officer in command of the hot air balloon detachment to mount a public demonstration and ride his balloon aloft for all of Cairo to see. On the appointed day the sheikhs and imams and their retinues were treated to a feast in shelters round an open square while Captain Conté and his men prepared their equipment.

There was an audible gasp from the French officers as Napoleon emerged from his quarters wearing a turban and silk robes over his shirt, trousers and boots. A bright sash ran round his middle, over which was fastened a sword belt from which hung a jewelled scimitar. He strode across to the largest shelter, under which Sheikh Muhammad el Hourad and his followers watched him approach, rising at the last moment to bow and make their greetings.

'General, you honour us,' the sheikh smiled. 'But I confess, I am a little confused by your attire.'

'Why, sir?' Napoleon glanced down at his robes, and the feather in the top of his turban dipped forward and bounced off his nose. A ripple of subdued laughter went round his guests, but when he glared at them they fell silent. Napoleon turned to the sheikh. 'I was merely trying to show you that we French are more than willing to adapt to your ways.'

'I see.' The sheikh smiled. 'And of course we appreciate the gesture. But tell me, why do you wear the turban of a Mameluke and the robes of a Bedouin?'

Napoleon glanced over his shoulder and glared at Junot. His aide shrugged helplessly and Napoleon resolved to give him a firm dressing down when the guests had gone. He turned back to the sheikh, trying hard not to blush with embarrassment and anger. 'I apologise. I was badly advised. Now, please, take your seats. The food will arrive shortly, and we can talk while Captain Conté makes his balloon ready for flight.'

Napoleon and his staff officers settled on to the divans prepared for them while the sheikh and his followers resumed their reclining positions. When everyone was settled Berthier nodded to one of the orderlies and the man hurried away to the kitchens.

The sheikh watched the officers and men laying the wood in the heavy cast-iron grate below the platform on which rested the round basket which would carry Captain Conté aloft. In the centre of the basket was a funnel which led up into the envelope of the balloon itself.

'General, can that thing really fly?'

'Yes. I have seen it myself, back in Paris.'

'By what magic does it work?'

'Not by magic, but by science.' Napoleon smiled, and then continued in a lecturing tone. 'By the principle that hot air, being lighter than the air surrounding it, will rise, filling out the balloon, and then causing it to lift, taking both basket and passenger with it. The balloon will continue to rise until the air inside has cooled and then it will descend safely back to the ground.'

'And you are sure you have seen this work, with your own eyes?'

'Yes.' Napoleon replied testily. 'I give you my word.'

'Then I am sure it will be so, if Allah wills it.'

'Speaking of Allah, or more broadly religion, I think it is a good time to mention to you that I have decided to enact a measure guaranteeing religious toleration in Egypt. I wondered what your views on the matter were.'

The sheikh stroked his beard. 'I assume that you mean that Jews and Christians should be allowed to practise their rites freely, alongside those of Islam.'

'Yes. That would seem to be the best way to encourage good relations between all the faiths. France wants peace and prosperity for all the peoples of Egypt.'

'And would you enforce such tolerance?' the sheikh asked wryly.

'Indeed.' Napoleon nodded, and his feather tipped forward again. With a grimace he quickly reached up and savagely plucked it out of the turban and tossed it on to the divan behind him.

The band suddenly struck up as the doors to the kitchens opened and a long line of servants emerged carrying platters of delicacies and exotic fruits. As the French officers and their guests began to eat, Captain Conté's crew finally lit the fire underneath his balloon-launching platform. The flames flickered into life and the timber crackled merrily. At first nothing seemed to be happening and then, as Napoleon watched, the balloon envelope rippled and began to fill, with painstaking slowness. After a while he lost interest in the display and idly glanced round the faces of those sitting at the tables set for the French.

In amongst them were a handful of women, and almost at once Napoleon's gaze fell upon a slim figure with fine tresses of auburn hair. She sat at the side of a handsome young lieutenant who frequently glanced at her in open adoration. It was easy to see why, Napoleon reflected. She was the most beautiful woman he had seen since leaving France. Since he last saw Josephine, he reflected bitterly, reopening the still fresh wound in his heart.

He lowered his plate and turned to Junot. 'Who is that woman over there?'

Junot followed the direction indicated by Napoleon and smiled. 'Ah! That is the delightful Pauline Fourès.'

'I don't recall seeing her before. Is that man her husband?'

'Yes, Lieutenant Fourès, one of our cavalry officers. A bit of a firebrand by all accounts. I'm not surprised you haven't noticed his wife before, sir. She disguised herself as a hussar to accompany her husband on the campaign. She only revealed her true identity after the battle outside Cairo.'

'Good God!' Napoleon shook his head in wonder. 'How could she have managed it? To have survived all that and kept her secret . . . She sounds interesting. I should like to meet her. Would you see to it, Junot? Supper, tonight at my mansion.'

'Yes, sir. An invitation to Madame Fourès, and the good lieutenant as well?'

'No. I think I would rather hear her story without any distraction.'

'I understand, sir. I'll see to it.'

'Good.' Napoleon looked at her for a moment longer and then turned his attention back to his meal. He was aroused at the prospect of meeting the woman, and at the same time felt a vague sense of shame at pulling rank over her husband, and the prospect of being unfaithful to Josephine, in spirit at least. Then his heart hardened. Let Josephine hear of this. Let her suffer the injury he had endured at her hands. As for Lieutenant Fourès? Napoleon shrugged. Perhaps it was time for Fourès to share his general's knowledge of the perfidy of women.

The sheikh coughed softly. 'I beg your pardon, General, but how long does this balloon of yours take before it makes its ascent?'

'What?' Napoleon shook off his thoughts of Josephine and Pauline Fourès. He looked across the square. Captain Conté was desperately piling more fuel on to the fire. Above it the material of the balloon had barely risen and resembled nothing so much as the flaccid, wrinkled breast of an old woman. Napoleon granted the captain a few minutes' grace, then discreetly gestured to Junot to come closer.

'Sir?'

'Have a word with Conté. Nothing too harsh, you understand, but tell him he'd better get that thing up in the air before he makes complete fools of us.'

'Yes, sir.'

Junot eased himself up from his divan, strolled across the courtyard and beckoned to the hapless Captain Conté, who emerged from under the platform with his face glistening with sweat and streaked with grime. He listened to Junot for a moment, looked past him towards Napoleon, and shrugged his shoulders helplessly.

'Is there a problem, General?'

Napoleon turned to the sheikh. 'Not at all. Demonstrations of such complexity take time, that's all.'

'It's just that your captain doesn't seem very happy. Does he really know what he's doing?'

'Who? Captain Conté?' Napoleon was hurt by the accusation and impulsively rushed to defend the reputation of his officer. 'Captain Conté has one of the most brilliant minds in the French army. That's why I personally selected him for this campaign.'

'Really?'

'Yes,' Napoleon said irritably. 'The man is a genius. He invented the pencil, you know.'

'The pencil.' The sheikh nodded slowly. 'Then, truly, he is not a man to be underestimated.'

Napoleon could not take the humiliation any more. He rose, and made an excuse that he had work to attend to and was sorry but the demonstration would have to wait for another day.

'I quite understand, General,' the sheikh responded with a kindly expression. 'Perhaps when Allah is more willing to permit men to behave like birds.'

'Yes, quite.'

As soon as the last of the sheikhs and imams had departed Napoleon tore off the turban and hurled it to the ground. 'So much for appeasing their sensibilities! The smug bastards. Laughing up their sleeves at us!' He whirled round and stabbed a finger at Conté. 'It's your fault! You and that worthless balloon of yours! Take it down. Get rid of it. Get it out of my sight before I have it cut to pieces and wipe my arse on it.'

'Sir!' Captain Conté tried to explain. 'It was the day's heat. I could not make my balloon more buoyant than the surrounding air. It works best in cooler climates.'

'Really?' Napoleon snapped. 'Cooler climates? Then you'd better pack it up and fuck off back to France with it, Captain.'

'Sir! I . . . Yes, sir.'

Napoleon glared at him a moment, then turned round to look for Junot. 'Junot! Over here! At once, man!'

Junot ran across the courtyard and stood stiffly to attention before his general. 'Yes, sir?'

'That other business. Concerning Madame Fourès. See to it now, please.'

'Tonight, sir?'

'Tonight. I need something to take my mind off this disaster.' A smile flickered across Napoleon's face. 'I think that she will prove a most diverting companion.'

The door closed behind the woman as Junot left the room and for a moment Napoleon watched her from his seat on the balcony outside. Pauline Fourès was wearing a sheer silk gown that hid little of her fine figure in the wan glow of the oil lamps burning in a bracket hanging from the ceiling. For a moment she simply stared round the room; then she darted across to a small side table and helped herself to a piece of baklava. Napoleon could not help chuckling and she froze at once.

'Who's there? General?'

Napoleon rose and entered the room.

'Madame Fourès, a pleasure.' He bowed and kissed her hand. 'Thank you for coming to see me.'

'How could I refuse?' She smiled, and her full lips parted to reveal perfect teeth. 'Colonel Junot was most insistent. And, after all, you are the most powerful man in Egypt. Your word is law.'

'It is. Please sit down.' He gestured to the two chairs beside the side table. 'Since you have started on the delicacies, feel free to continue.'

'Ah . . .' She laughed. 'Now I am ashamed.'

They sat and Napoleon poured them each a glass of wine, and they picked at the baklava as he asked her to tell the story of her adventures since the expedition had left France. When she had finished Napoleon reflected for a moment before he spoke.

'I envy a man who inspires such devotion in his wife.'

Pauline stared back at him. 'I love my husband, General, but I loathed life as an officer's wife back in France. I have not sacrificed anything to follow him. In truth I escaped the drudgery of eking out a life in a rented room while waiting for him to return. There has to be more to life than that. There has to be adventure.'

'Indeed.' Napoleon leaned closer to her. 'And have you found it?'

'I thought so, for a while. But now I am a mere lieutenant's wife once more.'

'Yes . . . A woman of your beauty deserves better.'

She looked at him for a moment and then tilted her head slightly. 'What are you saying, General? Are you going to offer my husband a promotion?'

'No.' Napoleon felt uneasy about what he was about to suggest and his eyes fixed on hers. 'A general's position is an isolated one. I cannot acknowledge any man, any friend, as an equal. Yet I need companionship . . . the comfort of intimacy. You understand? I need a woman. A special woman.'

'But you are married.'

'Yes,' Napoleon replied bitterly. 'And as you have no doubt heard, my wife has found a companion of her own. I will deal with her when I return to France. Under the circumstances I do not feel obliged to remain faithful to her. And I find that I am uncommonly attracted to you.'

'I see.' Pauline nodded. 'And what exactly are you offering me?'

'A palace here in Cairo. The company of the finest officers and scientific minds in Egypt. Is that not adventure enough for you, Madame Fourès?'

She considered this for a while before replying. 'And what of my husband? What becomes of him?'

'I will send him back to France. It would be best for all three of us.'

'Yes.' She licked her lips. 'A palace, you say?'

Napoleon nodded.

'And what happens when the campaign is over?'

'I don't know yet. Let's see what happens. But I will make no promises.'

'No promises, then.' She took his hand and kissed it. 'Please, call me Pauline. And when can this . . . adventure begin?'

Napoleon felt his heart beating faster as he gestured towards the arched doorway on the far side of the room. The night suddenly seemed unbearably hot. 'My bedchamber is over there. The choice is yours.'

Pauline rose from her chair, and staring down at Napoleon she reached up and pulled the pins from her hair, so that it cascaded down over her shoulders. Then she turned away and glided across the room towards the bedchamber.

Chapter 40

'You have to admire their sense of humour.' Napoleon smiled as he laid down the dispatch from Alexandria and reached across the bed to stroke her back. 'Who would have thought the English were capable of it?'

'Oh, yes, it's very funny,' Pauline snapped. 'I can hardly control the mad desire to laugh like a lunatic.'

'Be fair, my little Cleopatra.'

'Don't call me that! That's what the common soldiers call me. I won't have it, not here in my bedroom.'

'Very well, then, Pauline it is.' Napoleon eased himself closer to her and kissed her bare shoulder as his fingers traced their way down the gentle groove in the flesh above her spine and crept towards the upward curve of her buttocks. But she did not respond with her usual animal purr to his touch, and he withdrew his hand.

'What's the matter?'

Pauline opened her eyes and stared at him. 'What do you think? You contrive to send my husband on an errand back to Paris so that we can be together without complications. Then the wretched Royal Navy capture him, hear his tale, and politely return him to Egypt. Bastards! So what are we going to do? He'll be back in Cairo any day.'

Napoleon sighed. Another problem to deal with. The very least of his problems, he reflected. Despite his best efforts to convince the *fellahin* that the French were determined to improve their lot, the natives were still ambushing patrols and murdering any stragglers, or any soldier who dared to venture out of barracks on his own. The collection of taxes was bringing in a fraction of what it should, and even though the task had been subcontracted to local tax officials the natives were adept at concealing their wealth and making any excuse to avoid paying their dues. The difficulty of winning over the local people was exacerbated by the behaviour of his own men. Despite the declared ideals of the revolution, the French soldiers were inclined to pay mere lip service to the high moral values that France was supposed to be spreading through this corner of the world. As soon as they were out of sight of their officers they were liable to loot the nearest village, and were not above raping any women who caught their eye. Napoleon had issued orders that any men found responsible for such deeds must be tried and shot at once. Already he had been obliged to sign two death warrants, and hoped that this would deter any more crimes.

'Well?' Pauline nudged him with her hip. 'What are we going to do?'

'Do?'

'About my husband!'

'You must divorce him. There is no other way of dealing with it.'

'Then I will have nothing. Can't you send him away again? Somewhere dangerous . . .'

Napoleon propped himself up on an elbow and stared at her. 'Lieutenant Fourès is a good officer. He doesn't deserve such a fate. I will not send him to his death. Not even for you, Pauline.'

'Don't tell me you're feeling guilty about what's happened? I don't believe it.'

Napleon shrugged. 'I have done the man an injustice. I will not compound it with murder. So you must divorce him. I will see that the procedure is as swift as possible. Then I will move you into quarters next to mine, and settle an allowance on you. You will live well enough, Pauline.'

'And when you tire of me? What then? I shall be alone, with no family, no honour. What do you imagine will become of me?'

'Pauline, how could I grow tired of you?' Napoleon reached

over to her back again and continued his caresses where he had left off, running the tips of his fingers over her buttocks and letting them slide down into the cleavage. She shut her eyes and moaned, pushing back against his touch. He leaned over her, easing her auburn tresses aside so that he could kiss the fine hairs at the nape of her neck.

'Yes,' she whispered. 'Oh, yes . . . Like that.'

He eased Pauline on to her back and entered her gently.

'My love,' she muttered. 'Do you love me?'

'Of course,' Napoleon said. 'Now that's enough talk. More than enough. We can talk later. Much later.'

Pauline's divorce was rushed through with what would have seemed indecent haste back in Paris, but the world of the army was less demanding in its values and barely noticed the legal formality. Except for Eugène, who served on Napoleon's staff and for a while regarded his stepfather with frosty disdain every time they had occasion to confer. Much as he liked the young man, Napoleon felt no compulsion to try to hide his relationship with Pauline. Not after suffering the hurt and humiliation he had endured at the hands of Eugène's mother.

Pauline continued to affect her taste for military clothing and wore the uniform of a general when she accompanied Napoleon on his tours of the province. Lieutenant Fourès accepted the situation with good grace, as a man must when he has lost out to an officer of such lofty rank with the status of a national hero. He quietly returned to his regiment where his fellow officers and his men regarded him with shaming pity until he could take it no longer. One morning he took a horse and rode into the desert, and neither man nor horse was ever seen again.

In the new year the resistance to the French occupiers increased in both scale and ferocity, despite the measures that Napoleon had taken to win over the *fellahin* as well as their religious and political leaders in the towns and cities.

'Nothing we do makes a difference,' Napoleon complained bitterly to his staff at one of his weekly briefings. 'Now they attack us almost every day.'

Berthier coughed. 'With respect, sir, the peasants are not involved in the resistance. It's mostly what's left of the Mameluke forces and the Bedouin, raiding from the desert.'

'But who is supporting them?' Napoleon shot back. 'Who is feeding them? Who is passing on intelligence about our movements and the strength of our patrols? The peasant scum, that's who.'

'They probably have no choice in the matter, sir. The *fellahin* are caught between us and the enemy. They'll swear that they are loyal to us, and the moment we pass on and the enemy turn up they'll swear loyalty to Murad Bey. You can hardly blame them.'

'I'm not going to blame them, Berthier. I'm going to teach them a lesson. A very hard lesson, and if they are sensible they will profit from it. I want a declaration issued. I want a thousand copies of it printed off and sent to every town and village in Egypt. From now on, if any French soldiers are murdered, there will be reprisals. If it occurs in the cities or towns then ten natives will be executed for each French life taken. If our patrols are attacked in the country then the nearest village will be burned to the ground and all livestock slaughtered. The heads of those we execute will be prominently displayed as a warning to others.' Napoleon paused to let his words sink in, then he continued. 'We will establish order in Egypt, gentlemen. However many lives it costs. And then we shall have peace.'

Some of the staff officers shifted uncomfortably under his gaze, but no one raised any protest, and then Berthier nodded. 'Very well, sir. I'll see that to it that the declaration is drafted.'

'Good.' Napoleon felt some of the tension drain from him, and he crossed over to the window and gazed out over the rooftops of Cairo. 'The sooner these people are on our side the better. Especially given the wider situation. Speaking of which . . . Junot, are you ready to make your report?'

'Yes, sir.' Junot rose to his feet and cleared his throat before he began. 'According to our spies, the enemy still fighting us in lower Egypt amounts to some fifteen thousand mounted Arabs, and perhaps as many as fifty thousand infantry. Fortunately for us they have not evolved any effective tactics for engaging our columns. They cannot break our infantry squares and they cannot endure against our massed volleys. So they are limited to the raids that we have been dealing with. They are further weakened by internal disputes between various tribes and religious factions. Accordingly, they do not pose a significant danger to us. The real danger comes from outside.' Junot approached the large map of the region that had been painted on to the wall of the staff officers' briefing room. He picked up a cane and raised it up to the eastern coast of the Mediterranean and lightly tapped the name of a coastal town. 'I speak of Ahmad Pasha, the ruler of Acre and the Turkish province of Syria. Our latest report, from a merchant who called into Acre for supplies a month ago, is that Ahmad Pasha has amassed an army of fifty thousand men, together with a sizeable artillery train. He has also been feeding supplies and men across the Sinai to support the rebels opposing us in Egypt. That is why they have become more ambitious in their attacks on our forces recently. As a result the general sent a message to Ahmad Pasha demanding that this cease, and offering to agree a peace treaty.' Junot paused. 'The merchant reports that the officer sent to deliver the message has been executed.'

There was a ripple of angry muttering from the officers and Junot waited until they were silent again before continuing. 'A formal protest has been sent to the Turkish Sultan in Constantinople, demanding that he censure Ahmad Pasha. That might not count for much, but if Ahmad Pasha can be made to think that he is threatened from Turkey if he leads his army against us, then at least he might think twice about throwing his lot in with Murad Bey.' When Junot sat down, Napoleon was gazing into his courtyard. Pauline and a few of the other officers' wives and mistresses were sitting by a fountain chatting happily. He felt tired, and in need of a break from his official duties. More than anything he desired to be in the arms of Pauline. Then at least he would be spared the weighty concerns of commanding his isolated army.

'That is all for today, gentlemen. You are dismissed.'

Chapter 41

'The Sultan's declared war on France?' Napoleon stared at Berthier as his chief of staff lowered the dispatch he had been reading to his general. 'How can that be? Talleyrand is supposed to be in Constantinople concluding a treaty.'

Berthier indicated the report. 'He never left Paris, sir.'

Napoleon breathed in sharply through his nostrils and then hissed. 'The bastard . . . So now we're at war with the Sultan as well as Ahmad Pasha.'

'It's more than just a war, sir. The Sultan has issued a *firman* to all Muslims declaring a holy war against France.'

'A holy war, eh?' Napoleon clasped his hands behind his back and turned to the map on the wall. 'He can have his war, then. No doubt he will try to attack us on two fronts. From Syria in the east, together with a landing near Alexandria, a pincer movement. I'm sure our friends in the Royal Navy will be lending the Turks their full support, so we must deny the English the use of the harbours at Jaffa and Acre. If we move swiftly, Berthier, we can advance to Acre, deal with Ahmad Pasha and destroy the Sultan's army at Damascus, then fall back to Egypt to counter the other pincer. In the longer term, of course, we will need to occupy Syria to act as a buffer between Turkey and Egypt. And from there we could even march east to India.' Napoleon's mind recalled a report he had read in a bundle of newspapers taken from a merchant ship by one of the frigates that had survived the slaughter in Aboukir Bay. 'The sooner we can turn our attention towards India the better.

The British have appointed a new Governor General, the Earl of Mornington. The man has ambitions to extend British power right across the subcontinent, if newspaper reports are to believed. France cannot permit that. But first we must take Syria.'

'Yes, sir,' Berthier replied evenly. 'Provided we have the reinforcements we have requested from Paris.'

'It's always a question of reinforcements. If those fools in Paris could see any further than the ends of their noses, we would have received more men long ago. They seem to think we can achieve miracles, Berthier.'

'You have before, sir.'

'Yes, well, the magic will run out one day.' Napoleon laughed. 'But not for a while yet, eh?'

Ten thousand men were left behind in Egypt to keep order and guard against any attempt made by the Turks to land an army by sea. Napoleon gave orders for the four depleted divisions of Reynier, Bon, Kléber and the recently promoted Lannes to gather at the frontier depot of Katia, together with Murat's cavalry and the engineering and artillery trains. The army was not ready to advance until early in February, when General Reynier and the advance guard started their march across the Sinai desert. Napoleon joined the main body a week later, and was greeted by Berthier as he wearily swung himself down from the saddle and beat the worst of the dust off his jacket.

'Sir, it's good to see you.'

'And you, Berthier. What news have we had from Reynier? He must have reached Syria by now.'

'No, sir. He hasn't.' Berthier looked agitated.

'What's happened?'

'He's been forced to stop at El Arish, about fifty miles from here. The enemy have built a strong fort, with a large garrison. Reynier is besieging it.'

Napoleon whacked his hat against his thigh and swore. 'Very well, show me on the map.'

Inside the headquarters tent Berthier led him to the map table where a large, but sparsely detailed, chart was spread out. Berthier pointed the village out to his general. 'As you can see, El Arish lies astride the route into Syria. We dare not advance and leave such a strong force to threaten our communications. We have to take the fort, sir. There's no alternative.'

'But Reynier's had five days to do the job already.' Napoleon fumed. 'What's holding him up?'

'He hasn't been able to get his guns forward, sir.'

'Why not?'

'It's the sand, sir. It's too soft. The artillery train is struggling to make more than five or six miles a day. And that's just the field artillery. The siege guns are still here.'

Napoleon thumped his fist on the table. 'I will not permit this delay! We have to strike at Acre as quickly as possible, before the enemy can react. Before they can land forces near Alexandria.'

'The guns are being moved up as fast as possible,' Berthier protested.

'Well it's not fast enough!' Napoleon took a deep breath and calmed his anger before he continued in a more reasonable tone. 'All right then, Berthier. It's not Reynier's fault, it's the sand. In which case you must make arrangements for the siege guns to be moved up to Syria by sea. Find some ships and we'll send for them the moment we reach Acre. Meanwhile, we must get the army moving. I'm riding forward to Reynier at once. I want you to give orders to break camp, and bring the rest of the army across the Sinai. Clear?'

'Yes, sir.'

'Then get to work. I'll see you at El Arish.'

He hurried from the tent, barking an order to the commander of his escort to get the mounted guides back into their saddles. Without waiting for them, he swung himself back on to his horse and spurred it into a gallop. As he raced through the camp Napoleon barely had time to acknowledge the cheers and greetings of the men he passed, but he was glad to see them in high spirits again after the frustration and boredom of the previous months. With the prospect of a campaign before them, and more of the rich pickings from their fallen enemies, the men had recovered their fighting spirit and Napoleon hoped that he could get the offensive moving forward once again while there was time to make the most of their élan.

When the escort caught up with him they rode on through the night, across a moonlit landscape of silky dunes interspersed with rocky massifs. At dawn they caught up with the artillery train, labouring along the route towards El Arish. The wheels of the gun carriages rotated for short distances before sinking into the sand so that the carriages had to be dragged forward. Berthier had been right, Napoleon reflected: this was no terrain for heavy wheeled traffic. He gave orders for the largest-calibre guns to be left behind and all available camels and horses to be harnessed to the mortar batteries and the lightest field pieces, and then drove them forward to join Reynier's division outside the fort at El Arish.

They arrived late in the afternoon and as they crested the last rise before the village Napoleon saw the fort, a large square constructed from solid-looking masonry. To the left the sea sparkled serenely in the sunlight. Leaving the artillerymen and his escort to haul the mortars into the camp, Napoleon rode ahead to find General Reynier. The division commander was in a small redoubt on a low escarpment beyond the fort.

'What the hell are you doing up here?' Napoleon demanded. 'Your men are facing the wrong way.'

'No, sir. We were attacked by a relief force yesterday. The advance battalion only just managed to hold them off until I could bring up support. Then the enemy broke and retreated up the coast.'

'Have you sent any scouts forward to see how far they've gone?'

Reynier paused, nervously. 'No, sir. Not yet.'

'Why not? If they've gone then your men have been sitting on their arses here for two days when they could have been down there assaulting the fort.'

'We've already tried frontal attacks. My men didn't even get over the wall before they were repulsed. With heavy losses, sir.'

'I see.' Napoleon frowned. 'Right, then, leave a battalion up here, just in case the enemy does come back. Get the rest down to cover the fort and make ready for another assault. Meanwhile, as soon as the mortars are in place, we'll give those Turks a shelling they won't forget in a hurry.'

The artillery teams dragged the mortars up to the fortified pits that Reynier's men had prepared for them. Napoleon joined the crews as they wrestled the awkward timber carriages into place and unloaded the shells and propellent charges. It was hot, exhausting work and the battery was not ready to open fire until late in the evening. There was still plenty of light cast by the moon, and the range had already been calculated by Reynier's artillery commander, so Napoleon gave the order to start the bombardment. The first mortar fired with a booming thud and the flash from the muzzle briefly illuminated the crew and the surrounding pit in a lurid orange glow, then all eyes snapped forward towards the fort. There was a short delay before the rampart was lit up by a brilliant flash inside the fort and a moment later the crash of the detonation carried across the intervening ground, slightly deadened by the sand.

'The range is good!' Napoleon called out. 'All mortars – open fire!'

The bombardment continued through the night and into the following day in a steady rumble of explosions that soon shrouded the fort in a thick cloud of dust, illuminated from within by the blooms of exploding shells. Hour after hour the bombardment continued and still the garrison showed no sign of surrendering. Napoleon sat on a rock and watched the shelling continue for another night. In between fitful snatches of sleep, he stood up and walked swiftly to and fro behind the battery, fretting about the delay this siege was causing to his advance on Acre.

As the sun rose out of the desert on the following morning, one of the gunners shouted out to Napoleon and pointed towards the fort. The gate had opened and two men made their way outside. The gate was hurriedly closed behind them, just as the last shell to be fired went off a short distance beyond the wall. The two figures threw themselves flat.

'Cease fire!' Napoleon bellowed. 'Cease fire!'

In the silence the two men warily rose to their feet; then there was a glint as one of them raised a trumpet to his lips and blasted out three notes. The other unfurled a small white flag and held it up in clear view as they advanced across the open ground in front of the fort.

Reynier came trotting up to Napoleon with an excited expression. 'Looks like they have had enough, sir.'

'Not before time. Those bastards have delayed us enough already. Right, offer them terms. If they surrender the fort they can leave with their weapons, under parole. Tell them they are forbidden from taking up arms against French forces for a year. If they refuse those terms then we will continue the shelling and there will be no prisoners taken when we assault and take the fort. If they agree, get them out of here as quickly as you can, then break camp and continue the advance. Got that?'

'Yes, sir.' Reynier saluted and summoned an infantry section to go forward with him to meet the Turkish emissaries. Napoleon turned away and strode swiftly back to the mounted guides who were holding his horse ready. He swung himself into the saddle and turned back down the track towards the rest of the army, still seething at the delay to his plans.

With the removal of the threat to his lines of communication Napoleon led his army north, and into Syria. At once Reynier's advance guard came up against Turkish cavalry, but as soon as he formed his men into squares the enemy attacked only half-heartedly before withdrawing. The weather was cold and sudden squalls of rain turned the tracks into slippery mud, and it was not until the beginning of March that the first troops moved into position around the port of Jaffa. The town was protected by a decrepit wall, erected long before the days of artillery, and Napoleon was content to use his field guns to breach the walls rather than send for his siege artillery. As the engineers constructed their batteries Napoleon sent an emissary forward to negotiate terms for the surrender.

'God, I hope they're not anything like that lot at El Arish,' Berthier muttered as Napoleon and his senior officers watched the French officer enter the gates.

Napoleon shrugged. 'If they are, then we'll bombard them into submission just as we did before.' He raised his telescope and examined the walls. 'You can see that the masonry is crumbling in many places. I'm certain that a few well-placed shots will soon bring down a section of the wall large enough for Lannes's division to make an assault into the town.' He lowered the telescope and turned round with a smile. 'What do you say, Lannes? Think your men can take that place?'

General Lannes grinned. 'Just try to stop them, sir.'

Napoleon punched him on the shoulder. 'That's my Lannes! Only this time, try not to get wounded, eh? You have more lives than ten cats, but even you will run out of them one day.'

'Not before my enemies.'

The other officers smiled, and then Berthier raised his arm and pointed towards the gates of Jaffa. 'That was quick.'

Napoleon, still smiling, turned towards the town and saw the French officer emerge through the open gate, between two Turkish soldiers. Close behind him emerged a third soldier.

'At last, they're being reasonable.'

As Napoleon and his staff watched, the emissary was suddenly thrust down on to his knees. Light glinted off steel as the man behind him drew his sword and swept it round in a glittering arc. The officer's head leaped from his shoulders and bounced a short distance from the gate as blood sprayed up from his neck. The swordsman kicked the torso over and then he and his two companions strode back through the gate and it closed behind them. Neither Napoleon nor his officers spoke for a moment. Then the sound of jeering echoed across the ground from the city walls and broke the spell. As Napoleon stared at the distant figures waving their swords and muskets above the ramparts he shook his head with disgust.

'Animals . . . Barbarians . . . Very well, then they shall be treated as such. Berthier!'

'Yes, sir?'

'I want our guns to open fire as soon as possible. I want a good breach in that wall and then, Lannes, when you enter that town, you show its people no mercy. Understand? No mercy.'

'Yes, sir.' Lannes nodded. 'No mercy.'

Chapter 42

Under the covering fire of occasional blasts of grapeshot from the batteries the engineers began to dig their siege trenches, steadily zigzagging towards the walls so as not to provide any chance of enfilading fire when the assault troops moved forward to make their attack. The army went about its work with a grim determination to avenge the butchering of the officer, whose head and body still lay before the gate. When the trenches had been completed the batteries were loaded with iron shot and the bombardment of a length of wall close to the gate began in earnest. As Napoleon had suspected, the masonry was weak and within hours the ramparts had been blown away. Soon the rubble had formed a scalable slope, almost up to the level of the breach. The gunners turned their attention to the wall on either side of the initial gap and proceeded to widen it by stages until ten men could charge through it abreast.

As the guns fell silent, Napoleon went forward along the trench, nodding a greeting to the men lining each side as he passed. General Lannes was crouching with the first wave of troops, waiting for the order to attack. At his side was Eugène Beauharnais.

Napoleon's eyes widened in surprise. 'What are you doing here? You're supposed to be at headquarters.'

'Sir, I volunteered to join the attack,' Eugène protested.

'I don't care. Your place is at headquarters.'

'Not today. It's time for me to become a proper soldier.'

'A staff officer is every bit as important as a field officer.'

'Really, sir?' Eugène smiled. 'Did you think that when you led the charge at Arcola?'

Lannes roared with laughter. 'Ha! He has you there, sir! Go on, give the lad a chance to win his spurs.'

For a moment Napoleon was tempted to order Eugène to the rear, but there was truth in what the boy had said. An officer, above all men, must prove himself in battle if he was to win the respect and loyalty of his comrades, common soldiers and officers alike. He nodded slowly. 'Very well, then. But promise me that you will not take any unnecessary risks. If anything happens to you, your mother will never forgive me.'

Eugène smiled. 'I'll be careful then, sir. For your sake.'

'You rascal!' Napoleon pinched his cheek. Then he turned to Lannes. 'God bless you and good luck, my friend.'

Lannes patted the musket lying beside him. 'Fuck that. I'd rather put my faith in a stout heart and a good weapon, sir.'

'Then I'll see you in hell.' Napoleon slapped him on the shoulder and started to make his way back to the nearest battery to watch the assault as General Lannes rose up, musket in hand.

'Soldiers of the 8th! On your feet!' Lannes waited until they were ready, faces tense and bodies poised, and then raised his arm and punched it towards the breach. 'Charge!'

From the battery Napoleon watched as Lannes and his men surged forward over the narrow strip of ground between the end of the trenches and the town wall. Their cheers and throaty war cries echoed back off the masonry as they reached the rubble and began to scramble up. The Turks on either side of the breach began to open fire on their attackers, and were quickly wreathed in puffs of smoke. Several soldiers had fallen by the time Lannes and the first of his men gained the breach, where the Turks surged forward to defend the town. Napoleon strained his eyes as he tried to spot Eugène but the impetus of the charge quickly carried Lannes and the others through the gap and into the streets of Jaffa.

Once the sounds of the fighting had died away Napoleon made his way down the trench and up on to the ground in front of the breach, accompanied by fifty of the guides, who watched the walls on either side closely as they guarded their general. The rubble shifted under his boots and he had some difficulty in scrambling through the breach. There were bodies in the streets, scores of them. Mostly Turks, cut down in the ferocious assault mounted by Lannes and his men. Napoleon encountered only a handful of wounded Frenchmen as he passed through the town. Near the harbour Dr Desgenettes and his men were treating a group of severely injured soldiers, stretched out in a row on the street. The doctor looked up from his work as Napoleon and the guides marched by, but quickly wiped his brow and turned back to his patients. The main street through the town gave out on to the harbour, and Napoleon stopped in surprise at the sight that met his eyes. On the beach next to the harbour were thousands of Turks, huddled tightly together as they sat under the watchful eyes of the French guards. As Napoleon approached the exhausted French troops slumped on the foul-smelling quay, another batch of prisoners was marched out of a side street to join their comrades. They wore the distinctive red and green turbans of the men who had surrendered at El Arish. Napoleon felt a cold rage seep through his veins.

He found General Lannes sitting on a divan that had been hauled out on to the quay and dragged into the shade cast by the wall of a mosque. Napoleon was greatly relieved to see Eugène sitting on a chair nearby, talking animatedly with some of the younger officers of Lannes's division.

Napoleon thrust his arm towards the prisoners. 'What is the meaning of this?'

Lannes rose to his feet and stood stiffly before his commander. 'Sir?'

'I take it that they are prisoners.'

'Yes, sir.'

'I told you not to show the enemy any mercy.'

'I know that, sir. But they fought hard and fair before they were forced to give up.'

'Fine. And what do you propose to do with them now?'

'I don't know, sir,' Lannes admitted. 'I hadn't considered that yet. We've only just finished mopping up the last of the resistance.'

'We can't have any prisoners.' Napoleon spoke with quiet intensity. 'We have no spare supplies to feed them with, no spare troops to guard them, and, in any case, those from El Arish have broken the terms of their parole . . .'

Lannes stared at him with a pained expression. 'What do you want me to do, sir?'

'I want you to dispose of the prisoners. All of them.'

Lannes glanced round at the figures packed on the beach. 'But there must be nearly three thousand of them.'

'I'm not interested in the number, General, just the outcome. You have your orders, now carry them out.'

'Wait!' Eugène called out, striding towards Napoleon with an angry expression. 'You can't do it, sir. I took the surrender of the men from the citadel. I gave them my word that they would be well treated.'

'On whose authority did you make such a promise? Not mine.'

'I . . . I gave them my word they would be spared, sir.'

'Then you gave them what was not in your power to give. The dishonour is yours, Eugène, and you will be responsible for the consequences,' Napoleon said coldly. 'General Lannes, you will take the prisoners in batches to the beach on the other side of the harbour from here, and there you will dispose of them. I don't care what method you use as long as the job is done. The execution parties will be under the command of Captain Beauharnais.'

'Yes, sir.'

Napoleon leaned close to his stepson. 'Let this be a lesson to you. Next time you will obey my orders to the letter.'

'Yes, sir,' Eugène replied through clenched teeth.

'Good.' Napoleon turned to Lannes. 'Carry on then, General.'

They exchanged a salute and then Napoleon and the guides turned and marched back through the town. As they reached the street where they had earlier encountered Desgenettes, the doctor emerged from an entrance into a courtyard and hurried over to Napoleon. He looked afraid as he saluted his general.

'Sir, I've found . . . something. You must come and see.'

'What? What is it, doctor?'

Desgenettes glanced past Napoleon to the ranks of the guides behind him. 'Please, sir, come with me, and tell these men to stay here.'

Napoleon was still furious with Lannes and Eugène and he shook his head. Whatever it was the doctor wanted to show him would have to wait. The army had to be readied for the advance to Acre. But there was an imploring look in the man's eyes and after a moment's hesitation Napoleon nodded irritably.

'Very well, then, but make it quick.'

Desgenettes turned and led the way back through the arch into the courtyard beyond. To one side there was a narrow doorway leading into some kind of storage room and as they approached it Napoleon could hear groaning, and the fevered mutterings of sick men. He paused on the threshold and saw that the floor inside the storeroom was covered with crude mattresses on which men lay, covered with soiled rags. The stench of the place was overpowering and Napoleon raised a hand to cover his mouth and nose.

'What is this place? A hospital?'

'No, sir.' Desgenettes leaned over the nearest man and carefully lifted the corner of the blanket that covered him. The man's jaw was slack and hung open and his eyes gazed sightlessly at the ceiling and Napoleon realised he was dead. Then he saw the swollen lumps on the man's neck and round his armpits. Some had burst and glistened with blood and pus. The stench hit Napoleon like a blow and he had to struggle to keep himself from vomiting.

'Buboes,' Desgenettes explained, and let the blanket drop back over the body. He gestured to the other men in the room, most still moving fitfully as they mumbled and cried out. 'They've all got the same symptoms.' He turned to Napoleon. 'This isn't a hospital, sir. It's a plague house.'

Chapter 43

'That delay at El Arish is about to cost us dearly,' Napoleon said as he surveyed the new earthworks and other fortifications that had been erected around Acre. Some of Ahmad Pasha's engineers were still toiling away digging a ditch in front of the large bastion that dominated the city's walls. The enemy was in a strong position indeed, he reflected. Acre was built on a spur of land that thrust out to sea at an angle to create the harbour. A mole protected the harbour and at the end of the mole stood a lighthouse. The landward side of the city was defended by massive walls and outer works and through his telescope Napoleon could see the barrels of artillery pieces, positioned to sweep the open ground before the city the moment the French launched an assault. Two British warships were anchored outside the harbour, out of range of Napoleon's field guns in case the French decided to use heated shot.

'This is going to be tricky. We can only attack on a narrow front, and they can use the mole and the English ships to enfilade our positions. We cannot blockade them, which means the English can bring in supplies and reinforcements at will. Well then, if we can't starve them out, we'll have to blast them out. This has to be settled by an assault on the city.' He turned to Berthier. 'Any sighting of Admiral Perée's ships?'

'Not yet, sir. But they should reach Haifa any day. The artillery train is already there and will bring the siege guns up to Acre the moment they are landed.'

'Good. Then we'll see how tough those walls really are.'

Napoleon's telescope picked out a group of men who had appeared on top of the main bastion. Most were in flowing robes and turbans, and there were a few Europeans amongst them in blue coats with gold epaulettes. Two of the figures stepped on to a platform just behind the ramparts and gazed out towards the French lines. With a thrill of excitement Napoleon realised he must be looking at Ahmad Pasha himself, the man the Turks called *Djezzar* – the Butcher – a sobriquet awarded in recognition of the man's legendary ferocity and the abject cruelty he visited on his enemies. That Ahmad Pasha had survived into his seventies in the brutal world of Turkish politics was tribute to his ruthlessness.

Two can play at that, Napoleon reflected coldly. News of the massacre of Turkish prisoners at Jaffa must have reached Acre by now. Ahmad Pasha and his forces would be in no doubt about the merciless nature of their opponent. Although he took little pleasure in the deed, Napoleon knew that it would unsettle many of the enemy soldiers and he needed every advantage he could wring out of the situation. The French army might well be a match for any soldiers the Sultan and his allies could field, but it was terribly outnumbered and right at the end of a slender line of communications stretching all the way down the coast towards Egypt. Just one setback might shatter Napoleon's army. The men's morale was low enough as things stood. The climate, the hostility of the native peoples, and the exhaustion and discomfort of the desert marches together with the bloody assaults on El Arish and Jaffa, had all taken their toll on the French soldiers.

And now the plague had broken out in their ranks. Napoleon had forbidden Dr Desgenettes and his staff to breathe a word about the plague victims they had encountered at Jaffa. The plague house had been sealed off and placed under guard so that its unhappy occupants would die in secret. But, somehow, somewhere in Jaffa, the plague had found its way into the blood of the French soldiers as they looted the city. Already nearly fifty men had been diagnosed with the terrible disease and the first of them had died that morning. Desgenettes had taken over a Greek Orthodox monastery off the road between Jaffa and Acre, and new cases were hurriedly taken out of the sick tents and moved to the makeshift hospital. It was only a matter of time before the secret was out and the men would have one more dread to add to their burden.

Napoleon switched his attention from Ahmad Pasha to the naval officer standing beside him. That must be Sir Sidney Smith, the commander of the small squadron that Admiral Nelson had detached to the Levant to harry the French army. The English naval captain was obviously determined to win a reputation for himself. Even here on the fringe of the civilised world, Napoleon pondered, it came down to a conflict between France and England. It was amusing, Napoleon reflected, that even though they were separated by only a narrow stretch of water, they were obliged to fight each other in conflicts spread right across the world.

The naval officer raised his telescope and swept it over the French lines until it foreshortened into a glinting dot and then he stopped. For a moment the two foes scrutinised each other down the lengths of their telescopes, until the Englishman lowered his glass and waved cheerily before turning away to confer with Ahmad Pasha.

'We'll see who's still smiling in a week's time,' Napoleon muttered.

Berthier looked up from his notebook. 'Pardon, sir?'

'It doesn't matter.' Napoleon snapped his telescope shut and turned to his chief of staff. 'I want the approach trenches and the batteries prepared as soon as possible. When the siege guns are in position they will commence firing at once. That central bastion is the key to their defences. If we take that and mount some guns on it, then we can bombard any point of the city at will. See that the orders are given, Berthier.'

For the rest of the day the trenches crept towards the walls of Acre, under constant bombardment from the guns mounted in the towers and the main bastion. Napoleon noted that none of the enemy's pieces seemed to be heavy guns and was thankful for that small mercy at least. Some time could be saved on the earthworks being thrown up to protect the siege guns. Napoleon returned to his observation point from time to time to check on the progress and watched impatiently as his engineers struggled to break up the hard ground and dig deep enough to provide enough soil to bank up the sides of the trenches and make them safe for the men to approach the walls of Acre. As night fell Napoleon retired to his tent and reviewed his progress. It had taken longer to reach Acre than he had thought, but now the army had begun its siege the end of the campaign was a matter of weeks away. Within days the siege guns would be pulverising the walls until a breach was made. As at Jaffa, his men would pour into the city and sweep the defenders aside. With Acre in French hands Napoleon could return to Egypt, and the warm embrace of Pauline, and prepare to counter the Sultan's other pincer arm. He went to bed with a warm feeling of satisfaction. It was true that the campaign had been dogged by delay, some misfortune and the bad feeling that had arisen after the massacre of the prisoners on the beach at Jaffa, but in the end they had reached their goal and soon the French flag would be flying above Acre. When word of the victory reached Paris there would be further public acclaim and laurels for his reputation.

Junot woke his general at dawn, an anxious expression on his face.

'What's the matter?' Napoleon sat up. 'What's happened?'

'The men have heard about the plague, sir. The rumour spread through the camp last night. They're saying that this land is cursed. You should give up the siege and lead the army back to Egypt.'

'What good would that do?' Napoleon snapped. 'We can hardly leave the plague behind. Besides, the men are overreacting. The victims have been isolated and the plague will run its course soon enough.'

'I doubt that is going to satisfy the men.'

'You may be right,' Napoleon conceded. 'Then we must act now to reassure them. They have to be shown that there's nothing to fear. Have my staff officers summoned. I think it's time for a little demonstration.'

'What kind of demonstration, sir?' Junot asked warily.

A smile flickered across Napoleon's lips. 'You'll see soon enough, and I pray to God we live to tell the tale.'

As soon as he had dressed, Napoleon and his staff officers mounted up. He had given them no explanation and just wheeled his horse and trotted out of camp. The staff officers and a squadron of the guides followed him back down the road towards Jaffa before turning off into the hills a few miles from the camp. There on a small rise stood an old monastery with weathered walls. Outside stood several carts, tended by French soldiers. As Napoleon reined in outside the monastery the orderlies hurriedly rose to their feet and stood to attention.

'Where is Dr Desgenettes?'

'Inside, sir. With the patients.'

'Well, send him my compliments and ask him to join me out here.'

'Yes, sir.' The orderly hurried inside and Napoleon turned back to his staff officers. 'Junot, tell the guides to dismount and rest their horses. The rest of you are coming with me.'

'Where, sir?' Berthier asked nervously as he stared at the monastery. 'Not in there, surely?'

'You're not afraid, are you, Berthier?'

'Sir, I know what this place is. It would be madness to remain here another moment. We should leave. At once.'

'Not until I've made my point.' Napoleon turned at the sound of footsteps crossing the threshold of the monastery's arched entrance, and saw Dr Desgenettes emerge from the dim interior. He looked exhausted and the surgeon's apron he wore was soiled and stained with blood. He saluted. 'I must say, I'm surprised to see you here, sir.'

'Good. My staff and I have come to inspect your field hospital, doctor. Would you be kind enough to show us inside?'

'Inside?' Desgenettes's eyebrows rose in surprise. 'Very well then, sir. If you'd follow me.'

Napoleon turned to his staff and was amused to note their horrified expressions as he beckoned to them. 'Come, gentlemen.'

Inside the monastery it was cold, despite the small braziers burning at each end. On both sides of the main hall was a line of palliasses on which lay the sick. Most were still and quiet, but here and there men moaned in agony.

'This end is where we keep the recently admitted cases,' Desgenettes explained. 'If the symptoms progress, as they almost invariably do, then we move them to the far end. When they die they are taken out of the monastery for burial.'

'What can be done for them?' asked Napoleon, glancing down at the nearest man, a youngster no more than twenty. He had fine features and a shock of light brown curly hair and would have cut a handsome figure in his uniform. Already there were blackened swellings about his neck.

'We try to keep them warm and comfortable, and alleviate the pain when the sickness gets to its most advanced stage. The men with the strongest constitutions might survive, but their recovery will be slow. If they show arrested symptoms they are moved to another room where we can minimise the risk of further infection – in theory.'

'Aren't you at risk, doctor?' Junot asked.

'Of course. So is any man in close contact with the sick.'

'Then why haven't you caught it?'

Desgenettes smiled. 'How do you know I haven't?'

Some of the men were still well enough to recognise their commander and tried to sit up.

'No!' Napoleon waved his hand at them. 'Lie still, soldiers. You must conserve your strength, or I'll have you back on latrine duty in double time.'

Some managed a smile at that, but most stared at Napoleon with a lucklustre expression of despair and even resignation to their awful fate. He stopped at the foot of one of the makeshift beds and stared at the man lying there.

'This one's dead.'

Desgenettes came over and knelt beside the man, and felt for his pulse. After a moment he rose up and called out, 'Stretcher bearers! Here!'

Two men came from outside carrying a stretcher and set it

down beside the dead man. One took the body by the heels while the other lifted him under the shoulders and they hoisted him awkwardly across on to the stretcher. The blanket slid from his body, and there was a sharp intake of breath from Junot as the bare flesh of his torso was revealed.

'Good God, look.'

Some of the buboes had burst and the discharge was smeared across his neck and chest.

'Shit . . .' muttered one of the orderlies, turning his nose away from the foul odour and instinctively stepping back a pace. His companion had already grasped his end of the stretcher and looked up angrily.

'Come on, we have to get him out.'

'Wait,' Napoleon interrupted. 'Let me.'

He pushed the reluctant orderly aside and grabbed the stretcher handles. 'Ready? Let's go then.'

The body was heavier than he expected and Napoleon strained his muscles to hold up his end of the stretcher. The other orderly backed out slowly and the staff officers followed behind them, looking at their general in surprise and awe.

'Over there, sir.' The orderly nodded towards a mound of earth to one side of the main hall, and they set off across the broken ground. As they drew closer, Napoleon breathing heavily from the strain and fighting the nausea threatening to well up in his stomach, it became apparent that the mound was the spoil from a large open grave. They paused at the edge and Napoleon glanced down on half a dozen soldiers sprawled in the pit.

'Sir, when I say, we tip the stretcher. Ready? One . . . two . . . three!'

The body rolled off and tumbled down the side of the hole on to the other corpses. At once the orderly led the way back to the side of the monastery and they laid the stretcher down.

'Thanks for the help, sir.'

'The very least I could do.' Napoleon nodded and turned to make his way back to the staff officers and Dr Desgenettes. 'Time we got back to the siege, gentlemen. Doctor!'

'Sir?'

'If there's anything you need, just send word to Junot, and he'll deal with it. In the meantime, since the army knows about the plague outbreak, there's no point in remaining here. I noticed a small hill not far from the camp. Make arrangements to move your hospital to that site.'

'Yes, sir.'

'Carry on, then.' Napoleon strode over to his horse and swung himself into the saddle. He was well aware of the astonished looks from his staff and the men of the escort, and had to stop himself from smiling. He knew that word of his act would spread round the army just as quickly as the news of the plague, and the men would, once again, take him as one of their own, enduring every risk that they did in the common bond that made them march as hard and fight as hard as they did. He knew it had been a risk, but a calculated one. He had not come into direct contact with the body and hoped that would spare him from infection. He would find out soon enough, he reflected, and then wheeled his horse about and spurred it back towards the camp.

When Napoleon and his staff returned to his headquarters he found the commander of the artillery train waiting for him. The man jumped to his feet and shuffled to attention as his commander rode up to his tent. With a weary sigh Napoleon realised that something had gone wrong. Steeling himself for the man's report, he dismounted.

Chapter 44

'Colonel Pesset, you're supposed to be at Haifa, waiting for the siege guns.'

'Yes, sir,' the colonel replied unhappily.

'Then explain yourself. What are you doing here?'

'Sir, I beg to report, the guns have been lost.'

'Lost? How?'

'The ships carrying them from Egypt were intercepted by the Royal Navy, just off Mount Carmel, and captured.'

Berthier and the other staff officers exchanged glances and watched Napoleon closely for his response.

'Captured?' Napoleon responded evenly. 'All of them?'

'Yes, sir.'

'I see.' Napoleon lowered his head for a moment and took a deep breath. He felt a rage born of pure frustration welling up in his veins, and knew that if he surrendered to it he would turn into a screaming, hysterical monster, a side of his character he had no wish to display to this officer or the wider army. Not when his men needed him to be strong and impervious to the misfortunes that assailed them. He cleared his throat and looked up. 'Thank you for letting me know, Colonel. You may return to your men.' He strode towards his tent, glancing back over his shoulder. 'Berthier, Junot, inside now.'

As soon as they were seated around Napleon's campaign desk he leaned forward, folded his hands and rested his chin on them. 'So, what are our options, gentlemen?'

Berthier spoke first. 'We cannot continue the siege without heavy artillery, sir.'

'Granted. So we must send word back to Kléber to send us more siege guns.'

'But, sir, that will take weeks, months perhaps. In the meantime, the plague will claim more men.'

'And it will give the Sultan a chance to send a relief force to Acre,' Junot added. 'What if we are caught between Ahmad Pasha and the Army of Damascus? The longer we are here, sir, the longer we invite disaster.'

'It's a risk,' Napoleon conceded. 'But then all campaigns are risky ventures. However, given the past performance of the enemy, I think we can handle any relief force they send to Acre. That need not concern us unduly. The immediate problem is how do we overcome Acre's defences without siege artillery?'

'We still have the army's field guns, sir,' said Junot.

Berthier shook his head. 'Field guns are no good against those walls.'

'We don't know that, unless we give it a try,' Junot countered. 'It's possible the walls are not as strong as you seem to think. If they're anything like the defences of the other fortifications we've dealt with, we should be able to complete the job with our field guns.'

'I don't think so,' Berthier insisted. 'The weight of the shot is too light.'

Napoleon intervened. 'All very true, Berthier, but we must continue the siege with the tools that we have, while we send a message to General Kléber to ship us some more siege guns. Until they arrive we'll use the field guns, and we'll just have to resort to more traditional methods of siegecraft. The engineers will tunnel under the wall and use a mine to try to bring down that bastion.' He leaned back and ran a hand through his hair. 'That's all, gentlemen. Berthier, send that message to Kléber at once, and Junot, get our field pieces moved forward into the siege batteries.'

As they left to do his bidding, Napoleon sat still for a moment, and only when he was quite alone did he pound his fist down on the table.

'Fuck!' The word exploded through his clenched teeth. Why did his lucky star have to abandon him now, just when he needed it most? Had his life's share of good fortune been consumed already? If he and his army were defeated before the walls of Acre, people back in France would barely notice. Yet if he could take Acre, and win a notable victory, then he might yet derive some advantage from this unfortunate campaign. He nodded to himself as he firmed his resolve. They would remain before the walls of Acre until Ahmad Pasha surrendered or the walls were breached, and then Ahmad Pasha and his garrison would pay a bloody price for defying Napoleon Bonaparte.

For several days the field guns bombarded the walls of Acre, and Napoleon watched with growing frustration as his guns caused only superficial damage to the defences. Just one heavy gun would have smashed a large hole in the wall in the same time, Napoleon fumed. Meanwhile, the trenches progressed slowly, thanks to the rocky ground the engineers had to work through to approach the city. Then, at the end of March, his patience ran out and he gave the order for the army to prepare an assault. The night before the attack the battalions chosen for the task filed into the trenches with their scaling ladders and moved into position as quietly as possible. There was still a gap of over a hundred paces between the trench and the wall, and the open ground would be swept by the cannon and muskets of the defenders. The attack would be preceded by an intense bombardment by Napoleon's field guns and then the ramparts would be scourged by grape shot as the infantry rushed forward.

As the sun rose behind the French army and lit up the walls of the city Napoleon gave the command to open fire. The quiet stillness of the dawn was torn apart by the violent stabs of flame and the crash of artillery. Napoleon watched through his telescope as the Turkish gunners on the wall fired their weapons in reply. A small breach had been opened in the wall by the bastion which looked to be well within the reach of the scaling ladders, and the battery immediately in front of the gap continued to pound away at it, trying desperately to enlarge it before the assault began.

Berthier, standing beside his commander, tapped his watch. 'It's time.' He nodded to the signalman standing to one side and the man lifted a red flag into the air. The French guns fell silent and there was a brief pause before their drums beat the attack. From his vantage, Napoleon watched as tiny figures spilled over the lip of the trench and ran forward. The ladder bearers went in the first wave, stumbling forward under their burdens. As soon as the Turks realised the attack was under way they appeared at the ramparts and small puffs of smoke blossomed along the length of the wall. Below, on the open ground, the first Frenchmen began to fall, while their comrades hurried on without stopping as musket balls slapped into the soil all around them. The French gunners replied with grape and Napoleon smiled with satisfaction as each blast knocked large gaps in the dense ranks of the Turks manning the wall.

There was a deep, rolling boom from his left and he and his staff glanced towards the harbour as a salvo of heavy cannon fire crashed out from the lighthouse mole.

'What the hell?' Berthier muttered.

'Concealed battery,' Napoleon muttered as he swung his telescope towards the mole and saw the muzzles pointing out through the makeshift breastwork that the defenders had erected at the start of the siege. They must have moved the guns up the previous night, to enfilade the French attack, he realised. As he watched the enemy gunners reload he saw that they weren't Turks, but sailors from the British fleet. Then it struck him. 'Those are our captured siege guns!'

He lowered his scope and glanced down the slight incline towards the French batteries. Whoever was in charge of the sailors knew his business; within a few shots they had the range of the nearest of Napoleon's batteries and the heavy balls tore through the earthworks and smashed into the weapons beyond. The crews did not have a chance and were mown down along with their guns. After a few more rounds there was a short pause before the English trained their cannon on the next target and opened fire.

Napoleon turned his attention back to the desperate charge across the open ground. The first men had reached the city's defences and were struggling to lean their ladder up against the wall beneath the breach. The top rung was some distance below the gap and even as the first man scrambled up Napoleon realised that the engineers had miscalculated. Reaching the top of the ladder, the soldier valiantly stepped on to the top rung, and flattened himself to the masonry while his hands groped up towards the lip of the breach. The distance was too great, and as Napoleon and his staff watched in silence, willing the man on, a Turk leaned out from the bastion, took careful aim, and shot the French soldier in the back. He spasmed, arched and tumbled off the ladder on to his companions below. As the sailors' guns knocked out the batteries on the left flank, the assault on the defenders began to slacken and all along the wall musket fire poured down on the attackers as they threw their ladders up against the walls only to discover that none of them was long enough. Seeing that his men were being relentlessly cut down, Napoleon shook his head.

'It's no good. They're getting cut to pieces. Sound the recall.'

The moment the notes from the bugles cut across the battlefield the French troops turned and ran for their lives, pursued all the way back to their trenches by musket fire. At the same time Napoleon ordered the guns on his left flank to be abandoned. As the crews hurried out of range the British sailors methodically knocked out one battery after another until they ran out of targets, and it seemed as if stillness and quiet returned to the scene, until the combatants' ears recovered from the numbing effects of the previous din and could pick up the thin cries and shrieks of the wounded and dying men still out on the battlefield.

'What now, sir?' Berthier asked quietly as he surveyed the wrecked batteries and the bodies scattered before the walls of Acre.

Napoleon shrugged. 'Now we have to try something else.

We'll attempt another assault when the sappers have mined that bastion.'

It took another five days for the tunnel to be dug under the foundations of the bastion. The engineers packed the small space with barrels of gunpowder, laid a fuse and withdrew from the tunnel. Once again the approach trenches were filled with assault troops as they waited for the moment to attack. When all was ready, the chief engineer lit the fuse and fell back as it sputtered brightly into the darkness of the tunnel. Every man in the French army watched in tense silence, necks and shoulders strained as they braced themselves against the blast. When it came there was a sheet of flame from the end of the tunnel and the ground at the base of the bastion blew up into the air. A shower of rock, stones, soil and dust shrouded the scene. Napoleon felt the tremor pass through the ground under his feet and then the air was filled with the roar of the detonation.

At once, every man on the staff and the assembled senior officers strained to pick out the detail through the slowly clearing pall of dust. Then a puff of wind from the sea cleared the view and Napoleon's heart sank. The only sign of damage was the collapse of a stretch of the battlements and a small crack that ran only halfway up the wall. There was nothing for it but to call off the attack, and the men trudged back from the approach trenches to their tents in the camp.

The field guns resumed their bombardment of the wall, with the same dispiriting lack of effect, day after day, until Berthier brought it to Napoleon's attention that their stock of ammunition was running dangerously low. The next day the army headquarters issued a proclamation offering a bounty on any enemy cannon balls that could be retrieved from the ground in front of the walls. Those men who still had enough spirit of adventure amused themselves with daring sprints from their trenches to grab the nearest ball and then hurry back to safety before the Turks could respond with a fusillade of musket fire. A few did not make it, but the steady flow of recovered shot went some way towards supplementing the dwindling supplies in the army's stores.

The replacement siege guns were landed at Haifa in the middle of April and hauled overland to the siege lines. New, better protected, batteries were constructed on the right flank, and sweating crews manoeuvred the heavy guns into position and brought up the powder and shot ready for the renewed attack on the bastion. They opened fire on the last day of April and Napoleon noted with satisfaction that they were immediately having an effect. Each heavy ball smashed into the city's defences, dislodging a small fall of masonry. Within a day a practical breach had been opened and the French army prepared itself for another attack.

In those first few days of May the increasingly weary French battalions launched one assault after another, only to be repulsed by the Turkish troops, who fought with a tenacity that the French had not encountered before. There were severe losses on both sides. General Bon was shot dead in the breach as he urged his men forward, and the irrepressible General Lannes was wounded, once again, as he and two companies of grenadiers managed to break into the city, only to discover that Ahmad Pasha's men had built an inner line of defences.

In the middle of the month Napoleon called his senior officers to a meeting in his tent late in the evening. He watched as they filed in through the flaps and quietly took their seats. The strain and exhaustion of the last sixty days was etched into their faces, and even before he asked them for their views Napoleon knew that the fight had gone out of them and he would have to perform a miracle to persuade them that Acre could be taken. The trouble was, he felt as bitter and tired as they did and he was momentarily tempted to break off the siege and return to Egypt without even asking for their assessment of the army's chances. Then some inner reserve of determination stirred in him and he resolved to try to persuade them that the fight could yet be won.

'Gentlemen . . .' Napoleon smiled faintly. 'Friends. Berthier tells me that the men are at the end of their endurance, that some of you are openly saying that we cannot take Acre, and that we must retreat. Does any man here wish to say anything?'

Junot stirred uncomfortably. 'Sir, it's been two months and we're no nearer taking Acre than we've ever been.'

'No nearer? I think you seriously underestimate what we have achieved so far. We've breached their walls and must have killed thousands of their men. One last—'

'Sir,' Lannes interrupted. He wore a bloodstained dressing around his head and looked pained and drawn as he spoke. 'They have built an inner wall. I've seen it. We'd have almost as much difficulty overwhelming that as we did the outer wall. And what does it matter how many of them we kill? Yesterday – we all saw it – a flotilla of ships dropped anchor out to sea and they've been ferrying in fresh supplies and troops all through the night and the following day. Sir, I'd follow you anywhere, you know I would. But this is a fight we cannot win.'

'General Lannes is right, sir,' added Berthier. 'While the enemy can keep being supplied by sea, we are running out of supplies here on land. We're also running low on ammunition and powder. More worrying still is this morning's report from Desgenettes. Nearly two and a half thousand of our men are now on the list of sick and wounded. Sir, the army is being bled white by this siege and the assaults we have attempted so far.' He would have said more, but he caught the wild glint in his commander's eye and the words died on his lips.

Napoleon stared round the table at his officers. 'Is there no man here who considers it our duty to continue the fight? Well?'

No one spoke and Napoleon suddenly realised he had lost them. If these men . . . if General Lannes, of all people, had lost faith in victory, then the attempt to take Acre truly was finished. He lowered his head into his hands for a moment and then looked up slowly and nodded.

'Very well . . . I accept your views. If *you* will not fight then no man will. I'll give the order . . . We'll break camp and march back to Egypt. The siege of Acre is over.'

Chapter 45

'*Having maintained ourselves in the heat of Syria for three months, with only a handful of men, after capturing forty guns and six thousand prisoners; after razing the fortifications of Gaza, Jaffa, Haifa and Acre, we shall return to Egypt. I am obliged to go back there because it is the season of the year when hostile landings may be expected.*'

Junot finished reading the proclamation aloud and Napoleon nodded with satisfaction. 'It strikes a suitably uplifting tone, I think.'

'Of course, sir,' Junot agreed in a measured voice. 'But the fact is that Acre is still in Turkish hands. I wonder if the men will really share your view of our, er, success?'

Napoleon frowned at his subordinate. 'I'm not a fool, Junot. I know we've failed. But I can hardly say that to the men, particularly as we face a hard march back to Egypt. But if they believe that I believe we have achieved something it will put some heart back into them. Got it?'

'Yes, sir.'

'Then have that copied and distributed to the army at once. On your way out, send Dr Desgenettes in.'

Junot saluted and strode through the tent flaps. Napoleon shifted uneasily on his chair. The next interview was going to be a difficult affair but there was no putting the matter off. As soon as the heavy guns had exhausted their ammunition they were to be spiked before the rearguard pulled back, following the rest of the army. Once the French army began to retreat the enemy would close up on them and harass the column all the way back to the fortified depot at Katia. The army would have to march as fast as it could, and that meant some sacrifices would have to be made, Napoleon reflected. He glanced up as a figure entered the tent.

'You sent for me, sir.' Dr Desgenettes stood hat in hand before Napoleon's desk. He looked pale and exhausted and there was several days' growth of stubble on his face.

'Yes. Sit down, doctor.' Napoleon clasped his hands together as he continued. 'You know that the army is about to break camp?'

Desgenettes nodded. 'Junot told me about the retreat, yes.'

Napoleon smiled faintly. 'The correct term is withdrawal, doctor . . . We will be abandoning the heavy guns, and any other burdens that might slow us down, and that's why I need to speak to you.'

Desgenettes looked confused for a moment before he realised what his commander was implying, and then his expression instantly changed to anger. 'The men in the hospital. You want to leave them behind? Have you any idea what the enemy will do to them, sir?'

'They could be treated fairly.'

'After what happened to the prisoners at Jaffa? If we left them to the Turks we'd be committing murder, sir.'

'Then, if we cannot take them with us, let's not leave them to the Turks.'

Desgenette's eyes narrowed. 'What are you suggesting, sir?'

Napoleon paused, frustrated that the man was forcing him to spell it out. 'I'm suggesting that for those men who are too sick to move, or who would slow us down, an overdose of opium might be the most humane solution.'

'You would kill our men?'

'Not me. You. I want this task carried out by someone who knows what to do.'

'Sir, I am a doctor – a healer, not a killer.'

'Is it not the case that a doctor's duty is to alleviate pain and suffering?'

'Do not dissemble with me, sir.' Desgenettes shook his head. 'I refuse to do it.'

'It is not a request. It is an order. If you disobey me you will be committing mutiny.'

Desgenettes slapped his chest. 'Then shoot me! I will not kill our countrymen.' He paused a moment and looked at Napoleon shrewdly. 'But then I'm forgetting. They're not your countrymen, sir.'

Napoleon took a sharp intake of breath. 'How dare you speak to me like that! Doctor, you forget yourself. I am your general and while you wear a uniform you are a soldier first and a doctor second.'

'My medical oath takes precedence, sir. In any and all circumstances. And you will have to shoot me and my staff before you reach my patients. Then you'll have to murder them yourselves. I hardly think the rest of the army will approve of such actions, however much they revere General Bonaparte.'

Napoleon glared at him for a long time, wanting more than anything to have this man immediately taken outside and shot for his insubordination, but he knew that the army would not stand for that. Desgenettes, like most doctors, enjoyed the respect, gratitude and open affection of the common soldiers. It would be dangerous to harm the man, Napoleon realised. He forced himself to smile.

'Very well, doctor, there are now over two thousand men on the sick list. How do you propose to move them?'

'A good number of them are walking wounded. The rest can be carried on horses, camels and stretchers. At least as far as Jaffa, where we can put them on ships.'

Napoleon considered the proposal. The siege would be lifted in three days. Time enough to move the sick and wounded to Jaffa. He looked at Desgenettes and nodded. 'Very well, doctor, you have convinced me. Make the arrangements immediately. You can draw on men from Lannes's division to act as stretcher-bearers. Now, leave me.'

The rearguard had spiked the siege guns during the night, and as dawn broke on 20 May huge columns of smoke billowed into the sky as General Reynier's men set fire to the supplies and equipment that were being abandoned by the French army. As soon as the rearguard pulled back, the Turks in Acre swarmed out of the gates to pursue them, forcing Reynier to skirmish all the way to Jaffa. Napoleon had arrived in the port a day earlier and was shocked to discover that only a handful of small ships remained. The houses and merchants' storerooms along the quay were packed with sick and wounded men.

'Where is Admiral Perée?' he demanded.

'The admiral sailed for Alexandria yesterday, sir,' Berthier replied.

'Why? I gave him orders to take Desgenette's patients on board.'

'The admiral said he could not risk having any plague victims on his ships. He also said that he must leave before the Royal Navy blockaded the port.'

'Damn the admiral to hell,' Napoleon muttered in fury as he gazed at the men slumped in the shade along the quay. The transfer of the sick and injured from Acre had exhausted the patients, and those assigned to help them. Only a small number of them could be found berths in the vessels that remained in the harbour.

'Tell Desgenettes to have the worst cases loaded on to these ships as soon as possible. Those who are too sick to move, and those who are least likely to recover, are to remain in Jaffa. Tell him that they must be dealt with humanely after all.'

Berthier looked at him curiously but Napoleon just shook his head. 'Don't worry, he'll understand the order well enough.'

As the last ships put to sea Napoleon and the rest of the army began the march south along the coast. The wounded who were forced to walk did their best to keep up, and for the first few days their comrades did all that they could to help them along. Then, as exhaustion, hunger and thirst began to take their toll on the men, the weakest were left to fend for themselves, and the tormented cries of stragglers taken and tortured by the enemy haunted the men gathered round the campfires each night. The army trudged into Gaza on the last day of May and filled their canteens and haversacks with the remainder of the rations as they steeled themselves for the crossing of the Sinai desert.

By day the Sinai was smothered by blistering heat that sapped the very last dregs of energy from the men as they limped forward with cracked lips and parched throats. Those of the injured who died were unceremoniously pitched into the sand and left to feed the carrion that swirled in lazy circles as they followed the army across the wasteland. Discipline became as fragile as the bodies that depended on it, and the hostility of the men was evident in their glares and the bitter tone of their muttering whenever Napoleon and his staff rode by. So Napoleon gave up his horse to help carry the wounded, and ordered his staff to do the same, and they walked the rest of the way, alongside the straggling columns of their men.

At last, four days later, the first soldiers arrived at Katia, under the horrified gaze of those watching from the walls of the fortified village. The men of the army that had invaded Syria were barely comprehensible as they croaked their requests for food and water, and when these were brought to them they tore at the food and drank like wild animals.

As Napoleon watched them emerge from the desert and sink down in the shade of Katia's buildings he had little doubt that the army bore the brand of defeat. Nearly two and a half thousand had died in battle or of the plague. A similar number were sick or wounded, and would not be fit to serve again for some weeks, if at all. Over a third of the army that had set out in high spirits to carve a swath through the Turkish empire had been lost, and would not be replaced.

That much was clear now. There would be no fleet sent from France with reinforcements. Napoleon and his army had been abandoned by the Directory, something the men would realise soon enough. And when they did his authority over them would be tenuous at best. Napoleon had no desire to let Egypt be the end of his career. The future, his future, lay back in Europe. The question was, how could he justify leaving his army and returning to France?

As he pondered this question, Napoleon let his shattered army rest for several days. Uniforms were cleaned and patched.

Weapons were issued to those who had lost theirs and the men set to polishing their buttons and whitening their cross belts in preparation for the triumphal entry into Cairo that Napoleon announced to his men shortly before the understrength battalions began their march from Katia across the Nile delta to the capital. The celebrations, speeches, awards of decorations and presentations of swords and prizes lasted the whole day, and then the men were issued with the very last of the wine and spirits that had been landed with the army nearly a year ago. As the streets of Cairo echoed with the shouts and laughter of drunken revellers Napoleon retired to his bechamber with Pauline Fourès.

'Can't you have someone tell them to be quiet?' Pauline nodded to the shutters as she unlaced her bodice, and flung it across the back of a chair. 'Thank God I'm out of that. I thought those ceremonies would never end.'

'Pauline, right now I need to give them anything I can to help bolster their spirits. After the Syrian experience, and the revolts Desaix had to deal with in my absence, their morale has never been lower. They've not seen France for over a year, and as things stand they don't know when they will again. So you do as I say and humour them.'

'Very well.' Her lips opened in a seductive smile. 'Now, can I humour you, my general?'

Napoleon crossed over to her and enclosed her bare body in his embrace, relishing the smooth skin of her back as he ran a hand down towards her hip.

'You've no idea how much I have missed this.'

'This?' She laughed playfully and reached a hand behind to pat her bottom. 'Just this?'

'Just that.' He laughed, and she playfully swatted his shoulder. 'And all that is attached to it.'

A sudden outburst of singing rose up from the street outside Napoleon's garden and Pauline turned towards the shutters again. 'I can't be passionate with that racket going on.'

'Then don't be passionate.' Napoleon led her towards the bed and started pulling off his clothes. 'Get on the bed.'

Pauline raised her eyebrows in amusement, but did as she was told. As she lay bathed in the moonlight that pierced the shutters, Napoleon tore off his boots, then stockings, trousers and underwear in one, and climbed on top of her, pushing her thighs apart and penetrating her with a gasp of pleasure, and then making love to her as vigorously as he had ever done to any woman before.

'I think you really needed that,' Pauline smiled shortly afterwards. 'I take it there weren't too many available women on campaign?'

'Not enough to go round. In any case, I was busy fighting a war.'

Pauline was silent for a moment, before she continued softly, 'Was it as bad as they say? I've heard some terrible stories in the last few days.'

'They're all true.' Napoleon rolled off her, made himself comfortable on his side and then rested his head on her soft stomach. 'The Army of the Orient is all but finished. We can hold on for a few more months, maybe a year. But disease and the fighting will see to us all in the end. Unless we quit Egypt.'

'Quit Egypt? How? We have no ships and the Directory will not send us any more.' Pauline stroked his head. 'Anyway, is it so bad here? I've never been happier, living in a palace, with a famous general as a lover. All that would be lost if I returned home.'

'Unless I return to France I will not be a famous general much longer,' Napoleon replied quietly. 'I must get back to France. I am needed there.'

'You're needed here. I need you. Your men need you. If you left, how long do you think they would last?'

'France's need is greater.'

'Your need, you mean.'

Napoleon shrugged. 'It is the same thing at the end of the day. Or will be.'

'What do you mean?'

'Nothing.' Napoleon propped himself up and looked at her with a grin. 'I need you again.'

'What a romantic you are.' Pauline narrowed her eyes. 'You've spent far too much time in the company of that lot.' She jerked her thumb towards the shutters.

Napoleon chuckled and eased himself on to his back, pulling her over on top of him. As Pauline felt his penis hardening, she ground herself down on him and whispered, 'Promise me. When you leave Egypt, you'll take me with you.'

'Who said I was leaving?'

'Just promise me.'

'All right then, I promise.' Napoleon smiled. 'Now, no more teasing. Make me forget everything that exists outside this room.'

Just three weeks after the celebrations of the army's return to Cairo a Turkish fleet, escorted by Sir Sidney Smith's squadron, anchored in Aboukir Bay and began to land troops. As soon as General Kléber's messenger arrived he was ushered into Napoleon's presence. Napoleon glanced through the dispatch and looked up at the dusty messenger. 'You are to return at once. Tell Kléber not to confront them. He is to wait in Alexandria until I join him with the rest of the forces we can spare. He is to avoid battle under any circumstances. Clear?'

'Yes, sir.'

'Then go.'

As the messenger saluted, turned and strode away Napoleon rapped out a series of orders to Berthier to prepare the army to march immediately. They left Cairo the same day that the news had arrived, ten thousand infantry and a thousand cavalry under Murat. They took six days to march up the Nile as far as Rahmaniya and then cut across the desert towards Aboukir. At any moment Napoleon was expecting news that the enemy had marched on Alexandria, yet there was no message from Kléber and Napoleon could not help wondering if that was because Kléber was already under siege, or, worse, had already been overwhelmed. As they drew near to Alexandria, Napoleon rode ahead with his staff until they had Aboukir in view. The bay was filled with Turkish ships, and towering above them were the masts and spars of two warships of the Royal Navy. On the point overlooking the western approach to the bay stood a fortress.

Clearly visible on its ramparts, and teeming across the narrow strip of land that linked the fortress to the mainland, were the enemy forces.

'It doesn't look as if they've moved since stepping ashore,' Berthier mused. 'There must be ten . . . maybe fifteen thousand of them. They could have taken Alexandria with ease. What the hell are they still doing here?'

'I can't see any horses,' Napoleon said as he gazed through his telescope. 'There's your answer. Their cavalry must still be at sea.'

'No cavalry?' Murat sounded disappointed and Napoleon smiled.

'Never mind, Murat. You will have to content yourself with the enemy's infantry. Berthier, go back to the army and order the men to march on Aboukir. We'll attack as soon as they are in line.'

'What about Kléber's division, sir? Shall I send for him?'

'No. We can't afford to wait. If any of those ships in the bay are carrying horses, they'll have a chance to land them if we wait for Kléber.'

Berthier turned his horse and galloped back towards the faint column of dust that marked the head of the French army approaching across the desert. As Napoleon continued to examine the Turkish positions it was clear that they had made extensive additions to the defences of the fortress, and dug three lines of trenches, supported by several bastions, across the neck of land, each of which was defended by thousands of soldiers. Janissaries, Napoleon surmised, if this army had been transported from Turkey.

He lowered his telescope and shook his head. 'It's hard to believe that they have just sat on their backsides and handed the initiative to us. What kind of general would be so foolish?'

'One who is about to be kicked into the sea,' Murat grinned.

As the French army deployed in front of the first trench the Turkish troops began to beat their drums and the harsh blare of trumpets sounded across the dusty open ground between the armies. Some of the enemy guns, mounted in the nearest bastions, opened fire but the range was long and the heavy iron balls merely kicked up plumes of sand and grit well ahead of the first French line. The moment the last unit was in position Napoleon gave the order to attack, starting with Lannes on the left flank. The guns of Lannes's division advanced towards the enemy and unlimbered. Moments later the first cannon boomed out across the open ground as they pounded the embrasures of the nearest bastion. Once the enemy guns were knocked out General Lannes gave the order to advance, and with colours unfurled and drums beating the battalions of his division rolled forward.

As the French bombardment ceased the janissaries rose up in their trenches and raised their muskets. There was no attempt to hold fire until the French had approached to within lethally close range and the Turkish troops wasted their first shots in a ragged crackle of musketry that felled only a handful of men before Lannes's division reached the first trench and halted to pour a single devastating volley into the dense ranks of the enemy massed before them. The effect was just as Napoleon had envisaged and as the gunpowder smoke cleared in the sea breeze, he saw that the enemy had broken and were streaming back towards the second trench. The panic spread along the first line, so that General Destaing's brigade did not even have the chance to fire at the enemy opposite them before they too broke and ran to the shelter of the next line of defence.

From his horse Napoleon could see that the men of the second line were made of sterner stuff and withheld their first volley until the attacking columns were close. The shattering effect of their fire stalled Lannes's men a short distance from the second trench, and they deployed into line and exchanged fire with the janissaries. As he watched, Napoleon noticed a peculiar aspect of the fight. Every so often, a janissary would leap out of his trench and race towards the nearest French body. Most were shot down before they reached the corpses, but one, faster than his comrades, raced forward, swung his curved blade down and cut off the head, which he tucked under his arm as he turned and sprinted back to his own lines. He didn't make it. A shot caught him in the centre of the back and he pitched forward and twitched feebly on the ground.

Even though he did not doubt that the enemy's second line would cave in before the disciplined fire of the French troops, Napoleon did not want to lose any more men than necessary and decided the time had come for Murat's cavalry to deliver the blow that would shatter the enemy's will to continue the fight. As soon as the order was received, Murat trotted his horse to the front of the cavalry formation and bellowed the command to advance. It was as brave a sight as Napoleon had ever seen, and he felt his heart swell with pride, and only a little anxiety, as the lines of horsemen walked forward, slowly gathering pace as they crossed the abandoned first line of defence, then breaking into a trot before finally charging the enemy.

Murat's cavalry tore into and through the second line, scattering the Turkish forces before them. Sabres glittered in the midday sun as the horsemen hacked and slashed at the fleeing men. Fear preceded them and the Turks in the last trench turned and ran without even firing a shot. Clambering out of their positions, some made for the safety of the fortress above them; many more ran towards the beach and waded out into the surf, hoping to swim to safety. The cavalry rode after them until the sea was up to the flanks of their mounts, and all the time the riders were cutting down the men in the water around them, turning it red as the day wore on.

The killing stopped late in the afternoon and Napoleon rode forward with Berthier to inspect the battlefield. Thousands of enemy dead lay piled in the trenches and scattered across the open ground between. Mingled with them were the French dead and wounded and Napoleon hurriedly detailed the nearest soldiers to help their injured comrades down to the dressing stations Desgenettes had established just behind the army's original battle line. Over a thousand of the enemy had managed to reach the fortress and even now General Menou was busy reversing the defences of the last trench so that the defenders were now trapped there. As night fell, Napoleon returned to his tent to dictate a report of the battle to be sent to the Directory aboard the fast packet ship that communicated between France and Alexandria, when it could be assured of a route clear of English warships. The victory at Aboukir had smashed the Sultan's chances of driving the French out of Egypt for the next year, or possibly two. Napoleon phrased his report with the usual glowing praise for the gallantry of the men and their commanders. It was true the French had suffered nearly a thousand casualties, but they had smashed the cream of the Sultan's forces.

The next day an envoy landed from the Turkish fleet still anchored in the bay, asking permission to collect the Turkish wounded and take them on board the ships to carry them home. At first Napoleon was tempted to deny the request. But there had been more than enough suffering already, and he relented. As the Turkish seamen began to load the wounded janissaries aboard the ships' boats being held steady in the surf, the envoy approached with a package of newspapers bound with string tucked under one arm. He paused a short distance from Napoleon as the guides relieved him of his sword, knife and pistol, then continued forward, proffering the bundled newspapers.

'My master, Sir Sidney Smith, bids me to offer these to you in gratitude for the return of our wounded. They are the latest editions to reach the fleet, and are as current as anything that General Bonaparte's army has read in months.'

'The Directory is losing the war,' Napoleon announced to his inner circle of senior officers: Berthier, Lannes and Murat. He had summoned them to his office as soon as he had returned to Cairo. The contents of the newspapers Smith had sent him had been carefully sifted before being circulated via the army's official journal, and only a handful of men had been permitted to know the full details of events in Europe. Napoleon did not bother to hide his bitterness as he continued. 'Almost everything that we gained in Italy has been lost to Austria. In Germany our armies have been beaten back towards the French border and in Paris the factions plot against each other with no thought of the men fighting and dying for France. The war will be lost, the revolution will be crushed and France will return to the tyranny of the

Bourbons, unless the situation changes.' He paused and glanced round at the others. 'Or unless the situation is changed, by us.'

Berthier coughed. 'By us? How can we change anything from here, sir? You've said it yourself, we have been abandoned by the Directory. They might as well have forgotten we exist.'

'Very well, then,' Napoleon responded. 'If we can't influence events from Egypt, then we must return to France.'

Murat laughed. 'Return to France? And how do you propose we do that, sir? March the army back into Syria, through Turkey, across the Balkans, over the Alps, and back through Italy? I warrant we'd get as far as the Sinai before the troops mutinied and shot us all.'

'Then we go by ourselves, and leave the army here.'

The three generals looked at Napoleon in shocked silence. It was Lannes who responded first. 'Abandon the army?'

'They would hardly be abandoned,' Napoleon countered. 'I will leave Kléber in command. After the defeat at Aboukir Bay it'll be a while before the Turks mount any further invasions. If the situation here worsens then the army can be evacuated at a later date. I give my word on that.'

'As long as you can persuade the Directory to send the ships.'

'My dear Lannes.' Napoleon smiled. 'I think the Directory is a spent force in France. The people, and more important the army, are desperate for a change. They crave a government with the will to act decisively and save the revolution. France needs strong men, now more than ever. It is our patriotic duty to return to France and do what we can to save her.'

There was a moment's silence before Berthier said, 'My general, you know I would follow you anywhere, but what exactly do you intend to do if . . . when we reach France, when we reach Paris?'

'It's impossible to say exactly. We'll have to see what the situation is when we arrive. But let's assume, for the moment, that conditions are ripe for leading France in a new direction.' Napoleon's eyes glinted as he opened his hands to gesture to his three subordinates. 'Why should it not be we who determine the course of that new direction? Are we not patriots? Have we not risked our lives for France on the battlefield? Who better, or more deserving, to lead the nation forward to victory, and peace?'

Lannes shook his head. 'You are talking treason, sir.'

'Treason? What have I ever done to betray France? No. This is not treason. Treason is what those corrupt politicians in Paris practise every day they mismanage the war and drive our people into poverty.' Napoleon stabbed his finger down on the table. 'The time for change has come, Lannes. All that matters now is to determine which side you are on.'

Lannes looked at Napoleon with a hurt expression. 'General, I am on your side, and at your side, whatever happens, until the day I die.'

Napoleon nodded. 'Thank you. And you, Berthier? Murat? Are you with me?'

'Yes, sir.'

'Then it is settled. Never forget, my friends, that we do this for France, and for no other reason.'

'When do we leave?' asked Berthier. 'I will need time to plan for the transfer of authority to Kléber, and to brief my replacement here.'

'There will be no mention of this to anyone outside this room,' said Napoleon. 'If word got out then the morale of the men would sink like a rock. We'd risk a mutiny.' He lowered his voice a little. 'There are two frigates at Alexandria, provisioned and ready to sail at a moment's notice. In addition to you three, I will be taking my personal servant, Roustam, some of my household staff, a few good officers and two hundred picked men of the guides. None of them are in the know. Tomorrow, we leave Cairo, ostensibly on a tour of our outposts on the Nile delta. We will make straight for Alexandria, board the ships and set sail.'

Berthier was stunned. 'But when will you inform Kléber?'

'I will send him a message as we embark.'

Lannes took a sharp breath. 'Can you imagine how he will react? The man will be incandescent.'

'That can't be helped,' replied Napoleon. 'We have to put France first, ahead of our friends and comrades. It is painful, shameful even. I accept that, but it is necessary. I am sure all of you understand that. Now, time is short, my friends. You must take as little away with you as possible; we cannot afford to arouse suspicion. Be ready to leave at dawn tomorrow.'

'How long will you be away?' asked Pauline as Napoleon dressed himself beside their bed by the light of a lamp. Outside the sun had not yet risen.

'No more than two weeks.'

'Good. After last night, I can hardly wait to have you back in my arms.' She smiled dreamily, recalling the frenzied lovemaking, and the tenderness of her general as she lay in his arms afterwards. She raised her arms towards him. 'One last kiss, before you go.'

Napoleon hesitated as he looked down at her. Pauline lay there, in the twisted sheets, with all the drowsy beauty and allure of the recently awoken, and he felt his passion for her stirring again. Only now it was tempered by the imminence of his betrayal. Still, it was better that she suspected nothing. Napoleon smiled, climbed on to the bed and kissed her on the mouth, responding in kind as Pauline's tongue darted between his lips. At length he eased himself up, picked up his hat and sash and made for the door.

'Don't take too long, my love,' Pauline called softly after him. 'Return as soon as you can.'

'I will,' Napoleon replied, and then the door closed behind him.

Outside, in the courtyard, the rest of the officers and men were waiting for their commander. Napoleon mounted his horse and urged it forward. As the small column headed out of the gate, he glanced back once, and saw, as he knew he would, Pauline's silhouette at the window of their bedchamber. She waved and blew him a kiss, and he lifted his hat, and then turned his back on her and spurred his horse into a trot as he led his companions down the darkened street.

Chapter 46

Arthur

Amboor, India, February 1799

When General Harris and his army reached the range of hills known as the eastern Ghats they found the reinforcements sent by the Nizam waiting for them. True to the word of the new treaty he had signed with Britain, the Nizam had sent the six Company battalions in addition to several of the units formerly commanded by French officers, and over ten thousand cavalry. The army was under the command of the Nizam's senior minister, Mear Allum, and was almost as large as that of General Harris. When they marched to war against Tipoo, Harris decided, they would advance in separate columns so as not to make the entire force too unwieldy.

As the general explained at a briefing to his senior officers, 'This is the first time that a British army has been able to operate independently in India, thanks to the arrangements that Colonel Wellesley was able to make with the *brinjarri* merchants. The difficulty is that, in addition to the soldiers, we will have over a hundred thousand camp followers. If we marched in one formation the vanguard would have made camp and turned in for the night long before the rearguard even struck their tents.'

It was no exaggeration, but even so a number of the officers smiled at the image and Harris indulged them before reluctantly moving on to the unavoidable implication of marching in two columns. He coughed, then looked around the tent before his gaze fixed on the slight figure of Mear Allum, neatly dressed in flowing white robes. 'Even though the Nizam places great faith in Mear Allum, as do I, we have agreed that the Nizam's army would benefit from having a King's regiment assigned to it, and a British officer to act as adviser to its commander, Mear Allum.'

The Nizam's senior minister nodded politely. 'I thank you for your most courteous and generous description of my role, but I will be commander in name only. The day to day running of the Nizam's army, and the command of it in battle, will be the job of the British officer.'

'As you say.' General Harris bowed his head and smiled at Mear Allum. 'And I thank you, and the Nizam, for your forbearance in this matter. While I have every confidence in the men and officers of the Nizam's army, it is essential that they are commanded by someone familiar with the operational practices of the British army. My original intention was to appoint Colonel Ashton to the post, and since – tragically – he is no longer with us, the logical choice for the position is Colonel Wellesley.'

Arthur had been honest enough with himself to admit that he craved the appointment, but since there were several officers senior to him in the army, he had thought that his aspiration was futile. Now he was genuinely surprised and started in his seat.

'Me, sir?'

General Harris smiled. 'Yes, Colonel. Of course, I am aware that there are officers here with more experience, and seniority, than you, but in my view such men will be most needed in the main column, under my command. Since they are in charge of more than one regiment, to detach any one of these officers would disrupt the order of battle, whereas you are a regimental commander, and therefore both you and the 33rd can be detached without undue restructuring of the chain of command.'

It was a carefully worked response and Arthur quicky realised that the explanation was designed to appease those officers who held higher rank than he did.

'Begging your pardon, sir,' a deep voice boomed from the side of the tent, and everyone turned towards the massive figure of

Major General David Baird. Baird was well known to those who had served in India for any length of time. He had a reputation as a fine soldier: brave, strong and with an endurance that had seen him through three years of captivity in the dungeons of Seringapatam.

'You have something to say about the appointment?' asked General Harris.

Baird's neck stiffened as he folded his arms and responded. 'Indeed, sir. The scope of responsibility offered by the post is far from insignificant. Why, the man chosen would be in effective command of a force of over twenty thousand men! That is no command for a mere colonel, sir.' Baird paused and glanced towards Arthur. 'No offence meant there, Wellesley. You're as fine a young fellow as any man who might make general one day. But this ain't the time.' He turned back to Harris. 'It's a job for a more senior officer, sir. That's as clear as day.'

'Someone like yourself, perhaps?'

Baird shrugged his broad shoulders. 'Me, or an officer of my rank. But since I have had some experience of Mysore I'm confident that I am the best man for the job.'

'Your experience was largely confined to Seringapatam, if you'll pardon the pun.'

Baird frowned for a moment. 'I've seen more than just Tipoo's capital, sir . . . Ah, I see now.' Now that he had the quip, Baird bristled indignantly. 'Prisoner I may have been, but that stain on my memory is one that I am more than keen to wash away with the blood of my enemies. You could hardly ask for a soldier more dedicated to crushing Tipoo, sir. That's recommendation enough.'

'Desire for revenge might be an admirable quality in certain situations, my dear Baird, but not now. I have made my decision and you must accept it.'

'I'm damned if I will, sir!' Baird thrust his head forward. 'I'll not be passed over for the younger brother of—'

'That is enough, Baird!' General Harris slammed his hand down on the table. 'You will still your tongue, sir!'

Baird seemed on the verge of losing his temper, but through sheer force of will managed to clamp his mouth shut as he sat back heavily in his chair. Harris took a deep breath. 'Gentlemen, the briefing is over for today. Be so good as to take your leave. Major General Baird, please remain. And you, Colonel Wellesley.'

The other officers rose and left the tent quietly, and when the last of them had disappeared through the tent flaps Harris beckoned the two remaining men to move closer.

'Now then, Baird.' He spoke with forced civility. 'I do not want to witness such a display in front of the other officers ever again. Do I make myself clear?'

'Yes, sir.'

'Good. If ever you think you have reason to disagree with me, then you may make your protest in a private interview. Nowhere else. I will not have my authority questioned in front of other officers. If you disappoint me in this way again, Baird, then I will have you sent back to Madras to fill in requisition forms for the rest of the war. That would be a shame, of course, as the army could well use your fighting qualities.'

'Then give me command of the Nizam's column, sir.'

'Damn you, Baird. Have you not listened to what I've said? I have made my decision,' he added, with deliberate stress on each word.

'Aye, and I don't suppose that decision has anything to do with this laddie's being the brother of the Governor General?'

Arthur blushed and turned towards Baird with a frigid expression of disdain. 'If I thought for a moment that I was being preferred for reasons of nepotism, then I would have no hesitation in turning down the position, sir.'

'And what other reasons might there be, I wonder?' Baird sneered.

'Very well then!' Harris snapped. 'I'll tell you the reasons. Wellesley has taken the time to learn one of the languages of the natives. He has befriended some of them, and many others respect him and hold him in high regard. He has moulded his regiment into the finest body of men on this continent, and I trust he will be a fine commander of the Nizam's army.'

'So what if the lad speaks the darkies' tongue, sir,' Baird

protested. 'So what if he's chumming up to them? We're here to fight the bastards, not fraternise with them!'

Harris stared at his fiery subordinate with icy contempt. 'It's that attitude which disqualifies you, above all men, for the job. I need a man with tact, with a diplomatic touch, every bit as much as I need an officer who can lead men into battle. And I'm lucky that all those qualities abound within Colonel Wellesley. If you want the truth, Baird, I chose him because he is simply the best man for the job, and I will not let another man supersede Wellesley after all he has achieved simply because he is out-ranked. Now, there is no more to discuss. I have made my decision and you will accept it. You are dismissed, Baird. Please leave my tent.'

Baird stood up abruptly, knocking his chair back on to the ground. He nodded curtly to his superior, ignored Arthur point-edly, and strode outside fuming with indignation and hurt pride.

Once he had gone General Harris's shoulders slumped and he took a deep breath before he spoke to Arthur. 'It is a shame to have to address him in such a fashion. Baird's a fine soldier, and the men look up to him like a father. But in a sensitive situation he has all the social skills of a fighting dog. Worse still, he makes no attempt to hide his dislike of India and every native that lives here. If he was placed in charge of the Nizam's army I fear we would be at war with the Nizam before the first day's march was out.' Harris leaned forward and looked closely at Arthur. 'You, on the other hand, have precisely the qualities needed for the job: patience, diligence and integrity. I've been a soldier long enough to know that you are rather more than a cut above most officers, Colonel Wellesley. That this is so evident to others may well be more of a curse than a boon to you. I am well aware that many officers in this army are inclined to believe the worst of you, simply because you are Mornington's brother and a better man than the rest of them. Another general might have used that as an excuse to hold you back.' Harris's smile returned. 'But I am not another general. I'm a general with a war to fight and win, and everything is subordinate to the bloody defeat and destruction of my enemy, no matter whose feelings I have to hurt.'

Arthur grinned. 'Thank you, sir. I won't let you down.'

'You had better not,' Harris said seriously. 'This is your chance to do great things, Wellesley. You richly deserve it. But if you fail, there will never again be an opportunity like this. You will ruin yourself utterly, and in doing so you will fail your brother, and fatally damage his chances for greatness along with yours.'

'Why, sir? Any mistakes I make are surely my own.'

'No,' Harris said sadly. 'That is not how it works. By taking this command you lay yourself open to charges of nepotism. If you succeed, men will only think that if you could have done it, then so could any man. If you fail, then men will say you were unfit for the task, and that your brother put family above country, and for that there is no forgiveness or pity.'

Arthur pondered this for a while, and then he nodded. 'I understand. And I accept the position willingly.'

'You accept?' Harris looked bemused. 'There is no question of your accepting the position. It is an order.'

Arthur laughed. 'Yes, sir.'

Chapter 47

The army advanced along the Baramahal valley, which led west from Amboor. The floor of the valley was wide and flat and dotted with small low-rising groves of trees, or topes, so that the army made good progress. Arthur's column marched on the left, three miles from Harris. In between the two forces sprawled the vast train of *brinjarris*, the families of the sepoys and merchants and traders of all kinds. With them lumbered strings of bullocks, horses, camels, mules and here and there the grey swaying masses of elephants. A huge cloud of dust rose up in the wake of this host, announcing the approach of the army for a great distance. Each day they covered ten miles before camping for the night. Then the merchants moved through the tent lines selling curried tripe, sop, and boiled sausages to the hungry soldiers.

In the morning the sepoys used straw to light the morning fires, and fuelled the fires with cow dung that filled the air with its rich cloying odour. The shrill chatter of the women camp followers rose up on all sides as they hurriedly prepared a morning meal for their families, and then packed their belongings for the day's trek to the next camp.

Arthur regarded the apparent chaos of the camp with a degree of tolerance, since the writ of British military discipline extended only to the 33rd Foot and the six Company sepoy battalions. The rest were native levies with their own customs. The men of the 33rd were enjoying the status of being the elite formation in such a large force and marched with a swagger that pleased their colonel greatly. When the time came to fight they would inspire the other battalions and the Nizam's men to hold their places in the line.

When they reached the Ryacotta pass the wagons and guns ascended the slope on the road prepared for them by Harris's engineers, while the infantry and camp followers climbed over the broken ground on either side. Once through the eastern ghats the army was in the territory of Mysore and at once small groups of enemy horsemen began to shadow the columns. Tipoo's strategy was apparent the moment the army approached Kellamungallam. A huge pall of smoke hung over the remains of the city. Vast swaths of buildings had been burned and the defences pulled down or blown up. Beyond the city the route before General Harris's army had been torched.

'Tipoo has clearly decided to pull his soldiers back to defend Seringapatam,' General Harris concluded, as he addressed his senior officers once the army had camped a short distance from the charred ruins of Kellamungallam. 'He aims to lure us through his lands, denying us forage on the way, in the hope that we will fail to lay siege to his capital for long enough to take it, just as Cornwallis failed the last time a British army attempted to defeat Mysore.'

Baird interrupted. 'And what will make our attempt succeed where Cornwallis failed, sir?'

'I was coming to that. Or rather, I was about to ask Colonel Wellesley to outline the progress of the campaign from this point, since he and his staff were largely responsible for the plan. Colonel?'

'Thank you, sir.' Arthur stood up and paused a moment to collect his thoughts before he spoke. It still felt strange to be addressing a gathering of senior officers, most of whom were his superiors and older and more experienced than he was. Yet he did not doubt himself, since every possible contingency had been considered when the campaign was still in its planning stage. He cleared his throat. 'Tipoo knows that he would be defeated if he risked a pitched battle against us. So he has adopted the strategy of trying to starve our draught animals. I've spoken to the *brinjarri* chiefs and they assure me that their bullocks can eat a wide variety of grasses and plants. Tipoo's men cannot possibly destroy all edible matter growing in our path. Nevertheless, they will eventually restrict the supply. Therefore, I have advised the general that, if forage runs short, the army will be obliged to move outside the corridor of land that Tipoo's men have burned. Meanwhile, in order to prevent our forage parties from venturing off the cleared land, we can expect Tipoo's cavalry to launch harassing attacks from now on. Your men will need to take the necessary precautions once we leave Kellamungallam. The ground favours the enemy. It is flat and open for the most part, with scattered groves of trees for cover. We will need to keep our wits about us as we close on Seringapatam.'

'Thank you, Colonel.' General Harris gestured to him to resume his seat. 'From now on, gentlemen, the enemy will be surrounding us. It is our duty to make sure we do not present him with the smallest opportunity to wreck our enterprise.'

The advance continued steadily through Mysore, over the ground that Tipoo's men had burned, until late in the month, when Harris ordered the army to turn south-west and make directly for Seringapatam. Within a few miles they moved out of the belt of destruction and into country where there was abundant forage. The sudden change in direction threw off the harassing parties of enemy horsemen and it was two days before they were sighted again. After their early losses the enemy kept their distance and made no attempt to close with Arthur's column. There was no sign of any of Tipoo's infantry or artillery and it seemed to Arthur that these must be waiting in the enemy capital to repulse the British army when it finally laid siege to the city.

For four days the army marched towards Seringapatam, along a road hemmed in by dense jungle interspersed with flat country thickly dotted with clumps of trees. As his column advanced Arthur was constantly on the watch for signs of the enemy. This was the kind of country where Tipoo's men could hold up the British army with ease. Long enough to prevent them from reaching and taking Seringapatam before the monsoon season struck. But there were no ambushes, no attacks of any kind, and the army continued its march without interruption until it approached the large village of Malavalley late one afternoon.

The jungle had given way to land that was largely clear of trees. Arthur was riding near the head of his column when he heard the dull thud of distant guns, and a moment later a divot of earth flew into the air some distance beyond his foremost troops. Spurring Diomed forward he drew out his telescope and trained it on the low hills on the far side of Malavalley. The puffs of smoke that hung in the still air gave away the enemy artillery positions. As Arthur turned his attention to the enemy guns he saw dense formations of infantry on the slope below the guns and, on the top of the hill, the unmistakable shapes of elephants.

He lowered his telescope and pulled out his pocket watch. If Tipoo's forces stood their ground there was still time to attack them before the day was out. He turned to his small group of staff officers. 'Lieutenant Beaumont!'

'Sir?'

'Ride to General Harris and tell him that I have sighted the enemy. He may have reports of the sighting from his own men by the time you arrive, but tell him that I respectfully suggest that we attack the enemy at once, before they withdraw under cover of night.'

While he waited for a response Arthur quickly gave orders for his men to prepare for battle. The 33rd Foot and the six sepoy battalions marched forward and deployed in company columns facing the hills where the enemy waited, occasionally chancing a long shot from some of their heaviest guns. The Nizam's infantry units formed up to the left of the 33rd and the cavalry took up their position on the flanks. As he watched them manoeuvre Arthur prayed that General Harris would seize the chance to attack the enemy. Given that there were only a few hours of light left in which to fight a pitched battle, it was possible that Harris might wait until dawn, by which time the enemy could easily have melted away.

The army was just completing its deployment when General Harris rode up.

'Wellesley!' He smiled as he greeted his subordinate, then gestured to the men drawn up on either side. 'You're a step ahead of me. I got your message and my men are forming to your right. Baird's brigade will be closest to you. I had thought to camp for the night and tackle them tomorrow. But, as we have the enemy in sight, it would be foolish not to give him a thrashing.'

Arthur felt a surge of relief at his superior's words, and nodded. 'Very well, sir. What are your plans?'

'Nothing clever. No need to do much more than let good training and stout hearts have their way. We'll advance on the ridge and take it. The cavalry will screen our flanks and keep Tipoo's rascals at bay with those galloper guns you allocated to our lads.'

'Very good, sir.'

'All right then, Wellesley. I'll be off to take up position in the centre. As soon as you hear our guns fire, you can begin to advance. Don't waste any time. We have to force the enemy to fight before they lose their nerve.'

Once the general had gone, Arthur and Fitzroy rode up and down the line to make sure that the men were properly spaced. Almost at once there was the crack of a light gun away to the right.

Fitzroy muttered, 'Bloody hell, that was quick. If it was the signal, that is.'

Arthur glanced to the right and saw that Baird's brigade had started forward. 'Well, if it wasn't the signal, it is now.' He filled his lungs and called out, 'Fix bayonets!'

The men neatly reached for their bayonets, drew them out and slotted them on to the ends of their muskets. Back in Europe bayonets would only be fixed once it was clear that any exchange of fire was over. But here in Mysore, where the enemy cavalry could appear and disappear in an instant, Arthur decided that his men might only have the chance to fire once before they were charged.

'The line will advance, at the quick step!'

The men advanced as one, weapons resting on their shoulders as they stamped through the calf-high grass towards the ridge. Once again, Arthur rode down the line and returned to the 33rd, delighted to see that they had pulled ahead of Baird's brigade. Up ahead of them the men of Tipoo's army were chanting their war cries, and brandishing their weapons. The artillery on the hill continued to fire, and as the gap narrowed they drew first blood as a ball ricocheted off the hard-baked soil and ploughed through a file of men on the flank of Baird's brigade. Arthur tore his eyes away from the mangled bodies sprawling on the ground and looked ahead to calculate the point at which he would order his men to deploy into a firing line as they closed on the enemy. There was a slight fold in the ground three hundred yards from the nearest enemy unit and as soon as the 33rd reached it Arthur shouted the order to form line. At once the regiment slowed and the rear companies doubled obliquely to the left and forward to catch up with the right flank until, in a matter of minutes, the whole regiment was in a line, two men deep. The sepoy battalions formed up on the left, in echelon, as the 33rd continued forwards.

Arthur felt a surge of pride as he watched. The years of training and nurturing his men were paying off handsomely. There had been skirmishes before but this was their first pitched battle as part of an army, and suddenly he felt a thrill of pleasure and excitement that he had never experienced before. All those years of playing at being a soldier, and being painfully aware of it, fell away from him and at last Arthur truly felt that he belonged in uniform and that this was his calling.

There was a great roar from the crest of the hill and Arthur instantly abandoned his reverie as he saw a large mass of Tipoo's men, perhaps as many as three thousand, surge forward down the slope, directly towards the men of the 33rd Foot. This was it then, he realised. The moment for which he had been preparing his men, and himself. The redcoats did not hesitate for an instant when they saw the wave of enemy warriors rushing towards them. Arthur was about to shout some words of encouragement to his men, but realised that none were needed. They knew their profession well enough to be above the influence of platitudes and homilies. Any words he offered would only be taken as a sign of his nervousness. Arthur smiled. He had no nerves, no fear in the slightest, just a desire to see the job done and done well.

The two sides closed on each other, and Tipoo's men came on with a heedless courage that Arthur could only admire. When they were no more than a hundred yards away Arthur reined Diomed in and shouted an order, straining his voice to be heard above the din of the charging enemy.

'33rd! Halt! Make ready!'

On they came, now close enough for Arthur to make out individual features in the faces of the men gathering speed as they sprinted to close the distance with the thin line of redcoats.

'Present!'

The glittering steel of the long barrels and the wicked spikes of the bayonets swept out towards the enemy. The lines were staggered so that the entire regiment would fire its volley as one. Just over sixty yards away the first of Tipoo's soldiers missed a step as they eyed the wall of foreshortened musket barrels, and flinched before the imminent hail of lead shot.

'Fire!'

The fizz from the priming pans was swallowed up in a great crash as flame stabbed from every musket in the regiment. Above the smoke, standing in his stirrups, Arthur saw the entire front of the enemy charge collapse as scores of men tumbled to the ground, or reeled back under the impact of the musket balls. So crushing was this first volley that the bodies of the dead and wounded formed a solid obstacle that stopped the charge in its tracks. More men slammed into the backs of those who had been forced to halt and knocked many more to the ground, in piles of tangled, struggling limbs.

'Face front! . . . Advance!'

Arthur's regiment marched forward, in step, towards the enemy, still trying to recover from the terrible effects of the volley fired at point-blank range. Now the relentless approach of the redcoats behind their gleaming bayonets proved to be too much for the nerves of the men who just a moment earlier had been charging towards the British line with such reckless exhilaration. Individuals, and then small groups, turned away and began to thrust back through the ranks of their comrades, fleeing up the slope. The sudden collapse in fighting spirit spread through the enemy like a wave and the entire formation broke and ran, many abandoning their weapons, and leaving their wounded comrades to their fate.

Arthur was about to order his men to charge when a pounding of hooves made him look to his right. Charging across the face of the slope was a brigade of cavalry from Harris's column. Dragoons. Their sabres were out and flashing brilliantly in the sun as they charged home, tearing through Tipoo's broken infantry and cutting them to pieces as they hacked and slashed at the men streaming up the hill.

'33rd! Halt!'

With his regiment stilled, the rest of the units in the line caught up and took up their position on the flank. As the last of the cavalry continued the pursuit up the hill, Arthur turned his attention to the right flank. Baird's brigade was still advancing and had pulled a short distance ahead of Arthur's line. The centre regiment of the brigade, the King's 74th Foot, was at the front of the line and as Arthur watched it broke into a trot as it neared the crest of the hill. Arthur frowned. The commander of the regiment was bound to get a roasting from Baird for letting his men disrupt the formation. Already, the tall figure of the brigade's commander was visible galloping his mount forward to catch up with the 74th. But before Baird could reach them, the crest of the hill above was suddenly filled with horsemen as they poured forward, charging straight at the 74th. The regiment halted as one and just had time to loose off one volley before they were struck by the swarm of enemy cavalry. Arthur could just make out Baird as he reined in and took charge of his errant regiment. As the flanking regiments came forward they too were forced to halt and engage the enemy cavalry. The sounds of pistol and musket fire crackled across the slope of the hill and then Arthur saw that, behind the cavalry, a column of infantry had appeared. While their cavalry attacked the 74th they would have the chance to approach Baird's infantry without coming under fire. Then it would be a question of hand to hand fighting in which the enemy would have a good chance of carrying off a victory against Baird's men.

Arthur turned back to his regiment. 'The 33rd will advance at the double!'

The red line rippled forward, up the hill, a short distance from the struggle engulfing Baird's brigade. As they advanced Arthur kept glancing to the side, gauging the distance between his men and the desperate melee away to his right. When the 33rd had advanced a quarter of a mile beyond Baird's formation Arthur halted them and, leaving the light company to protect his flank, he wheeled the rest of the regiment to the right, in a line facing the enemy column hurriedly marching down the slope towards Baird's brigade. With bayonets fixed there was risk of injury when loading and Arthur knew it was best that it was done before they closed on the enemy.

'Reload!'

The men grounded their muskets and pulled out fresh cartridges, biting off the end with the ball and holding it in their teeth as they primed the pan and dropped the charge into the muzzle. Then they spat the balls in and rammed the lot home before taking the weapons back in both hands ready to advance again. As soon as the reloading was complete Arthur gave the order to advance, and the regiment moved along the slope towards the column of Tipoo's infantry, already drawing near to Baird's men who were still in close formation as they fought off the enemy cavalry. Some of Tipoo's men closest to the 33rd were shouting and gesticulating towards the new threat but their officers drove them on, knowing that their one chance of achieving some measure of success in the battle lay in charging directly into the ranks of the redcoats.

Arthur hurried his men on at the double, their kit thudding up and down as they trotted forward. He did not halt them until they were no more than seventy yards from the flank of the enemy column and then the familiar sequence of orders rattled out again.

'Make ready! Present! Fire!'

The volley burst out in a storm of smoke and shot and all

along the side of the enemy column men buckled and fell to the ground. The blow stopped their advance dead in its tracks, and at the same time unnerved the enemy cavalry who turned away from Baird's men at the sound of massed musket fire. At once the redcoats, who had been beleaguered a moment before, let out a shout and surged forwards.

Arthur grabbed the chance at once. '33rd! Charge!'

Theatened from two directions the enemy instinctively recoiled, then broke and ran, streaming back up the hill at an angle from the two British formations. The enemy cavalry were heedless of their infantry and ran scores of them down in their bid to escape. Not wishing to repeat the mistake of the 74th, Arthur halted his men, and wheeled them back to the ridge to face any further attacks over the hill. But the battle was over. From his vantage point near the crest Arthur saw that the slopes of the nearby hills were also cleared of the enemy and red-coated battalions were moving forward to secure the ridge above Malavalley, stepping over the bodies of hundreds of Tipoo's warriors as the daylight began to fade.

Although the enemy had been beaten there was no question of continuing the pursuit into the night. Tipoo still had a strong force of horsemen in the field and General Harris knew it would be folly to attempt a pursuit which would scatter his cavalry in the face of such a danger. As the army and camp followers settled around the large village for the night in a vast square of tents and glittering fires, Arthur, accompanied by Fitzroy, rode over to General Harris's headquarters to make his report. The 33rd had only lost two men, victims of lucky shots fired from the enemy column they had shattered with their first, close range volley.

'Did your boys get a chance to take 'em on with the bayonet?' Harris asked.

'No, sir.' Fitzroy smiled. 'The enemy didn't quite stand up to that.'

'Hah!' Harris grinned with derision. 'So much for the tiger warriors of Mysore. After today, I doubt that we'll see much more of them before we reach Seringapatam.'

'I hope that's the case, sir,' Arthur replied.

'Of course it is. They'll not dare to chance their arm against massed volleys again, mark my words.'

He clapped Arthur on the shoulder and turned as Major General Baird entered the tent to make his report. He had lost twenty-nine men from his brigade, but Harris was content with the estimated tally of enemy dead accounted for by Baird's men and did not censure the reckless advance of the King's 74th. As Harris moved on to the next officer Baird approached Arthur.

'Good evening, sir.' Arthur saluted.

'Wellesley,' Baird acknowledged in an even tone. He was not smiling and his brow was faintly furrowed as he continued, with evident reluctance, 'I suppose I should thank you for intervening earlier. The timing of the flank attack was well judged.'

'Thank you, sir.'

Baird stared at him for a moment, then nodded. 'Yes, well, I just wanted to express my gratitude, Wellesley. That's all. Good evening to you. And you, Fitzroy.'

He turned and walked away, back to the cluster of officers from his brigade.

'Cheerful soul,' Fitzroy muttered. 'And so gracious in his appreciation of being rescued.'

'Baird's a tough one,' Arthur replied. 'It wasn't easy for him to offer his thanks. He'll have his chance to prove his worth once we reach Seringapatam.'

'What makes you think that?' Fitzroy smiled. 'After today's thrashing, I doubt Tipoo and his men will stand their ground a moment after we start firing at them.'

'Don't be too sure,' Arthur replied. 'Today was just a delaying action. Once we reach Seringapatam Tipoo and his men will defend their city to the death. Then I fear we'll discover just how dangerous the warriors of Mysore can be.'

Chapter 48

Seringapatam, April 1799

The army came in sight of Tipoo's capital on the afternoon of 3 April. Arthur climbed on to the roof of one of Tipoo's hunting lodges, to the south-east of the city, and carefully examined the defences through his telescope. Seringapatam occupied an island in the Cauvery river, the main course of which passed to the north of the city, while a narrow channel flowed round the south, creating an island a little less than three miles long and just over a mile wide. The city had been built on the western end of the island and was surrounded by thick granite walls, outside which lay a large fortified camp where Tipoo's army was massed, ready for the coming siege. Within the walls of the city the two minarets of the mosque gleamed in the distance, like ivory against the rich emerald green of the surrounding landscape.

Arthur turned at the sound of footsteps climbing the stairs behind him, and saw Fitzroy emerging on to the roof.

'Ah, there you are, sir.'

'Come and have a look, Fitzroy.' Arthur indicated the distant city and passed his telescope to his aide. 'It's an impressive sight.'

There was a moment's pause as Fitzroy squinted down the telescope and slowly panned it along the perimeter of Tipoo's defences. 'Good God,' he muttered. 'There must be over fifty . . . sixty guns along this side of the city.'

'I counted over ninety. But you'll note that the construction of the walls follows the usual eastern style, and will not permit effective flanking fire on any attackers. Clearly Tipoo's French advisers haven't had time to improve the city's defences. That, or

Tipoo is arrogant enough to believe that he knows better.'

'So, sir, do you know how the general intends to crack this nut?'

'It's straightforward enough. The island is too big to besiege; our forces would be spread far too thinly to stop Tipoo's men getting in or out of the city. Harris has decided to march round the city and set up camp to the west. From there we can batter the walls with siege guns and launch an assault across the south Cauvery channel. Our scouts reckon that the water is shallow enough at this time of year to wade across, crocodiles permitting.'

'Crocodiles?' Fitzroy stared at him. 'You're joking.'

Arthur smiled. 'Not afraid of a few reptiles are you, Fitzroy? I thought you would have grown used to them what with your father being a politician.'

Fitzroy raised his eyes. 'Very funny, sir. Very droll. Nevertheless, I think I shall tread exceedingly carefully when the time comes to make our attack.'

'Most wise.' Arthur turned back to examine the defences. 'Of course, time is against us. We have a little over six weeks before the monsoon season. When that comes, the south Cauvery will be unfordable until November. If we don't take the city before the middle of May, then we'll have to retreat all the way back to Vellore empty handed.'

Fitzroy glanced at his superior. 'In which event, I doubt the Governor General will be in the best of moods.'

'You can't imagine.'

The site chosen by General Harris for the army's camp was three miles from the ford. The wide expanse of the Cauvery protected them from the north. The Nizam's army was positioned to the south of the main force and Arthur's men were given the task of constructing a defence line to guard the camp from any attacks from the south and west. Meanwhile, Tipoo had not been idle. Having seen the direction from which Harris would attack he moved quickly to fortify the mainland side of the south Cauvery with a series of trenches and earthworks on which he mounted some of his artillery. Between the two armies the ground was open except for a nullah, an earth aqueduct that snaked across the landscape, rising several feet above the surrounding rice fields. To the right of the British position it looped around a tope in one direction before winding back round the village of Sultanpettah.

As light faded the day after the army had encamped, General Harris summoned Arthur to his headquarters and both men leaned over a map of the territory around the enemy's capital. Harris pointed to the tope. 'The enemy have been firing rockets into our lines from these trees all afternoon. I want them cleared out of there. If you can take and hold this area then we can get some guns forward to enfilade their defences this side of the south Cauvery.'

Arthur looked at the map. 'What do we know about the nullah, sir? Is it fordable?'

'I imagine you'll discover that soon enough,' Harris replied tersely.

Arthur straightened up. 'Would it not be a good idea to send out a small party to reconnoitre first, sir? Before we try anything with the whole regiment in the dark.'

Harris frowned. 'Colonel, we do not have the luxury of time to do that. Now you have your orders, so carry them out.' He paused and then added shrewdly, 'Unless you would like me to give the job to Baird.'

'I'll go, sir.' Arthur replied stiffly.

'Good. Then you'd best prepare your regiment right away. I want that tope in our hands by first light.'

'Where's this bloody tope then?' Major Shee muttered as he strained his eyes to try to make out the details of the ground ahead of them. The night was dark and ahead the nullah rose up as a black mass. It was impossible to pick out any trees. He turned back to the other officers. 'Sir?'

Arthur had been trying to identify some landmarks to fix his position from what he recalled of the general's map, but the night had defeated him. At first they had been guided towards the tope by the continuing rocket fire, but then the enemy had ceased their attack and Arthur had done his best to keep his men moving in that direction, advancing ahead of the main body of the regiment with the two flank companies. He had decided to leave Major Shee in command of the rest of the battalion, where hopefully his difficult nature and predisposition to drink would not endanger the men. Arthur was aware of the nervousness of the soldiers around him, particularly young Lieutenant Fitzgerald of the grenadier company.

He cleared his throat and spoke calmly. 'The tope should be just the other side of the nullah. There's only one way to be sure, of course. That's why we're here. It's time to go forward, gentlemen. Mr Fitzgerald.'

'Sir?'

'Pass the word back down the line and tell the men to move as quietly as possible. Then come forward with me. I'll need a runner once we reach the tope.'

'Yes, sir.'

Arthur turned to Shee. 'Major?'

'Yes, Colonel?'

Arthur could have sworn that he smelt traces of spirits on Shee's breath.

'Return to the other companies and bring the regiment up in support. If we do engage the enemy on the far side of the nullah, we'll need you on the scene quickly.'

'Yes, sir. You can rely on me.'

'Of course, Major. I would expect nothing less.'

Shee saluted then turned and half walked, half stumbled across the broken ground back towards the rest of the 33rd. Arthur put the chances of the man's losing his way at about evens and was grateful that he had thought to appoint Fitzroy as the major's second in command for the night's operation.

Arthur waited for Fitzgerald to return and then he called out softly, 'Flank companies . . . advance.'

They moved forward as quietly as they could but Arthur winced as his finely tuned ears caught the sound of boots scuffing the ground and the faint chink of loose equipment. The land began to slope upwards as they reached the nullah and Arthur's senses strained to pick up every detail of sight and sound. Somewhere on the far side of the aqueduct the enemy were waiting and he suddenly felt terribly vulnerable. Then the realisation hit him.

There was a faint loom along the horizon behind the regiment and they would be silhouetted against lighter sky the moment they reached the top of the nullah. They would be easy targets. He drew his pistol and held it close to his chest as he scrambled up through the grass. Then, as the ground levelled off, he stopped and glanced round. The water in the aqueduct was ink black and stretched out on either side.

'Fitzgerald. Bring the men up. Light company to the left. Grenadiers to the right.'

'Yes, sir.'

As Fitzgerald whispered the order down the bank Arthur eased himself forward, slipping his boot into the water. The footing was soft and sloped steeply and in moments he was up to his waist. He held the pistol high and waded forward, hoping that the crocodiles confined themselves to the river. He moved slowly towards the far bank, fifteen yards ahead, and then climbed carefully out. Arthur looked round, listening, but all was still and quiet amongst the low trees of the tope below the nullah. He felt a wave of relief that they seemed to have found the right place, and stood erect, forcing himself to set the appropriate example to his officers and men.

'Fitzgerald, bring the flank companies over.'

The men moved forward into the water, muskets held overhead as they waded across. Above the faint splashes Arthur could clearly hear some muttering, before a sergeant growled, 'Keep yer bloody mouths shut.'

The dark shapes were clambering up on to the bank on either side of Arthur when there was a blazing pool of light from a short distance away down below amongst the trees, and a loud roaring hiss.

'Rocket!' someone just had time to yell before the missile arced out of a gap in the trees, towards the bank of the nullah, and buried itself in the ground so close to Arthur that he blinked as a shower of loose soil spattered his face. At once more rockets were fired, brilliantly illuminating the tope so that Arthur had brief glimpses of the tangled mangrove that lay ahead of him. Muskets joined in, flaring in the darkness as they went off.

'The bastards are everywhere!' Fitzgerald shouted and ducked as a rocket fizzed overhead.

'Stand up!' Arthur took his arm and forced Fitzgerald to his feet. 'You're an officer, Fitzgerald. You must set the standard.'

'Yes, sir.'

Arthur turned to his men. 'Get down the bank! Into the tope. Quickly!'

The soldiers of the flank companies slithered and clambered down the bank and moved forward towards the trees, still under fire from the enemy troops and rocket crews. Arthur veered right, towards the grenadiers, who, true to their role as the teeth arm of the regiment, had fixed bayonets and were charging towards where the enemy fire seemed most concentrated. With a sick feeling of anxiety Arthur noticed that the men were already separating and he cupped a hand to his mouth.

'Flank companies! On me!' Around him the crackle of gunfire and the hiss of rockets and the shouts and cries of the men drowned out his order. 'On me! On me, damn it!'

'Sir! Watch out!' Fitzgerald called out as half a dozen shapes suddenly materialised out of the darkness. Arthur drew his sword and raised his pistol, tensing as he prepared to fight. Then, by the dim flare of a rocket passing a short distance away, he saw that they were grenadiers.

'It's the colonel!' one of the men said, in a relieved voice. 'Thank Christ.'

Arthur waited until they were gathered round him, then issued his orders. 'We're going forward. We still have to clear the enemy out of the tope. There's plenty of our lads out there, and the rest of the 33rd will be here soon, so watch your targets before you use the bayonet.'

'Yes, sir,' the men muttered.

'Follow me then.'

They set off, Arthur leading from the front, followed by

Fitzgerald and then the grenadiers. Arthur made for a small group of Tipoo's men that he had seen a moment earlier and went forward as quickly as he could through the tangled roots and undergrowth of the dried-out mangrove. It was impossible to make any speed in the pitch black and the men had to hold their weapons carefully for fear of injuring their comrades if they tripped or slipped as they struggled through the tope. Meanwhile sounds of firing and fighting continued on all sides. Arthur was furious. There was no sense in sending men forward into such terrain on a dark night. The disciplined cohesion that had made the 33rd such a deadly weapon on the battlefield was shattered. His men, so carefully trained to stand and fight in ordered ranks, were scattered across the tope. Leaderless and no doubt fearful of the unfamiliar conditions, they had lost any advantage they might have had over Tipoo's men at Malavalley. Arthur vowed to make a protest to Harris the moment the attack was over.

'Sir!' Fitzgerald called out as loudly as he dared. 'Up ahead. The enemy.'

Arthur stared into the darkness, and thought he saw shapes moving amongst the dark tangle of trees ahead of him. Then there was a flash as one of the enemy fired his musket towards the nullah and in the orange glow Arthur saw another five or six men frozen as they raised their muskets. As the light blinked out one of Tipoo's men shouted out in alarm. The same light had clearly illuminated Arthur and his men.

'We're seen! Get at them!' Arthur lurched forward, sensing clear ground under his feet as he entered an open space between the thickets. Another musket flashed out, no more than twenty feet away, and Arthur felt the rush of air as the ball passed close by his cheek. Instantly he raised his pistol and fired in the direction of the muzzle flash. By its light he saw the man, looking up from his musket. At once there was a cry of pain and Arthur shoved the pistol into his belt and went forward with his sword, slashing at the dim figure of the man he had shot. The blade connected with a jarring thud and the enemy soldier collapsed with a grunt. Then there were more figures all around him in the darkness and only the vague shapes of turbans or shakos allowed the combatants to identify each other. There was no chance for skills learned in bayonet drill or fencing practice to be used in the deadly game of blind man's buff as the redcoats and Tipoo's warriors fought it out, thrusting with their bayonets and swinging heavy musket butts, while the two officers made sword cuts at the swirling black forms to their front.

'Bastard's got me!' one of the grenadiers cried out in surprise and terror, then added in astonishment, 'It's me shoulder!'

Then the sounds of fighting stopped, and Arthur could hear bodies crashing away through the undergrowth. Then there was only the hard breathing of those who remained, and a thin keening whine from the badly wounded man.

Arthur swallowed and drew a deep breath. 'On me,' he said quietly. 'Fitzgerald?'

'Here, sir.'

'You grenadiers, over here.' Arthur moved over to the wounded man and knelt down. 'Who is this?'

'Private Williams, sir,' the man groaned. 'Oh, God! It bloody hurts . . .'

Arthur turned to the others. 'Get Williams up. We have to take him back to the nullah.'

'Yes, sir.' Two of the men leaned over and raised Williams from the ground, while another picked up his musket. Williams groaned in agony.

'Keep yer bloody mouth closed,' one of the men grumbled. 'Or yer'll 'ave all of 'em down on us in a flash.'

'Quiet there,' said Arthur, and then looked round. It was a moment before he realised that he had no idea in which direction the nullah lay.

'Sir?' Fitzgerald whispered. 'Which way?'

'Damn it, man, I don't know!' Arthur glanced round to try to make out some landmark, something familiar. Then he saw the faintest loom in the sky which had earlier revealed his men to the enemy concealed in the tope. 'There.'

They made their way out of the small clearing and back through the dense undergrowth, all the time listening for the enemy. There were still occasional shots and rockets much further off, and shouts from men who were fighting, lost or wounded. Arthur was tempted to try to rally them again but paused when he heard the sound of several men passing through the trees a short distance away.

'Down,' he hissed, and then Williams let out a groan. The other men stopped and fell silent and Arthur felt his heart beating against his chest like a mallet.

'33rd!' he called out, tightening his grip on the handle of his sword. The sounds resumed, growing closer, and one of the grenadiers laughed nervously. 'Come on, you bastards, who is it?'

A musket fired close by and in its glare Arthur saw a handful of the enemy. Almost at once there was another shot and a blow struck him just above the kneecap, knocking his leg out from under him. Arthur fell back with a shout of surprise rather than pain. At once the enemy let out a cry and charged the grenadiers.

'Let's have 'em!' Fitzgerald bellowed and ran forward. The grenadiers went after him with their bayonets lowered. Struggling back on to his feet Arthur ran his spare hand down his breeches until they came to a ragged tear over his knee. The cloth was sodden and when his fingers probed further a searing pain made him gasp. He stood up and limped towards the sounds of the fight nearby: the scrape of metal, the thud of blows and the groans of the combatants. A figure rose up in front of him, sword raised ready to strike. Just in time Arthur recognised the shape of the man's hat.

'Easy, Fitzgerald. It's me!'

The young lieutenant froze for a moment and then laughed. 'Sorry, sir.'

'Where are the others?'

'That way, sir.' He turned and raised his arm, barely visible in the dark. 'Over—'

Someone burst through the undergrowth just beyond Fitzgerald and then the lieutenant let out an explosive gasp as he was borne back, past Arthur, under the impact of a pike. An enemy soldier snarled with triumph as he drove the weapon on into the officer's body and then, too late, he noticed Arthur, and the sabre scythed through the air and into his neck with a wet, crunching thud. Abruptly he released his hold on the pike and snatched at his throat, sinking to his knees before he toppled to one side with a gurgling sound. Arthur sheathed his sword and knelt beside Fitzgerald.

'Oh, God . . . God . . .' Fitzgerald moaned as his body trembled. 'Sweet Jesus . . . it hurts.'

Arthur groped towards the shaft of the pike, felt along until he sensed Fitzgerald's jacket and then fixed his grip on the pike. 'Hold steady there.'

'Sir?' Fitzgerald writhed as the pike moved inside his stomach. Arthur gritted his teeth and wrenched the shaft and head of the weapon out and felt a rush of blood over his hands as the other man screamed.

'Grenadiers!' Arthur called out. 'Over here! On me!'

There was a rustling as the men came back, breathing hard. 'There you are, sir. Thought we'd lost you. Where's Mr Fitzgerald?'

'Here. He's been injured. Did you deal with them? The enemy?'

'Two down; the others ran for it. Not a scratch on us, sir.'

'Good. Now, you, help Mr Fitzgerald. Get him over your shoulders. The rest of you find Williams and let's get out of here. There's nothing more we can do.'

'What about you, sir?' asked one of the grenadiers. 'I heard you fall.'

'I'm all right.' Arthur replied through gritted teeth. 'Don't worry about me. Get moving.'

The nullah was closer than he had thought and shortly after the brief skirmish they emerged from the trees to see the bank rising up above them. As they struggled up the slope several figures rose up on either side.

'33rd!' Arthur snapped. 'Colonel Wellesley. We've got wounded men here. We have to get them across to the other side. Lend a hand.'

The small party clambered into the water, helping Williams and Fitzgerald across to the other side. The lieutenant groaned in agony as he was manhandled over the nullah on the shoulders of three men, and he passed out before he reached the far bank. Arthur glanced back towards the impenetrable mass of the tope. There was still fighting going on in there, further off now, and he shook his head in pity and anger for the fate of his men before he turned and waded across the nullah.

'Twenty-four casualties?' Harris mused. 'Not as bad as it could have been, Colonel. Too bad about Fitzgerald. He was a fine young man.'

It was shortly after midnight and Arthur stood before the general in the headquarters tent, still in sodden, muddy clothes. A bloodstained dressing had been tied round the flesh wound just above his knee. His face was rigid with barely suppressed rage as he replied. 'Twenty-four of my men is bad enough, sir, considering they never should have been sent into the tope in the first place.'

'It was a risk,' Harris admitted. 'And it failed. The tope is still in enemy hands. I had hoped we might save time by taking it tonight, but we'll just have to make another attempt tomorrow, in daylight. I'll give the job to Baird.'

'Sir, I respectfully submit that I should command the second attempt.'

'But you're wounded.'

'It was my task, sir. I deserve another chance.'

'Really?' Harris stared at him for a moment, and Arthur was sure that he would refuse. Then the general shrugged. 'Very well, Wellesley, as you wish. The command is yours. But the 33rd needs a rest. You'll have the Scottish Brigade for the job. Make sure you see it through.'

'I will, sir. You have my word.'

'Good. Now go and clean yourself up and get some sleep.'

'Sir.' Arthur saluted and turned painfully to stride out of the tent, only resorting to a limp when he was out of the general's sight. As he rode Diomed back to the encampment of the Nizam's column he decided that if the night's disaster had taught him one thing, it was never to conduct any operations under cover of darkness, if it could be avoided. Never again would he lose control of his men in that way. The spectre of failure haunted him through the early hours. He tried to rest, but the vision of Fitzgerald's face, as he died by the light of the surgeon's lantern, returned to Arthur again and again, and robbed him of any sleep.

Chapter 49

Throughout April the army pushed its siege lines forward, capturing the enemy positions on the western bank of the south Cauvery river. The tope was taken in daylight and most of the bodies of the 33rd's grenadiers were recovered, but eight remained unaccounted for and Arthur feared that they must have been taken prisoner. Once the enemy outposts had been cleared from in front of Seringapatam's walls General Harris gave orders for the construction of strongly fortified batteries for the heavy siege guns that Arthur had procured while the army assembled for the campaign. At a range of nine hundred yards the guns methodically knocked out the enemy cannon along the western wall of Seringapatam before turning to pound the corner bastions into rubble. Then on the second day of May the batteries were aimed at the point along the wall that General Harris had chosen to be breached. An intense bombardment followed over the next two days, until a wide section of the city's wall had been smashed through and Harris was satisfied that an assault could be made over the rubble.

That night he assembled his senior officers and announced his plan of attack. 'It's important that we take the city on the first attempt. The first of the monsoon rains might arrive in the next two weeks and the *brinjarris* tell me that their food supplies are starting to run down. So I have decided to throw as many men into the attack as can be spared from defending our camp. There will be three formations in the attacking force: two assault columns and a reserve. Major General Baird has volunteered to lead the assault. Given the antipathy between Tipoo's men and our Madras sepoys I pray that we do not have to deploy them in the battle for Seringapatam. They will be held in reserve.'

'Who is to command the reserve, sir?' Arthur asked. He already knew that the 33rd had been selected for the assault force and was looking forward to leading them into the attack.

'You are.'

'Me?' Arthur started and some of the other officers could not help smiling at his surprised expression. Arthur fought back a flush of irritation with himself. 'But who is to lead my regiment, sir?'

'Major Shee.'

'Sir, if my regiment is to be part of the attack, then I should be with them.'

Harris shook his head. 'I need a steady head to control the reserve column. As soon as the attack goes in, you are to march your column across the river and wait outside the breach. I'm trusting you to use your judgement as to whether Baird needs any support. Is that clear, Wellesley?'

There was little chance of altering the general's mind at this stage and Arthur accepted his role in the coming battle with as much grace as he could muster.

'Yes, sir.'

'Very well then, gentlemen. The men will move forward in the trenches before dawn and keep out of sight until the signal to attack is given at midday. Make sure all your officers are thoroughly briefed on the attack, and try to get some sleep, if you can.' Harris gave them a wry grin, and then gestured towards the tent flap. His officers rose from their chairs and filed out.

'Wellesley?'

Arthur turned back. 'Yes, sir?'

'A word, if you please.'

Once the last of the other officers had quit the tent Harris spoke. 'I have good reasons for assigning you to command the reserve.'

'I'm sure you do, sir.'

Harris looked at him sharply. 'Don't try to be ironic, Colonel. It doesn't become a senior officer in my army.'

'No, sir.'

Harris sighed. 'The fact of the matter is that I need an officer with sound judgement to command the reserve. The assault column is a different matter. Baird is a born fighter and he wants revenge for the years he spent chained in the dungeons of Seringapatam. Who better to command the attack?'

'Baird's the man right enough, sir. But why am I to be denied my place at the head of the 33rd?'

'If the attack goes badly I'll need you to retrieve the situation. And if the attack fails, then it is vital that a path is kept open through which Baird and his men can retreat. That is why you are the best man to command the reserve, just as Baird is the best man to lead the attack.'

Arthur's heart was warmed by his superior's praise. 'I apologise, sir. I should not have questioned your orders.'

'No. You shouldn't. Besides, there is another reason for keeping you out of the assault column.'

'Sir?'

'You'll find out soon enough, assuming that we defeat Tipoo tomorrow.'

The last men of the assault columns were in position shortly before dawn rose across the lush green landscape surrounding Seringapatam. They carried only their muskets and a haversack for their cartridges to ensure that they were not encumbered as they negotiated the rubble that sloped up to the breach. As soon as they were in place, their officers ordered them to sit down and stay still. The sun rose up out of the light haze that hung over the verdant landscape, but as soon as it was high enough for the warmth of its rays to be felt the temperature rose quickly. Within an hour the men in the trenches, huddled together, began to stew in the heat of the Indian day. Around them, in view of the enemy, the engineers began work on a new battery close to the river's edge in an attempt to mislead Tipoo about the imminence of an attack. The siege guns continued a monotonous bombardment of a section of the wall some distance upriver of the breach, while a handful of sepoy pickets patrolled the banks of the south Cauvery to discourage any attempt by the enemy to probe the lines of General Harris's army.

Just after eleven in the morning Arthur made his way forward. He found Baird with the men of the 'forlorn hope': a handful of volunteers led by a sergeant whose task it was to rush the breach and hold it long enough for the main column to advance through the gap. Baird had brought a jug of arrack with him and it was being passed around the men as Arthur squatted down beside the massive Scottish officer. Baird eyed him suspiciously as they exchanged a quick salute.

'What can I do for you, young Wellesley?'

Arthur stiffened slightly at being addressed in this manner, but then held out his hand. 'I came to wish you good luck, sir.'

'Good luck, eh?' Baird nodded, then took Arthur's hand in his great fist and squeezed it firmly as he shook. 'That's damn good of you. Thank you. Here, Sergeant Graham, give me that jug.'

'I'll not be Sergeant for much longer, sir!' the man grinned as he handed the arrack back to his commander, and patted the standard resting across his knees. 'It's Lieutenant Graham, the moment I plant this in the breach.'

Baird smiled. 'Och, you'll be dead before you even make the breach, you bloody fool.'

The men of the forlorn hope laughed nervously and Baird passed the jug to Arthur. 'Have a drink, Wellesley.'

Arthur was about to refuse. He was tired, he had a headache and the last thing he wanted was any drink to cloud his mind. Then he looked at the men sitting round him and watching his reaction. Most of them were as good as dead, he realised with a stab of pity. So he made himself smile, as he instinctively wiped the rim of the jug on his sleeve and raised it.

'Your health, gentlemen!' He nodded and then took a steady draught of the fiery liquid before lowering the jug and handing it back to Baird. The Scot gave him a hearty wink and took a gulp before passing the jug on. 'I'll try to save a few of Tipoo's men for you, Wellesley.'

'If you wouldn't mind?' Arthur grinned for a moment, then his expression became serious again. 'Good luck then, sir.'

'Aye.' Baird was reflective for a brief moment. 'We'll need it sure enough.'

Arthur returned to his command post. Behind him, over four thousand men in the reserve column were crouched in the sweltering discomfort of the rear trenches. He pulled out his fob watch and dabbed his brow on the back of his sleeve. It was almost time. The siege guns continued their relentless pounding and all seemed quite still on the walls of Seringapatam. Only a handful of tiny figures were in view on the ramparts, keeping watch on the English forces.

As the hands of his watch closed together at noon there came the shrill call of a whistle and at once a wave of redcoats erupted from the forward trenches, as if they were bursting up from the very earth itself. The men of the forlorn hope dashed forward behind Sergeant Graham as he held the rippling standard aloft, then they surged across the shallow current of the south Cauvery and up the far bank, dripping and glistening as they sprinted towards the ragged gap in the city wall.

The main column had swiftly formed up in companies, and rippled forward across the river as the first of the defenders to appear on the walls began to fire on the attackers. Arthur saw Sergeant Graham clamber on to the highest point of the rubble piled in the breach. He thrust the standard down and beckoned to his men, and then lurched to one side and collapsed. The standard slowly began to topple, before one of the men of the forlorn hope snatched at it and held it up. Beyond the wall, Arthur glimpsed scores of men in flowing white tunics armed with muskets scrambling up to the crest of the debris, and a vicious and unequal struggle began.

Already, Baird and his first company were emerging from the river and surging up into the breach. Arthur caught a brief glimpse of the Scot, swinging his claymore, before he disappeared beyond the wall, closely followed by his men. Not a single enemy soldier still lived in the breach or on the ramparts immediately either side of it. Redcoats appeared on the battlements, fanning out to the left and right and charging into the dense ranks of the defenders who were only now spilling out of the bastions further along the wall. For an instant Arthur could not help but envy those who were storming the Tipoo's defences. All the months of painstaking preparation, long marches across inhospitable country and the back-breaking labour of trench-digging would be forgotten amid the explosive exhilaration of being part of that wild attack.

Arthur stared towards the trenches. The last of Baird's men had cleared the near bank and there was no chance now of confusing the columns. He cleared his throat and shouted the order. 'The reserve will advance!'

Sergeants relayed the order and the sepoy battalions and the Swiss de Meuron regiment of mercenaries that fought for the Company clambered out, grateful to quit the fetid misery of the trenches. As soon as the reserve was formed up Arthur led them down to the river and they waded across, muskets held high as the slack water eddied about their waists. On the far bank they halted in front of the wall to await further orders while Arthur went ahead with his aide, Fitzroy, and the grenadier company from the Swiss regiment. The rubble was loose beneath their boots and Arthur had to use a hand on the masonry to steady himself as he made his way up into the breach. The crest and reverse slope were covered with bodies, mostly Tipoo's men, taken with the bayonet or shot down at point-blank range. Sergeant Graham lay sprawled on his back, slack-jawed, staring lifelessly towards the heavens. Gunfire crackled on either side and Arthur could see distant figures fighting at close quarters for possession of the bastions and towers along the wall. Ahead of him the streets of Seringapatam were silent and still as its people took shelter in their homes and prayed to their gods for deliverance, or mercy.

The two men climbed the nearest steps on to the wall to gain a better view of the fighting. Away to the north, the action seemed concentrated around the water gate on the wall that looked out over the main channel of the Cauvery. In the other direction, Arthur could already see a swarm of redcoats surging towards the Mysore gate.

'Looks like Tipoo's men are on the run,' Fitzroy said as he shaded his eyes, squinting in the same direction as Arthur.

'It looks that way,' Arthur conceded after a moment. 'In which case, we must take measures to ensure that the slaughter doesn't get out of hand. Go down to the reserve and order the sepoys to stand down. They are not to be allowed to enter the city.'

Fitzroy raised his eyebrows. 'They're not going to like that, sir. You know the rules of war. The place has been taken by assault. By rights they should have a free hand.'

'That's not going to happen,' Arthur replied firmly. 'Tipoo's people had nothing to do with his decision to wage war on us. They are not going to share his fate. And I am certainly not going to throw them on the mercy of Madras sepoys. I want the de Meuron regiment drawn up in front of the breach. They are not to let any soldiers into the city. Clear?'

'Yes, sir.' Fitzroy saluted and climbed down from the wall to relay Arthur's orders. Meanwhile Arthur stared out over the city. The sound of gunfire was already fading away, apart from occasional bursts as the attackers discovered a few remaining pockets of Tipoo's men. Rising above the city was the palace and Arthur realised that if the ruler of Seringapatam could be found and persuaded to surrender, then the city might yet be spared the worst ravages of defeat. Otherwise, the marauding bands of redcoats would unerringly find their way to stores of drink and then, fuelled by arrack and the fire in their blood, they would carry murder, destruction and rape to every corner of the city.

As soon as Fitzroy returned they set off towards the palace, stepping round the bodies that lay behind the wall. When they turned into the avenue that led to the palace gates they saw several companies of redcoats waiting outside.

'It's the 33rd.' Fitzroy pointed. 'And over there – Major Shee.'

Arthur hurried across to Shee. 'What news?'

Shee stiffened his back as he made his report. 'Enemy's beaten, sir. Just winkling out the last few of 'em. There's a few hundred still sheltering in the palace. General Baird has asked them to surrender.'

'Baird? Where is he?'

'Through there, sir.' Shee nodded at the gate.

Arthur and Fitzroy made towards the arch and cautiously

walked through into a large courtyard. Baird had his back to them, and was staring at the façade of the palace. Several of Tipoo's men stared back warily from the palace entrance. More men stood at the windows of the building. At the sound of boots crunching on gravel Baird glanced back over his shoulder, and then turned to greet Arthur. There was no triumph in his expression, just weariness.

'Ah, Wellesley, it's all but over now. I'm just waiting for the *killadar* to send out word that he's accepted my terms.'

'Terms, sir?' Arthur asked. 'What terms?'

'Surrender of the palace and the men sheltering there, including two of Tipoo's sons. In exchange, the palace and all those in it will be placed under the protection of your regiment.'

'What about Tipoo, sir? Where is he?'

'The *killadar* claims he doesn't know. The last time he saw Tipoo was over by the water gate.'

'We have to find him, sir. If he escapes then he'll continue the war from somewhere else. If he's been killed we must find the body.'

'I'm no fool, Wellesley. I know damn well what's at stake.'

'I apologise, sir. I meant no offence.'

'Never mind. Anyway, here's the fellow now.'

Arthur looked up and saw a thin man emerge from the shadows behind the main entrance, walking swiftly down the steps towards them. He bowed his head formally as he stood in front of Baird and spoke, in good English. 'The *killadar* accepts your conditions, and your word as a *pukka sahib* that no harm will come of the household if we lay down our arms.'

'Those were the terms offered, and I stand by them, with these officers as witnesses.'

'There is one other thing,' Arthur interrupted. 'You must take us to the body of Tipoo, or at least to the last place he was seen.'

'As you wish, *sahib*.'

'Very well,' Baird growled at the palace official. 'Those are the final terms. Take 'em or leave 'em.'

'We accept, *sahib*. I will tell my master.'

'I want everyone in the palace brought out here,' Baird

ordered. 'They are to leave their weapons – all of them, mind you – stacked in the hall over there.'

'Yes, *sahib*.' The native bowed and trotted back towards the palace.

Baird turned to Arthur. 'Bring your men in. They can guard the prisoners and take up position in and around the palace.'

'Yes, sir.'

Shortly afterwards, as the redcoats stood waiting, the first of the enemy came out of the palace and cautiously made their way across the courtyard towards the men of the 33rd, to be herded together in one corner of the courtyard. A steady stream of warriors emerged, and then the Tipoo's sons and scores of his wives. When the *killadar* appeared Arthur approached him to ask if any of his men had been taken prisoner during the night attack on the tope early on in the siege. The *killadar* had been held hostage by the company, in the days of Cornwallis, and spoke some broken English.

'We show you,' he replied nervously. 'Prisoners? Please come.'

'Show us?' Arthur muttered. 'Show us what?'

'You must see. Come!' The *killadar* started towards the door to a smaller courtyard to one side of the palace. 'This way!'

'What's over there, I wonder?' Fitzroy asked suspiciously.

'The dungeons,' Baird replied quietly. 'Where they held me for over three years.'

Baird summoned several men to accompany them. The party followed the *killadar* cautiously and once through the door they found that they were in what looked to be some kind of training ground. To one side a flight of steps descended to two rows of barred cells. At the far end was a pit. Fitzroy leaned closer to Arthur. 'What do you think he means to show us?'

'How should I know? Anyway, we'll find out soon enough.'

The *killadar* led them across the courtyard and down the steps. As they made their way between the cells Arthur saw that the gates were open and the cells were empty. Except for the last one. As they approached four enormous figures emerged from it and bowed to the allied officers

'Who the hell are they?' Arthur said in a strained tone. The men were all superbly muscled and looked as if they could break a man's neck with their bare hands.

'*Jettis*,' Baird explained quietly. 'Strong men. They performed tricks and feats of strength for Tipoo and his father.'

'What kind of tricks?' Fitzroy asked with a trace of anxiety.

'I've seen them twist a man's head right round. And worse.'

The *killadar* was standing close to the edge of the pit and beckoned to them. As they drew closer Arthur caught a glimpse of an animal's skin as it prowled round the far side of the pit: a tawny yellow with darker stripes.

'Tigers! It's a tiger pit.'

They approached the rim of the pit carefully. Three huge tigers were sitting chewing on what looked like the remains of a man. Arthur felt sick. Then the full scale of the horror hit him as he reached the edge of the pit and stared down. There were perhaps a dozen mauled bodies scattered across the floor. The tattered remains of their red uniform jackets was proof enough of who they were. The men who had accompanied the three English officers began to mutter angrily at the sight.

'Prisoners,' Arthur realised. 'The men we lost in the tope.'

'What have they done to them?' Fitzroy asked quietly.

Arthur looked more closely and saw that most of the necks of the dead were twisted round at horrible angles. Some of them had what looked like huge nails sticking out of the top of their skulls. He stared at the bodies a moment, as nausea welled up in his stomach. Then he glanced at the *jettis* again. Surely not, he thought. God, please not that.

Baird had been watching his expression and read his thoughts precisely. 'That's right, Wellesley. These men did it. Beat the nails into the skulls of our men with their bare hands, while our men still lived. I know, I saw them do it when I was a prisoner here. Indeed, I lived with the thought that they would do that to me one day.' Baird looked pale as he spoke.

'Bastards . . .' one of the soldiers growled as he stared on the bodies of his comrades. Suddenly he swung round, lowered his bayonet and drove it into the stomach of one of the *jettis*. The man doubled over with a deep explosive groan under the impact.

While the officers watched, too shocked to react, the soldier withdrew the weapon, reversed it and swung the butt against the *jetti*'s head, then kicked the man over the edge of the pit. He landed with a thud and a crack as his arm broke under the weight of his muscled body. At his cry one of the tigers roused itself and padded cautiously towards him, and despite the pain from his wounds the man screamed in terror.

The soldier turned to his comrades. 'Finish them all, lads! Kill these bloody butchers. All of them.' He turned and pointed at the *killadar*.

'No!' Arthur bellowed and drew his sword, hurriedly stepping between his men and the *killadar*. 'Stand still, damn you! Stand still, I said.'

For a moment there was a tense confrontation and then the soldier lowered his musket and grounded it. The others followed his lead and stood waiting for orders. There was a piercing shriek of pain from the pit, and then some more, and growls, before the man was silenced with a powerful snap of a tiger's jaws. One of the surviving *jettis* dropped to his knees and began to beg, huge glistening tears pricking out of his eyes as he wailed for mercy.

'You'd better go and find Tipoo's body.' Baird spoke calmly. 'That oily-looking bastard of a bureaucrat can identify him. I'll take care of the situation here.'

Arthur looked at him suspiciously. 'What are you going to do, sir?'

'The *jettis* will be executed. We'll have to shoot the tigers to get at the remains of our men for burial. I'll attend to it. You go and find Tipoo.'

'Yes, sir.'

Arthur gestured to the entrance to the courtyard and told the *killadar* to lead him to the last place Tipoo had been seen. As they left the courtyard Arthur looked back once. Baird stood off to one side, simply watching, as the men dragged the first of the *jettis* over to the edge of the pit and thrust him over the edge.

'You saw what they did to our men,' Fitzroy said through clenched teeth. 'They deserve what's coming to them.'

'No man deserves that,' Arthur said firmly, and gently eased his friend out of the courtyard. They followed the *killadar* along a wide thoroughfare that led to the water gate. A company of the 73rd Foot had been left to hold the position and they roused themselves as the officers and the native approached. It was clear that some of the fiercest fighting of the day had taken place here. Bodies of English and native warriors were sprawled across the terreplein and the mouth of the passage that ran through the gate was piled high with dead and wounded, some still struggling weakly as they moaned. A lieutenant was leading the company and he saluted as Arthur stopped in front of the gate and surveyed the scene.

'Looks like a hard fight, Lieutenant.'

'Aye, that it was, sir. They made a final stand in the passage there, and fought to the last. Brave lads they were.'

Arthur turned to the *killadar*. 'Was this the place?'

'Yes, *sahib*. This was where I last saw Sultan Tipoo. He sent me back to the palace to protect his wives while he defended the gate.'

'Very well.' Arthur nodded and turned to the lieutenant. 'I want the native bodies taken out of there and placed in a line by the wall.'

As the sun dipped towards the horizon and cast deep shadows behind the wall the redcoats reluctantly went about the distasteful task. The bodies, limp and slippery with blood, urine and ordure, were pulled out of the tangle of limbs and carried to one side. The *killadar*'s expression filled with grief as he recognised companions and friends from Tipoo's court who had fought and died alongside their ruler. As the light faded, Arthur ordered a torch to be lit so that the *killadar* could examine the bodies in its wavering glare. At last, two men emerged from the passage carrying a small portly man in a richly embroidered silk jacket. He was darker skinned than the others and had fine small hands.

The *killadar* swallowed and nodded. 'That is Sultan Tipoo.'

'Put him down,' Arthur ordered, and the two soldiers gently lowered the body to the ground. Arthur leaned closer and saw that apart from a few scratches and smears of blood, and a bullet wound to the shoulder, Tipoo seemed to have no lethal wound. Arthur undid some buttons on the jacket and tore open the silk shirt to reveal the dark smooth skin of the chest. He leaned his ear against it and listened for a moment, but there was no hearbeat.

'He's dead.'

The lieutenant came over. 'Is that him, sir? Tipoo?'

Arthur nodded.

'I remember this one. I saw him up there on the bastion, taking shots at us while his servants loaded his guns. He killed Lieutenant Lalor, shot him through the head. A fine shot at that range. That was before they went down to the passage to make their last stand. He was fighting it out with a sword when I saw him fall. How did he die?'

Arthur glanced over the body. 'It's hard to know for certain. Perhaps he fell and was knocked senseless. He was found near the bottom of the pile. It's likely that he suffocated.'

'Jesus . . .' The lieutenant shook his head. 'That's no way to die.'

Fitzroy muttered, 'There are worse ways, believe me.'

'Take the body to the palace,' Arthur ordered. 'His sons can confirm the identity. Once his men know that he's dead, there will be no reason to continue the fight.'

They returned to the palace, the body of the Tipoo being carried by a small detail of the men from the water gate. Tipoo's sons, his wives and the surviving courtiers gathered round the body and began to grieve, their anguished cries echoing back off the walls of his audience chamber. Baird came, in response to the news, and stood to one side looking over the scene. There was no pity in his eyes, just a cold look of satisfaction.

'I'll shed no tears for that brute,' he muttered to Arthur. 'Nor his family, nor the people of this wretched city.'

'What are your orders, sir?'

'Orders?' Baird frowned for a moment, and Arthur realised that the Scot was as exhausted as himself, and tiredness was dulling their minds. 'Your men are to guard the palace. Take Tipoo's sons back to General Harris, then return to the reserve column.'

'Yes, sir. What about the city?'

'What about it?'

'Should we not take steps to establish order here, sir? In case our men get out of control.'

'No. The men have earned their prize. The city is theirs.'

'Sir . . .' Arthur paused a moment. He could imagine the horrors that awaited the people of Seringapatam once the British soldiers, drunk on victory and arrack, began to vent their rage and lust on the inhabitants. 'Sir, it would be an unconscionable wrong to let our men sack the city.'

Baird shrugged his broad shoulders. 'Rules of war, Wellesley. Nothing I can do about it. Nothing I will do about it. Not after the way I was treated by these bastards. Now, if you please, you have your orders.'

'Yes, sir.' Arthur saluted and turned away.

He left the city with a company of his men to escort Tipoo's sons to the headquarters of General Harris. Already the sacking of Seringapatam had begun. Occasional gunshots echoed across the city, together with the drunken shouts and singing of the soldiers, and screams and pleas for mercy from its people. A fire flared up in one quarter, casting an orange loom over a corner of the city, and Arthur regarded the scene with disgust and a leaden sense of despair in his heart. Then he turned away and followed his men down through the breach and across the dark waters of the south Cauvery. If there really were crocodiles in the river, they would be feasting on the dead who had been killed while trying to flee from the island.

General Harris received Tipoo's sons graciously and promised that they would be well treated the moment they had given their paroles. As they were led away Harris joined Arthur as he stood gazing through the tent flaps towards Seringapatam. Listening to the distant pop of gunfire and faint shouts and screams both men were well aware of the horrors unfolding in the city.

'Baird's not holding his men back, then?'

'No, sir.'

'A pity. This is going to make the job that much more difficult for the man who is to take charge of the city. There will plenty of work to be done winning the natives over to our side. It will require a man with uncommon powers of persuasion and organisation. Major General Baird is not that man,' Harris concluded sadly, before he turned to Arthur. 'That is why it must be you, Colonel Wellesley.'

'Sir?'

'I've made my decision. I want you to be the first Governor of Mysore.'

'Me, sir?' Arthur was too tired to hide his shock and surprise.

'You. Now get back to your tent and get some sleep. You take charge of the city first thing in the morning.'

Chapter 50

Napoleon

Paris, October 1799

Josephine entered the house as quietly as she could and closed the servants' door behind her. Even though it was early in the evening the house was silent. She knew that Napoleon had already arrived. The coach he had travelled in from Marseilles was in the yard beside the stable at the back of the house, and the horses were quietly munching on their feed. She had instructed the driver of the carriage she had borrowed from Barras to drop her at the end of the street. As soon as word reached Paris that Napoleon had returned from Egypt, Josephine had been thrown into a panic. Enough people in the city already knew of her unfaithfulness for word to have come to the ears of her husband's family, and it was certain that he would discover the truth soon enough, if he had not already. So Josephine had gone to her old friend Paul Barras and begged him to lend her his best carriage and horses so that she might meet Napoleon on the road to Paris and tell him the truth, before the rest of his family could fill his head with their version of events. She had resolved to find him, seek his forgiveness, promise to be faithful for ever more, and get him into bed. A night of passion would win him over so completely that no amount of sordid scandalmongering from his family would tear him from her. Unfortunately, the damned driver had lost his way on the road from Paris and after two days of confusion Josephine had ordered him to return to the capital.

She stood a moment on the threshold of the hall and listened. The only sound she could hear above the muffled noises from the street was the ticking of a clock. Swallowing nervously, she made her way along the hall, wincing as a floorboard creaked beneath her. A lamp burned above the front door and the warm glow of a fire in the hearth of the sitting room cast its orange hue in a slant across the hall. By the feeble light she noticed a large mass crowding the corner by the door. As she approached, the shape resolved itself into a pile of chests, hatboxes and bags, neatly stacked. With a stab of anxiety Josephine realised that these were her belongings, all of them, packed and ready to go.

'Oh, no . . .' she moaned. Then, steeling herself, she glanced into the sitting room. But it was empty, even though the fire had only recently been built up and the wood crackled and hissed as it burned.

'Mother?' The voice came from directly behind her and Josephine's heart leaped as she spun round. Hortense stood at the entrance to the kitchen. In the glow of the lamp Josephine could see that she had been crying.

'My God, he hasn't hurt you, has he?'

Hortense shook her head.

'Where is he?'

'Upstairs, in your bedroom.' Hortense swallowed nervously. 'He was in a wild rage when he arrived. Shouting and calling you all sorts of names when he discovered you weren't here. He called you a . . . a whore, and smashed all the mirrors in your dressing room. Then he told his servant to pack all your belongings. He says he wants you out of his house for ever.'

'Only when I'm good and ready,' Josephine muttered and turned to the stairs, hurriedly climbing to the first floor where the main bedroom was at the rear of the house. Skirts rustling over the floorboards she strode to the door and turned the handle. The door did not yield and she realised that Napoleon had locked her out.

'Napoleon. Open the door.'

'Go away!'

She smiled. At least he had spared her the pretence of ignoring her. 'Go away? From my house, and from the side of my husband? Why would I want to do that?'

'So you can be in the arms of your lover, you traitor!'

'What lover?'

'The one you were with when I reached Paris. When you should have been here.'

A wave of relief swept through Josephine. She took a breath to calm her nerves, and lowered her voice. 'I wasn't in Paris. I was on the road looking for you. My coachman took a wrong turning and we must have missed you.' It sounded false even as she said it, but it was true, and she could prove it easily enough.

'Liar!'

'It's true!' she called back. 'I swear it on the lives of my children. As soon as I heard you had landed in France I set off to meet you. I could not wait to be back in your arms again. And if that damned coachman had known his business that's where I would have been three days ago. Oh, Napoleon, my love, open the door. I beg you!'

'No. Now go. Please.'

Please? She smiled to herself at the first sign of his weakening.

'I cannot go. I love you. I would die if I could not be at your side.'

'Then you can die for all I care.'

She felt anger rising inside at his words, but forced herself to maintain her pleading tone. 'Very well, my love. I will go. But only if you let me see your face one last time. I will not say goodbye to a door, Napoleon. Open it and make your farewell face to face.'

There was a short pause, before he said suspiciously, 'Why?'

'We are adults, my love, so please let's behave with the dignity of adults.' She made her tone as gentle and reasonable as possible. 'Now, open this door.'

There was silence, then the soft padding of bare feet. Her heart beat fast against her breast as a key turned in the door and a moment later the handle twisted and the door opened slowly.

★

Next morning Lucien arrived on the doorstep of his brother's house and rapped the knocker. A moment later the door was opened by the preposterously dressed servant Napoleon had brought back with him from Egypt.

'Has my brother risen?'

'No, sir.' Roustam stood aside to let Lucien pass, and Lucien could not help smiling as he saw that the hall was empty of all the baggage that had been there when he had called the day before. 'Ah – she's gone then.'

'Sir, I—'

'Just get some coffee brewing and take it to the study. My brother and I will be in conference this morning.'

'But, sir . . .'

'Just prepare the coffee!' Lucien repeated. He climbed the stairs two at a time. He felt elated by the departure of Josephine. Now his brother would be able to concentrate his full energies on other, far more important, matters. Reaching the door at the end of the landing, he did not knock, but turned the handle and entered the room.

'Napoleon, it's late. You were supposed to be at my house an hour ago. As it is I've come to you and—'

He stopped abruptly and stared towards the bed. Napoleon was propped up on a pillow, his pasty white chest naked and his dark hair as rumpled and untidy as the tangled bedclothes that covered his lower body. Resting her head on his shoulder was Josephine. Lucien took a deep breath and clenched his teeth to hold back his surprise and anger. He took a step back towards the door.

'I apologise, madam. I had no idea you were here.'

'Evidently,' she smiled. She leaned further into Napoelon and nuzzled up to his breast, kissing his flesh.

Lucien flushed with irritation and embarrassment. 'I, er, need to speak with my brother. At once.' He fixed his eyes on Napoleon. 'It's very important. I'll wait for you down in the study. Don't take too long.'

He turned and left them, shutting the door behind him. As the sound of his footsteps retreated along the landing Josephine smiled to herself.

★

'Now that you're here,' Lucien said testily, 'we can finally begin.'

Napoleon did not reply, but smiled and helped himself to a cup of coffee and sat down. He took a careful sip and grimaced as he realised it was cold. He set the cup down and looked at his younger brother. 'Well?'

'You have picked a good time to return. A very good time indeed, brother.'

'Good?' Napoleon's brow rose in surprise. 'France is at war with England, Austria, Naples, Portugal and Turkey. The only enemy who is willing to discuss peace is Russia, and then only because Tsar Paul hates the English even more than he hates us. Our army is still recovering fom the defeat at Novi. Most of the departments of France are on the verge of rebellion, our troops haven't been paid for months and the treasury is almost empty, and the Jacobins are pushing for a new Committee of Public Safety. What have the Directory done with the country that I left so powerful when I sailed to Egypt? The situation could hardly be worse.'

'And therefore the opportunities for change could hardly be better.' Lucien smiled. 'Especially as those who govern us at present are so hopelessly divided. Talleyrand is in disgrace since he tried to get a bribe out of a treaty with the Americans. General Bernadotte is hardly making a secret of his schemes to seize power. Barras, so my informants tell me, is even plotting a coup to return the Bourbons to power. And now you arrive in Paris, on the crest of a wave of popularity thanks to your victory at Aboukir. That's about the only news the people have had to celebrate for months. They are desperate for change.'

Napoleon eyed him shrewdly. 'And you are keen to give it to them, no doubt.'

'Me, and others like me,' Lucien admitted. 'I've managed to stay clear of political scandals, and I command the support of a large number of the deputies, but I lack the affection of the people. If something is going to happen, if my comrades and I are to change the government, then we'll need a figurehead to lead the movement. It has to be someone untainted by the politics of the capital. Someone who is popular with the mob, and who can command the respect and loyalty of the army.'

'Someone like me, I imagine.' Napoleon smiled.

Lucien's expression remained serious. 'It has to be you. Any other choice would be too divisive. You'd only have to be the public face of the new government. Once things have settled down, you could return to the army and retire from public life.'

'I might not want to,' Napoleon said carefully.

'It's possible that your . . . retirement from public life, might not be in the best interests of France. But I wouldn't express such a view in front of those whose help we will need in the days to come.'

'I understand.' Napoleon eased himself back in his chair. 'Who else is in on your plans?'

'Two of the Directors, Sieyès and Ducos. We've sounded out Talleyrand, Joseph Fouché and some of the other ministers. They're all for a change in government and want a new, more powerful executive in its place. The thing is, many of them are afraid of using a soldier as the putative leader of the coup.'

'Very wise of them. And at the same time they're being foolish. They want a centralised government with the authority to act swiftly and decisively, and at the same time they're afraid of the consequences of such a move.' Napoleon shook his head with contempt. 'They can't have it both ways.'

'They know that,' said Lucien. 'That's what has been paralysing them for months. The trouble is with Bernadotte and Barras circling like wolves their hand is finally being forced. You weren't their first choice. Sieyès wanted Joubert, but he was killed at the battle of Novi and you're our last chance. Sieyès isn't keen on you. He is worried about your "incendiary temperament" as he put it, and your ambition.'

'Then he's no fool.'

'We must handle him carefully, brother.'

Napoleon nodded. 'When do we make our move?'

'I've thought about that. Not until after your official reception by the Directors. We have to see how they react to your popularity. They might question your reasons for abandoning the army in Egypt. They may try to fling some shit at you and hope enough sticks to taint your public image.'

'A compelling vision, Lucien, but hardly poetic.'

Lucien slapped his hand down on his thigh in irritation. 'This isn't a game, Napoleon! We are playing for the highest possible stakes. We foul this up and it might cost us our lives.'

'You know, if we succeed, it might also mean the fall of the revolution.'

'Perhaps, but anything is better than a return to the monarchy. Almost anything.'

Two days later, Napoleon presented himself, in full uniform, before the Directors in the audience chamber of the Luxembourg Palace. There were far fewer officials there to witness the meeting than there had been on his last such appearance. The president of the Directory, Louis Gohier, greeted Napoleon cordially and offered him the congratulations and gratitude of the Directors, on behalf of the people of France. Then he glanced at Barras, and Napoleon noted that Barras gave a slight nod before Gohier turned back and continued.

'The Directory, like all France, greets your unanticipated return with pleasure mingled with a little surprise. Only your enemies, whom we naturally regard as our own, could put an unfavourable interpretation on the patriotic motives which induced you to abandon your army.'

Napoleon felt his blood surge with anger but managed to keep his tone calm and respectful as he replied. 'Citizen, the news that reached us in Egypt was so alarming that I didn't hesitate to leave my army, but set out at once to come and share your perils.' Napoleon grasped the hilt of his sword. 'I swear that this sword will never be drawn except in defence of the republic, and its government.'

Barras leaned forward and smiled. 'We are comforted to hear that, General. And we will endeavour to find a new command suited to a man of your talents and ambitions just as soon as we can, so that you might be spared the interminable politics that bedevil Paris.'

The words were spoken with such deliberate emphasis that Napoleon suddenly felt that his façade of loyalty was as transparent as the finest blown glass and that his ambition was on view for all to see. The ceremony ended and he approached the Directors and embraced each one of them in turn, in a frosty gesture of fraternity. As he left the palace the sentries at the gate presented arms and chorused, 'Long live Bonaparte!' The cry was echoed by the dense crowd of civilians who pressed around his coach as it passed through the gates and on to the street. Napoleon smiled and waved to his public and wondered how many of them would still be so enthusiastic in their support for him in a month's time.

'It has to be soon,' Napoleon said firmly as he looked round at the men in his study. 'The Directors dare not discipline me now, for fear of the public reaction. But the moment my popular support fades they will move against me, and I will have no chance of leading the coup.'

Sieyès stirred uneasily. 'This isn't about your salvation, General Bonaparte. It is about the salvation of France.'

'Of course it is,' Napoleon agreed readily. 'I understand that, citizen, as I understand that I am merely the instrument through which our cause will achieve its aim. No man shall rise above his peers.'

'Quite,' Lucien intervened. 'And that point must not be forgotten, whatever else happens. But my brother is right. We cannot wait any longer. Bernadotte is building his support amongst the Jacobins in the Council of the Five Hundred. Unless we move first he will be ready to act within a matter of weeks. Of course, the Directors will oppose him, but if he has the Council, and the mob, then they are finished, and we will have lost our chance. That being the situation, I say we make our move early in November. I have already won over General Moreau to our cause and most of the other generals in Paris will follow my brother.'

'Until we have a new constitution,' Sieyès reminded him firmly. 'Then the general will step aside and return power to a civil authority.'

'Of course.' Napoleon nodded.

Sieyès gave him a searching look for a moment and then turned his attention back to Lucien. 'When do we do it?'

'November the ninth. My brother will be breakfasting with the officers of the Paris garrison before he goes on to inspect some new regiments. That will keep him at a distance while we neutralise the Directory.'

'How can we achieve that?' Ducos spoke for the first time, and Napoleon had to hide his instinctive dislike of the man. Thin and wheedling, Ducos embodied the worst of the politicians who had undermined the revolution. 'We need three of the five Directors to authorise any votes put in front of the deputies and the senators. Sieyès and I can't do it by ourselves.'

'You won't need to.' Lucien smiled. 'On the day, you two will go to Barras. You will offer him a deal. Bribe him if necessary. He is to resign his office for a suitable fee, or be placed under arrest along with Gohier and Moulin. Either way you two will be able to initiate the votes we will need to push our reforms through. November the ninth,' Lucien repeated. 'Are we agreed?'

There was a brief silence as the plotters considered the plans. One by one they nodded their assent, and Lucien stood up. 'Then there is no more to be said. On the tenth, if all goes to plan, France will wake to find itself with a new government.'

'If all goes to plan?' Sieyès shook his head ruefully. 'When does anything ever go to plan?'

'Well, pray that it does.' Napoleon forced himself to smile. 'Otherwise that day may well be our last.'

Chapter 51

'Barras cost us more than we anticipated,' Lucien explained. 'He wouldn't go for less than two million francs.'

'Two million!' Napoleon whistled appreciatively. 'I had no idea that a man's principles were worth so much.'

'Neither did he, I suspect.'

'What about the others?' Napoleon asked anxiously.

'Moreau has placed Gohier and Moulin under house arrest. Lannes and Marmont have troops in place covering the entrances to the Tuileries. Moreau has the Luxembourg Palace surrounded and we have troops at Versailles and Murat's cavalry detachment at St-Cloud. The Jacobin club has been closed and Bernadotte and the ringleaders of his group are being held on the premises. There have been no reports of any resistance so far. So, all is going well, and it's time for your appearance before the senators.'

Napoleon looked at his brother. 'Are you certain that they will support us?'

'Of course! We'll have a clear majority, but there will be a few opponents. As for the rest, they won't know which way to jump and won't cause us any problems. Are you ready to go?'

'As ready as I ever will be.'

'Good. Come then, brother, it's time to change the world.'

They left Napoleon's study and made for the front door as Josephine emerged from the sitting room opposite. Napoleon had not told her about the plot, but the frequent comings and goings of politicians and generals at all hours of the day and night had made it quite clear that something was being hatched and Josephine stared at him with an anxious expression.

'Whatever happens today, my love, I pray you have good fortune.'

Napoleon went to her, drew her into his arms and kissed her on the lips. 'I'll send word to you as soon as there is an outcome.'

'Napoleon!' His brother beckoned to him. 'We have to go, now.'

Napoleon kissed her once more and broke away from her, hurrying out of the house without a backward glance. Josephine followed him as far as the door and watched as he climbed into Lucien's carriage. With a crack of the driver's whip, it lurched forward and rattled down the street, in the direction of the Tuileries.

The soldiers outside the National Assembly cheered as soon as they saw Napoleon descend from the carriage. He wore his finest uniform and his new bicorn hat with a large revolutionary cockade attached. A broad red sash was tied round his waist and a jewelled sword hilt glittered in the clear autumn sunlight. The two brothers entered the building and made for the chamber where the senators sat in tense expectation. As Napoleon entered the room the senators rose to their feet and applauded, many only half-heartedly, he noted. The president of the chamber indicated the speaker's lectern and Lucien stepped up, and opened with the text he had agreed with Napoleon the previous night.

'Senators! The Directors have met and agreed the following motion which is to be put before the house. That the existing constitution be suspended and that, while a new constitution is drawn up, three Provisional Consuls, General Bonaparte and Citizens Sieyès and Ducos, will be charged with the government of the republic. Furthermore, that both legislative assemblies are temporarily relocated to St-Cloud where they will be safe from any attempt by the Jacobin-inspired mob to intervene in the processes of government. There is no need for any debate of this matter and voting will proceed at once.' He turned and bowed to the president of the chamber and did not move from the lectern as the vote was called. A clear majority of the assembly showed their support and after due prompting a number of waverers raised their hands.

'The motion is carried,' announced the president and Lucien raised his hands to silence the muttering that echoed round the hall. 'This session is now suspended. It will be resumed at St-Cloud tomorrow. Honoured gentlemen, I would ask you to leave the chamber at once and make your arrangements for transfer to St-Cloud.'

As the senators began to mutter to each other, Napoleon edged closer to his brother and spoke softly. 'That seemed to go well enough.'

'For now, but there may well be a few problems tomorrow, once they wake up to the true scope of the new arrangements.'

'And what will my part be? I felt a bit like a tailor's dummy just standing there.'

'It's better that you say nothing. It's important that you are seen to be above the debate. Leave that to the politicians and it will seem that the army is not forcing the issue. Otherwise the Jacobins who are still at large will have the mob on the streets before you know it.'

'The mob will not be happy once they get wind of the changes.'

'Once we secure the support of both houses tomorrow everything will seem perfectly legal and democratic. There will be no justification for opposing us, and any who attempt it will be arrested and dealt with according to the law, whatever we decide the law is after tomorrow.' Lucien smiled, and slapped his brother on the shoulder. 'Rest easy, Napoleon. We've done all that we set out to achieve. Tomorrow's votes are no more than a formality.'

'I hope so,' Napoleon replied as he watched the last of the senators file out of the hall. Some looked back at him with nervous expressions, some with defiant glares.

The next day, the debates at St-Cloud were delayed as the halls chosen to act as makeshift debating chambers were not fully prepared, and the deputies and senators walked the grounds in small groups, talking quietly under the gaze of the grenadiers who guarded the building. Lucien and Napoleon were watching them from a balcony above the garden.

'I don't like the look of this,' Lucien said quietly. 'The delay is giving the Jacobins a chance to get organised. They could cause us a problem in the house of deputies.'

'But you're the president of the chamber,' said Napoleon. 'You can control the debate, make sure it goes our way.'

'I'll do my best, of course, but the vote will be close. I think it best if you remain outside the chamber today. This lot have more balls than the senate and won't be quite so easily impressed by your presence.'

As soon as the halls were prepared Lucien and his followers ushered the deputies inside, and as they took up their seats it was clear that many of them regarded him with open hostility. When the last of them was in position, the doors to the hall were closed and Napoleon joined the officers and men waiting in the courtyard of St-Cloud. As soon as the debate opened the cheers and roars of protest occasionally carried outside to those waiting for the outcome, where Napoleon paced anxiously up and down the flagstones round the long ornamental pond. At noon, Junot rode into the courtyard and dismounted. He marched to Napoleon's side.

'What's the news, sir?'

'Nothing! They sit there on their fat lawyer arses and talk and talk. God! It's a wonder that the government ever decides on anything.' He shook his head in frustration. 'And Paris, Junot? What is the reaction on the streets?'

'They're tame enough. Rumours are circulating, but that's all. We control all the streets around the Tuileries and the National Assembly. There won't be any uprising, or protest that we can't handle.'

'Good . . . That's something at least.' Napoleon stared at the hall housing the deputies and slapped his hand against his thigh in irritation. 'Damn it, why can't they just get on with the vote?'

Junot was silent for a moment, then glanced round to make sure that he would not be overheard before he spoke in a low voice. 'Sir, may I ask what the orders will be if the vote goes against us?'

Napoleon looked at him. 'It won't go against us.'

'But what if it does, sir? What then?'

'I tell you it won't, and I'll make sure of that right now.' Napoleon turned to the nearest group of grenadiers, who were talking quietly as they puffed on their pipes. 'You men, form up! You're my escort to the debating chamber, so put those pipes out and smarten yourselves up!'

'What are you doing, sir?' Junot muttered.

'It's time I spoke to our worthy deputies myself, and put them right on a few issues.'

'Is that wise, sir?' Junot asked anxiously. 'If you intervene, they will be calling you a tyrant on the streets of Paris before the day is out.'

'Better that, than let those fools ruin everything that we have gained so far.' Napoleon turned to the squad of soldiers formed up at his back and snapped his fingers. 'Follow me!'

He led them inside the house, and up the flight of stairs that led to the debating chamber. Two men from the national guard stood outside the doors and they moved uncertainly to block Napoleon's path.

'Out of my way!'

'General, you cannot enter. The chamber is in closed session.'

'Then it's time we opened the debate up,' Napoleon replied and pushed the men aside. They were too shocked to react as he grasped the handles of the doors and thrust them open, so hard that one crashed back against the doorframe. Inside the ballroom hundreds of faces turned towards the doorway. Lucien, sitting on a large chair at a long table on a dais, glared at his brother. The speaker at the lectern pointed towards Napoleon. 'What is the meaning of this intrusion, General Bonaparte? Why are there soldiers with you?'

Napoleon ignored the speaker as he marched into the chamber and indicated that his soldiers should form up beside the platform on which the lectern rested. He turned to Lucien. 'I request permission to address the assembly.'

Lucien glanced round the hall. Most of the deputies seemed too stunned by the intervention to react. Several of the Jacobins were talking quietly to each other as they shot hostile looks towards his brother. If he denied Napoleon the chance to speak, then his brother would leave the chamber humiliated. Lucien realised that his hand had been forced. He cleared his throat.

'The Assembly recognises General Bonaparte, and will hear him speak.'

Napoleon bowed his head. 'Thank you, President.' He climbed the three steps to the platform and strode towards the lectern. The speaker still stood there, and Napoleon gestured to the steps on the other side of the platform. 'Return to your seat . . . please.'

For a moment Napoleon was worried that the man might defy him and refuse to give up the platform, but then he took a pace back and retreated towards the steps, causing a ripple of whispering and angry muttering to sweep through the hall. Lucien banged his gavel down several times until the chamber was silent again. When all was still, Napoleon gripped the edge of the lectern and stared out over the anxious white faces that surrounded him like a field of tennis balls. He felt a surge of contempt for these men who sat on their fat arses and talked while he and his men marched and bled for France. He drew a breath and began.

'Citizens, my soldiers and I have been waiting for a decision for over three hours. I . . . we cannot understand the reason for the delay. Nor will France understand the reason.'

A man in the front row of seats to the left of the platform jumped up and stabbed his finger towards Napoleon. 'You do not speak for France! You are a soldier, a subordinate of the state. We are the voice of France!'

As the chamber filled with cries of support for the deputy, Lucien hammered his gavel furiously until silence returned. 'I am sure that General Bonaparte is aware of the authority of the Assembly of Deputies. He will not need reminding again. Please continue, General.'

Napoleon gave the deputy who had interrupted him a

withering stare, then resumed. 'Every man in this room, from the president of the chamber down to the most junior of my grenadiers there, speaks for France, and desires only that she might vanquish her enemies and improve the lot of her people. For that to happen there must be change. That was accepted yesterday by the Directors and the members of the senate. All that remains is for this chamber to complete the process by voting for the provisional government.' He thrust a hand out and pointed at the audience accusingly. 'If you fail to do that, and do it immediately, then you fail your people and you fail France herself!'

The deputy was on his feet again, and took several steps towards the platform as he shouted, 'How dare you address the house in such a fashion!'

More cries of protest echoed round the chamber and several of the Jacobins stood and waved their fists in the air. Napoleon regarded them with a cold expression and folded his arms while he waited for them to fall silent again as Lucien hammered away. But the clamour just grew and now most of the deputies were on their feet and pressing forward towards the platform. The sergeant in charge of the grenadiers glanced round at Napoleon, waiting for instructions. For the first time Napoleon felt a prickle of anxiety at the base of his spine and he nodded to the sergeant and indicated the front of the platform. The sergeant barked an order to his men and they thrust their way through the crowd until they formed a cordon between Napoleon and the deputies. Lucien gave up his attempt to restore order and hurried over to his brother.

'We have to get out of here. Now.'

'I'm not afraid of these fools.'

Lucien grabbed his arm and hissed, 'It's you who are the fool! Because of you we risk losing everything! Now let's go before they tear us to pieces.'

Napoleon glanced back at the deputies and saw that a number of them had drawn knives and were brandishing them overhead, their faces contorted with anger. Their cries of rage and protest filled the hall and assaulted him from every side. He turned to Lucien and nodded. 'Let's go.'

It took an effort to walk calmly to the edge of the platform and descend to the floor. The grenadiers used their muskets to push the crowd back and create a small cordon round the two brothers, and then they forced their way back towards the door. Napoleon stared straight ahead and did not look at the angry faces shouting at him from only a few feet away. He felt something strike his cheek and realised that someone had spat on him. Abruptly he stopped, but Lucien took his arm and forced him on, towards the door. 'Keep going!'

They were pursued out of the chamber and the deputies only gave up when Napoleon, Lucien and their escort hurriedly retreated down the stairs. Shaken, the two brothers emerged into the courtyard where hundreds of other soldiers and officers had gathered in response to the deafening howls of protest from the chamber. They stared at their commander in shock and Lucien gripped his arm.

'Speak to them! Say something quickly!'

'Say what?'

'Napoleon, for God's sake, all will be decided in the next few minutes. We've lost the debate. Now we must use force. The men are waiting for a lead. You'd better give it right now, or everything is lost.'

He gave his older brother a gentle push and Napoleon stepped forward, on to the edge of the flight of steps that looked out over the courtyard. Napoleon drew a deep breath and thrust out his arms towards his men.

'Soldiers! We are betrayed. The deputies have defied the will of the Directors, the senators and the people of France! They would seek to sell their loyalty to our enemies. They even attempted to assassinate the president of the chamber and me just a moment ago. I wanted to speak to the deputies and they answered me with daggers!' Napoleon beat his fist against his chest. 'I have served the revolution since the first. I have shed my blood on the battlefield for the revolution and you all know how many victories I have won for the honour of France. Yet they call me traitor! They are the traitors! The crisis is at hand, my comrades. If we hesitate now then all France is lost! We must clear out that nest of traitors.' He stabbed a finger towards the debating chamber and many of the soldiers cheered.

Lucien noticed that a good many still did not look convinced. He stepped forward and drew Napoleon's sword and held it aloft. 'Soldiers! Soldiers, hear me! I am Lucien Bonaparte, brother of the general. I love him as dearly as my life itself, yet I swear to you that I would run him through with this blade if ever he threatened the liberty that we have gained through the revolution!' His voice trembled with emotion and the men in the courtyard were visibly moved by his words. Lucien pressed on. 'The revolution is in grave danger, soldiers. The royalists are on the verge of victory. Only we can stop them. The cry once more is, To Arms! Long live General Bonaparte! Long live the revolution! Long live France!'

The soldiers took up the cheers and the deafening roar filled the courtyard. While it continued, Napoleon found the officer in command of the grenadiers and hurriedly gave his orders. The men formed up quickly and with a drummer beating the advance they tramped into the building and up the stairs towards the debating chamber. The deputies, who were busy debating a motion to declare Napoleon an outlaw, turned nervously towards the sound. As the doors were flung open by the soldiers panic gripped them and they ran from the hall, knocking chairs and each other over as they scrambled towards the other exits and even the windows, dropping down into the gardens below before streaming away from St-Cloud.

Only a handful remained. Those who were the most loyal supporters of Lucien and his brother. As night fell the president returned to the chamber. He stared at the rows of overturned chairs and abandoned notebooks and papers. Then he calmly resumed his seat on the platform. A company of grenadiers guarded the entrances with orders not to admit anyone. Lucien had prepared a document which he now read out to the handful of deputies gathered before him.

'The motion before the chamber of deputies is that this house approves the decisions of the Directors and senators of the republic to dissolve the government, pending the drafting of a new constitution by a provisional body.' He looked up. 'All those in favour?' His words echoed round the hall with a hollow sound as his supporters raised their hands. There was a brief pause before Lucien smiled. 'The motion is carried unanimously.' He banged his gavel. 'I declare this session closed, and the house dissolved. My thanks to you, gentlemen. My thanks, and the gratitude of the nation.'

Lucien was the last to leave the chamber and he paused to take a final look round before he smiled and went to find his brother, who was waiting in one of the drawing rooms with the other senior officers, as well as Sieyès and Ducos.

'It's done,' he announced simply. 'All authority has now passed into the hands of the provisional consulate.' He bowed his head to Sieyès and Ducos. 'May I be the first to offer you my congratulations?'

Then he turned to Napoleon. 'First Consul, what are your orders?'

Chapter 52

'Moreau?' Napoleon eased himself lower into his bath so that the water lapped over the edge of his chin. He shook his head. 'And what does General Moreau have to say to me today?'

Bourrienne broke the seal and unfolded the dispatch. He held it carefully so that the perspiration that glistened on his brow did not drip on to the paper and make the ink run. The steam that filled the bathroom of Napoleon's apartment at the Luxembourg Palace was bad enough already for the documents that Bourrienne was obliged to bring in to read to the First Consul, while Napoleon spent up to two hours at a time immersed in the hottest water that he could stand. Peculiar working conditions, Bourrienne thought to himself, but then Napoleon was a peculiar individual. Since the December plebiscite had confirmed popular support for the new constitution, Napoleon had drawn to himself the workload of almost every major office of state. The First Consul worked seventeen or eighteen hours a day, not counting his baths, and there seemed to be no detail, however small, that ever escaped his phenomenal memory. With a mind like that in charge of France's affairs the other two consuls had soon proved to be superfluous. Sieyès and Ducos, after some faltering efforts to stand alongside Napoleon, had accepted the inevitable and given up their posts at the heart of the new government. But not everyone supported Napoleon's rise to power. Many politicians and army officers were uncertain about the bloodless coup of November, and none more so than Moreau.

In the weeks that followed Napoleon had been careful to reward his followers and make peace with his rivals. Murat had been appointed commander of the Consular Guard – a hand-picked corps of tough veterans whose duty it was to protect Napoleon. Murat had also been permitted to take Caroline Bonaparte as his bride, and while Napoleon was glad to have such a formidable soldier for a brother-in-law he could not help thinking that Murat had his work cut out with the most shrewish of Napoleon's sisters. Fouché was now head of police and Talleyrand was in charge of foreign affairs. Masséna was in command of the Army of Italy, Berthier would shortly be in command of the Army of Reserve and Moreau had the most prestigious command of them all – the well-equipped and hard-fighting Army of the Rhine. Which was where Napoleon's chief difficulty lay.

Bourrienne quickly scanned the note and then began to read it through. 'He's taking issue again with your plan for the coming campaign.'

Napoleon was silent for a moment, his brow gradually tightening into a dark scowl as he stared at the chandelier overhead. At length he muttered, 'Damn the man, what does he think he is playing at? We must beat Austria and we must beat her swiftly. To do that we must destroy her armies and take Vienna before autumn sets in. Any fool can see that. But not Moreau. No, he wants to creep forward like a tortoise, and duck back into his shell the moment he senses danger. Bastard . . .'

Bourrienne refrained from comment, and waited a moment before coughing lightly. 'Do you wish me to take down a letter to him, sir?'

'No . . . Wait.' Napoleon's head rose a little higher above the steam swirling off the surface of the water. 'He's reviewing a new cavalry formation near Montmartre, is he not?'

'Yes, sir.'

'Then send for him. I will meet him here this evening, with Berthier and Talleyrand. See to it at once.'

Bourrienne stood up, collected his papers and bowed, greatly relieved to quit the stifling humidity of Napoleon's bathroom. As he made for the door there was a splash of water from the overfilled bath as Napoleon raised an arm. 'And send Roustam in. It's time I was out of here and got dressed.'

'Yes, sir.'

Once he was alone again Napoleon raised his hands to his face and relished the sensation of moist warmth against his eyes. He was tired. More tired than he had ever been and more tired than he should permit himself to be, he reflected. In truth, the seemingly endless difficulties facing the government could only begin to be solved if there was peace with England and Austria. But that seemed more unlikely than ever, now that the two powers had curtly rebuffed his offers to talk peace. If only that wretched man William Pitt could put the interests of his people above his personal abhorrence of France there might be peace, Napoleon considered. However, there was little hope of that, and Napoleon resigned himself to the prospect of the English Prime Minister obstinately dragging out the war for years to come, defying France, and Napoleon, from the other side of the Channel. Meanwhile, Austria was the only enemy that France could close with and destroy. So it was against Austria that the full fury of France's army would be launched.

'Sir, your gown.'

Napoleon glanced up with a start. Once again his intense preoccupation with policy had driven out all awareness of his surroundings and Roustam had entered the room without his realising. He stared at his Mameluke servant and wondered if this blindness to minions was what happened when a man became a ruler of his nation. If so, it was a dangerous development, and Napoleon had no intention of ending up like Marat. He rose up, shedding water in a steaming cascade, and stepping out of the bath he took the gown that Roustam proffered to him, anxious to get dry and dressed in his uniform so that he would no longer feel naked and vulnerable.

'Would you like breakfast, sir?'

'Yes. No, wait. Is my wife still in bed?'

'I believe so, sir.'

'Then I'll have breakfast later. You may go.'

Roustam bowed and backed out of the room. Napoleon

rubbed the gown against his flesh as he made for the door that led to his sleeping quarters. First Consul he might be, but his needs were the same as any other young man's.

Dinner, like all meals shared with Napoleon, was eaten in a hurry. The First Consul resented spending any more time than was necessary on consuming food, especially when there was important business at hand. The stewards cleared away the plates, dishes, cutlery and glasses and left the four men to themselves, quietly closing the door on the room.

'Well,' Talleyrand said as he dabbed at his lips with a napkin. 'The food was good, what little of it I had the chance to taste. So what is the purpose of this meeting, Citizen First Consul? Since I assume we weren't just invited to enjoy your hospitality.'

Napoleon made himself smile at the foreign minister's manner. Talleyrand represented much of what Napoleon despised, and admired, of the ancient regime. His manners were refined to the point of being an art form, and his offhand manner left people in no doubt that he considered them to be beneath him. His dry wit chafed Napoleon's nerves, and yet if ever there was a man who was destined to deal in the duplicity of diplomacy it was Talleyrand, and therefore Napoleon was grateful that he had accepted the appointment. But he still loathed the man.

'No, indeed. And now that we have eaten it is time to talk.' Napoleon gestured round the table. 'It falls to the four of us to decide what direction France is to take in the coming months. What does France need?'

'Peace,' Talleyrand said at once. 'Citizen Consul, if you are to cement your hold on France then we must have peace. The people are tired of war. Our navy is in a deplorable state, the army is not much better and the treasury is all but empty. We need to make peace in order to consolidate the gains of the revolution.'

'I have tried to make peace,' Napoleon said wearily. 'You know what the English said in their reply to me? "Peace is impossible with a nation that is against all order, religion and morality." ' He shook his head. 'While that is their attitude there can only be war between us, and we can be sure that England will continue to subsidise any nation that stands against us.'

Talleyrand smiled. 'It seems that the English are preparing to fight to the last Austrian.'

'Quite,' Napoleon continued, irritated by the interruption. 'And while their navy controls the seas then we have to turn our attention towards the Austrians. What realistic chance is there of peace with Austria?'

Talleyrand was still for a moment, as he considered the question. Then he shrugged. 'Not much. They are keen to keep the territory they currently occupy in Italy and they wish France to give up the Low Countries. We would only have peace if we consented to both demands.' He looked closely at Napoleon. 'Of course, if you are serious about peace, then you could always meet their demands.'

'No!' Moreau slapped his hand down on the table. 'That would be an insult to France, and our armies. I would not stand for it, and neither should you.' He spoke directly to Napoleon. 'If we conceded so much the people would be outraged. Given their present ill humour, a diplomatic reverse on that scale might trigger another coup.'

'That is possible,' Talleyrand conceded. 'And we'd probably end up with yet another general in charge, and be back where we started.' He paused. 'I wonder who that general might be, in the unlikely event of a coup.'

'Thank you, Talleyrand,' Napoleon cut in. 'I think we are agreed. There can be no compromise with Austria, and the war must be ended as swiftly as possible. In which case, it is time to consider the means by which that can be achieved. Berthier, the map.'

Berthier rose from his chair and crossed to a chest of drawers. He retrieved a large map and returned to the table, where he spread it out between the four men. They gazed down at a detailed rendering of central Europe. Talleyrand's quick eye immediately picked out the preliminary dispositions of the forces that Berthier had marked out.

'I see now that this meeting was not to seek our advice, but to give us orders, Citizen Consul.'

A frown flickered across Napleon's face. 'While I value the opinions of my . . . colleagues the time for a decision has come. Now then,' he tapped the map, 'to business. Despite the recent setbacks in Italy and Germay we are in a good position to end the war decisively, thanks to our occupation of Switzerland. You are all aware that a new army has been gathering around Dijon – the Army of Reserve. In the next few days I will announce that Berthier is to be its commander.'

Berthier nodded slightly, since he was already aware of his appointment.

'Who is to replace him as Minister of War?' asked Moreau.

'Carnot.'

'Carnot? I thought he had been disgraced.'

Talleyrand smiled. 'Of course. That's what makes him so suitable for the job. He will be no threat to the new regime, especially if . . .' Talleyrand turned to look searchingly at Napoleon. 'I assume that means you will be taking the field against Austria.'

Moreau shook his head. 'The new constitution forbids that. The First Consul is prohibited from holding an army command.'

'That's true,' Napoleon agreed. 'I shall simply be accompanying Berthier in an advisory role. The command of the Army of Reserve is his.'

'Or at least that's how it will be presented to the people of France,' said Talleyrand. He dipped his head in acknowledgement of Napoleon's neat circumvention of the new rules.

'It seemed the obvious thing to do,' Napoleon replied off-handedly. 'It should be safe enough for me to leave Paris for a few months. The people will be loyal to the new regime for a while yet.'

'I can imagine,' said Talleyrand. 'Fouché is busy censoring the newspapers and I hear that soon all theatre owners must have their plays approved by him as well. Meanwhile, your brother Lucien has been hard at work commissioning patriotic songs and monuments to the glorious dead.'

'Your cynicism is misplaced,' Moreau responded coldly. 'Whatever you may think, the dead sacrificed their lives for France, which is more than you have done, citizen.'

Talleyrand shrugged. 'I have devoted my life to the service of my country. That is my sacrifice.'

Moreau snorted. 'What does a civilian know of sacrifice?'

'Did not Danton, Desmoulins and Robespierre know the meaning of sacrifice?' Talleyrand replied with icy calm.

'Gentlemen!' Napoleon raised a hand. 'That's enough. We do not have time for such petty altercations. Now then, to details. The plan was forwarded to the senior army commanders before Christmas. It was my intention that General Moreau's Army of the Rhine would deliver the main blow. To achieve this it was to deploy one of its corps to pin the Austrian army in the region of the Black Forest, while the other three corps crossed the Rhine near Schaffhausen, turned the enemy flank and fell on the rear of the Austrian army.'

'It sounds like a viable scheme.' Talleyrand raised his fine eyebrows. 'So why the past tense?'

'Because General Moreau has pointed out what he believes are unwarranted risks in the original plan,' Napoleon replied calmly. 'If you wouldn't mind, Moreau?'

'Indeed.' Moreau stood up and leaned over the map. 'It's a bold plan, Bonaparte, I grant you that. But it's too bold. There's not enough room for three corps to manoeuvre at Schaffhausen. Besides, if the enemy got wind of the plan they could defeat my army in detail.'

'Assuming they could march fast enough,' added Berthier.

'It is still a significant risk,' Moreau insisted. 'With all due respect to Bonaparte's plan, in my view it would be wiser to advance on a broad front on the north bank of the Rhine. And that is what I shall do,' Moreau concluded, and resumed his seat.

'Thank you, General.' Napoleon smiled. 'I'm sure you are wise to be cautious, given that you command by far the largest and best of our field armies. Consequently, I have amended the campaign plans, and now, instead of striking the main blow in Germany, it will fall in Italy instead. Gentlemen, it is my intention that the Army of Reserve will advance into Switzerland, and when it is fully equipped and provisioned – no later than the end of April – it will turn south, cross the Alps and cut across behind the Austrian army of General Melas so that the enemy will be crushed between the forces of Masséna and those of Berthier.'

'Cross the Alps in May?' Moreau shook his head. 'It can't be done. The passes will still be covered in snow and ice. It would be impossible to get the guns over the mountains, and what of the danger of avalanches? It would be the height of folly to attempt it.'

'The Austrians would never expect it,' Napoleon replied. 'That is why it must be done. That is why it will be done. And that is why we will defeat them . . . decisively.'

Moreau was silent for a moment. 'I can't approve of this plan.'

'I don't believe anyone asked you to,' said Talleyrand and Moreau glared at him.

'Yes, well that is the plan in any case.' Napoleon tapped the map. 'It will go ahead according to schedule, and I will be requiring you to release Lecourbe's division to reinforce Berthier the instant we open a route across the Alps.'

Moreau thought it over. 'Lecourbe commands one of my best divisions.'

'That is why I need his men.'

'Of course.' Moreau nodded. 'I will reinforce Berthier, as you suggest. Now, if you don't mind, Bonaparte, I must go. I have to leave for my army at first light. I will send you word the moment I begin my campaign.'

'That would be appreciated, General.'

The small meeting broke up as Talleyrand took his chance to leave with Moreau. Once they had left, Berthier stared at the door that had closed behind them.

'I don't trust those two.'

'Nor do I,' Napoleon agreed. 'But I need them both, and I dare not antagonise Moreau, not until it is clear to every French soldier which one of us is the master. So I must win this campaign, Berthier. If I lose, those two will throw me to the wolves.'

Chapter 53

The air was as clear and fresh as any Napoleon had ever tasted and he breathed deeply and filled his lungs as he gazed down the length of the Great St Bernard Pass. It was late in the afternoon and the sun was sinking behind the mountains to the west, making the snow-capped peaks appear blue in the watery light that remained. Napoleon gazed back along the narrow track he had ascended. A long line of soldiers, dark against the snow, snaked down into the treeline. Here and there several men struggled to help mules and horses haul small wagons and empty gun carriages up the slope. The barrels of the cannon, the most awkward of burdens to be taken over the pass, had been tied securely into hollowed-out tree trunks, each one harnessed to a hundred men who were tasked with hauling them up the pass, and then gingerly steering them down the far side.

It had been Marmont's idea, and Napoleon felt pleased that his choice for the Army of Reserve's artillery commander had been vindicated. So many of the officers who had served with Napoleon since the early days had turned out to be fine commanders, in spite of humble origins in many cases. Men like Masséna, and Desaix. Thought of the latter made Napoleon smile. A day earlier he had had news that Desaix had broken the blockade of Egypt and returned to France. Napoleon had sent for him at once; a man of Desaix's talent could be vital to the success of the present campaign. That was the real triumph of the revolution, Napoleon thought with a slight nod. A man might rise as high as any on the basis of merit alone, and not because of some accident of birth. That was why France would win, in the end. For what nation could hope to stand against a nation of men free to pursue their ambitions?

For a moment the cares and concerns of leading an army were forgotten as Napoleon marvelled at the view afforded him from the top of the pass. To one side of the track the hospice of St Bernard squatted in the thick snow, and its monks stood at the entrance passing bread, cheese and wine into the hands of the soldiers as they tramped past, wrapped in coats and blankets, hands in gloves or bound with strips of cloth to save them from the cold, and frostbite. Napoleon watched as a company of the Consular Guard stood and ate their rations, stamping their feet and breathing plumes of steamy breath into the gloomy blue twilight.

Even though Napoleon was wrapped in a large fur coat he felt the sting of the icy air, and the perspiration that he had shed in the final climb up to the top of the pass now chilled his skin.

'God, it's cold,' he muttered.

Junot turned to him. 'Sir?'

'I think we'd better get moving again, before it gets dark.'

'Yes, sir. A lodge has been prepared for us a few miles down the path. We will eat and sleep there.'

Napoleon nodded. For the soldiers there would be no shelter. They would only rest when they reached the treeline, having marched for over two days in the numbing cold with no chance to sleep.

The staff officers moved on to the track and began the descent. Napoleon swapped greetings with the soldiers who made way for them as they passed. Despite their exhaustion he was pleased to see that they were still in high spirits and greeted him with the same rough informality the men had used when he took command of his first army. As night folded over the mountains they proceeded by the light of the braziers that had been set up at regular intervals. Soldiers clustered round each blaze, stretching out their hands to the flames until they were moved on by a sergeant or an officer. At last Napoleon and his small group of staff officers reached the lodge, a solid timber construction with a few small shuttered windows. It smelt musty, but a fire had been built up by the men sent ahead to prepare the shelter for Napoleon. A simple meal of onion soup steamed in a cauldron and the new arrivals fell on it hungrily.

As Napoleon sipped at the scalding brew he read through the reports from the leading division of the army, commanded by Lannes. The news was not good. Thirty miles further on, the valley became very narrow at the village of Bard. Above the village, on a rock, was a fortress with a strong garrison whose cannon covered the route into Italy. Lannes had taken the village without any difficulty, but the fortress was impregnable. Leaving a small force to cover the enemy, Lannes had taken his infantry on a winding track around the fortress and was moving on towards Ivrea. Lannes would be vulnerable without artillery and Napoleon felt his heart sink a little at this first obstacle to his plans.

Time was more important than ever. Shortly before leaving Geneva he had received news that the Austrians had attacked Masséna and divided the Army of Italy. While half the army was driven back towards the French border, the rest, along with Masséna, were under siege in the port city of Genoa, caught between the Austrian army and the Royal Navy. Even though Masséna was short of supplies, Napoleon had sent an order to hold on until the middle of June, long enough to divert the enemy's attention away from the Army of Reserve closing on them from the Alps. It was a bad situation but Napoleon was reassured by the fact that Masséna was in command at Genoa. He could be counted on to fight for as long as possible.

However heroic Masséna might be, Napoleon reflected, everything depended on getting the Army of Reserve into position in the shortest possible time, and the delay at Bard might yet cost him dearly. He set his spoon down with a sharp rap on the table and stood up. 'Junot, Bourrienne, come with me. We must keep going. The rest of you follow first thing in the morning.'

He led the way outside, and explained briefly about the situation at Bard as they continued along the icy track, joining the dark string of soldiers trudging south. The night sky was clear and stars gleamed brilliantly in the velvet heavens as they marched as fast as they could. As soon as the ground became level and firm enough to ride a horse, Napoleon and the others commandeered some mounts from a cavalry regiment and rode on, passing Aosta before dawn and from there following the Dora Baltea river towards Bard where they arrived at the headquarters of General Berthier late in the afternoon.

Napoleon saw at once that Lannes had not exaggerated the problem presented by the fortress. It completely dominated the ravine through which the main route passed. Berthier pointed out a number of shattered wagons and cannon littering the track below the fortress, togther with the bodies of several horses and men.

'We tried to get some artillery and supplies through to Lannes last night, sir. But they heard us, and rolled some burning faggots into the ravine and shot the column to pieces. The only other route past the fortress is up there, sir. The engineers have started work on widening the track, but it will take several days.'

Napleon followed the direction indicated by Berthier and saw a string of tiny figures picking their way along the side of a cliff. There was not even room for a horse, he realised. That meant that, with the exception of the infantry, the army was bottled up by this fortress and its garrison of no more than a few hundred.

'Well, we must make an attempt to assault the fortress,' Napoleon decided. 'Tonight.'

'We already tried a direct assault two days ago, sir. The only approach to the fort is up that road from the village. The road is covered by several guns and they cut our men down with grapeshot before they even got near the walls.'

'Then we might have a better chance under the cover of darkness,' Napoleon responded. 'And while the enemy are distracted by the attack, we'll try to send another column through the ravine. I admit it's risky, but we have to get the guns through to Lannes.'

Berthier opened his mouth to protest, but he saw the familiar set expression in his superior's face that indicated there would be no further discussion of the situation. Berthier turned to his staff with a sigh and gave orders for the attack.

Two hours after the sun had set behind the mountains and darkness has filled the valley, Napoleon and Berthier stood on a small spur of rock to watch the assault. An infantry battalion, with several ladders, was already picking its way up the road from the village. Each man was carrying only his musket and a cartridge pouch, although none of their weapons was loaded yet, in case some fool fired by accident and alerted the garrison. Down in the village, a column of supply wagons and a battery of limbered guns were ready to move forward the moment the attack began. Once night had fallen, engineers had crept down the road, smothering it with straw and dung to muffle the sound of the vehicles' wheels, which had been wrapped in sacking.

A blazing wicker bundle suddenly flared up on the gatehouse of the fort and then it arced out across the road, landed in a shower of sparks and began to roll down the slope, illuminating the attackers as they dived aside to avoid being mown down by the flaming ball. At once the Austrian guns blasted a storm of grapeshot into the ranks of the French infantry racing towards the walls with their spindly-looking ladders. As Napoleon watched, scores of his men were struck down by the withering fire from the fortress and only a small party reached the outermost bastion and threw their ladder up against the wall. But they died to a man in the crossfire from the other squat towers that projected from the wall.

Napoleon turned his attention to the road that passed down the ravine. The column there had been ordered to move forward the moment the firing began. It was too dark to trace their progress amid the snow-laden trees that ran beside the track, and Napoleon nodded his satisfaction with that. If the Austrians missed them, then Lannes would have enough artillery to continue his advance. But even as the thought passed through his mind, more flaring bundles tumbled down from the fortress and the startled men driving the wagons and gun carriages were lit up in the red glow the flames cast across the gleaming snow on the ground. Tiny stabs of light rippled along the wall as the defenders fired their muskets down into the ravine.

'At least their guns can't be trained on the road immediately below the fortress,' Napoleon commented.

'They don't need guns,' Berthier responded grimly. 'Look there.'

A spark, like a star, arced down towards the road and a moment later there was a brilliant explosion as a grenade blew up close to one of the gun limbers, dropping all but the lead horses. By some miracle the driver escaped injury and stood up and stared down at his dead and dying horses in their traces. Then he was hit and toppled to one side and lay still on the ground.

Napoleon had seen enough to know that the attack and the attempt to sneak past the fortress had failed.

'Berthier, call your men back, and whatever is left of the supply column down there. We'll have to try something else, or try it again tomorrow night.'

Berthier gestured towards the fort. 'We'll never take that place by force, sir. Perhaps we should have chosen a different route.'

Napoleon's eyes narrowed as he replied, 'What help is that observation to me now, eh? We are here, Berthier, and we concentrate our minds on what is before us. Nothing else matters. So, pull your men back, rest them, treat their wounds, and send them back against the fort tomorrow. As for the artillery, we'll have to try again tonight. This time with just two guns. We'll set off at midnight.'

'We?' Berthier looked at him sharply, his face dimly visible by the loom of the snow.

'Yes. I'll be going with the guns. I have to reach the vanguard as soon as possible.'

Berthier was silent for a moment, while he considered protesting that Napoleon should not take such a risk. But he knew his commander well enough to realise any such protests were pointless. They always had been since that suicidally brave charge at Arcola. Berthier nodded wearily. 'Yes, sir.'

Napoleon turned away and softly crunched through the snow as he made his way down to the village of Bard where a room awaited him in the modest inn by the small square in the heart of the village. He sat and warmed himself by a fire as he drank some soup and then, leaving orders that he should be called at eleven thirty, he closed his eyes and eased himself back in a chair. He did not sleep. His mind was filled with a torrent of thoughts: anxiety about the stability of the government he had left in Paris; the threat presented by General Moreau's popularity throughout the army; Josephine, naked, with arms outstretched towards him, then a fleeting image of her in another man's arms; he banished the image from his mind and hurriedly concentrated on the current campaign.

Napoleon pictured the map of the Alps and northern Italy, superimposing his forces on the landscape, and those of the enemy gleaned from the latest intelligence reports. He shook his head as he saw that the delay at Bard would give the enemy plenty of warning that the French army was attempting to cut across their communications with Austria. If they moved as slowly as they had done in the past, then there would still be time for Napoleon to concentrate his army and face the enemy on favourable terms. If, however, General Melas seized his chance, he could defeat the French forces piecemeal. The spectre of defeat haunted his thoughts and made rest, let alone sleep, impossible over the following hours.

Napoleon took a last look at the dark mass of the fortress looming above the ravine. The roar of cannon fire from the French lines rumbled across the valley, echoing back from the sides of the surrounding mountains. More than enough noise to help conceal the sound that the gun carriages and their limbers would make in the next few minutes.

'Time to go,' he muttered to Junot. 'Ready?'

Junot nodded.

Around them were the men of the hussar squadron Napoleon had chosen to act as his bodyguard while he rode to join Lannes at Ivrea. Behind the mounted men, two four-pounder horse-guns were ready to move off, harnessed to the best horses that could be found in the artillery train. This time Napoleon had decided to gamble on speed, rather than subtlety. His heart beat against his breast like a caged eagle as he lifted his chin from the fur collar of his coat and called out, 'Advance!'

He spurred his horse forward. Junot and the hussars followed him, and behind them the tackle and timber of the guns jingled as they slowly gathered speed and caught up with the trotting cavalry just as they emerged from the village on to the track running into the gorge. Napoleon glanced up at the fortress, and could just make out the line of the battlements against the sky. They rode on, into the gorge, and the rocky spur jutting out from the cliff opposite the fortress forced them towards the enemy. Just as they came to the point closest to the walls there was a faint shout, audible even above the boom and echo of the French guns.

Napoleon steered his mount to the side and reined in.

'Go! Go!' he shouted to the hussars and then again to the artillery riders as they came up. Above them, flames flared up and once more a wicker bundle roared down the cliff. This time Napoleon was almost beneath it, and the sight was terrifying. He kicked his heels in and raced after the others, and there was a crackling thud and explosion of sparks as the bundle landed close behind him. Shots cracked from the wall above and he heard them whip down into the snow on either side as he leaned forward and rode on, urging his horse to gallop as fast as it could until he had passed beyond the loom of the burning wood and caught up with the others. More blazing bundles roared down towards them like fiery comets as they passed through the ravine, but they stayed just ahead of where the enemy guessed they must be and only one of the shots fired wildly into the darkness from the fortress struck home, into the haunch of one of the hussars' horses. It reared up with a shrill whinny before its rider regained control and urged it on with whispered curses.

Once clear of the gorge they rode on for another half-mile, the cannon jolting across the rough track, and then Napoleon gave the order to slow down and continue at a walk. He paused, with Junot, to look back towards the fortress.

'We did it!' Junot shook his head in wonder. 'We did it, sir.'

Napoleon grinned. 'Did you ever really doubt that we would?'

'The thought crossed my mind.'

'Ha!' Napoleon reached over and slapped his friend on the shoulder. 'Come on then. We must find Lannes and get these guns to him.'

As June began, over fifty thousand of Napoleon's men had crossed the Alps and were massing north of the River Po. The fort at Bard was still holding up his artillery train and the army had only a handful of cannon that had survived the hazardous passage of the gorge. A few more cannon had been taken from the enemy garrisons following the capture of Ivrea, Pavia and Milan. As Napoleon entered the city the Milanese turned out in their thousands to cheer the arrival of the French army.

Napoleon turned to Junot with a smile. 'Seems that any grievances they might have nursed from the last time I was here have been forgotten.'

Junot nodded as he gazed warily round at the crowd. 'Let's hope they remain friendly long enough for us to defeat the Austrians.'

'Of course. Now smile and wave at your adoring public, as any good liberator should.'

The following night, as Napoleon and his staff settled into the mansion formerly occupied by the Austrian governor of the city, a messenger arrived from Murat, scouting ahead of the main army with his light cavalry. The hussar was exhausted and mudstained, and as he took the dispatch from the man Napoleon ordered that he be fed and given good accommodation for the night. Once the messenger had gone, he returned to the dining table where the staff officers were noisily celebrating the capture of Milan: the latest prize to fall to the French army in this campaign that seemed to be succeeding so gloriously once they had left the Alps behind them. Their spirits were even higher now that Desaix had joined them, and was entertaining his comrades with tales of his adventures in Egypt.

Napoleon broke the seal and quickly scanned the contents.

He read it again, more slowly, before folding it and setting it down on the table. Picking up his fork he rapped the side of the tureen in front of him. The conversation died away instantly and the gold-braided officers turned towards him, some still smiling.

'Gentlemen, Murat has captured some dispatches sent from General Melas to Vienna. It seems that General Masséna has been obliged to surrender Genoa.'

There was a brief silence before General Lannes thumped his fist down, clattering the cutlery and dishes around him. 'Shit!'

'Quite,' Napoleon responded. 'As of yesterday, Masséna was still discussing terms. That will hold an element of the enemy in place around Genoa, but the bulk of their army is now free to face us. The question is, will they try to slip past us and re-establish their lines of communication with Austria, or will they fight?'

'Fight?' Lannes snorted. 'They'll run all the way back to Mantua and duck down behind the walls.'

Napoleon nodded. 'I agree. In which case we must make them fight. As soon as possible, before they can concentrate their forces. Lannes, your division is closest to Masséna. You will cross the Po at once and march on Genoa. Make contact with the enemy as soon as possible. The rest of the army will force march to catch up with you. Desaix!'

'Yes, sir.'

'There's no more time for tall tales.'

Desaix grinned. 'No, sir.'

'Then you will take two divisions and set off after Lannes. Gentlemen!' Napoleon stood up and leaned forward across the table, resting his weight on his knuckles. 'If we can bring the enemy to battle then this campaign can be decided in a matter of days, weeks at the most. Make sure you let every man in the army know it.' He poured himself a glass and raised it. 'To victory!'

Marching through driving rain the Army of Reserve crossed the Po and closed on the enemy. As they marched Napoleon read the reports from Murat. It was clear that the Austrians were advancing north from Genoa towards the fortress city of

Alessandria. If they reached it first then they could make for the north bank of the Po and threaten Napoleon's supply lines leading back through the Alpine passes. Then, on 13 June, Murat's scouts reported that the enemy was retreating on Genoa.

'Are you certain?' Napoleon stared at Berthier in surprise.

His chief of staff gestured to the map that covered the table between them. All the latest sightings of enemy formations had been pencilled in. 'It's difficult to be sure, sir. The enemy cavalry is stronger than ours, and is doing a good job of screening their army. But, from what Murat's scouts are reporting, I can think of no other explanation.'

'Then we must stop them, at once.' Napoleon leaned over the map and stabbed his finger at one of the blue boxes Berthier had marked on the map earlier. 'Desaix . . . Order Desaix to march south towards Novi. He is to try to hook round and cut across their line of march. If he can do that, then we can close the trap on Melas.'

Berthier glanced up with a questioning look. 'Are you sure that's wise, sir? To divide our army when we're so close to the enemy?'

Napoleon patted him on the shoulder. 'Berthier, if our enemy was advancing, then of course I would concentrate our strength. But he's not. He's in full retreat, and we cannot afford to let him escape us. If Melas does reach Genoa then we'll be obliged to lay siege to the town and the campaign will drag on for months. So,' he tapped the map, 'we'll make for this village, Marengo, while Desaix blocks his line of retreat. Then we will have our battle.'

Berthier stared at the map. 'I hope so, sir.'

The next morning dawned clear and bright and Napoleon rose early. He was in high spirits. Patrols had been sent towards the small enemy force covering the bridge across the Bormida river. On the far bank, the reports said, lay the bulk of the enemy's army. Now that he knew where they were, it only remained to cross the river and fight the battle. If things went true to form, the Austrians would be preparing defensive works and waiting for the enemy to come to them, Napoleon mused, as he leaned over the map. He ate a leisurely breakfast, making notes for the coming battle.

He looked up at the faint sound of a few cannons being fired, over towards the Bormida. The sounds did not increase in intensity and he put it down to a skirmish around the bridgehead between the enemy and General Victor's men, and turned his attention back to the map. Around him the tents of Watrin's division stretched out in ordered ranks. After the tiring marches of recent days the men were enjoying their rest and their relaxed chatter and singing drifted across the camp. At length, Napoleon was satisfied that he had worked out the details of his attack and was about to call for Berthier when a staff officer strode up towards his table and saluted.

'Message from General Victor, sir.'

'Well?'

'He asks you to come at once. The enemy is attacking.'

'I know. I heard the guns earlier. I'm sure that General Victor can contain the enemy's bridgehead.'

The officer shook his head. 'General Victor says the entire enemy army is crossing the river.'

Napoleon stared at him for a moment and then laughed. 'Oh, come now! The man must be exaggerating. The Austrians wouldn't dare . . . surely.' A cold feeling of anxiety pricked the base of his spine, and he stood up. 'Oh, very well, I'll have a look. Fetch Junot and have our horses readied.'

As they rode up the road towards Marengo, Napoleon was still thinking over the plans of his attack, and was frustrated that he had not been able to commit them to paper. If this alarm proved to be over little more than a feint to cover the Austrian retreat on Genoa, then General Victor would deserve a firm dressing down for wasting Napoleon's time instead of dealing with the matter on his own. He reached the far side of the village and rode up to the small rise that gave fine views towards the Bormida. There he suddenly reined in, his back stiffening as he surveyed the flat plain in front of him. A mile away, the men of Victor's corps, some ten thousand men, were forming up to face the enemy. A short distance beyond them, and spreading out along the bank of the

Bormida river, were dense columns of Austrian infantry marching directly towards the French lines. To the right large cavalry formations kicked up clouds of dust as they edged towards the French flanks. His experienced eye calculated that over thirty thousand of the enemy must be across the river already. Within moments they would attack, and the anxiety he had felt shortly before now became fully fledged fear for the fate of his divided army, surprised by the sudden advance of the Austrians.

He turned to Junot. 'A message to Desaix. Take it down.'

While he waited for Junot to take out his notebook and pencil Napoleon cast a last look at the enemy wave closing on the thin ribbon of Victor's men, and he felt rage at himself for underestimating his enemy so fatally. He turned back to Junot, saw that he was ready, and dictated. 'I had thought to attack Melas. He has attacked me first. For God's sake come back to the army if you still can. Or all is lost . . .'

Chapter 54

Marengo, 14 June 1800

The Austrian attack rolled forward just as Lannes's and Murat's hastily roused divisions began to arrive on the battlefield. Napoelon glanced at his watch. Just gone eleven in the morning. The enemy would have enough time to break the French army and begin a pursuit long before the fall of night obliged them to break contact. He clenched his fist and struck his thigh.

Why did I not see this?

They were outnumbered at least two to one. Worse still, the Austrians completely outgunned them and their cavalry was better mounted and far more numerous. Already they were manoeuvring to Napoleon's right towards the village of Castel Ceriolo. The flat dry landscape around Marengo would be ideal for large, sweeping movements of cavalry and Napoleon saw at once that his goal in the imminent battle was not to achieve a victory, but simply to avoid annihilation.

A signal gun fired from the Austrian forces massed to the west and, an instant later, the batteries formed up in front of the infantry spat tongues of flame and were instantly swallowed up in a bank of smoke. A moment later the sound of the discharge rolled across the battlefield like thunder as roundshot carved bloody paths through the ranks of Victor's men.

Only a handful of French guns were positioned at the centre of Victor's line and they spat back their defiance, trading shots with the batteries immediately opposite. All the time Victor's guns were whittled down by the enemy until, no more than a quarter of an hour after the cannonade had begun, the last French eight-pounder was struck squarely on its carriage and a hail of splinters cut down half of the gun crew. The survivors turned and ran for the lines of infantry waiting behind them.

The Austrian guns fell silent, then a moment later the sound of drums and trumpets reached Napoleon. Through the dense bank of gunpowder smoke emerged columns of enemy infantry, the sun glinting off their musket barrels and the officers' gorgets and swords as they waved their men forward. There was a lull in the noise of battle as the enemy came on, and the French waited, grimly. Then, when it seemed that the two lines could not get much closer, Napoleon heard the order to present arms echo down the French line. Thousands of musket barrels swept up and out, aiming at the enemy no more than seventy paces away.

'Fire!' Victor bellowed, his booming voice carrying across the battlefield. Stabs of light and swirls of smoke billowed out along the French line like a ribbon of soiled cotton. From his slightly elevated position Napoleon could see the leading ranks of the enemy column tumble down as the volley of musket balls tore into them. But they held their ground, re-formed and marched a short distance closer before deploying into a firing line. Victor's men managed to get off two more volleys before the Austrians returned fire. Then the fight was swallowed up in an ever-thickening bank of acrid yellow smoke that hung across the battlefield.

Napoleon waited until he was certain that the French line was holding along its front, and then rode forward to General Victor. The veteran greeted him with a salute and a wry shake of the head. 'They caught us out nicely, sir.'

Napoleon ignored the comment as he returned the salute. 'You must hold here for as long as possible. Lannes and Murat are moving up to support you. I've sent for Desaix.'

'Desaix? He won't be able to reach us until long after this battle is over.'

'Perhaps,' Napoleon conceded. 'But he might. Meanwhile we have to hold the Austrians back as long as we can, until tonight at least. Then we'll concentrate our forces and go on to the attack tomorrow.'

'If there are any forces left to concentrate,' Victor said quietly. He glanced towards his men, now firing by companies in a continuous rattle of musket fire. 'Besides, we're going to run out of ammunition before long. Then we'll be at their mercy.'

'If that happens, we'll fall back on the main camp and resupply the men from there.'

'Yes, sir.'

'Remember, Victor.' Napoleon thrust his arm towards the ground. 'Hold here for as long as possible. That is our only chance of surviving this day.'

'Yes, sir.'

Napoleon wheeled his horse round and rode along the rear of his line. Whenever the men noticed him, a cheer rose up, before the sergeants and officers bellowed at them to face front and keep firing. The first of the walking wounded were already staggering back from the foremost ranks, clutching their bloody injuries as they made for the rear. When he reached the end of the line it was clear to Napoleon that the main weight of the enemy attack was being thrown at General Watrin's division, on the right flank. The dead and wounded lay thick on the ground and as the survivors closed ranks, the gaps in between units were growing all the time. So that was the enemy's plan, Napoleon nodded to himself. Melas intended to crush the French right, then send his cavalry in a sweeping arc to trap the French army against the Bormida and crush them.

Watrin was having his arm bandaged as Napoleon rode up to the small cluster of divisional staff officers.

'Not serious, I hope.' Napoleon gestured towards the injury.

'A flesh wound, sir. That's all. Nothing compared to what's happening to my men.' He glanced at the smoke shrouding his line. Only the rear ranks were clearly visible. In front of them the men in the front lines were no more than dim grey shapes, firing, reloading and firing again. 'They're carving us up, sir. I doubt we'll be able to hold this position for another ten minutes.'

'You have to,' Napoleon replied bluntly. 'Reinforcements will be on the way. You have to hold the enemy back until they arrive. Whatever the cost. Is that clear?'

'Yes, sir.'

'Then God be with you, General.'

'And you, sir.'

By the time Napoleon had returned to his command post on the raised ground behind Marengo, the Austrians had pulled back their battered assault columns and were preparing another attack. As the smoke dispersed and lifted from the battlefield the perilous situation of the French army was clear for all to see. The ground was littered with the dead and wounded of both sides, but whereas the battered units of Napoleon's army were spread thinly across the ground the enemy were able to mass fresh battalions to continue the fight, and these were forming up, preparing for the next assault.

Berthier approached him, clutching a scribbled note. 'Victor's men are down to their last few rounds, and we have only fifteen pieces of artillery left. Victor asks for permission to withdraw before the next attack begins.'

'No. He must stay where he is.'

'But, sir, Victor cannot hold them back.'

'Then he must delay their advance for as long as possible.'

'At least reinforce him then. We still have Monnier's division in reserve.'

Napoleon turned and pointed towards Castel Ceriolo. 'We need Monnier there. He must hold the flanks. Watrin's division is all but finished. Give the order for Monnier to advance immediately.'

'What about Watrin, sir? Should I pull him back?'

Napoleon shook his head, even though he knew that Watrin's division must collapse under the next attack, unless they were supported. But Monnier's men were the only forces available to send into the battle and they had to hold the flank. Then Napoleon's gaze fell on the men of the Consular Guard, two thousand strong and every man a tough veteran.

'Berthier, send the Guard forward to support Watrin.'

His chief of staff was shocked. 'The Guard? But, sir, if the army breaks and routs, who will protect you?'

'If the army breaks then I will be beyond need of protection,' Napoleon replied quietly as he gripped the hilt of his sword. 'Send the Guard forward.'

Berthier nodded solemnly and turned back to his campaign desk to hurriedly write the orders and hand them to the waiting dispatch riders. As the last of them rode off, he returned to Napoleon's side.

'That's it then, sir. We've no more men to put into line against the enemy now. We're in the hands of fate.'

'Fate won't decide this,' Napoleon replied. 'It's a test of courage and endurance . . . And numbers.'

Berthier smiled mirthlessly. 'Fate has a way of favouring the bigger battalions.'

Napoleon did not reply, but stared out over the battlefield at the Austrians surging forward to attack his thinly stretched army. Could they weather another assault, he wondered? If not, then only Desaix could save them from utter destruction.

After a fresh cannonade the Austrian columns came on again. To the right, opposite the end of Watrin's division, a large body of cavalry was forming up behind the columns of Austrian infantry. The Consular Guard formed into a square before it marched steadily forward to fill the gap between Watrin's and Monnier's divisions. As the enemy saw the guard moving towards them, they turned their attention away from the remnants of Watrin's division and opened fire on the square. At such close range the veterans were shot down by the score under the withering volleys of the enemy. But each time they steadily closed ranks and continued forward, until at last the order was given to halt, and open fire.

For the moment the Guard was holding its own and Napoleon turned his attention to the far right of the line. The sacrifice of the Guard had not only taken the pressure off the shaken survivors of Watrin's division, but also given Monnier the chance to form his men up on the right flank, and now his fresh columns rolled forward towards Castel Ceriolo. As Napoleon had hoped, the Austrians began to break contact with Watrin and the remnants of the Consular Guard as they turned to face the new threat. The firing died away for the moment as the French soldiers fell back a few hundred paces and re-formed their line.

A rider approached Berthier, and leaned forward to hand him a note. Berthier glanced at it before turning to Napoleon. 'Victor is pulling back, before he is destroyed.'

For an instant Napoleon was on the verge of shouting an order that Victor should hold his line to the last man, but then cold calm reason asserted itself. Such an order would be madness. Inhuman madness. Instead he nodded. 'He has done enough. Tell him to withdraw towards the main camp at San Giuliano. Pass the order down the line to all the other commanders.'

Berthier hurried back to his desk. Now that defeat seemed unavoidable, Napoleon felt a tired calmness fill his body. His men had done all they could to stem the Austrian assault, and it was his duty to try to save as many of them as he could. With luck, Desaix might arrive in time to cover their retreat. The loss of this battle would give heart to France's enemies, and destroy his reputation. The fault, he accepted, was his own. He had misjudged the character of his opponent – the classic mistake of an arrogant commander blinded by faith in his infallibility. Once news of this defeat reached Paris, his days as First Consul were numbered. Bernadotte and Moreau would circle like vultures ready to pluck the power from his bones.

The French army retreated from the battlefield, marching back down the road towards the village of San Giuliano. The men trudged along in silence, the injured being helped by their comrades. As they passed him Napoleon noted the exhausted and anxious expressions on their grime-streaked faces and knew that their travail was not over. Glancing at his watch he saw that it was not yet three o'clock in the afternoon, still early enough for the enemy to mount a pursuit. Beyond Marengo he could see that the centre of the Austrian line was forming into a column whose intention was all too clear. Melas was sending his army after them, determined to complete his victory with one final crushing blow to his defeated enemy. He would do it too, Napoleon realised. A short while earlier he had seen a dense cloud of dust on the far side of the river as one of the Austrian cavalry columns moved out to swing round the retreating French and cut off their escape route. A similar force was massing this side of the river, ready to march towards Novi to act as the other pincer arm.

'Sir!' Berthier called out to him and pointed down the retreating column in the direction of the camp. A small party of horsemen was galloping towards them. At their head was a figure with gold braid on his uniform coat. 'It's Desaix!'

Napoleon made himself smile as his friend rode up and reined in. Desaix had ridden hard and his horse's flanks heaved like a blacksmith's bellows.

'Sir, it's good to see you.' Desaix gestured to the retreating column. 'I assumed the worst.'

'I fear the worst is still to come.' Napoleon pointed out the dust from the enemy cavalry columns. 'They aim to block our retreat while the main body of the enemy army pursues us down this road. Not a good situation for us, I fear.'

Desaix quickly took stock of the situation and then pulled out his watch before he turned back to Napoleon. 'This battle is completely lost.' Then he raised his head defiantly. 'But there is still time to win another. My leading division is close behind me, sir. If we can form a new line, before San Giuliano, and put every gun we have to the head of the enemy column, then we can stop them dead in their tracks, and take them in the flanks.'

Napoleon considered the idea for a moment and nodded. Desaix was right. If the army continued to retreat they would only be falling into the enemy's trap. Their only chance was to turn on the pursuit column and attempt to break it.

He cleared his throat. 'Very well. One last throw of the dice.'

The late afternoon sun slanted across the fields surrounding San Giuliano. The French line was strung out across the plain in a shallow S formation. On the right flank Monnier and the remnants of the Consular Guard were tasked with holding back the enemy column advancing from Castel Ceriolo. The rest of the army was drawn up facing the road to Marengo. In front of San Giuliano Marmont had massed the remaining eighteen guns, and concealed them behind the stone walls and hedges of the villagers' smallholdings. Beyond them, Desaix and his men stood ready to attack the enemy column. The battered divisions of Victor and Lannes' stood formed up parallel to the road, but far enough away to remain out of sight. As they waited for the Austrian column to march into view Napoleon rode down the line to offer encouragement to his troops. Every so often, he halted to deliver the same message.

'Soldiers! You have retreated enough. The enemy thinks we are beaten! He thinks that he is, at last, our master. He thinks that he has beaten us into a corner like a whipped cur. Well, he should know the danger that comes from cornering a wild beast. He is about to get his arse well and truly bitten off!'

The men raised a laugh, and he moved on, until he reached the survivors of the Consular Guard, drawn up in a neat line. They raised their muskets and presented arms as he reined in before them. Napoleon felt his heart sink as he realised that less than half of the men who had so gallantly marched to Watrin's rescue still remained. He swallowed and took a deep breath as he addressed them.

'Men of the Guard, you have proved today that you are the bravest of the brave in the French army . . . in any army. If we win this day then all France shall hear of your courage, and the men of the Guard will for ever hold the place of honour wherever I lead our armies into battle.' He took off his hat and raised it above his head. 'Your general salutes you!'

Unlike the other units he had addressed the men stood still, staring ahead as if they were on a parade ground, and there was no outburst of cheers. A sergeant at the end of the front rank suddenly shouted out, 'Chins up!'

The men strained to raise themselves up to their full height and Napoleon could not help smiling at their fearless and fierce sense of elan. He replaced his hat, wheeled his horse about and galloped back to his command post, just behind the centre of

Desaix's line. They did not have long to wait for the enemy column. With drums beating the pace the Austrians marched straight down the road from Marengo. They did not falter for an instant when they saw the French lines waiting for them before San Giuliano, no doubt taking them for little more than a rearguard left behind to delay the Austrians for as long as possible while the main body of the French army fled.

Desaix shook his head. 'They're in for a surprise.'

'That they certainly are,' Napoleon replied quietly. 'Signal Marmont to open fire.'

A staff officer relayed the order to a signalman and the flag fluttered up, held aloft for a moment and then swept down. The artillery crews rose up from their places of concealment and hastily cleared away the straw and cut branches hiding their guns. An instant later the cannon roared into life, belching deadly cones of grapeshot into the leading units of the Austrian pursuit column. Gun after gun fired in a rolling cannonade. The leading companies of the white-uniformed enemy were shredded by grapeshot and as the bodies piled into bloody heaps along the road the column stalled. Shocked by the sudden hail of destruction, they stood and endured the slaughter for some minutes before a senior officer attempted to take control. Slowly, too slowly, the head of the column began to deploy to either side of the road, still under heavy fire from Marmont's guns, which were being worked as swiftly as their crews could manage. The target was so big there was no need to aim carefully and the guns discharged their grapeshot the moment they were reloaded.

After twenty minutes of terrible carnage, the Austrians were still attempting to draw their men up in a battle line. Napoleon realised that this was the moment to strike the decisive blow.

'Order Marmont to cease fire. Tell Desaix to charge home!'

'Yes, sir,' Berthier nodded.

As soon as the last of the guns fell silent, the leading battalions of Desaix's men marched through the dense bank of smoke and emerged a short distance from the enemy. Napoleon watched as Desaix ordered his men to halt and volley fire, before they advanced to point-blank range and halted to reload and fire again. Volley after volley rang out from both sides, each one wreaking terrible carnage. As he watched Napoleon sensed that the impetus was quickly draining from the French attack. Unless the Austrians broke soon, he doubted that they ever would.

A sudden sheet of flame tore up into the sky a short distance behind the head of the enemy column and Napoleon saw scores of men hurled aside by the blast. The red flame of the explosion faded and a rolling mushroom cloud billowed above the Austrian lines. He saw a crater in the road and scores of blackened bodies and body parts lay scattered around it.

'Jesus,' Napoleon muttered in horror. 'What was that?'

'Must have been an ammunition wagon,' Berthier replied. 'Lucky shot from our side must have set it off.'

The explosion caused a brief lull in the fighting. The Austrians had turned towards the sound of the blast, dazed and frightened. At that moment a trumpet call sounded from Napoleon's left and he turned and saw that the small body of cavalry covering the left flank was moving, picking up speed as it surged forward down the side of the enemy column, and then wheeled inwards towards the Austrians, still shaken by the blast.

'The young fool!' Berthier said through clenched teeth. 'He'll get himself killed.'

Napoleon strained his eyes and realised that the cavalry formation belonged to Kellermann, the son of the hero of Valmy, and one of Murat's most promising officers. Napoleon shook his head. 'No, he's done the right thing. It's perfectly timed. Look!'

Kellermann's troopers launched themselves into a charge, trumpets blaring and colours rippling in the wind as they spurred their mounts forward, extending their heavy swords until the glinting blades pointed directly at the terrified Austrians in front of them. A few had the presence of mind to turn and fire their muskets at the charging horsemen; then they were engulfed by the French cavalry and the Austrian column shattered. Men threw down their heavy muskets and ran, fleeing back down the road towards Marengo, and away from the advancing lines of the men of Victor's and Lannes's divisions. As far as Napoleon could see the battlefield was covered with white-coated figures streaming away from their French pursuers. Large bodies of men, still in column, laid down their arms and surrendered and their colours were snatched from their hands by jubilant Frenchmen.

As dusk gathered over the battlefield Napoleon made his way forward with Berthier. There was a thick belt of bodies where Marmont's guns had torn into the leading battalions of the enemy column and then two lines of corpses where Desaix's men had exchanged volleys with the enemy before they had finally broken. From the earliest reports to have reached headquarters it seemed that over five thousand of the enemy had been killed and an even larger number taken prisoner, along with forty guns, fifteen colours and General Zach, the second in command of the Austrian army. Nightfall, and the presence of strong detachments of Austrian cavalry, had ended the French pursuit and across the plain the exhausted men were re-forming their units and marching back to camp.

Amid all the reports there had been no word from Desaix and Napoleon felt a growing concern for his friend as he edged across the battlefield. Then, just outside the hamlet of Vigna Santa, he saw a group of officers gathered beside the road. Amongst them stood an Austrian general, head bowed in shame. Napoleon strode across the corpse-littered ground towards them and saw that they were clustered about a body sprawled on the ground. Napoleon pushed his way through and looked down.

Desaix lay on his back, head flung to one side, eyes wide open. A bloody hole had been torn through his breast. His sword lay at his side.

Napoleon knelt down. He stared at the body, and his throat tightened. No words came to him. His heart felt heavy and he reached forward and closed Desaix's eyes as Berthier approached the group.

Berthier clapped his hands together as he gazed round the battlfield. 'My God! We've won! We've beaten them. Sir, you've won a geat victory . . . sir?' Then he saw Desaix. 'Oh, no . . .'

'Excuse me,' a voice interrupted, in accented French. 'General Bonaparte?'

Napoleon glanced up and saw the Austrian officer standing

over him in the gloom, holding out his sword, handle first. Rising to his feet, Napoleon faced his enemy. General Zach stood stiffly as he surrendered his weapon.

'To you the victory, General Bonaparte.'

Napoleon took the sword, noting its finely wrought hilt and jewelled guard. He held it for a moment and then shook his head.

'The victory is not mine. Had it not been for Desaix I would be presenting you with my sword. No, the victory is not mine. Truly, it belongs to another.'

He knelt down again, and placed the sword across Desaix's chest, and folded the dead man's arms across the blade. Then he stood up and pushed his way through the cordon of officers and strode back towards his headquarters before anyone could see the first tears welling up in his eyes.

Chapter 55

Arthur

Seringapatam, May 1799

As the sun rose on Tipoo's capital, the day after the city had fallen, it revealed the men of General Baird's assault column still plundering the city and wholly out of control. Smoke billowed up from several fires that were spreading, unchecked by the British forces inside the walls.

As he waded across the south Cauvery river with Captain Fitzroy Arthur looked at the columns of smoke billowing up into the rosy sky with growing anger. His companion sensed his mood and muttered, 'What the hell does Baird think he's playing at? If those fires aren't put out we'll lose half the city.'

'Yes,' Arthur replied quietly. 'That's something we'll have to put right as soon as I take charge.'

He unconsciously touched the bulge in his jacket, where he had put the orders from General Harris authorising him to take command of all British forces in the city. The same orders required Baird and his staff to quit Seringapatam and return to Harris's camp two miles to the west. Arthur had already given instructions for his regiment, the 33rd Foot, to be formed up and ready for action the moment he assumed command of the forces inside Seringapatam and restored order to end the looting, raping and murder.

By rights, as brigadier of the day, Baird should not be relieved until midday, but General Harris realised that the sacking of the city had to be ended as soon as possible. Baird was not the man to do it. His dislike of Indians generally, and his vengeful hatred of the people of Mysore in particular, meant that he was the very last man in the British army who could be trusted with bringing order back to the city and steering it towards a long-lasting alliance with Britain and the East India Company. By contrast, there was hardly a man more suitable for the job than Arthur Wellesley. He spoke the native tongue, and had the necessary tact and respect to work alongside the people of Mysore. More shrewdly, Harris was aware that the younger brother of the Governor General would be sure to do his utmost to implement Richard's policy of expanding British power in India by way of treaties, alliances and, where necessary, force. A policy of which Harris wholeheartedly approved.

Arthur and Fitzroy emerged on the far side of the crossing and entered the wall through the breach. Baird had sent word that he had moved his headquarters to the Dowlut Baugh, Tipoo's palace on the far side of the city. The streets were quiet, as most of the looters were sleeping off the debauchery of the previous night. The inhabitants of Seringapatam were still hiding, behind locked and barricaded doors, hoping that their homes would prove too much of a challenge to the looters and encourage them to search for easier pickings amongst their neighbours. There were some men, more resilient or simply more sober than their comrades, who were still looking for booty, women and drink, and they made no effort to stand to attention and salute as the two officers strode past. For his part, Arthur ignored them. There was no sense in getting caught up in an ugly scene that might well result in harm to him and his companion. The British soldiers were not the only looters on the street. A number of natives were breaking into shops to steal whatever they could while the city was lawless. The situation was made worse by the prisoners who had escaped from the city's dungeons during the assault.

Those killed in the looting as well as the fighting lay in the streets and Fitzroy looked in disgust at the body of a dark-skinned native girl, no older than twelve or thirteen, who lay on her back, her sari thrust up around her waist and her legs apart.

'That has to stop,' Arthur said firmly. 'At once. If ever I take another enemy city, then I'll hang the first man I catch who commits rape and murder.'

The Dowlut Baugh had been built just beyond the wall of the city on the bank of the north Cauvery. It was surrounded with ornamental gardens. Unlike the palace in the city, the Dowlut Baugh was airy and spacious and seemed more suited to a philosopher king than a warrior tyrant like Tipoo. The gate was guarded by the grenadiers from Arthur's regiment who had taken part in the assault. Major Shee emerged from the guardhouse as soon as he had word of Arthur's arrival.

'Good to see you, sir!'

'And you. Where are the rest of the men?'

'They're gathering at the mosque. I've had the officers and sergeants rounding them up since we got your orders, sir.'

'Very well.' Arthur nodded approvingly. 'You had better join them. I want twenty-man patrols ready to scour the city as soon as I take command.'

'Yes, sir.'

'Where's General Baird?'

'At breakfast.' Shee nodded to the palace. 'In the banquet hall. You can't miss it, sir.'

'Right. Come, Fitzroy.'

They left Shee and crunched up the gravel path to the ornately carved white stone of the entrance portico. The palace was guarded by more of the grenadiers, who stiffened to attention as their colonel entered the building. Inside the entrance was a large reception hall with arched doorways leading to other chambers. The sounds of light-hearted conversation could be heard through the door to the left and Arthur led the way over to it. Inside, the walls rose up to a domed roof decorated with hunting scenes. The room was perhaps thirty yards across, and on a dais on the far side Baird and his officers were sitting at a table. Several of the palace servants were serving them freshly prepared mangoes, oranges and other small fruits. As Arthur and Fitzroy crossed the hall Baird and his officers turned at the sound of their footsteps. Baird rose up, cigar in hand, and waved towards the table.

'Wellesley! Come and join us!'

Arthur ignored the invitation with a shake of his head. 'Sorry, sir. I have orders to carry out.' He reached inside his jacket for the folded letter and handed it to Baird. 'From General Harris, sir.'

Baird tore open the wafer seal and unfolded the sheet of paper. Holding it in one hand as he lifted the cigar to his mouth with the other, his eyes scanned the document. Then he glanced up.

'What's the meaning of this? I'm brigadier of the day, and as commander of the assault I should be left in charge of the city.'

'I didn't get the impression that anyone is in charge when we made our way through the streets just now, sir.'

'The lads are just having some fun.' Baird waved. 'They've earned it. Rules of war are clear enough. If a town or city does not yield before the breach is practical, then it's fair game for the besiegers.'

'These people had no part in Tipoo's war against us. They're little more than bystanders. To subject them to the full horrors of an unrestrained army is immoral, General. The looting has to stop.'

'Does it?' Baird smiled. 'On whose authority?'

'Mine. General Harris has appointed me acting Governor of Mysore with immediate effect. As it says in the letter.'

Baird glanced at the sheet of paper again, until his eyes found the phrase. 'Immediate effect . . . So it does.'

For a moment Baird stared at Arthur, with a glowering expression. His officers looked on in uncomfortable silence, ignoring their food. Then Baird leaned forward and stubbed his cigar out on his plate. 'Damn you, Wellesley! You've been up to your bloody tricks again.'

'Tricks, sir?' Arthur responded icily.

'You know damn well what I'm talking about! Milking your family connections for all they're worth.'

'I can assure you, sir, that I had no part in making this decision.' Arthur felt his pulse racing as he responded to the attack on his honour. 'If you are suggesting that I have not acted as a gentleman should in this matter, then you would leave me little choice but to ask for satisfaction.'

Baird rose to his feet, towering over Arthur, and jabbed a thick finger at him. 'You impudent fool, I could swat you away like a fly. But we all know what harm that would do to my career with your brother running the show. So there'll be no duel.'

'As you please, sir,' Arthur replied. 'Now, with these men as witnesses, I hereby relieve you of command of the forces in Seringapatam.'

Baird glared at him, then flicked Harris's letter aside and turned to his officers. 'Come, gentlemen, it seems we are not wanted here.'

Arthur felt his anger and frustration boiling up inside him. So far he had managed to contain it, but now, at Baird's petulant behaviour, his reserve snapped.

'Oh, finish your damned breakfast!' He turned about and strode away, followed by a bemused Fitzroy. Outside in the hall he stopped and whacked his palm against his thigh. 'As long as there are men like that exercising any kind of power in India, we cannot hope to win her people over.'

'I rather thought we were here to defend the Company's interests,' said Fitzroy. 'Not to court popularity amongst the natives.'

'You cannot have one without the other.' Arthur turned to look his friend directly in the eyes. 'Besides, there are bigger issues at stake. These lands may yet become the greatest prize that any empire has ever won.'

The first challenge to face Arthur was to bring order to the ravaged streets of Seringapatam. As soon as he had assumed authority over the city he joined Major Shee and the 33rd Foot. Summoning the officers he swiftly briefed them on his intentions.

'It is vital that the people here can resume a normal life as soon as possible. That can only happen if they believe that we will not tolerate any further indiscipline.' Arthur paused to make sure that his next words would be clearly understood. 'To that end you will each be assigned a section of the city by Captain Fitzroy. You will enter your areas and detain any soldiers you encounter. They are to be escorted outside the city walls at once. Those caught in the act of looting will be flogged on the spot, before being thrown outside. Any man caught in the act of murder or rape will be taken to the nearest city gate and hanged. I want no one to be in any doubt about the consequences of indiscipline. Any questions?'

Major Shee nodded. 'Does that apply to our lads as well as the natives?'

'It applies to all soldiers, without regard to race or regiment. That includes the men of the 33rd.'

One of the younger officers nervously raised his hand.

'Yes?'

'Begging your pardon, sir. But won't hanging white soldiers damage morale?'

'Perhaps. But if we don't do it, then far more damage will be done to the reputation of our army and the Company. You have your orders and you will carry them out. Understand?'

The officer nodded.

'Then, go to it, gentlemen. I want order restored on the streets by no later than the end of the day. Dismissed!'

By dusk, the fires had been put out, a curfew had been established on the streets and the city was firmly under the control of the acting Governor. The last remnants of Baird's assault force had been turned out of the city, some bearing the red stripes of a recent flogging, and four red-coated bodies hung from a gibbet over the Mysore gate. The next day, Arthur turned his attention to another pressing issue: the disposal of the corpses that littered the streets and walls of Seringapatam. They had already been exposed to the heat of the Indian sun for nearly two days and the stench of putrefaction filled the still air. Hundreds of the prisoners were ordered to dig mass graves on the eastern end of the island and for five days carts and wagons loaded with bodies trundled out of the city and deposited their grisly burdens into the pits. Over nine thousand of the enemy had been killed in the assault, dwarfing the British losses of little more than three hundred dead.

Tipoo was spared the indignity of a mass grave and granted full honours of war the day that Arthur took control of the city. He organised the burial rites in person. Tipoo's sons, his surviving ministers and officers from his army were permitted to attend and followed the gun carriage bearing his body to the pyre in a corner of the grounds of the Dowlut Baugh as dark clouds thickened overhead. An honour guard of men from the 33rd lifted the body on to the carefully built layers of wood, decorated with flowers and ornately patterned shrouds. Then, as the first flames licked up around the body, the guns on the city wall boomed out one by one in a solemn salute to the fallen ruler. As his followers wept, rain began to fall, accompanied by jabs of forked lightning that stabbed down from the heavens in blinding daggers of dazzling light.

More than one man had fallen, Arthur reflected as he watched the smoke swirling up into the sky, where it was quickly lost against the heavy black clouds hanging overhead. Tipoo would be the last of his line to rule Mysore. His sons were to be sent into exile in Vellore and the throne of Mysore was to be restored to its original line of Hindu rajas, the sole survivor being a five-year-old boy. Since Krishna Wodeyar was too young to rule in his own right, a regent needed to be found. Another problem that vexed Arthur, since the man in question must have the respect of the native population, as well as the trust of the British.

Two weeks after the fall of the city Henry arrived with a small entourage of officials. He had been sent to report on the situation as soon as Richard had received news from General Harris that Seringapatam had fallen. As he dismounted Henry cast an appreciative eye over the Dowlut Baugh.

'You seem to have found yourself decent enough lodgings,' he mused as he shook hands with his brother.

'Oh, this?' Arthur smiled. 'I'm sure it will do for now. Until I can find something better. But do come inside and take some refreshment.'

'Yes, I will, but first I have something for you.' Henry reached into his saddlebag and pulled out a small package. 'Some letters from Kitty. I swear that woman will have created a national paper shortage by the time you return to Ireland.'

While Henry had a bath and changed into some fresh clothes, Arthur sent word of his arrival to General Harris, still encamped to the west of the city, and as daylight faded the three men met on a terrace overlooking the gardens. After admiring the view as the sky turned a brilliant fiery red, they sat at the table Arthur had prepared for the meeting and Henry turned immediately to the notebook he had brought with him.

'I'm sure you are aware how delighted the Governor General was to hear that the campaign had been concluded quickly and with minimal losses. He asked me to extend his personal gratitiude to you, General Harris.'

Harris bowed his head in polite acknowledgement. 'Most kind, I'm sure. But there is still some ground to cover, I'm afraid.'

'Oh?'

'Not all of Tipoo's commanders have yet surrendered to us. Some are still at large, and have fallen in with local groups of bandits. It will take some time to stamp them out.'

Henry frowned. 'Will that entail keeping your army in Mysore? I'm sure you appreciate that John Company is keeping a close eye on the cost of this campaign, and will not be pleased to hear that there will be a delay in dispersing your forces.'

'It can't be helped,' Harris replied evenly. 'War is an expensive business. We will need to maintain a force in Mysore sufficient to crush the rebels. And one in particular.'

Henry raised an eyebrow as he held his pen poised above a fresh page of his notebook.

'The man's called Dhoondiah Waugh,' Arthur explained. 'He was one of Tipoo's prisoners, but he escaped during the attack on the city. Since then he has been enlisting the support of other prisoners, and those who used to fight for Tipoo. So far he has contented himself with brigandage. But his following seems to be growing by the day, and the man has taken to calling himself the King of Two Worlds.'

'Sounds like a modest, unassuming fellow. What do you propose to do about him, Arthur?'

'Me? Surely this is a matter for General Harris?'

Henry could not help smiling slightly. 'I should have told you before, but it seemed only decent to raise the matter once General Harris was with us.'

'What matter?' Arthur said irritably. 'Speak plainly.'

'Very well. Richard is minded to confirm your appointment as Governor General of Mysore on a permanent basis. That is, if General Harris has no objections.' He turned to Harris with a questioning look.

'Objections? No, none whatsoever. Colonel Wellesley has performed his temporary duties with commendable efficiency. The city is back under control, the markets have reopened and he has established good working relations with the local officials. You have my full support for his appointment.'

'Good!' Henry nodded with some relief, and Arthur sensed at once that the situation could have been very tricky if Harris had taken any exception to the appointment. 'Then it merely remains to set out the scope of his authority.' He flicked back a few pages in his notebook and scanned some written comments. 'Richard has decided that the new Governor of Mysore should have supreme political power in Mysore, and to have command of all troops serving between the western and eastern ghats.' Henry glanced up at Harris. 'That is to say, once you have led the army back across the border to Vellore. Obviously Richard does not want to cause any difficulties over protocol.'

'Obviously,' Harris replied. 'And what kind of force does your brother propose to leave here in Mysore?'

'Given the need to clear out the remaining nests of rebellion, and that fellow . . . what was his name again?'

'Dhoondiah Waugh,' Arthur answered patiently.

'Of course.' The pen dipped into his inkwell and scratched out a brief note. 'Now, as I was saying, the force will need to be sufficient for the job. According to the advice Richard sought in Madras, two regiments of King's cavalry, another two of the Company's native cavalry, and three battalions of King's infantry and six of the Company's should suffice. In addition to a decent complement of artillery, of course.' Henry looked up innocently. 'That should be sufficient, wouldn't you say, General?'

'From a military point of view, yes.'

'Is there any other point of view I should be aware of?'

'Only that the command of such a large force would normally be assigned to a general. I can think of one or two men who might feel aggrieved by the appointment of Colonel Wellesley to such a prominent position.'

'I assume you are referring to General Baird? We had a copy of his official protest before I set off from Madras. He was . . . how shall I put it? Intemperate in his remarks.'

General Harris smiled. 'I can well imagine. He made his first protest to me in similar terms. I advised him to moderate his opinions, or seriously consider leaving the army.'

'Did you, by God?' Henry looked pleasantly surprised. 'That must have nettled him.'

Harris folded his hands and stared back at Henry. 'Young man, I'll have you know that I have nothing but admiration for General Baird as a soldier. In that respect he has no peer. But the man is no diplomat, nor a strategist. If he had at least some ability in those skills, I would have no hesitation in supporting his application for the post of Governor of Mysore. Even over your brother.'

'I see.' Henry had the grace to blush and continued in a far more respectful tone. 'I thank you for your candid words, sir.' He paused a moment, then referred back to his notes. 'Which leaves the question of the choice of regent for the new Raja.'

'I believe we have the right man,' said Arthur. 'A fellow called Purneah. He's a man of his word and proved to be an able enough administrator under Tipoo. In my opinion he's the best choice for the post of *dewan*.'

Henry frowned. '*Dewan*?'

Arthur smiled faintly. 'Henry, you are going to have to make greater efforts to learn the local language. *Dewan* is their term for the principal minister of Mysore.'

'Ah, a kind of prime minister then?'

'There, you have it.' Arthur nodded.

'When can I meet this man, Purneah?'

'Tomorrow. I've requested the opportunity to address the senior officials and civic leaders of Seringapatam and the surrounding towns – those we hold, at least.'

'Very well,' Henry shut his notebook with a quiet snap. 'Tomorrow, then. And once you've spoken, then I have a few words to communicate to them from the Governor General of India.'

'And what might they be?'

'You'll see.'

The next morning the audience chamber of the Dowlut Baugh was filled with the nobles and notables of Mysore. They had been told they were to hear a message from the highest-ranked *sahib* in India and they attended in their finest clothes. Henry had decided to address them from in front of the throne so that there would be no doubt as to who was the new power in Mysore. The five-year-old Raja was almost invisible as he perched on the throne and already looked thoroughly bored with proceedings.

When the last of the guests had arrived Henry took his place on the dais and waited until the murmuring came to an end. Arthur stood to one side of the throne, in his best uniform, the scarlet and gold braid brilliantly illuminated by a shaft of sunlight streaming in through one of the tall windows that ran along the side of the audience chamber. As he looked over the faces of the men in front of him he could see the anxiety in their expressions, and he could well understand it. They had been freed from a tyrant, but had only the vaguest notions of what British rule would entail. The previous history of the Company's involvement in India was one of naked exploitation and corruption, and would not inspire confidence in these men. It would be up to Arthur to prove to them the benefits of British rule. A victory had been won on the battlefield, but a much harder fight was about to begin in order to win the loyalty and trust of the natives.

Henry coughed lightly to clear his throat, and began. 'I know that some of you speak my tongue, but my brother will translate what I have to say into Hindoostani so that there will be no misunderstanding.' He paused while Arthur passed on his opening comments, then continued. 'The Governor General of India sends you his greetings, and a promise. That this day marks the birth of a new commonwealth . . . that no nation in this continent, or any other, will ever rival in its greatness . . . He promises an end to corruption and an end to brigandage so that every man, woman and child in Mysore shall be free to travel without hindrance, and without fear. Trade will flourish and there will be peace for all . . . The Governor General pledges his word that the Golden Age of India is about to begin.'

Chapter 56

'I am honoured, *sahib*.' Purneah bowed his head. 'But why ask me?'

'For a number of reasons,' Arthur replied. 'You have a reputation for honesty, and plenty of administrative experience. You speak many languages fluently.'

'Not least of all, English,' Henry added with a smile. 'And you were a loyal servant of Tipoo.'

Purneah bowed his head for a moment at the memory of his former ruler. 'Which will make me appear not to be some kind of British placeman, in the eyes of my people.'

'Precisely,' said Henry, and turned to Arthur. 'As bright as a button, just as you said.'

Arthur winced at his brother's words. From the previous occasions when he had met Purneah he had come to realise the quality of the man, and now was embarrassed by Henry's gauche manner and quickly attempted to gloss over it.

'I would be honoured if you accepted the post of *dewan*, and worked with me in making Mysore into a peaceful and proud kingdom.' Arthur leaned forward and looked at the man frankly. 'Will you accept?'

Purneah's dark eyes gazed back, and then he nodded. 'Very well, I will accept. However, I imagine there will be conditions attached to the powers I will have at my disposal.'

'Naturally,' replied Henry. 'We did not fight a war against Tipoo just to have another enemy rise up in his place. As with other territories allied to Britain, you will be required to have a resident here. The man the Governor General has chosen for the post is Barry Close. He's an old India hand; I'm sure you will have excellent relations with him. In addition, Arthur will be required to remain in Mysore as military governor until the remnants of Tipoo's warriors are dealt with, and the widespread banditry is suppressed. Once that has been achieved most of the British forces will be withdrawn. Even so, there will need to be a permanent garrison of Company troops in Seringapatam, to ensure the security of Mysore. That means the new Raja will not have need of a standing army. Of course, you will be required to pay for the upkeep of the soldiers.'

'And who will these soldiers answer to?'

'The Raja, in the first instance, but the ultimate decision on issues relating to their deployment and use will be a matter for the East India Company.'

'Ah.' Purneah smiled. 'So, in other words, we will bear the costs of our own occupation.'

'You could express it that way,' Henry admitted. 'But the presence of a Company garrison in Mysore will guarantee its security from outside invasion.'

'As long as there's a profit in it for the Company.'

Arthur shook his head. 'That attitude belongs to the past. The British interest in India has reached a stage where we can no longer simply regard this continent as a trading post. We have an obligation to ensure that India is ruled wisely, in the interests of all its peoples. In that way everyone can profit from the arrangement, even the East India Company,' he added with a wry smile.

'Such idealism would be welcome,' Purneah replied, and continued in an ironic tone, 'and, of course, it would have the additional benefit, for Britain and the East India Company at least, of keeping French interests at bay.'

'Yes, it would. Let's not be coy about this. If Britain did not move to establish herself in India, then another European power would step in without hesitation. It is not a choice between independence and submission to Britain, but merely a choice between which power Mysore accepts as its overlord. From that point of view, it is my belief that it is in the best interests of the people of Mysore to bind their future to that of Britain.' Arthur paused to let his words have their effect, then continued. 'There is another aspect you need to consider. In the past, I grant that the representatives of the East India Company have not always conducted their business with sufficient rectitude.'

'That has been noticed.' Purneah smiled.

'I'm sure. But that must and will change now that the administration of India is conducted by the British government and not the Company. Corruption and lawlessness will no longer be tolerated. That applies to Europeans as much as the natives of this continent. However, if this new order is to be made to work your people need to embrace the same values.' Arthur looked at Purneah earnestly. 'That is what I ask of you, and what you must ask of the people you appoint to serve in the government of Mysore.'

'I see,' Purneah said doubtfully. 'I will do all that I can to work successfully with you, *sahib*, but the people will need proof that you really mean what you say about this new order.'

'Very well, then you shall have it,' Arthur replied, then turned to Henry. 'I assume that I will have the full backing of the Governor General with regard to any measures I take in this respect?'

'Yes,' Henry said solemnly. 'Richard made that quite clear when he briefed me before I left Madras.'

Arthur nodded with satisfaction.

Once Henry had gathered enough information to present a detailed report on the situation in Mysore he returned to Madras to present his findings to Richard. Shortly afterwards General Harris re-formed his army, less the contingent left behind in Seringapatam, and with the host of camp followers retraced his steps to Vellore. The moment he quit the borders of Mysore, Arthur assumed full military and political authority in the new province. His first priority was to win the trust of Purneah and the people of Seringapatam, and not long after his appointment the opportunity arose.

From the outset, Arthur made it clear to his officers and officials of the Company that there had been too many beatings of Indians on the flimsiest of pretexts. He had witnessed Europeans thrashing water-carriers for being too slow in their duties, or even for failing to understand an instruction. They had been beaten with a wanton cruelty that would not have been tolerated if it had been given to a dumb animal back in England. In future, Arthur ordered, all such beatings would result in disciplinary action and the victims would be paid damages. His decree was met by vocal resentment amongst the officers of the Company battalions, who had grown accustomed to casual brutality after long years of service in India. Then, one day, Purneah came to the Dowlut Baugh in the company of a native woman. As soon as Fitzroy announced their arrival Arthur had them admitted to his office, bowing his head respectfully to each in turn.

'How may I help?'

Purneah indicated the woman. '*Sahib*, this is the widow of Basur, a goldsmith who was one of General Harris's camp followers. He died of his injuries last month. She wants justice.'

'Injuries?' Arthur raised his eyebrows.

'He was attacked by a customer for failing to deliver a commissioned piece on time,' Purneah explained. 'He had been ill, and could not work for several days. When he returned to his workshop, the English officer who had paid for the piece was there. He was angry, very angry, *sahib*, and picked up one of Basur's tools – a mallet – and began to beat him with it. Only when Basur was insensible did the man stop and leave the workshop.' He nodded to the woman. 'His wife found him there when he did not return home at the end of the day. There was not much that could be done for him and he died a few days later.'

Arthur felt sick, before he felt fury at the officer who had done this. He called out for Fitzroy and when his aide entered the office, he instructed him to take notes, before turning his attention back to Purneah.

'What is the name of this officer?'

'Lieutenant William Dodd, of the East India Company, *sahib*.'

Arthur vaguely recalled the name, but could not put a face to him. He spoke to the woman. 'Do you know which battalion Lieutenant Dodd belonged to?'

She glanced up quickly, momentarily surprised to be addressed in her own tongue by a white man, then her gaze dropped again and her hands picked at the folds of her sari as she replied. 'Yes, *sahib*. After the attack I complained to the colonel. He said he would investigate. Then, two days ago, I heard that Dodd *sahib* had had his pay suspended for six months.' She looked up again, and Arthur saw that tears were flowing down her cheeks. Her lips trembled as she continued. 'Six months pay, *sahib*, that is all Basur's life was worth ... Now I have no husband; the children have no father. We want justice,' she concluded defiantly.

'I understand.' Arthur nodded, rising to his feet. 'And I thank you for bringing this to my attention. You have my word that it will be dealt with at once.'

His guests stood up and Purneah spoke softly to the woman. She nodded and bowed to Arthur and turned and walked out of the office. When the door had closed behind her Purneah fixed Arthur with a penetrating stare. '*Sahib*, this is a most serious situation. Word of this killing has filled the markets and streets of the city. The people are watching and waiting to see how much weight the promises of Wellesley *sahib* carry.'

'I am aware of the gravity of the offence,' Arthur replied formally. 'And it will be dealt with according to the law.'

Purneah gazed at him a moment, before bowing and leaving the office.

Arthur turned to his aide. 'Find out which battalion Dodd is in, and then I want to see both him and his colonel, at once.'

It was late in the evening before Fitzroy returned to the Dowlut Baugh with the two Company officers. Arthur was watching the gravel drive from his office window and saw them approaching the palace. Several hours had passed since he summoned them and the initial anger he had felt had given way to a cold, calm determination to make this man Dodd pay for his crime. He returned to his desk and waited until the sound of boots echoed down the corridor outside his office. They stopped and at once there was a rap on the door.

'Come!'

Fitzroy led the way, stood aside to let the officers pass, closed the door behind them, and then took his place at the smaller desk to the side of the office to take notes. Arthur did not speak for a moment as he stared at the two Company officers. The colonel he already knew: Sanderson, who had served over two decades in India, and had eight years of service as a regular back in Britain before that. He was heavily built, with a bright red complexion that told of a fondness for spirits. Beside him stood a younger man, of approximately the same age as Arthur, he guessed. Dodd was tall and slender, with cropped blond hair and brilliant blue eyes. Handsome would be the word for him, Arthur mused. It was clear that he had been drinking as well, and that he was one of those men for whom the only effect of alcohol was to render them bitter and cruel.

'Fitzroy, where did you find them?'

'At the Company's officers' mess, sir.'

'So I can see.' Arthur interlaced his fingers on the desk in front of him. 'Now then, gentlemen, it seems you are both at the heart of a miscarriage of justice.'

'Miscarriage of justice?' Sanderson feigned surprise. 'Sir, I don't know—'

'Quiet!' Arthur snapped. 'You will be silent, sir, until I give you leave to speak.'

Sanderson opened his mouth with an angry expression, thought better of it and clamped it shut. Dodd just gave a small bitter smile, that quickly vanished like a wisp of smoke.

'I was visited today by the *dewan*, in the company of a woman. She claims that Dodd killed her husband, and that when you were asked to investigate the matter you merely suspended the lieutenant's pay for six months. Is that true?'

Sanderson shrugged. 'Yes, sir.'

'In which case was that suspension based upon finding the lieutenant guilty of the charge?'

Sanderson glanced sidelong at his subordinate. Arthur slapped his hand down on the desk. 'Don't look at him! Answer me!'

Sanderson's eyes steadied on the wall behind Arthur's head and he shuffled to attention. 'I decided on the evidence presented to me that Dodd was guilty of a serious misdemeanour that might bring disrepute to the reputation of the Company, sir.'

'A serious misdemeanour,' Arthur repeated coldly. 'Is that what a brutal, cold-blooded murder is?'

'Murder, sir?' Sanderson shook his head. 'He simply beat a fellow for failing to provide a service. Hardly an uncommon event, given the laziness and dishonesty of the natives we have to deal with. Of course, it was unfortunate that the man died. An accident was what it was, sir. Nothing more.'

'An accident is what happens when you barge into someone, or drop a plate on their foot. What an accident is not is a systematic and cold-blooded beating with a mallet. Do you deny that is what happened, Dodd?'

'It wasn't like that, sir,' Dodd said evenly. 'It was, as my colonel says, a mishap. The man had wronged me. I had been drinking. He refused to repay me and there was an argument. I lost my temper. I reached for the nearest thing to hand. It happened to be a mallet. After that, things were something of a blur. I had no idea the man was badly injured when I left his shop.' Dodd shrugged. 'That's all there is to it, sir. Naturally I regret that the man died.'

'Naturally,' Arthur repeated with heavy irony. 'Murder is murder, Lieutenant Dodd.'

'But he was only a native, sir,' Dodd protested.

'What of it? He was a man, and you were responsible for his death by your own admission. And you will face the consequences.'

'Sir?' Colonel Sanderson interrupted. 'You go too far! This is not the first incident of its kind. With good reason. These natives need to be ruled with a firm hand. Once in a while it is a useful thing to set an example.'

Arthur stared at him with open contempt before he continued. 'That is precisely the kind of example that can only win us the eternal emnity of the people of this continent. That is the kind of example set by the very tyrants with whom we are at war. That is why we have to set a better example. One that will win the respect and loyalty of these people. There are too few Europeans in India to rule by coercion. So we must rule by consent. And that means setting the right example. You, Lieutenant Dodd, will be made an example of.' Arthur leaned back in his chair and gestured to Fitzroy to take dictation as he concluded in a formal tone. 'It is the decision of the military governor to overrule the disciplinary process of Colonel Sanderson with respect to the case of Lieutenant Dodd. With immediate effect, Lieutenant Dodd is dishonourably dismissed from the service of the Honourable East India Company. Subsequent to his dismissal, proceedings will commence to try William Dodd for murder in a civil court. By order of the Governor.'

As he finished Arthur turned back to the two Company officers whose faces expressed anger and disbelief. Sanderson recovered first.

'This is an outrage, sir!'

'I'm aware of that,' Arthur replied coolly. 'Which was why I had to act.'

'Sir, I pray you, do not dissemble. You know what I mean. It is not justice to weigh the life of a native against the life of a Company officer, not to mention a British subject. I shall of course be forced to appeal to a higher authority.'

'As military governor, I am the highest authority. My decision stands, and you two *gentlemen* are dismissed.'

Arthur ensured that a proclamation about his decision was posted in every quarter of Seringapatam to serve notice to all Europeans and the people of Mysore that no man was above the law. Dodd was duly stripped of his rank and forced to undergo a ceremonial drumming out of his battalion. A large crowd had gathered outside the Dowlut Baugh to witness the event, and as he emerged from the gates Dodd was pelted with rotten fruit and ordure before he could escape into the city. Then, a week before his civil trial was due to begin, Arthur received news that he had fled the city. Sanderson claimed not to know anything about his flight, but Arthur knew that Dodd's options were limited. Since he was denied access to any British settlement, he would end up having to sell his services to one of the rulers of the Mahratta states, for ever exiled from his countrymen.

And good riddance, Arthur concluded, although he would have preferred that the man had stood trial and been convicted. Still, the lesson had been delivered and none of the British soldiers and officers under his command could be in any doubt about the consequences of their mistreatment of the local people from now on.

Throughout the summer Dhoondiah Waugh continued to attract brigands and the remnants of Tipoo's army to his side, and the number of raids on the outlying towns and trade routes of Mysore continued to increase. When Arthur sent columns after the raiders, they arrived in the area long after Dhoondiah Waugh's men had left. It became clear to Arthur that a more systematic approach was needed to remove the threat and he began to make his preparations for fresh campaigns. A breeding programme was set up to provide a stock of the white bullocks that had proved so useful in carrying supplies and hauling guns during the campaign against Tipoo.

The officer Arthur selected to track down and destroy Dhoondiah Waugh was Colonel Stevenson, a Company officer of long experience who proved adept at responding quickly to the enemy's raids. However, as soon as the enemy became aware of the columns closing in on him, Dhoondiah Waugh simply crossed the border into Mahratta territory where Stevenson was not permitted to follow.

'It's no good, sir,' Stevenson complained after returning from his latest attempt to catch the rebel leader. 'He can outmarch my men, and the moment he crosses the border he's away scot-free. You have to give me permission to pursue him into Mahratta territory.'

'I have written to the Governor General to explain the situation,' Arthur replied. 'I am waiting for his reply. Meanwhile,

I have decided to take the field against him. The situation in Seringapatam is stable enough to bear my absence for a while. It's time we put every available man and gun into the effort against Dhoondiah Waugh, if that's what it takes to destroy him.'

'Yes, sir.' Stevenson nodded in satisfaction. 'I had hoped for your involvement.'

'Oh?'

'Well, sir, I doubt that there are more than a handful of officers in India who fully appreciate the difficulties of campaigning here. You're one of them. If anyone can put an end to Dhoondiah Waugh, it is you, sir.'

Arthur felt the pride swell in his breast, and indulged the sensation for a moment – after all, it was his due after the success of the campaign against Tipoo. Then he fought down the emotion and hardened his expression. It would not do to let others see him respond to praise, let alone flattery. That would surely lead to his undoing. He needed honesty and objectivity from his subordinates. Anything else was superfluous. He cleared his throat and addressed Stevenson. 'Yes, well, I shall do my best. But before we can be sure of defeating him, we need permission to pursue him across the border. Until then, the initiative is his, and there is nothing we can do to stop his raids on Mysore.'

Chapter 57

'At last,' Arthur muttered as he finished reading the dispatch from Richard. He laid it down and looked up at the small team of officials he had gathered in his office to discuss the coming campaign. In addition to Fitzroy, there was Stevenson, Close and Purneah. 'The Governor General has concluded a treaty with Goklah, the Mahratta warlord whose territory borders Mysore. It seems that Dhoondiah Waugh has been carelessly indiscriminate about whose lands he preys on. Now he has another enemy, and we shall crush him between our forces and those of Goklah. The Governor General's final instruction is that when we take Dhoondiah Waugh he is to be hanged from the nearest tree.'

'Good!' Stevenson exclaimed heartily. 'Now we surely have the man caught between the beaters and the hunters. All that remains is to stick him.'

'Quite,' Arthur responded with an amused smile. 'Now then, gentlemen, let's turn our minds to the plan. We've seen that Dhoondiah Waugh cannot be stopped by defending the trade routes that pass through Mysore. We simply have not got enough men for that. So what I propose is the offensive control of those routes. We'll send a strong column against him, consolidating our gains as we push on, driving him up towards Goklah. We'll do all we can to deny him access to men, arms and supplies. My *hircarrah* scouts report that Dhoondiah Waugh has a number of strong forts in the border areas. To start with we will ignore his raiding columns and concentrate on reducing those forts. Without them, he'll be forced to keep on the move. Without supplies, I suspect that his followers will begin to melt away. Eventually, he will be cornered and finished off. And then we'll have peace in Mysore.'

The Company's resident in Seringapatam, Barry Close, leaned forward as he responded. 'That's fine in principle, sir, but as long as Dhoondiah Waugh has gold and silver to pay for supplies, then we can be sure that the *brinjarris* will sell him grain, and other goods, even weapons.'

'I have thought of that,' said Arthur. 'I think it's time we made the merchants aware of the dangers of dealing with Dhoondiah Waugh.' He turned to Purneah. 'A hint might be given to them that I am in the habit of hanging those whom I find living under the protection of British and Company forces and dealing treacherously towards our interests. I shall spare neither rank nor riches in this respect.'

Purneah nodded. 'I shall see to it, *sahib*.'

'Very well.' Arthur indicated the bottle of arrack on the table. 'Fitzroy, if you would do the honours?'

When every man had a full glass, Arthur raised his to make the toast. 'Gentlemen, the hunt is on. To the day's fox.'

Early in June Arthur led the small army he had formed into the northern region of Mysore, the stronghold of Dhoondiah Waugh. In addition to two King's battalions there were five Company battalions. Each unit had been allocated two small field guns, since grapeshot had proved to have a profoundly demoralising effect on enemy warriors more used to small arms fire and hand to hand fighting. In order to move swiftly enough to counter the enemy's moves, Arthur also took along two King's regiments of cavalry and three of the Company's mounted units.

The villages the column marched through all bore evidence of Dhoondiah Waugh's cruel regime: the blackened shells of burned buildings and the pinched faces of those who had lost all their animals and crops to the brigands. All that he saw made Arthur more determined than ever to crush Dhoondiah Waugh and give some peace and order to the desperate natives who stared at the passing soldiers and held out their hands as they begged for scraps of food. The *hircarrah* scouts soon found the first of the enemy's strongholds on the border with the Mahratta federation. The defenders were offered terms, and when they contemptuously turned them down Arthur ordered his guns to blow the gates open with roundshot before his soldiers stormed the fort and killed every man under arms within. The rest were released, and Arthur had few doubts about their fate if they ever passed through the lands they had once preyed on.

One by one the enemy's strongholds fell to the British forces, and the stores of arms and food that could not be carried off were set on fire. As the summer heat beat down on the parched landscape the campaign assumed a steady rhythm of marching during the cool hours before dawn and into the morning, before lying up during the suffocating midday heat, and then resuming their progress into the early evening before making camp for the night. The only relief from marching came when they encountered each stronghold, which fell in less than a day, and then the column moved on.

As July began with still no sighting of Dhoondiah Waugh and his army Arthur began to doubt that his campaign plan was working. The British were steadily whittling down the enemy's supply bases and reducing his strongholds and yet Dhoondiah Waugh resolutely refused to give battle, even though he surely knew where Arthur's column was from day to day, since his horsemen were nearly always in sight somewhere in the hazy distance, keeping a watch on the column's progress.

'The bloody man is going to retreat to the ends of the earth,' Fitzroy grumbled one morning early in the month. He was riding at Arthur's side, and squinting in the harsh glare of the sun. The dust kicked up from the column filled the air and settled on the jackets and crossbelts of the battalion marching beside them so that it seemed as if they had all passed through a pool of ochre dye.

Arthur licked his lips and spat out the grit that had got caught in his saliva. 'He can't go too far. If Goklah is true to his word then even now he will be moving towards us with his army. Dhoondiah Waugh will have a battle on his hands whichever way he turns. There will be no escape.'

'I pray so,' Fitzroy muttered. 'Before we all choke on this wretched dust. I imagine you'll be looking forward to returning to the comforts of Seringapatam as much as the rest of us, sir?'

'Yes. I suppose so,' Arthur replied. His mind went back to one of the final communications he had received from Richard, shortly before setting off on the present campaign. Another attempt was to be made to take Java, to secure the trade routes from French privateers. Richard had asked him to consider taking command of the expedition once he had dealt with Dhoondiah Waugh. Although the idea attracted him, Arthur had been forced to set it aside while the present campaign was under way. His thoughts were interrupted by the sudden pounding of hooves as a rider came galloping down the column.

'Wellesley, *sahib*?' the man called out. 'Colonel Wellesley?'

'Here!' Arthur raised his hat and waved it from side to side as he halted Diomed.

The rider yanked his reins and veered his mount towards Arthur. It was the chief of the *hircarrah* scouts, a man whose reliability Arthur had come to trust. He had been sent ahead of the column to gain knowledge of Goklah's movements and report back. Now he reined in and Arthur saw at once that both the man and his mount were exhausted from days of hard riding.

'What is it?' Arthur asked in Hindoostani. 'What's happened?'

'Goklah has been defeated by Dhoondiah Waugh, *sahib*. Six days ago.'

'Defeated?' Arthur shook his head. It could not be true. Goklah had over fifteen thousand men and eight guns. He looked closely at the scout. 'How did this happen?'

'*Sahib*, I was not there,' the scout replied carefully. 'I met some survivors hiding in a nullah. They told me what had happened. They were ambushed as they camped for the night. I rode on to the battlefield to see with my own eyes, and it was true, *sahib*. A shallow valley filled with the dead.'

'And Goklah? What of him?'

'Dead, *sahib*. The men saw it, and they said that Dhoondiah Waugh himself dyed his beard in the blood of Goklah.'

Arthur continued to stare at the man for a moment, as the

column tramped past. He was aware of Fitzroy at his side, fretting to know the nature of the news the scout had brought. He told the scout to join the column, but not to speak a word of the fate of Goklah. As the man rode off he turned to Fitzroy and spoke in an undertone.

'Goklah is dead. His army is destroyed.'

'Good God . . . What now, sir?'

'What now? We carry on with the plan.'

'Sir?' Fitzroy looked surprised. 'How can we? Goklah's army was three times the size of ours. If Dhoondiah Waugh can defeat Goklah, what chance have we got?'

'Man for man, our forces are more than a match for any army on this continent. As long as we hold the column together we have little to fear. Besides, with such a victory under his belt, Dhoondiah Waugh might become reckless enough to face us in battle. And if he does, then he is doomed, Fitzroy. Hold to that thought.'

'Yes, sir,' Fitroy replied uncertainly.

Arthur turned his mount back towards the head of the column and with a click of his dry tongue he gently urged Diomed forward.

They continued to reduce the enemy's strongholds until, at the end of July, they stormed the final fortress of Dummul late in the afternoon. As dusk settled over the surrounding hills Arthur's men went through the fort with firebrands, systematically torching everything that could burn. Brilliant sheets of red and orange flame crackled up against the rouge glow of the sunset. A thick plume of smoke gathered over the blaze, billowing gently into the gloom as it rose steadily higher. Even though they had burned several of Dhoondiah Waugh's strongholds in the previous weeks the soldiers still regarded the spectacle with fascinated awe for a while before returning to their camp and preparing their evening meal.

'That's it, then, sir,' Fitzroy announced. 'The last of them. There's nowhere for Dhoondiah Waugh to run now.'

'True enough,' Arthur agreed.

'What will he do now, sir?'

'There's not much he can do, apart from keep on the move. We've destroyed his supplies, so there will be little food to sustain a large force. He'll have to divide his army. Very soon, the prospect of continually being on the march without rest and further spoils will cause his men to melt away. At which point, Dhoondiah Waugh will be little more than a common criminal on the run. The days of the King of Two Worlds are numbered. It has come to the final act.'

Chapter 58

As Arthur had anticipated, Dhoondiah Waugh divided his army into three smaller forces, each one to fend for itself while trying to evade the British pursuit. But with the *hircarrah* scouts scouring the landscape looking for signs of the brigands it was only a matter of time before they were discovered. The first of the forces was surprised as it camped for the night and was annihilated by a column led by Colonel Stevenson. Arthur posted a thirty thousand rupee reward for information leading to the death or capture of Dhoondiah Waugh and within days a report on the precise location of the enemy was received. The rebel chief was leading the larger of his surviving columns away from Stevenson. On his present line of march he would be passing across the open ground at Conaghull – a mere ten miles from the main British column.

It was shortly after noon, and Arthur's mind raced as he grasped the opportunity that lay before him. As well as the bulk of the infantry and artillery he still had two regiments of King's cavalry and two native mounted regiments, nearly fourteen hundred horsemen in all. 'Fitzroy, I want the cavalry ready to ride at once. They are to leave their kit behind. All they will need is one day's rations and their weapons.'

'Yes, sir.'

'Hurry, man! We must move quickly.'

Within half an hour, the cavalry column had left the main body and was riding hard across the landscape in the direction of Conaghull. Just over two hours after he had first received the report, Arthur spotted a dense cloud of dust a few miles distant and he felt relief wash through his heart. At last, they had pinned Dhoondiah Waugh down. He indicated the haze to Fitzroy and called out, 'We'll attack as soon as we reach them.'

'Yes, sir. If you think that's wise.'

They rode on, until they were no more than a mile from the enemy force, now visible through gaps in the clumps of trees that dotted the plain. As the enemy drew into sight, Arthur halted his men and with Fitzroy rode over to a small hummock for a better sighting of the ground ahead.

From the crest they had a fine view across the plain. Fitzroy's expression steadily became more concerned as his eyes took in the mass of men and horses moving across the landscape. 'Sir, there must be nearly . . . five thousand men over there.'

Arthur nodded as he squinted through his field telescope. 'At least. But no more than half are mounted.'

'They still outnumber us, sir.'

'Yes. But, as ever, this is is a test of quality over quantity, and the superiority of our men has not failed us yet.'

'There's always a first time, sir,' Fitzroy responded quietly.

Arthur lowered his telescope and turned to his aide with a smile. 'And that time is not now.' He turned back towards the enemy army and pointed to an open stretch of ground. 'That's where we'll take them. We'll form a single line parallel to the enemy and charge.'

'A single line? No reserves, sir?'

'No. We need to strike with maximum impact. If we don't succeed with the first charge there will be no need for a reserve. It's all or nothing, Fitzroy.'

'Yes, sir.'

'Then let's go!' He wheeled Diomed round and galloped back down the slope to the long column of mounted men waiting impatiently in the harsh glare of the afternoon sun. They moved off at a tangent to the enemy and had closed to within half a mile by the time they reached the position Arthur had indicated. As they caught sight of their pursuers, Dhoondiah Waugh's warriors halted and prepared to fight for their lives. Arthur drew his men up in one long line. The two King's regiments were in the centre while the native cavalry formed up on the flanks.

It was a brave sight, Arthur reflected as he glanced either side at his cavalrymen. He loosened the straps on his saddle holster, checked his stirrups were secure, and then drew his sword and bellowed the order, 'Draw sabres!'

The order was relayed down the line and the air was thick with the rasp of blades scraping from their scabbards. When the noise had died away, Arthur raised his blade high and then swept it forward towards the enemy to signal the advance.

He nudged his heels in and Diomed paced forward. On either side the line rippled into motion as the horses began to cross the open ground, half a mile from the waiting enemy. The officers and their sergeants kept shouting orders to keep the line dressed, and Arthur noted with professional satisfaction that the men were maintaining their positions almost as well as if they had been on an exercise at Horseguards.

Ahead he could see the enemy infantry raising their muskets, no more than four hundred yards away.

'At the trot!'

The line lurched forward, slightly more uneven now as the pace increased. Ahead, the first of the enemy opened fire, flashes and puffs of smoke pricking out along the face of the mass of men awaiting the British cavalry. At that range Arthur knew the chances of any ball hitting a target were remote, but he felt his pulse quicken none the less, and as soon as they had closed to within three hundred yards he raised his sword again.

'Gallop!'

Beneath him the ground shook as the iron-shod hooves thundered over the baked soil. The air was alive with flashes of sunlight glinting off blades and buttons and buckles. Before them the enemy line disappeared behind a curtain of gunfire and out of the corner of his eye Arthur saw a horse pitch forward as blood burst from a wound in its skull. Then it was gone, and Arthur guessed that they must be within a hundred paces of the enemy.

'Charge!'

As soon as he gave the order, the trumpeter at his shoulder

blasted out the notes and the signal was echoed down the line as the men let out a roar and spurred their horses on. The stench of gunpowder filled Arthur's nostrils, and the world was swallowed by a thick swirl of pallid smoke, before a figure on horseback leaped into view almost in front of him. Arthur's sword had been poised, point forward, and he just had time to flex his arm and swing a cut as Diomed ploughed into the enemy's mount with a panicked whinny, knocking the smaller horse aside. The blade swished through the air, the tip slicing across the bridge of the man's nose, severing the bottom section. As he recovered and lifted the blade for the next cut, Arthur jerked the reins to the left, swerving Diomed towards half a dozen foot soldiers who scattered. Arthur swung at the nearest, who threw up a round shield just in time to deflect the blow into the arm of one of his comrades. The sabre cut through bare flesh and bone. The man with the shield thrust out his sword, aiming the blow at Arthur's side, and he just had time to throw himself back in his saddle so the blade stabbed past his stomach, tearing through the leather cuff of the glove that held the reins. Arthur swept his blade up in a desperate unorthodox blow that smashed into his foe's elbow, and the sword clattered to one side.

For a moment, he was clear of the fight and no one faced him. Snatching a glance around him, Arthur saw that his men had shattered the enemy line completely, and were engaged in personal duels with other riders in a loose melee that stretched out for nearly a mile across the plain. Most of Dhoondiah Waugh's foot soldiers had already broken and were streaming away from the fight, run down here and there by some of Arthur's men who had cut their way right through the enemy line. A short distance away he saw a party of enemy horsemen gathered round a standard and realised he must be looking at Dhoondiah Waugh and his bodyguard.

'Follow me!' Arthur called out, waving his sword overhead to draw attention. 'On me!'

Several dragoons immediately rallied to the call and spurred their mounts to the colonel's side. As soon as he had a score of men ready Arthur pointed his sword at the enemy horsemen.

'That's Dhoondiah Waugh, boys! He must not escape. Charge!'

Diomed burst forward, with Arthur rising up in his stirrups as he leaned forward, sword raised. He sensed the men charging just behind him on either side and was lost in the mad thrill of the action. All the long weeks of marching under a hot sun, the razing of enemy strongholds, and the constant stream of intelligence reports and redeployment of forces – all that vanished from his mind as he charged straight through the melee at Dhoondiah Waugh and his bodyguards, heedless of any danger as his heart thudded in his breast.

The British mounts were far heavier than the native horses, and the charge of the small party of redcoats crashed into the enemy warriors, knocking three from their saddles and scattering the rest before the air resounded with the clang, clatter and scrape of blades. Arthur found no foe to his immediate front and saw that he was cut off from the fight by some of his own men who had swept past him. Over the back of a horse he caught sight of a tall enemy warrior in fine silk robes. His light brown beard was streaked with red and Arthur knew at once who it must be. Quickly he sheathed his sword and drew one of his pistols, thumbed back the cock, and raised it, taking careful aim on his foe. At the last moment Dhoondiah Waugh turned and saw the muzzle pointing straight at him over the back of a riderless horse, and his eyes widened.

Arthur pulled the trigger. There was a spark from the frizzen, a flash from the pan and then the charge exploded in the barrel with a gout of flame and smoke. He saw his target reel back in the saddle as Dhoondiah Waugh grimaced and clutched a hand to the shoulder of his sword arm. The blade dropped from his fingers. Arthur holstered the pistol and reached for his second, but the men who had charged with him now swarmed round Dhoondiah Waugh and the last of his bodyguard, obscuring the enemy leader. Their blades flashed in the dusty air, hacking and chopping at the enemy, and then it was over.

As soon as the enemy's standard toppled into the dust, the rest of them turned and ran for their lives, chased down by the jubilant British cavalry. Arthur let them continue their pursuit as he surveyed the battlefield. Bodies littered the ground in a long strip spread across the plain. The vast majority of them were brigands, and their riderless horses dotted the dried earth. Arthur nudged Diomed with his knees, steering his mount towards the spot where the rebel leader had fallen. Dhoondiah Waugh lay curled up on his side. His turban had been flicked off his head by the tip of a dragoon sabre and his body was covered with sword cuts. Around him lay half a dozen of his bodyguards, also hacked to death in the last furious assault by the men Arthur had led towards them. He stared at the bodies for a moment, taking in the realisation that the struggle to bring peace to Mysore was over at last.

Chapter 59

When news of the death of Dhoondiah Waugh reached the Peshwa of the Mahratta federation he immediately sent a message of gratitude to Arthur, for avenging the death of Goklah. At once Arthur saw the opportunity to improve British relations with the Mahrattas, and as his column was crossing the southern stretch of their lands he sent word asking if the Peshwa might resupply his men since they had grown short of rations in the last weeks of the pursuit of Dhoondiah Waugh. As Arthur hoped, the Peshwa saw a similar opportunity and threw open the doors of his nearest fortified town, Moodgul, and bade his British ally take whatever food was needed, and rest there as long as he liked.

It was only a few days after the column had arrived, and while it was still enjoying the hospitality of the local Mahratta warlord, that the Peshwa himself – Bajee Rao – arrived at Moodgul to greet his ally. The local warlord, Holkar, was given little warning of the arrival of the Peshwa and hurried to prepare the town to greet him. Arthur gave orders that the dragoons were to make ready to parade before the ruler of the confederation, and horses were hurriedly groomed, saddles and equipment polished and buffed and uniforms cleaned so that the regiment would look its best. Even though the Peshwa was accompanied by only a small retinue and a regiment of his cavalry, his entrance through the town gate took on the ambience of a state procession as the Mahratta people cheered and bowed as he passed by. He made his way through the town to Arthur's camp on the far side, and the

515

moment he was sighted the officers and sergeants hurriedly inspected the ranks of mounted men drawn up in squadrons.

Arthur and Fitzroy were in full uniform and sat uncomfortably in the stifling heat as the Peshwa and his entourage walked their horses slowly across the large clear area lined by tents and horse lines. Arthur nodded to the colonel of the dragoons who drew a deep breath and bellowed the order, 'Present!'

The dragoons drew their sabres and rested them smartly on their shoulders, guards held out so that there was a right angle between upper and lower arms. It was a spectacular display and one that Arthur hoped would impress his host.

The Peshwa was a young man with a ready smile and he bowed his head in response to Arthur's salute, then reined his horse in.

'Colonel Wellesley.' He spoke softly with a slight lisp. 'I am delighted to meet the man responsible for the defeat of Dhoondiah Waugh.'

Before one of his courtiers could translate Arthur replied in Hindoostani. 'The pleasure is mine, sir.'

The Peshwa's expression revealed his surprise and he smiled again. 'You speak our tongue well, Colonel.'

'You are very kind, sir.'

'No, it is you who are kind, Colonel. Not many of the white men in India have made an effort to learn the local tongues.' He laughed. 'They just speak louder in the hope that volume will compensate for clarity.'

Now it was Arthur's turn to laugh. 'You have the measure of my people, sir. It is a peculiarity of the British that they find it hard to speak other languages.'

'And yet you do, Colonel.'

'I try to make up for the shortcomings of others, sir.'

'How admirable of you. But I wonder, can one such as you make up for the depredations of so many of your fellow countrymen? Or at least the Honourable East India Company?'

'I can assure you that British affairs in India are no longer the sole responsibility of the Company. The world is changing, sir.'

'Yes, it is,' the Peshwa replied thoughtfully.

Arthur gestured to the dragoons, still waiting in their squadrons. 'Would you care to inspect my men, sir?'

'Indeed.'

The Peshwa rode down each line of horsemen and surveyed them with a genuinely curious expression. At the end he turned to Arthur. 'Thank you, Colonel. A fine body of men. I only wish I had such soldiers in my army.'

There was a hint of feeling that went beyond politeness and Arthur felt his pulse quicken as he replied. 'All India knows that the Mahratta people field the finest native soldiers in these lands.'

'That is true, but some of my warlords abuse that advantage by waging war on each other, and occasionally on me. Sometimes, I fear, I am ruler of the Mahratta federation in name only.'

'Then you might consider a more formal alliance with Britain, sir.' It was a bold suggestion and Arthur feared that he might have overstepped the bounds of diplomacy. For a moment the Peshwa stared at him, and then he shook his head sadly.

'An interesting thought, Colonel, but with so many Frenchmen advising the Maharatta warlords, I fear that I would not long survive such an alliance. But come now, we are not here to bewail the ways of the world. I am your host and you and your men are here to celebrate the end of Dhoondiah Waugh.'

While Colonel Stevenson led the column back to Mysore, Arthur and a small escort remained the guest of the Mahrattas for several more weeks. He took every opportunity to explore the lands and get to know the most prominent of the warlords. He entered notes of his observations in a small book in a private code he shared with his brothers. Then, in November, he returned to Seringapatam.

Now that the brigands had been defeated, the kingdom was enjoying newfound prosperity and the routes that linked the towns and cities flowed with merchandise and travellers. Arthur was greeted with respect and gratitude in every settlement he passed through and it seemed that the vision of the Wellesley brothers was at last taking root in Mysore.

He reached the capital just after sunset one night, and rode quietly round the walls of the city until he reached the Dowlut Baugh. There was sure to be a mass of paperwork and other duties awaiting his attention, but Arthur promised himself a good night's rest before he resumed his duties as military governor.

There was one letter he did attend to. It was from Richard in his own hand and Arthur broke the seal and read it while a servant prepared a bath for him. Richard was delighted by his success against Dhoondiah Waugh. No one in India could now doubt Arthur's potential as a military commander. He had brought peace to a land larger and more populous than all the islands of Britain. His return to Seringapatam was fine timing, since the need to mount an expedition to seize Java was more pressing than ever. Richard offered his brother the task of planning the operation, preparing the men and supplies required, and ultimately commanding the force. He concluded, in words that warmed Arthur's heart:

I employ you because I rely on your good sense, discretion, activity and spirit. I cannot find all those qualities united in any other officer in India.

Arthur set the letter down and leaned back in his chair to gaze out of the window. Outside, the moon gleamed in the starry sky, bathing the ornate gardens of the palace in a silvery loom, and the Cauvery flowed like a black ribbon across the lush landscape of Mysore. The feeling of being at peace was overwhelming, and Arthur realised that, finally, he had achieved a recognition he could be satisfied with.

Chapter 60

Trincomalee, Ceylon, January 1801

Out in the harbour the transports lay at anchor, while around them the placid waters teemed with small craft from which the natives sold fruit, carvings, jewellery and jugs of spirits to the sailors and soldiers aboard the ships. Despite the fact that the ships had arrived in the harbour some weeks earlier trade was still thriving and at least it gave the men something to do while the preparations for the expedition continued. Arthur and his small staff had been obliged to make their headquarters in the offices of a burgher trader, since the Governor of Ceylon – the Honourable Frederick North – had declined to offer them accommodation at the fort. Indeed, his lack of hospitality and helpfulness was causing considerable delay in making Arthur's small flotilla ready to sail.

There were over five thousand soldiers aboard the transports and North had refused to allow them permission to land, not even to carry out exercise and training. The reason he gave was that Ceylon had been in British hands for less than five years and the last thing the Governor needed was for some insensitive, or inebriated, soldier to cause offence to the natives or the local population of Dutch traders and their families. So the men remained crowded in the transports while Arthur did his best to complete the loading of supplies into the transports' holds. There were still shortages of biscuit, salt beef, medicines, spirits and above all ammunition. Once again, the officials of the Company were proving reluctant to authorise the release of their stocks of powder. At first Arthur had tried to persuade North and his officials to see reason and co-operate with him, but after a week he gave in and sent a message to Calcutta, begging Richard to intercede and make it quite clear that Arthur should have unrestricted access to whatever resources he needed to prepare the expedition. It would take at least three weeks for a reply and Arthur had to resign himself to yet more delay.

In the meantime, he did his best to repair relations with the Governor and his staff by hosting a dinner aboard his ship for the senior officers of his command, those of the garrison at Trincomalee and Admiral Rainier and the captains of the squadron assigned to support the expedition. The warships were anchored slightly further offshore where they would be free to put to sea in the event that any French vessels appeared on the horizon. Arthur was aware that there was a strong animosity between the Governor and the admiral, but he braced himself to doing his best to repair relations all round. It frequently surprised Arthur how often personal differences of opinion were permitted to stand in the way of the vital interests of the state, as if such men felt that they were more important than the nation they professed to serve.

On the morning of the appointed date, Arthur's mood was not improved by the receipt of a private message from Richard, which had crossed the letter he had sent to Calcutta. Once he had decoded the message Arthur's brow creased into a frown. There was a possibility that the Java expedition would once again have to be cancelled. The situation in the Mediterranean was such that the expeditionary force might be enlarged and redeployed to Egypt instead. Arthur was told to make the force ready to sail either to the east, towards Java, or west, towards Red Sea. The final decision would be communicated to him as soon as possible.

The message made Arthur uneasy. The last news he had had of the situation in Egypt was that the French still had a considerable army there. If Arthur and his men were sent to

Egypt they would be outnumbered and would have to face a well-trained and well-armed enemy. Arthur did not doubt that his men were a match for any French soldiers that lived, and he was confident enough in his abilities to confront them, but a campaign in Egypt was a more uncertain prospect than the capture of Java, and it would have to be tackled with great care. He could not help but be scornful of the politicians back in London who could redirect thousands of men from one theatre of war to another on a whim.

The air in the great cabin of the East India Company ship *Suffolk* was hot and humid, despite the attempt to create a through draught by using windscoops over the skylights and opening all the stern windows. The officers of the army and Navy were in their best uniforms and the Company officials in their best coats, and everyone attempted to endure the heat with stolid indifference. A long table had been laid with spotless cloths and gleaming silverware and cut glasses, and the odours of the cooking wafted through from the captain's galley.

'What's that, Wellesley?' Admiral Rainier sniffed.

'A saddle of mutton, sir. My steward, Vingetty, cooks it in a rich sauce and serves it with a salad. Accompanied by a Madeira.'

'Salad?' Rainier frowned. 'I don't know about a salad. Mutton deserves something more wholesome, like boiled vegetables.'

Arthur stopped himself from wincing at the idea. He nodded tactfully. 'Of course, sir, but Vingetty makes a better salad than he boils a vegetable, so there we are.'

'Hmmm. Well, needs must.'

'Yes, sir. Now would you care to take your seat?'

As the guests took their places Arthur made sure that the Governor was seated at the head of the table with Rainier on one side while Arthur sat opposite. Frederick North was a stout, sour-faced man with a pale complexion despite the years he had served in Ceylon. Once everyone was seated he picked up a soup spoon and rapped the table until the other diners fell silent.

'Grace . . .' North clasped his hands and shut his eyes and some of the others followed suit. Rainier caught Arthur's eye and looked to the heavens with an exasperated expression, but said not a word as North began.

'Divine Lord, who watches over us all, bless us here today that we might serve our King and country well, and prosper by the fruits of our own efforts. Amen.'

'Amen,' echoed round the table, as North picked up his napkin and tucked it into his neck cloth.

'An interesting grace,' said Rainier. 'One of your own?'

'Yes. And suitable to the occasion, given that you and Colonel Wellesley will soon be sailing off to war.'

'If ever the order comes,' Rainier grumbled. 'Been telling 'em for years that we have to take Java.'

'I know,' North replied tartly. 'As you keep telling me. And as I keep telling you, we should be concentrating our efforts on Mauritius. As your superior, I would expect you to carry out my orders.'

Admiral Rainier shrugged his shoulders wearily and Arthur realised that this had long been a bone of contention between the two men. Rainier replied in a bored tone, 'You are the senior civil authority with power over all forces stationed here, but the moment the squadron leaves these waters control of the vessels reverts to me. I will only carry out operations against Mauritius under Admiralty orders.'

'Which I am certain are on the way. Assuming my powers of persuasion have made their lordships see reason.'

'We shall have to wait and see, won't we?' Rainier smiled, then looked across the table at Arthur. 'What's the first course?'

'Turtle soup.'

'Fish, or as near as.' Rainier wrinkled his nose.

'I'd have thought a sailor would be fond of fish, sir.'

'And I'd have thought a soldier would be fond of bloody boiled vegetables. Especially a man from Ireland. That is where your family is from, ain't it?'

'Yes, sir.' Once again Arthur felt the implied slight, and wondered if the family would ever shake off its history.

'That's right,' North added. 'And I am sure that your brother must be delighted with the peerage conferred on him following the victory in Mysore. But I forgot, the news reached here only yesterday. He will not know yet.'

'A peerage, sir?' Arthur felt his breast lift with pride for his brother, and at the same time there was a tinge of jealousy that no reward had come his way.

'Oh, yes. He has been given a title, in the Irish peerage.' North spoke the last words with emphasis and some relish. 'But still, a peerage is a peerage, eh? I am sure your brother will be delighted with the honour.'

Arthur knew that Richard would see the reward as a very poor second to the British peerage he aspired to, but he smiled at North. 'Of course, sir. Delighted.'

'And I imagine that you look forward to emulating his triumph. Though I dare say you will admit that your path to success is being smoothed by having a brother who is the highest authority in India.'

Arthur felt his cheeks flush at the naked accusation that he was benefiting from nepotism. It was a charge that he knew had been levied against him in the past by other officers, and no doubt was still bandied about to explain his various appointments. But had he not proved worthy of every task that had been assigned to him? He had ably commanded one wing of General Harris's army. He had brought peace and prosperity to Mysore, and thanks to his system of supplying his forces in the field he had led his forces further into the heart of India, and marched faster, than any British commander before him. And still his accomplishments were written off as the product of family connections. *Good God, when will this end*, he thought furiously. He forced himself to keep a calm exterior as he turned to North.

'I can assure you, sir, that the Governor General would never put his family above the needs of his nation. Nor would I actively seek preferment on such a basis.'

'Of course not.' North nodded. 'Your achievement is a credit to you, young man. To have assumed such a command as your present one, while still only a colonel, is tribute enough to your talent. I can only imagine how many officers of superior rank serving in India must regard you as something of a prodigy and toast your continued success. However, experience would suggest that there might be some resentment at the positions of authority that have come your way.'

Admiral Rainier coughed. 'Steady on, North. You go too far. I have it on good authority that Wellesley is the right man for the job. Of course there will be some old soaks who grumble about his success. There always are.'

'Some?'

'Enough of this!' Rainier blustered, grabbing his glass. 'It's time for the toasts! Gentlemen! To His Royal Majesty, King George III!'

'The King!' the others responded.

'I give you one more toast,' Rainier continued. 'To our good host, Colonel Wellesley, and may glorious victory attend him . . . wherever the bloody government decides to send him in the end!'

A few days later another message arrived from Richard. The situation in Calcutta was becoming more vexed, his brother told him. He had decided that if the expedition was to be sent to Egypt then it would need to be reinforced, in which case it would be extremely difficult for Richard to justify maintaining an officer of Arthur's rank in command of so large a force. Worse still, Richard wrote, it seemed that General Baird had designs on securing the command for himself and had been busy canvassing all the senior military officers in India to support his application. Indeed, the Commander in Chief of the forces at Calcutta, Sir Alured Clarke, had strongly urged Richard to give the command to Baird. Arthur must prepare himself for the possibility that he would be required to hand over the command to a superior officer.

As Arthur read this, a sense of bitter betrayal entered his soul. Had not Richard himself told him that he prized Arthur above all officers in India? Now, here he was, buckling under the pressure of opinion from men motivated by little more than professional jealousy, and, in the case of Baird, a more personal rivalry. The same evening Arthur sat down to write a reply with a heavy heart. He told Richard that he must make a clear and final decision on the matter. Either he must confirm Arthur's command of the expeditionary force, or he must choose another officer. Any doubts about his ultimate authority would only serve to hamper Arthur's attempts to collect the supplies he required, and undermine his standing with subordinate officers. He asked Richard to respond as soon as possible and resolve the matter.

The days passed slowly as he waited for a reply, and the more he reflected on the situation the more he realised that Richard had staked more than was sensible, or at least politically wise, on the appointments he had given him. If an official as far from Calcutta as Frederick North was aware of the resentment arising from Arthur's preferment, then such a feeling must be widespread indeed. And who knew, perhaps the envious muttering of those in India had already reached the ears of Parliament and the board of directors of the East India Company back in London? After the prosecution of Warren Hastings, all subsequent Governor Generals had to be wary of being seen to wield power too partially, or for personal gain. Richard had already risked enough in making Arthur Governor of Mysore. Elevating him over the heads of military officers of higher rank and greater experience would be to court political ruin. Richard's hands were tied, Arthur realised, and he gloomily awaited the inevitable news of his replacement from Calcutta.

But before any such message could arrive, a frigate docked at Trincomalee bearing a dispatch from London. Arthur was summoned to the office of the Governor shortly afterwards. As he entered the room, he saw that Rainier was already seated opposite North's desk. The Governor waved him towards a spare chair, and began the meeting at once.

'Dundas has decided to send the expedition to Egypt,' he said bluntly. 'The transports, and Admiral Rainier's squadron, are to sail to Bombay to meet up with other forces before making for the Red Sea. Are your men and your ships ready?'

Arthur had taken the news to be confirmation of the loss of his command. But almost at once he realised that it raised another problem. One that could do untold damage to his reputation.

'Sir, there are still a few supply issues to resolve, but nothing that can't be settled once we reach Bombay. However, I am waiting for the Governor General to make a final decision over the command of the force. If he has decided to replace me, then I can hardly quit Trincomalee before the new commander arrives . . .'

Admiral Rainier nodded as soon as he got the point. 'No. I can see how that would look. You going off in high dudgeon, taking your army with you. I know that's what the orders say, but it won't count for much once tongues start wagging.'

'Precisely, sir.' Arthur turned to North. 'I should wait until I hear from Calcutta.'

'But you can't wait.' North tapped the dispatch. 'It says you are to set sail immediately.' He smiled. 'Whatever the cost to your reputation.'

Chapter 61

The fleet set sail early in February and arrived at Bombay in March. During the voyage the fleet was overhauled by one of the fast packet ships used to carry dispatches. Arriving too late at Trincomalee, the ship had set off after the fleet. There was a message from Richard to inform his brother that Major General Baird was now in command of the expedition. Arthur hurriedly wrote a dispatch to Baird explaining his actions and sent the packet ship back to Ceylon. For the rest of the voyage he slipped into a melancholy mood and upon reaching Bombay began a detailed report of his preparations and advisory notes for his replacement.

Baird finally caught up with the expeditionary force at the beginning of April. He immediately summoned Arthur to meet him in the Governor's residence. Arthur took his reports with him, and entered the ornate entrance to the building with a sense of foreboding. His mood was not helped by an itching sensation that had begun a few days earlier and now affected most of his body. The army surgeon he had consulted had served long enough in India to recognise the symptoms at once.

'It's the Malabar Itch, I'm afraid, sir,' Dr Scott said as Arthur buttoned up his shirt. 'You're in for an uncomfortable time over the coming weeks.'

'How does this Malabar Itch develop?'

'Once the skin irritation covers your body you can expect blisters to follow. They will erupt and spread the infection which will make sleep all but impossible.'

Arthur swallowed. 'And then?'

'Well, if it doesn't drive you mad enough to kill yourself, you can expect the blistering to recede after two or three weeks. Full recovery will take some months and you will need to rest, sir. No soldiering.'

'Damn it, man, I'm supposed to be leaving to fight in Egypt within a month.'

'A month?' Dr Scott shook his head. 'Believe me, sir, in a month's time you will be bed-bound. There's no question of your embarking on a campaign for a long time.'

'We'll see about that,' Arthur snapped as he pulled on his coat and made for the door. He paused, and turned back. 'Is there anything to do to treat the illness?'

'The usual treatment is an ointment composed of lard and sulphur.' Dr Scott pursed his lips. 'I've heard that some of my colleagues have had more success by having their patients bathe in diluted nitric acid.'

Arthur winced. 'Sounds painful.'

'It is, sir. But you might want to consider it.'

'I might,' Arthur muttered as he left the dispensary.

Now, a few days later, he felt the hot prickle of the blisters chafing against his clothes and it took a great effort to resist the urge to scratch viciously at the irritation. He took a deep breath and entered the office assigned to Baird. There were a number of men present, some of whom Arthur recalled from the day he had assumed control of Seringapatam. One or two of them glanced at him with barely concealed smugness in their expressions. Baird was seated behind a large desk and looked up the moment Arthur closed the door behind him.

'Wellesley. How are you?'

'I'm well, sir.' Arthur considered asking if Baird's voyage had been pleasant, but thought better of the impulse, under the circumstances. 'I take it you received my letter, sir.'

'Yes,' Baird replied. There was a silence and Arthur braced himself for a harsh dressing down. 'As far as I am concerned you did the right thing, Wellesley. If you had left it any longer the winds would not have been favourable for the Red Sea.'

'Yes, sir.' Arthur felt the relief wash through his body at the general's words. He approached the desk and handed his document folder over. 'My report, sir. And the plans and documents pertaining to the campaign.'

Baird took the folder and placed it on his desk. 'I'll read through that as soon as possible, and consult you again then. In the meantime, I have one question for you.'

'Sir?'

'I know that there have been some differences of opinion between us in the past, Wellesley, but I'm not foolish enough to bear a grudge. I'd be grateful if you would serve as my chief of staff. Well, will you do it?'

'Yes, sir,' Arthur replied. 'Of course. I'd be honoured.'

'Good!' Baird smiled genuinely. 'I'd hoped you'd agree. Now then, I'll read through your report and then we'll talk again.'

The chance did not arise, as the illness took its hold on Arthur. The blisters spread across his skin until his whole body was encrusted in white protrusions the size of peas. If he scratched at them, the blisters burst and spread their foul contents, and left him in even more discomfort. Arthur attempted to distract himself by reading as much as possible, and writing a long letter each day to Kitty. As Dr Scott had said, sleep became impossible since every point of his body that was in contact with the bedding felt as if it was on fire. After a few days Arthur finally consented to try the nitric baths and substituted one kind of agony for another as the treatment left his skin feeling almost unbearably sore and tender.

General Baird came to see him early in May. He stood a short distance from the bed and shook his head sadly as he gazed down at Arthur.

'The fleet is sailing tomorrow. I wish you were coming with us.'

'So do I, sir.'

'I can understand that. After all the work you have put into preparing this army, you deserve to be there when it goes into action. You've done a fine job, Wellesley. I have no doubt that your brother's confidence in your abilities is fully justified.'

'Thank you, sir.'

'There is a ship, the *Susannah*, which is waiting here to pick up the last consignment of powder. She leaves in ten days. If you have recovered by then, you can leave with her and catch us up. After that, the shift in the trade winds pattern will make it almost impossible to reach the Red Sea in time.'

'I understand, sir.'

'Once again, my thanks.' Baird smiled. 'I think you'll understand if I refrain from shaking your hand.'

Arthur laughed, then winced as the movement brought on a fresh wave of fiery irritation.

'I hope to see you in Egypt, then.'

Arthur nodded. 'Goodbye, sir.'

His recovery proceeded slowly, too slowly to re-join the expedition, and Arthur watched sadly from the window of the hospital as the *Susannah* slipped her moorings and headed out to sea.

Three days later a cargo ship arrived with the news that the crew had witnessed the *Susannah* founder in a storm, taking every soul aboard with her.

When Arthur heard this, he could not help wondering at the perversity of fate. To have given him a reputation-making command only to take it away, then make him too ill to join the expedition, and thereby miss a terrible death at sea. It was impossible to know if there was any divine design to his life. Rather, he seemed to be swung from fortune to misfortune with the regularity of a metronome. As his health slowly recovered Arthur's grievance against Richard for his decision to replace him continued to fester after an exchange of letters failed to resolve their differences. Richard refused to acknowledge that he had been pressured into withdrawing Arthur's command, and maintained that the reason for his decision was his need for Arthur's services in India.

Once he was well enough to travel, Arthur took a ship to Mangalore and then rode inland back to Seringapatam. He arrived early in May, as a thunderstorm lashed the city. Arthur's illness had turned his hair grey at the temples, and his skin was still acutely sensitive as a result of the painful treatment he had undergone to cure the Malabar Itch. Vingetty did his best to make his master comfortable as the humidity of the monsoon season continued to aggravate his condition. He resumed his duties as military governor and summoned Barry Close to a meeting as soon as he returned to his office.

'It's good to see you back, sir.' Close smiled warmly as he entered the office and shook Arthur's hand.

'I trust that Mysore has been running smoothly in my absence.'

Close cocked his head to one side. 'We have peace, trade and taxes, but there are still a few malcontents out there trying to stir up bad feeling against the Company.'

'Thus it ever was,' Arthur replied wearily. 'But nothing to concern us unduly, I take it?'

Close hesitated a moment before he replied. 'I'm not so sure, sir. I've had some disturbing reports from my agents in the Mahratta federation.'

'Well?'

'It seems that some of the warlords have hired themselves a number of French mercenaries to train scores of battalions of new recruits.'

'Which warlords exactly?'

'Scindia and Holkar. At the moment Holkar is remaining loyal to the Peshwa, but Scindia?' Close shook his head. 'I've no idea what the devil's up to.'

'But you have some suspicions,' Arthur prompted.

'Yes, sir. Yes I do.' Close stroked his chin. 'I believe he intends to rise up against the Peshwa, and impose a puppet ruler of his own. Scindia's men have also been raiding into Hyderabad. It's possible he plans to seize control of Hyderabad as well.'

Arthur quickly thought through the implications. 'If that happens, Scindia will pose a far greater threat to our interests than Tipoo ever did.'

'That's my fear, sir.' Close nodded. 'And we would have a war on our hands, the like of which has never been witnessed on Indian soil.'

Chapter 62

Napoleon

Paris, July 1800

'I gave them a great victory!' Napoleon slammed his fist down on the desk. 'What more do they want of me?'

The First Consul and his closest advisers had just returned to the Luxembourg Palace after the celebrations of the anniversary of the fall of the Bastile. There had been the usual parades by the National Guard units, a few speeches to remember those who gave their lives for the revolution, and then the entry into the arena of over a hundred of the veterans of Marengo. Lucien had planned the moment carefully. The men wore tattered uniforms, some were bandaged, and they carried the colours of the Austrian regiments that had surrendered in the rout that followed Desaix's heroic counter-attack. When the soldiers appeared the band struck up a specially composed piece of uplifting music, and the tens of thousands of Parisians who had gathered to watch the spectacle were supposed to burst into wild patriotic cheers. Instead they remained stonily silent and the final fanfare sounded flat and false as the notes faded. Napoleon had barely been able to contain his fury as the carriages made their way back to the palace, and finally gave vent to his rage as they entered the First Consul's private apartments. Lucien, Talleyrand and Fouché had sat still through the tirade and now waited a moment to be sure that the storm had run its course before daring to respond.

Lucien kept his voice calm as he answered. 'Victories are all very well, but the people want peace, brother.'

'Peace?' Napoleon pressed a hand over his heart. 'Don't they understand that I want peace too? There is no man in France who yearns for peace more than I do. But we can only have peace once our enemies are defeated. At the moment they will not accept anything less than the restoration of the Bourbons and the destruction of all that the revolution has achieved.'

Talleyrand coughed lightly and Napoleon rounded on him with a cynical smile. 'Are you ill, or is it that you have something to say?'

'Citizen Consul, I am merely concerned about the notion of having peace only when our enemies are defeated.'

'Really? I would have thought it was axiomatic.'

'There is another way. We must negotiate a peace.'

Napoleon sighed wearily. 'That's precisely what we are trying to do. Even with their armies defeated and an armistice agreed, the Austrians are delaying moves towards signing a peace treaty at every opportunity.'

'They will see reason, in time,' Talleyrand offered.

'If they don't see the gleam of English gold first, to lure them back into war.'

'Precisely,' Talleyrand countered. 'The problem is England. While we are at war with England there will be no prospect of peace for France. We must deal with England.'

'Oh, we'll deal with them all right.' Napoleon nodded. 'The moment we land a French army on their shores. We'll dictate peace terms from their houses of Parliament.'

'You misunderstand me, Citizen Consul. I meant that we must deal with them in the sense of making peace with England.'

'Oh.' Napoleon looked disappointed. 'But there can be no chance of peace while Pitt is Prime Minister. That man has made the destruction of our revolution his life's mission. He denies us peace, and is prepared to ruin his country to bribe other nations to oppose us.'

'True,' Talleyrand conceded. 'So we must wait until he is replaced, and, provided that we proceed shrewdly, that could happen rather sooner than you might suppose.'

Napoleon narrowed his eyes. 'Explain yourself.'

'England's strength relies on her trade. She needs customers for her goods, so we must attack her trade in order to hurt her enough to compel her to negotiate.'

'How?' Lucien asked. 'You know the state of our navy. Most of our fleet is laid up, the best officers fled during the revolution, and man for man, ship for ship, they are no match for the Royal Navy.' He glanced at Napoleon. 'That was made perfectly clear at Aboukir Bay.'

'Thank you for reminding me,' Napoleon replied coldly.

'Then we don't attack their sea trade,' Talleyrand continued. 'We cut them off from their customers instead. We make treaties and alliances with whatever nations we can, and at the same time we make sure that we use our diplomatic contacts to undermine England at every opportunity.'

'Easier said than done,' Fouché muttered.

Talleyrand turned to him with a faintly amused expression. 'You surprise me, citizen. I had thought you and your agents have had commendable success in your efforts to undermine and slander the opponents of the consulate. I merely wish to imitate your methods on the diplomatic stage.'

As Fouché frowned Napoleon struggled to hide a smile and nodded to the foreign minister. 'Go on.'

'We must move quickly, while the example of Marengo is fresh in the minds of the rulers of Europe. Spain is weak, and will bow to pressure to return to France the territories she seized in North America. She is also concerned about English rivalry in the Americas and the Pacific ocean. We might yet persuade King Carlos to join us in the war against England. Prussia has no desire to echo the Austrian defeats and, in any case, they are rivals for control over the German principalities. The Tsar of Russia is furious about England's claiming the right to search all ships at sea. My agents in St Petersburg say that Tsar Paul is even now trying to coax the Prussians into a joint war against England for that reason alone. Even America is losing patience with the Royal Navy's interference with their shipping. Of course, while England is allied with Austria, that means the Tsar will be obliged to fight Austria as well. So, as you can see, the international situation is replete with advantages for us to seize.' Talleyrand clasped his hands together. 'If we can make peace with Austria, and put our efforts into diplomacy, then we can isolate England. In time she will be forced to accept peace on our terms.'

'You make it sound easy,' Napoleon remarked.

'I did not say it would be easy, Citizen Consul. But it will work.'

Napoleon nodded thoughtfully. Talleyrand's advice made sense. And his scheme had the virtue of granting Napoleon time to reorganise and rebuild France's exhausted armies for when they were needed again – as he had no doubt they would be. Until England was utterly crushed, any peace treaty would be little more than a breathing space before the struggle continued. But France desperately needed a period of peace. The mood of the public earlier that day was eloquent proof of that, and Napoleon's mind turned from the wider sphere to the more immediate problems within France's borders.

'Very well, Talleyrand. Do all that you can to isolate England. That is the goal of our foreign policy from here on, and every other consideration is subordinate to that aim. Clear?'

'Yes, Citizen Consul.'

'Good. Then while our diplomats do their work abroad, we shall provide proof of our desire for peace here in France. We will make a new nation. We will consolidate the gains of the revolution so that our enemies see the futility of their desire to restore the Bourbons and all that they stand for. And we must convince our people that they have a stake in the future of France. All our people.'

'What do you mean by all?' asked Lucien.

'I mean that we cannot succeed unless we resolve those issues that divide the French people.'

Lucien stirred uncomfortably. 'There are good reasons why the people are divided, brother. Class, religion and politics are the very stuff of society. And there are those who are for the revolution and those who are against. It is our duty to see that the latter are suppressed and eventually eradicated.'

Napoleon sighed. 'Can't you see? That will never happen. As long as we drive people into the ranks of those who oppose us, France will never be at peace with itself. The process of revolution will never end. We will always see enemies about us, and be locked into one bloody purge after another.'

'Then what are you saying?' Lucien asked suspiciously.

Napoleon stared at him for a moment before replying. 'Perhaps it is time that the revolution came to an end. Perhaps it is time that we embraced those who opposed the revolution.'

'We once called them enemies of the people.'

'But they *are* the people,' Napoleon countered earnestly. 'They always were, even when the Committee of Public Safety was drawing a line between those who supported the revolution and those who opposed it. That was the Committee's mistake. There was hardly a peasant in the land who was not a revolutionary, until the Committee turned their sights on the church. The moment they began to attack the priests, they drove a wedge between their own supporters. It is the same with the nobility. Many of them were radicals, yet because of their birth they were branded enemies of the people.' Napoleon uttered the last phrase with contempt. 'It was the same in Corsica, Lucien. You remember how our people embraced the revolution? You recall those times at the Jacobin club in Ajaccio?'

'I remember.'

Napoleon smiled. 'Every one of us was a fervent radical . . . until the French government decided to suppress our Corsican identity. They lost Corsica because they did not embrace us as Corsicans. Such a little thing, and yet, people being people, there was a conflict where there never should have been one. That was the great mistake. That is what we must resolve.'

Lucien shrugged. 'How? There has been too much blood shed for people to even imagine resolving their differences.'

Napoleon knew that Lucien was right. But unless they tried to draw the French people back together their foreign enemies would not be able to resist exploiting the issues of religion and class that divided France. As long as there were émigrés who claimed to speak on behalf of the downtrodden church and nobility, then France would be at war with itself even as it was at war with other nations. That must end, Napoleon decided firmly, before France devoured itself and left England gloating over the ravaged carcass of its longtime enemy.

'So, then, what do you propose, Napoleon? An amnesty for the priests and aristos?'

Napoleon took a deep breath. 'I propose that we abolish the laws proscribing the nobles and allow them to return to France. Furthermore, we return their property to them.'

'Not the land already in the hands of the peasants, surely? If we did that there'd be another revolution. One we'd not survive.'

'Very well,' Napoleon conceded. 'We return as much property as we can. And one other thing. We must make a treaty with the Church of Rome.'

'What kind of treaty?'

'We have to restore the church in France.'

'Are you mad, brother? After all that the church has done to the common people over the centuries? After all the money it has taken from their purses? After all the food it has taken from their mouths? The radicals would not stand for it. In case you hadn't noticed, most of those radicals happen to be in the army. Are you prepared to put their loyalty to the test?'

'No. That is why any such treaty must be negotiated in secret. And the church must be subordinate to the state. The common people can have their religion, they can have their Catholic church, as long as it is controlled by us, and not by Rome.'

'Forgive me, First Consul,' Fouché said quietly, 'but your brother is right – my agents keep me briefed on the feeling amongst the soldiers. It is too dangerous to even attempt it.'

'It is too dangerous not to,' Napoleon replied. 'We need the common people behind us. We need to deny them any reason to offer their loyalty to our enemies. Besides, soldiers forget their politics the moment they march off to war.'

Talleyrand stirred. 'That sounds like an argument for making war.'

'Not this time.' Napoleon reflected for a moment. 'But war does serve a purpose as much within a society as without.'

'Until a society grows weary of it. As weary as France is now.'

'We'll know if that's true soon enough,' Napoleon concluded. 'In the meantime we must deal with Austria. If they play their game as they did before they will drag the negotiations out for as long as possible while they prepare to renew the fight. In which case there will be more war, whether our people like it or not. It is your job, Fouché, to silence those we cannot win round.'

'I will see to it,' Fouché replied evenly.

'Good.' Napoleon nodded. Fouché's slightly reptilian features unnerved him. Napoleon had no doubt that the Minister of the Interior would use any measure needed to suppress opposition to the new order. It was regrettable, thought Napoleon, but the need for repressive action had been forced on him by the enemies of France. Political freedom was a luxury at the best of times. Besides, what did the common peasant or soldier in the ranks really care about such refined notions as a free press? As long as they were fed and entertained then they were content. And, better still, they could be counted on to support Napoleon against the lawyers, philosophers and radicals who formed the core of those opposed to the consulate. In time, when there was true peace, there might be occasion to let people express themselves more freely.

Until then France must be saved from herself before she could be saved from her enemies.

Having signed the peace preliminaries the Austrians delayed moves towards a peace treaty when negotiations opened at Lunéville, just as Napoleon had expected. The Austrian envoys presented a long list of their terms, few of which Napoleon could agree to. Nevertheless it granted the French armies a chance to rest through the long summer months. Meanwhile, in Paris, Napoleon worked feverishly to reform the governance of the country.

A commission was set up to frame a new legal code that would sweep away all the regional anomalies and update the civil, criminal and financial laws of France. Napoleon attended as many meetings as he could, driving its business forward until the first draft was ready four months later. Plans were made to improve roads, ports and canals. Theatres were to be subsidised to help keep the people entertained and provision was made for the care of more than ten thousand wounded veterans who had returned from the wars. Joseph led a small party of church figures to Rome to open negotiations with the Pope for the restoration of the Catholic church in France. Before Joseph left Paris, Napoleon made it clear to him that the final concordat would not include any provision for priests to collect tithes, nor would any property of the church be returned, and the appointment of bishops would have to be approved by the French government.

All this frantic activity consumed much of Napoleon's time. He rose before dawn and was dressed and had breakfasted by six in the morning. Then he went to his private office, read the pile of documents prepared for him by Bourrienne and scribbled notes in the margins, and dictated his responses to the team of secretaries standing by, pens poised. At noon he had a brief lunch and moved on to attend some of the committees he had instituted to rebuild the nation along more modern, efficient lines. Then there would be a late dinner, after which, if there was no pressing business that still needed attending to, Napoleon joined Josephine and a small inner circle of his family and friends for entertainment. Sometimes it was cards, Napoleon favouring pontoon or whist, at which he invariably cheated.

'Why do you do that?' Josephine asked him irritably, one evening in early autumn, as they said good night to their guests and retired to their sleeping quarters.

'Do what, my love?'

'Cheat at cards. You do it every time we play.'

'Do I?'

She dug her elbow into his side. 'You know you do. Why?'

He shrugged. 'It means that I win every time.'

Josephine paused to look at him as they entered her bedchamber. She placed her palm against his cheek and gently caressed it. 'Is it so important to you to win at everything? To be the best all the time?'

'What else is there? Why should a man aim any lower than the best in his ambitions?' He eased her gently inside and closed the door behind them. Then he slipped his arms round her waist and pulled her towards him. The scent of her perfume filled his head as he kissed the curve of her neck, marvelling at its silken texture. He whispered, 'I want to be the best lover that you have ever had . . .'

'You are,' she purred, tilting her head aside as she enjoyed the sensation of his lips grazing her flesh there. 'You are the best.'

Napoleon wanted to believe it, more than anything he had ever believed in his life. Yet the knowledge of her infidelities twisted in his mind like a blade and his body trembled with rage.

'What is it?'

'Nothing. Take your clothes off.'

She pulled away and looked at him. There was a wild glint in his eye that she took for passion and she murmured, 'Yes, my love.'

He stood and watched as she hurriedly removed her dress, her bodice, her stockings and finally undid the lace straps of her underwear. Then she stood before him, naked, and trembling in the cold air even though a servant had lit the fire in the corner of the room. He took one of her small breasts in his hand and rolled his thumb over her dark brown nipple, all the time staring into her eyes. Then he let his hand slide down her ribs, over her stomach and in between her legs. Josephine shut her eyes and bit gently on her lip.

He suddenly withdrew his hand and wrenched at the buttons of his jacket. Josephine took the opportunity to draw away from him and jump into the bed, sliding down under the thick coverings and curling into a ball. It took him a fraction of the time it had taken her to undress and then he clambered in beside her. There was no preamble. He mounted her, thrust himself inside and worked to a swift, vigorous climax and then collapsed on to her with a groan.

'That was quick,' she muttered with a trace of disappointment evident in her tone.

'I'm a busy man,' he replied huskily as his heart pounded.

'Too busy to pleasure me it seems.'

Napoleon rolled off her and lay on his back. They had had

this discussion several times before in recent months, and he knew the steps by heart. She would accuse him of sparing her no thought, of no longer being the partner of her soul. He would promise that he would give her all of his attention the moment he could afford the time. He genuinely meant it. He loved her more than ever, but thanks to his public duties there was very little time to share that love with her. But the argument would go round and round until she had obtained a promise to join her at the theatre, or the opera, or spend an evening at one of the salons of Paris. The latter were tiresome affairs where men and women either toadied to him or went out of their way to try to impress upon him their greater intelligence or better breeding. And all the time he would be thinking about the pressing difficulties facing France.

It was becoming clear that the Austrians had no intention of signing a peace treaty and Napoleon had ordered Moreau to mass his forces on the Rhine. If there was no treaty by December Napoleon had resolved to renew the war. Then there was a fresh outbreak of rebellion in the Vendée, led by the royalist Georges Cadoudal. Fouché had given orders that Cadoudal and his followers were to be hanged on the spot if they were captured. Yet they were still at large and plotting to spread their rebellion, and there were even rumours of an attempt to be made on Napoleon's life.

He pressed his head back into his bolster and yawned.

'I bore you then?'

He swore under his breath and leaned over her. 'You are the centre of my world, Josephine, but there are demands made of me from every direction of the compass. What can I do? France depends on me, and I cannot ignore her, even for you. Surely you can see that?'

'I can see where your priorities lie well enough.' She turned on her side, away from him, and Napoleon was left looking at the shallow arch of her spine for a moment before he kissed the nape of her neck.

'As soon as I can, I will spend an evening with you.'

'When?'

He thought quickly. There was a new production of Haydn's oratorio *The Creation* opening in December. He would take her to that, and make a lavish evening of it. There would be a dinner at the Luxembourg, and then the guests would proceed to the Opéra in a convoy of coaches. Napoleon made a mental note of the details and resolved to have Lucien make arrangements for the event first thing in the morning.

Towards the end of November, Napleon's patience with Austria finally gave out and he gave the order to General Moreau to march towards Vienna. He was eating dinner with Josephine one evening early in December when they were interrupted by Berthier. Napoleon noticed his chief of staff's excited smile at once.

'What is it, Berthier?'

'A great victory, sir. The Austrian army blundered into Moreau's forces at Hohenlinden and was cut to pieces. They lost over eighteen thousand men.'

'What is Moreau doing now?'

'He's sent two of his generals, Ney and Grouchy, to pursue the Austrians.'

Napoleon recalled the names from the personnel records in the Ministry of War. Both were aggressive commanders who were far more likely to keep the pressure on the enemy than Moreau. He nodded with satisfaction, before turning his gaze back to Berthier. 'I want a full report on the battle as soon as possible. Make sure that Lucien gets a copy, and that he gets an announcement into the papers for tomorrow. If all goes well, the war will be over before Christmas. That will give the people more than enough cause to celebrate.'

'Yes, sir. Will that be all?'

'No.' Napoleon's eyes glittered as a new thought struck him. 'Tell Moreau that if he can force an armistice on the Austrians, it is to be signed on Christmas Day. That will be a fine story for the newspapers. And the day before, we shall attend the Opéra.' He grinned at Josephine. 'That will give the people of Paris a Christmas to remember for years to come.'

★

The carriages set off from the courtyard of the Luxembourg Palace shortly after six in the evening. The First Consul's carriage led the procession. Those that followed carried friends, including Josephine's son and daughter, Eugène and Hortense. A cold night had closed in over the capital and a mantle of freezing fog lay across the tiled roofs. Even so, the streets were crowded along the route to the opera house. Details of the procession had been published several days before and the people had turned out in their thousands to catch sight of the First Consul and his wife. Many had already been drinking and the streets echoed to the sound of singing and cheers. Torches had been lit along the route and cast a rosy glow in the fog that added to the gaiety of the scene. A squadron of dragoons rode ahead of the carriages, the breastplates of the riders gleaming, and the horses' coats shining as they snorted plumes of breath into the night air.

Napoleon was wearing the scarlet coat of the First Consul, heavily patterned with gold braid. He smiled as he waved to the crowds. He felt happier than he had in many years. Earlier in the day he had received news that the Austrians had asked for an armistice, and guaranteed to sign peace preliminaries as soon as possible. They could hardly do otherwise with Moreau's army poised to take Vienna. At long last, peace in Europe was in his grasp. And then England would be on her own. Napoleon's celebratory mood, and that of the people of Paris, were as one. He reached a hand across to Josephine and entwined his gloved fingers about hers. She turned to him, and even though she wore a thick fur coat he felt her hand tremble.

'Cold?'

'No.' She smiled. 'Excited. And proud. So very proud of you.'

The carriage suddenly lurched as it turned into the Rue Saint-Nicaise, pressing them together, and they laughed in surprise, and Napoleon darted his head towards Josephine and kissed her lightly on the lips.

'I love you,' he said softly. 'This night more than ever.'

'And I love you.' She kissed him back and squeezed his hand.

'I just wish Eugène and Hortense could have shared the carriage with us.'

'I'm sure they are happy enough where they are. Besides, if they were with us, I rather fear that everyone's gaze would be drawn to them. They certainly have their mother's fine looks.'

Josephine shook her head, but smiled all the same at the compliment. Then her eyes lit up as she glanced at something over Napoleon's shoulder. 'Oh! Look there!'

He turned and saw that two small children had climbed on top of a large barrel resting on a wagon, parked at the side of the street. Between them they held up a tricolour flag with his name embroidered on it. Napoleon waved at them and they shouted with delight and waved back frantically. Just before they passed out of sight he glimpsed a glittering spark below them in the wagon. Then the carriage jolted as it passed by and the children and the wagon were gone.

Josephine chuckled. 'It seems your public loves you.' Then she noticed the faint frown in his brow. 'What? What is it?'

Napoleon shook his head. 'I'm not sure.'

He leaned out of the window and stared back towards the wagon at an angle. The children were still waving. He shrugged and settled back against the seat cushion. Josephine was still staring at him and he forced himself to laugh. 'It's nothing. Really.'

Outside in the street the world dissolved into a brilliant flash of white, then orange, and an instant later there was a deafening roar, and the carriage was slammed forward as if a giant fist had struck the rear. Napoleon and Josephine were hurled against the seats opposite, amid a shower of broken glass. For a moment Napoleon could hear nothing, and his head felt as if it was stuffed with wool. The light from the torches outside had gone and thick black smoke smothered the street. He shook off the glass and groped towards Josephine, his heart beating in panic and dread. He felt her body, and as she stirred a wave of relief swept through him. His ears filled with a dull roaring sound that slowly resolved into specific noises: the shrill whinny of an injured horse; screams and moans and the shouts of people frantically calling out for their friends and family.

'Napoleon?' Josephine's voice sounded slightly muffled as she pulled herself up on to a seat and held his face in her hands. He saw that her cheek was bleeding from a cut. She spoke again, and he heard her more clearly this time as his hearing recovered. 'Are you all right?'

'I'm fine . . . I think.' Napoleon glanced over his body and flexed his limbs. There was no pain and no blood. Then he turned to the shattered window on his side of the carriage. 'An explosion. A bomb.'

At once he recalled the convoy of carriages behind them and pushed down the handle of the door. It swung open and Napoleon scrambled down into the street and stared back along the convoy. The cart and barrel on which the two children had stood to greet Napoleon had vanished. The street was filled with the bodies of people and horses and the shattered remains of carriages. Every window as far as Napoleon could see had been shattered and the buildings immediately around the point of the explosion had collapsed. An officer from the Consular Guard ran up and took his arm.

'Sir! Get back in the carriage. We have to get you out of here!'

'Leave me alone.' Napoleon gestured towards the blackened figures stirring amid the carnage. 'Help those people!'

The officer stared at him briefly and then nodded, turning to his men. 'Follow me!'

'My God . . .' Josephine mumbled.

Napoleon looked round and saw that she had followed him down from the carriage. She stared past him, and then thrust her gloved hand to her mouth as her eyes widened in terror. 'My children! My children . . . My Eugène. Hortense. Where are they?'

She brushed past him and ran back towards what was left of the following coaches and Napoleon went after her, his heart heavy with dread. Only a miracle could have spared those caught in the full blast of the explosion.

Chapter 63

Napoleon followed Josephine as she went from the remains of one carriage to the next, picking her way over rubble, fragments of wood, shattered limbs, and the carcasses of horses. Some of the bystanders and men of the Consular Guard had found some torches from further up the street and moved over the scene in their search for the survivors.

'Mother!' a voice cried out and Josephine snapped towards it.

'Eugène! Is that you?'

A shape waved to them in the gloom. 'Yes, over here.'

Napoleon and Josephine clambered across a pile of rubble from one of the collapsed buildings and found that the carriages towards the rear of the convoy were still intact. The horses and driver of Eugène's carriage had all been killed by flying masonry and splinters from the carriage ahead of them. The door hung on one bent hinge and Eugène beckoned to them desperately. 'In here. Quickly.'

When they reached the carriage Napoleon and Josephine looked inside and saw Eugène cradling his sister in his arms. There was a livid streak of blood down the silk material of her dress and she looked up with a dazed expression at her mother and stepfather.

'Oh, God.' Josephine's voice caught in a choke before she continued, 'She's hurt. Out of my way!' She hauled herself into the carriage and pushed Eugène to one side as her hands traced the flow of blood up to the torn flesh of the girl's wrist. A jet of blood arced into the carriage and splashed on Josephine's cheek.

'Get some pressure on the wound!' Napoleon snapped as he squeezed in beside his wife. 'Eugène. Find a doctor. At once.'

'Where?'

'Just do it!'

Eugène stumbled away and Napoleon hurriedly unwound the fine scarf from round his neck and began to tie it round the injury, as tightly as he could. Hortense gasped at the pain and Josephine glanced furiously at her husband.

'I have to stop the flow of blood,' he explained gently. 'It's her only chance.'

But even as he spoke the blood continued to well up through the material.

'Mama, I'm cold.' Hortense's eyes fluttered. 'So cold.'

Her body began trembling violently and Josephine grasped her chin. 'Oh, God, please, no. Not Hortense. Please God.' She shook her daughter. 'Hortense . . .'

The girl moaned faintly in her throat and her whole body was shaking.

Josephine glanced up. 'She needs help.'

'Eugène is finding someone.'

'Mother . . .' Hortense's voice was little more than a murmur. 'I'm cold. Hold me.'

Josephine drew her daughter in close to her, nuzzling her soft hair as she stroked Hortense's cheek. 'My baby . . . My baby.' The first tears glistened in Josephine's eyes, and rolled down her cheeks, smearing her make-up. Napoleon tied off the dressing and held the girl's cold hand. Josephine was rocking her daughter gently in her arms, as if the girl was an infant. She continued to whisper endearments and comforting noises until Eugène returned.

'I've cleared a path for your carriage, and sent word for a doctor to go to the palace at once.'

'Good boy.' Napoleon patted his stepson on the arm. 'Now we must get your mother and sister away from here.' Napoleon eased Josephine away from her daughter, who had passed out. Slipping his hands under the girl's shoulders, Napoleon turned to Eugène. 'Here. Give me a hand.'

★

The study was lit by the fire alone, and Napoleon sat in a chair staring into the flames as the wood hissed and crackled. He was still smeared with smoke and black smudges, and his formal coat was unbuttoned and hung open. He held a large glass of brandy in his hands. As he gazed into the wavering orange glare at the heart of the fire he saw the explosion, and its terrible aftermath, playing out in his mind, almost as if it was happening again.

After he had helped carry Hortense back to his carriage and settled Josephine in beside her with her son, Napoleon ordered his driver to return to the Luxembourg Palace at once. Then he turned back to the scene of the attack and helped the men of the Consular Guard to pick through the wreckage looking for any more survivors. It was as bad as any battlefield Napoleon had ever seen; so many of the casualties were women and children. Those closest to the explosion had been blasted to pieces. Fouché had rushed to the site, anxiously searching for his master, and his expression was a picture of relief as he seized Napoleon by the arm.

'Thank God! There are already rumours that you had been killed.'

Napoleon glanced round the devastated street. 'I was lucky.'

'No.' Fouché shook his head. 'France was lucky. We have to move fast, to quash the rumours. The people have to know that you are unharmed, before anyone tries to take advantage of the situation. Come, sir.' He gently pulled Napoleon towards the end of the street.

'Where are we going?' Napoleon muttered.

'To the Opéra.'

Napoleon stopped dead, and pulled himself free of Fouché's grasp. 'The Opéra? After what's happened? Are you mad?'

'We have to show your face in public, sir,' Fouché insisted. 'The Opéra is as good a place as any. And it's nearby. Come on, sir. There's no time to waste.'

They collected some of the Consular Guards as they went and by the time they reached the steps leading up to the main entrance an anxious crowd had spilled out from their seats to try to find out more details of the explosion. The Guards cleared a path through the crowd and Napoleon mounted the steps and turned at the top. At once there was a sound, as if the whole crowd shared a sigh of relief, and then excited muttering broke out before a lone voice cried. '*Vive Napoleon!*'

The cry was quickly taken up and echoed off the tall façade of the Opéra. Napoleon raised his hand and waved to the crowd in response to their open affection and relief that he had been unharmed. The cheering continued, minute after minute, until Fouché touched his shoulder and spoke loudly into his ear. 'I have commandeered a carriage for you, just round the corner. You'll be taken back to the palace and your wife.'

Napoleon nodded mutely, then lowered his arm and followed Fouché down the steps and along the front of the Opéra to the corner. The carriage was just past the turning and guarded by several of Fouché's mounted policemen.

'You can trust them,' Fouché said, noticing Napoleon's expression. 'You'll be safe with my men.'

He helped Napoleon up into the cab. 'I'll join you once I have given the orders to begin a hunt for the people behind the attack.'

Napoleon nodded and shut the door. At once the carriage lurched into motion and rattled over the cobbled street as the mounted policemen cleared a path through the crowd, warily looking about them for any sign of further danger to the First Consul.

At his private apartments, Napoleon went immediately to find his wife. She was in her private sitting room, with her son, her physician and some of her closest friends. Her face was streaked with tears as she watched the doctor tend to Hortense's wound. Napoleon stared at them for a moment, before the doctor noticed him and called out softly, 'She will be fine, sir. She's lost a lot of blood, but she is a strong girl.'

Napoleon nodded his gratitude and then quietly slipped away to his study. He felt guilty. The bomb was meant for him, not Josephine's daughter, and she would not have been injured if he had not become the First Consul, or if he had not decided to arrange the trip to the Opéra. Reaching his study, he ordered a servant to light the fire, and then he poured himself a drink and sat down to wait for Fouché.

Shortly after midnight, the door to the study clicked open and Napoleon glanced up as the Minister of the Interior entered the room. He nodded towards a chair on the other side of the fire and Fouché sat down.

Napoleon cleared his throat. 'What was the butcher's bill?'

'Over fifty casualties so far, half of them dead.' Fouché paused a moment before he changed the subject. 'But you're alive and unhurt, and that's the main thing. I've primed the newpaper editors with the story I want to run tomorrow. I've told them it's the work of royalist and Jacobin agents.'

Napoleon sniffed faintly. 'An unlikely combination.'

'Maybe, but this outrage may provide the excuse we need to crack down on both parties. I've given orders to start rounding up all those we suspect of being their ringleaders. Someone will know something about the plot. It's just a matter of asking the questions in the appropriate manner.'

'You're talking about torture.'

'Torture? Not the word to use, I think. We'll call it something like coercive interrogation, to help keep the newspapers on our side. We might possibly discover who was behind the plot, but we are sure to uncover a great many pieces of useful information while we are at it.' His eyes glinted at the prospect, before he assumed a more sombre expression and leaned forward towards the First Consul. 'I heard the news about your stepdaughter a short while ago. I am told she will recover. That must be a comfort to know.'

'I don't want comforting words,' Napoleon replied quietly. 'I want you to find the men behind this. I don't care what it takes. I don't care how many people get hurt to produce information about the bastards who tried to kill me. Find them, Fouché. Find them and bring them to justice. They will pay for this with their heads.'

*

The Minister of the Interior's network of agents and informers scoured the streets, cafés and salons of the capital and within weeks they had uncovered the identities of the two men who had improvised the explosive device. They were quickly arrested and taken before Fouché and his interrogators, who knew every refinement of the art of extracting information. Fouché reported to Napoleon that the men were working for Cadoudal, and had no connection with the Jacobins. Nevertheless, that fact would be suppressed in order to justify the arrest and exile of hundreds of political opponents that had taken place in the weeks immediately after the explosion. The two men had broken down under the relentless pressure of Fouché's interrogators and had implicated a number of leading royalists in the plot, including many émigrés. Once they had given up all they knew, the men were summarily tried, sentenced to death and shot before dawn in the courtyard of Fouché's ministry.

It came as no surprise to Napoleon to learn that the attack had been planned in England, and paid for with English gold. His heart hardened towards the most resolute and ruthless enemy of the revolution. That the English government had resorted to such underhand terrorist methods was a clear sign to Napoleon of the lengths they were prepared to go to defeat France.

There was little time to nurse his grievance, however. Once again the Austrians were using delaying tactics at the Lunéville negotiations and, when the peace preliminaries had still not been signed by the end of January, Napoleon sent a curt warning that unless they were signed at once the French armies would resume their march on Vienna. The Austrians hurriedly recanted, agreed to French terms and signed the Treaty of Lunéville early in February. A month later a treaty was signed with the King of Naples which closed the ports of his kingdom to English ships. William Pitt's coalition had failed and in March he was forced from office. England had at last run out of allies. Napoleon drew cold comfort from the fall of his adversary. France dominated Europe and could afford to wait until the English were humbled enough to beg for peace. Meanwhile, he continued to work every hour that he could to change France for ever, so that there could never be a return to the gross inequalities of the years before the revolution.

Corruption by government officials was exposed and punished. Ministers were constantly called to account for their failures and set new tasks. A system of grain silos was established to safeguard the people against failed harvests, and the newly established Bank of France became the sole source of paper currency, replacing the hated and almost worthless assignats. Mindful of the need to appeal to the patriotic spirit of the people Napoleon made plans for laying down new streets and avenues in the capital – to be named after the recent victories of the army, and the victories yet to come. At the same time, the plans had the additional benefit of creating thoroughfares wide enough to be easily commanded by a handful of cannon in the event of any uprising.

The constant stream of new initiatives that poured from the office of the First Consul steadily eclipsed the role of the other branches of the legislature set up by the new constitution, and while the senate broadly approved of Napoleon's actions the assembly of tribunes resented his abrogation of power. Napoleon knew that the time would soon come when he would be forced to remould the constitution in his favour. Before then he would need to do everything in his power to win the support of the people. The thing they desired above all was peace, and with that achieved on the continent at least, France began to enjoy the benefits of order and prosperity as spring blossomed across the land.

It was then that the situation began to change.

'The Tsar assassinated?' Napoleon rose from his chair. 'When?'

'Three weeks ago, at the end of March,' Talleyrand replied. 'Tsar Paul was killed by a group of his generals and senior members of his own household. Including his son, Alexander, who is now the new ruler.'

Napoleon gave a wry chuckle. 'I doubt there has ever been a more dangerous family to be born into.' His expression became more serious. 'What do we know of this Alexander? What are his intentions towards us?'

'Our ambassador says that Alexander is keen to mend relations with England. It's bad timing. Just when I thought we might make an alliance with Russia.'

Napoleon was silent for a moment as he walked over to his window and stared down into the gardens of the palace. 'Damn those Russians. They will ruin everything for us one day.'

The news added greatly to his concerns over the report that an English army had landed in Egypt. The last hope of any French intervention in India had been crushed by the Governor General and his brother, a more than capable soldier who had done much to turn the military situation to England's advantage. Then there was the matter of an uprising in the colony of San Domingo, and Spain was unwilling to return Louisiana to France. As long as the enemy controlled the seas, France would be denied ready access to her colonies. The time had come to cut cards with the devil, Napoleon concluded reluctantly. He turned towards his foreign minister.

'We must have peace with England, as soon as possible. We need time to settle our overseas affairs. Time to build our navy up to strength.'

'To what purpose?' Talleyrand asked quietly.

'So that when the conflict begins again – which it will – we can clear the Channel of enemy warships and land an army in England.'

'I see.' Talleyrand shrugged. 'So it is not a lasting peace we shall be seeking, then?'

'There can be no lasting peace with England. Either France prevails or England does. The world is too small for us to share.'

'What are your instructions, First Consul?'

'Send an envoy to Prime Minister Addington. Tell him France wants peace. I imagine that the English will be in no mood to turn down such an offer. They have been at war as long as we have.'

Napoleon had gauged the English mind well. The new Prime Minister agreed to begin talks, and as summer wore on the tentative negotiations gradually resolved into the drafting of a preliminary agreement. Napoleon was eager to sign the document, but the English managed to find one excuse after another to delay. By the end of the summer Napoleon had had enough. Just as he had done with Austria, he issued an ultimatum. The agreement was to be signed by October, or France would break off negotiations and renew the war. The English gave in. The document was signed and hostilities ended. In the weeks that followed, the representatives of France and England met at Amiens to settle the final details of the peace treaty.

Finally, at the end of March 1802, when the First Consul and his wife had retired to the château at St-Cloud for a brief rest from his duties, Talleyrand arrived one evening. He was shown into the orangery where Napoleon and Josephine were having tea and cakes beside a small stove. Talleyrand bowed graciously to Josephine before he gave his news to Napoleon.

'The treaty has been signed.' He smiled warmly. 'The English put their seal on it a few days ago.'

'No last-minute alterations to the terms?' Napoleon asked in an equally good humour.

'We have what we asked for. England is to return the colonies they seized from us, as well as those taken from Spain and Holland. The only territories they get to keep will be Trinidad and Ceylon. They've also agreed to hand Malta back to the Knights of St John, and Egypt is to be returned to Turkey. In return we are to pull our troops out of Naples and the papal territories.'

Napoleon clapped his hands together and rubbed them happily. 'Wonderful! If only I could see Mr Pitt's expression now! It could not have been better.'

'No, the timing is perfect. Next month we'll have the Concordat with Rome in our hands. There will not be a man in France who won't be rejoicing.'

'I can imagine there will be one or two who might not. But this news will bury any arguments about the legitimacy of the new constitution. I have provided order, economic revival and international respect. Who dares to question me now?'

For a moment the foreign minister's expression registered

surprise, then the mask slipped smoothly back into place. 'You are right, of course, Citizen Consul. The nation owes you far more than it can ever repay. But, surely, for the sake of appearances, it is best that the success be seen to be due to the efforts of the consuls, senators, tribunes and deputies collectively?'

'Why?' Napoleon responded bluntly. 'Only a fool would not be able to detect my guiding hand behind all of this. The improvements to France's fortunes are largely due to my efforts, Talleyrand. I see no harm in letting the people know it.'

'The harm is that some people – disposed to jealousy and mendacity as they are – will start rumours that it is a sign of your dictatorial ambitions.'

'Then let them.' Napoleon dismissed the idea with a curt wave of his hand. 'The people know that I am no dictator. I do not seek power for myself. I seek only to express the general will of the French people. They understand that.'

Talleyrand's eyelids flickered. 'Let us hope so, Citizen Consul. Now, if you will forgive me, I must return to my ministry to ensure that news of the treaty is dispatched to our embassies. I came here because I just wanted to tell you the news in person. Madame Bonaparte.' He bowed to Josephine again.

Napoleon nodded. 'My thanks, Talleyrand. For all that you have done.'

'As you say, citizen, it is we who must thank you, for all that you have achieved.'

He bowed his head, turned, and left the orangery, closing the door gently behind him before he crunched away along the gravel path to the stables.

Josephine stared after him for a moment and then poured herself and her husband another cup of tea. 'That man sees through you, Napoleon. You must be careful of him.'

'Careful?' Napoleon seemed vaguely insulted by the idea. 'Don't worry about him. I know exactly what he is. Every inch an aristocrat, but at least he has his country's interests at heart. I can trust him that far at least.'

Josephine pursed her lips. 'Perhaps . . .' She sipped her tea and then continued. 'This peace. Do you think it will last?'

'No,' Napoleon replied bluntly. 'The English have given up more than they would like, and it has not resolved the issues which caused the war in the first place. In truth this treaty is doomed. But at least there will be a short peace for all Europe to celebrate. That, at least, is a good thing.'

Josephine looked at him steadily. 'Does that mean that you will have more time to spend with me? It seems, since the attempt on your life, that you have been working harder than ever. It feels as if . . . as if you have been avoiding me for some reason.'

Napoleon stared at her. He saw the hurt look in her eyes and suddenly realised how much he had been taking her for granted. Yet he did not want to assume the mantle of blame. 'It is not my fault, Josephine. France needs me. I must devote myself to the nation. It is my duty. There is so much to do. So much still to be done.'

She raised a hand to stop him. 'I know. I know all of that. It's true. But I am your wife, Napoleon. Is there no obligation to me? What about your duty to me? When Hortense was injured you know whom I had to turn to for comfort? My son. Because my husband was too busy.'

The words were spoken in a cold, harsh tone that wounded him.

Josephine continued. 'You are too busy because you choose to be. There is not one branch of government that you do not oversee and interfere with. I overheard a comment made by one of your officials the other day. As you were dictating a letter, he leaned to one of his companions and muttered "God created Bonaparte, and then He rested." I wouldn't be flattered by that, if I were you. I got the distinct impression that he was ridiculing your ambitions.'

'Who said that?'

'I will not tell you,' she replied firmly. There was a tense silence between them for a moment before Josephine continued in a more concerned tone, 'I don't think it is healthy for one man to work so hard. Not for you and not for France.'

'Why?'

'If you shoulder every responsibility that you can, then what happens to France if you are taken from us? You cannot guarantee immunity from sickness, or from a bomb for that matter. The country would be thrown into anarchy if you were lost.'

Napoleon nodded. 'I had thought of that.'

Josephine leaned forward and took his hand. 'Then you must find some men to share the burden with you. Men you can trust.'

'No. Power shared is power weakened. The only guarantee of a stable future for France is for me to remain in control of the government, and the army.' He stared at his wife, wondering how far he should trust her with his thoughts. Then her barbed comments about his failings as a husband cut into his heart again. He owed her his trust at the very least. Napoleon pressed her hand between his and lowered his voice. 'I've already made up my mind. France needs me to remain her master. I must become First Consul for life, and I must have the power to choose a successor. Only that will guarantee a better future for our people.'

Josephine shook her head. 'You are mad. All this power has turned your head. Do you think for a moment that all those politicians in the assemblies will agree to that?'

'No, I don't,' Napoleon conceded, and then smiled faintly. 'And that is why I have no intention of asking for their agreement.'

Chapter 64

The cardinal from Rome began his delivery in Latin and the words, read in a monotone, echoed round the interior of Notre-Dame. Most of the guests had little understanding of the language and looked on with feigned expressions of interest and respect as the Holy Father's message was delivered. The consuls were sitting to one side of the pulpit, while the rest of the audience sat in neat ranks facing the cardinal, dressed in their finery. Napoleon had already been shown a translation and was reassured that there were no unpleasant surprises in the Pope's greeting to the Catholics of France and his expression of great happiness over the reconciliation of the French people and the Church. In truth, Napoleon thought it a rather dull document with little of the fiery passion of the great speeches of the leaders of the revolution. Still, if it gave the peasants what they wanted and helped to draw the people of France closer together, the Concordat would prove to be very useful. For a moment he marvelled at the power that religion wielded over the minds of men when science and philosophy offered so much more insight into the workings of the world and the people who populated it. Religion was little more than the codification of sundry superstitions and prejudices, he decided. It was not amenable to reason, much like the spirit that animated those who persisted in their loyalty to the Bourbon monarchy. In due course, compulsory education of the masses would put paid to religion – Napoleon already had the outline of a national system of schools sketched out in his mind. For now, religion served his purpose and he would embrace it until such time as it could be consigned to the midden heap of history.

The cardinal droned on, and Napoleon's gaze wandered round the interior of the cathedral, over the ranks of the military officers and politicians in the front rows of the seats facing the pulpit. He was well aware of the anger and resentment this treaty with the Pope had engendered in their ranks. It had been a closely calculated risk to appeal over their heads to the people of France, but it was more important to divide the royalists from the church than worry about the ideological concerns of the intellectuals and radicals of Paris society. Besides, he would need all the popular support he could muster in the months to come.

Napoleon frowned, and lowered his head as if bowing it in thoughtful reflection on the Pope's message. In reality he sought only to hide his face from the other members of the audience since he feared that some amongst them might read his mind from his troubled expression. He was burdened with anxiety over the reaction of the tribunes' assembly towards the peace he had brought to France. Talleyrand, Fouché, Lucien and their followers had been busy preparing the ground for a vote to make Napoleon First Consul for life. Instead the tribunes had offered to renew Napoleon's current office for another ten years.

Was this his reward for bringing the first peace that France had known since the revolution? He fumed and clenched his fist, then thrust it inside his jacket to keep it out of sight. Did the fools really think he would quietly accept this sop when so much work still had to be done to drag France back to the summit of European power? Did they really think that there was anyone else who could have achieved as much as Napoleon had in the short time since he had risen to power? France needed him. More than she needed the ingrates of the tribunes' assembly. When the time came for the people of France to make their feelings clear Napoleon would make sure that the spiteful and petty spirits who stood between him and the glorious realisation of France's ambitions would be swept away with all the other dead weight that was holding the nation back.

He took a deep breath and looked up again. The cardinal had

reached the end of the Pope's message and was descending from the pulpit. He made his way, at a solemn pace, towards the altar and prepared to offer the sacrament to the consuls. Napoleon had been expecting this moment; the Catholic Church would hardly pass up the opportunity to use the ceremony to establish its preeminence over even those who ruled France. As the cardinal turned round, wafer in one hand and goblet in the other, Napoleon rose to his feet, bowed curtly and marched boldly down the aisle between the ranks of France's most powerful men. He kept his chin up, and his gaze fixed on the arched exit from the cathedral. Even so, he was aware of the looks of astonishment, and amused admiration, from those on the periphery of his vision.

'Was that wise?' Talleyrand asked, as they stood on the balcony of the Luxembourg Palace a short time later, acknowledging the cheers of the vast crowd that had gathered to celebrate the Concordat. The First Consul and his foreign minister were basking in the adulation of the people.

'It was necessary. It was important to show the Pope, as well as our people, that the state owes no allegiance to the Church.'

'Yes, well, I imagine that's exactly how His Holiness will see things the moment he receives a report from the cardinal. I just hope it doesn't sour the Concordat so soon after it has been signed.'

'It won't,' Napoleon replied confidently. 'The Church needs the agreement as much as we do.' He glanced at the foreign minister. 'The real difficulty that faces us is keeping the peace with England. It is vital that you win us as much time as possible before war breaks out again.'

'I will do what I can,' Talleyrand responded evenly.

'No.' Napoleon shook his head. 'You will do what I say. The fate of us all depends upon it.' He turned back to the crowds and gave them a final wave before turning away and striding back through the tall glazed doors into his office, followed by Talleyrand. Fouché was sitting to one side of the desk waiting for them. Napoleon had thought it wise not to share the public acclaim with Fouché, who had become a sinister figure already, and was likely to become hated and feared in the months to come. Napoleon took his seat behind the desk and Talleyrand found a chair as far from Fouché as was politely possible.

'Half of Paris must be out there.' Fouché smiled. 'It seems that the people have come to love you, First Consul.'

'Love?' Napoleon shrugged. 'Perhaps that is what they feel for me. Now. But the mob is a fickle beast. We all saw that during the revolution. So I care little about their love. What concerns me is not providing the people with any reason to oppose the new order. That is our mission, gentlemen. As long as we succeed in that we can do as we will to remake France, and carry her influence into other lands.' He paused to let his words sink in. 'They have the peace they wanted. They have law and order. We must extend the benefits of the consulate even further. I want every man in France to have the chance to rise through his own merits rather than because he is the son of an aristocrat. I want us to provide the people of France with the means to gain an education and an opportunity for advancement. We will have a national system of education. We will also have a national system of public reward to celebrate achievement.' His mind raced ahead. 'A decoration for achievement in all fields, civilian as well as military. We'll create a body of men who will be honoured by the nation, a legion of honour if you will.'

'Legion of honour?' Talleyrand pursed his lips. 'A laudable notion, though I am not sure that our military recipients will be pleased to rub shoulders with scientists, artists and the like.'

'Maybe, but they will have to get used to it. What matters is that we tie everyone into the new regime.'

'And what of those people who would rather not be part of it?'

'That is where our friend Fouché plays his part.'

Fouché bowed his head politely.

Napoleon continued. 'While the government offers the carrot, Fouché will wield the stick. There will be tight censorship of the newspapers, the theatres and public meetings. No one will be permitted to spread ideas that undermine the regime. At the same time Fouché will be empowered to set up a system of military tribunals in the areas where there is any kind of unrest. As far as anyone needs to know the purpose of the tribunals is to provide summary justice to any rebels who are captured. In practice, they will provide us with a means, and a justification, for arresting any troublesome royalists and radicals.'

'I see. And when were you planning to put all this into effect?'

'As soon as I become First Consul for life.'

Talleyrand could not help an amused smile. 'Do you really think the assemblies will permit you to assume such power?'

'Not for a moment,' Napoleon admitted. 'That is why you and the rest of my followers are going to propose an amendment to the tribunes' motion offering me a renewal of my term of office.' Napoleon folded his hands. 'You will accept the motion, on condition that there is a plebiscite on my assuming the post of First Consul for life, with the right to choose my successor.'

For a moment the other men were silent, and then Fouché leaned forward with an excited glint in his eye. 'Brilliant . . . Quite brilliant. They can hardly protest if the decision is passed over to the people. Not without making it look as if they were betraying democracy. They'll have no choice but to vote for the amendment.'

Talleyrand nodded his appreciation. 'They'll be completely outflanked.'

Napoleon kept his silence as the other men reflected on his masterstroke. It was the perfect political manoeuvre and the fact that his opponents would be forced to support the plebiscite gave him a thrill of added pleasure.

'There is one thing we must keep in mind,' said Talleyrand. 'The need to move swiftly. The public adulation will inevitably die away once they get used to peace. The amendment can be pushed through quickly enough, but we must insist that the popular vote takes place as soon as possible.'

'Of course,' Napoleon agreed. 'There is no reason why it could not happen as early as August.'

Talleyrand considered this for a moment and nodded. 'By August, then.'

★

As Napoleon had foreseen, the amendment was carried by a clear majority. When it was over his political opponents slunk out of their debating chambers seething with fury that they had been compelled to vote for it thanks to their own loudly proclaimed support for the voice of the people. Better still, the announcement of the result was scheduled for August, just as Napoleon had wanted.

In the following months he made sure that the people of Paris were provided with plenty of entertainment and military parades. He gave clear instructions that his subordinate officers were to appear in full dress, with flowing plumes fixed to their gold-braided bicorns. By contrast, he wore a plain coat, as an officer might wear on campaign, and fixed a revolutionary cockade to his hat. Newspapers throughout the country praised the improvements the First Consul was bringing to almost every sphere of French life. Behind the façade of peace and prosperity Fouché moved to silence his critics and enemies. Outspoken royalists and Jacobins were quietly arrested and taken before the military tribunals where their cases were hurriedly processed with little regard to legal niceties. Many were deported, or exiled. A handful of unrepentant prisoners were sentenced to death and taken to barracks outside Paris, shot and buried in unmarked graves.

Despite every precaution taken by Napoleon and his followers there was never any doubt that the people would endorse the hero who had swept away the corruption of the Directory and devoted his life to improving the lives of the people of France. In the middle of July long queues formed at the polls across the country as people cast their vote. While the votes were counted Napoleon remained in Paris, hard at work on the plans to regulate the price of grain so that the poorest citizens would never fear hunger again.

Or so the newspapers reported. In truth, Napoleon fretted over the size of the majority he would achieve in the popular vote. If it was not large enough, his enemies would gain heart from the sizeable minority of the people who still opposed

Napoleon. Only an overwhelming majority would settle the matter beyond dispute and prove to France, and the rest of Europe, that Napoleon ruled with a moral authority that the Bourbons had never enjoyed in the centuries that they had been kings of France.

On the last day of July, after the final results had been conveyed to the capital, Napoleon attended a picnic with Josephine and her friends in the gardens of the Tuileries. She had intended to hold the party on the banks of the Seine away from the sweltering heat and bustle of the capital but Napoleon could not bear to be away from Paris when the result of the vote was known. So the party sat on spotless sheets amid the clipped precision of the flowerbeds overlooking the river. The fouled water glided by, bearing the shimmering reflection of the crowded slum houses looming over the far bank. A company from the Consular Guard formed a loose cordon around the guests and their presence detracted from the pastoral idyll that Josephine had intended to create.

'Must they stand there?' she asked quietly. 'They're making us look like prisoners.'

'Hmmm?' Napoleon glanced at her, and realised at the same time that he had been holding the same slice of cheese and ham tart for several minutes. He took a bite and answered her as soon as he had finished chewing. 'They're here to protect us.'

'Protect us from whom? I thought everyone loved you.'

'Just try to ignore them, my dearest, and then I'm sure your guests will as well.'

'Ignore them?' Josephine turned her head round to the nearest section, standing stiffly at attention fifty paces away. Each man wore a tall bearskin hat that only emphasised his natural height. 'Hardly. Besides,' she continued insistently, 'who are they protecting us from? I'd love to know.'

'The usual malcontents, and those hired by foreign agents to stir up trouble.'

'Now you sound just like one of those toadying newspapers which relish attacking anyone who criticises you.'

'It's not that bad. People are still free to say what they like.'

'As long as they don't say it too loud, or to too many people.'

Napoleon sighed. 'Who has been slinging the mud this time? Your friend Barras? Or that jumped-up perfume platform, Madame de Staël?'

Josephine was quiet for a moment before she continued. 'Did you have to banish her from Paris?'

'I didn't. That was the decision of the Minister of Police.'

'That dog Fouché.' Josephine sneered. 'He's little more than your pet.'

'He's a lot more than that. If Fouché exiled de Staël then you can be sure he had a good reason to do so.'

'Really? Are you sure? There have been quite a few people disappearing from Paris society in recent months, none of whom I'd describe as a dangerous enemy.'

'They had to go. For the public good.' Napoleon reached for some grapes and popped one into his mouth. 'They'll be allowed back, once they've seen reason and can keep their opinions to themselves. Who knows how far they would take their conspiracies if we permitted them to remain in Paris?'

'Oh, come on. How many of them do you suppose are actually dangerous?'

'I don't know. But the men who tried to kill me and you, and injured Hortense, came from somewhere.'

It was a harsh reminder, and Napoleon felt guilty about his words almost as soon as he had uttered them. Josephine turned away from him indignantly, but he saw through the gesture as she quickly wiped a tear away on her sleeve.

'I'm sorry, my love. I did not mean to upset you.' He reached out and gently placed his hand across her shoulder. 'Really I didn't.'

'It doesn't matter,' she replied, her voice catching. 'You are probably right. You usually are.' She turned back towards him, and forced herself to smile. Then her expression froze as her gaze swept over his shoulder. 'Here comes your nasty little policeman.'

Napoleon swivelled round and rose to his feet as he saw Fouché striding across the gardens towards the picnic guests. As soon as he saw Napoleon he broke into a smile and quickened his pace.

'The result?' Napoleon asked at once. 'Is it in?'

'Yes, citizen.' Fouché laughed lightly. 'Or should I say, First Consul for life?'

Napoleon grasped his arm. 'The numbers. Tell me the numbers.'

'Three and a half million votes in favour . . . eight thousand against.'

'Good God,' Napoleon muttered. 'Is that true?'

'Trust me, if it had been rigged they wouldn't even have got eight hundred votes.'

'That's it then. France is as good as mine.'

Chapter 65

Despite the Treaty of Amiens, Napoleon kept a wary eye on the activities of the English as the months passed. Although most of the provisions of the treaty were respected by both countries, the remaining differences between them were as deep as an ocean. Even as Napoleon strove to improve the governance of France with all manner of reforms, his mind was always drawn to the confrontation with the oldest enemy of the revolution. There was little doubt in his mind that the war would be renewed, but if there was any chance, however small, of a lasting peace, then he would take it.

That hope was grasped with fervour by Talleyrand, who spent every waking hour striving to find some means of preventing Europe from sliding back into a bloody conflict. The foreign minister was adamant in his opposition to war, and for the first time Napoleon sensed that there would come a time when the man's principles would outweigh his usefulness. Napoleon did not trust him. His suspicions were confirmed when Fouché showed him the police file that had been kept on Talleyrand.

As Napoleon scanned through the documents the Minister of Police sat so still and silent on the other side of the desk that Napoleon was almost unaware of his presence. As he flipped the last page over he drew a deep breath and leaned back in his chair.

'Most interesting . . .' Napoleon pushed the file back across the desk and smiled. 'But I'm not sure it amounts to treason.'

Fouché raised his eyebrows momentarily. 'Perhaps not. But the names of his associates, and lovers, are suggestive, wouldn't you agree?'

'They're simply the flotsam of the Paris salon circuit.' Napoleon waved his hand dismissively. 'They present no danger to us.'

'That's possible.' Fouché paused and looked straight at the First Consul. 'But we should not ignore the risk to you . . . and your family. After that infernal device that nearly killed you on the way to the Opéra, who can say what treachery exists out there? You must be on your guard, citizen.'

Napoleon frowned at the memory as Fouché paused to let his words sink in before continuing. 'With your permission I will have Talleyrand watched day and night so that we can have a full list of his contacts.'

'With my permission?' Napoleon mused. 'And if I don't give it, then I assume you'll have him watched anyway.'

'Of course not, citizen,' Fouché replied in a pained voice. 'I am your loyal servant. I would never deceive you.'

'I wonder.'

'It is my duty to make sure that any threat to the government, and to the people of France, is identified and dealt with before it can do any harm.'

'And you think Talleyrand is a threat?'

'I doubt it, sir. Not at the moment. My worry is that he is not sufficiently discreet in terms of the company he keeps, nor in what he might say at an unguarded moment.'

Napoleon could not help laughing. 'Talleyrand is the most discreet man I have ever met! Besides, he would never betray France.'

'No. Not France. But given that he's a noble, it is possible that he favours the old order over the new. It is possible that his vision of France is not the same as ours, citizen.' Fouché shrugged. 'It's understandable enough, given his past.'

Napoleon thought it over. It was true that Talleyrand was an aristocrat. Yet his beliefs, as he voiced them, demonstrated a radical frame of mind. Even though he had been abroad during the revolution, Talleyrand had served his country loyally since his return. It was mainly due to his deft touch that the Treaty of

Amiens had worked out so well in France's favour, and it was thanks to him that France was at last enjoying peace with the rest of Europe. And yet . . . What if Talleyrand was plotting to undermine Napoleon, in favour of the royalists? What if there was more to his social circle than there seemed? Certainly some of those named in the report numbered amongst Napoleon's severest critics and political opponents. As Fouché had said, Napoleon should be on his guard.

'Very well. Have him watched. But make sure that he knows nothing about it. I would not want Talleyrand to think I had lost faith in him. Just in case there is no proof of disloyalty.'

'I understand, citizen.' Fouché leaned forward and retrieved the folder. 'I'll see to it at once.'

There was something in his tone that made Napleon look sharply at his Minister of Police. There was a note of triumph there and Napoleon suddenly wondered if Fouché was genuinely concerned about Talleyrand's loyalty, or whether he was playing a deeper game of position, undermining a potential rival in his play for greater power and influence at the heart of government. The lean face stretched over the skull and the hooded, knowing eyes did not engender trust, and Napoleon realised that Fouché – lacking public affection – was obliged to plot and scheme to secure his advancement. In the same way, Talleyrand was obliged to use his charm and wit to achieve his aims. Two sides of the same coin then, Napoleon concluded wearily. Was this how it would be from now on – a constant war of position amongst his subordinates as they plotted against each other?

'Fouché,' he said quietly.

'Yes, citizen?'

'I appreciate the conscientious, not to say zealous, manner in which you have carried out your duties. However, perhaps it might not be necessary to arrest so many of our people now that the popular vote has been taken to empower me for life.'

'You still have enemies, citizen.'

'And I'd prefer it if you did not provide me with any more. Understand?'

'Yes.'

'So tread very carefully around Talleyrand. He has powerful friends.'

'Maybe, but that won't save him if he commits treason.'

'No,' Napoleon conceded. 'It won't. Just make sure you have enough evidence if the moment comes.'

In the following months Napoleon regarded his chief ministers warily. Fouché continued his campaign against the rebels of the Vendée as vigorously as ever, but operated in a more restrained manner in Paris, relaxing some of the restrictions on popular entertainments and imprisoning newspaper editors less frequently. For his part, Talleyrand continued to work hard to persuade the foreign ambassadors that France was sincere in its desire for peace. His task was not made easier by the intransigence of the English and the opportunism of the First Consul. Although the British had undertaken to return Malta to the Knights of St John within three months of the treaty, the island remained in their hands. As summer ended and the British garrison remained in place, Napoleon summoned his foreign minister and the English ambassador to the château at St-Cloud that had been refurbished to act as a diplomatic residence away from the noise and grime of the capital.

In order to lend the meeting a less tense ambience Talleyrand had suggested that a buffet of regional delicacies should be laid out in the drawing room overlooking the ornate gardens. A small party of dignitaries had also been invited, and while Josephine hosted the main party the three men slipped away to a small arbour at the end of the main lawn and sat in the dappled shade of trellised vines as they talked. Lord Whitworth was tall, over six feet in height, and stiff-necked with the casual bluntness, bordering on rudeness, that seemed to characterise so many of his high-born countrymen. At least he had a decent command of French, Napoleon admitted as they swiftly moved from polite informalities to the real business of the day.

'I have to confess,' Lord Whitworth crossed his legs as he drawled, 'His Majesty's government is perplexed by France's refusal to sign a commerce treaty between our nations.'

'How can I agree to that, when you still remain in Malta?' Napoleon responded. 'Surely you can see that it is hard to justify a new treaty to my people while the previous one remains to be honoured?'

Whitworth tipped his head slightly to one side. 'The situation has changed.'

'No it hasn't. Your forces are still there. A handover within three months, you said. Then you said you could not leave until a Grand Master of the order had been named. When the Pope sanctioned the new Master, you refused to ratify the appointment. When I offered to permit Neapolitan troops to provide a neutral force of occupation, you refused to let them land on the island.' Napoleon paused and sighed. 'Lord Whitworth, France has acted with great patience in this matter, but her patience is not without its limits. So, tell me, when will England return Malta to its rightful owners?'

'Ah, well,' the ambassador responded awkwardly. 'The thing is that His Majesty's government has decided that since the initial period of three months has expired the terms of the treaty no longer apply.'

'What?' Napoleon responded sharply. 'Explain yourself.'

'It is, of course, our honest intention to quit the island. However, given that the terms of the treaty have failed to cover the present situation, England asserts that it is within its rights to retain possession of Malta.'

'What rights?' Napoleon snorted. 'You have no right to be there.'

'I beg to differ, sir.'

'Your continued occupation breaks the spirit and the letter of the treaty and you know it.'

'That is your opinion.'

'It is the opinion of every rational man in Europe!'

Before Whitworth could respond to the sudden flaring up of Napoleon's temper Talleyrand interrupted. 'The First Consul is right, my lord. There is no worth in your government's position, and everyone knows it. Yet I can understand your attachment to Malta. It holds a certain strategic importance to the Royal Navy, and as the new Grand Master happens to be Tsar Alexander, you are understandably nervous about providing Russia with access to the Mediterranean, especially given her interest in the disintegration of the Turkish empire.' Talleyrand paused, and then smiled. 'Is that a fair approximation of your government's concerns?'

Whitworth gave a slight nod of assent. 'I will agree that it is, for the sake of argument.'

'Then, for the sake of argument, will you not also accept that the possible benefits of continued occupation would be as nothing compared to the vast cost in lives and wealth – should your failure to honour the treaty provoke a renewal of hostilities?'

'Are you threatening England, sir?' Whitworth's tone was angry. 'Do you desire war?'

'No, my lord. Do you?'

'Of course not.'

Napoleon stabbed a finger at him. 'Then give up Malta.'

Whitworth shook his head. 'England will not agree to that. Not yet at least.'

'If not now, when?'

There was a brief pause before Whitworth replied, 'Not for seven years.'

'Seven years?' Napoleon's eyes widened in surprise and anger. 'Seven years! You are joking, my lord. Surely?'

'I assure you I am not, sir.'

'This is an outrage!' Napoleon clenched his hands into fists and leaned forward in his chair so suddenly that Talleyrand feared he might strike the ambassador. He rose to his feet and stepped between them.

'Gentlemen, for pity's sake, lower your voices.' He gestured towards the lawn where some of the guests had turned to look towards the arbour following Napoleon's outburst. Talleyrand continued, 'We must subordinate our tempers to reason. The fate of Europe depends upon it.'

Napoleon glared at him for a moment, then, lips pressed together in a thin line, he forced himself to sit back and loosen his fists. Talleyrand waited a little longer, until calm seemed to prevail, then turned back to the ambassador.

'My lord, it seems to me that Malta is not the real issue of substance here. Perhaps your country feels that France poses some kind of threat to the interests of England. If you might try to explain your grievances in more detail then we might yet progress to a better understanding.'

Whitworth considered the idea and nodded. 'Very well, sir. But be aware that, even though I know the mind of my political masters, I do not speak for them. What passes between us here is no more than an informal exchange of views. Agreed?'

Talleyrand turned to Napoleon with a questioning look. 'That is agreeable, citizen?'

Napoleon nodded, still frowning at the ambassador. 'Go on.'

Whitworth cleared his throat and began. 'Despite the treaty, England is concerned that France is not resolved to make peace. We need to trade with Europe, yet we find that the First Consul seems determined to place every obstacle he can in the way of English commerce with the Continent. Then there is our concern over the territorial ambitions of France. In recent months you have annexed Piedmont, Elba, Holland and Parma. We wonder what lands will be gathered into your arms next. Especially since you seem determined to reduce the number of German principalities and draw them into the sphere of French influence. And what of your wider interests?' He stared directly at Napoleon as he spoke. 'Our ambassador in Spain has noted how you have resorted to the most undiplomatic threats in order to get the Spanish to return your territory of Louisiana in the Americas. As we speak, a large French army is busy putting down a slave revolt in San Domingo. Surely you must undestand our anxiety over so strong a force in a region where we have far fewer troops? From our side of the Channel, it seems that France is merely using the peace to prepare the ground for war. Put yourself in our position and you must surely agree that our concerns appear to be well warranted.'

'I understand that well enough.' Talleyrand nodded. 'But I assure you, France relishes the current peace, and is merely settling outstanding affairs in order that she can enjoy the benefits of the growing harmony between the interests of our nations.'

'What harmony?' Whitworth shook his head. 'Whatever harmony remains is withering, not growing.'

'Then it is urgent that we do all we can, as swiftly as possible, to repair the situation. So tell us, what would His Majesty's government ask of France in order to ease the tension between us?'

Napoleon watched Whitworth carefully as the Englishman collected his thoughts and responded. 'Open the ports of Europe to our ships and our merchants. Settle your revolt in San Domingo and bring your army home. And return those lands you have annexed to their former owners.'

'He asks for the moon!' Napoleon protested to Talleyrand, then rounded on the ambassador. 'And if we gave in to those demands, would you return the favour? Would you abandon Malta? Would you stop sheltering the émigrés who spill their bile into the foul pamphlets that appear on our streets? Oh, don't think I don't know who is funding their lies. The same source of money that buys arms for the Vendée rebels, and no doubt provided the means for those bastards who tried to assassinate me. You shelter them in the Channel Islands, and it's your ships that land them on our shores to spread their mischief. Is England prepared to accept that France is no longer the land of the Bourbons? Is England prepared to recognise that France is at last a free nation?'

'A free nation?' Whitworth smiled mockingly. 'A free nation, under Bonaparte. What exactly is the difference between an absolute monarch and a First Consul for life?'

'The difference is that *I* was elected by the people.' Napoleon raised his chin. 'I embody their will.'

'Really? And who is to say that His Majesty does not embody the will of our people?'

'Then why don't you ask them?' Napoleon smiled coldly. 'Why don't you ask your people? Unless you are afraid of what they might say.'

Whitworth stared at him in silence for a moment before

replying. 'The common people are not in possession of the knowledge or the will to act in their own interest. Until they are, their social superiors will determine their best interests, and those of England as a whole.'

Napoleon shook his head. These aristos were all alike, from one side of Europe to the other. Arrogant, greedy and desperate to hang on to the power handed to them by their ancestors. They would fight to the last breath rather than permit a man like Napoleon, with all his natural advantages of intellect and ambition, to remake their archaic nations into more efficient and fair societies.

Talleyrand looked from one to the other with a growing sense of despair. There was no shred of reconciliation between them, and his heart felt heavy at the inevitable fate awaiting the peoples of France and England. There was nothing more he could do to try to bridge the gap this day. He would have to wait until the immediate tension had bled out, and then try again.

He stood up. 'Gentlemen, we have spoken enough. The other guests will fear there is something amiss unless we return to the party. For their sakes, I beg you, we must behave with cordial affection, while peace still has a chance.'

He gestured towards the distant gathering of guests, clustered around Josephine on the lawn. Napoleon bowed his head curtly towards the ambassador and left the arbour, striding back across the neatly cut grass. Whitworth stared after him, and muttered, 'I rather fear that man may prove to be as much your problem as he is ours.'

Then he set off at a far more leisurely pace, as if he was idly admiring the features of the garden as he ambled back towards the other guests. Talleyrand was still for a moment, his eyes fixed on Napoleon as he contemplated the last words of the ambassador.

The year ended with no sign that the English were willing to quit Malta. In January Napoleon decided to increase pressure on them and gave orders for the preparation of an expedition to the last remaining French territory in India at Pondicherry. There might still be a slender chance of winning back some ground from the Earl of Mornington and his brother, Arthur Wellesley.

The public delight over the previous year's peace treaty was daily turning into fear of the outbreak of a new war and Napoleon felt compelled to address the senate and the assemblies of the tribunes and deputies on the matter of the relations between France and England.

Standing before them on the podium, as the dull grey light of a winter's day filtered through the windows, Napoleon sensed their anxiety and need for reassurance. He set out the grievances of France and stressed the danger of England's continued support for those who sought to destabilise the consulate and undermine all the benefits that Napoleon and his government had brought to the people. At the end, as grey clouds thickened over Paris and ushers began to light the candles inside the hall, Napoleon concluded his address.

'You all know me best as a soldier, and yet I tell you there is no greater ambition in my heart than that France may enjoy everlasting peace and prosperity. There could be no greater gift to this nation of ours than a generation that has never known the ravages of war in its lifetime. But what value is such peace if the honour of our nation is debased by the pernicious propaganda and provocations of England?' He paused and turned his gaze on Lord Whitworth sitting in the visitors' gallery, so that no member of the audience could be in any doubt where his final remarks were aimed. 'It is the tragedy of England that her houses of Parliament are riven by two factions. On the one side there is a peace party, dedicated to the benefits and rewards of a universal peace. On the other side is the war party, comprising mean and bellicose spirits in whose hearts there resides an implacable hatred of France. If the war party seizes control in the coming months then the blood of countless innocents will be on their hands. If there is war, then history will judge that the cause of it will be England, not France. And if there is war, then I give my word that France will prevail and our armies will utterly humble those who have forced us to take up arms.'

The applause was muted and solemn, as Napoleon had

anticipated. This was no rallying call for an attack, but a grim warning that France must be ready to fight an enemy who seemed utterly relentless. As he acknowledged the clapping that echoed round the chamber Napoleon saw Whitworth rise from his seat. Their eyes met and Whitworth shook his head with regret before he turned and climbed the steps towards the exit.

It did not take long for reports of Napoleon's address to reach London and the King quickly made his own appearance before Parliament. King George tersely rejected Napoleon's warning, and authorised the calling up of the militia and the expansion of the Royal Navy to place it on a war footing. Napoleon responded by issuing orders for the massing of an army of over a hundred thousand men on the Channel coast. In April Talleyrand concluded negotiations with representatives of the American government for the sale of the vast swath of land in North America that formed the Louisiana territory. The price was sixty million francs. Never had land been sold so cheaply, but then again, Napoleon reasoned, never had France needed money so badly.

At the end of the month Lord Whitworth formally requested an audience with the First Consul. They met in the Luxembourg Palace. There was little attempt to exchange more than perfunctory courtesies before the English ambassador proffered a document to Napoleon. Talleyrand stood to one side, hiding his despair behind his customary mask of detachment.

'What is this?' Napoleon demanded.

'A message from Prime Minister Addington, on behalf of His Majesty. He considers that the presence of so large an army on the coast directly opposite Britain constitutes a direct threat. The Prime Minister therefore requires that the army is to disband. Failure to accede to this request will be considered a hostile act.'

Napoleon took the sealed letter and laid it on his desk before he replied. 'Might I ask how France is to interpret His Majesty's rapid enlargement of the Royal Navy? It seems that a new ship of the line appears off our coasts almost every day. If I disband my army, will he disband his ships?'

Lord Whitworth ignored the question and gestured towards

the letter. 'I am instructed to wait until the eighth of May for your response. If you refuse to comply, then I am to leave Paris and return to London.'

Napoleon felt his heart quicken. 'Then you will declare war on France.'

'I did not say that, sir.' Whitworth drew himself up so that he looked down on Napoleon as imperiously as possible. 'As all men know, England desires nothing more than peace.'

Napoleon felt some last measure of restraint snap inside him as he stared back at the haughty English aristocrat. He slammed his fist down, making the letter jump. 'Respect the treaty then! Leave Malta at once!'

For a moment, they glared at each other. Then the ambassador bowed his head and backed a few steps away. 'I shall return to the embassy. I will await your reply. Until the eighth.'

Once he had gone, Talleyrand turned to Napoleon and asked, 'Will you disband the army?'

'No.'

'Then it's war.'

'So it seems,' Napoleon replied evenly. 'Though we shall give England the ignominy of declaring it.'

'Do you think they will?'

'I am certain of it.'

'Then God help us all.'

Lord Whitworth waited in Paris until the appointed day and then, having received no response from Napoleon, left Paris with his meagre household in a small convoy of carriages. Four days later he boarded a ship at Calais and set sail for England. In Parliament the Tories, urged on by the revitalised fanaticism of William Pitt, proposed a motion to declare war on France.

One morning, late in May, Napoleon was at breakfast with Josephine when a footman entered the room and approached the table carrying a sealed message. Napoleon broke the wafer, unfolded the single sheet and read the hurriedly scribbled message. He set it down with a frown and stared fixedly at the window for a moment before Josephine gave a light cough.

'What is it, my dear? That letter.'

'Hmmm?' Napoleon turned to her, as if he was unsure of her words for a moment. Then he glanced at the paper. 'Oh . . . It's from Talleyrand. He received an official dispatch from London this afternoon. The English declared war on France on the sixteenth.'

'War?' There was a protracted pause before Josephine continued, 'How long do you think it will last, this time?'

Napoleon considered the question briefly. 'I've no idea. All I do know is that this time there can be no peace until England, or France, is utterly crushed. We have exhausted any other possibilities. As the saying goes, it will be a fight to the bitter end.' He stared at the letter. It seemed an age since the last time he had gone to war. Then it had seemed glorious and he had revelled in it. But now? Napoleon felt the weary weight of his heart as he contemplated the coming conflict. There would never be a war like it. Two great powers, one dominating the land, the other master of the oceans, locked in a struggle that would embrace Europe and spread its dark wings to the far corners of the world. It would be a war on a scale that no one had ever seen before.

Chapter 66

Arthur

Poona, August 1803

Arthur laid down his razor and began to rinse the remains of the soap from his face. When he had patted away the last drops he laid down his towel and stared into the mirror. At thirty-four years of age his body still had the trim athleticism of a man ten years younger. That was down to the hard exercise that he took every day, the same regimen he insisted on for his men. Even so it had taken many months to recover from his illness, and there was grey hair at his temples. He shook his head sadly at the toll India had taken on his body. To be fair, these lands had given him the chance to develop his ideas about the best methods for waging war. If he had remained in Europe, then he would never have had independent commands on the scale of the forces he had wielded in India.

His promotion to Major General had come through the previous year and now he was leading an army of nearly twenty-five thousand regular troops and sepoys. Some months earlier, as the British had anticipated, war had broken out between the Mahratta states and the Peshwa, Bajee Rao, had come to the Governor General begging aid to help restore him to power in Poona. Richard had made good use of the opportunity to draw up an advantageous treaty before authorising Arthur to take command of the army that would place Bajee Rao back on his throne. The Governor General had learned from his embarrassment over the affair with General Baird and had first offered the command to General Stuart. But Stuart had gracefully declined and stated that Arthur should be in command since he had equipped, organised and trained the finest army ever assembled in India. Those were the very words, Arthur recalled. His professionalism and ability had been recognised and there was no longer any grudging resentment, nor the muttered accusation of nepotism, to besmirch his reputation.

So he had led his army north from Mysore and entered Poona early in May, and returned Bajee Rao to his palace. Far from being a useful ally, Bajee Rao was detested by his people and his kingdom was destitute and disintegrating. Despite being restored to his throne by the English, the Peshwa had at once begun to plot with Scindia to oust his rescuers. Such was the man's ineptitude in the arts of deceit that Arthur had come to hear of the plot almost at once and had remained in Poona to discourage Bajee Rao from any attempt to renege on his treaty with the Governor General. At the same time, attempts to negotiate treaties with Scindia and Holkar were proving difficult. Reports from Arthur's network of agents had revealed that Scindia was trying to forge alliances with other Mahratta chiefs to wage war on the British. Meanwhile Holkar had declared war on the Nizam and had invaded the lands of Hyderabad, claiming that the Nizam owed him money. As a result Arthur had been obliged to divide his command and send Colonel Stevenson to protect Hyderabad with ten thousand soldiers.

Arthur had other problems. The men and horses he had brought with him from southern India were used to a diet of rice, yet the Mahrattas fed their beasts on *jowarry* – a coarse grain that was not suitable for the men in Arthur's army. So his supply lines ran all the way back to Mysore. That was bad enough, but worse still was that many of the contractors had made off with much of his rice supply. That difficulty could be resolved by hiring new contractors, but in the meantime the army had advanced slowly from Poona to threaten Scindia's fortress at Ahmadnagar. The monsoons had turned the tracks into glutinous mud that meant the army could progress no more than three miles a day. Arthur had left his men briefly to collect more bullocks and ensure that the situation in Poona was stable. The peace between France and England had changed the strategic situation in India overnight. Under the terms of the Treaty of Amiens the government in London had agreed to return Pondicherry to the French. Already a number of French soldiers had turned up in India, looking for employment under the local rajas and warlords. Hot on their heels had come a steady flow of French merchants eager to compete with the trade of the East India Company. Just when it seemed that the influence of France had been driven from the subcontinent, the French were back in play.

Arthur took a last glance at his image in the mirror. How much longer would his constitution hold out, he wondered? He had endured the strain of several years of campaigning in this unforgiving climate, and the odds against his returning home to England in good health were lengthening all the time. Besides, there was always the memory of Kitty at the back of his mind, and he yearned to return to her. The last letter he had received from her was some months ago. She said her heart was still his, and that she had successfully fended off the suitors her older brother had attempted to foist on her. That was small comfort to Arthur while he was on the far side of the world. He was familiar enough with Dublin society to know that the Viceroy would have a plentiful stock of dashing young staff officers to catch the eyes of the local dignitaries' daughters, and that included Kitty.

'Damn,' he muttered in frustration and reached for his shirt, thrusting his head through the collar and hurriedly fastening the buttons. His servant had laid out the rest of his uniform on a chest beside the basin, and with a last moment to savour the cool loose fit of the shirt Arthur wearily began to dress. He made his way to the veranda of the residency where Barry Close had just sat down for breakfast. Even though Close had only recently been transferred from Mysore, he had made useful connections with the most powerful men in Poona.

'Good morning, sir.' Close nodded. 'Dare say you had a better night's sleep than you've had in a while, eh?'

'More comfortable, at least.' Arthur beckoned to one of Close's stewards. 'Lamb chops, if you please.'

The steward bowed. '*Acha, sahib.*'

Once the man was out of earshot Arthur lowered his voice. 'Any further developments with the Peshwa?'

'Only that he is as treacherous as ever. My informants at the palace say there is a regular exchange of messages with Scindia and Holkar. I had a word with him last night about it. I mentioned that it was somewhat unseemly for a man beholden to our side to be in communication with his former enemies.'

'He didn't deny it then?'

'Of course he did, sir. But you know Bajee Rao – the man is a compulsively bad liar. He insists that any communication he has with the other side simply demands that they bow to his authority once more. He swore, by all his gods, that he remains a steadfast and loyal ally of Britain.'

'It's conceivable he might be telling the truth,' Arthur mused wistfully.

'Only to the same extent that porcine aviation is conceivable,' replied Close. 'The Peshwa is a black-hearted knave, motivated at any moment by what he fears most.'

'Well, yes. Quite.' Arthur stared across the compound towards the main gate of Poona and the distant domes of the Peshwa's palace, gleaming in the rays of the early morning sun. 'Well, we must do what we can to discourage him from playing both sides. I think it's time that you let him know that if there should be any more of this underhand opposition, I shall be obliged to take possession of the country solely in the name of the Company.'

Close stared at him. 'Would you carry that threat through, sir?'

'I would. I am empowered to act in the name of the Governor General, and I will not shirk from doing anything necessary to bring peace and order to the Mahrattas. You must make sure that he is convinced of that.'

'Well, I'll do my best, sir.'

'I'm sure you will. In the meantime, we'll continue our efforts to remove Holkar from the Nizam's territory and get him and

Scindia to disband their armies and accept the authority of the Peshwa.'

'That's a tall order, sir.'

'I understand that, but we hold Poona, we have the Peshwa and have set a precedent for decisive action when it is required.' Arthur leaned forward and poured himself some tea. 'If they're sensible, then they'll meet our demands sooner or later.'

'And if they don't?'

'Then there will be war, and my army and I will hunt them down and destroy them.'

The resident ran a hand slowly over his thinning hair. 'The latest reports say that Scindia has over forty thousand men, and eighty guns. And the Raja of Berar is marching to join him with another twenty-five thousand men and forty guns.'

'I read the reports too, you know,' Arthur said testily. 'Our army is more than a match for them.'

'I'm sure you are right, sir.'

The door to the kitchen opened as the steward returned with a platter of lamb chops and strode towards them. Arthur glanced at the man before addressing his final comment to Close on the matter. 'I am right, as I will prove to you, and the whole of India, before the year is out.'

As Arthur ate the conversation turned to more light-hearted matters and the news that the Peshwa was planning to hold a tiger hunt later in the month. Arthur was minded to attend, given the slow progress of negotiations with Scindia and Holkar, and they fell to discussing the merits of various firearms. As breakfast ended and Arthur dabbed his lips with a napkin, a small party of horsemen came trotting up the road leading towards the city gate. They were covered in dust from several days of hard riding and were only recognisable as Europeans by the cut of their clothes and uniforms. A squadron of dragoons and a handful of civilians. As they turned off the road and made towards the entrance of the compound Arthur and Close sat up and scrutinised them more closely.

'Who the devil are they, d'you suppose?' Close grumbled. 'Bound to be the bearers of bad news.'

There was a brief silence before Arthur nodded. 'You can count on it. The man riding alongside the troop commander is my brother Henry.'

'So it is. By God, you have fine eyesight, sir.'

'Not really.' Arthur smiled. 'Only a select few men in India have a nose like that.'

Henry left his escort as they entered the compound and continued towards the residency as the troopers dismounted from the exhausted horses and led them to the troughs by the line of tie rails beside the entrance. Arthur got up and descended from the veranda, waving a greeting to his brother.

'Henry! What brings you here?'

'Charming greeting, I must say. After such an arduous journey, and not having seen you for so long, I'd have expected something better.' Henry reined in and slid down from the saddle. A servant darted out from the side of the house and took the reins as he stretched his back and rubbed his seat. He nodded to the servant. 'Have him watered, fed and groomed.'

Arthur raised his eyebrows. 'You're not staying?'

'Only long enough to brief you. Then I'll carry your reply back to Richard.'

'Brief me? Why, what's happened?'

Henry gestured to the table where Close was still seated, and they exchanged a brief wave. 'Let me take some refreshment first. I swear I have half the dust of India lining my throat. We've ridden directly from Madras, only stopping to rest when the nags were on the verge of collapse. Not a pleasant experience.'

Arthur smiled at his brother's affected insouciance before replying in kind. 'I beg your pardon, how inhospitable of me. Do please be my guest.' He gestured to the table and they climbed the steps to join Close. While Arthur ordered the steward to bring a jug of pressed juices, Henry beat some of the dust from his coat and eased himself into one of the cane chairs.

'So.' Arthur turned to him. 'Tell me. What brings you here?'

'It's the French. You know that Richard has been holding off their claims for their colony at Pondicherry to be returned to them.'

'I had heard about it.'

'The situation has changed. A French frigate arrived to reclaim the colony on the fifteenth of June. Over two hundred men landed and took possession of the fort. They say that a powerful squadron of warships is sailing to join them, together with a general and a division of French soldiers.'

'Most awkward. Who else knows about this?'

'Richard sent me as soon as he found out, but you can be sure that word will have reached most of our Mahratta friends by now.'

'Which means they will be making speedy efforts to contact the French and come to some arrangement to inconvenience our interests.'

'To put it mildly.' Henry leaned forward and his tone became serious. 'We can't delay the inevitable a moment longer. Richard wants you to move against Scindia at once. He's already given orders to General Lake to advance into the land between Jumna and the Ganges. Everything turns on a decisive defeat of the Mahrattas. Then we can enforce British influence across the breadth of the subcontinent.'

'You have to admire our brother's ambition,' Arthur responded drily. 'The situation is rather more complicated here in the field. My army is stuck in mud and my supplies are tenuous.'

'Now is not the best time to start a new campaign,' said Close.

'There never is a best time,' said Henry. 'Anyway, those are his instructions.'

Arthur raised an eyebrow. 'Instructions, or orders?'

'Richard gave you his full authority to act in this matter. He has every confidence that you will make the right decision.'

'I see,' Arthur replied coldly. If the campaign failed, Richard would be absolved of blame. Of course, if it succeeded then he would claim the credit for his grand strategic vision. Besides that, Arthur sensed that his loyalty to his brother was being tested. The expansion of British interests in India had cost a fortune, and the government in London and the directors of the Company would be certain to call the Governor General to account in the near future. It would be natural for Richard to want to know how far he could depend on his brother's support. Yet Arthur deeply resented the ploy.

He let out a weary breath. 'Very well, tell him that I will destroy Scindia's army.'

The monsoon rains continued to slow the army's march as Arthur led his forces towards the fortress of Ahmadnagar. Mud sucked down the wheels of his guns and the drivers of the artillery trains whipped their bullocks on as soldiers, often knee deep in mud themselves, braced their shoulders against the spokes and strained to shove the guns and the limbers back on to firmer ground. Even that had its hazards as the rain, and lighter deposits of mud, made the ground slippery and the men had to avoid the slithering motions of the bullock-drawn vehicles while struggling to remain on their feet and trudge on towards Ahmadnagar.

As soon as Henry had left Poona to carry Arthur's response back to Calcutta, a message was sent to Scindia declaring that he bore responsibility for the coming conflict thanks to his unwillingness to negotiate. Scindia's reply blamed the British in turn, saying that their pre-conditions had made any meaningful negotiations impossible. Scindia's message ended with a rallying cry for every native of the subcontinent to rise up and throw off the British yoke. It was a hollow ambition, since the inhabitants of lands already under British rule realised they had more to lose than to gain by rebelling. But Arthur knew that the real audience of Scindia's call to arms was the French. If they could supply enough advisers and arms, then the Mahratta armies might yet overthrow the British.

Four days' march brought the British army to Scindia's fortress at Ahmadnagar. Arthur, and a small escort, rode ahead to examine the enemy's defences. At first light that morning the rain had finally stopped. By the time they found a small hill close enough to give a good view of the walls the sky had cleared and the rising sun was quickly warming the lush landscape, causing steam to rise up in a faint haze. Before them lay the *pettah* – a small walled town – and to one side the fortress itself. Ahmadnagar was circular with massive walls of solid stone with formidable-looking towers at regular intervals. A deep ditch, filled with water, surrounded the fortifications. Arthur flicked back his drenched cape and reached for his telescope. Around him, the staff officers followed suit as the escorting dragoons allowed their mounts to wander a short distance off to graze.

'The scouts say that between the *pettah* and the fortress there is a garrison of a thousand Mahratta troops, and another thousand Arab mercenaries, under the command of French officers,' Arthur commented as he scanned the walls of the *pettah* closely. 'Looks like the usual combination of brick, mud and masonry surrounding the town.' He squinted as he focused on a party of enemy soldiers watching them from one of the towers. 'About twenty feet high, I should say.'

'The town walls should be breached easily enough, sir,' commented Captain Fitzroy. 'Once we get the heavy guns out of that damned mud.'

'We're not going to lay siege to it,' Arthur replied. 'There's not enough time for that. We'll take the town by direct assault, before we turn our attention to the fortress. The key thing is not to let the soldiers garrisoning the *pettah* escape to the fortress.'

Fitzroy examined the walls of the latter for a moment. 'That's going to be a tough nut to crack. The heaviest guns we have are twelve-pounders. It'll take weeks before we can batter a hole in those walls. We could always bypass Ahmadnagar, sir.'

'No. I need a forward supply base, and somewhere to fall back on if the campaign goes against us. So we must take the place. There's no avoiding it. But don't be too daunted by those walls. They look old and weathered to me. I doubt they'll stand up to much. Our twelve-pounders will be perfectly adequate for the job.'

He collapsed his telescope and pushed it back into its saddle holster before turning to Fitzroy.

'Return to the column at once. I'll use three battalions for the attack, the 74th, the 78th, and a battalion of the Company's natives. Have them assemble assault ladders and bring up one of the guns to blow the gates open.'

'Very good, sir. What time shall I give them for the attack to begin?'

'What time?' Arthur paused to stretch his back muscles. 'Why, we shall attack the place at once.'

Chapter 67

'There's nothing complicated about it, gentlemen,' Arthur explained. 'We haven't got time for a textbook siege of the town. I want it taken at the first attempt, understand?'

The officers nodded.

'It is vital that as much of the garrison is destroyed as possible. Our cavalry pickets will cover the perimeter of the town to prevent any attempt to reach the fortress. Now, remember, although I want your men to go in hard and fast, they are to respect the townspeople. Any man caught looting or raping will be hanged.'

'Sir?' One of the Company officers spoke up.

'What is it, Captain Vesey?'

'My lads are from Madras, as are most of the sepoys. There's plenty of bad blood between them and the Mahrattas. It'll be hard to stop them taking their revenge.'

'I don't care about that,' Arthur replied firmly. 'Those are my orders, and you will carry them out, to the letter.'

'Yes, sir.'

He paused to make sure the officers were certain of his sincerity. Arthur had seen enough of the suffering of the poorest natives during his time in India to know that if they were only treated humanely they would openly welcome British rule. However, he did not expect many of his officers and men to share his long-term vision for India, and discipline would have to be enforced pitilessly if British forces were to win the favour of the natives of these vast tracts of land. He glanced round at his officers and continued the briefing.

'Colonel Wallace will be attacking the main gate of the *pettah*. The other two columns will scale the walls on either side. If either of those attempts succeeds in crossing the walls they are to make for the gates and open them, if Colonel Wallace hasn't already managed to. To work then, gentlemen.'

The three columns moved into position to begin the attack. Colonel Harness was commanding the left-hand column and, as Arthur looked on, Harness began advancing before the other columns were ready. In front of the column the men from one of the light companies kept up a steady fire on the defenders in the bastions on either side of the targeted length of wall. As yet there was no sign of the enemy on the rampart and Arthur felt a vague twinge of anxiety.

Beside him, Fitzroy grumbled, 'Bloody Harness is bolting towards the wall like a March hare. The other columns aren't even ready yet. The attack will go in piecemeal.'

'It doesn't much matter,' Arthur replied. 'It will unsettle the enemy as much as us, so do calm yourself, man.'

Fitzroy stirred guiltily. 'Yes, sir.'

All three columns were led by companies of King's soldiers and supported by sepoys. It was the same throughout Arthur's army. The most reliable units were brigaded with native soldiers to stiffen the latter's resolve. Harness led a mixed force of men from the 78th and one of the Madras battalions. The 78th was from Scotland and was the only kilted regiment in India. With their colours raised at the head of the column the men marched steadily through the line of skirmishers towards the wall. An occasional puff of smoke appeared on the flanking bastions as the Arab defenders risked quick shots at the approaching column before ducking down out of sight. As soon as they reached the wall the leading ranks hurriedly raised their ladders and leaned them up against the rampart and the first of the men began to clamber up the rungs.

'Where are the defenders?' Fitzroy spoke quietly. 'Surely there are men on that wall. Why don't they show themselves?'

Arthur did not reply, but strained his eyes to follow the

progress of the left-hand column. The first of the men had reached the top of the ladder and swung themselves on to the rampart. Only they did not jump down on to the walkway behind, but froze for an instant, before being jostled to the side by more men coming up behind them. Soon a half-dozen men were poised on top of the wall as still more came up the ladders.

'What the devil is happening?' Arthur snapped, and then instantly clamped his mouth shut and forced himself to adopt the imperturbable expression that he knew impressed other men. Suddenly he realised why the men were not jumping down on to the walkway behind the rampart – there was no walkway. Just a sheer drop inside the wall on to the ground behind. As he watched, one of the men lurched to one side under the impact of a musket ball and toppled back down the wall amongst his comrades. A moment later another man was shot down by the defenders behind the wall. Then someone at the base of the walls must have realised what was happening and slowly the men began to descend the ladders and fall back from the wall, under fire from the bastions.

Arthur clenched his fist in irritation at the setback, and then relented. In the event it was just as well that Harness had hurried forward ahead of the other columns. Turning to Fitzroy Arthur indicated the right flank column. 'Get down there and tell Vesey what's happened. Tell him to raise his ladders against the bastions. He is to avoid the wall at all costs.'

'Yes, sir.' Fitzroy saluted and spurred his mount forward towards the ranks of men marching up to the right side of the *pettah*'s gate, which Wallace's column was boldy approaching, dragging a six-pounder cannon with them. Once Fitzroy had passed on the warning the right-hand column split into two as they made for the bastions at each end of the length of wall assigned to them.

Arthur pulled out his telescope to watch the progress of the attack as closely as possible. One of Harness's grenadier officers had rallied some of his men and they had moved towards the nearest bastion and thrown up a ladder. The first three men and the officer hurriedly began to climb. As they neared the top a handful of defenders suddenly appeared and thrust the ladder away with poles so that it toppled back, throwing the climbers on to the ground. At once the officer was up on his feet. His hat had been knocked off and a livid red streak ran down his face from an injury in his scalp. He helped his men replace the ladder, and while the skirmishers turned their fire on the defenders above he raced back up the ladder, followed by his men. He didn't pause at the top. Drawing his sword as he reached the rampart, he clambered across the battlements and fell upon the Arabs in the bastion. His sword flashed brilliantly as he carved a path through his enemies. The grenadiers surged up the ladder and joined him to clear the top of the bastion. The struggle was brief as more grenadiers piled into the fight and then disappeared into the bastion. Colonel Harness was hurriedly directing his men towards the place and they began streaming over the top as the distant pop and crackle of musket fire sounded over the *pettah* walls.

Over on the right Vesey's men had reached another bastion and were locked in a desperate fight with its defenders. With two bastions out of action Colonel Wallace faced little danger as the central column waited on the track before the main gate. Ahead of them the six-pounder had been loaded and the artillery crew was running it up to the gate so that the muzzle pressed against the stout but aged timbers.

Arthur spurred Diomed forward to join the men waiting to assault the town. He was determined to be there when they did enter to make sure that the officers restrained their men from looting or attacking the civilians within the walls. As he rode along the column towards the gate an artillery sergeant carrying the portfire suddenly shouted. 'Back, lads! They're opening the gates!'

There was a dull clatter from beyond the timbers and then they began to swing inwards. Arthur had a glimpse of armed men under the gate tower, then the sergeant swept his portfire down on to the paper cone of the fuse. Even as it flared briefly, Arthur felt a cold fist clench in his stomach, but it was too late to do anything. The gun went off with a boom as a jet of flame and smoke gushed through the *pettah* gatehouse. Colonel Wallace thrust his sword out and shouted to his men. 'Forward! Forward, you devils!'

Arthur dismounted and pushed his way through the men and under the gatehouse. The cannon had gone off right in the faces of some of Vesey's sepoys. One man, who must have been directly in front of the muzzle, had been torn in two and his head, chest and shoulders lay several feet from his pelvis and buckled legs. In between, his guts and pools of blood lay spashed across the ground. Several more men were injured and were staggering out of the way of Wallace's soldiers as they charged into the town. Beyond them Arthur caught a glimpse of a handful of the Arab mercenaries disappearing into one of the narrow streets. Then he saw Vesey and indicated the injured men.

'Have them taken back to our lines to get their wounds tended.'

'Yes, sir.' Vesey saluted.

'By the way, Captain.' Arthur clapped him on the shoulder. 'That was fine work.'

'Yes, sir. Thank you, sir.'

Arthur drew his sword and entered the base of the gatehouse. He stepped over several enemy bodies on the stairs as he made his way up and emerged on to the paved top of the bastion where the grenadier officer had carved a path through his enemies. The small area was littered with the bodies of the mercenaries, all killed by savage sword blows or thrusts from the bayonet. Amongst the dead were two of the grenadiers, and a third, injured, man was slumped against the inside of the rampart clasping his hands over a wound to his stomach. As he saw his general he raised a bloodied hand to salute. For an instant, Arthur felt a compulsion to tend to the man, but compassion was a luxury a commander could not afford until after the battle. So Arthur returned the salute and made his way to the breastwork to look over the town.

British troops were pouring through the tangle of streets pursuing small bands of the enemy, some of whom still had enough of their wits about them to turn and fire occasional shots. A few had already emerged from the far gate and were desperately running for the cover of the nearest topes to escape the groups of cavalry that encircled the town ready to ride down any Mahratta warriors that came their way. Once he was satisfied that only a handful had managed to reach the fort Arthur turned away from the scene. The grenadier leaning against the parapet was staring at him with a frozen expression of agony. Arthur leaned over him and touched his shoulder. There was no reaction and he realised that death had claimed him only a few moments earlier. Arthur straightened up and gazed sadly at the man. An hour ago he had been marching towards this small unregarded town, no doubt swapping tall tales and jokes with his companions; an earthy vibrant being, perhaps with a wife or sweetheart waiting for him back in Scotland. Now, thanks to an order from Arthur, he was dead.

He pulled out his watch and glanced at the hands. It was barely twenty minutes since the attack had begun and already the town had fallen. The enemy had suffered hundreds of casualties, and there would be many British wounded as well. But if, as Arthur intended, the swift and decisive assault served to discourage the defenders of the fortress, then a greater number of lives could be saved in the long run. It was a peculiar train of thought and he wondered if other generals indulged in such moral computations to justify their decisions. Now that the action was over, a familiar weariness settled on him and with a sigh he turned his mind to the capture of the fortress as he descended the stairs inside the bastion.

Over the next two nights a battery was constructed three hundred yards from the fortress. Arthur and his engineers had examined the fortifications in some detail through their telescopes before settling on a section where the masonry appeared to be weak and crumbling in places. The *killadar* commanding the fortress was clearly unversed in modern siege warfare, or had chosen to ignore the advice of the French officers serving under him. There was no attempt to fire on the British engineers and by dawn on the second day the battery was complete and guns, powder and ammunition had been hauled into position. As soon as there was enough light to gauge the fall of shot Arthur gave the order to open fire. There was a rolling crash as the twelve-pounders belched flame and smoke while Arthur stood to one side and squinted through his telescope at the fortress. He saw the iron balls strike home and chips of masonry explode from the face of the wall. Lowering his telescope he nodded to the officer in command of the battery.

'The range is good. Keep firing, but don't rush the job. The guns must be loaded carefully. I don't want a single shot wasted, understand?'

'Yes, sir.'

Arthur returned the officer's salute and returned to his tent for breakfast. Once he had eaten, he turned his attention to the latest intelligence reports that had come in from the *hircarrah* agents. Here in the northern part of India they could not hope to pass through the Mahratta camps unnoticed, and had to report on enemy movements from a distance. Already it was quite clear that they had little ability to judge the size of enemy formations and Scindia was reported to be in command of anything between fifty and a hundred and fifty thousand men. By contrast, Arthur knew exactly how many men he had in his army. In addition to two and a half thousand regulars there were another seven thousand sepoys and four thousand Mysore cavalry. Colonel Stevenson's slightly smaller force was already marching to join them. Combined, they should be a match for Scindia's horde.

All day the guns boomed out in a slow rhythm and by early afternoon there were signs that the walls were beginning to crumble as each impact brought a shower of mortar and rubble tumbling down into the outer ditch. The bombardment continued the following morning and a breach finally opened. More shot widened the gap until finally the ammunition gave out late in the afternoon.

The chief engineer returned Arthur's telescope to him and pursed his lips for a moment before he gave his judgement. 'I'd say that the breach was practical, sir. We could fire a few rounds of case shot in to clear away the enemy before our boys go in. Do you wish to make the assault today, sir?'

'Of course.'

'Then I'll have the guns made ready.'

'Very well,' Arthur agreed. 'See to it.'

As the sun dipped towards the horizon, burnishing the landscape in a fiery glow and casting long dark shadows, Arthur formed the bulk of his army up opposite the breach. Only the leading battalions would make the actual assault, but he had calculated the impression such a show would make on his enemies and shortly before the attack was due to begin a white flag appeared on the nearest bastion, hurriedly waved from side to side to attract the attention of the British. Arthur went forward and met the *killadar's* representatives in front of the battery. In addition to a man bearing a makeshift white flag, there was a Mahratta official and a French officer. The latter saluted Arthur as they approached. Arthur spoke first, in French.

'If you wish to spare yourself from my men, then the fort must be surrendered at once.'

'My commander, the *killadar*, wishes to know what terms you will offer.'

'I've already stated my terms,' Arthur replied. 'Surrender now, or perish.'

There was a brief exchange between the Mahratta and the Frenchman before the latter continued. 'The *killadar* wishes to negotiate.'

'The negotiations are over. I will not permit the *killadar* to play for time. I will give him ten minutes to make his decision, from the moment we finish speaking. You may tell him that he and his men will be permitted to quit the fort and I will give them two days' grace before I advance from Ahmadnagar.'

'That is a generous offer,' the French officer conceded. 'I will do my best to see that it is accepted, sir.'

Arthur nodded, and then drew out his fob watch and looked at it pointedly as he muttered, 'Ten minutes, then.'

★

Just as the hands on the watch crept towards the deadline, the gates of the fortress were thrown open and the garrison began to file out, glancing nervously at the massed ranks of the British troops formed up in front of them. As the Mahrattas formed a makeshift column, a few hastily loaded wagons and carts trundled over the bridge across the ditch, and finally the *killadar* and his senior officers emerged. Accompanied by the French officer they approached Arthur and bowed their heads respectfully, before the *killadar* looked at the British general in frank admiration and spoke briefly, pausing to allow his French officer to translate.

'He says that there is no dishonour in surrender to an army that could make such short work of the *pettah* and its garrison . . . He says the British are a strange people. You came here in the morning, looked at the *pettah* wall, walked over it, killed all the defenders, and returned to breakfast. What enemy can withstand you?'

Arthur forced himself to keep his face expressionless, and the French officer laughed before he continued. 'I doubt any native army has seen anything like it before. I can imagine the effect it will have on Scindia's men when the *killadar* tells the tale,' he concluded shrewdly. 'You are a formidable adversary, General. I fear we may meet again soon.'

'Not if you leave India,' Arthur replied firmly.

'Even if I did, sir, I am sure that a man of your talent will be called back to fight in Europe and I fear for my countrymen.'

'You are most generous in your praise, sir,' Arthur replied tersely. 'Now, if you would be so kind as to ask the *killadar* to move his column out, I have a fortress to occupy and a campaign to fight.'

The French officer saluted and then translated for the Mahratta commander before they strode off to join their column. The moment the Mahrattas shambled away to the north, Arthur led his men into the fortress of Ahmadnagar.

With a secure base to his rear, garrisoned by a battalion of Company soldiers, Arthur moved north across the Godavery river, while Colonel Stevenson marched towards him across the territory of Hyderabad. As the summer sun baked the landscape the two British columns marched deeper into enemy territory, closely following reports of the movement of Scindia's army. Such was the heat during daytime that the army broke camp while it was still dark and covered as much ground as possible before late morning, when they made camp and rested in whatever shade they could find. Then, late in September, news came that Scindia was at the village of Borkardan, two days' march away. Arthur hastily sent a message to Stevenson instructing him to join Arthur's column there to confront the enemy and force a battle. As word spread through the ranks that the enemy was close to hand the sense of excitement and tension was palpable.

On the morning of the 23rd the army ended their march at the village of Naulniah. If their intelligence was good, the enemy was camped another day's march away, but already the soldiers were scanning the surrounding landscape for any signs of enemy horsemen. While the dusty columns of infantry, gun limbers and cavalry tramped into the area marked out for the camp the usual cavalry pickets were sent out to cover the approaches to the camp.

Arthur had just retired to his tent for some refreshment when he saw through the tent flaps a patrol from the 19th Dragoons come galloping up to the array of tents that formed the army's headquarters. Their cornet hurriedly dismounted and beckoned to a *brinjarri* merchant riding with them. Arthur set down his cup of tea and rose to meet the dragoon officer.

'What is it?'

'Sir, this man ran into our patrol three miles from here. He says he was on his way to sell food to Scindia's troops in their camp, nearby.'

Arthur's attention snapped to the *brinjarri* merchant. He questioned him in Hindoostani. 'Where is Scindia?'

'Two or three *coos* from here, sahib.'

No more than six miles, Arthur calculated, his pulse quickening.

'How many men are in this camp?' he asked, and then realised that there was no question of the merchant's being able to judge the number accurately. He tried another tack. 'How big is this camp, then?'

The merchant paused a moment before he replied, struggling to work out the scope of what he had seen. 'Sahib, they are camped along the Kaitna river, for a stretch of three *coos*.'

'Three *coos*?' Arthur repeated, astonished. He made a quick estimate and felt his heart beat fast with excitement as he realised that the enemy force must be at least a hundred thousand men strong. He had found Scindia's army. Better still, he had caught them in camp. Arthur looked over his army arriving to make camp for the night. They had already marched fourteen miles. Stevenson was still several miles distant and could not hope to reach the enemy camp before the end of the day. Yet there was not an instant's hesitation as he made his decision. Turning back to the tent he called out to Fitzroy.

'Pass the word. I want the battalion commanders to have their men stand and prepare for battle.'

Chapter 68

Assaye, 23 September 1803

'Good God . . .' Fitzroy muttered as he gazed at the host stretched out along the far side of the Kaitna river. His mount shuffled as he and his general surveyed the enemy camp from a small hill half a mile from the river. The strongest position was to the east, where Scindia's regular battalions were forming up on raised ground covering the far bank of the river. Interspersed amongst the enemy infantry were scores of artillery pieces. 'I've never seen anything like it.'

Arthur smiled. 'Nor have I. They must outnumber us fifteen or twenty to one. But now we have them. Scindia can't escape a battle without having to abandon his guns.'

'With those odds I doubt that escape is on his mind, sir. Any frontal attack across the river would be suicidal.'

'Well, don't be too troubled by those horsemen at least. They're nothing but rabble.'

Fitzroy stared across the river. To the west tens of thousands of mounted Mahrattas were slowly saddling up and massing in their war bands. To the north of the village of Assaye, on the far side of another river, the Juah, another host of mounted men was gathering. Fitzroy cleared his throat. 'Even so, sir, if we meet them in the open, those horsemen will surround us in an instant.'

'Perhaps,' Arthur mused. 'One thing is for certain, they know we are close. They're already breaking camp and taking up positions for battle. So there goes the element of surprise. Get back to the column and bring the army up. Tell Maxwell to have his cavalry deploy on this side of the river. He's to screen the movement of our infantry and guns. Tell them all to hurry. We've no time to lose.'

Once Fitzroy had galloped off Arthur hurriedly assessed the position. He was committed to an attack now. If he failed to strike then the British reputation for invincibility in India would be shattered. Worse still, an emboldened enemy would make any retreat a desperate business with the army operating at some distance from its supply base at Ahmadnagar. Arthur would have to win this battle if his army, and the reputation of his country, were to survive. But to get at the enemy he would have to cross the river and charge up the steep bank on the far side, straight into the muzzles of Scindia's muskets and cannon. The casualties in such an attack would be horrific and the English army might well be broken before it ever came into contact with the Mahrattas.

As he looked again at the enemy line and followed the course of the Kaitna to the east he saw two villages on opposite banks of the river, a mile beyond the enemy's left flank. A track led across the river plain to the nearer village and then seemed to resume on the far bank before it headed towards Assaye. His *hircarrah* scouts had assured him that the only place where the Kaitna could be crossed was at Kodully, almost opposite the centre of the enemy camp. Yet it seemed there must be a ford between the two villages to the east. Why else would they be there? In which case, that was where the army must cross. Once on the far bank Arthur's battalions could form up across the narrow strip of land between the Kaitna and the Juah. If they moved swiftly enough then they might attack Scindia's flank before his cumbersome forces could be redeployed to face the new threat.

By the time Fitzroy returned, Maxwell's cavalry had reached its position and spread out across the plain between Kodully and the two villages Arthur had spotted. Behind them the infantry columns and guns marched towards the Kaitna, kicking up choking clouds of dust as they came on. As Fitzroy reined his horse in Arthur gave his orders.

'We'll have to hit them where they are strongest – over there on the right. If we can break Scindia's best troops, and destroy his artillery, the rest will flee of their own accord. But we can't risk a frontal attack. So,' he turned and indicated the settlements either side of the river, 'we'll cross the river between those villages.'

Fitzroy frowned. 'The scouts didn't mention a ford there, sir.'

'I know, but there has to be one. Trust me.'

'But what if there isn't, sir?'

'There will be,' Arthur replied calmly. 'Now go and tell our battalion commanders to make for the ford, then join me there. And pass the word for my groom. I'll need a fresh horse ready during the battle. Diomed, I think.'

Fitzroy saluted. 'Yes, sir. Pray God that you are right about the ford.'

Arthur examined the battlefield one last time from his vantage point. Swarms of enemy horsemen had crossed the Kaitna and approached Maxwell's cavalry screen. Every so often one of the English galloper guns would fire a charge of grapeshot at any Mahrattas who drew too close, and they would turn tail and trot back out of range. There was no sign that they were willing to take the English cavalry on, Arthur noted with satisfaction. Then he turned his bay horse away, galloped down the gentle slope towards Maxwell's small reserve and ordered a squadron to escort him while he examined what he hoped would be the ford between the two villages.

As the small column reached the first houses on the near bank it was clear that the Mahratta horsemen had thoroughly pillaged the place. Some of the houses were burned down and several bodies still lay in the street. At the sound of horses the remaining inhabitants scuttled inside their hovels and closed the doors behind them. Arthur led the way round the fringe of the village until they came to the track leading down into the river. The current flowed past gently enough but the water was a muddy brown so that it was impossible to gauge its depth from the bank.

Arthur tapped his heels into the flanks of the bay and urged his mount into the water, taking care to stay in line with the entrance and exit of the ford. The water splashed about the bay's legs as the mare waded further into the current, yet even by the middle of the crossing the water barely came up to her belly. With a growing sense of relief Arthur urged her on until he approached the far bank and the river grew shallow again. Then he wheeled the bay round and kicked his heels in, and the mare surged back to the southern bank where the dragoon escort stood waiting. He called an order to their officer.

'Get across and form a picket line two hundred yards from the far bank. Report any sign of enemy movement towards the ford immediately.'

He rode back until he could see the infantry columns approaching down the track and turned his attention to the enemy camp once more. It was clear that they had abandoned their original battle line and were moving to counter Arthur's move on their flank. He tapped his riding crop against his boot for a moment, until he was aware that he was betraying his nerves and quickly stopped it as Fitzroy came riding up, gesturing towards the enemy.

'Sir, have you seen? They have almost formed a new line already.'

'Let them,' Arthur replied. 'They will not be able to bring more than a fraction of their forces to bear on us. Then we'll see their true quality.'

Just after he spoke there was a dull roar close overhead and then a cannon ball smashed through the second floor of a house at the heart of the village, showering the street with mud plaster and rubble.

'That must have been a twelve-pounder, at least,' Fitzroy muttered.

'More likely an eighteen-pounder,' Arthur replied as he gauged the distance to the enemy. 'From the direction of Assaye, I think.'

'God help us if they get the range of the crossing.'

'They won't,' Arthur replied calmly. 'They can't possibly see it.

There's a slight rise between us and them. They're firing blind.'

Even so, more shots passed overhead and some crashed into the village, unnerving the soldiers as they marched quickly through the main thoroughfare and down to the river. The first of the battalions and a few cannon hurried across to the far bank and marched straight on towards the Juah to take up their position on the right flank of Arthur's battle line. As the second battalion thrashed across the river one of the dragoons from the picket came galloping down the far bank into the river and approached his general. He drew up, glistening from the spray that his mount had kicked up, and saluted.

'My officer sends his compliments, sir, and begs to inform you that the enemy have completed their change of facing. They have also fortified the village of Assaye with batteries and some rough earthworks.'

'That was quick,' said Fitzroy. 'Their commander knows his stuff. He's trained them well.'

'Yes,' Arthur conceded. 'But they'll be no match for our men when the fighting starts.' He turned back to the dragoon. 'Was there any sign of movement from their battle line?'

'No, sir. They were holding their ground when I left the picket.'

'Good.' Arthur nodded. 'Then we still hold the initiative. You can return to your squadron now. Well done.'

The dragoon smiled with pride and raised his hand to salute. Then there was a wet crack and Arthur's face was sprayed with warm fluid and what felt like lumps of mud. He instinctively wiped the mess away with his gloved hand and saw a thick red smear on the beige leather.

'Christ Almighty!' Fitzroy exclaimed.

Arthur looked up and saw that the dragoon was still sitting bolt upright in his saddle. Only his head was gone, and jets of blood spurted up from the tattered flesh at the stump of his neck. An enemy cannon ball had smashed it off and sprayed blood, brains and bone across the jackets and faces of Arthur and his staff. The man's last spasm had alarmed his horse and it pranced skittishly, until, at last, the body slumped to one side and toppled from the saddle. Arthur recovered from the shock first and glanced at the frozen expressions of those around him.

'Anyone else hurt?'

His staff officers hurriedly checked themselves, but they were uninjured and Arthur breathed a sigh of relief. 'A freak shot, gentlemen. Nothing more. We must continue with our duties as calmly as possible, please. Do not unnerve our men. They already have enough to concern them.'

As soon as the infantry and artillery were across, Arthur ordered two companies of sepoys to defend the village on the north bank of the Kaitna and sent a message to Maxwell to bring his cavalry across the river to join the rest of the army. The Mysore cavalry was to be left to counter the Mahratta horsemen on the southern side of the river, in case they made any attempt to attack the rear of the British army. Then Arthur rode forward to make sure that his infantry line was ready to advance. The regular battalions were positioned on the flanks with the Company soldiers formed up in the middle, with cannon filling the gaps between the battalions, which now stood in two lines. Before he gave the order to advance Arthur rode forward with Fitzroy on to the slight rise in the ground that stood between the two armies. From there Arthur could see that the neck of land between the Kaitna and the Juah became wider as the two rivers diverged. Which was just as well, he reflected, as he looked towards Assaye and saw that it was ringed with cannon, and its crude walls were packed with enemy soldiers. Any English troops who ventured within range of Assaye were bound to be mauled and Arthur determined to make it clear to his unit commanders that they were to stay well clear of Assaye in the coming attack. The enemy line had finished its manoeuvre and now stood ready to receive the British attack.

'It seems that I have underestimated Scindia's professional soldiers,' Arthur commented wryly. 'This is going to be a bloody action. We'll keep our left flank close to the Kaitna as we advance. That will leave only the right flank to cover. Maxwell can manage that.'

A distant rumble and rattle drew their attention to a dozen

British guns being hauled into position opposite the enemy line.

'About time,' said Fitzroy. 'Now they can have a taste of their own medicine.'

But even as the artillery crews urged their draught bullocks forward the Mahratta gunners were shifting their aim from the ford and a moment later the first rounds landed around the limbered British guns and their crews, chewing up the soil in small explosions of earth and grass.

'They're using grapeshot,' Fitzroy observed.

An instant later the enemy gunners hit their first target as the leading pair of a team of bullocks shuddered under the impact of the heavy lead balls and collapsed dead in their traces, bringing the rest to an abrupt halt. Two more guns were knocked out before the British could reply and it was clear to Arthur that any intention he had of destroying the enemy artillery before his infantry advanced was doomed to failure. The Mahratta artillery crews knew their business well and were firing almost as fast as the remaining British guns. It was clearly a desperately unequal exchange and as chain shot shattered the wheels of yet another of his guns, Arthur realised that the time had come for his infantry to advance into the teeth of the enemy fire.

'Give the order for the artillery to withdraw.'

As Fitzroy spurred his mount over to the guns Arthur turned the bay back to his waiting infantry and rode down the line giving his orders to each battalion commander in turn to make certain they knew exactly what was expected of them. The officer commanding the pickets on the right flank, Colonel Orrock, was a florid-faced Company veteran. As Arthur explained about the danger of approaching too close to Assaye he was certain he smelled spirits on the man's breath. But there was no time to upbraid the man and once Orrock confirmed that he understood his orders Arthur rode on to the other battalions, finally taking up position behind the kilted Scotsmen of the 78th on the left flank. He nodded to Colonel Harness and the latter bellowed the order to advance, and the rest of the line followed suit, tramping up the slight rise in echelon.

As the line reached the crest the British regiments had their first sight of the dense mass of the enemy line waiting for them five hundred yards away. The Mahratta guns stood a short distance in front of the infantry, spread across the ground from the Kaitna to Assaye. The survivors of the first guns Arthur had sent forward had lost most of their horses and bullocks and could not join the advance. Arthur knew that meant that all he had available to him now was a handful of the guns assigned directly to the regular battalions.

The fire of the enemy guns slackened for a moment as they saw the approaching line of redcoats, and then flame-stabbed smoke rippled along the line again. Some shot went high, ripping through the air close overhead; some fell short and ripped up the ground ahead of the British infantry. But those that were on target cut bloody paths through the British line, which were hurriedly closed up as the battalions continued forward at the same measured pace. The air was filled with the booming roar of cannon and the whirr of iron shot passing close by, and still Arthur's men did not flinch, but advanced with stolid determination towards the enemy guns. Then, at sixty paces, Colonel Harness ordered his men to halt and make ready to fire. Just ahead of them the Mahrattas, with equal courage and discipline, still worked their guns, firing into the British line at point-blank range.

Primed and cocked, the British muskets rose up, aiming at the gun crews.

'Fire!' Harness shouted.

There was a deafening crash and a blanket of greasy smoke blossomed in front of the 78th and at once the muskets were lowered as the Scotsmen drew another cartridge from their pouches, bit off the ball and tipped the powder into their muzzles, together with the waxed paper, spat the ball in after and packed the lot down firmly with their ramrods. Pans primed, they raised their muskets again and Harness cried out the order to unleash another volley.

Even as the sound of the last shot died away, Harness called for his men to fix bayonets and advance. Arthur rode forward with them, through the swirling smoke, emerging to see that the guns directly in front of the 78th had almost all been silenced. Miraculously, two full crews still remained, and still stood by their weapons, loading another round of grapeshot. As soon as he saw them, Harness increased the pace and the redcoats with their feathered bonnets and flapping kilts charged home. The Mahrattas snatched up their ramrods, handspikes and any other weapons that were to hand and threw themselves at the British. Despite their courage, the fight was over in a moment and the gunners lay where they had fallen around and under their cannon.

'The 78th will re-form and reload!' Harness yelled, and his men quickly closed up to face the block of enemy infantry behind the guns, barely more than a hundred yards away. The din of their shouted war cries and beaten drums contrasted sharply with the cool silence of the British ranks.

To his right, Arthur saw the battalion of sepoys halt to fire a volley at the gun crews in front of them and then they too charged home with the bayonet. Meanwhile, as the 78th began to advance again, the enemy infantry raised their muskets and fired a volley. The range was long and most shots missed, but some found their mark and men spun round and collapsed under the impact, before tumbling on to the trampled grass. Arthur felt the bay lurch beneath him and begin to topple to one side. Instantly he dropped the reins, kicked his feet free of the stirrups and threw himself clear just before the horse hit the ground and rolled over. The impact drove the breath from his lungs and for a moment he crouched on hands and knees, gasping for air.

'Sir!' A hand lifted him under the arm and pulled him up. 'Are you hurt?'

Arthur waved his hand as he struggled to breathe. 'Fine . . . Just winded.'

He glanced round and saw that it was the young grenadier officer who had carried the bastion at Ahmadnagar, Lieutenant Campbell. 'Thank you, Campbell. Now, my hat, if you please.'

The officer plucked it from the ground and handed it to Arthur. 'I need to re-join my men, sir.'

'By all means.'

Campbell trotted forward a few paces to catch up with his men just as Harness halted the 78th fifty paces from the enemy and calmly called out the order to fire another volley, as if it was just another parade ground exercise.

'Fire!'

The volley thundered out and a withering storm of lead slashed through the Mahratta troops so that most of the men in the front line went down. This time there was no second volley and Harness immediately followed up with the order to charge with the bayonet. The enemy, having already witnessed the slaughter of the artillery crews, shuffled back several paces, and then the first of them turned to run, and in moments the panic was contagious and they broke and ran. With a roar of triumph the 78th ran after them, bayoneting the few who were brave enough to stand their ground.

As he caught his breath Arthur looked to the right and saw the sepoy battalion next in line charge home, and the panic from those men who had fled from the 78th communicated itself along the line so that those opposite the sepoys also broke and fled before the redcoats. Arthur felt a moment's satisfaction at the sight of his plan bearing fruit. No native unit in India could have withstood the large, fierce men of the 78th, and once they broke Scindia's line the other units had collapsed, just as Arthur had hoped they would. He turned to look for the groom who had been told to follow his general at a discreet distance with a remount. The man had already seen the bay fall and was trotting forward, leading Diomed by the reins. Retrieving his pistols, sabre and telescope from the dead bay, Arthur climbed into the saddle and ordered the groom to return to Maxwell's reserve regiment of native cavalry.

From the vantage point of the saddle Arthur could see that Harness had managed to recall his men and the 78th was once again forming up as it waited for further orders. The Company officers were having less luck with their men who, having broken the Mahratta line, were excitedly running down and killing their enemies. For nearly a thousand yards the enemy line was destroyed and the ground between the two rivers was covered with figures streaming away from the British regulars and sepoys. To Arthur's delight he estimated that thirty or forty guns had been captured. Without artillery, Scindia's power would be broken and the best he could hope for was a war of brigandage against his British opponents.

Beyond the fleeing enemy Arthur noticed several large groups of Mahratta cavalry riding forward, heedlessly knocking aside their fleeing compatriots on the ground. He looked round and saw that the two four-pounders allocated to the 78th were trundling up a short way behind the regiment. Turning Diomed, he rode over to the officer in charge of the guns.

'See those horsemen approaching? I want you to unlimber just ahead of the 78th and fire grape into any body of horsemen who venture within range, understand?'

'Yes, sir.' The Company officer saluted and turned to urge his contractors to goad the bullocks forward at a faster pace as the guns bumped across the uneven ground behind the limber. Once they were in position the crews quickly unhitched the trails, manhandled the guns round towards the advancing enemy horsemen and loaded with grapeshot. The first gun fired with a loud crack and the ground close to the nearest body of Mahratta horsemen was torn up. At once they stopped, wheeled their mounts round and galloped away until they were well out of range.

But even as Arthur began to feel that victory was firmly in his grasp the air reverberated with a sudden furious barrage of cannon fire from the direction of Assaye. His stomach clenched in anxiety. His orders had been clear enough: the place was to be avoided, yet there was no mistaking the direction of the cannonade. He spurred Diomed forward and rode to the sound of the guns. To his left the officers of the Company battalions had finally reined in their men and were forming them up to wait for new orders. In front and to the right of Arthur the ground was strewn with the bodies of Scindia's men, together with a sprinkling of redcoats, a clear sign that Arthur's confidence in the training, discipline and courage of his troops was not misplaced. He smiled as he took a moment's pride in what had been achieved. Then his expression hardened as he reached the right flank of the British line and came across scores of redcoats sprawled across the bloodied ground; torn to pieces by grape and chain shot from the guns around Assaye.

It was clear what had happened. Some fool had blundered towards the village instead of closing on the main body of Scindia's troops. With a sinking sensation he recalled Orrock's appearance a little earlier on, when he had given the man his orders. It was too late to berate the man now; the damage was done. Looking around Arthur realised that hundreds of men had been cut down before the village. The survivors of Orrock's pickets, and the 74th, which had been following him, had formed a square to protect them from the Mahratta cavalry that had charged from the enemy positions around Assaye, emboldened by the carnage their gunners had wrought on the British formations. The redcoats had held their own, firing volleys into the horsemen that swirled around them, all the time adding to the bodies of men and horses heaped about them. But already the Mahratta commanders were trying to gather their men in, ready to advance against the British flank from the direction of Assaye. Arthur saw the danger at once.

Five hundred yards behind the 74th's square Maxwell's cavalry stood formed and ready to charge. Arthur saw that Maxwell and his staff were advanced a hundred yards ahead of their men. There was not a moment to lose. Arthur snatched his hat from his head and waved it frantically from side to side to attract Maxwell's attention. Then one of the staff officers edged his mount alongside Maxwell and pointed in Arthur's direction. Arthur waited a moment until he was certain that his cavalry commander had seen him, and then drew his sabre and thrust it in the direction of the enemy forming up around Assaye. For a moment he was not sure that Maxwell had understood, and then the shrill notes of a trumpet carried across the battlefield and the dragoons and native cavalry eased forward into a trot, slowly gathering pace as they swept across the ground, bypassing the cheering men of the 74th, and then charged the horsemen and guns around Assaye. All along the line glinting steel glittered in the late afternoon sun as they drew their sabres and spurred their mounts into a full gallop to close the final gap between them and the Mahrattas. They were bigger men and far better mounted than their enemy, and the impetus of the charge shattered the Mahratta forces around Assaye. The men of Maxwell's three regiments slashed about them as they carved a path through the enemy formations, striking down gunners, horsemen and the infantry at the other end of Scindia's battle line.

It was an impressive enough sight, Arthur reflected, but he knew all too well that the same spirit that made men choose to join the cavalry made them live for precisely this moment: the mad gallop at the enemy, the shattering of his formations and then the thrill of the pursuit afterwards. Even as he watched, the British cavalry swept on through the flank of Scindia's army, scattering their enemies who turned to flee across the Juah river. Maxwell and his men were carried away by their success and charged on after them, across the river, leaving the battlefield.

Arthur's relief at the impact of their charge abruptly turned to frustration and anger. The army was small enough as it was without a significant part of it losing their heads and charging off when they were most needed by their general. As he rode up to the 74th his anger was interrupted by a distant cannon shot from the rear of the British position. He reined in and turned to look. Some of the enemy cannon had been recaptured by Mahratta gunners and they were now firing at the 74th.

'How the hell . . .' Arthur began before he realised they must have been feigning death when the British line swept over them. Some Mahratta horsemen had also managed to work their way round the right flank, no longer covered by Maxwell's cavalry, and were helping to serve Scindia's guns. As Arthur looked, another gun fired, and this time the shot was true and cut down two men at the corner of the square as it tore through their chests and flung the bloody remnants at the feet of their comrades.

There were only two formations ready for action, Arthur realised. The 78th and the 7th Native cavalry in the reserve. He turned Diomed about and galloped back across the field of bodies to Colonel Harness.

'We have enemy to the rear!' Arthur gestured back towards the guns.

'I wondered what the noise was.' Harness frowned. 'But those guns were taken, sir.'

'Evidently not. We'll have to do the job again. Get your men back there as quickly as possible.'

'Yes, sir.'

Arthur left the colonel to bellow his new orders and galloped back across the rear of his re-forming infantry battalions to the cavalry reserve, still behind the rise that the rest of the army had crossed just over an hour earlier. Explaining the situation to the regiment's colonel, Arthur took over the command and ordered the regiment to form a line. As the manoeuvre was complete he ordered the men forward. They crested the rise and Arthur saw the 78th marching towards them. In between the two British forces Scindia's men were firing their guns with the same dedicated efficiency as they had before, bombarding the remains of the 74th as that regiment fell back towards Assaye.

Drawing his sabre, Arthur indicated the guns and gave the order to increase pace to a trot as they flowed down the gentle slope towards the Mahrattas. They were spotted at once and the horsemen abandoned their guns and ran for their mounts, leaving the gunners to snatch up whatever weapons they could as the British converged on them. Once they had closed to within the last three hundred yards of the line of guns, Arthur shouted the order to charge. Diomed's hooves drummed on the baked ground beneath him and her mane flickered in the wind and Arthur felt his heart pounding like a hammer as the cavalry thundered towards the enemy.

They smashed through the loose mass of Scindia's horsemen, hacking and slashing with their sabres. The crude *tulwars* of the Mahratta horsemen were no match for the well-forged steel of the English blades, often shattering under the impact. Arthur saw a man to his side and made a cut to the head with all his strength. The edge of the blade struck the man on his turban, cutting through some layers of cloth and knocking him cold. He grunted and slipped from his saddle, while Arthur recovered his sword and rested it against his shoulder as he slowed Diomed and looked round. The enemy horsemen were already routed, riding their small beasts away from the melee as swiftly as they could as they raced for the safety of the Juah river.

'Keep moving!' Arthur called out. 'Go for the guns!'

He urged Diomed forward and the native cavalry followed, charging in amongst Scindia's artillery crews, who had finally ceased firing and were preparing to make their final stand. Arthur's eye fixed on a richly dressed officer and with a twitch of the reins he steered Diomed towards the man, extending the tip of his sabre as he spurred the mare into a canter. The Maharatta officer saw him coming, and snatched up a handspike from the nearest gun and held it ready, as if it was a spear. At the last moment, Arthur swerved slightly and made a cut with his sabre. But the officer was too swift and dodged aside and at the same time rammed the handspike into Diomed's chest with all his might.

A shrill whinny of agony and terror burst from the mare's muzzle and she reared up so abruptly that Arthur was nearly unseated. He clamped his thighs round Diomed's girth and threw his weight forward. The horse dropped to four feet again, the shaft of the handspike protruding from the bloody wound. The Mahratta officer had drawn his *tulwar* and darted forward to attack the British general. Arthur parried the blow, flicked his sword and cut at an angle into the man's neck, severing muscles and arteries before the blade cut into the bone. The enemy officer had a startled expression on his face as the blood gushed from his wound in thick jets, then, as Arthur yanked the blade free, he toppled to the ground. Diomed was staggering dangerously, and Arthur sheathed his blade and slipped down from the saddle.

'Easy, girl,' he said softly as he worked his way forward to her head. 'Easy.'

The handspike was lodged solidly in her chest and flecks of blood sprayed from her muzzle as her nostrils flared. She had been piked through a lung, Arthur realised. There was nothing he could do for her now. Such a wound was usually fatal, in which case the merciful thing to do was end the animal's agony. Arthur drew a pistol from the saddle and his lips pressed into a thin line as he eased the muzzle to the side of the horse's head and pulled the trigger. Diomed bucked to one side, legs tensing briefly before she died.

Arthur stared at Diomed for a moment before he took one of the few mounts that had been made available by the loss of its rider during the skirmish. From the saddle he saw the last of the gunners being shot down by Harness as they tried to flee towards the bank of the Kaitna. Arthur's third mount of the day was a poor replacement for his previous horses and was badly blown by the long marches it had endured over the course of the day and the previous night.

By the time Arthur reached the infantry line every battalion had formed up in a line that ran across the spit of land. Ahead of them the remains of Scindia's army formed their third line of defence for the day, with their backs to the Juah river. Most of Maxwell's cavalry had drifted back across the river and was re-forming to the east of the British line, just outside Assaye.

Arthur steered his new mount towards Maxwell and his tired, but elated, troopers.

'One last task for you today.' Arthur forced himself to smile, aware that their initial exchange would be overheard by the nearest men.

'Name it, sir.' Maxwell was grinning, clearly having the time of his life. 'Did you see my boys charge, sir? We tore them to pieces, by God! Would have chased them all the way to the Himalayas if the lads had had their way.'

'Then I'm thankful that they didn't. I need you here and I need you now. When the final attack goes forward, you must charge their flank and break them. Once the flank goes their whole line will collapse. I'm sure of it.'

'You can count on us, sir.' Maxwell saluted.

'I *am* counting on you.' Arthur lowered his voice. 'And this time I'd be obliged if you retained greater control over your men. There are tens of thousands of enemy horsemen still in the field and I need every damn trooper I can lay my hands on if this battle is to end well for us. Do I make myself clear, Maxwell?'

'Yes, sir. Amply.'

'Then you have your orders. Carry them out.'

Once again, Arthur took a position beside the 78th and a peculiar stillness hung over the plain. The sun was sinking towards the horizon and a golden slanted light threw long shadows across the flattened and bloodstained grass of the battlefield. He drew a deep breath and raised his hat in the air.

'The line will advance!'

Harness bellowed the order to his men, and then it was repeated across each battalion as the redcoats marched towards the enemy, in echelon as before. On the far right of the line the shrill cry of cavalry trumpets sounded as Maxwell, at the head of his men, charged towards the men closest to Assaye, now held by the survivors of the 74th. In his excited state Maxwell had led his men at an oblique angle to the enemy line and before he could correct the direction his men instinctively edged away so that the whole force charged along the front of Scindia's remaining battalions, under fire, before they reached open ground some distance beyond.

Arthur cursed the man, but at least the cavalry had inadvertently covered the advance of the infantry and they emerged from the clouds of dust kicked up by the horses close enough to halt and deliver a crashing volley before the enemy could react. The shock was too much for Scindia's men and before the British battalions could decide the final stage of the battle with the bayonet, the enemy turned and fled in a single mass, surging into the waters of the Juah. The redcoats pursued them to the water's edge and halted, too tired to go any further and with their bloodlust finally sated after the day's awful slaughter. Instead, they set down their weapons and drank greedily from the water, before refilling their canteens for the first time since the previous day.

Arthur watched the fleeing enemy for a while longer as they disappeared into the twilight. Then he turned to survey the battlefield, strewn with bodies and abandoned guns. In the distance there was still an occasional explosion from the enemy's ammunition tumbrils where some slow fuses had set fire to the gunpowder-laden vehicles abandoned by the enemy. Scindia's army had lost every artillery piece. The trained battalions of regulars he had set so much store by had all been shattered and driven from the field. The victory was as complete as it could be, Arthur reflected. His men had proved their superiority over the enemy beyond any doubt, and word of this battle would soon reach every corner of India, and beyond. It took a moment for his exhausted mind to register that more than a battle had been won. Britain was now the undisputed master of the subcontinent.

There was still much to do to cement the victory, to settle scores with the remnants of the Mahratta warlords still opposed to Britain, but the end was inevitable. As Arthur turned away from the river to give orders for the men to camp in the open near Assaye a leaden weariness settled on him. At last, long after night had fallen, he stumbled through long lines of slumbering and snoring men towards the small farmhouse he had chosen for his headquarters. The men's sleep was far from peaceful and several times he heard voices cry out suddenly as men woke with a start, troubled by nightmare visions of the battle.

By then Arthur had been given a provisional butcher's bill. Over a quarter of his army had been killed or wounded, including Maxwell who had been shot from his saddle as he led his men in their final, poorly executed charge. Seldom had a victory been won with such a high proportion of losses, he reflected sadly as he finally settled down on some straw in a corner of the barn with the other senior officers. But then seldom had a new empire been created for the loss of so few men. For it was true. Between them, he and Richard had forged an empire from this vast expanse of land. When they had arrived, British possessions had been but small inroads on the map of the subcontinent. Now British influence, British trade, British law and British armies would cross India at will and bring peace and order on a scale to equal all the lands and peoples of Europe.

It was a heady vision. Almost too great a success for Arthur to comprehend, and at length his weary mind slipped into a deep sleep even as he sat, leaning against the rough mud plaster wall. There Fitzroy found him a short while later, once he had completed the battle report in his notebook. Fitzroy gazed down at the tired face, and realised for the first time the great strain that the campaign had placed on his friend. He smiled as he took off his jacket and laid it gently over his commander.

'Rest, my general,' he said softly. 'You have earned it.'

Chapter 69

Arthur allowed two days for his army to recover their strength. While the survivors rested, the injured – over a thousand men – were loaded on to carts and wagons and escorted back to a makeshift hospital at Naulniah. Soldiers scoured the battlefield to collect abandoned weapons and equipment. The engineers dug graves for the British dead outside Assaye. The enemy fallen were counted and then piled into great pits and covered over. Scindia's artillery was examined and the best guns were incorporated into the British artillery train, while the rest were loaded with a double charge and wedged shots and then had their barrels burst after Arthur's gunners lit delayed fuses and retired to a safe distance. On the third day Arthur formed the army up and set off in pursuit of Scindia.

The route the warlord had taken was marked by a wide trail of abandoned equipment and baggage carts, and the bodies of those who had died from injuries taken at Assaye. There were more casualties inflicted by the villagers lining the route who had endured many years of raids at the hands of the Mahrattas, and now took their bloody revenge on the stragglers who fell behind what was left of Scindia's army. As the enemy fell back, Scindia divided his force in two, sending a large body of men to defend his fortress at Gawilghur while the remainder finally turned to face the British once again on the plains of Argaum.

The redcoats formed lines and moved forward with their artillery in close support, pausing at close range to blast gaping holes in the dense mass of Mahratta troops, and then charging home with the bayonet. The experience of Assaye had badly shaken them, and now their resolve crumbled completely and the army of Scindia was shattered for ever. Gawilghur was taken in December and then, at the end of the month, Scindia's envoys signed a peace treaty. His army was to be dissolved and a garrison of several Company battalions was to be established at his capital. Large expanses of Mahratta territory were ceded to Britain and henceforth Scindia was obliged to accept British arbitration over any disputes that might arise between him and the rulers of neighbouring states.

As Arthur composed his report to Richard there was little emotion left in him to celebrate the end of the war. There was no doubt, even in his mind – so resolved to underplay his achievements – that the victories his army had won were as great as any achieved by any British army in India, or beyond. But Arthur was wise enough to realise that when word of Assaye reached London the newspapers there would scarcely believe that such a victory could be achieved against such great odds. Therefore he took great care that his report did not seem boastful or in any way vain. Besides, Arthur felt that there was little to celebrate when so many good men had been killed and mutilated in order to defeat Scindia's host. At length he completed his account, sealed the document and placed it in the hands of Captain Fitzroy to convey to the Governor General at Calcutta.

While the defeat of Scindia had left Britain the virtual master of the subcontinent, there were still a number of minor threats to deal with. With Scindia out of the way, Holkar assumed the mantle of the handful of rulers still opposed to British rule and he at once demanded that Arthur hand over Scindia's lands to him. It was a bold threat, but one that Arthur knew he could counter with ease. Such was his reputation, and that of his men, that no Mahratta force dared face them in battle and the conflict with Holkar was marked by a wearying series of small raids and skirmishes that dragged on into the early months of the new year.

Then, early in spring, as Arthur was inspecting one of his

sepoy battalions in the glare of the sun, his head began to spin, and his legs buckled under him. He lost consciousness so swiftly as he collapsed on the ground that he had no recollection of it when he came round.

His eyes flickered open and for a moment Arthur's mind was hazy as he struggled to understand what had happened to him, and even where he was. The room was shaded and overhead a punkah swayed from side to side and stirred the air over his face.

'Ah, awake at last.'

Arthur turned his head and saw Colonel Stevenson smiling at him from a chair beside the bed. Arthur swallowed and spoke softly. 'At last? How long have I been here?'

'Three days.'

'Three days!' Arthur repeated in horror. 'And where is here exactly?'

'Our supply base at Dimlah, sir. You're in the hospital.'

Arthur frowned. 'Was I injured?'

'No, sir. Bless you, you collapsed. On the parade ground. Surely you recall?'

Arthur shook his head, furious with himself, and ashamed. He struggled to rise and found that it required all his strength merely to prop himself up on his elbows.

Stevenson looked concerned. 'Sir, please lie back. I sent for the doctor the moment you began to stir. He will be here any moment. Just rest.'

For a moment Arthur was determined that rest was the last thing he would do, especially since he had been out of action for over three days. Then his strength gave out and he slumped back on the bed, breathing hard. He waited a moment until he had recovered and then turned his head to Stevenson.

'What's happened since I was brought here?'

'Nothing, sir. There's been no news of any raids, and the frontier with Holkar is holding fast, as far as I know. He's given us little trouble for nearly a month now. I think the danger from that quarter has passed. For now, at least.'

'Thank God,' Arthur replied quietly. 'I think I am about done in this country. One more campaign would break me.'

The door to the room opened, admitting a shaft of light that made Arthur squint, before the new arrival closed it and strode across to his bed.

'Ah, so you're with us again, sir?' The doctor leaned over the bed, grasped Arthur's hand in a powerful grip and pumped it. 'I'm Hollingsworth, a Company surgeon. You're probably a bit too dazed to recall me, eh?'

Arthur nodded. 'I'm sorry.'

'No matter.' The doctor straightened up. 'Have to say I was very worried about you when they brought you in, sir. Looked like you was in a bloody coma.'

'What is wrong with me?'

'Same thing that's wrong with most men who have served in this land for long enough. Exhaustion, that's what. It's time for you to quit India. While you still can. You need a long rest and a change of climate, sir.'

'I just need a rest. A few days and then I'll be back on duty.'

'Ah, no, sir. Not at all. I know the symptoms. Trust me, you either take my advice and take the first ship you can back to Britain, or have yourself measured up for a coffin.'

'Balderdash.'

The doctor smiled kindly. 'India has broken your health, sir. You must accept that and return home, or you will die here. Now, as you are back with us, I'll see to it that you're started on a diet of good broth. I'll see you again later, sir.'

Once the doctor had left the room Arthur closed his eyes for a moment. There was no denying how his body felt. How his mind felt, for that matter. He found it an effort to merely think, let alone talk.

'Sir?'

'Yes, Stevenson.'

'Is there anything I can do for you?'

'Not now. I need sleep. But when I wake, I'll need you to take down a letter for me, to my brother Richard . . .'

As he slowly recovered and gradually resumed his duties, Arthur waited for a response to his request. But none came, and it was not until he had sent a second letter that a reply came, late in May, summoning him to Calcutta. Before he quit his army, Arthur made sure that it was amply provisioned and carefully deployed to counter any attacks by Holkar, and then set off in a palanquin with a small cavalry escort. He reached Fort William in August and immediately made his way to the office of the Governor General.

Richard was in a meeting with senior officials from the East India Company and Arthur was kept waiting in the anteroom for almost an hour. At times there were heated exchanges from the Governor General's office but Arthur sat and stared out of the window heedlessly. Below the ramparts the sprawl of Calcutta teemed with life and industry. It was over five years since Arthur had last seen this view and much had already changed. The increasing control that Britain had over India had brought further commercial expansion in its wake and scores of new houses had been built for Company employees, merchants and native traders, clear proof of the success of the enterprise of Richard and his brothers. Yet as Arthur gazed out over the thriving city he recalled the men he had known and fought alongside, who had died to make this possible.

At length the door to the Governor General's office swung open and a half dozen civilians trooped out, barely acknowledging his presence. Then Richard was standing at the door. Five years had marked his face with more lines, yet Arthur noted the look of anxiety that flitted across his brother's expression when he saw him. It came as no surprise. He had seen his gaunt expression every day in his shaving mirror, and knew all too well how exhausted and ill he appeared.

'Arthur . . . God, you're thin. I had no idea . . .'

'It's good to see you too, Richard.' Arthur smiled. 'I take it you did not read my letter. Letters I should say.'

'Of course I read them,' Richard replied quickly, but betrayed himself when he failed to meet his brother's eye. 'But it's hard to retain every detail of all the correspondence I have to deal with. Anyway, come in and have a seat.'

Arthur followed him into the office and eased himself into

one of the chairs that had just been vacated by the Company officials.

'God, you have no idea how those penny-counting pedants vex me,' Richard grumbled as he pushed aside a sheaf of papers. 'After all that we have done for the Company you would think they would be more grateful. But no. It seems that they are plotting to have me recalled to England . . . I'm sorry, Arthur. I shouldn't regale you with all this. You have your own concerns.'

'It's been five years since we last met,' Arthur said quietly. 'I am your brother, yet I feel like a mere item on your agenda . . .'

Richard frowned. 'I hardly think—'

'Please, Richard. Hear me out.' Arthur took a deep breath and continued, 'I am exhausted. Utterly exhausted. I want to leave India. I want to go home. I told you this in the letters I wrote. If you did read them, then surely you are not surprised.'

'Go home?' Richard shook his head. 'But Arthur, I need you here, at my side. You are my right arm.'

'You don't need me any more.' Arthur nodded to the map on the wall behind his brother, now almost all under the sway of England and the East India Company. 'It's over, Richard. We have achieved all that we set out to achieve here. We have won an empire for England, and for the first time many of the native races have known peace and prosperity. What is there left for me to do? I have beaten every army that opposed us. Now I wish to leave. You should consider it too, before you overstay the reputation you have forged for yourself.'

'But I need you here,' Richard persisted.

Arthur shook his head. 'General Lake is more than capable of taking over my command. Besides, I feel that I've outgrown India. I've learned my craft and when I return to Europe I believe I will be a match for any general amongst our enemies.'

'Even that fellow Bonaparte?'

'Even him,' Arthur replied firmly. 'England needs me, Richard. And, thanks to the years I have dedicated to our interests here, I need England. I need rest.'

Richard stared at him, thin-lipped, for a long while before at last he sighed. 'It seems you have fixed your mind on this. Is there nothing I can say that will change your opinion?'

'No.'

'Very well, then. I will have your authority to quit India drawn up. I take it you will need a few months to settle your affairs here?'

'Yes.' Arthur felt a surge of pure relief flow through his body now that the decision was made. 'Thank you, Richard.'

'I should thank you. Without you, none of this would have been possible.' Richard gestured towards the map. 'All England should thank you.'

Arthur rose from his seat. 'It's been a long journey. If you don't mind?'

'Of course not. I'll have some rooms made ready for you at the fort. You can wait in the mess until they're ready. Will you join me for dinner tonight?'

'Yes. I'd like that.' Arthur smiled and then turned to leave the office. As he wandered down the corridor, past the line of offices filled with clerks feverishly struggling to cope with the new empire, Arthur gazed out across the ramparts, over the river, following its course to the horizon where it eventually flowed into the sea. There would be much to do before he could finally leave this land, but before all that there was one pressing matter he had to attend to with all his heart. He took his seat at a desk in the corner of the mess and placed a sheet of paper on the surface in front of him. Several newly arrived officers, pink-faced and flush with youthful energy, cast curious glances at him but he ignored them as he dipped his pen in the inkwell and began to write.

My dearest Kitty, I am coming home . . .

Author's note

One of the most fascinating aspects of writing this series has been recreating the origins of two of history's greatest generals: where they came from, what their background was and how their historical context helped determine their characters and defined the opportunities open to them. *The Generals* covers that vital part of their careers where Bonaparte and Wellesley learned their craft as commanders of armies. And what formidable armies they proved to be!

The men that Napoleon encountered when he arrived in Italy were hungry, sick, poorly equipped and unpaid, and outnumbered by a better-armed and better-trained enemy. Yet, like Robert E. Lee's Army of Virginia, they won tremendous victories because they marched and fought harder than their enemy, and had a terrific sense of elan besides. For this they had Napoleon to thank. Right from the outset he knew what motivated men and made every effort to win their respect. He made sure that good service and bravery were rewarded, and he tolerated a level of informality with his men that warmed their hearts and made them identify with his military goals, and ultimately his political ambitions.

By contrast, Wellesley was an utter professional who quickly grasped that relentless training and preparation would provide him with an army that would stand firm in the face of far larger enemy forces. When the British troops closed with the enemy their discipline and training completely outclassed their opponents, with the result that a handful of Europeans were left the masters of India by the time the Wellesley brothers quit the subcontinent. While Napoleon was a shrewd leader of men, Wellesley was a master of every detail of supply and manoeuvre, on the battlefield as well as off it.

It is important when considering their careers not to lose sight of the different circumstances in which each man sought advancement. Napoleon was very fortunate to be in Paris at the time of the royalist uprising. That made him a reputation he was quick to exploit. Indeed, he wore good fortune like a second skin in his meteoric rise to the rank of First Consul. For Wellesley, mired in a far less flexible political and military context, the prospects for promotion were much more limited than his great rival's – at least until he arrived in India where British ambitions to extend the influence of the East India Company at last provided him with the chance to experiment with and perfect his ideas about generalship. His natural flair, and tireless dedication to his calling, were soon appreciated by his superiors who often manipulated the rigid rules of military precedence to secure him a commander's role in the campaigns in which he fought. Unlike the fiery Napoleon, Wellesley was the embodiment of calm collected command, as his officers and men frequently commented in reports and letters home.

With Napoleon now master of France and a formidable power within Europe, and Wellesley the hero of India, the stage is set for each man to carve out his place in history. While Napoleon seeks to make France the undisputed power in Europe, Arthur is just as strongly resolved to defeat France and save his nation from the chaos and bloodshed of revolutionary ideals.

For those who wish to flesh out their knowledge of the background to *The Generals* I thoroughly recommend the following titles. David Chandler's compendious *The Campaigns of Napoleon* provides detailed accounts of the campaigns and battles and a fascinating analysis of Napoleon and his methods. There are ample maps and diagrams to permit the reader to follow the action and some sound judgements about Napoleon's motives and ambitions. For Wellesley, I would recommend Jac Weller's *Wellington in India*. Again, it is a detailed and racy account of the young British officer's rise to fame as he develops a successful means of waging war across India that had eluded all his predecessors. Weller is one of those historians who has walked the ground and his book is a useful guide to anyone who wishes to explore the battlefields in person. For a wonderful appreciation of the experiences of the British military in India I heartily recommend the delightful *Sahib* by Richard Holmes. Finally, an honourable mention must go to Paul Strathern for his excellent upcoming work on *Napoleon in Egypt*, a proof of which unfortunately arrived just after I had completed this book.

I'll conclude with the usual caveat. While *The Generals* is a work of fiction I have made every effort to be faithful to the facts. However, there are occasions when I have had to bend the history and tweak time to make the story work. I apologise to the purists for this, but I wanted to share my excitement about these two towering historical figures in as pacy and readable a way as possible. They lived in extraordinary times and were both extraordinary individuals, and it is those aspects that I wanted to do full justice to in this book.

Simon Scarrow
January 2007

SIMON SCARROW

Young Bloods

Arthur Wesley was born and bred to be a leader. With a firm belief that the nation must be led by a king, red-coated British officer Arthur throws himself into serving his country and heads for battle against the French Republic to restore the fallen monarchy.

Napoleon Bonaparte joins the French military on the eve of the Revolution. Shunned as an outsider for his Corsican heritage, he believes leadership is won by merit, not by noble birth. When anarchy explodes in Paris, the young artillery officer is thrust to the forefront of a revolutionary army poised to march against Britain.

As two mighty Empires embark on a bloody duel, Wesley and Bonaparte prepare to face a sworn enemy. One fuelled by ambition, the other by a sense of duty, they are unaware that the fate of Europe will one day lie in their hands.

Praise for Simon Scarrow's highly acclaimed Eagle series:

'It's *Spartacus* meets *Master and Commander* in this rip-roaring, thoroughly entertaining tale of swashbuckling adventure from one of the most exciting writers in historical ficion' *Daily Record*

'I really don't need this kind of competition' Bernard Cornwell

'A good, uncomplicated, rip-roaring read' *Mail on Sunday*

978 0 7553 2434 7

headline
review

The Eagle In the Sand

Simon Scarrow

Trouble is brewing on the eastern frontier of the Roman Empire. The troops are in a deplorable state, while the corrupt behaviour of their senior officers threatens to undermine the army's control of the region. To restore the competence of the men defending a vital fort, two experienced centurions are dispatched to Judaea from Rome.

On their arrival Macro and Cato discover that there is an even more serious problem to deal with. Bannus, a local tribesman, is brewing up rebellion amongst the followers of Jehoshua, who was crucified in Jerusalem some seventeen years earlier. Now Bannus is pushing the faction towards violent opposition to Rome.

As the local revolt grows in scale, Rome's long-standing enemy Parthia is poised to invade. Macro and Cato must stamp out corruption in the cohort and restore it to fighting fitness to quash Bannus – before the eastern provinces are lost to the Empire for ever . . .

Praise for Simon Scarrow's EAGLE novels:

'It's *Spartacus* meets *Master and Commander* in this rip-roaring, thoroughly entertaining tale of swashbuckling adventure' *Daily Record*

'Scarrow's legionary adventures have put guts back into historical writing' *Northern Echo*

'A good, uncomplicated, rip-roaring read' *Mail on Sunday*

978 0 7553 2775 1

headline

Now you can buy any of these other bestselling books by **Simon Scarrow** from your bookshop or *direct from his publisher*.

FREE P&P AND UK DELIVERY
(Overseas and Ireland £3.50 per book)

Young Bloods	£6.99
Under the Eagle	£6.99
The Eagle's Conquest	£6.99
When the Eagle Hunts	£6.99
The Eagle and the Wolves	£6.99
The Eagle's Prey	£6.99
The Eagle's Prophecy	£6.99

TO ORDER SIMPLY CALL THIS NUMBER

01235 400 414

or visit our website: www.headline.co.uk

Prices and availability subject to change without notice.